MEMORIES

OF PROPHECIES

MEMORIES

OF PROPHECIES

Davis Ashura

MEMORIES OF PROPHECIES

Printed in the United States of America

Trade Paperback ISBN: 979-8-7290494-0-0

Hardcover ISBN: 978-1-7329780-5-8

First Printing: 2021

DuSum Publishing, LLC

Books by Davis Ashura

The Castes and the OutCastes:

A Warrior's Path

A Warrior's Knowledge

A Warrior's Penance

Omnibus Edition (only available on Kindle)

Stories for Arisa (short-story collection)

The Chronicles of William Wilde:

William Wilde and the Necrosed

William Wilde and the Stolen Life

William Wilde and the Unusual Suspects

William Wilde and the Sons of Deceit

William Wilde and the Lord of Mourning

Instrument of Omens

A Testament of Steel

Memories of Prophecies

To my Amma and all the wonderful lessons she gave me. Who I am as a person is because of her.

Contents

Acknowledgements

As always, the focused and solitary pursuit of writing doesn't happen for me without the wonderful support that I'm blessed to receive. It begins with my wife and family, who understand that when I wander into my study to write, it means I'm getting lost in a strange wilderness and it's probably not a good idea to bother me.

There are also my friends from my writer's group, which we've somehow managed to maintain despite the craziness of the season of misery that was 2020.

Then there are my alpha readers without whom this book simply wouldn't be nearly as good. It begins with Edmund Milne and Brady West, who were my first true alpha readers and have kindly kept on with this book. Ticiana Marques, who continues to make sure my horseriding writing is more accurate than I can manage on my own. Stephen Kutz who catches a truly massive number of errors and typos. Jay Jenkins, whose passion for the characters has made me think about them in ways I'd never considered. And finally, Richard Larraga, who helps polish the manuscript.

I owe a debt of gratitude to all of you.

Author's Note

I am still in a state of shock over how well *A Testament of Steel*, the first book of *Instrument of Omens*, has been received. I never expected it, but I'm also grateful beyond measure. All in all, it's been nothing short of a stunning, surreal experience.

Of course, writing *Memories of Prophecies*, the sequel to such a successful book, has presented its own set of challenges. It wasn't just the difficulty of laying down one word after another, which never gets easy. It was also the maddening struggles of making sure to consistently unite all the different aspects of the worldbuilding—be they historical, philosophical, or magical—into my other series; to build one cohesive whole and not contradict myself.

By now, it's likely obvious to most people that all my books are linked. The Anchored Worlds is a sprawling web of storylines and timelines, and while each series can be read separately, they also possess such a mass of inertia that it's not easy keeping the various elements in line.

And they surely want to fall apart.

There is also the uncertainty of a writer's mentality and having to live up the reputation of *A Testament of Steel*. That book is a hard act to follow, but it's not impossible. It took some elbow grease and lots of nose-to-the-grindstone mentality, but in the end, I managed it. And looking back on the process and the finished product, I'm so glad to have experienced it all. The book has been a joy to write, and I'm surprisingly pleased with how well it turned out.

So, I think I'll keep writing this love letter to *Wheel of Time* and *Lord of the Rings* and be grateful for this long journey there.

Davis Ashura

P.S. There is also a glossary in the back to help you keep track of all the various names, places, etc. It's not exhaustive but creating it was exhausting. Who knew Seminal was so complex?

The Trials So Far

Cinder Shade is a young man, born in the poor, remote village of Swallow. His expectations in life are few. Despite the love of his loyal parents, Cinder's clubfoot and withered right leg leave him with a limited future. This seems certain during an afternoon of hard labor when a deadly snowtiger enters their farm and kills his parents. But Cinder manages to escape the beast. He hides in the family well, seemingly saved until he loses his balance and falls into the water, losing consciousness. When he finally rouses, Cinder has no recognition of himself, his remaining family, or anyone else.

The difficult decision is made to send Cinder to the nation's seaport capital of Swift Sword, to the orphanage of Our Lady of Fire, named after jade-eyed Sira, a mythic heroine from the world's past. Legends say she, along with her husband, the warrior-servant, Shokan will rise again one day...

During the journey to the orphanage, Cinder's club foot and withered leg are miraculously healed. Once there, Cinder makes several friends, including the brother and sister, Riner and Coral Strain, and several enemies, a foul-mouthed group of thugs, older boys who bully Riner. Cinder's guiding sense of right-and-wrong won't allow him to simply stand by and watch. He fights off the bullies, earning their further enmity, but additionally gaining the trust and admiration of Coral.

This brings Cinder to the attention of Lerid File, the martial master of Steel-Graced Adepts, a fine martial arts academy in Swift Sword. Master Lerid tests Cinder and accepts him as a student, but until the moment he heard of Steel-Graced Adepts, the notion of becoming a warrior had never entered Cinder's mind. Now that he knows about it, there is nothing more he wants than to become a warrior worthy of the name.

However, his initial time at Steel-Graced is difficult. The other students are far more advanced, and Cinder, despite his healed disability, is small for his age and physically weaker. Though whilst here, he discovers an inner strength: he doesn't quit. No matter the hardship, he endures, forcing himself to outwork all other students.

Settling into this new life, Cinder bonds with his brother cadets, training daily and learning more about his vast, ancient world, such as the differences between humans and the other sentient species. All other races, such as the dwarves and elves, are able to source their *lorethasra*, allowing them to increase their speed and strength and perform unimaginable feats. It is only humans that cannot draw on this power—although there was a time when they could. The reasons for this are lost in the legends of the past.

Cinder also discovers another unexpected talent. He can play the mandolin, a skill he indulges with Coral. Although uncertain of their relationship, he plays while Coral sings, in a rough tavern where he often must fight to survive, defending her honor and his own.

His training progresses, and Cinder rapidly improves, overtaking most of the other students. His improvement becomes so obvious that he is chosen to represent Steel-Graced at the Maker's Tournament, the annual competition for admittance into the Third Directorate, the most prestigious military academy in the elven empire of Yaksha. Cinder, along with Bones, another student at Steel-Graced, end up as members of the chosen four. However, before leaving for the elven island, Cinder promises Coral that he will return to her.

At the Third Directorate, Cinder finds his place and makes good friends—including the short-tempered dwarves—and certain enemies, such as most of the elves. Cinder refuses to accept their boastful assertions of superiority. Instead, he believes in true brotherhood and equality. This faith causes friction, especially with the elven prince, Estin and his follower, Riyne.

Cinder meets others, such as a troll, who somehow recognizes him, and he delves deeper into the truths about *lorethasra*, and the human equivalent of *Jivatma*. He learns information about the fallen, burning-eyed god, Shet, and how humanity lost the ability to conduct *Jivatma*. He also meets Anya, Estin's older sister. She is a rare, green-eyed elf with honey-blonde hair, second in line for the imperial throne, a ranger, and the finest warrior amongst the elves. The two form an unexpected friendship, which causes further tension with Estin: close bonds between elves and humans are frowned upon. But Cinder disregards the prince's antipathy…

Instead, he focuses on his training, and his work pays off. He tames one of the fabled Yavana horses and masters the bow. He also visualizes a strange sight whenever he is at his most calm. Filling his mind's eye, it is a perfect pool of water, and in its presence, there comes an increase in his concentration and clarity of thought. The pool is most easily reached when in the Foe, a half-realm not entirely in Seminal, where the Firsters train against simulacra of the deadly spiderkin, the greatest of elven enemies.

But other issues continue to plague Cinder; strange visions, utterly real in the emotions they evoke. And the most haunting is that of a mysterious woman with honey-blonde hair. He hears her voice in glorious song—yet never sees her face.

As the year passes, Cinder matures in all the ways of a warrior. He triumphs in the end of year competition before facing the Unitary Trial, a challenging scouting mission within a deadly stretch of the Dagger Mountains. It is a disaster. The spiderkin attack en masse. Many of Cinder's brother Firsters are slaughtered, and he survives only through the use of *Jivatma*, the perfectly reflective pool of water, which increases his speed and strength, allowing him to defeat a number of spiderkin.

But it is Anya, in command of the Unitary Trial, who ultimately saves him, sensing the location of a gravely wounded Cinder in a way she doesn't yet understand and which she keeps secret from everyone else.

Afterward, the surviving cadets limp their way home, stopping for rest at Swift Sword. There, Cinder reunites with Coral, a bittersweet meeting. Recognizing the dangers of his chosen profession, he realizes it isn't fair to make any further promises, not when death might claim him so easily. Regretfully, he ends his young relationship with the heartbroken Coral, in favor of his life's chosen path.

When the Firsters finally return to the Third Directorate, Anya steps in to sponsor Cinder next year for the harsh Secondary Trial. Cinder isn't certain of her proposal, but he promises to consider it.

Meanwhile, deep in the Dagger Mountains, a titanic figure rustles. Menace pours off him like the black smoky chains shackling him. He slouches in his slumber, briefly awakening. His eyes flash open, but his right eye is filled with flames. The world knows him. Shet. And he knows his enemies even if they don't yet know themselves.

Cinder Shade's journey is far from over…

1

The cadets' common room at Krathe House felt strangely quiet to-night, lonely despite the presence of everyone in one area. It was understandable. Nineteen Firsters had set out for the Dagger Mountains in the Unitary Trial, but only thirteen had returned. Thirteen young men who still mourned their friends recently killed in combat against the spiderkin. Thirteen young men whose spirits were sapped by the absence of their fallen brothers.

Lost forever was Nathaz and his bold, brash personality. Dorcer's steadying influence. Joria's and Rorian's burgeoning competence. Cinder shied away from his memories of the terrible battle that had stolen the life of his brother warriors. Especially Nathaz and Rorian, who had died in his arms. Recalling the life leaving their eyes…

Cinder shuddered. The memorial service for the fallen had been earlier in the day, and the pain still too new. It still cut too deep and was too sharp.

The elves had also lost two of their own. Crail Valing and Farin Eshanwe. While Cinder had barely known either of them, he reckoned their deaths had dealt a similarly painful loss to their kinsmen. At least it appeared so based on their vacant, sorrow-filled expressions.

He glanced around the room. The commons currently contained more students than it ever had prior to the Unitary Trial. Before their departure for the Daggers, this part of Krathe House had been set aside for only the Firster humans and dwarves, with the elves having separate living quarters. But given the losses their class had suffered in the Unitary Trial, the academy's administration had decided the cadets should share one living space. Thirteen newly promoted Seconds now shared the quarters that had once held twelve Firsters.

Cinder's vision carried to the broad, open windows opposite the room's main entrance. It was night, and an evening breeze stirred the gauzy curtains. An owl hooted somewhere in the depths of the night, the sound somehow forlorn and distant. It reflected the stifling and heavy quiet of the common room. Everyone separated into their own islands of grief, which still felt crushing and new.

Cinder cleared his throat, thinking of what might break the tension. "Right now, Nathaz would be telling us to stop crying so fucking much. He'd tell us to pick ourselves up and carry on with living."

Some of the humans and even the elves smiled, while the dwarves, who had known Nathaz best, chuckled softly.

"And he'd be right," Derius said. The dwarf was heavily built for even one of his kind and woven into the braids of his long, dark hair and near waist-length beard were tiny, silver bells. They tinkled like whispering wind chimes when he spoke.

"Farin would say the same thing," Riyne said, eyes distant as he smiled in fond remembrance. The blond-haired, dark-eyed elf noble, Cinder's foe and possible enemy, didn't seem so deadly right now. Right now, he appeared like a young man lost to grieving.

Cinder tried to see him in that light rather than as the bully who had ambushed him in the dark of night in the Quad, or the deceitful warrior who had delivered illegal blows during the Grand Melee. Both times, Riyne's attacks had left Cinder injured and requiring a physician's care in the hospital.

As a result, given their history, maybe it was foolish to think of

Riyne as anything other than an enemy. And maybe he still was and always would be, but how much better if he could earn a measure of forgiveness? After all, wasn't it true that in battle, all men were brothers? Cinder believed so, and perhaps Riyne would also learn this truth, especially given the losses they had all suffered in the Unitary Trial.

Then again, sometimes bullies remained who they always were.

Mohal, a tall elf, dark-haired, blue eyed, and handsome—there was no other kind of male elf but handsome—nodded agreement. "Farin wouldn't curse, though. He never did. Even hearing it from others made him uncomfortable." Mohal was also an elf noble, but one of lower status than Riyne. He was also someone Cinder had once considered a friend, but maybe not anymore. Mohal had been distant and curt following Cinder's unexpected victory in the Grand Melee, the annual competition meant to determine the finest warrior in the Firster class.

In the over twenty-five-hundred-year history of the Third Directorate, no human had ever won the Grand Melee. Cinder was the first, and the elves had not been pleased at his victory, Mohal included. However, after the battle against the spiderkin, the elf had sought him out, and they'd spoken. Cinder hoped it meant they could resume their friendship.

Estin laughed as well, and Cinder tried not to scowl. If Riyne *might* be an enemy, Estin most certainly was. The prince—the blond-haired, blue-eyed son of Empress Sala Yaksha—had hated Cinder from their first meeting, and the sentiment was mutual. Their interactions weren't helped by Cinder's friendship with Estin's sister, Princess Anya, a relationship the prince considered unseemly.

"He always winced when someone cursed," Estin said. "He said it made us sound like dwarves."

Sriovey, the red-bearded leader of the dwarves—the others were all dark-haired—puffed. "What does that mean? You think we're barbarians because of our *foul* language?"

Estin wore confusion on his face. "No. That's not what I meant," he said, his voice placating for once, rather than filled with arrogance. "But dwarves do curse a lot."

"Maybe we have a lot to curse about. You ever think about that?" Sriovey's eyes flashed, and he rose out of his chair, continuing to glare at the prince. The other dwarves stood as well.

Estin's prior mollification transformed into righteous indignation. He climbed to his feet, and the other elves moved to back him up. "Or maybe you deserve your lot in life. You ever think about *that*?"

A fight looked to be in the offing as the two groups faced off against one another.

"Hold on now," Bones said. The tall, dark-skinned, almond-eyed warrior was Cinder's oldest friend at the academy, dating back to when they had been apprentices in *Steel-Graced Adepts*. He stepped between the two groups. "Let's not get carried away."

Cinder was proud of Bones' attempt to keep the peace, although it seemed to be falling on deaf ears.

Estin's lip curled. "What do you know about it, human?" the prince demanded. "Your kind are a stain on creation. You bring nothing but death and misery."

Ishmay, a tall, lanky human from Gandharva with hazel eyes, moved to Bones' side. "We are who we are, and we won't apologize for it."

Wark and Depth, two more of Cinder's fellow countrymen from Rakesh with features similar to Bones' but not his height, stood now, too, confronting Estin.

Bones addressed the elven prince. "Plus, you better understand. You have a problem with the dwarves, you have a problem with us."

Sriovey's glare now turned to Bones. "We didn't ask for your help."

Bones glared back at him. "We're supposed to be brothers. Remember?"

Sriovey didn't reply, and the three groups formed a tense triangle. Jaws clenched. Fists formed.

Cinder sighed. Instead of an argument, it seemed like a brawl might break out. *Fragging idiots.* Fighting? Tonight of all nights? Only hours after the memorial for their fallen brothers? A memorial where the masters of the academy had spoken movingly on behalf of the dead, proclaiming uplifting sentiments of fraternity. Those same sentiments had been echoed by the fools gathered here now.

Anger built within Cinder, a cresting emotion of redness and frustration.

Apparently, the words spoken at the remembrance hadn't penetrated the thick skulls of the Seconds.

Devesh-damn it. Just for once, why couldn't they see their commonality rather than their differences?

Without intending it, a perfectly reflective pool sheathed in blue-and-green lightning formed in his mind's eye. It was his *lorethasra*, the strange source of power wielded by all woven—every sentient being other than humans.

But Cinder had managed it, early on since his time at *Steel-Graced Adepts* and also during the Unitary Trial. He'd used it to kill a half-dozen spiderkin.

However, his *lorethasra*'s appearance in this moment surprised Cinder. Always before, he had only been able to draw it forth when he was calm or when his life was threatened. Not when he was furious.

Whatever the reason, it didn't matter. As long as he could use his *lorethasra* to cut short the incipient argument, he'd be happy. He allowed the smallest amount of his *lorethasra* to leak into his body.

All of his senses sharpened. His sight brightened; his hearing enhanced. Smells were more powerful. Even touch and taste. In addition, his muscles twitched as a readiness to explode into motion was made available.

And this was the barest trickle. He wondered what he might be able to accomplish with more, although he knew not to try to for it. Attempting to push past the blue-and-green lightning always left him scoured with fiery pain.

Cinder forced his way into the center of the three angry groups, the heart of the triangle. "Enough!" he shouted. "Whatever disagreements we have can wait for the morning. Tonight, we're supposed to be honoring our fallen brothers."

Sriovey spoke. "Hotgate, this doesn't concern you, and—

"Shut up," Cinder barked at him, not wanting to hear anything from the dwarf.

Sriovey's mouth closed with a snap.

Estin's didn't. "Who are you to claim fraternity with an elf?" he sneered. "Peasant human. Move out of the way, or you will be moved."

Cinder remained rooted in place, doing his best to rein in his anger as he faced the prince. "Now isn't the time for this."

Before the final word left his mouth, Estin's fist flew at him. Cinder watched it approach. With *lorethasra* fueling his muscles and senses, the fist came at him at a crawl. Cinder easily caught it in one hand.

Estin tried to withdraw his fist, but Cinder didn't let go. He squeezed until the prince gasped in pain. Cinder flung Estin aside, and the prince landed gracelessly on his ass. He rolled over on his side, gripping his hand and clearly in pain.

Cinder glared about at everyone. "I said enough. We will not brawl. Not on this night. Not on the night when we eulogized the dead."

Movements and sounds penetrated his anger and disgust. The flicker of Riyne's shocked, wide-open eyes. Derius' sharp intake of breath.

"How the hell did he move so fast," he heard Ishmay whisper to Bones.

Derius stepped forward, appearing calm now rather than angry from a few seconds ago. Cinder still tensed, but the dwarf held up his hands in appeasement. "I just want to say my piece." He addressed the entire room, but especially the elves. "Now you know who's in charge of the dorm. Don't fuck with Hotgate."

Estin had gathered himself, rising to his feet, but he still clutched his hand against his abdomen. "Elves are in charge of their own kind," he spat. "The Blessed Race answers to no one."

Cinder really wished the prince would shut the hell up. He got directly in Estin's face. The *lorethasra* still trickled into him, and a buzzing sound reached his ears. For a second, he imagined seeing the lightning flicker across his face, a reflection seen in Estin's eyes.

The prince's face went slack with fear, and he stumbled back. "What are you?"

Cinder stared after the prince, confused and unsure why he

suddenly seemed so afraid. What had the prince seen? Had that really been lightning?

"He's Hotgate," Sriovey said in answer to Estin's question, piercing Cinder's uncertain musings. "And like Derius said, you best not fuck with him."

Cinder woke early the next morning, got dressed, and exited his room, strapping his shoke to his hip. The commons were empty since no one else was awake, and everyone still had their doors closed. He decided to leave Krathe House—*Vanquisher's House* in *Shevasra*—and go for a morning run. He was yet to fully recover from the injuries he'd suffered in the Unitary Trial, but day-by-day, he was getting stronger, and the best way to gain further improvement was to push himself even harder.

This morning he meant to cover his usual five-mile run, but he'd go as hard as he could, extend past his body's limitations. There would be no allowances made for the lingering pain in his shoulder or his decreased stamina.

His resolve was tested several miles into the run. Perspiration poured off his forehead, dripped off his nose, drenched his stomach and the small of his back. Worse, his heart pounded, and he could barely get enough air in his lungs. He wanted to pant, but he forced himself to take deep respirations. He recalled the lessons from his time at *Steel-Graced Adepts*, his first martial school, on the necessity of regulating his breathing. *Deep breath in. Deep breath out. Controlled and steady.*

He continued on, denying the need to slow down. His lungs burned, his heart pounded, and a hitch twisted like a knife into his side. On he pressed, ending up completing the five miles only a few minutes off his usual pace. But as soon as the run was complete, he fell into a squat, gasping. His flanks ached, and his throat was sore. Nausea curdled his stomach, but he managed to hold down his gorge. He sat there for a few minutes, next to the still-empty Quad, struggling to recover and hoping he hadn't gone too hard.

Eventually his thudding heart eased off enough for him to stand, and he shuddered when he rose to his feet, inhaling deep and yawning mightily. Hunger gnawed at his insides, and he took halting steps toward the cafeteria. He needed food. However, his progress proved slow. His legs were like limp noodles, his heart remained tachycardic, and he had no energy left within him.

He had no option but to bear the discomfort and press on. He eventually made it to the cafeteria where he went straightaway to the buffet. He collected a hearty breakfast of eggs, bacon, and dosas—lots of dosas—and flopped down at an empty table. Sweat still poured off of him as he tucked into his meal. Afterward, his stomach was still rumbling with hunger, and Cinder grabbed a few idlis on his way out the door as he headed to the library.

The corridors of Firemirror Hall were empty—the new school year had not yet started—and Cinder's footsteps echoed. He passed a number of empty classrooms, their blackboards bare, and the spaces darkened since the *diptha* lamps inside were turned off. The hallways, though, were bright as sunshine beamed through the panes of large windows facing the Quad.

Cinder's eyes automatically went to the massive figure centered within the square, the living statue of the Titan, Garad Lull, one of Shet's great captains and the author of untold misery, no matter that it was three thousand years in the past. As always, an unreasoning anger stirred in Cinder's heart, like embers whipped to life by the wind. He hated the figure, the cruelty evident on the Titan's face, the sneering contempt. How he'd like to wipe the smirk off Garad's face.

He started when he realized he'd come to a halt, glaring fury at the Titan. *Where does the hatred come from?* He often wondered the same question, over and over again. But now wasn't the time to think about it. He had other things to do today. Cinder got going again, moving at a fast clip down the corridor.

Seconds later, he encountered Master Nuhlin Genhim, who was frowning as he ambled along, hands clasped behind his back, staring at the ground, and likely considering some matter of importance.

Typical. Master Nuhlin was brilliant, an expert in multiple fields, and the Firsters' instructor in Tactics and Strategy, although he had never served in the Yaksha Army. He was of middle years for an elf and also the only unkempt one Cinder had ever met, his long dark hair rarely combed or placed in a proper ponytail.

Cinder tilted a bow of respect to the master and received a distracted nod of acknowledgment in return. He expected the master to pass him by without commenting, but the instructor jerked to a stop when he came abreast of Cinder.

"You spoke well last night," Master Nuhlin said. "Your words about how we should strive for unity. It is a sentiment we should all hope to achieve." He inclined his head. "Carry on." Without another word, he strode off.

Cinder watched the master depart, gladdened by the compliment. He only hoped the Seconds could eventually achieve some semblance of what he had spoken—unity—because based on last night, they seemed more interested in arguing with one another than getting along.

With an annoyed grunt, he dismissed his worry. It was a problem for another day. He had other questions to address this morning. Questions relating to his *lorethasra*. About whether it was truly *lorethasra* and not something else. About what it might mean for who he was as a person. He'd struggled with these questions for the past year, gaining little traction, but he sensed the truth was out there. He hoped the library possessed more of the answers.

On he went, eventually coming across an open breezeway. Crossing it allowed him to reach the library, which he entered through a pair of heavy brass doors engraved with the imagery of books and scrolls.

As always, he paused within the library's entrance, closing his eyes and breathing in the dusty aroma of old paper. No sounds ruined the library's quiet, which seemed to reverberate with the pent-up expectation of a journey's beginning or undiscovered knowledge. One more inhalation, and Cinder opened his eyes. In front of him extended the familiar sight of long, dark tables, several stories of groaning shelves, and the weight of history represented by an assortment of books.

A knowing chuckle interrupted his purple-prose thoughts. It was Master Molni Cirnovain, the head librarian, and currently, the library's only other occupant. "You always look like a penitent kneeling at the feet of holiness when you walk into the library," the old master said.

Cinder grinned and walked to where the elderly, bespectacled elf sat at his typical spot, rooted behind the main desk, directly left of the entrance. Cinder had gotten to know the librarian well during his first year at the Third Directorate and considered him a friend. Currently, Master Molni had a finger placed in a book to hold his location, and Cinder guessed it was probably a historical text about *lorethasra*, the master's area of specialty.

"I wonder what your face must look like when you first enter," Cinder said in reply. "You're probably praying when you come into the library every morning."

Master Molni laughed, stepping out from behind his desk. "As old and crusty as I am, you'll likely find me scowling at all the re-shelving I have to do."

"I know you better," Cinder said, reaching the librarian and drawing him into a hug. "You love books too much to ever be angry with them."

"True," Master Molni said, still smiling, hands on Cinder's shoulders. "It's good to see you, young man." A moment later, sorrow filled his features. "I heard of the Unitary Trial. I was there last night during the memorial. I would have talked to you and offered my condolences, but you were speaking to the princess."

An undercurrent of suppressed curiosity filled Master Molni's voice, and Cinder kept his face motionless, not reacting to the old librarian's interest. How would other elves react when they learned of Anya's proposal to take him on his Secondary Trial, the offer she'd made last night at the memorial? He had thought about what they might say and figured they would probably make her life more difficult, and he didn't want that for her. He didn't want Anya to suffer anything on his account. He'd hold tight the privacy of her proposal.

"She was our commander during the Unitary Trial," Cinder said. "I would have died if she hadn't found me after the action. She ensured I was well."

Master Molni gave a bright smile. "Of course. A simple explanation is generally best," he said, somewhat enigmatically.

Cinder eyes narrowed, and he viewed Master Molni with a hard gaze. "Sir?"

The old elf waved aside his question. "I'm sure you didn't come here to tell me about the princess," he said. "What can I do for you?"

Cinder continued to peer at Master Molni, trying to discern what the elf might have intimated. Or was it all in his imagination?

Master Molni continued to wear a patiently innocent expression, and Cinder realized he wouldn't learn anything by staring. "I was hoping to find information detailing the relationship between *Jivatma* and *lorethasra*."

Master Molni chuckled. "Didn't you already look into that last year? You did read the version of *Revelatory Dreams* kept in the reserve section, did you not?"

"Yes, but it didn't tell me much. I was hoping you knew of a book that describes the appearance of *lorethasra*."

Master Molni frowned. "As far as I know, there is no such descriptive passage. No one knows what *lorethasra* looks like. It's a potential power, but no one can actually see it."

The information was unexpected, and Cinder hid his surprise. He had read a book last year, a supposed biography about Sapient Dormant that *did* describe the appearance of *lorethasra*. Master Molni must not have remembered it. "No one?"

"No one," Master Molni confirmed. "Why do you ask?"

Cinder shrugged. "I figured knowing what it looks like might help me reach mine," he said in as nonchalant a manner as he could manage.

"Well, I've never seen mine, and I know of no one who can or has."

Cinder nodded understanding even as his mind raced. He *could* see his *lorethasra*. He had seen it every time he reached for it, as recently as last night, in fact, but he kept the information to himself. He wasn't sure what it meant or how the elves and dwarves would react if they knew of his ability.

He mentally groaned. Anya knew about it. He'd told her about it once, in passing, after a small-unit drill a few months ago. He hoped she'd forgotten, but he doubted it. Anya also knew he could conduct his *lorethasra*, another secret he'd shared with only her, and he had no intention of sharing it with anyone else. It was a talent only the rarest of humans could claim, and even then, only temporarily from what he'd read. Again, who knew how the woven would react to it?

Master Molni tapped his chin, frowning. "If anyone could have described the appearance of *lorethasra*, it would have been the Mythaspuris. They knew much we will never learn, and if there is an answer to your question, you might find it in one of the various biographies of Sapient Dormant and Manifold Fulsom."

Cinder's lips tightened in a momentary grimace. He had already read about Sapient's possible accounting of *lorethasra*. He didn't want a repetition of what he had already learned. "I don't think I can take another biography about those two. Isn't there anything else? Any*one* else?"

The old librarian shrugged. "There are some journal entries from a few lesser known Mythaspuris, such as Indrun Agni." He gestured for Cinder to follow him. "Follow me. I know one of possible interest."

Cinder trailed Master Molni to the third floor and a small section of dusty tomes. Most of the books in this area had unusual titles, some of them blasphemous, and he found himself smiling.

"Here we are," Master Molni said, withdrawing a thick volume, passing it over to Cinder. *The Mythaspuris Improbability*. "Some of what you seek might be found in chapter ten."

Cinder sat at a table reading the book Master Molni had pulled for him and quickly discovered that *The Mythaspuris Improbability* was a controversial text. It argued that most of what was known about the Mythaspuris was conjecture, hyperbole, and likely wrong. There was even a section questioning whether the Mythaspuris might have been entirely fictional.

However, the chapter Master Molni had brought to Cinder's notice was a critique of several documents said to have been written by Indrun Agni, one of Sapient Dormant's most trusted lieutenants and a Mythaspuri somehow lost to history. He had several interesting declarations to make. Indrun claimed there existed an infinity of Anchored Worlds, a term he used to depict the various aspects of creation. The Realms he called them—such as the Realms of the Rakshasas—and some of them existed in close conjunction to Devesh, while others endured nearer to His great enemy, the Empty One.

The Empty One. The name alone caused Cinder to shudder, and a cold dread like maggots crawled up his spine. There was also a passing reference to the Empty One's son, Zahhack. Cinder frowned. *Zahhack.* The same name as the creatures in Shet's hordes. There had to be a connection. The same allusion stated that only Zahhack could safely speak the Empty One's true name. Anyone else would earn His Father's terrible attention.

There were a few more passages, mostly critiques, but Cinder skimmed those parts. He landed instead on another interesting item, a supposed explanation of the supernatural. According to Indrun, *Jivatma* encompassed *lorethasra*, but it included the additional Element of "mind," and it stemmed either from Devesh, reflecting His glory, or from the Empty One and involved His ruinous power. But when it originated from the Lord, some viewed it as a shimmering pool.

Interesting.

The rest of the chapter proved less thought provoking, and when he finished with it, Cinder glanced out the window. His eyebrows rose when he realized he'd spent the better part of the morning reading in the library. It was time to get some other work done, like training at the Cauldron. He re-shelved the book and headed out the door, pausing long enough to thank Master Molni for his help.

"You're welcome," Master Molni said. "Did you find what you were looking for?"

"Not entirely, but it helped," Cinder said.

"Well, let me know if you need anything else."

"I will. See you tomorrow."

Cinder exited the library and re-entered Firemirror Hall. His head was bent as he considered the notion of *Jivatma*. He knew the term, encountering it last year, and thought it was a synonym for *lorethasra*. Now, it seemed that it possibly wasn't. He'd have to investigate the matter more thoroughly.

A few turns of the corridor later, he ran into Anya.

As always whenever he saw the princess, he took a reflexive sharp intake of breath. Given her warrior's bearing and build, everyone who met her likely thought her striking, although some idiots—elves, mostly—thought her merely pretty. They were wrong. Anya was breathtaking, young for her kind—in her early one hundreds—with honey-blonde hair, sparkling, emerald eyes, and a playful smile that almost always lit her face.

She gave him a crooked grin containing her usual undertone of teasing. "You appear to be pondering a matter of great consequence."

Cinder smiled at her, surprised anew that he was taller than her. It hadn't been the case this time last year. Anya was a tall woman, but Cinder had grown quite a bit since his entrance to the Third Directorate. "I was thinking about something I read."

Anya tilted her head. "You're always wanting to learn. Gaining knowledge is an admirable goal."

"A better one is to grow in wisdom."

She arched a single brow. "A curious outlook." She gestured to the shoke at his hip. "Were you planning on sparring?"

"I was, and it looks like you were, too," he said, noticing her own shoke and the pair of leather helmets she held. Governors, they were called. For humans, they served to protect their heads. For woven, they did the same, but they also regulated their ability to source *lorethasra*.

Anya nodded. "I was, but only if I can find a worthy opponent."

Cinder laughed. "A worthy opponent? For you? I'm not sure one exists, except maybe Lisandre." He shrugged. "But until one shows up, I will happily volunteer my services."

She chuckled in response. "We'll see. Most folk don't enjoy a beating."

Cinder gave her a sneaky grin. "I've learned some new tricks."

"New tricks? This I have to see. Are you free now?"

Cinder nodded. "I was actually on my way to the Cauldron."

"Perfect." Anya indicated for him to lead the way.

They made their way through the Quad, which was bathed in sunshine. Birds warbled, and a gentle breeze blew, whispering through the leaves and brush. A few other members of the Directorate were about, mostly faculty or elven warriors who had come to the academy for further training.

Cinder greeted those he and Anya came across with a quick dip of his head. The third time one of them gave him speculative glance, he glanced askance at the princess. "I'm thinking your people are wondering why I'm walking at your side. Should I drift back two paces as is considered decorous?"

"They aren't thinking about me. It's you they're wondering about. They know what you did in the Grand Melee and the Unitary Trial."

It made sense. Cinder had defied so many odds by all that he had accomplished in the Third Directorate, but the increased scrutiny made him uncomfortable. He offered a joke, more to resolve his own discomfort than to help with anything Anya might be feeling. "And you're sure it's not because I should be walking two paces behind you as is considered decorous?"

Anya gave him a wry smile. "That's only for the empress. It's considered decorous to walk two paces behind her. No one else."

Only the empress. Cinder would have thought it true for all members of the royal family, at least in formal settings. "Not even for you, a princess?"

She shook her head, still smiling. "Not even the heir to the throne."

"The heir is your sister, right? Enma."

Anya nodded, her smile transforming into a slight tightening of her lips. Clearly, there was tension between her and Enma, and Cinder wondered about it. Why would Anya have issues with her sister? And would it be considered impolite to ask about matters related to the two of them.

Anya surprised him. "You want to know about Enma."

Cinder started. *How had she known?*

Anya chuckled. "Your curiosity was obvious."

Cinder held his tongue, not sure how to respond.

"And I won't tell you much about Enma, except to say that she is beautiful, intelligent, and intense."

"It sounds like she will make an impressive empress," Cinder said, speaking cautiously and still not knowing what bounds he might be crossing. He wished he had never brought up Enma.

"You don't need to be so careful about speaking about my sister," Anya said, apparently trying to set his mind at ease.

"I was worried I might have overstepped my bounds."

"You didn't, and if you do, I'll let you know. You have nothing to worry about."

They walked the rest of the way to the Cauldron in silence, arriving at an area of grass and wildflowers where rings of stacked stones formed sparring circles, each one roughly thirty feet in diameter. Most were floored in dirt or sand, others in grass, and a few in flagstones. This was the Cauldron, a place where warriors sought greatness.

"Are you ready?" Anya asked, going to a sparring ring. She had her shoke in hand, and the governor on her head.

Cinder followed suit, standing on the opposite side of the training circle, watching Anya, focusing on her stance and posture, trying to determine what she intended.

"Begin," Anya said. She came at him hard, giving him no opportunity to decipher her plans.

Cinder lost within five strokes, a hard crack to his left bicep, and he dropped to the ground, biting back a scream of anguish. No blood flowed, and the worst he'd be left with was a bruise, but that wasn't the reason for his reaction. It was because a shoke caused a phantom pain that was identical to the injury a bladed weapon in a similar situation would have delivered.

Anya glared at him, clearly annoyed. "What was that? I know you can do better. I've seen it. Focus. If you plan on earning the privilege of accompanying me on your Secondary Trial, you will have to give a greater display than what you just offered."

"I have to earn the privilege of accompanying you?"

"Of course."

Cinder reviewed his schedule for the coming year. Seconds underwent a more rigorous training program than they did in their first year. In two months, all of them would leave Yaksha proper again for the Autumn Trial, a months-long campaign in the Dagger Mountains. And following that, in spring and early summer, they would take part in the Secondary Trial.

The latter required a sponsor, and for humans and dwarves, the simplest solution was to join their home armies. The elves, on the other hand, would each travel with a ranger during their Secondary Trials. Anya had offered to do the same for Cinder by sponsoring him, but apparently, matters weren't as simple as he thought.

"How do I earn your sponsorship?" he asked.

"By training hard and proving yourself against everyone and anyone, no matter what skills they use. I won't take you otherwise. You can defeat any Second with your sword. You did it in the Grand Melee when it was skill-on-skill alone. But unless you can also do so while your opponent is wielding *lorethasra*, you're of no use to me. You would be a danger to yourself, to me, and your unit."

Cinder frowned. What Anya asked was impossible. The elves possessed strengths and powers he couldn't hope to compete against. They had insurmountable skills and abilities…

His concerns trailed off, and he reconsidered what he knew about the elves. Maybe their powers weren't insurmountable. After all, he'd defeated six spiderkin by himself during the Unitary Trial. It was a feat few elves could duplicate, and it had been due to his *lorethasra*.

"You're scowling at me," Anya said, sounding disappointed in him. "Being angry with my decision won't change it."

"I wasn't scowling at you," Cinder said. "I was thinking about the Unitary Trial and when I killed those spiderkin. When I conducted my *lorethasra*. I need to learn how to do so more regularly."

Anya nodded. "A good start, but you need to learn to do so in the midst of combat. Better yet, before combat even starts. Not just when you're calm. You need to—"

"I think I can manage," Cinder interrupted, annoyed with what felt like condescension on her part. He went to the other side of the sparring ring. Prior to readying his shoke, he reached into the depths of his core. Soon enough, he saw it, the perfectly reflective pool he knew as his *lorethasra*—or was it really his *Jivatma* since he could visualize it?

He reined in his wandering ruminations. Whatever it was—*lorethasra* or *Jivatma*—it glistened in his vision. So did the familiar and painful blue-and-green flashes of lightning. By now, he was wise enough to simply hold it in his mind, do nothing more with it as it enhanced his senses.

"You have your *lorethasra*?" Anya asked.

"I'm ready."

"Thirty-three."

Cinder blinked in uncertainty. "What?"

"It took you thirty-three seconds to conduct your *lorethasra*." Without another word, she came at him.

Cinder met Anya's attack, his intuition guiding his movements. He slapped aside a thrust, evaded a follow-up side kick, and slid to her left. She sent more attacks. Cinder defended, keeping up with her ever-increasing speed. Surprised pleasure lit Anya's features, then concentration. She moved more quickly. Cinder felt his form fraying. He couldn't keep up with her, even with his *lorethasra* leaking into him.

The end came in a slash he was late in defending, followed by a trip, and her shoke tapping his neck. "Dead."

He'd done better than the first time, but it still wasn't good enough. He had to be superlative in order to win a place next to Anya. It wouldn't be easy; likely the hardest thing he would ever do. "Were you conducting your *lorethasra*?"

"A small weave only."

Cinder grunted. *Good.* It meant she hadn't beaten him through skill and physicality alone. She had needed her *lorethasra* to win.

It was progress on his part.

"Again?" Anya asked, standing at her starting position in the training ring.

Cinder answered by resuming his starting position. While he walked toward it, he tried to punch through the blue-and-green lightning to more fully conduct his *lorethasra*. The immediate slice of agony had him retreating. He would have to settle for his usual bare trickle.

"Begin," Anya said.

They shuffled toward one another, but this time Cinder initiated the action. He pushed her, trying to gain a better sense of her timing. He stayed with her until she accelerated the action. He held on, keeping up with her. Their shokes clashed, and they separated.

She came faster on the next pass. Another clash of shokes, and he darted back from a front kick.

Faster still, and Cinder began to struggle. Anya moved in a blur. He could barely see her attacks coming. His form disintegrated as he desperately fought to stay ahead of her. He managed for a few seconds, right until she got him off-balance. A trip he never saw coming and a tap of her shoke to his chest and it was over.

Cinder grimaced. "Dead."

"So you are," Anya said.

Cinder rose to his feet and resumed his place in the training circle. The path to excellence required failure more than success, and it seemed his path would be very long indeed. He made a decision then. He might never overcome Anya's speed and strength, but he could at least close the distance in skill and experience.

Anya smiled at him, seemingly understanding the strands of his thoughts. "Good. Fight to improve. Fight for what you want."

Cinder nodded. "How else will I earn a place by your side?"

She nodded. "This is the way.

2

Aweek later, classes for the Seconds began, and their first was
Equitation.

Cinder stood at attention between Bones and Wark as Master Halin
Dorund, their instructor, prepared to address all the human and elven
Seconds. Their mounts rustled restlessly behind them.

Clouds drifted across an endless expanse of blue while a warm summer
sun shone on the flat field on which they waited. This was part of
the racecourse they had completed during the Grand Melee, a set of
obstacles—barrels and low-lying hedges—meant to test the ability of
a rider and mount to take tight turns and maintain speed. Cinder and
Fastness hadn't done well in this section of the course, mostly because
Cinder wasn't very good in the saddle.

Cinder glanced around, searching out any differences in the course,
but a quick perusal revealed no changes.

Master Halin continued to gaze at them from where he sat, mounted
upon a roan gelding, graceful when astride a horse and giving no
hint of the limp left to him by the severe battlefield injury he'd suffered
decades, or centuries ago. The master was of middle years for an

elf—in his late two hundreds—but his hair remained black, and his eyes were clear and observant as he assessed them.

Cinder's white Yavana stallion, Fastness, nickered. *"I'm bored,"* the horse said. Rather than clear words, his statement was more a set of impressions that only Cinder, as the stallion's rider, could interpret.

Such a link wasn't common. Most Yavanas didn't speak to their riders. It only happened on a handful of occasions, but the talent was part of what made the breed so special. That and their uncanny intelligence. Add in their size, speed, and endurance, and it was easy to recognize why Yavanas were considered the finest species of horse in the world.

Too bad they only bred true in the Cord Valley of Devesth, a Sunset Kingdom to the uttermost north and west of Yaksha Sithe.

Cinder, though, was limited in how he could reply. The skin of his thoughts couldn't be directly conveyed. They had to be spoken. He patted the stallion's muzzle. "I know," he said in reply to the white's complaint. "We'll ride soon."

Fastness shook his head, shoving Cinder with his head.

Cinder took an involuntary step forward, grunting. He regained his balance and glanced in irritation at the stallion, who whinnied laughter.

Cinder shook his head. He was one of the few people at the Directorate with a pure-bred Yavana. All the other Seconds except for Estin had horses of mixed ancestry. It meant their mounts weren't Fastness' equal, but at least they were more biddable. The white was too intelligent for his own good, and when he was bored, he descended to playing annoying jokes and pranks. Be it gently nipping at Cinder when he wasn't looking, flicking him with his tail, or tipping over a water pail, the young stallion could be a pest. In fact, Cinder often figured "Pest" to be a more fitting name for the big Yavana.

But he wouldn't trade Fastness for any other horse at the Directorate. He loved the stallion, and by now, he considered Fastness more of a friend than merely his mount.

Of course, having the white as his horse was a temporary matter. The stallion was too valuable to risk in the world at large, and after

Cinder completed his time at the Third Directorate, Fastness would
likely be retired to stud since he allowed no one else to ride him.

Master Halin cleared his throat, finally ready to speak. "You all did
reasonably well in the Grand Melee, and for that reason alone, I applaud you. And reports indicate that your performance in the Unitary
Trial was exemplary, and for that, you have my respect."

The line of Seconds shifted as heads lifted, shoulders straightened,
and they shared glances of pride. Cinder caught Bones' questioning
gaze, and he nodded in reply. Six of their own had died, but in the face
of all they had encountered in the Unitary Trail—the hordes of spiderkin—they *had* performed well.

Master Halin raised his hands, calling for quiet, and the shifting
ceased. "But your performance in the Grand Melee and the Unitary
Trial is part of the past. We can learn from it, but it provides nothing
more than education." He met all their eyes, his air grave. "Any glory
earned doesn't linger. By now, it's gone. It is this day and every day following which are more important."

Cinder found himself nodding in agreement. Master Halin spoke
the truth. The past was finished. Any successes or failures achieved a
day, a week, or a month ago were immaterial. What truly mattered was
learning from those events and growing.

"As I said," Master Halin continued, "you did reasonably well in
the Grand Melee, but here at the Third Directorate we expect mastery,
not 'reasonably well'. Starting today, we will begin bridging the gap between what was and what should be. You'll ride out in groups of three.
Your goal: complete this portion of the race as swiftly as possible but
as a unit. It will be a random drawing, so don't bother looking for your
friends."

His decision made sense. A warrior couldn't always expect to work
with those with whom he was familiar. Many times, a stranger would
be the one fighting at his side.

Master Halin called out the initial set of three Seconds: Mohal,
Depth, and Riyne. All three were skilled riders, and the trio completed
the course in good time. Next came Wark, Estin, and Ishmay. They

didn't do as well since Wark wasn't at the same level as the other two. It also didn't help when Estin's Yavana stallion, Byerley, bared his teeth at Ishmay's mare and lunged at her, causing her to shy off course.

Cinder was up next, riding alongside Bones and Loriam, a black-haired elf with whom he might have shared a half dozen words in their first year.

He mounted Fastness, patting the white's neck. "Come on, old son. Let's go wide open."

The stallion nickered excited agreement. Most of the time, he could be a pest, but when work was needed, he was willing to get it done.

Cinder had Fastness ride to the outside of the two. His Yavana was unmatched on a straight run, but the two of them couldn't take the barrels as quickly. Cinder lacked the skill to lean into the turns well enough. They'd be better off taking the longer route around the course whenever possible.

"Go!" Master Halin shouted.

Cinder flicked his reins, and Fastness shot off. Hooves pounded. Clods of dirt and grass blasted into the air.

Cinder only noticed it in passing. His attention was entirely focused on running the obstacle course.

They were a stride ahead of their partners in the run when they hit the first barrel and swung smoothly around it but still lost ground on the turn. Same with the next three barrels.

They were a full length and a half behind the others when they exited the barrel run. *Finally.*

Loriam shot him a frown. "Keep up."

Next came a short straightaway and the hedges. Cinder focused, hunching down and silently urging on his horse. Fastness could make up ground here.

His Yavana stallion surged after Bones and Loriam, vaulting over a hedge. Fastness landed, dug deep, and accelerated. A second leap. A third. Cinder matched the stallion's movements on each jump, and they reached the shoulder of Loriam's mount by the end of the straightaway.

One circuit down. Two more to go.

It was the barrels again. Fastness churned the ground, striving to keep pace with the others. Cinder had the stallion maintain his speed deeper into the turn, trusting the white to have the strength to slow harder than the other horses.

Fastness managed it, and Cinder leaned into the turn, his balance much better than the first time through. He squeezed with his heels, guiding the white with his shifting weight, reins relaxed. They shot toward the next barrel, nearly abreast of Bones and Loriam. All through the barrels, Fastness remained close to the other two horses. They hit the straightaway again, and this time, they nudged into the lead.

In the final circuit, they finished the barrels alongside the others, and at the hedges, Cinder had to rein in Fastness, holding back his top speed to allow the others to keep pace with him.

"Well done!" Master Halin shouted when they finished. "Well done, indeed."

They rode in a line back to where the other Seconds waited. Fastness blew hard, and his coat was covered with a light sheen of sweat. Cinder made a note to give the horse an extra measure of grain tonight.

"You've become a better rider," Loriam noted, "but right now it's your horse doing most of the work. Keep practicing and become worthy of him."

"I plan on it," Cinder said, accepting the charitably proffered advice, which was what he already intended. He leaned forward to pat Fastness' neck. "You hear that, old son? We'll practice more and no one will be able to keep up with us."

Fastness nickered in approval.

Master Halin had them out longer than usual, and after Equitation, the Seconds quickly got their horses settled in the stables before hustling off to Firemirror Hall and their next class, History. No one spoke as they rushed along. They didn't even have time to straighten their mussed uniforms—dark blue pants, gray shirts, and blue, knee-length jackets.

The sun was warm, and a mild breeze carried their stink. Cinder took a whiff of himself and the others and grimaced. A miasma floated about them, a rank mix of sweat, dirt, horse, manure, and feces. The latter was from one of the elves—Mohal—who had stepped in an unidentified type of scat somewhere outside the stables. He was frantically scraping a boot against the ground every few strides trying to get it off.

"Come on," Cinder urged Mohal when the elf paused again to scrape his boot against the ground.

Mohal finally managed to remove most of the scat, and he rejoined the others. In a bunched cluster, they reached Firemirror Hall, and racing up the stairs, they got to their destination: a second-floor classroom—the same one as last year for History.

Cinder blew out in relief. They'd made it. He paused to take in the space. Light flooded the room, pouring through a wall of windows, and through them was a view of Garad Lull lording over the Quad. Further on, there were the tall hills and mountains soaring around the academy.

The dwarves, who must have arrived minutes earlier, were spread out around the seven heavy, rectangular tables within the room. With only thirteen cadets remaining, there would be only two at each one this year.

Sriovey took a whiff when the humans and elves entered, and he scowled in disgust. "The hell did you dipshits do? Make mudpies with horse patties?"

"Shut it," Cinder said, sitting next to the dwarven leader. "Just be glad you're too short to ride a horse."

"And ugly," Ishmay added from the table directly behind. "No proper mount would ever let you ride."

Sriovey grinned. "That's not what your sister said."

Bones, seated at one of the frontmost tables, warned them. "Sisters are off-limits," he said, replaying an old admonition. For some reason, while Bones might mock someone's mother, grandmother, and even great-grandmother, he'd never do the same about someone's sister.

Estin, sitting at the other frontmost table, twisted in his chair, facing backwards. He managed to peer down his nose at Sriovey, wearing a pinched-mouth expression of distaste. "If we combed through every human and dwarf currently at the Directorate, do you think they would have enough civilized bones in their bodies to form a skeleton?" he asked the room at large.

"Fuck off," Sriovey said, still smiling.

"Are you cursing so much to make up for Nathaz's absence?" asked Riyne, who sat at a table adjacent to the dwarf's.

Sriovey's humor died. "Don't talk about Nathaz. You're not worthy to say his name. *Ghrina.*"

Riyne tensed. "What did you call me?"

Cinder perked at the sudden strain in the room. Another fight was in the offing, and he cursed under his breath. "Fragging jackholes."

"You heard what I said," Sriovey replied, appearing nonchalant in the face of Riyne's rising temper. "We all know what you did in the Grand Melee against Cinder. You couldn't beat him with skill, so you sourced *lorethasra* and tried to injure him, maybe disable him."

Riyne made to stand. "You'll eat those—"

Cariath Gelindum, the elf who had come in second in the Grand Melee, was seated next to Riyne and tugged frantically on the noble's jacket. When he had his attention, he whispered something to the other elf. Riyne gave a reluctant nod and sat back down.

Cinder eyed Cariath, who still had the same wild, curly hair as always—brown like brambles—and soft eyes of the same color. Cinder speculated on what the elf had said to Riyne. Maybe he'd ask him later. He and Cariath had generally gotten along well in spite of their differences; mostly centered around the fact that Cinder was a simple human and Cariath was an arrogant elf.

Lieutenant Capshin Sonsing marched into the room, breaking the tableau. The aide-de-camp to General Arwan was an elf in his early middle years, black haired, fit, and well groomed. Cinder had never seen him wearing anything other than an immaculately pressed officer's uniform. It was identical to the ones worn by the cadets, except in one regard. Rather than the bronze-eagle pins worn by the cadets, Lieutenant Capshin's was silver. It evidenced his status as an officer, and his rank was marked by a gold star on each of the two stripes on his left shoulder.

"We learned much about Yaksha Sithe last year," Lieutenant Capshin said without preamble. "This year, we'll expand our areas of interest to include the nations of Rakesh, Gandharva, and Surent. However, before we get to those places, I thought we'd start the lecture with a discussion about wraiths."

Cinder had read about wraiths, and he recalled some of what he knew. They were powerful creatures, humans once, who could somehow wield their *Jivatmas*. Yesterday, he had made the decision to privately insist on using the older term rather than *lorethasra*, the name used by the elves, dwarves, and other woven.

"I thought most all wraiths lived north in the WraithLands," Depth said, interrupting his recollections. The shorter Rakeshian sat sandwiched between Bones and Jozep.

Lieutenant Capshin smiled. "Most isn't the same as all." He clasped his hands behind his back and faced the class. "Let's see how much you remember from last year. *Porash nazah loni, telemarr rul.* What does it mean? Cinder."

Cinder didn't hesitate. "It's *Shevasra*. It means 'if you want peace, prepare for war.' It's the adage of Yaksha Sithe."

The lieutenant nodded. "Correct, and when it comes to war, an enemy of all peoples are the wraiths. Who can tell me the history of the wraiths? Where did they come from?"

Cinder knew the answer, and he raised his hand, a grin on his face. "No one knows."

Lieutenant Capshin sighed heavily, clearly unamused. "Thank you for your utterly unenlightening answer, Mr. Shade."

Cinder's grin fell away. In his mind, he figured the lieutenant would think the joke was funny. Obviously not. He raised his hand again, wanting to fix his earlier mishap. "No one knows because they appeared after the *NusraelShev*. Right after humans lost the ability to wield our *Jiv*—I mean, our *lorethasras*."

"Humans could never wield *lorethasra*," Estin said.

"There is no hard evidence that they could," Lieutenant Capshin said to Estin, "but the historical documents describing the state of Seminal prior to the *NusraelShev* would indicate that they likely could. We covered some of it last year when we discussed the founding of Yaksha Sithe."

Estin leaned forward, prepared for an argument. "Many historians disagree with those supposed stories of our founding. They think they're fables."

"So what?" Bones said. "What difference does it make? We're talking about wraiths. Not whether humans can or ever could wield *lorethasra*."

"But it is about humans wielding *lorethasra*," Estin countered. "Cinder was the one who brought it up."

Cinder didn't feel like arguing, and he waved aside Estin's words. "Fine. Pretend I didn't say anything about humans conducting *lorethasra* before the *NusraelShev*."

"Source," Estin corrected. "We *source lorethasra*. We don't conduct it."

"Fine. You *source* it." Cinder said, emphasizing the word and making sure Estin noted his mocking eye roll. "Forget I said anything about it, but the fact remains, that's when wraiths showed up. Right after the ending of the *NusraelShev*."

"What else can you tell me?" Lieutenant Capshin asked.

"They were once human, but now they're insane."

"Sounds about right for the species," Estin muttered.

Cinder ignored him. "They're also powerful. Most believe they *can* wield *lorethasra* given some of the things witnesses have seen them do, like call up earthquakes, wield balls of fire, shoot arrows out of thin air."

"Anything else?"

Estin, of all people, elaborated. "They're unthinking horrors filled with bloodlust. They shamble along, mostly as individuals but some-times in large herds, and their only goal is to feast on the flesh of any sentient being they come across. They don't feel pain or discomfort. The cold of the icy north doesn't bother them, and the best way to kill one is to stab them in the brain or decapitate them. Individually, they're more powerful than any woven but a holder, a troll, or a yak-shin, and they're one of the few things the zahhacks fear."

"An excellent summation," Lieutenant Capshin said. "Let's now dig a little deeper into what causes a human to transform into a wraith." He went to the blackboard and wrote a single word: pain. He underlined it. "In most every interview of the family and friends of someone who turns, it is clear that pain, a deep-seated emotional anguish, such as the murder of a child, is the spur that causes the transformation. And Mr. Shade is right. They *can* source their *lorethasra*. They must. In fact, some believe it is that exact action that causes their transformation."

Cinder shifted in his seat, frowning in unease. Lieutenant Capshin's explanation spurred disquieting thoughts. He recollected again the pain needed to conduct his *Jivatma*. The razor-sharp whipping of the blue-and-green lightning. He'd experienced the pain most fully during the battle against the spiderkin when the alternative to conducting *Jivatma* had been death. Now, he considered another more worry-ing possibility. What if the agony of pressing through the lightning had some deleterious consequences? What if it turned a person into a wraith?

The day progressed, and Cinder found himself falling into the normal routine of the academy. The unchanging nature of his work helped set-tle his mind and take it off of his fallen brothers, and it seemed to help the others also. Some, like Wark, Jozep, and Depth, who had generally been quiet and reserved ever since the Unitary Trial, spoke more often as the day wore on, and they laughed a little more easily.

After a quick lunch, the unified group of Seconds went to the

Cauldron for training in weapons. The sunny day persisted into the early afternoon, and puffy, white clouds graced a bright, blue sky. A playful wind shifted the air, lofting the scent of wildflowers.

At the Cauldron they met Master Absin Morewe, their by-now-familiar instructor. He was an older elf, his age apparent based on his white hair and seamed face. While the years had stolen some of Master Absin's skills and speed, they had done nothing to defeat his knowledge. Cinder had sparred against the old elf on many an occasion during his first year at the Directorate, and those hours of training and instruction had been invaluable. They were the reasons Cinder could hold his own against any Second, and for those reasons alone, he would be forever grateful to the old blademaster.

The first time the once-Firsters had met Master Absin, he had held a switch in his hand. Never afterward, but for some reason this afternoon, he clutched it again. "Fall in," he barked.

The Seconds instantly obeyed, lining up based on their rank in the Grand Melee. As the Prime, Cinder held pride of place at the head of the line, and to his left was Cariath, followed by Estin and the rest of the elves, except for Riyne, who stood bracketed between Sriovey and Derius. His disqualification in the final event of the Grand Melee when he'd attacked Cinder with *lorethasra* had cost him a huge drop in the final standings. Worse, it had earned him a second black mark on his record.

Riyne came from a celebrated line of warriors, and the black marks might very well doom his chance for future glory. An *insufi* blade, a sword given to only the finest of warriors during the holy *Upanayana* ceremony, was the minimum of what others of his lineage had achieved. Several had even managed the exalted title of *Sai*, an ancient honorific from Shokan's time. Currently, less than a dozen elves could lay claim to the title. And Riyne might forever be denied such acclaim. In fact, the *insufi* blade itself might be beyond his reach.

Cinder studied Riyne, his mouth curled down in disappointment. How could someone so smart not yet learn life's hard lessons, especially when so many of those lessons had been piled atop his head? How was it he had yet to absorb the wisdom of humility and acceptance? Was he truly so stupid? *What a waste*. Riyne was skilled in all weapons, possibly the best overall warrior among all the Seconds, but his arrogance and his lickspittle attitude toward Estin had led to his downfall. As a result, there he stood, seventh in line when he should have been no lower than second.

Master Absin tapped the switch against his thigh, seemingly examining them. "You are the survivors of a catastrophic Unitary Trial, and for that alone, I applaud your courage and skill." He paused. "But you also need to continue your work and progress onward as warriors. This year, the woven must obtain further mastery in the use of their *lorethasra* in battle." Excited murmurs arose from the elves and dwarves, and Master Absin smiled, one promising pain rather than pleasure. "Yes. There is much you have yet to learn. The instruction is often harsh. Prepare yourselves." His smile faded. "As for the humans, you will master your weapons as few of your kind can." He hesitated. "I would also ask you continue to reach for your own *lorethasra*. Use the breathing technique I taught you last year."

Less excited murmurs met this declaration, including a snort of derision from Estin.

After the Seconds quieted, the prince spoke. "Will we get to spar today?"

Master Absin addressed him. "Why do you ask?"

"I was denied a match in the finale of the Grand Melee," Estin replied, nose high and tone haughty. "One in which our kind can go full out with our skills."

"And whose fault was that?" Sriovey muttered, loud enough to be heard by everyone.

Estin glared at the dwarven leader.

Cinder in turn glared at the prince. He knew what Estin wanted. He wanted a fight. A rematch from when Cinder had destroyed him during their duel.

Fragging prick.

After everything Estin had done last year, he had the audacity to act affronted? He had the audacity to remain selfish, unable to see past his own needs and desires. How was it possible for one person to be such an unredeemable jackhole?

Cinder had fought alongside Estin in the Unitary Trial, bled alongside him. They had both seen their brother warriors die. Did their shared mourning mean nothing? The memorial for the fallen had occurred only a few days ago, and Estin's behavior was unchanged.

Cinder clenched his jaw. Fine. He'd give Estin a rematch. He owed him a beating anyway. "I'll fight you. It's what you want, right?"

Estin slowly turned to face him, smiling in predatory satisfaction. "You're a fool to accept."

"Silence!" Master Absin shouted. "This is my class, and in my class there will be no duels. If the two of wish to spar for honor or presumed glory, do it on your own time."

Cinder recognized the validity of Master Absin's admonishment, but he continued to eye Estin in challenge. The prince never backed off.

Master Absin threw his hands in the air in disgust. "Fine. If you two wish to spar, then you'll spar. It'll be the same rules as the Grand Melee, but only for two points, not four." He stabbed a finger at Cinder and Estin. "But this will be the end of the matter. Should either of you choose to test my patience again with this rivalry, you'll be cleaning latrines with your bare hands. Am I clear?"

"Yes, sir," Cinder said.

"Yes, sir," Estin said a beat later.

"Then get ready."

Cinder rid himself of his jacket and entered the sparring ring. He stood opposite Estin, never taking his eyes off the prince. Anger didn't cloud his mind. Only resolve. Cinder allowed nothing else. He was cold as a winter pond as he viewed Estin, evaluating his balance, the placement of his feet, the angle of his shoke. His eyes narrowed as his innate sense of a warrior's likely movements whispered to him.

He knew what Estin intended. The prince was as easy to read as a children's primer. Estin had already lost. He just didn't know it yet.

Cinder tightened his grip on his shoke.

"Fight!" Master Absin shouted.

Cinder allowed Estin to charge forward. As expected, the prince feinted a thrust. His balance shifted. *He's going to attack with a horizontal slash, step inside my guard, and follow-up with a knee to the abdomen.*

He parried the expected slash, slid to the side when Estin tried to close the distance. Cinder's counter diagonal chop landed. A hammer blow to the thigh that had the prince screaming. An unnecessary follow-up kick to the gut blasted out Estin's breath and all the elf could do was lie on his back and gape like a fish, the agony clear on his face.

"Two points and match for Cinder," Master Absin said.

Cinder stepped over Estin, an utterly disrespectful action, but then again, he didn't respect the elf. He paced toward the other Seconds, stopping in front of Riyne and staring hard. "Do we have a problem, too?"

Riyne looked away and said nothing.

Loriam thrust out his jaw belligerently. "You might be better than us with the sword, but you aren't a better warrior. If we were allowed to use the full array of our skills, you'd be dead inside of a single stroke."

Cinder was tired of elven arrogance. "Keep believing that," he said. "You're supposed to master your talents this year. So will I. All your skills will be meaningless against me. I'll destroy you. Every one of you."

"Big words from a weak human," Estin growled. He must have gotten back his breath and recovered from the pain of the shoke.

"I never ambushed anyone, nor did I ever fight from behind someone else's skirts."

"I hid behind no one," Estin snapped.

"Coward!" Cinder snapped. "Riyne might never earn an *insufi* blade because you convinced him to do what you couldn't. You hid."

Estin's face went white, but he had no chance to respond.

"That's enough," Master Absin said, getting between the two of them. "You've both earned the privilege of ten laps around the Quad.

Go!"

Cinder set off without another word. Estin fell in behind him. Neither spoke. Cinder knew the fight with the prince had been childish. He'd given in to his baser instincts, but he didn't regret what he'd done. Estin had needed another reminder of a simple fact: Cinder wasn't a weakling to be bullied. He hoped the lesson stuck this time.

3

After the laps around the Quad, Cinder returned to the Cauldron and studiously ignored the prince for the rest of the class. He was glad Estin graced him with the same sentiment. By silent accord, they stayed on opposite sides of the Cauldron. Cinder ended up paired up against Derius, and he trusted the dwarf enough to try something new. While he sparred, he sought out his *Jivatma*. He failed every time, and his inattention cost him. He ended up losing every match to the dwarf.

"What's the problem?" Derius asked after the third such defeat. "Before the Unitary Trial, you used to crush me, and I just saw you kick Estin's ass."

Cinder paused, considering what to say. He wasn't ready to divulge his secrets, but perhaps a bit of them? After all, Derius was a trusted friend. "Sometimes I can do things I shouldn't be able to. But it only comes to me when I'm utterly calm or facing death. I need to be able to do it when I'm in the crucible of combat."

Derius grunted. "Must be some weird human thing. You'll figure it out. Now, shut up. We have time to get in one more match."

They sparred again, and as before Cinder lost.

Then it was time for them to return to Firemirror Hall for their next class: Tactics and Strategy, held in the same classroom as the one for History. The mid-day sun shone through the windows, leaving the room warm. Cinder's sight went to the wall of windows, and he gazed at Garad Lull. The familiar fury rustled like an uncoiling snake, and he shifted his attention away from the Titan.

He took a seat next to Sriovey, and they talked about the day so far. The dwarven leader was disappointed in how the second year seemed to be an extension of the first one. "We're not doing anything different."

"You will be," said Master Nuhlin Genhim. He walked into the classroom, a broad smile on his face, and his blue eyes had the wide-eyed appearance of a youth. "Attend." He rapped his desk with his fist, quieting the room. "Today will be the start of a different class than the one you are used to." He stared at Sriovey. "From this point forward, we will examine *your* tactics and strategy in the small unit engagements you'll soon be facing. You have a little over two months before you ship out again for the Autumn Trial. You'll be in the wilds of the Daggers for a four-to-six week period of time, assigned to a unit of the Yaksha Army while you gain experience in killing spiderkin, zahhacks, and possibly wraiths. We will have you prepared as best we can for the dangers of the world beyond this academy."

Cinder wasn't sure what Master Nuhlin had in mind, and he shared a quizzical glance with Bones seated across the aisle. They shrugged at the same time.

Master Nuhlin folded his hands behind his back and began pacing, head bowed. "Let us review what occurred and try to ascertain how the deaths of our warriors could have been avoided." He addressed Riyne. "Tell me. What do you think might have saved our warriors?"

Cinder didn't think anything could have saved their brothers. There had been far more spiderkin, older and more dangerous than Loial Company had originally thought. The lack of accurate information was what had doomed their campaign, leading to a sequence of errors, each one piling on top of the other. The disaster started, though, when the Firsters had ventured into the cave. Everything after that fateful moment had been reactionary, choosing the best choice from a set of terrible options. It's how a battle was lost before it began, then all that was left was deciding the least bad course of action and hope the other side selected a worse one.

Riyne didn't speak up to answer Master Nuhlin's question, and the silence stretched. A few of the elves shared uncertain looks.

Master Nuhlin appeared to grow impatient. "Does no one have anything to say?"

Cinder, who had been unconsciously slouching, straightened in his chair. "The only way to have saved our warriors would have been if we never went into the fragging cave."

"You see no other options?" Master Nuhlin asked.

Cinder shook his head. "We went in. We discovered the enemy vastly outnumbered us, and they became alert to our presence. Once that happened, it was all over but the bleeding."

"Indeed," Master Nuhlin said. "What lesson can you take from this? Tell me." His gaze went to the rest of the room. "Someone other than Cinder."

Sriovey exhaled heavily. "It means if you aren't rightly prepared, prepare to be fucked."

"There are no good options," Estin of all people added.

Master Nuhlin gave a sorrowful nod. "Yes. Sometimes you do the best you can and have to live with the consequences."

Consequences. A long word yet utterly incapable of encompassing the depth of what it was meant to convey. *Consequences.* Death of loved ones. *Consequences.* Judgments to deliver justice for some and anguish for others. *Consequences.* Go into a cave and experience suffering. *Consequences.* Or don't go inside and be branded a coward.

"I didn't mean to bring up painful memories," Master Nuhlin said, "but this is an important lesson you should all ponder. There was no good outcome for what happened. Once you engaged based on Loial Company's faulty scouting report, your fate was sealed. There was no escape afterward."

Cinder slouched into his seat again. He'd already come to this realization on the journey back to Swift Sword. Even worse, this wouldn't be the last time he would have to live with such an outcome. It would happen over and over again. More friends, more brothers would die, and he'd have to watch it happen while he lived on. Or maybe he would be the one to die because of insurmountable odds. It was all-too possible given the life he'd chosen.

The knowledge left him feeling old and tired, longing for an easy life of ignorance. Or at least for the class to be over, so he didn't have to think about it anymore.

Unfortunately, Master Nuhlin wouldn't shut up. He insisted on pressing home his point, inserting it like a dagger. "The moment you stepped ashore at Swift Sword, you courted death. Perhaps the commander of the Loials could have organized his men in a different way. Sent scouts up ahead and back on your company's trail. Then others would argue about how those scouts would have been easily over-powered by the spiderkin and prevented from passing along any useful information to the commander. The company's warriors would have been whittled down with nothing to show for their deaths."

Bones spoke. "The way you describe it makes it sound futile."

"It was futile," Master Nuhlin said. "Futility. That is today's lesson. Learn it. Master it. Overcome it." He held up a finger. "Because I promise you, you will witness it many times in the years ahead."

His statement had the strange pressure of prophecy.

Tactics and Strategy ended soon thereafter, and the Seconds departed for their next shared class, Unarmed Combat. Just like last year, it took place in the Cauldron and was taught by Master Jovick Sonsen who waited for them at the sparring rings.

Master Jovick was a truly ancient elf, whose elderly appearance was belied by his hair. It should have been white, but instead it was dark like shoe polish. Otherwise, Master Jovick possessed wizened features, eyes cloudy with cataracts, and the blunt, surly affect of the truly old, the kind of folk who had no patience for foolishness.

"Hurry up," Master Jovick snapped when the Seconds didn't hustle as quickly as he would have liked. "Get your asses in formation." In addition to his surly demeanor, Master Jovick could bellow as loudly as a bull, and he had a barbed tongue that was perpetually ready, willing, and able to quickly exclaim his disgust.

Cinder stretched his legs, quickly getting to where Master Jovick stood scowling. The others sped alongside him, and they lined up just as they had for Master Absin. Cinder faced forward, squaring his shoulders and coming to attention as Master Jovick had always required in the past. The old elf silently scrutinized the line of Seconds, still glowering.

Cinder kept himself unmoving, and sweat beaded on his forehead. The earlier breeze had died down, and the afternoon sun blazed heat from a cloudless sky. It baked the sparring circles, causing the Cauldron to live up to its name and boil hot as an oven. It was unusual weather for the Directorate.

Master Jovick finally broke the quiet. "You'll pair up. I'll decide who. My decision." His glare settled on Cinder and Estin. "And I won't be having two dumbasses fighting for pride in my class. You want pride and glory? Go to Swift Sword. Go be a gladiator and join their stupid circuses. Am I clear?"

"Yes, sir," Cinder shouted, offering the only correct response.

Estin's reply echoed his statement.

"Good. Now let's see if you remember why you're here. The motto of this school. *Mastha par! Krathe lomon!* Tell me what it means."

As one, the Second shouted. "Cultivate perfection. Vanquish foes."

A smile cracked the façade of Master Jovick's irritation. "Damn excellent. It's time to work." He pointed to Cinder. "The first ranked dumbass from this morning can spar against Sriovey. Wrestling only. No punches or kicks."

Cinder silenced a groan. Wrestling a dwarf, any dwarf, was often an exercise in futility. Given their heavily muscled frames and unreasonable strength, it was akin to wrapping up against a silverback.

He mentally shrugged. No help for it now. Plus, the only way to improve was to accept pain and push for growth.

The other Seconds were paired off while he and Sriovey went to a grass-covered sparring circle. Cinder did some quick stretching, loosening up before they got started.

Sriovey did the same and glanced his way, his expression firm. "Just because you're the Prime doesn't mean I'm going to take it easy on you."

"Would never have expected you to," Cinder replied. Of course, he expected the dwarf to go all out. Didn't it go without saying?

"Let's see what you can do," Sriovey said. He bent his knees and hunched over a bit at the waist.

Cinder mimicked the dwarf's posture.

Sriovey stalked forward, and Cinder circled, trying to keep his distance. He watched Sriovey, trying to figure him out. The dwarf tried to hide it, but he shot several furtive glances at Cinder's lead leg.

Cinder knew what to expect.

Sriovey shot forward, looking for a single leg.

Cinder whipped his leg out of the way. He tried to get behind Sriovey, but the dwarf spun around too quickly. Cinder shoved him away and angled off, regaining distance. He continued to study Sriovey's posture, working to determine what the dwarf planned next.

Sriovey twitched his shoulder, thrusting his arms, like he was going to shoot for another single leg. Cinder bit and realized his mistake an instant too late. It was a feint. *Shit.*

Sriovey took advantage of his momentary lapse and shot again, deep this time.

Cinder had no choice except to sprawl. It wasn't a good position. He pressed his chest against the dwarf's back, pushing him into the ground, trying to control his movement. Sriovey tried to stand, and Cinder pushed down on the back of the dwarf's neck. Sriovey relaxed, and Cinder congratulated himself on his success so far.

Sriovey exploded, getting his knees and feet under his torso. He launched upward. They were chest-to-chest now. The dwarf's gorilla-strength arms went around Cinder's waist and squeezed.

Cinder had a moment to gape in dismay before his feet left the ground. He dug for underhooks, got a leg between Sriovey's, doing anything to prevent the dwarf from sending him for a body-slam.

It worked, but Sriovey still rode him to the ground, landing in top position.

Cinder immediately locked Sriovey in full guard, and once sure of his control, he shrimped, twisting to get out of the dwarf's grip. He might as well have tried to unwrap steel chains. The ground itself seemed to tighten about him. Cinder got his feet on Sriovey's hips, pushing him off before he could gain side control. The dwarf twisted with the motion, getting his hips out of the way. He braced his feet under him and pushed down on Cinder's left knee, levering it out of place. It gave Sriovey the room to scuttle into side control.

Damn it.

Cinder felt Sriovey's weight shift, and he recognized what was coming. He drew in his arms, preventing an armbar. The dwarf shifted again. An attempted front choke this time. Cinder fought for wrist control, but Sriovey was too strong. A few seconds of applied brute force later, and Cinder was forced to tap.

Sriovey rolled off of him and clambered to his feet. "You've gotten better."

Cinder was too caught up in the annoyance of defeat to appreciate the compliment. He hated losing, even when he knew he stood little chance of winning. *Show me someone who accepts losing, and I'll show you someone who will lose.* He didn't know who might have said the aphorism to him, but it was the truth.

There was one other thing he needed to know, though. "Were you conducting *lorethasra*?" he asked the dwarf.

Sriovey grinned. "Against a puny human? Why bother?"

Cinder didn't let Sriovey's needling bother him. "How about against an elf? You need it then?"

Sriovey's grin drooped. "Of course. They aren't as strong as us, but they have their own abilities. And I was joking before. I *was* sourcing against you. I even used a weave of Earth to trap you against the ground."

It was an unanticipated admission, one that left Cinder wondering what talents he might have if he had unfettered access to his *Jivatma*.

"You ready for round two?" Sriovey asked, interrupting his ruminations.

"Only if you give me your all, including your *lorethasra*."

"You'll have it."

"Then I'm ready as rain."

They fought three more matches, and each time Sriovey wore Cinder down and won. But each time, the dwarf had to use a weave of *lorethasra*, always Earth, which was the strength of all dwarves.

Cinder didn't mind. He was starting to sense when Sriovey was sourcing his *lorethasra*. There was a sound, like ivy rustling. Plus, he had the dwarf working, and by the end of their matches, both of them were gassed and in need of a breather. They joined Ishmay, Wark, Mohal, and Depth, who all sat on a set of stone bleachers, also taking a break.

The six of them watched the others continue to wrestle. Riyne was locked up with Bones, and for once, Cinder's friend appeared to be getting the better of the match. His self-confidence generally fled whenever he faced an elf, but not today. Bones currently had Riyne in a front headlock, threatening a standing choke, which Riyne had to accept by tapping.

Cinder loudly applauded his victory. Bones grinned in reply.

Next, his attention went to where Derius was locked up with Jozep. It was a close match, and the two dwarves crashed against each other, each one straining for an advantage. They broke apart, but an instant later, they went right after one another again, swift despite their bulk. Cinder shook his head in disbelief at their speed. How did they move so fast with all that muscle?

A stray recollection occurred to Cinder, and he spoke to Sriovey without thinking. "I remember a long time ago when Master Absin talked about who you once were. Soothing those in need, soothing their hurts. I asked Derius about it one time, but he wouldn't say anything."

Sriovey's eyes glittered in annoyance. "I told you. We don't talk about it."

"I know. I'm sorry. Derius said the same thing. I was only hoping..." He trailed off. He didn't know what he was hoping. This was clearly sensitive ground, but there was also a mystery here, one to which he felt drawn. Who had the dwarves really been? The books he'd read on the topic had been singularly unenlightening.

"I know you're only being yourself," Sriovey said, speaking into their silence. "Curious, but you have to understand. It's a painful topic. We don't talk about it to those who aren't family."

"I get it," Cinder said, holding back his disappointment.

Sriovey hesitated. "Nathaz told me once he was planning on sponsoring you to visit our crèche. I'm willing to make the same offer in his honor. We could tell you then."

Cinder frowned in confusion. "But don't merchants visit the crèches all the time?"

"They don't have a sponsor. Sponsored folk are considered family while they're visiting."

Cinder smiled as realization swept over him. An instant later, his eyes misted. *Nathaz.* He missed the dwarf. "Thank you."

Sriovey grunted. "Thank Nathaz. If I had my choice, I'd slam the front door on your ass."

The words might have sounded harsh, but Cinder wasn't fooled. There was an undertone of generosity and affection to them."

Cinder grinned. "Does this mean I get to meet your family?

Sriovey laughed. "Sure it does. I only hope they don't hate me. Introducing them to a jackass and all."

In a dark corner of the world there existed a dead city. Ancient and proud, but now its great streets were cast into shadow and gloom. Its winding parks and scenic views given over to coldness and hollow winds. And along those once-magnificent boulevards, within creeping darkness, Rabisu hungered. He had hungered for countless turnings of the wheel and the sun, for ages before coming to this realm.

His true home was a pallid place, bereft of life and food, and here, in this Realm of Seminal, he had thought to find satiety for his endless appetite, his all-consuming lust to imbibe every being he came across. Heremisth had told him it would be so, but Heremisth had lied.

True. Upon this world there existed an abundance of delicious food and wondrous creatures to feed his cravings, but none were available to him. Not often. Not unless they ventured near him, for otherwise he was trapped, locked within the walls and bounds of this dead city, held in place by a creature shining bright, who hid in a dark-souled temple in the heart of this place.

The creature was wise to do so, keeping within the wards of the only building where Rabisu feared to go. He knew when to give way. He recognized the power of the dark soul at the center of the city; the dark soul that might consume him. And surely it would, should it ever break free of the temple.

Rabisu shuddered. He wished to be long gone before that ever happened.

And now, there was a chance, an opportunity. He had scented a specific aroma on the winds, the heart of one Heremisth had told him could satisfy his hunger for a thousand years. Rabisu had thought that, too, was a lie. It hadn't been present when he first entered this world.

But now here it was.

The soul whose potency had shivered the tides of *aether* was here, upon this world, and Rabisu *hungered* for him.

And he knew how to lure him here.

Rabisu chuckled at his plan. In his original realm, he had been gifted with the power of prophecy, and many times had he twisted prophecies to suit his own needs.

And in this, the irony of what he intended was delicious. His freedom would come about through the unwitting work of Aranya. She would send the soul to this dead city and never realize she would be opening the doors to Rabisu's freedom. The soul would grant him the power to break his bondage, and, oh, how he would feast then.

It would all start with an *aether*-cursed creature; not one to be consumed, but one to be commanded. And one had answered Rabisu's call.

A bear. There it stood within the walls of the city, cowering and fearful. It would have shown wisdom to stay clear of this place, but Rabisu's will would not be denied. He would even help the helpless beast. He couldn't reach far into the world, but he could reach far enough.

Rabisu concentrated, and a vertical line split the world, rotating on its long axis and exposing a door swirling with rainbow hues. *Perfect.* Next, he bent closer to the bear and whispered his needs into the ears of the terror-struck ursine.

The words nearly shattered any semblance of the bear's intellect, and it howled in terror and pain.

4

The first week of school passed in a blur, and the Seconds soon settled into a familiar routine. Rise before dawn, go for an early morning run, share their classes and meals, finish any required research, and then relax for the evening in the common room. It was no different than what they had done as Firsters.

Most of the elves quickly found their footing as well, developing nascent friendships with the humans and dwarves. It was remarkable since they would have scorned those same individuals only a few months prior. Laughter flowed again in the commons as the humans, dwarves, and elves grew used to one another's presence.

Estin and Riyne, however, remained the exception to this growing warmth and fellowship. They persisted in holding onto what was a standoffish demeanor at best and prickly and arrogant attitude at worst. The two were usually huddled together, alone in an island of their own choosing.

Cinder wished it didn't bother him so much to see them like that, but if they wanted to isolate themselves from their fellow cadets, then so be it. It was their choice to make. But with their self-centered outlooks, they would ultimately fail in whatever they hoped to achieve. Giving, not receiving, was the key to healthy living. It was as true for the blacksmith, the accountant, and the baker as it was for the warrior. The best people gave rather than received and doing so made the world a better place.

Those had been Cinder's final thoughts at the end of the first week as he readied for bed. Darkness had fallen, and quiet blanketed the Directorate and the dorm. Before shutting off his *diptha* lamp, Cinder sent a silent prayer to Devesh, asking for a dreamless sleep. Recollections of Roria, Joria, and Nathaz continued to haunt him, and he hoped not to see his fallen brothers tonight. He shut off the lamp. Minutes later, he was asleep.

A powerful being stands upright on sturdy, powerful legs, which end at cloven hooves. Eight-feet in height and midnight-black in hue, his head is crowned with the curving horns of a bull. Red-eyes glow. A chained whip is coiled at his hip, and he clutches a massive trident like a lifeline. A Bael is the breed's name, and he chants:

> *By Her grace are we born*
> *By Her love are we made*
> *By Her will are we shorn*
> *By Her fire are we unmade*
> *And are reborn once more*

Cinder tossed restlessly in his sleep, coming close to awakening. The poem was familiar, achingly so, and he hated it. It was spoken by beings who…

Somnolence, warm and heavy, fogged his mind, and he lost the train of his thought. Sleep weighed on him like a warm blanket, and his restiveness softened. Other dreams beckoned.

Rumbling cries rise, a lion on the hunt. More than one. The sounds draw near.

My head snaps in the direction of the sounds. "Just our fragging luck."

"What in the unholy hells was that?" a golden-haired woman asks.

"Our deaths," says a Bael. The creature holds his trident in a steady hand and uncoils his chained whip, setting it alight. The flames crackle.

"Why don't we Blend?" a man asks, one close enough in appearance to the woman to likely be family.

"They see right through them," a familiar-looking, plain-faced man answers.

I address the two Baels. "Can you keep them off of us with your whips?"

"Doubtful," one of the Baels replies. "They are too swift."

"That fast?"

"Faster than you would believe."

The ghrinas—the woman and the man—form up.

Again, Cinder rolled in his sleep. The woman… He knew her. Or he thought he should. Same with the others. A tear leaked unnoticed down his cheek.

He might have fully awoken, but darkness shrouded his room. He inhaled deeply, and on his exhalation, the dream re-captured him.

Two lions enter my vision, and details emerge. The cats are golden furred, except on their backs where they bear a mottled black and yellow pattern.

Not lions then. Something else.

They near, and I inhale sharply. Each feline is thick and powerful, standing over seven feet at the shoulder and twenty-five feet from head to tail. They run with breathtaking swiftness. Their over-sized tails point straight back as they cover yards with every bounding leap.

Shylows. That is their name.

They are only seconds away.

I meld with three others, all close as brothers, joining with the plain-faced man and the two who share features similar to my own. My thoughts dim, and I become one with the other three. We form a Quad, a single group consciousness.

The Quad moves Primary to point. Secondary and Tertiary flank him. Quaternary holds the rear.

Quaternary throws a barrage of Fireballs. They streak toward the Shylows and miss entirely. Instead, they hit the ground in a dull roar.

The Shylows split apart, charging forward.

Primary steps forward to meet the attack of one of the great cats, but his straight thrust, usually so lethal, catches nothing but air.

The Shylow leaps over Primary.

Secondary and Tertiary are ready, but the Shylow dodges past them as well.

Quaternary faces a great cat alone. No one is near enough to support him. The Shylow lands and guts Quaternary.

The Quad becomes the Triad.

Dimly, the Triad recognizes the anguish of its members. They mourn the death of their friend, but the Triad is untouched by grief. It is charged with a mission: defeat the Shylows. Nothing else matters.

Tertiary charges from the right; Secondary from the left.

The cat spins and Tertiary catches a blow to his arm. It shatters, and he's sent soaring through the air. He crashes down, losing consciousness as his head smacks hard against the ground.

The Triad becomes the Duo.

Secondary manages to land a deep cut into the cat's shoulder.

The Shylow howls in pain and anger even as he spins about and rakes Secondary across the leg, causing it to buckle. Primary races in low and slashes the Shylow's rear leg, hamstringing the cat before it can deliver a deathblow to Secondary.

Secondary leaps straight up, stabbing through the cat's lower jaw and into its brain.

The animal keens a nerve-jangling scream as it dies.

The Duo turns to face the other Shylow, which is engaged with the others, the ghrinas and the Baels. One of their members is dead, a man. The woman lays face down as well, long hair matted with blood. Duo considers its options. Secondary's leg is damaged. He will be slow. The Duo can't attack as fiercely as it would like. Secondary needs protection and support. The Duo moves toward the battle, keeping Primary close to Secondary.

As the Duo nears, a Bael is crushed. He lands with an unmoving thud. Primary slashes at the remaining Shylow's unprotected haunch, but somehow the cat's tail, hard as bone and quick as a viper, strikes him, knocking him onto his back.

The Shylow howls in outrage. The other Bael has wrapped his blazing whip around the creature's neck. Smoke rises as fur singes and flesh burns. The Shylow pulls hard against the whip, yanking the Bael off his feet and toward the cat where the beast swats him into the ground.

Secondary uses the distraction to attack. He is too slow. The Shylow catches Secondary on his claws. With the last of its focus and the last of Secondary's strength, the Duo stabs, pressing Secondary's sword to the hilt in the Shylow's chest.

The animal screams, loud and terrible, before falling over dead.

The Duo dissolves, and I crash to my knees, sobbing in grief.

Cinder sat up with a shout, barely restraining a scream as terrible grief and terror coursed through him. What was happening to him? What did these vivid dreams mean? What were Baels? Who was the woman? Those people?

Tears streaked down his face. The dream… This one was different than any other he had experienced. The battle had seemed so real. He knew the men who had died, loved them like brothers. Their names were… He wracked his mind, but he couldn't bring them forth.

His fists gripped the sheets, and his jaw clenched—

Wait!

He latched onto the image of the woman. She was the same one from his dreams of the glorious city. The one who sang. He had seen her face in this dream, and he desperately sought to recall it, clawing at his memory.

Seconds passed, but her image wouldn't come, and he wanted to howl his fury. Who was she? Who were—

He realized all the images from the dream were pouring out of his mind like water draining from an upended bucket. In mere seconds, he couldn't recall any of the images. He couldn't remember anything but the notion of having a dream. One in which he'd been engaged in battle and those close to him had died.

And a woman with honey-blonde hair. Who was she?

And more importantly, who was he? Was he someone who had really lived and experienced these strange, impossible dreams?

Cinder remained awake well into the night, still struggling to make sense of the dream. Those images and people… they seemed so real. Who were they? And how was he connected to them?

He couldn't resolve the mystery of the dream's meaning, and after tossing and turning for a few more hours, fatigue eventually took hold, and he went back to sleep.

Early the next morning, well before dawn, he awoke. But the dream—or the remnants of the dream since he could no longer recall any details—continued to burden him. He decided to go on a run to clear his mind.

He exited Krathe House, entering a crisp morning where the sun was a mere gleam on the eastern horizon. Tall, black lampposts provided pools of light, and his breath fogged. He shivered. Yesterday's unseasonable mugginess had given way to colder weather, but at least the world was quiet. No sounds broke the morning's meditative calm.

Cinder was glad for the silence. He always loved this hour of the day, when everything was at rest and no one else was about. It was peaceful, and his world needed peace.

He started his run, initially moving slowly, not much faster than a brisk walk. He let his muscles loosen in the cool air, and after a hundred yards of slow jogging, he quickened the pace. His heart began beating harder and faster, his breathing deepened, and he focused on it, making sure to take deep inhalations and exhalations. No panting. His form required attention as well. He held his head upright. He kept his eyes straight ahead, maintained a slight forward lean while leaving his hands relaxed, shoulders pulled back, and arms pumping.

Faster. His breath plumed more heavily.

He accelerated, and while doing so, he reached for his *Jivatma*. It wouldn't come to him at first, but after closing his eyes for a few strides, the still pool became evident. It glistened just out of reach, wrapped in the blue-and-green lightning. Cinder didn't try to conduct it, though. He simply held his *Jivatma* in his sight, knowing an invisible thread of it was wafting into him.

He ran even faster now, pushing onward to the speed of an elf. He knew he couldn't maintain this pace, not for long anyway, but every day, he was determined to hold it for a little longer. The hypnotic nature of the run centered his mind, and his thoughts drifted. He recalled again the dream from last night, and it only cemented a truth he had long since recognized.

He wasn't normal. He only had two years of memories. Nothing of his current life extended past the well in which he'd awoken. Nothing except these strange visions of people existing in impossible places, but which nevertheless struck a resonance within him. They felt real, and Cinder was starting to wonder if they were.

The contemplations disturbed his smooth gait, and he stumbled. Long practice allowed him to recover his pace. On he went, but this time he forced aside the indecipherable nature of his troublesome dreams and visions. He couldn't answer their meaning, at least not now.

He chose to bend his thoughts toward a different matter. It was one General Arwan, the commandant of the school, had mentioned several days ago. The new Firsters would arrive soon. In two days, and Mirk Bassang, a fellow apprentice from *Steel-Graced Adepts*, was one of them. Gorant Sin Peace, another student at *Steel-Graced*, had almost succeeded in gaining admission into the Directorate, but an unfortunate slip in his second entrance match had cost him. Hopefully, he would make it next year. Both him and Sash.

But for now, it was Mirk who had earned a place at the Third Directorate. Mirk, who worked harder than anyone Cinder knew. Mirk, who fought for every last scrap of ability, using the very dregs of his Devesh-given talent to improve himself. He'd served as an inspiration for Cinder during his time at *Steel-Graced*, and he smiled when thinking about seeing Mirk again.

Only two more days.

Until then and thereafter, Cinder needed to continue training. He ran on, maintaining the pace of an elf for another mile until the speed grew taxing. He was finally forced to slow and finished the final few miles at his normal pace.

He re-entered the Quad and headed straight for the cafeteria. He was famished.

By now, the sun was fully risen, sending fingers of golden light beaming through a thin cluster of clouds, but no one was yet about. A quick glance at lights shining from a number of windows told him people were starting to wake up and start the day.

Inside the cafeteria, he discovered no one else but the servers, who shared hushed conversations, occasionally laughing. Cinder greeted them and grabbed a tin plate, piling it high with eggs, grits, and several dosas. He also grabbed a tall glass of milk, sat at a table, and set to eating.

Anya showed up a few minutes later, sweat glistening on her brow. She must have been out running, too. For once, she wasn't armed. She gathered her own breakfast and joined him. There was still no one else around.

"You look out of sorts," she noted after taking a seat. "Have a samosa." She passed him one. "They make everything better."

"They do, but I like dosas better than samosas."

Anya laughed. "That's a silly rhyme."

"It is, but sometimes you need silliness," he said, "especially after a restless night and bad dreams."

A flash of surprise flitted across her face.

"What?" he asked.

"Some woven believe dreams are our minds' way of making sense of the world."

Cinder didn't think her statement applied to the dreams he was talking about, and Anya must have noticed his doubt.

"You disagree?" she asked.

"No," Cinder replied. "It's not that. I think you're probably as right as anyone about the nature of dreams, but in my particular case, I don't think it applies."

Anya quirked a half-smile. "It sounds mysterious. Am I allowed to know about these dreams, or is it a secret?"

Cinder didn't see the harm in telling her and explained about the visions he'd been experiencing ever since waking up in the well two years ago. He kept his report short and to the point, omitting the woman with honey-blonde hair, though. Anya's hair was the same color, and he didn't want her—or anyone—thinking his dreams were in any way related to her.

Anya tapped her lips. "What you say is interesting but not unexpected. You do have an unusual history, after all. It stands to reason that your dreams would be similarly unique."

"You think they're just dreams then?"

"What else could they be?"

Cinder shrugged, embarrassed now at explaining what in the light of day sounded trite and silly. He had vivid dreams. So what? "Nothing, I guess," he replied. "Just the result of too much time on my hands."

Anya's eyebrows lifted. "Don't let any of the other instructors hear you say that. I'm sure they would find plenty of ways to fill up any extra time you might think you have." She rose to her feet. "I have matters to attend, but do you have *time* to see me after your classes?" She grinned. "I have something which might help with your dreams. In the past, it has helped me. Meet me after supper at the Foe."

"I'll be there."

The rest of the day didn't contain any surprises, and after classes and dinner, Cinder collected his shoke and went to a special part of the basement of Firemirror Hall. There, he entered an old, familiar space. It was a broad cellar, musty and dank, barely illuminated by a couple of dull *diptha* bulbs.

However, the room's main feature was the hulking circular doorway hunkered in a corner and leading into a small alcove. Misery Gate was its name. It was black and made of a mysterious stone carved with strange symbols. They were the letters or words of a dead language— *Shevasra*—and no one alive could read it.

However, if manipulated in the proper sequence, the markings— chevrons—activated Misery Gate and led to the Foe, a strange half-world. There, warriors could train against spiderkin simulacra. They could battle at full speed and power, take any level of damage, including death of a sort, and yet exit the place healthy and hale since the injuries received in the Foe weren't real. They were like those delivered by a shoke, temporary and with no lingering aftereffects, no truer than the world of the Foe itself.

Anya hadn't yet arrived, and he chose to wait for her rather than activate the Gate. While biding his time, he studied the chevrons on the Gate. He'd examined them many times in the past, but their meaning always eluded him. Nevertheless, he persisted in his study whenever he was down here. There was something entrancing about the carved symbols, something that drew the eye.

Minutes later, Anya trotted down the stairs, and he ended his examination of the chevrons. He noticed she was unarmed, and he eyed her in unsurety. "We're not sparring?" He had thought that was what she intended. In the Foe, he could more easily reach his *Jivatma* and actually conduct it since the painful blue-and-green lightning didn't surround it there. He figured she wanted to see how good he was when he had unfettered access to it.

"We aren't sparring," Anya confirmed. "I want to teach you about Chakras. What do you know about them?"

Cinder allowed himself time to formulate his answer. He'd done some reading about Chakras, and he had his own notions about them. He just wasn't sure how she'd take his response. "I know what I've been taught, and what I think is more likely to be true."

Anya appeared intrigued. "What do you mean?"

"Woven source their *lorethasra* and purify it further through whatever Chakras they've managed to open. From there, they cycle it through their *nadis*—it's like another arterial tree—and into their bodies."

Anya nodded. "Everything you say is true, so what about it is wrong?"

"Nothing, but I don't think it applies to humans. According to accounts I've read, humans used to source their *lorethasras*, but they didn't need Chakras to use their power. They were able to directly weave Elemental threads from their *lorethasra*: Fire, Earth, Air, Water, and Spirit."

Anya crossed her arms. "I've read similar accounts, but no other race can make such a claim."

Cinder shrugged. He hadn't expected her to accept his words without dissent. "Every record about Shet states it's what he did."

"Shet was a god."

"He was a human first, and they say he was once an *asrasin*, a type of ancient human—

"I know what *asrasins* supposedly were," Anya cut in sharply. "But regardless of what you think, there's no proof." Cinder was about to reply, but she waved him to silence. "We're drifting afield of what I asked. I asked you about Chakras. What else can you tell me about them? Do you know their names and their location?

Cinder wanted to discuss his theories in greater detail, but since Anya didn't want to hear them, he acceded to her request. "There are seven Chakras. Opening one allows a woven to send a more purified form of *lorethasra* into their *nadis,* thereby granting them greater powers. The first one is *Muladhara,* the Root Chakra. It's a red, four-petaled lotus and is supposed be located in the pelvic floor. It signifies Earth and allows for acceptance, confidence, and security. More is known about *Muladhara* than any other Chakra, but even then, only one in a thousand manage to open it."

Anya nodded. "Very good. Continue."

"The second one is *Svadhisthana,* the Sacral Chakra. It's an orange, six-petaled lotus and located in the lower abdomen. It allows for the heightened mastery of fluids and senses. It's related to Water. Even fewer woven manage to open it. Around one in a hundred thousand. Next is *Manipura,* the Solar Chakra. It is behind the navel and is represented by a ten-petaled, yellow lotus. Only one in ten million manage to open it."

"Woven don't necessarily open the Chakras in order from *Muladhara* to *Manipura,* but you are correct. It is only one in ten million who can open any three Chakras."

Cinder dipped his head in acknowledgement. "*Manipura* is supposed to allow for mastery of the body and movement through Fire."

"What about the rest of them?"

Cinder had a question of his own. "Why are we doing this?"

"Because I need to know what you don't know before we enter the Foe. We're not going to fight spiderkin tonight. I'm going to teach you how to open your *Muladhara.*"

Cinder frowned in surprise. Was opening a Chakra even possible for a human? And what might it mean for him if he could? How would it help him?

"If you can source your *lorethasra* as you did when you fought the spiderkin during the Unitary Trial, you also then need to open your *Muladhara*. It may be the only way for you to escape the limitations of your species. The only way to forge yourself into the warrior you were meant to become."

Again, her answer was unexpected, and this time it had the strange cadence of prophecy.

"There's more to tell," Anya said, "but finish listing the Chakras and I'll explain the rest of what I mean."

"The fourth one is *Anahata*, the Heart Chakra. It is located at the level of the heart, and is a green, twelve-petaled lotus, somehow related to Air. The fifth one is *Vishuddi*, the Throat Chakra, and it's in the throat. A blue, sixteen-petaled lotus signifying *aether*."

"Or *lorethasra*," Anya said. "We're not sure which."

Cinder shrugged. "The sixth Chakra is called *Ajna*, the Third Eye Chakra. It's in the middle of forehead. It's an indigo, two-petaled lotus." He halted his recitation. "I always thought *Ajna* was strange. Each Chakra has more petals than the ones below it, but not *Ajna*. It only has two."

Anya appeared amused. "Consider it part of the mysteries of life," she said. "Continue."

"There's only one left," Cinder said. "*Sahasrara*, the Crown Chakra. It has one-thousand-petals, is violet in color and exists in the space immediately above the mind."

Anya smiled in pleasure. "Well done. You're ready to learn." She gestured to Misery Gate. "Do you know the sequence which opens the Foe and produces no spiderkin?"

Cinder answered by pressing the chevrons in the prescribed sequence.

He stepped to the side and watched as the symbols began to glow golden. A flash of light lit the room, followed by the explosion of something that had the appearance of bubbling water. Whatever it was, the liquid blasted out from Misery Gate, extending twenty feet into the basement as a single, bulbous mass before collapsing on itself in a rush and forming a watery, mirrored film, which filled the black doorway.

"Follow me after a count of five," Anya told Cinder. Once he affirmed her instructions, she took a deep inhalation, preparing herself for Misery Gate. She stared at the watery screen, knowing what was coming and hating it. Everyone did.

Not allowing herself any further weakness, she pushed through the film filling the Gate. The instant she did, an icy chill passed through her, one reaching to her core. Her muscles involuntarily tightened, but the cold instantly dissipated when her next step brought her into the Foe. Now, it was nausea souring her stomach, and she had to work to keep from vomiting. It only required a few seconds of eyes-closed deep breathing to manage the task. Given how often she had been to the Foe, she was used to it by now.

Anya moved away from Misery Gate and examined the place in which she found herself, a small glade, quiet and peaceful until the spiderkin arrived. They wouldn't this time, though. Cinder had activated the chevrons in the correct sequence. The two of them would have the Foe to themselves, only sharing it with the towering evergreens of the nearby forest and the mountains looming in the distance. Cinder could have set the Foe for twilight, dawn, or night, but he'd chosen noon. Nevertheless, while the sun might have stood at its zenith, it couldn't rightly be seen as anything but wan gold light, one containing the pallid light of an eclipse.

Seconds later, Cinder entered the Foe, and his reaction surprised her. He didn't grimace from the bone-deep cold of the crossing or the nausea present on arriving here. He simply glanced around, fully recovered from one step to the next.

Impressive. Then again, Cinder *was* impressive, not least because of his ability to match one of the Blessed Race when it came to combat. He also had many other admirable qualities. His intelligence, his generosity, and his desire to lead rather than merely command. It also didn't hurt that he was handsome.

Very handsome.

"What now?" Cinder asked, interrupting her ruminations.

Anya shut off her considerations about Cinder and refocused on the matter at hand. "Now we sit, and I show you what you need to learn. What you said about the Chakras was correct, but what you have is only information. What you require is practical knowledge. Do what I do." She eased herself to the ground and assumed a cross-legged position, one foot on each knee.

She waited for Cinder to copy her posture.

"How will learning about Chakras help me with my dreams?" Cinder asked. "At breakfast, you said you had something that might help me with them."

"Learning to open a Chakra, any of them, brings a certain peace. I used to have troubling dreams, too, but once I opened *Muladhara*, they…" She sought her words. "…became less frequent. I still have them, but not nearly as often."

She caught Cinder viewing her skeptically. "What kind of dreams?"

"The kind that woke me up at night, terrified."

"Nightmares?"

"Somewhat," Anya allowed, not wanting to divulge the truth about her human past life and her husband, Rukh. "Now. Learning to visualize your Chakras takes practice, and it becomes increasingly difficult to open another one."

Thankfully, Cinder let the matter about her dreams drop. "How do I view them?" he asked.

"Through quiet contemplation," Anya said. "Close your eyes and center yourself. Let no stray considerations cause distraction. Feel the world around you. The ground underneath you. Imagine your body filled with a desire to grow, to expand its potential. Feel your breath bringing life to you. Recognize the steadiness of your heartbeat. When you've done this, you're ready. Seek inside. The easiest Chakra to open is *Muladhara*. Search for the potential place in your sacrum. It will feel like a place of fertility, and within it, you will see a red peach pit primed for growth."

She watched as Cinder did as she asked. His eyes closed, and his breathing steadied. He appeared to be at peace, but after a few moments, a frown creased his forehead.

Anya smiled. Everyone frowned the first time they tried to reach *Muladhara*. She was glad to see Cinder do so as well. At least in this matter, he was no different than everyone else. "You can't force it," she chided. "It's best for now if you simply practice the breathing and the recognition of your heart's stability."

"I'm trying," Cinder said, sounding for all-the-world like a petulant child.

Anya's smile widened. She found it endearing, seeing him struggle since he so rarely did.

"I can tell you're grinning," Cinder said, eyes remaining closed.

Anya chuckled. "It took me a full year to see my *Muladhara* and two more to imbue it with enough *lorethasra* to actually purify and open it. Considering this is your first time, and you've only been trying for five minutes, I hardly think what you've done counts as failure."

Cinder's eyes snapped open, his features filled with shock. "It took you a full year to see it? Does everyone else take so long?"

"A single year is fast," she replied. "Most people require ten or more."

"Oh." Cinder blinked. "I'm sorry. I didn't mean to insult you."

"You didn't." Anya offered a faint smile, touched by his apology. "Now close your eyes and try to see your *Muladhara*."

Rather than do as she instructed, Cinder chose to question her again. "What about the other Chakras? Do woven visualize them the same way."

Anya shook her head. "No. Each one needs to be reached in their own way."

"But why do it like that?" Cinder asked. "Why is it necessary? Why not weave directly from *lorethasra* or conduct straight from *Jivatma*."

Anya frowned. In another life, she might have been able to conduct *Jivatma*, but no longer, and it didn't matter anyway. As far as she was concerned, it was a term from her dead past, unimportant to her life today whether it really was different from *lorethasra* or not. She said as much to Cinder.

"Yes, but what if someone could conduct *Jivatma*?" Cinder asked. "*Lorethasra* contains the five Elements: Earth, Water, Fire, Air, and Spirit. But it doesn't contain mind. *Jivatma* does. Or at least some Mythaspuris said so. They also said it was the true soul. It seems like it would be more powerful."

"Maybe so, but conducting directly from *Jivatma* is a waste. It grants you abilities, true. But utilizing it in such a fashion causes it to diffuse through and out of your body. You lose the greatest portion of its potency." She enjoyed Cinder's surprise. "After our conversation about *Jivatma*, I did some reading. There is a journal supposedly written by Manifold Fulsom. Tell Master Molni I said you could read it."

Cinder leaned forward. "What does it say?" he asked, enthusiasm evident in his voice.

Anya laughed. She always forgot how charming and persistent Cinder could be when he was excited. "The reason to conduct *Jivatma* or *lorethasra*—I'm not yet convinced they're as different as you say— and send it through the Chakras is because you can then cycle it as *prana* through your *nadis*. It captures the full potency of what you can accomplish without losing so much to the air and *aether*. You can also then use your *lorethasra* on a more subconscious level."

"What do you mean?"

"I mean you can simply think about what you want to accomplish. Chakras allow your talents to become automatic. It becomes like breathing. You don't have to consciously think about taking a breath. It just happens, but you can control it to a certain extent. It's the same with *lorethasra* sent as *prana* through a Chakra. Once you manage to do so, you then can simply create the weave you have in mind without all the required mental preparation the *asrasins* apparently had to do. All their separating of Elements and connecting them and such."

Cinder wore a thoughtful expression. "I always thought woven just used Chakras to remove toxins from their *lorethasras*."

"Chakras do much more than purify," Anya said. "Now, can you please close your eyes and try to visualize your *Muladhara*?"

She hoped Cinder would acquiesce to her request, but as usual, he proved incorrigible.

"Can you demonstrate it?" he asked.

Upon hearing his tenacious questioning, Anya didn't know whether to laugh at him or shake him. She chose neither and decided to do as he asked. Through long practice, she easily centered herself and reached for her *Muladhara*, her Root Chakra. It existed in a potential space in her sacrum, and it swiftly came into her mind's eye, appearing like a blood-red nut. She then sourced her *lorethasra* and sent a pulse of it to her *Muladhara*. The red, four-petaled flower opened like a rosebud reaching for water. She sent more *lorethasra* into the Chakra, and it was transformed into *prana*, a golden fluid, a color richer than honey and glowing from within which spread through her *nadis*, suffusing her body. Her senses increased in clarity, and her limbs twitched with the need to burst into motion.

"Amazing," Cinder said. "Did you know your skin glows when you're sourcing your *lorethasra*. Your cinnamon scent is more prominent, too."

Anya had forgotten Cinder could sense her natural fragrance. She still didn't know how he could, and it embarrassed her. It was too intimate. Only the closest of her family could smell her cinnamon scent, and even then, only rarely. For Cinder to do so left her feeling vulnerable. "Close your eyes," she ordered, an adamant tone in her voice.

This time—thankfully—Cinder did as she instructed. While he tried to visualize his Chakra, she wondered about the future. During his Secondary Trial, when she took him into the Daggers, would he still pester her with so many questions?

5

The day after his time with Anya in the Foe was one supposedly meant for rest, but Cinder chose to spend it in training. It was his usual habit. While the rest of the Seconds scattered to Certitude to enjoy some time off, Cinder went back to work. After what Anya had taught him last night, he was intent on visualizing *Muladhara*, sooner rather than later.

He went back to the half-world of the Foe, but his hours spent there proved unproductive. Not only did he fail at bringing *Muladhara* to light—an expected outcome—he also received a mild headache for his trouble. Nevertheless, he didn't let his lack of success disappoint him. After all, Anya, who was said to be a prodigy, had taken a solid year to visualize her *Muladhara*. He had to take inspiration from that.

Afterward, Cinder went to the library and researched the infor mation Anya had relayed to him last night. He found the journal she mentioned, the one said to have been written by Manifold Fulsom himself, and the details in the small volume confirmed much of what the princess had said and left Cinder with much to think about.

After lunch, he went to the Cauldron where he sparred against Master Absin. Lisandre wasn't present, which was disappointing.

Cinder wanted to test himself against the elf, who was said to be the finest warrior in Yaksha—other than Anya.

And finally, to close out the day, he spent an hour at the archery range and a few more riding Fastness.

By then, it was evening, and everyone else had returned, regathering in the commons. Several of the dwarves and humans were playing darts. Others were discussing what they'd seen and done during the day while Ishmay and Jozep were teaching Mohal and Riyne how to play euchre. The presence of the latter at a table with a human and a dwarf was shocking. Estin sat in a corner by himself, reading a book, an island of quiet and unhappiness, given the looks of betrayal he kept shooting in Riyne's direction.

Otherwise, relaxed laughter filled the room.

Cinder was glad of it, and he smiled to himself as he sat on the couch positioned under the room's large window. Outside, the sun had set, and both moons had risen—white Dormant and golden Fulsom. Slivers of their lustrous light washed the world in an ethereal glow. Down below in the courtyard garden on the back side of Krathe House, flowers bloomed, and their perfumed scent carried on a cool, clean breeze. Anya was down there, too, tending to her plants. She was often gardening when she wasn't training.

Cinder might have stared while she worked, but he knew she'd catch him at it. She always did.

Making a wiser decision, he returned his attention to his mandolin, strumming a few chords and considering what to play.

"Don't be giving us any of your boring-ass, maudlin shit," Sriovey said from the other side of the room where he was playing darts with Bones and Derius.

Cinder grinned at the dwarf's common complaint, making sure to meet Sriovey's eyes and begin a song he knew would elicit an aggrieved protest.

Right on cue, Sriovey groaned. "Devesh, no! Anything but that fragging song."

"You said fragging," Bones chortled. "You dumbass."

"Shut up," Sriovey replied. "Besides, your sister made me promise to stop cursing."

Bones inhaled sharply, scowling. "For the last time, sisters—especially my sister—are off limits, you dickhead. Or should I bring up *your* sister."

It was a sore point for Sriovey, and he reddened, his face matching the hue of his beard.

Mohal interrupted their squabbling. "A mandolin on its own is fine, but wouldn't it be better if there were two instruments? Riyne can play the fiddle."

Cinder stared at Mohal in speculation. What was he trying to do here? Did Mohal really expect Cinder to play music with Riyne? Or was this some elven ploy meant to embarrass him? After a brief consideration, he decided to place his trust in Mohal's good intentions.

"Tell him to join me if he wants to," Cinder said to Mohal.

"You can tell *him* yourself," Riyne said, sounding irritated. "I'm sitting right here."

"Then get your fiddle if you want."

Riyne met his gaze, his expression inscrutable. After a few seconds, he shrugged. "Sure. Why not. I'll be right back." Riyne went to his room.

"But we need a fourth for the game," Ishmay complained upon Riyne's departure.

"I'll take over," Depth said. He'd already been lingering at the table, offering advice to the new players.

Riyne returned a short while later, fiddle case in hand. He sat down on a nearby chair, angling it toward Cinder. "Give me a second to get it in tune and warm up."

"Take your time," Cinder said. The moment felt surreal. What the hell was going on? Was he really about to play music with Riyne? The person he despised above all others, except maybe Estin.

Riyne adjusted the pegs of his fiddle, getting it in tune. He then loosened his fingers, running them along the strings. After a few minutes, he glanced at Cinder. "Ready?"

Cinder didn't answer at first, his mind still lost in the unreality of the circumstance. Waking up this morning, he'd never have expected to finish the day by playing music with Riyne Coushinre. Riyne the bully. The arrogant jackhole. The craven sycophant.

But here Riyne sat. Patient and waiting and without the slightest hint of mockery on his face. What was going on?

Cinder didn't know, and he mentally shrugged, deciding to give Riyne a chance. "Tell me if you know this one." He strummed the first few chords of a song he liked.

Riyne smiled. "Good choice."

Jozep jumped up from the euchre table. "Wait! I want to play. Let me get my tabla." The excitable, young dwarf darted out of the commons, heading to his room.

"Damn it!" Ishmay exclaimed. "Now we need another fourth."

"I'll take over," Wark said. He left the couch where he'd been talking to Loriam.

"Mind if I join you?" Loriam asked. "I've always wondered about this card game you humans and dwarves enjoy so much."

Wark shrugged. "Sure. I'll teach you."

Moments later, Jozep returned, settling himself on the couch next to Cinder. "On three," he said.

Three claps of Jozep's hands, and they were off, playing one of Cinder's favorite songs. It was about a group of strangers who bond over a time when all of them are trapped in an inn during a storm. They initially detest one another, but over the hours of their time together, they end up sharing their troubles and doubts, finding commonality. By the next morning, they've bonded, and they make a promise to always recognize and never forget one another or simply walk on by.

Riyne was smiling after they finished. "I love that song," he said.

"Do you know this one?" Jozep asked, setting a slow tempo.

Riyne answered by playing the accompaniment.

"Too slow," Sriovey complained. "It's a fragging ballad."

"It's not a ballad," Cinder said. The tempo slowly increased, and on a silent beat, it pounded like thunder, becoming ferocious.

They played on, but a few songs later, they needed to take a break.

Jozep went to get a drink of water, and after he left, Riyne spoke to Cinder. "I need to apologize to you," he began, "for what I did in the Grand Melee." He appeared to vacillate. "And for other things. I behaved dishonorably."

Cinder blinked in shock. On a night filled with surprises, an apology from Riyne was the last thing he would have ever expected. "Thank you for the apology," he said, still dumbfounded.

Riyne grimaced. "I made the mistake of listening to Estin. I shouldn't have."

"He is your prince," Cinder said.

"And I have my own mind. He made the suggestion, and I was the moron who agreed to his plan. It was wrong. I know it now. I should have known it then."

Cinder stayed silent, sensing there might be more to what the elf wanted to tell him.

Riyne didn't speak at first, and a pregnant expectation filled the air. "It doesn't mean we're friends," he said at last, "but I respect you."

Cinder accepted Riyne's statement. "Respect is probably the best the two of us could ever hope to share."

Fastness roused when a gentle wind swirled through the sweltering horse barn at the Third Directorate. The breeze was annoying, lofting stray stalks of straw into the air, some of which flicked him in the face. He snorted in irritation, shaking his mane and turning his back to the irritating wind.

And yet…

Fastness eased back around. His nose lifted, and he whickered softly.

The wind also delivered the distant scent of pine-freshness, of deep snow, and mountain coldness. The chill of autumn and winter were his favorite seasons. It was bred into him, in the soft snows and high country of Cord Valley in Devesth, and he oftentimes missed his home. He missed running to his heart's content, of racing the young stallions and fillies of his herd, of leaving them breathless and behind as they were unable to touch his speed.

He was Fastness, and none were faster.

Not even the wind.

Fastness stuck his nose out of his stall, breathing in the loveliness of the coming cold. And just as the wind filled his lungs, a strange understanding filled his mind. Or better to say, a strange wisdom swelled over his usual thoughts of running, eating, and sleeping.

This wind wasn't a beginning or an ending. It was timeless, and like an unheard song, it struck a chord of dimly recalled feelings and memories.

Fastness shook his head, unsure from where these bizarre thoughts were originating. He would ask his rider. Cinder was young, but he knew much. In that way, he was wise, although he sometimes lied and pretended to know something when he really didn't. Fastness remembered when his rider had told him about dragons. *Dragons.* Fastness nickered in amusement. Dragons weren't real.

Thoughts of Cinder reminded Fastness of their afternoon run today. They had handled the turns better, swift as any, including Byerley, the annoying black Yavana ridden by Estin, Cinder's hated rival.

Fastness snorted hard. He was faster than Byerley. He could take any turn swifter, and any straightaway more rapidly.

But he couldn't do so with Cinder on his back and Estin on the black Yavana. Cinder simply wasn't a good enough rider, clumsy and poorly balanced as he was. However, he was steadily improving, and soon he would do well enough for Fastness to lose no ground to Byerley on any portion of their runs. They would leave the black Yavana far behind them, unable to do anything but eat their thrown dirt and turf.

Fastness whickered in contentment. Byerley deserved many mouthfuls of dirt.

As he continued to stare out into the darkness, the serenity of the evening filled Fastness' mind, and his amusement faded. All thoughts of racing Byerley drifted away from his mind like dandelion seeds on the wind.

The night was fine, and he enjoyed the depthless silence of the darkness, remaining in place with his head outside his stall, at peace with the world beyond the barn. Insects made their noises, leaves on trees rustled, and the grass bent as the wind continued to blow.

But eventually, the wind died, and Fastness made ready to settle down and sleep some more. He halted, however, when the gleaming yellow moon in the dark sky captured his attention. He stared heavenward, at the drifting clouds high above; at the brilliant stars like a casting of gems; and the golden orb of the moon like a great eye peering down at him.

Fastness shifted about, uneasy for reasons he couldn't express. *Fulsom.* It was the name of the moon. Cinder had once told him so.

Fastness' mind went elsewhere. *Fulsom.* The name resounded in his mind, striking a familiar note. It reminded him of someone mighty, a friend from the past.

The next day, a slow, steady excitement built and percolated amongst the Seconds. All of them felt it, a burgeoning sense of expectancy. The new Firsters were coming, and the eagerness to meet them washed over the second-year cadets. The excitement carried into their classes as well, making it hard to concentrate.

Cinder would catch himself or one of the other Seconds grinning for no reason. All of them smiled more easily today, laughed more readily.

The instructors, too, except for Master Jovick. His dour demeanor was unchanged in the face of everyone else's excitement. Cinder reckoned the unarmed combat instructor had forgotten how to crack a smile.

The day progressed, and word came of the appearance of a few carriages entering the grounds of the Third Directorate. Cinder had seen one of them pull up and disgorge a cluster of confused-looking dwarves. A few Thirds at the Directorate had swiftly taken charge of the newly arrived cadets. Otherwise, Cinder had yet to meet any of the Firsters.

That would soon change. It was time for the welcoming ceremony in the banquet hall. Formal attire was required, and all of the Seconds, the Thirds, and the visiting warriors were already situated in the large room. The space was lit to brightness by large wagon-wheel chandeliers glowing with dozens of *diptha* bulbs. In addition, stray beams of the setting sun highlighted the many murals decorating the walls of the hall. Most of the images depicted famous elves from the past caught in a moment of martial prowess.

Four tables ran lengthwise across the room, one for each class-year and another for the elves here for extended training. The seating was determined by a warrior's standing. As Prime, Cinder sat at the head of his class-year's table, Cariath across from him, and Estin to his left. The rest of the Seconds progressed down the table. The Thirds were similarly organized.

There was also a fifth and final table. It stood upon a raised dais, positioned perpendicular to the others and was for the administration, special guests like Anya, and the senior instructors. Three flags hung on the wall behind it. The central one had a fiery golden crown on a field of red—Yaksha Sithe's flag—while the other two were black banners. The right hand one contained a simple symbol, a silver aum, and the left hand one, the Directorate's symbol, a stylized eagle clutching a sword.

Cinder's stomach rumbled when the servers brought in trays of food, and the spicy aroma filtered through the hall.

The Firsters wouldn't be long in arriving now.

Minutes later, just as he predicted, the doors leading to the banquet opened, and in strode the Firsters. Cinder's eyes immediately went to Mirk, who appeared to be doing his best not to grin in delight. The other humans wore similar expressions of awe and amazement as they gazed about the banquet hall. Cinder caught Mirk's attention and gave him a fist-pump of enthusiasm. From down the table, so did Bones.

Mirk's attempt at maintaining a dignified pose shattered. He broke into a broad grin and gave an involuntary shout of joy. Laughter followed his exclamation.

"I can't believe the goof made it," Bones said, his voice loud enough to carry.

A chorus of chuckles met his statement, and Mirk might have reddened, but his grin never left him.

Shortly afterward, the administration, instructors, and special guests entered the room—Anya among them—and they took their seats. Everyone, that is, except for the school's commandant, General Sylve Arwan, an elf of middle years. Fit, strong, and with white streaks in his russet-blond hair, he remained standing, tall and straight, his piercing blue eyes assessing the students.

The commandant greeted the Firsters and like last year, he explained the Third Directorate's history and its mission; his expectations and those of the instructors at the academy, and the long, storied legacy of warriors who had trained in these halls. His call to glory.

Cinder remembered the speech's content from last year, but he still listened closely. It remained inspirational, and he found his heart swelling with pride. A grin spread across his face, mirroring the surging desire to make real General Arwan's rousing words.

As soon as the commandant finished his speech, the room broke out in applause. Cinder's excitement crested, and into the bedlam, he shouted, "*Mastha par!*"

The room answered in a deafening roar, "*Krathe lomon!*"

"Well said," General Arwan said, clapping in approval. "Now feast. Tomorrow we begin the work of forging warriors."

Cinder tucked into his food as soon as it was placed in front of him. He was hungry. Everyone else ate in much the same fashion. They were growing young men, and minutes of minimal conversation passed as the cadets and other warriors focused entirely on their food. Cinder caught General Arwan muttering something about piranhas and a feeding frenzy.

The meal continued, and after the meats and vegetables, there came dessert and another round of eating.

When it was done, Cinder sighed in appreciation, full and satisfied.

"Where do you plan on serving for your Secondary Trial?" Cariath asked.

It took Cinder a few seconds to realize Cariath was addressing him. "I'm not sure," he answered, forcing himself not to glance at Anya.

Estin snorted derisive laughter. "You'll be joining Raksha's cavalry or our own fast infantry. It's what all humans do."

Cinder might have answered, but Riyne's brother, Ranger-Lieutenant Lisandre, one of their commanders in the Unitary Trial and seated nearby, must have over-heard their conversation. He spoke first. "Not necessarily. Cinder is your Prime, ranked first among the Seconds. Historically, everyone who is ranked first earns a sponsorship from a ranger."

"Those have all been elves and a scattering of dwarves," Estin countered in an airy fashion.

"Which makes taking on a human all the more interesting," Lisandre said.

While the conversation was about him, Cinder didn't see a need to step in and defend himself. Lisandre was doing it for him.

Estin's amusement faded. "Why would any ranger take on someone so"—his mouth made a moue of disgust—"limited?"

"Because he's the Prime," Lisandre said. "He's defeated every elf and dwarf he's faced, doing so as handily as I've ever seen since your sister's time here. And in the Unitary Trial, he handled himself with aplomb."

"Fine," Estin said, waving aside Cinder's achievements as if they were meaningless. "But he's only won against us—elves and dwarves alike—because we weren't allowed to use the full measure of our abilities."

Cinder had to interrupt. "You keep telling yourself that. Your abilities give you an advantage, but just like I figured out how to overcome your speed, I'll figure out how to defeat your other skills."

"Care to wager on it?" Estin challenged.

Cinder didn't want to, but he decided to humor the prince. "What are the stakes?"

"At the end of the year, if you defeat me when I use everything I have, I'll beg my mother to grant you an *insufi* blade, forged specifically for your needs."

"And if I can't?"

"You drop out of the Third Directorate." Estin smirked, leaning back in his chair, hands cupping the back of his head as if he'd managed a checkmate.

Cinder laughed in Estin's face. "You're an idiot. I gain a blade if I win, and only if you can convince your mother to give it to you, but if I lose, I give away my future? Those are terrible stakes."

Estin scowled. "Then what do you suggest?"

Cinder considered it for a moment. "Let's make it simpler. Whoever loses our year-end bout has to call the other person 'Exalted Lord and Master' for all of next year."

Estin's scowl became a vindictive smile. "Deal."

"Heard and honored," Cariath said.

"Heard and honored," a handful of other voices declared, including General Arwan and Anya.

The wager was now made formal, and Estin no longer had a chance to back out of it. Cinder intended on making him pay.

Shortly after making his bet with Estin, Cinder left the Seconds' table and went to talk to Mirk. Bones, Depth, and Wark joined him. They all had friends in the incoming class of Firsters. For Depth, it was Garlin Fairsent, a handsome Rakeshian, well-built and several years older than Cinder. He was also the person Cinder had defeated in the first round at the Maker's Tournament last year. Wark's friend was Brow Cowl, a fellow student from *Jasmine Waters*—his martial school—and also a warrior Cinder had overcome in the Maker's Tournament.

The four of them made their way to the Firsters' table. Cinder grinned wide the entire time, glad to see Mirk, who stood up, wearing a matching smile. They laughed, hugging one another.

"Welcome to the best damn school in the land," Cinder said.

Their reunion was a jumble of exuberant exclamations. Mirk didn't look like he'd changed a bit. He was a year old than Cinder, a few inches shorter, and had the typical appearance of someone from Rakesh: medium build, black hair, and dark, almond eyes.

"What exactly happened to Gorant?" Cinder asked after they finished embracing. "I never got the full story."

Mirk's mirth faded. "Bad luck. He was up on his opponent in the second round, but he slipped during an exchange and got clipped in the temple. Concussion and he was done."

Cinder sighed. "Too bad. It would have been nice to see him here."

"He'll make it next year," Mirk said, sounding utterly confident. "Him and Sash both."

"He's bound to," Bones said. "After all, with you here, it's looking like they'll let anyone in."

"Fuck off," Mirk said to Bones, his grin returning. "Give me a year, and I'll be taking you down a peg. Just like Cinder did."

Wark broke off his conversation with Brow. "Good luck with that," he said with a snort. "It takes someone special to handle Bones, and you ain't it."

Brow, who had been listening in, grinned. He was older than Cinder by a year or two, bearded and with a lean but well-muscled build. Last year, he'd been taller than Cinder, but this year he was inches shorter. "What kind of special?" Brow asked. "The special, badass kind, or the special, stupid kind who drools on himself."

Cinder eyed Brow in disappointment.

Wark had a younger brother. Touched in the head they called it in Rakesh. Whatever the case, Wark's brother would always remain a child, and Wark clearly didn't think the joke was humorous. "That's not funny," he said, not smiling in the least.

Brow must have realized his mistake because his features immediately collapsed into contrition. "I'm sorry, Wark. Really, I forgot."

Wark shrugged, trying to recapture some of his prior joy. "It's alright," he said, but Cinder could tell it wasn't. "But in answer to your question, Cinder is the first kind of special."

Garlin, Depth's friend, must have overheard the last part of the conversation because he interjected. "Special, my ass. I'm not impressed." He addressed Cinder directly. "You're bigger and taller than the last time we fought, but we both know you got lucky against me. It won't happen twice."

Cinder found Garlin sizing him up, and he couldn't tell if Depth's friend was looking for trouble. Nevertheless, better safe than sorry. He locked onto the other man's gaze, not backing down and giving him a quick once over as well.

Brow nodded agreement. "He got lucky against both of us. I saw him across the sparring circle. This scrawny little shit. I thought I'd run him over like a runaway wagon." He chuckled softly. "Next thing I know, the little fucker eliminates me."

"He ain't so little anymore," Garlin noted, carrying himself like someone itching for a fight.

Cinder had heard enough. "Anytime either of you want a rematch, you let me know."

Garlin smiled. "Music to my ears. I've been waiting all year for another go against you."

"I'm standing right here," Cinder said. This wasn't how he envisioned the welcoming ceremony, but he also wouldn't back down from Garlin. This was a test to see if Cinder was an easy mark, someone the other man could intimidate.

Cinder wasn't, and if Garlin needed a beating in order to learn that lesson, then so be it.

"Now isn't the time," Depth said. He put a hand on Garlin's chest, trying to guide his friend away.

Garlin didn't budge an inch. He kept his eyes locked on Cinder's, only disrupting contact to briefly glance at Depth's hand on his chest.

Depth silently withdrew it.

Wark chuckled. "A sparring match between a Firster and Hotgate wouldn't be worth his time."

Garlin glared at Wark. "He might have got here before me, but give me six months, and I'll crack him over my knee. He got lucky when we fought."

Cinder snorted derision. "I beat you because I'm better than you. You try to win by trickery. Pretending you're injured. It's a coward's approach."

Garlin reddened. "You give me my rematch, and we'll see who gets beat."

Cinder nodded. "I'll give you a rematch at the end of the year, after you've learned some. We'll see what you have for me then."

"I have plenty now."

Cinder feigned a yawn. "No, you don't. You've got nothing. Like Wark said, you're not worth my time."

Garlin's jaw clenched, and he pushed forward. Cinder eyed him, unworried. He already could tell what Garlin intended. *Nothing.* Everything the new Firster was doing was bluster.

"Garlin," Depth said, a warning note in his voice. "Cinder would wipe the floor with you. He'd wipe the floor with most anyone here."

Garlin scoffed. "That ain't saying much. So what if he can beat you and Bones—"

Mirk cut him off. "You're talking shit about things you know nothing about," he said, appearing upset. "It's a sad way to start your time at the Directorate. Be happy for what you've accomplished."

Garlin stared at Mirk. "It's sounding like you're telling me what to do," he said in an ominous tone.

Depth must have had enough. "Grow up," he snapped at Garlin. "Cinder has the only pin in our class with ruby eyes. You know why? Because he's our Prime. He kicked the ass of every elf and dwarf he's faced. You really think you can do better?"

"Yeah, but—"

Depth interrupted him. "He killed six spiderkin in our Unitary Trial. By himself." Depth snorted in contempt. "You're a fucking idiot if you think you can take him."

Garlin's confidence wavered. "Beating elves, dwarves, and

spiderkin… that ain't possible." He stared at the Seconds, like he was looking for the lie.

Anya chose that moment to come by their table. "I don't mean to interrupt you, gentlemen," she said, "but I'm glad to see you getting to know one another." She faced Cinder. "A moment of your time, Cadet Prime? Meet me outside in five minutes."

"Yes, ma'am."

Anya nodded, smiled at the others, and sauntered off. Cinder couldn't help but stare at the sway of her hips.

He wasn't the only one.

Garlin's eyes bulged, and his mouth gaped as he watched Anya depart. "Who was that?" he asked in a strangled voice.

Cinder empathized with Garlin's reaction. He often felt that way about Anya, too. "*That* was Her Royal Highness, Princess Anya."

"She's got a way about her, no doubt," Bones added, "but if any elf catches you staring at her like you just did, you better be ready for a fight."

Garlin didn't take the hint, and he continued to stare after Anya, who had briefly halted.

Cinder shook his head in annoyance at the idiot. *Jackhole.* "They'll beat you into the ground so deep, you'll need a lamp and a ladder to find your way out," he warned, hoping Garlin would finally figure it out. Anya was an elven princess. He and Garlin were run-of-the-mill humans. She was as far above them as the clouds in the sky.

Anya caught the human Firsters staring at her as she left the hall, and she shook her head in amusement. *Men.* They were the same no matter the species and no matter the Realm. Bree used to laugh about…

Anya stumbled to a halt.

Who in Devesh's name was Bree? She tried to force an answer, but none came to her. She had no idea who Bree might have been and chalked it up to another mystery from her prior life. After taking a second to collect herself, Anya continued on her way.

She stepped outside the banquet hall, exiting into a long corridor carpeted in rugs. It was dimly lit with clusters of wall sconces turned down for the evening. No one else was about, and the sounds from the festivities were diminished to a background hum. Large windows allowed a view of the northern mountains while paintings from the Directorate's illustrious history decorated the hallway's walls. The artwork was difficult to distinguish as anything but dark smudges given the dimness.

Seconds later, Cinder exited the banquet hall. "You wanted to see me, your Highness?" he asked.

Anya rolled her eyes. Cinder's address of her both in the banquet hall and now had been properly formal, but he maintained a teasing tone. She sighed. Why did he persist in talking to her in such an overly familiar manner? Nothing she said seemed to rid him of his bad habit. She figured it was how she'd treated him early on in their relationship, allowing him too much leeway in how he spoke to her.

Then again, Anya liked how fearless Cinder was around her. Too many men found her intimidating. Her martial skills were a puzzle they couldn't solve, and as a result, hardened warriors often wilted in her presence while others simply wanted her for their own gain. Money, power, influence. The fame of her status. In the seasonal galas, they often knotted about her like vultures. Her sister enjoyed such attention, but Anya found it detestable.

"Anya?" Cinder said.

She blinked, suppressing a start and ending her musings. "I wanted to tell you I'm leaving," she said without preamble.

"Where are you going?" Cinder asked.

"The Daggers. I've spent enough time at the Directorate. I need to explore the mountains. I worry for what might be occurring there." She poked him in the chest, a breach of etiquette since elven women weren't supposed to touch a human man in such a familiar fashion. Thankfully, no one was around to witness it. "While I'm gone, I expect you to continue your training, little *bishan*."

"*Bishan?*"

Anya grinned in anticipation. "It's *Shevasra*. It means '*incompetent person who has potential.*" She laughed when Cinder's mouth dropped in slack-jawed surprise. She laughed even harder when he reddened in embarrassment, not caring in the least.

"It wasn't that funny," Cinder said, sounding affronted.

"Yes, it was. You can consider my teasing repayment for all the times you called me 'Simply Anya.'"

"That's not the same at all," Cinder protested. "My nickname is charming. Yours is an insult."

Anya raised an eyebrow. "By 'simply' you never meant to imply I'm simple?"

Cinder was suddenly staring at the ground, abashed. "Fair enough," he muttered in the tone of a little boy caught out in a misdeed. "You're right."

"Of course, I am, and since we're in agreement about my wisdom—"

"I never said you were wise."

Anya overlooked his disagreement. "Since we're in *agreement* about my wisdom, I want you to keep on working at overcoming a woven fully engaged in a fight and using all their talents. Remember, you have to earn your place at my side."

The last of Cinder's boyish abashment slipped away. "Consider it done." He sounded utterly certain in himself.

Anya didn't know where Cinder's self-confidence came from, but she had to trust in it. So far, he'd done everything he set out to accomplish, achieving heights no human had ever managed. "I'll hold you to your promise."

She expected Cinder to ask her how he could overcome his limitations, but he surprised her by shifting direction. "Are you heading to the Daggers because of the spiderkin we encountered in the Unitary Trial?" he asked. "Such a large nest shouldn't have been found so far south."

"It's part of the reason," Anya said. "Mostly it's because I've a notion to travel. I'm not someone who likes to settle in one place for too long."

She didn't bother adding how her memories tended to grow more burdensome and problematic when she planted roots in one location for too much time. While doing so last year had given her back the name of her husband, Rukh—

With the sense of an arrow hammering into a target, the image of a beautiful woman slammed into her mind. *Bree.* For the second time this night, remembrances of a different life took away Anya's steadiness. Her vision went distant, to the past. To a glorious city. Her husband. She remembered his sister, Bree. His brother, Jaresh.

"What's wrong?" Cinder asked, face lit with concern.

"It's nothing. I'm fine," Anya said, still distracted. Bree and Jaresh were people she had loved. She knew it with a certainty that allowed for absolutely no doubts, but now wasn't the time to ruminate about them. "Remember to train."

Cinder still viewed her with concern. "I'll remember," he said at last, "but I'll miss our sparring sessions." A few seconds later, a narrow-eyed gaze stole across his face. "I've studied some *Shevasra.* If I'm your *bishan,* then you're my *Isha.*"

By now, Anya's heart was somewhat settled, and she pushed away her troubles as best she could. She could integrate her newly recovered memories later. "*Isha* means master."

"Is that what I need to call you during the Secondary Trial?"

"The short answer is yes. The long answer is that calling me *Isha* is an honor you'll have to earn. It won't be given to you free of charge."

"I understand. It'll happen."

Again, he said it with such conviction that Anya found herself believing him, believing *in* him. And why not? With everything else he had managed to achieve, why not win against a woven fully sourcing his *lorethasra*? Cinder had an iron will, working harder and with greater intensity than anyone she had ever met.

Anya nodded to him. "With an attitude like that, I have no doubt you will." She focused her gaze upon Cinder, wanting to impress the importance of her next words. "But don't forget about *Muladhara*? Your skills with a sword are impressive, but you need a greater edge if you want to win your heart's desire."

Cinder smirked. "Heart's desire is a bit much, don't you think."

Anya reddened, partly in embarrassment and partly in annoyance. "You know what I mean. Work on all facets of your training; the spiritual as well as the physical."

The bear had escaped its tormentor, traveling through a strange rainbow-hued rent in the world. Weeks of running, ever southward, ever away from that horrid, dark place, and now it stood on the shores of a vast body of water.

An ocean.

In its nearly full century of life, the bear had never before swum the ocean's currents. It would do so now, only making the journey because of an incomprehensible need, one implanted by that terrifying dark force of metal and smoke. The whispers spoken by the being still haunted the bear's days and nights.

It shuddered in remembrance.

But across the water, on an island, it knew it would find a measure of peace. A certain scent, one of iron. And maybe then it would also be rid of the aching hunger from which it had once thought itself free, so long ago in the early decades after its awakening. It hated the sensation but had no choice but to follow where it led.

6

After the welcoming ceremony, Cinder had planned on helping Mirk settle into the Directorate, but over the next few weeks, their busy schedules never seemed to mesh for much more than brief greetings. The Firsters were thrown into the deep waters of their schooling while the Seconds had to prepare for a small unit drill in the wilderness. It was supposed to be the focus of their instruction prior to the upcoming Autumn Trial.

As a result, Cinder didn't have much time to catch up with Mirk. Instead, he had to focus on his own training.

Soon enough, the day of the wilderness drill arrived, and Cinder packed what he figured he'd need. The instructors had been rather vague on what the cadets should take with them, so he packed a bedroll, his mess kit, bandages, a fat-bellied knife, several loops of rope, a canteen, hardtack, dried meat, and flint and steel. He tucked it all away in his rucksack before strapping the shoke to his belt, collecting his bow and quiver, and exiting his room.

Outside, he met his fellow Seconds in the commons, and once everyone was ready, they set off as a group for the cafeteria and had a hearty breakfast of spicy scrambled eggs, upma, and dosas. Afterward, they went to a corner of the Quad and waited for Masters Absin and Jovick, who had told them to meet them there.

Cinder set down his rucksack and wiped his brow.

The day was young, but it promised to be a warm one. The sun beamed down, and a humid heaviness seemed to suffocate the academy. An infrequent breeze desultorily moved the air, barely shifting the leaves and limbs of the nearby dwarf red maples, which shaded their area of the Quad.

Cinder fanned his chest with his shirt while waiting on the masters who arrived a few minutes later.

Master Absin cleared his throat, calling for attention. "I know you thought you would be undergoing small unit drills in the wilderness, but it isn't the case. You *will* be tested, but this is a survival drill, and you'll face it with just the items in your packs." His gaze became piercing. "This is the first expedition of your Second year, and it will also be the easiest. You'll be split into groups of two or three cadets, get dropped off somewhere in the mountains, and be expected back at the Directorate in no later than seven days." He smiled, thin and humorless. "You'll also be blindfolded on your way to the drop off point and bound when you get there."

Cinder understood the purpose of the blindfolding. The instructors wanted them lost in the wilds. It was similar to what might happen to them during their work as rangers or scouts when they would be forced to discover their whereabouts and trace their way home on their own. But what about the binding? That didn't make any sense.

Cinder shared a questioning look with Bones, who shrugged. He had no idea what was going on either.

"Head to the stables," Master Jovick ordered, arms crossed across his chest. "Master Halin will have horses saddled for you to ride—not your usual ones—and some pack mules." His typically stern demeanor somehow grew even more severe. "We leave in fifteen minutes."

After the masters left, the rest of the Seconds were discussing the situation amongst themselves while drifting toward the stables. Cinder called them back. He had already reviewed what he'd packed, and there were some changes he needed to make. He figured the others would have to do the same.

"Hold on," he said to the Seconds. "We've still got some time. What did everyone pack?"

"What difference does it make?" Estin grumbled. "We'll be fine. This is Yaksha. There are a few wolves and coyotes up in the highlands, but nothing too dangerous. Besides, elves have an innate sense of our location. Same with the dwarves. Just follow our lead, and everyone will be back with no problems."

"What about food?" Cinder challenged. "We aren't packing enough food to last a week. Same with water. We'll have to hunt, trap, fish, and gather what we need to survive. Do you have the equipment for it?"

Estin's mulish expression softened.

It was the answer Cinder expected. "Let's see what everyone has."

A quick inventory revealed that none of the Seconds had the proper supplies and gear. They dashed back to their quarters where a ruckus ensued as everyone tore about, some having to completely reorganize their packs.

"Devesh damn it!" Riyne cursed in annoyance. "I can't find my other canteen."

"I have a spare," Derius shouted to him. "But I don't have enough rope."

"I've got extra," Mohal said.

Cinder unstrapped his shoke and left it behind. He also didn't bother with the steel sword Master Lerid had given him. This was a wilderness trek. Knives and machetes would be more useful.

More trading and contributions were made until the Seconds got themselves sorted out and hurried off to the stables. There, they found all their masters and other senior warriors waiting for them.

"What in Devesh's holy name took you sluggards so long?" Master Jovick growled.

"We had to repack our rucksacks, sir," Cinder answered. "Some of us didn't have the right gear."

Master Jovick cracked a smile. "You're learning. Good."

Master Halin stood off to the side. "We've already got your mounts saddled and ready," he said, gesturing to the horses and pack mules the grooms had led out of the stable. "And don't worry about where we're dropping you off. The rangers have thoroughly scouted the areas. There are a few coyotes and a scattering of wolves, but nothing more dangerous. You should be able to handle them."

"Get your gear put away," Master Absin said. "We'll get you mounted and blindfolded and head on out."

He called out more instructions, and everyone was soon split into pairs; everyone except for Riyne, Derius, and Ishmay, who were to be grouped into a trio. Each small unit was led by a single master or a senior warrior. As for Cinder, he was matched with Jozep, and Master Absin would be the one to guide them to their drop-off point.

"Put this on," Master Absin told Jozep, handing him an unadorned steel bracelet.

"What is it?"

"It hinders your ability to determine the location of the Directorate." Master Absin gave Jozep a piercing stare. "Don't take it off. I'll know if you do."

Cinder glanced at Estin. There went the prince's confident declaration of this being an easy drill.

Jozep slipped on the bracelet, and Cinder shortly got his rucksack tied down. A groom blindfolded him and guided him to mount a placid gelding.

"Are you ready?" Master Absin asked.

"Yes, sir," Cinder and Jozep replied in unison.

"Let's go then."

They set out, traveling for most of the morning in silence with Master Absin leading their horses. Cinder could tell they followed a well-trod trail through a rocky wilderness. Their horses' hooves clopped off the stones, and warm sunshine continued to beam down upon them without any breaks. They were headed northeast then. It was the most likely direction based on the terrain and lack of trees to provide shade.

Hours rolled by, a steady clip-clop of the horses' hooves, occasional nickers, bird cries, and the rustling of brush. A short halt ensued for a lunch made of hardtack, cheese, and dried meat. Their blindfolds were removed while they quickly ate, but there were no visible landmarks present to clue them into their location.

On they went.

By now, it was mid-afternoon, and the sun baked the ground. It was the hottest part of the day. No breeze shifted the air, and sweat beaded on Cinder's forehead. Based on the sun's position in the sky and how it blared down, they were still heading northeast.

Cinder tried to figure out the easiest path back to the Directorate. River Revelant was west of their location and following it might be their best means of getting back to the academy. Although… Cinder frowned. In the foothills, the river was said to be rough with whitewater and lined with boulders. Traveling its banks would be a hard journey.

The sun's brightness and warmth cut off, and Cinder realized they'd entered the forest. After the day's heat and humidity, the abrupt coolness amongst the trees was a welcome respite.

They traveled on, eventually stopping for the evening. Cinder discovered a quickly darkening world when Master Absin removed his blindfold.

"We'll stop here," the elven swordmaster said. "Help me set up camp."

They had another cold meal and afterward, Cinder spent the last few moments of the day stretching and practicing his unarmed forms. Jozep joined him.

"You have any idea where we are?" Cinder asked.

Jozep shook his head. "None." He pointed to the bracelet Master Absin had given him. "Not while I'm wearing this thing."

"Get some rest," Master Absin said, interrupting their conversation. "We have many more miles to cover tomorrow."

Two days of riding later, early in the afternoon, Master Absin had them dismount. "We walk the rest of the way." He shuffled about, and it sounded like he was hobbling the horses.

Cinder found his hands suddenly full with his rucksack.

"Strap them on," Master Absin said.

Hours of hiking followed with Master Absin holding their hands and guiding them. It helped some, but it was still rough going. It was miles of plunging through dense foliage that left Cinder scratched and bruised, and the entire time, the blindfold remained in place. Despite Master Absin's aid, several missteps led to an occasional tumble. A crack of Cinder's head against a low-lying branch made him curse aloud. Another crack only a few hundred yards later taught him to hunch low.

At last, they passed out of the forest's damp coolness and entered sunshine. It was warmer, but not by much. They were likely in the high hills northeast of the Directorate, but at least they had exited the trees. For this, Cinder was grateful, and he straightened with a groan. His back ached from bending over for so long. They walked around some more, seemingly in circles.

"We're here," Master Absin said. "Shuck your rucksacks and spin around in place until you're dizzy."

"Can you tell us why, sir?" Cinder asked.

"Because I told you to."

A common military answer. "Yes, sir." Cinder spun in place, losing all sense of direction. He didn't know how many revolutions he managed, but the dizziness eventually caused him to fall over.

"Now put your hands behind your back," Master Absin ordered. "It's time to bind you."

Cinder still didn't understand the reasoning for why they had to have their hands tied, and Master Absin had not been forthcoming when asked. Was it to further slow them down? Make it harder for them to follow the master who had led them? It seemed like overkill.

Couldn't the master simply hide the rucksacks and tell the Seconds to wait for a count of several hundred before removing the blindfolds? The cadets would then have to scrounge around for their gear first, rather than immediately chase after the master. It seemed like it would make more sense to do it like that.

At least Cinder thought so.

Nevertheless, he did as ordered, and a rope went around his wrists, tightly binding his arms. Cinder tested the ropes. They had enough give so he could free himself, but it would take a bit.

Jozep was also bound. Scuffling sounds followed. Master Absin must have gathered their rucksacks. The elf's light footsteps drifted away from them. Apparently, he also intended on hiding their belongings.

Definitely overkill.

"See you in a few days," Master Absin said.

Cinder's blindfold was whipped away. So was Jozep's.

The mid-day sun blared down, and Cinder squinted his eyes to slits. The brightness was overwhelming. Tears blurred his vision, and by the time it cleared, Master Absin was long gone.

Cinder blinked away the last of his tears and took in his surroundings. He and Jozep sat in a small meadow. Wildflowers grew in profusion all around them, and beyond the field rose a towering evergreen forest, thick and verdant with a line of north-south running mountains standing tall in the distance. The scent of cedar and pine perfumed the air.

A deer hugged the border of the trees, noticing their presence and bounding away.

Cinder didn't like the deer's presence. Deer meant predators. He already knew there were wolves and coyotes up here, but what if the rangers had missed more dangerous animals, like mountain lions or bears. He and Jozep had to free themselves immediately.

Cinder shuffled to where Jozep sat tugging on his bindings. "If we sit back-to-back, I can loosen your ties. Once you're free, you can undo mine."

Jozep nodded. "Do it."

Cinder felt along the dwarf's ropes, located the knot, and worked to loosen it. Thankfully, Master Absin hadn't meant for their ties to be impossible to remove, and it only took him a little bit of yanking and pulling to get Jozep's bindings open enough for the dwarf to free himself.

Soon, he was unbound as well.

"Now what?" Jozep asked.

Cinder glanced at the sky. It was only a few hours to sunset. "Now we find our packs and get our camp set up. We'll start back for the Directorate in the morning."

Minutes later, they found their gear and the rest of their equipment under some brush at the edge of the forest. In addition, Cinder noticed a gnarly tangle of briars and thorns close to where they discovered their packs. It was a perfect place for rabbits and other small creatures to hole up. Since they didn't have enough food to get back to the academy, they could supplement their supplies here by setting some traps.

Of silent accord, Cinder and Jozep split duties. Jozep got the fire going while Cinder set a few spring snares and added a pair of drag nooses on what he figured was the main animal run. By the time he finished, night was swiftly settling over the land.

Cinder eased down next to the fire. "You have any idea where we are?"

Jozep shook his head. "No idea. The bracelet, remember."

Cinder grunted. There was no question of asking or allowing Jozep to take the bracelet off. It would be cheating. Honor was involved in this test, and they had to pass it based on the rules. It didn't matter if Master Absin really could or couldn't tell whether Jozep ever removed the bracelet.

They fell into quiet, sharing a small meal of dried meat and hardtack. All the while, Cinder stared into the fire, planning what needed doing in the morning.

A wolf's lonely howl broke him out of his considerations. Cinder glanced into the darkened woods. More howls rose from the hills around them. Apparently, not so lonely a howl.

Disquiet filled Cinder. It wasn't winter, and the land wasn't in drought. The wolves should have no trouble hunting their usual prey. They shouldn't have any reason to track down a human and a dwarf.

Still…

"I'll take first watch," he told Jozep.

The next morning, Cinder went to the traps and discovered a disturbing scene. Blood and fur in the briar patch but no dead animals. Several rabbits had been caught in the snares—likely four of them. A successful trapping, but a bear had stolen the kills. Its prints were clear in the soft soil. A big one, too, based on the size of the paws and the scat near one of the snares.

While he stared at the scene of thievery, a sense of being watched fell over him. A deadly malice that had him crouching low and instantly wary. Sunshine penetrated the forest's canopy, dappling the world in hazy, yellow beams. The day remained bright and warm… and yet gloom seemed to hide the light. A smell reached Cinder. The stench of musk and old blood.

Something studied him. Something wrong. Something filled with cunning and an abiding hunger.

Cinder's hand went to the hunting knife at his hip. He silently cursed, wishing he had his machete with him. Better yet, a spear or any kind of weapon with reach. His heart beat out the rhythm of his nervousness, and he slowly backed out of the woods, never lifting his eyes from the place where he sensed the danger lurking. Not even after he reached all the way to where Jozep stood by their campsite. The dwarf had already doused the embers from their fire and had their gear together.

"We're being watched," Cinder said softly, still staring at the forest.

Jozep glanced in the direction Cinder was staring, and his hand drifted to the warhammer he'd decided to pack. Cinder was glad to see it on the dwarf's person. Although when they had set out, he had thought Jozep stupid for bringing it.

"Wolves?" Jozep asked.

Cinder shook his head. "I saw bear tracks. A big one. It stole the rabbits I trapped last night. But there's something else out there. It's staring at us."

The sense of danger persisted, and Jozep must have picked up on it. He gripped his warhammer more tightly, knuckles going white. He and Cinder gazed at the woods, muscles tense and ready, observing the area from which the menace emanated.

Minutes of knotted nervousness later, the threat came apart like a tattered fog under the sunlight. Only then did they relax.

"It's gone," Cinder said.

Jozep appeared worried. "What was it?"

"I don't know, but we better be careful," Cinder said. "Whatever was out there felt old and powerful."

"We should keep our weapons close and get back to the academy as fast as possible. They need to know about this."

Cinder nodded. "Let's head southwest. We were riding northeast most of the way here."

"Sounds good," Jozep said, setting off an instant later.

Cinder followed him, but he halted at the edge of meadow, giving the distant woods one last look. *Nothing.* The trees appeared utterly normal. But the memory of killing danger persisted. Cinder hustled out of the meadow, eager to catch up with Jozep.

7

The day wore on, and they caught no further sight, scent, or sense of whatever creature had spooked Cinder so badly in the morning. He was glad of it, and he slowly relaxed since the feeling of danger didn't recur. Hopefully it meant that whatever beast had been eyeing him was still back at the meadow where they had started today's journey. Or maybe the wildflower field was its home, and it hadn't appreciated strangers in its territory?

Something simple like that.

Regardless, they trekked southwest, taking a winding path along animal trails and thick foliage. Their going was slow, but late in the evening, they reached a clearing next to a burbling stream, which rushed over stones and boulders. They stopped there and made camp. Thus far, all they'd eaten was their supplies, a tasteless concoction of dried meat and drier hardtack.

They needed water and fresh food, and the stream promised the former as well as the possibility of the latter.

"Gather the wood, and I'll get a line in the water?" Cinder suggested.

"You sure you know how to fish?"

"Of course," Cinder said, offhandedly. "We took a class on it last year, remember?"

"It was only one session, and I've forgotten most of it."

Cinder grinned. "Thankfully, young one, I didn't. We'll be fine."

Jozep scowled. "First, I'm older than you, and second, prove it."

"I'll prove it," Cinder said, "but why don't we put a wager on it. If I can catch us enough fish for supper tonight and lunch tomorrow, you have to clean any dishes we use today and all-day tomorrow."

"And if you can't?"

"I have to gather all the firewood tomorrow, set up camp, and also help gather food."

Jozep grinned, obviously thinking Cinder wouldn't be able to hold up his end of the wager. "Deal," he said, leaving to collect the firewood.

Cinder, meanwhile, scoured the area around the stream, searching for a likely limb. He wandered the bank, careful around the loose shale and slick rocks until he found what he was looking for: a thin branch with some give. He cut a length of thread from the spool he'd brought with him, dug out a few worms from the moist soil lining the stream, and found a comfortable boulder on which to sit. He was soon casting away.

Luck or Devesh was with him because within a half-hour he had a line of trout, enough for supper tonight as well as breakfast and lunch tomorrow. Jozep joined him by the stream once he had their camp arranged, and together, they scaled the fish. After cleaning up, they set the trout over a pair of spits and relaxed by the fire.

"Did you bring any salt?" Jozep asked, his hopeful tone revealing that he hadn't.

Cinder nodded, reaching into his rucksack and withdrawing a pouch of salt.

Jozep sighed in appreciation. "Thank goodness. Nothing is as bad as fish that tastes like fish." He tilted his head in consideration. "Except chicken that tastes like chicken."

Cinder laughed. "What?"

Jozep grinned. "You know. Chicken when it doesn't have any

seasoning. When it's just chicken. It has to be covered up with other flavors, or it's disgusting."

Cinder was prepared to laugh again, but when he deliberated on Jozep's explanation, he realized his friend was right. Chicken without seasoning—or fish for that matter—*was* disgusting.

The fire crackled, and while the fish cooked, they discussed their plans for tomorrow. They had to figure out what direction to take and how best to preserve the trout. Cinder tried not to stare at the sizzling fish while they spoke. Watched pots never boiled, and watched food never cooked. Still, it had been a long day, and he looked forward to the end of it. A full belly, and he was ready to sleep.

At last, the trout was done, cooked to a flaky finish, and Cinder groaned when he took his first bite. He hadn't realized how hungry he was. He wolfed down one of the fish, spitting out the bones. So did Jozep, and they split a third trout.

In the midst of finishing off the final fish, Jozep snapped alert and his head whipped to the woods.

The evening had lengthened, and twilight gripped the world, a prelude to full night. Visibility was dropping, but Cinder didn't need to see in order to feel the fell malice that had captured Jozep's attention. The same sinister sensation as earlier in the day. The same sensation of something wicked watching them.

As one, they rose to their feet. Cinder fetched his weapons, his machete, a stout knife, and his bow and arrows. Jozep got his throwing axes close at hand, and his hand rested on his warhammer. They looked to the small point from which the danger seemed to emanate.

"What is it?" Jozep asked.

Cinder had no idea, and he peered into the forest, trying to locate what had him and Jozep so rattled.

A snort. Twigs snapped. A snuffle and a careless rustle against the thick undergrowth. The creature was pushing through the forest, headed toward them.

"He's coming," Jozep said unnecessarily. "Fifty yards."

Cinder's heart pounded. His mind filled with terrible imaginings.

He nocked an arrow.

The noises drew steadily closer, louder. Cinder realized the world had grown silent, as if the forest animals recognized a danger and hid themselves low. The sound of movement stopped, and a low rumble echoed into the clearing.

A beast thrust out of the dense woods, only his massive head and powerful shoulders visible. *A bear.* An enormous one. Snarling. His snout was gray, his teeth yellow, and his eyes flashed silver in the gathering darkness. A wicked scar, marked by a line of white fur, tracked down his forehead and across his right orbit. It gave him an even more terrifying appearance.

This was an old king of the wild, scarred and tough. Cinder had heard of such creatures. Aged beasts robbed of speed and power. Ones who could no longer bring down their prey on their own and had to resort to stealing in order to live. The scent of cooking fish must have lured him.

The bear growled at them, a clear warning, a deep-toned rumble ending on a whoofing note.

Cinder stared at the creature, and his stomach dropped. This was no ordinary animal. Cruelty and danger wafted off the bear, thick like the stench of old blood mixed with musk. The aromas Cinder had scented in the morning. The bear snarled again, rumbled more loudly.

Cinder readied his bow, while Jozep clutched an axe. The tableau held still for a few pregnant moments until the monster of a bear snarled one last time and retreated into the forest. Neither Cinder nor Jozep relaxed, though. To be here now, the bear must have followed them, hunted them all day.

"We need to cross the stream," Cinder said, eyes still locked on the place where the bear had pushed out of the forest. "The water's deep in places. He might not be able to track us so easily. If nothing else, it might slow him down."

"Cross the stream at night?" Jozep said, sounding skeptical.

"We have enough moonlight." Dormant was full, and its ivory light illuminated the world in a lustrous glow. "Either we cross, or we stay on the same bank as the bear."

"We cross," Jozep said.

"We should also keep going," Cinder said. "I want a lot of distance between us and this camp."

"Agreed," Jozep said.

They gathered their rucksacks, wrapping the remaining fish in large leaves and quickly left the campsite. After crossing the stream, they put as much distance as possible between themselves and where they had seen the bear. All the while, they watched the woods. The bear remained a presence out in the forest, a deadly promise of spite and hunger.

A few miles later, they encountered a stone outcropping, a pointing finger of salvation rising a hundred feet. High up the cliff was a prominence, a relatively flat shelf, a place to watch the world, reachable only by a narrow path, one barely seen. It would be a hard ascent, but the bear couldn't follow them, at least not easily.

And the bear was following. He had crossed the stream and was trailing them, a couple hundred yards away and keeping his distance but matching their pace. A grunting, snorting sound of danger.

"Let's get up there," Cinder suggested.

"I can make it harder for him to get to us," Jozep said. "You go first."

They carefully climbed the steep slope, and when Cinder glanced back at Jozep, he noticed the dwarf pausing now and then. He was holding his hand behind him, and a gray mist drifted off his fingers. It defied the stiff breeze, refusing to dissipate. Instead, it plunged into the stone, and where it touched, the ground became smooth and glassy.

"Let's see him climb that," Jozep said, pleasure in his voice.

Cinder smiled. "I'm glad you're with me," he said.

"I'm glad I'm with you, too."

They reached the outcropping, and minutes later, the bear exited the pines and cedar. It seemed to stare up at them for a few moments before disappearing back into the woods.

Early the next morning, they left their stone perch and headed south-west again. Ever onward they went, and over the next two days and two nights, they caught neither sight nor sound of the beast. Jozep dared hope they had lost the monster.

But Cinder didn't believe it. A dark cloud permeated the air with danger and fear, and he could almost taste the bear's presence, far away but trailing. The old king hadn't forgotten them. Cinder knew it. The only question was when the bear would attack. It had to be soon. The creature wouldn't have followed them all these miles from his high-land home for no reason.

On their fourth day out from the meadow, late in the evening, they stopped an hour or so before twilight and set their camp at the base of a rugged hill. Its slope was a near vertical cliff. A ragged wind blew down from the heights, causing their fire to flutter like a flag. Sparks drifted into the night, falling short of the surrounding forest, and the wood crackled and snapped. The squirrels Cinder had managed to ar-row roasted over the flames. Fat occasionally sizzled.

There was still no sign of the bear.

"Can you sense him?" Cinder asked, not needing to explain who he meant.

"No," Jozep said, sounding irritated. "And I haven't been able to sense him for days now."

Despite his dismissive words, he never paused in his work. Jozep whittled spears. Cinder had insisted on it. They had a dozen of them by now, including one Cinder had tipped with his hunting knife.

Cinder fell silent, staring into the flames as he considered their sit-uation. They had made good progress so far, winding down from the slopes of the mountains and reaching the foothills where travel be-came easier. They only had to continue in their southwesterly course for another day or two, and they would be back at the Directorate.

Just one or two more days, but Cinder didn't think they'd make it there without having to confront the bear. He could taste the danger. The beast would soon strike. The old king was coming, and it was dif-ferent. The silver flash in the creature's eyes when it had stared at them.

Cinder couldn't remember his family, friends, or life in Swallow, but he remembered the *aether*-cursed snowtiger. Her eyes had flashed in the same way as the bear's, glowing like silver lanterns.

Aether-cursed.

They had to deal with an *aether*-cursed bear. Tonight probably.

A light drizzle began falling. *Perfect,* Cinder thought sourly. *Bad visibility and bad footing. What else can go wrong?*

"We need more wood," Cinder noted, glancing at their pile. He wanted a large fire ready for when the bear came after them. "Watch my back while I get some."

Jozep nodded.

Armed, they went a short distance into the woods. Cinder soon had his arms full of sticks, twigs, and occasional branches. It wasn't enough. They would need much more wood than this. Four more trips they made into the forest, penetrating deeper as required. All the while, Cinder's senses were alert, and his heart pounded, but not with fear; only adrenaline. Or if it was fear, it was for Jozep since fear for himself rarely touched Cinder.

By now, the rain thickened to a cold downpour. Mist rose, choking the world in a cloak of shadow.

Cinder readied for a final trip when Jozep hissed. "He's here." He gestured with his chin. "A few hundred yards. Coming at us. Slow."

"Get more fires going," Cinder ordered. The wood they'd collected was still dry inside. It would burn.

They quickly had the rest of the wood alight in four piles.

"He's coming faster," Jozep whispered, his face a mask of concern.

Cinder reached for his *Jivatma* and gathered his bow in hand, nocking an arrow. He noticed bizarre noises: crackling, hissing, rustling, and susurrations. The sounds distracted him, but he threw them off, peering instead in the direction Jozep indicated. Snuffling and a heavy grunt came from the woods, edging closer. Cinder focused on the shifting noise.

The bear was circling. Cinder followed the sounds. He couldn't see beyond the scope of the firelight. He wiped at his face, clearing his eyes of the downpour. Lightning briefly lit the skies. Thunder crashed.

The bear exploded out of the forest. Cinder only had time to get off a single shot. It took the beast in the chest, causing the bear to rear and roar in anger. When it did so, Cinder blinked in alarm. The creature was gigantic, fifteen feet tall and two thousand pounds or more.

Jozep must have noticed the same thing. "Devesh save us," he said in fear-filled awe.

The words helped Cinder shake off his shock. He grabbed a spear, the one with his hunting knife.

The bear stalked forward. His eyes glowed like white-hot fire, lit with intelligence. Jozep flung a throwing axe, but it bounced off the bear's tough hide. The creature might have paused long enough to offer a mocking smile before charging forward.

The ground trembled beneath the beast. *Jozep's talents, his* lorethasra.

But the bear leapt lightly, overcoming the shifting ground. He moved far too gracefully for a creature of his size. The monster reared again and swiped at them.

Cinder found his spear pushed aside, and he was forced to duck under a paw the size of a shield. The six-inch claws would have shredded him. He rolled away, gaining distance. Jozep fought the bear alone, managing to hold off the beast. Stone spears erupted from the ground, directly under the monster's paws. They should have punched through the creature, but it didn't happen. The bear's fur rippled, standing straight up, and the stone spears crumbled beneath the pressure of his heavy limbs.

"It's blocking whatever I do," Jozep said, panic in his voice.

Cinder's *Jivatma* finally came into his mind's eye, but so did the surrounding lightning. He recognized the danger he faced. If he pushed past the pain of the lightning, did he risk becoming a wraith? But what other choice did he have? Better to live than die.

He did a gut-check, preparing himself for the agony to come. *No hesitation.* He reached into the lightning.

Cinder screamed. The lightning flayed his mind. His bones felt like they were being ripped into splinters. But he refused to quit. Refused to fail. He pushed against the wall of lightning, using every last drop of will.

He punched through the barrier with a surprising suddenness, and the pain retreated. It tore away like fog ripped apart by a stiff wind. At the same time, everything within and around him took on a brighter sheen. The misting rain, the darkness and gloom, none of it impeded his vision or any of his senses.

The bear roared, and Cinder's attention returned to the battle at hand. Jozep was desperately keeping the bear at bay with a spear.

Cinder's muscles bunched, and he blurred forward. Knife-tipped spear aimed at the bear's haunch.

Somehow, impossibly, the beast grew aware of him enough to spin and slap aside the spear. Cinder barely evaded a return swing. If not for his *Jivatma*, he wouldn't have. The creature's speed was incomprehensible. How could something so huge move so fast?

Jozep used the distraction to switch weapons. He went with the warhammer and landed a heavy strike, a concussive blow cracking the bear's hind leg. The limb buckled but didn't break. But at least the monster fell on his side. It struggled to rise.

Cinder re-entered the fray, sending a *Jivatma*-powered stab of his spear hard into the bear's flank. He punched through, past the hilt of his foot-long knife blade. Cinder tried to rip the spear free.

But the bear roared, twisting and surging to his feet. The motion yanked the spear from Cinder's grip, leaving him defenseless. He backed off, retreating to get another spear.

While he did so, Jozep stayed in the fight, wielding his warhammer. He sent probing attacks, and the beast reared, swiping at him. Jozep tried to block with his hammer. He might as well have tried to hold back a rockslide. The bear blasted through his defense, and Jozep was flung through the air. He landed on his side. An audible snap and scream indicated he'd broken his arm.

Cinder grabbed another spear and rushed at the bear, shouting at it. He had to take the *aether*-cursed monster's attention off of Jozep. The bear viewed him, snarling and possibly smiling again. The beast fell back on all fours and stalked forward; head hung low. Cinder backed off. He distantly noted Jozep regaining his feet.

The bear rushed forward like an avalanche.

Cinder braced his spear into the ground. The bear ran onto it. The spear tip penetrated to a depth of four inches before the shaft shattered. Cinder was already moving. He threw himself underneath a swinging paw. The bear pressed forward. Another attack. Cinder retreated as fast as he could.

He sensed movement underneath him. The creature had access to *lorethasra*, and it was weaving. But training against the dwarves had taught Cinder what to look for with braids of Earth and how to evade them. He balanced on shifting ground, leapt away from a series of rocks meant to trip him, but in the end, the bear was too fast. The creature attacked with a swiping paw.

Cinder sensed it coming, and he ducked low, but the blow was only partially evaded. It crashed into him. His chest and abdomen were shredded, and he was launched through the air. He landed awkwardly, rolling his ankle. It gave way with a loud crack, like kindling snapping. Cinder fell over on his side, the pain immediate. His chest was scored like windrows. His abdomen a mess.

Get up. He had to get back to his feet. The bear was coming. Cinder levered himself upright, conducting more *Jivatma*. It allowed him to ignore the agony tearing across his chest and abdomen, the distant throb of his broken ankle. He needed a weapon. His gaze flitted about in panic, resting on the spears. He'd landed next to them. He re-armed himself.

Jozep re-entered the fray, working with only one arm. He managed another heavy strike against the bear, hitting the same leg as before. This time it broke. The bear roared, fury and pain evident. He managed to face Jozep, who had his hammer ready for a killing blow to the monster's head.

The bear blocked, though, taking the hammer strike on a foreleg, which cracked like a tree splitting in half. The limb flopped uselessly, but the bear didn't give up. Nearly crippled, the monster still managed to smack Jozep off his feet, hurling him into a boulder ten feet away. The dwarf hit with a sickening thud.

Cinder shouted again, distracting the bear before it could finish off Jozep. Thankfully, the beast paused, staring his way. Cinder conducted more *Jivatma* and hurled his spear like a javelin. He put every ounce of focus and strength into the throw. The spear blasted into the bear like the missile from a ballista, piercing the *aether*-cursed creature directly in the chest.

The bear roared in pain but still charged clumsily at him, running despite its broken limbs and terrible wounds.

Cinder had another spear ready. He fired it across the short distance. It landed inches away from the first spear, but still the bear came forward, dragging himself now. Cinder grabbed another spear. He thrust, trying to hold off the bear. The beast evaded and raked Cinder, laying his arm open to the bone.

Cinder gritted his teeth, accepting the pain. His strength was failing. He conducted more deeply from his rapidly emptying *Jivatma*. The bear prepared another attack, but Cinder got his thrust off first. He used the last of his *Jivatma* to power his attack. The spear punched through the bear's chest, driving three feet deep.

The bear keened, high-pitched and mortally wounded. It stiffened, and its silvery gaze met Cinder's. The glow from the eyes faded, transforming to a normal brown, and the bear stared at Cinder. It whoofed once, eyes full of confusion and anguish. The bear collapsed and didn't move.

Cinder's legs gave out.

It was done. Rain fell, but otherwise the world was quiet, and after the battle filled with terrible roars and cries, the relative silence felt strange and passionless. The bear lay dead. Steam drifted off his body, hissing and mixing with the falling rain and crawling mist. The creature's body shrank, transforming from titanic to withered in a matter of seconds.

Cinder recalled the bear's last moments. The pain and confusion. A simple animal unsure why it was dying. Unexpected pity for the animal rose in Cinder's heart.

Jozep!

Cinder's gaze shot to his friend, who still lay crumpled next to the boulder against which he'd broken. He quickly hobbled to where Jozep lay, hating what he knew he'd find.

"I'm in a world of hurt," the dwarf wheezed. His jaw was broken, misshapen and crooked. Same with both his legs and an arm. He was dying. They both were.

Cinder nodded blearily, eyes welling. He'd have to watch another friend die. "I know."

Jozep sighed, closing his eyes. "You won't die. Neither of us will." He paused, seemingly gathering his breath. "Cut out the bear's heart. It'll be rich with *aether*. We can use it to heal ourselves."

"Use it how?"

"By eating it raw. The *aether* inside will do the rest."

Eating the bear's heart sounded grotesque, but Cinder trusted Jozep. The dwarf knew more about *lorethasra* and *aether* than he did. There was a question he had. "Will we end up like the bear? Thirsting for *aether* or *lorethasra* or whatever?"

Jozep shook his head minutely. "No," he wheezed. "We should be fine. I think." His eyes remained closed, and his voice was growing faint. "The only problem is my jaw. I can't chew or swallow anything whole."

It was definitely a problem, but one that could be overcome. Cinder would find a solution for it. In the meantime, he lurched to his feet, careful to keep the weight off his broken ankle. A few limping, bleeding, gasping steps brought him to the bear's wasted carcass. No meat or muscle was left on its skeletal frame. It made it easy to carve into the beast and find the heart, which was similarly shrunken.

It fit easily in Cinder's hand, the rich, ruby-red color of a rosebud emanating off of it. The creature's blood, a thick soupy substance, pooled and dripped from his fingers, but he didn't allow the distaste of what he was about to do enter his mind. Cinder went to work. He bit down and chewed. Bit down and chewed.

On the fourth bite, after he'd consumed half the heart, he gasped. A fire rippled across his skin, like the pain of the lightning encircling his *Jivatma*. But this was somehow pleasurable. He felt lit from within.

The pleasure abated when the bones of his broken ankle shifted on their own. Cinder screamed in agony. His vision went white. The bones eventually stopped moving. His vision slowly cleared, and he could think again. He realized the bones had settled in their proper place. A soothing heat followed by a comforting coolness took away the pain, and seconds later, he stared in astonishment when his ankle healed. He twirled his foot, feeling not even the slightest twinge.

Contentment and security spread through his body, deep into his bones. His skin tingled, and Cinder's heart filled with awe. A prickling sensation drew his attention to his wounds. Spears of golden light lanced from his lacerations, fading away like a slowly shuttered lantern. When the light ended, the deep claw marks were similarly healed, leaving not even a scar.

Cinder took a deep breath, easy and pain free. His eyes went to the bear's heart, wondering. What was *aether* to so easily execute the miraculous?

He shook off the question. He had to take care of Jozep. Cinder darted to his rucksack and grabbed a mortar and pestle. He had an idea how to feed Jozep the heart.

He went to where his friend lay, and the rise and fall of the dwarf's chest was the only indication he yet lived. Cinder sat next to Jozep, supporting his head in his lap and praying this would work.

"Can you swallow water?" he asked.

Jozep managed a weak nod, his gaze hazy and distant. He might only be minutes from death.

Cinder used a spare knife to slice up the remains of the bear's heart, cutting it into small chunks. The terrifying likelihood of Jozep's pending death spurred him on, buzzing inside him like a trapped bee. As soon as he had the heart chunked, he ground the pieces in the mortar and pestle, working fast, praying all the while on Jozep's behalf.

It was finally ready.

Cinder placed a small curd of the bear's pasted heart into Jozep's mouth and offered him the canteen. "Drink."

Jozep took a swallow. He managed another before falling into a fit of coughing. Cinder waited for it to pass, canteen at the ready. Jozep's coughing ended, and Cinder encouraged him to take in more of the bear's heart and drink more water. More swallows followed, slow, spastic, and leaving Cinder too much time to think and fear for Jozep.

Why wasn't he healing? By now, Cinder was frantic. The bear's heart was nearly gone. There was nothing else to do. The imminence of Jozep's death left him terrified in a way that danger never did. A pit hollowed Cinder's stomach. What if there was no way to save Jozep?

Even as the question crossed his mind, the event he had been waiting for occurred. Jozep gasped as if salvation was upon him. His jaw straightened with a rough grinding of bones, and the dwarf screamed. The grinding noise continued. His fractured femurs were shifting. His wounds glowed golden. The healing only took a few seconds, but it seemed to last for far longer. Eventually it was done, and Jozep exhaled a shuddering breath. He closed his eyes, and he appeared to fall asleep.

Cinder watched it all in stunned disbelief. Eating the heart had healed them both. Consuming the bear's *aether*... Or was it *lorethasra*? *Aether*, after all, was the magic found in the world at large. *Lorethasra* was the magic within a person. Or in this case, an animal. Shouldn't such creatures be called *lorethasra*-cursed rather than *aether*-cursed?

His thoughts were rambling, but Cinder didn't care. He and Jozep had fought a deadly foe. They should have died, and yet they had won, claiming a hard-earned victory.

Cinder surged to his feet, facing the heavens and giddy with relieved joy. He roared his triumph.

He then glanced at Jozep, who had collapsed into a deep slumber, realizing only then that the dwarf's broken arm wasn't healed. The bear's heart apparently had its limits.

No matter. Cinder splinted Jozep's arm while his friend slept, still smiling.

They'd be home in a few days, and Jozep would live. It was enough.

8

It took two days for Cinder and Jozep to make it back to the Directorate; two days of hard, painful travel, especially for Jozep, who was limited by his broken arm. Worse, while the injury started out as merely swollen and painful, sometime during their journey, a seeping infection set into it, one resistant to the cleansing medications Cinder had packed.

By the time they made it home to the academy, Jozep could barely walk. He was lost in a fugue of light-headedness and weakness, and Cinder had to support him most of the last few miles, an exhausting trek.

It was evening by the time they entered the grounds of the academy. The Quad was quiet. A row of jasmine lined the path on which they walked, and the flowers were still in bloom. The lush fragrance floated like an unseen balm, and Cinder felt the stress of the journey begin to ease. A pair of doves crooned in a nearby bush, and Dormant and Fulsom shone overhead. Their light beamed through tattered clouds, lighting upon Garad Lull. Cinder paid the Titan no mind.

They'd made it, and although he had to basically carry Jozep—who was stout and heavy like all dwarves—he managed. They shuffled into the infirmary where the staff immediately took over, and Cinder could release a grateful sigh when they eased Jozep off his shoulder and carefully placed him on a gurney.

"We'll handle it from here," the physician in charge said.

"Thank you, sir," Cinder said. Worry over Jozep kept him from leaving. "Will he be alright?"

The physician smiled, easing the fear in Cinder's heart. "He's young and strong. He should be fine."

"Thank Devesh," Cinder whispered in reverent gratitude.

"He probably won't even miss the Autumn Trial," the physician added.

Cinder's heart unclenched further. "Thank you again, sir." He inclined his head to the physician and left the infirmary, making his way to Firemirror Hall. Despite his fatigue, he had to report to Master Absin and let him know what had happened.

He found the swordmaster in his darkened office, a square space containing a simple desk and a pair of bookshelves. A single *diptha* lamp burned on his desk, and Master Absin had his feet propped on it as he read a book. A painting of a woman in formal regalia graced one wall. *Empress Sala.*

Cinder had seen her image before. Most offices and rooms had her visage hung on at least one wall. She was a handsome woman, but the painting gave her a sense of unsmiling gravitas. As Cinder studied the image, he realized that Anya didn't resemble the empress. It wasn't merely because the princess' features were unique and beautiful rather than just handsome. It was also because the princess frequently had a teasing smile lurking at the corner of her lips. She wasn't severe in appearance like the empress' image.

"Welcome home," Master Absin said with smile, interrupting Cinder's considerations. "You made it back in time." There must have been something on Cinder's features because Master Absin's visage grew serious. "What's wrong?"

Cinder reined in his thoughts and shortly explained what had happened to him and Jozep in the survival drill.

Master Absin heard him out, only interjecting to ask a few clarifying questions. During it all, his features became ever flatter, his voice absent of emotion. It was as if he was trying to suppress ever growing fury or fear, and Cinder couldn't tell which emotion it was.

When he finished his report, Master Absin steepled his fingers under his chin, elbows braced on the desk. He spoke in a deadly quiet voice filled with an undercurrent of indecipherable passion. "You're telling me a fifteen-foot tall, *aether*-cursed bear nearly killed you and Jozep?"

"Yes, sir." Cinder tried not to take a backward step. The master appeared livid.

"Son of a whore!" the master snarled.

Cinder did take a step back then. Master Absin never cursed.

"Come with me," Master Absin snapped.

They set off through Firemirror Hall, and Cinder trailed silently after Master Absin, who pounded down the hallway, footsteps heavy. Other elves moved to the sides of the corridors as Master Absin passed them by.

They reached General Arwan's offices. The door was open, and Master Absin swept inside.

Lieutenant Capshin sat behind a tidy desk, relaxed and smoking a pipe while reading a missive of some sort. A pair of bookshelves flanked a window behind him, and to his right stood a closed door.

The lieutenant glanced up when they entered and must have immediately noticed Master Absin's anger. He straightened away any amusement from his face. "What happened?" he asked, momentarily eying Cinder.

"I need to see the commandant," Master Absin said. "It's important."

Lieutenant Capshin went to the closed door. He tapped on it once, opened it slightly, and bent his head inside. He held a brief, whispered conversation with the commandant before turning back to them. "The commandant will see you." He held open the door for them.

"You'll want to hear this, too," Master Absin told him.

They entered the commandant's office, a place Cinder had never before visited. He was astonished by what he found inside. The place was an utter mess. A hoarding of books, scrolls, old weapons, strange crystals, and ugly rocks of no particular use fought for space on crowded bookshelves. The commandant's desk was similarly untidy with not a single empty square inch. Every bit of it was occupied by... junk.

"You needed to see me, Absin?" the commandant asked, leaning back in his chair.

"Tell the commandant what happened," Master Absin said to Cinder.

"Yes, sir." For the second time, Cinder recited what had happened during his recent survival drill.

As he gave his report, General Arwan's face went red with anger, and Cinder had no idea why. After finishing his account, he hastened to add "I took Jozep straight to the infirmary, and the physician in charge thinks he'll make a full recovery. He won't even miss the Autumn Trial."

"Unbelievable," General Arwan said, sounding utterly disgusted. "An *aether*-cursed bear dangerous enough to nearly kill two of our own, living at our back door?"

"The rangers have grown complacent," Lieutenant Capshin said, his voice a low growl.

"I don't think so," Master Absin disagreed, his earlier fury or fear controlled now. "The rangers are our finest warriors. They swept the areas where we dropped off the cadets just a few days prior to when we dropped them off. I find it hard to believe they would have missed something so obvious as a monstrous *aether*-cursed bear of such power."

"You think something else is at work here?" General Arwan asked, worry in his voice. His glance flicked to Cinder.

"I don't know," Master Absin said. "This entire situation is bizarre."

There were undercurrents to their conversation that Cinder couldn't piece together or tease apart, some unspoken missive that neither was apparently willing to share in front of him, a mere cadet. It probably had to do with an unknown aspect of the political situation of Yaksha

Sithe and the rangers. Something like that, but he didn't care. He was bone-tired and just wanted to get some rest.

"It *is* bizarre," General Arwan agreed. "It makes no sense, and that makes me nervous." He addressed the lieutenant. "Send out the rangers. I want them scouring the wilds and making sure nothing else haunts our back door. They can spend a month out there for all I care, however long it takes. But I expect no other *aether*-cursed beasts wandering Yaksha's interior. Dismissed."

"Yes, sir," Lieutenant Capshin replied.

Cinder now recognized what likely had the masters so upset. Yaksha proper had been civilized for thousands of years. There weren't supposed to be any dangerous *aether*-cursed beasts living in the core of the island, but there had been. The rangers had either failed their duty, overlooking the *aether*-cursed bear, who was likely decades old, or… what exactly? He didn't know.

"You look worn out, cadet," General Arwan said to Cinder. "Get some rest."

His words spurred Cinder to straighten. He'd been swaying on his feet. "Yes, sir."

It was late evening, and a very tired Cinder wandered his way back to Krathe House where the rest of the Seconds had already returned to the Directorate. Most of them were still awake, however, and gathered in the commons. They huddled around him when he arrived, and for the third time, he explained what had happened.

"An *aether*-cursed bear attacked you," Riyne scoffed, voice full of disbelief.

"Are you sure it wasn't an *aether*-cursed chipmunk?" Estin said with a laugh.

Cinder faced the prince, face solemn, holding back a cutting rejoinder. This matter was too serious for childishness. "It was a bear, and it nearly killed us. We would have died if Jozep hadn't thought to consume the creature's heart. He's in the infirmary right now."

Sriovey blanched. "How bad is he?"

"He'll live," Cinder answered. "The physician in charge thinks he'll be fine. You can check on him in the morning. Right now, he needs some rest. So do I." With that, Cinder plodded to his room and collapsed on his bed.

The week after the encounter with the bear, an unsettling ennui weighed on Cinder. His stamina seemed stolen, and his strength and speed far less than they had been prior to leaving for the wilderness drill. It was a struggle to concentrate, and a challenge to care about his classes and training. He found himself easily distracted.

Plus, the weather was lovely, and Cinder was bored. As a result, he was barely paying any attention to Lieutenant Capshin's lecture on Gandharva. They'd actually been reviewing it all week, but none of the information was new. Last year, Cinder had made a point of reading extensively about the nations bordering Yaksha Sithe, and he already knew what Lieutenant Capshin was droning on and on about.

Cinder sighed in exasperation. The class was taking too long, and he wanted it over.

He stared wistfully at the warm sunshine and blue skies seen through the classroom's bank of windows, wishing he could enjoy the pleasant breeze and its promise of a crisp, cool evening

His mind drifted, and he wondered how Anya was doing. She was likely deep in the Daggers, probably killing zahhacks and spiderkin. And speaking of the Daggers, what could he and the others expect in their upcoming Autumn Trial? What would they encounter? Zahhacks? Wraiths? More *aether*-cursed beasts? All of the above? Hopefully, they would have better planning than they had in the Unitary Trial. How would he—

A hand smacked sharply onto the table directly in front of him. He started out of his reverie and found Lieutenant Capshin smiling mirthlessly at him. "Cadet Shade. Perhaps you can stop staring outside and rejoin the lecture."

Cinder squirmed in humiliation as everyone chuckled at his

discomfort. Most obvious in his glee was Estin, who snickered into his hand, doing little to smother the sound. "I'm sorry, sir," Cinder said. "My mind was elsewhere."

"Oh, really? Who knew?" Lieutenant Capshin said sarcastically. "You were day-dreaming. I expect better of you. You've earned an essay. Have it done by tomorrow. Explain to me how the current political situation in Gandharva impacts Yaksha Sithe."

"Yes, sir," Cinder said, offering the only appropriate answer. Nevertheless, the lieutenant's essay shouldn't be too hard.

"Unless you want to explain it to us now," the lieutenant challenged, eyes glittering and still standing next to Cinder's desk.

Cinder couldn't interpret the lieutenant's visage, and he swallowed heavily. "I can if you like, sir," he replied after a moment of silence. "But do you mean about the demographics about Gandharva, or the situation between the Unifier Party and the Moralists?"

"The former," the lieutenant said, sounding surprised, "but incorporate the latter while doing so."

"Yes, sir," Cinder said in a no-nonsense tone, not wanting the lieutenant to think he was making light of the situation. He took a few seconds to prepare his answer. "Demography is destiny. I don't know who said it first, but it's true. For the past fifty years, Gandharva, which is a parliamentary democracy under a constitutional monarchy, has essentially been ruled by one party, the Unifiers. However, over time, it has been the Moralists who have risen to challenge Unifier rule. The Unifiers take a hands-off approach to governance and economics. They believe people should do as they will so long as they don't cause trouble for others.

Cinder cleared his throat. "The Moralists, on the other hand, believe in a more vigorous approach to governance. They take the position that government should do everything it can to foster righteous and moral living. And only the Moralist way of life is righteous or moral. They also have an expansionist view about Gandharva. They wish to push the borders outward, and since the Moralists are having five children for every woman, while the Unifiers are only having slightly more than three, they might manage it. The Moralists are outbreeding their internal adversaries."

"Humans do nothing but breed," Estin stated.

"You sound jealous," Bones said, a mocking tone to his voice.

"Of humans? Hardly," Estin scoffed.

"Of our male potency," Bones replied, extravagantly stretching his arms. "Clearly, our women must like us if they're willing to bear us so many children. I wonder what it means that elves have such small families. A little more than two children per woman on average, right? Maybe you're doing something wrong. I'd be happy to teach you—"

"Enough," Lieutenant Capshin cut in. "We're not here to discuss such... crude matters." He turned to Cinder, a warmer expression on his face compared to when the presentation about Gandharva had first begun. "Please continue."

"Yes, sir," Cinder said. "The Moralists are outbreeding the Unifiers, but they likely won't outbreed anyone else. They are an expansionist party, but contradictorily, they also have a strong separatist streak."

While he spoke, Cinder glanced to Ishmay, wondering how he was taking his presentation. He didn't want to offend his friend by insulting Gandharva, but he also had to tell the truth. So far, Ishmay seemed merely attentive with no evidence of annoyance or indignation.

"The Moralists foster an unnecessary animus. They regularly expound about the physical differences throughout Gandharva. Moralism rose in the south, and it's still most powerful in the south. Southerners aren't as tall as northerners, and they tend to have fairer skin and features. A mix of Rakesh and somewhere else."

"You don't look like you're from Rakesh," Depth interjected, speaking to Cinder. "You look like someone from the Savage Kingdoms."

"That's because he's a savage," Estin said.

Cinder exhaled heavily and prayed for patience. Why couldn't Estin just shut up for once? "Were you dropped on your head as a child?" he asked the prince. "Or were you always this stupid?"

A few sniggers broke out.

Confusion roiled across Estin's face. "What do you mean?"

Cinder shook his head. "Nevermind. The Moralists use this difference in appearance to drive divisions among the people. They complain about northern arrogance, but they also are doing their best to drive out anyone who doesn't look like them out of their districts. Unfortunately, the Unifiers have also taken to using this same tactic. The situation risks spiraling out of control, and if the people can't see how they are being manipulated, Gandharva might fall into civil war."

Ishmay interjected, his voice filled with disgust. "In short, we've elected the finest politicians in our entire history but also our worst leaders. They're all a bunch of shits."

One more week passed before Jozep was released from the infirmary, and while Cinder was overjoyed to see him, a secret worry was now stealing his happiness. His ennui had broken, but now a new concern plagued his hours.

He could no longer reach his *Jivatma*. Ever since the battle with the *aether*-cursed bear, he hadn't been able to. Initially, he had hoped it was because he'd drained his *Jivatma*, and it was simply taking a long time to refill. That hope was starting to fade, and doubts were beginning to seep into his mind.

What if he'd burned out his *Jivatma*? He'd read accounts of it happening to woven who had used too much *lorethasra* and could never again source it. He feared he faced the same future. It would leave him broken. He'd never be the kind of warrior he had hoped to become.

Cinder wanted answers to his dilemma. He wanted to talk to someone who could help him. But who to trust? Who could he ask about his ability to conduct *Jivatma*?

He wavered in asking for help because of his readings about the *NusraelShev*. The histories and documents of the great war often spoke of an underlying theme of blame. The woven blamed humanity for the misery of the *NusraelShev*.

Their attitude, written in their scrolls and texts and spoken out loud by many elves even now, reinforced Cinder's notions of how they would likely fear his abilities. Anya hadn't, but she struck him as unique among her people. But what about the others? Elves like Estin or Riyne? Or even the other woven, such as the dwarves, trolls, or holders. What would they say if they learned what he could do? By now, they most likely recognized he was different from other humans and probably chalked it up to being able to source *lorethasra*. They seemingly didn't care since no one had called him out on the fact, but what would they say if they learned he conducted *Jivatma*, the same potency used by the ancient *asrasins*?

In the end, there was only one other person Cinder believed he could trust: Master Molni.

Cinder sought him out, late in the evening, only a few minutes before closing when no one else was likely to be present in the library. The *diptha* bulbs in the wagon-wheel chandeliers were already turned down, and Master Molni sat at his usual location by the front desk, alone.

The old elf smiled when Cinder entered. "What brings you here so late?"

"I have questions," Cinder said.

Some of his worry must have shown because Master Molni's smile dwindled. "Oh? Should I be concerned?"

Cinder didn't immediately reply. He continued to vacillate over whether to speak to Master Molni. "If I tell you a secret about myself, can I trust in your discretion? Will you keep it confidential?"

Master Molni offered an encouraging smile. "This does sound serious."

Cinder remained silent. Master Molni hadn't yet promised to keep his secret.

The old elf's features grew serious. "If this secret imperils you or other students, then I make no promises. Otherwise, yes, I won't tell anyone else what you tell me."

Cinder scrutinized the elf for a few moments longer, still unsure of the librarian's intentions, but in the end, what choice did he have?

After all, he'd come to Master Molni for help. Why bother if he let fear keep him silent. Cinder spoke without preamble. "I can conduct my *Jivatma*."

"You mean your *lorethasra*," Master Molni said with a knowing grin. "Many have noticed it. They've seen the speed with which you move. Amongst the staff, it's more of an open question than a secret."

Cinder shook his head. "No. Everyone thinks I can source my *lorethasra*. It's not true. I can conduct my *Jivatma*."

Master Molni frowned. "You aren't making sense. *Jivatma* and *lorethasra* are the same thing. I know there are records indicating otherwise, but they're wrong."

"No, they're not," Cinder said. "No one can see their *lorethasra*. I can see my *Jivatma*. It's like a pool of the purest water, reflecting a light I can't locate."

Master Molni leaned back in his chair, his features clearly troubled. He stroked his chin, eyes distant. Awareness returned. "I see. Have you told anyone else?"

"Only Anya," Cinder said. "It slipped out when she saw me fighting in the Foe. She wanted to know how I moved so fast."

"And you're certain this vision of water isn't an imagining of some sort?"

"It's not. And before you ask, I haven't found any definitive corroborating evidence. Just an account in a contested biography about Mythaspuri Sapient Dormant."

Master Molni's expression remained troubled. "You once asked me if I've ever come across accounts of someone seeing their *lorethasra*, and I hadn't. But since you asked, I've done some more reading and come across accounts similar to what you claim. Including in *Forever Triumphant*, our religious text."

Cinder blinked in surprise. "I thought *Forever Triumphant* was unreliable."

Master Molni's mouth twitched into a sour smile. "Corrupted, you mean. Written to obscure the truth rather than elucidate it. Regardless, there is an early section in the book, a verse discussing Shokan, *'His soul glistened like water under the Lord's brilliance'.* There are similar descriptions about the soul in some scattered accounts from Indrun Agni. Unfortunately, few give credence to the verse in question. And fewer to Indrun Agni, the least of the Mythaspuris. I certainly didn't."

"And now?"

"And now, I think I might have to revisit my preconceptions." Master Molni's scrutiny intensified. "You're certain of this pool you can see?"

"Yes, and when I conduct it, my senses sharpen. I can move faster. I can do things no one else can." He went on to explain all he knew of his *Jivatma*, when he'd first purposefully conducted it, the blue-and-green lightning... all of it.

Master Molni frowned. "Why is the lightning not present in the Foe?"

Cinder had already considered this, too. "I think it's because the Foe isn't entirely in this world. I think the reality of Seminal causes the lightning and locks away a human's *Jivatma*."

"Except for yours apparently."

"Except for mine," Cinder agreed. "I don't know why. Maybe it has to do with the injury I suffered when the *aether*-cursed cat killed my parents and injured me."

Master Molni grunted. "As good an explanation as any," he said.

"There's more. During the battle with the bear, I used the very last dregs of my *Jivatma*, and since then, I've been unable to reach it. My fear is that I burned it out, like some woven are said to do with *lorethasra*."

"What about in the Foe? Can you see your *Jivatma* there?"

"No. It was the first place I went. I can't see it there, either."

Master Molni eyes narrowed in thought. "Can't see it or can't reach it?"

Cinder equivocated. "I don't know. When I reach for it, I can't see it."

"They aren't the same," Master Molni said. "My advice is to go to the Foe and reach for your *Jivatma* as you used to do when you are at your calmest. See what happens before worrying about having burned it out. Even then, there are certain rare fruits—the Aushadha fruit of an Ashoka tree, for example—and water rich in *aether*, which might be able to restore what you've lost. Also, in some cases, it simply takes time for *lorethasra* to restore itself. No different than a person who needs to recover from any other sort of injury."

Cinder wanted to believe it could be as easy as what Master Molni indicated, but a quiet voice warned it wouldn't. Hope, however, was what he needed right now, and hope was what he clung to. "I'll go to the Foe." He hesitated before leaving the library. There was one last issue he had to ask about. "Will you tell anyone about this?"

Master Molni shook his head. "I see no reason to, but when you're ready I expect a full account." His face split in a smile. "I want to be the one to write your biography."

Cinder grinned. "If my life is worth writing about, I wouldn't want it to be anyone else." His smile slowly slipped. "Thank you, sir."

Master Molni waved aside the words. "Don't thank me yet. Go to the Foe and find out if I'm right."

"Yes, sir," Cinder said. "But thank you anyway."

Cinder's first stop after his discussion with Master Molni was the basement of Firemirror Hall and Misery Gate. During his walk to the portal, hope and trepidation brewed in equal parts.

Perhaps it would be like Master Molni said: he wasn't able to see his *Jivatma* because of a lack of calmness. Perhaps all he needed was the serene center Master Lerid had once taught to him. Maybe then, he'd have the success he was hoping for.

Anxiety, though, ate at his fading confidence. After all, hadn't he already tried meditative techniques? Sat still and unmoving with his mind adrift? And it hadn't worked. Not the slightest shimmer or sheen to indicate the presence of *Jivatma*. Why would it be any different this time?

His musings ended when he reached the cellar-like room containing

Misery Gate. He studied the large stones and the carved glyphs. What was the gate in reality? Who had built it, and was it true that it could take a person to distant parts of the world?

His unanswerable questions circled through his mind, and a moment later, he recognized he was intentionally wasting time. He shoved the queries aside and took several slow, settling breaths. He was ready.

Cinder activated the Foe, choosing only the glade. When the Gate opened, he stepped through the shimmering film filling it and immediately winced at the icy chill penetrating to his bones. On his next step, he entered the Foe and was struck by stomach-clenching nausea.

He breathed in through his nose and out through his mouth, willing the discomfort to assuage.

Several seconds later, it was gone, and he was able to gaze about. Nothing disturbed the glade, and the sourceless light filling the Foe seemed to rest at noon. Mountains towered in the distance, but closer at hand, a forest of evergreens contained the by-now familiar meadow. The scent of pine and juniper hung in the air.

Cinder sat on the grass, taking a cross-legged pose, one foot on each knee. He paused then, reconsidering why he was here. Would it truly be devastating if he couldn't conduct *Jivatma* any longer? After all, for thousands of years, humans had survived without *lorethasra* or *Jivatma*. Why couldn't he? He would still be a fine warrior. Bones, Ishmay, and Depth were. Same with Wark. They were warriors worthy of the name.

So, he tried to tell himself, but he was less than successful. After all, he'd touched his *Jivatma*, and could he ever truly be content with anything less?

Cinder shook his head. The questions were immaterial, and he shoved them away. He closed his eyes and focused inwardly. His breathing steadied, and he willed his heart to slow down. Aimless thoughts flitted through his mind, but he did nothing to rein them in. Doing so would only cause his mind to center on them. Better to let them drift away.

Instead, he kept his attention on his breathing, imagining his troubles emptying out of his mind, draining down his spine, and leaking through the small of his back and buttocks into the soft grass. More controlled breaths. *In through the nose. Out through the mouth.*

After a period, he felt the peace lay across his shoulders and mind, the lightest of touches but penetrating to his bones and relaxing him. Tranquility unshackled his final burdens, carrying them away into the wind and the earth.

Cinder was ready, and he opened his mind's eye, reaching for his *Jivatma*. He allowed it to take shape, urging it to bloom like the opening notes of spring, a state outside and beyond his control. All the while, his heart beat like a ponderous bass drum, pacing the motions of his life.

Time passed, and like a slowly revealed dawn hidden by thick clouds, an image skipped across his mind's eye. He wasn't sure what he was seeing, but it might have been the possible scintillation of light on water. A spark of excitement shot through him, and he didn't fight it. Instead, he let the enthusiasm surge and recede like a wave, and when it was gone, serenity resumed.

Again came the light. Another flash. This one a flickering view of the world at darkest night after lightning. A possible view of his *Jivatma*, but he wasn't sure.

He continued to breathe slow and deep, letting the peace lift away any hopes and fears.

Again came the flash, longer this time, blinking and flickering until finally the image steadied.

Cinder's throat clenched. His equanimity disappeared, but the vision did not. It persisted in his mind's eye, a sickening truth. Where he should have seen his *Jivatma*, there existed a desert-dry shell. Empty and absent of glory.

It was gone. His *Jivatma* was gone. Not even a puddle remained of the once-glistening pool.

Cinder swallowed convulsively, shuddering, his tranquility destroyed. Tears welled behind his closed eyelids, and sorrow stung like poison in his veins.

He had lost a truly wondrous aspect of himself, and he wept. What would become of him now? Without his *Jivatma*, who was he?

Even in the midst of his grief, Cinder kept his eyes closed, struggling to control his breathing, trying not to give in to hopelessness.

No. This isn't the end. I won't despair. He spoke the words over and over again to himself, trying to capture any kind of optimism.

In the end, while the soothing wasn't immediate, his heartache softened some, and Cinder wiped away his tears. He was able to think more clearly.

This wouldn't be the end. He was healthy and hale. It would be enough, and he'd make it so.

An epiphany occurred. Is this how he wanted to live his life? Afraid of what he'd lost rather than focus on what might be? Wouldn't it be better to focus on the likelihood of joy rather than fret over the fear of failure? Choose realistic hope over craggy cynicism?

In the midst of his reflections, odd noises intruded. He couldn't rightly tell if it came from within himself or the glade. A sizzling, snapping sound like a log burning, the hissing of the wind; odd shifting sounds, like ivy rustling, and the gentle whoosh of waves.

He'd heard them before, or at least he thought he had, especially when sparring with the woven in his class, but when Cinder focused on the noises, they fled.

9

Anya had been back at Taj Wada, the empress' palace and grounds, in Revelant for most of the past three weeks. She would have already left for the Dagger Mountains, but her mother had another task in mind for her. Upon her arrival home, Anya had been told that she would shortly be visiting Apsara Sithe and taking part in a formal diplomatic mission. Her father would also attend as the senior member of their party.

Part of their mandate would include negotiations on trade issues and cross-border taxes, but the majority of their focus would be on Redwinth Wheat, Apsara Sithe's only unmarried prince. He was a nephew to their empress, Quel Apsara, and his older brother, Starias, had already been married off a few decades ago to Shariah Tawaine, the crown princess of Heliar Sithe. Anya's mother believed Redwinth would make a good match for Enma. It was Anya's duty to determine if this was true.

Anya didn't want to go, but she never considered doing anything other than as instructed. She understood duty. In her first life, her husband had been a stickler for both duty and honor, and his attitude must have rubbed off on her. She smiled as she recalled the few details she could about her life with him. *Rukh.* At least she remembered his name. *Bree and Jaresh, too.* Rukh's sister and brother. *Sign.* Her own cousin. Some of their features had returned to her along with details of the life she'd once known.

Regret-filled remembrances for what had once been but could never again be filled Anya's mind as she stood in a gazebo overlooking a koi pond. She distantly noted the sun shimmering off the clear water; the fish darting about or swimming languidly; the reeds thrust like green spears amidst various bonnets of four-leaved lilies decorating the pond's surface.

Her gaze shifted to the left, to the gleaming white stone of the soaring palace. From its topmost turrets flew Yaksha's flag, a fiery crown on a field of red, rippling against a blue sky softened by a handful of puffy clouds. Her vision went to the right, this time to the area beyond the pond; the stables and even further, a wildflower field abutting a large copse of oak, maple, and elm. Closer at hand, a wood and stone bridge—its posts and pillars carved with fanciful figures—arched over the water and led to the gazebo. Upon it she only now noticed her parents' approach. They stepped lightly onto the span.

Her father, Avan Aruyen, was a dark-haired elf in his middle-years, his early three-hundreds, who had a background similar to Redwinth's. Avan, too, was a younger son, originally from Heliar Sithe's imperial family, and eventually he'd been bartered off to marry Yaksha's heir, Anya's mother, Sala. And here, a somewhat delinquent young man—or at least so the stories said—had found his footing, maturing as both a husband and a father, nurturing a family and mastering many different types of arts and crafts; a healer, a blacksmith, luthier, and a delver of deep thoughts. In addition, Anya and her siblings had taken their father's last name since, by tradition, only the empress could possess the surname "Yaksha."

Her father smiled greeting, and his blue eyes sparkled. "Why am I not surprised to find you alone," he said when he reached her side. "You always did like to wander the world's lonely places." He kissed her on the cheek and maintained a smile, one meant to remove any sting from his words.

Anya smiled in return.

Her mother, Sala Yaksha, reached her next, also smiling, her dark eyes warm. Of early middle years, the empress possessed no remarkable physical attributes. Her blonde hair had once been her finest feature, but the centuries had dissipated some of its luster. In fact, on initial inspection, the empress was utterly average, neither lovely nor ugly. At best, she was handsome. In fact, if not for her bearing and confidence—the empress easily commanded any room she entered by the simple force of her presence—she would have garnered few second glances. This was especially so in comparison to Enma, Anya's sister, who was beautiful and noticed by everyone.

"You and your father leave for Apsara in a few days," her mother said. "How go your preparations?"

"I've read everything we know about Redwinth," Anya said. "Every available piece of information, including Ambassador Semwil's private correspondences about him. The prince is ten years older than Enma and is said to be charming, intelligent, and charismatic. He is considered a fine warrior and an even better leader of men. If he matches his assessments, he should make a good match for Enma. Possibly soften some of her… abrasive qualities."

Anya had a complicated relationship with her sister. She loved Enma, but she didn't always like her.

Her father tsked. "You shouldn't say such things about your sister."

Anya quirked a grin in reply. "I'm sure I shouldn't, but sometimes I fail to think before speaking. Mother used to say the same about you."

Avan threw his head back and laughed, a deep belly-laugh full of life and pleasure. "I imagine she has had cause to say far worse."

Anya found herself laughing with her father but also staring at him in fascination. How did he manage to laugh so joyfully and without encumbrance? Rukh had been like that, too. Able to live in the moment. But then again, Rukh was special. He was incomparable. He could do many things most normal folk couldn't.

But not Anya. For her, a chronic worry always stole a part of her happiness. She was unable to live in the moment, the perfect place the scholars, philosophers, and gurus taught led to contentment.

Her mother shifted the conversation, surprising Anya. "Tell us about this human, Cinder Shade. His name is on the tongues of many. Not simply because he defeated Estin and Riyne nor because he took first place in the Grand Melee."

Anya schooled her features to polite interest. It wouldn't do for her parents to learn of her interest in Cinder, especially if they learned of the hours she'd spent training him. Hours alone that some might call inappropriate.

Her parents might try to forbid her having further contact with Cinder, which Anya couldn't abide. She was Cinder's instructor, and she had to spend those hours with him. How else could she train him? He had a chance to become a special warrior, and she wanted to be the one to help bring his skills to a polished sheen.

Plus, she liked Cinder, although she let none of those feelings land on her otherwise blandly curious features. "Oh? What has he done now?" she asked her mother.

"He and a dwarf were attacked by a powerful *aether*-cursed bear during an expedition into the heart of the sithe." Her mother shook her head in disbelief. "General Arwan sent scouts the moment he heard. They came across the carcass. Desiccated and little more than a bag of bones, but they were able to age it nonetheless. The beast was over a century old. Savage and powerful."

Anya's jaw dropped. A century-old *aether*-cursed bear on Yaksha proper? How? The creature should have been detected long ago. Even in the Daggers, it would have been. Such a beast would have been a terror, and it defied belief that the creature had been somehow over-looked. "And Cinder and the dwarf survived the encounter?"

"Which is the remarkable thing," her mother said. "Even a trio of elven rangers would have been hard pressed to defeat such a monster. The fact that a dwarf and a human were able to do so is next to impos-sible." She lifted her brows. "As I said, Cinder Shade's name is on many tongues."

Her father viewed her in curiosity. "I understand you've become friends with the boy. Why is this? You risk your name and reputation."

Anya silently cursed. Of course her parents had already learned about the time she had been spending with Cinder. General Arwan or anyone at the academy could have told them by letter or missive. "I have spent time with him, but only because he *is* special. I think he might be able to source *lorethasra*. I've been testing him to see if it's true." She didn't bother adding how Cinder claimed it was *Jivatma* he conducted, which was impossible. Such a talent had died with the Mythaspuris.

"Source his *lorethasra*?" Her mother said, sounding skeptical and yet unhappy. "I've heard the same suspicion from other masters at the Directorate."

"Master Absin continues to try and teach it to every human who enters the Directorate," Anya explained.

"And if Cinder can source his *lorethasra*, it would explain much," her father said, sounding thoughtful and as similarly unhappy as Anya's mother. "It would also raise a whole host of undesirable possibilities. What if all humans could do the same? They would be unstoppable, especially when they already outbreed us. They would be like locusts." He scowled. "Our borders would be overrun inside of a century."

Anya had also considered this, but she didn't think it would happen. She explained why. "Not necessarily. With *lorethasra*, they would have the time to seek out education, and as we know, societies with educated women naturally tend to have smaller families. The same would hold true to humans."

"Quite a gamble to bet on this, this so-called *natural* tendency," her father said.

"It's also possibly an unnecessary concern," her mother interjected, addressing Anya. "Have you learned if Cinder truly can source his *lorethasra*?"

Anya hedged her answer. She was certain he could—he had confirmed it, after all—but there was still a tiny possibility he was wrong.

His abilities *might* merely derive entirely from the work he put into mastering the sword. "Not entirely."

Her mother's eyes narrowed in suspicion. "*Not entirely* from you is *almost certainly* from others. You've always been too conservative in your estimations. I want him to meet Quelchon Ginala."

Anya's heart jolted, and she scowled in anger. "The seer who said I would betray you? You still trust her?" She scoffed. "You should have replaced her long ago."

Her mother wore a sour grimace. "If only quelchons could be so easily replaced. Their talents are rare. None have been born in Yaksha in several generations." Her jaw firmed. "I'll have Ginala recite Cinder at some point."

Anya still didn't like it, but there was also an expression to her mother's features, something she'd never before seen. Fear. Her mother was afraid, and it astonished her. "You fear Cinder. Why?"

Her mother sighed. "There are mysteries about Cinder Shade. What he's said to be capable of. It might mean nothing, but it could be the end of things we'd rather not lose. It concerns us."

Anya frowned. "What aren't you telling me?"

"There are passages in *Forever Triumphant* which give me pause," her mother said. "You should read them."

"Our holy book? I thought it was a fictionalized account of relatively true events."

Her father took up the explanation, speaking carefully, as if to avoid stepping on fragile eggs. "It *is* fictionalized, at least the versions open to the public, but there is also an uncorrupted copy. Your mother has one in her private library. Every empress possesses one. It will be made available to you. Read it when you have a chance. You'll discover the reason for our disquiet."

Anya quelled her astonishment. If they were this uneasy about Cinder Shade now, what would they think of him if he managed to open his *Muladhara*? It didn't bear commenting, and she also didn't think it wise to tell them about her decision to sponsor Cinder in his Secondary Trial.

"Prepare for your journey to Apsara," her mother ordered. She was the empress now, full of authority. "Do your duty to your sister, to your sithe, and your empress. I've also decided to recall Lisandre. He will accompany you." Her expression hardened. "You have a duty to this house as well, and it doesn't include risking your reputation training a human."

There was clear warning in her mother's words. Her time spent with Cinder had been noticed, and it was necessary to nip any resultant rumors in the bud. The best means to do so would be by placing her in close proximity to Lisandre, a man many—including her parents—believed would make a good match for her. At least on a temporary basis, since for marriage, Anya would likely be auctioned off to some other sithe's prince.

And while wisdom might have meant meekly acceding to her mother's will, Anya didn't see herself as meek, and she wasn't willing to cut Cinder loose. "My devotion to duty has never been in doubt," she said. "I've bled for this sithe, and I will do whatever is required to see it safe."

Her mother grunted, obviously hearing Anya's lack of promise at giving up Cinder's training.

Her father smiled, clearing his throat to interrupt the budding tension. "We'll leave you to your privacy then. We depart with the morning tide."

Her parents left the gazebo, and as Anya watched them exit the koi pond, a memory washed over her. Of a village carved into an escarpment, a lush land with curtains of water drifting off a gauzy waterfall, of myriad iridescent rainbows and soaring bridges, and of Rukh striding away from her; of him leaving for war.

Was that the last time she had seen him? She couldn't tell, but whatever the case, she wished Rukh hadn't died and that it didn't feel like he'd abandoned her. She wished he had joined her in this life like he had promised he would.

It had been a week since Cinder had realized his *Jivatma* was a burnt-out husk. A week of trying to set aside the grief of losing something precious. But bending unwilling feelings wasn't easy, and it centered on a simple fact: Cinder was no longer the warrior he had been prior to the survival drill, and he sorrowed for his lessening.

He'd grown used to the speed available from unconsciously conducting *Jivatma*, of moving as swiftly and smoothly as an elf.

He no longer had such an advantage.

Cinder was still quicker and more graceful than his fellow humans or even the dwarves, but not nearly to the same degree. His prior fleetness and fluidity had given him a certain confidence; confidence he now lacked. He could no longer easily defeat the dwarves and elves. They were once again a challenge for him, and in fact, he now lost more matches against them than he won.

Master Absin had made note of the changes, and he pulled Cinder aside during an evening of extra training at the Cauldron. "What is the problem? You seem… off these days."

They sat next to one another on a set of bleachers overlooking the sparring circles, watching other warriors train in the Cauldron. The sun dipped toward the horizon, but there was still plenty of light in the late evening. The muddled mix of laughter, annoyance, exhortation, and cursing—all the typical sounds of warriors in training—drifted across the sparring circles and the field.

"It's the fight with the bear," Cinder said. "I'm still recovering from it." Strictly, he hadn't told a lie, but it also wasn't the entire truth.

Master Absin peered at him, a crafty expression on his face. "I'm sure that's true, but are you sure some of it isn't related to an inability to source your *lorethasra*?"

Cinder gazed at Master Absin, somehow unsurprised at the elf's awareness. He had never discussed his abilities to the blademaster, but apparently there was no need. The man was smart, and he missed little. Given Cinder's speed, strength, and performance, Master Absin had obviously guessed his abilities stemmed from the use of *lorethasra*.

But guessing was one thing. Should he confirm Master Absin's supposition?

Master Absin watched Cinder, noticing how well the boy hid his emotions. Admirable really, but unnecessary. The boy's initial reaction, his flat affect, had betrayed him, blaring the truth. Cinder could source his *lorethasra*. It couldn't have been any clearer than if Cinder had shouted it out from the Directorate's rooftops. The silence stretched, and Master Absin took pity on the young human. "No one told me," he said, "and I will tell no one."

Cinder's inexpressive visage collapsed into a sour grimace. "I should have guessed you would have already known."

Master Absin smiled, glad Cinder was finally relaxing. "I've trained generations of warriors," he said. "There are those such as Lisandre, who were born special. Others, like Bones and Riyne, who with full commitment, might become special. Then there is you. You stand as far above those special warriors as they do above the ones who fail at entering the Directorate. *Lorethasra* would explain much of what you've managed to accomplish."

Cinder's frown persisted, and Master Absin found himself irritated when the young human seemed to disregard the immense compliment he had paid him.

"Couldn't it just be my talent at deciphering a warrior's intent?" Cinder asked. "My anticipation."

"You would still have to get your sword in place, your body aligned to take advantage of those insights," Master Absin said. "You need speed to manage it. Speed such as no other human enjoys."

"Speed isn't as necessary if my form and control are correct."

"Which they aren't," Master Absin. "They aren't even close."

That got a reaction. Cinder's eyes widened in outrage. "What do you mean? My form isn't perfect, but it's much better than it was when I first came here."

Master Absin nodded. "True, and most elves would be thrilled with your form and control, but you have a long way to go before you can say your execution is equal to your speed and balance. You need less width to your slashes. A shorter route to your parries. Better setups to your feints, and more commitment to your thrusts. You might potentially match Anya if you really dedicated yourself."

Cinder's demeanor grew distant.

Master Absin watched the young human, the emotions flitting across his face. Grief, anger, followed by hope, and finally pensiveness.

"Will you tell me what happened to you?" Master Absin asked. "What happened to your *lorethasra*?"

"Nothing. I never sourced my *lorethasra*. It was my *Jivatma*. I could conduct it."

Master Absin's eyes widened in surprise. "*Jivatma*? That is an old term, but from what I understand, it means the same thing as *lorethasra*."

"Everyone thinks so," Cinder said with a bitter chuckle, "but it's not true. They're not synonyms. I've done a lot of research about it."

"Really?" It wasn't what Master Absin had been taught, and centuries ago, he'd done his own reading. Nothing he'd encountered indicated *Jivatma* and *lorethasra* weren't different names for the same concept. However, one thing he'd learned in his life was to never be so bold as to entirely believe what he thought he knew. Be it as a warrior and his knowledge of combat, in what he considered to be Devesh's will, or in politics and how best to help those who required it. Especially the last.

In his estimation, a wise person always allowed for doubt. A wise person didn't unquestioningly accept their knowledge as being tantamount to absolute truth. As a result, he had an open mind for Cinder's beliefs. "Why don't you tell me where I'm wrong," Master Absin suggested.

Cinder flashed a faint smile. "It's a long story."

Master Absin smiled in reply. "I have time to listen."

Cinder cleared his throat and spoke of what he knew about the differences between *lorethasra* and *Jivatma*.

Based on his explanation, they boiled down to several key points, and Master Absin summarized them. "You say *lorethasra* contains the Elements we think make up the world, but it also includes the Spirit of a person?"

Cinder nodded. "From what I've learned. Yes."

"And *Jivatma* merges those Elements with the mind?"

"Yes. The will."

"And as a result, *Jivatma* must be the soul?"

"Some people think so."

"But you're not sure," Master Absin said rather than asked.

"It would make sense if it were true," Cinder said, "especially given its appearance."

The last part of his answer captured Master Absin's attention. "Appearance? No one can see their *lorethasra*."

"When I conduct my *Jivatma*—"

"Conduct?" Master Absin interrupted.

"It's how the Mythaspuris describe the use of their *Jivatma*. Same with some stories about Shokan, Sira, and *asrasins*, ancient human masters."

"Conduct," Master Absin mused. So many old terms used by such a young man. Odd. "Go on."

"When I conduct my *Jivatma*, I see a perfectly reflective pool of water. It shimmers under a bright, blue sky, but I can never see the sun."

Master Absin had no response to Cinder's statement. His description of *Jivatma*, if it was true and not a delusion, might lend credence to his beliefs. There was only one problem. "If *Jivatma* is the soul, then how can you have over-taxed yours? The soul is Devesh's love and grace seeded within us. It impels our motions, our intellect. Are you not still alive? Are you not still capable of thought?"

A crease troubled Cinder's brow, and once again, his gaze went distant. After a few moments, he twisted in his seat, facing about. "You don't think my *Jivatma* is gone?"

Master Absin chuckled. "No. I'm saying if *Jivatma* really is the soul—"

"The Mythaspuris believed it was."

"Just because they believed it doesn't mean it's the truth." Master Absin allowed annoyance to creep into his voice. He didn't enjoy being interrupted, especially when he had a point to make. "They weren't all-knowing or all-seeing. Only Devesh can claim such providence. As for *Jivatma*, if it's the soul, you can't overuse it and remain living. Since you live, it means you didn't overuse it. Either that or *Jivatma* isn't the soul. Don't believe everything you think."

A hopeful note entered Cinder's voice. "But if it *is* the soul, it might mean everything will ultimately work itself out."

Master Absin laid a companionable hand on Cinder's shoulder. He liked the young human. While other elves would immediately dart to the dangers posed by humans sourcing their *lorethasra*—dangers Master Absin recognized—he thought them overblown. Humans wouldn't overwhelm Yaksha Sithe or any other woven nation. He had faith in his people's power and Seminal's inherent balance. "I hope so, too. In fact, I know of some elves who even the physicians thought had burned out their *lorethasra*, but it wasn't true. They recovered, but it took them months to do so."

Cinder's lips thinned, and his gaze went to the ground. "I hope it's the same for me. It's strange being so weak when I thought I was gaining strength." He vacillated. There was another reason for his worry, one that over the past few days had taken precedence over all others. He hesitated to give it voice but felt he had to. "I don't want to be a burden to the unit. I don't want them expecting my strength, and I end up giving them my weakness. It'll get them hurt. Or worse."

Master Absin nodded. "It is a valid fear, but by now everyone has noticed your... regression. They've accounted for it. But your skill with a sword isn't your greatest attribute. It's your mind. Your skills as a tactician and strategist—areas where elves and dwarves struggle—are what will see your fellow Seconds come home alive." He leaned toward Cinder, his eyes intense. "And whatever else happens between you and your *Jivatma* you can still gain strength. Dedicate yourself to your talent, to your form and to your execution. Fight to live. Remember who you are. *Mastha Par! Krathe Lomon!*"

Cultivate perfection. Vanquish foes.

Cinder's jaw firmed, his spine straightened, and a weight seemed to lift off him. "Yes, sir," he said, the words ringing out like a vow.

10

Following his conversation with Master Absin, Cinder was able to put to rest some of his fears regarding his *Jivatma*… To a certain extent, anyway. He consoled himself, reminded that if *Jivatma* really was a person's soul, it had to be impossible to truly burn out. Which meant, he'd simply have to wait and pray for it to heal.

In the meantime, he still had some faint understandings of how to overcome weaves of Earth and Air; he still had his skills as a warrior, and he could yet improve them. For instance, archery didn't require *Jivatma* or *lorethasra*. It required concentration and dedication, and Cinder could concentrate, and he was most certainly dedicated. And even without *Jivatma*, he was one of the finest archers amongst the Seconds, and he aimed to become the best.

He forced himself to approach all his classes with that kind of determination, and by the time Archery rolled around the next day, he was feeling much better about his future.

"What has you so happy?" Bones asked as they trekked alongside the other human and elven Seconds toward the archery range.

Cinder smiled, at ease like he hadn't been in several weeks. "Just feeling like today is going to be a good day."

Bones snorted. "At least you aren't whining any more. No one likes a whiner."

Cinder laughed, somewhat abashed that Bones had noticed his despondency. Had everyone?

He figured they had, but it no longer mattered. Today he was happy. The talk with Master Absin had helped him tremendously, and his depression had dropped away like a damp, dirty coat he'd tossed aside. It left him feeling buoyant, full of energy and an excited desire to test himself.

The Seconds soon reached the archery range, a sunny field where man-sized and man-shaped targets stood at various distances from a single dirt stripe—the shooting line. Bales of hay were placed around and behind the targets to catch any stray arrows. A solitary tree, its trunk arching, crowned a single hill rising yards past the range, and its leaves rustled as a gentle breeze blew through its branches. A blue sky speckled with fluffy clouds encapsulated the scene.

Their instructor, Master Serwil, waited for them. He was a whipcord-slim elf, blond haired, older, and generally plain spoken like Master Jovick, but rather than addressing them with brusque impatience, a bitter undercurrent often bled through his rough words. Perhaps it was because Master Serwil's life had been full of tribulations—his family had been killed by a horde of zahhacks. Nevertheless, Cinder generally found the archery master to be unstinting with his teaching, no matter how he might phrase the instruction. Just as important, Master Serwil was fair. He didn't see humans as the natural inferior to the elves, and he expected excellence from all of them.

"Line up, cadets," Master Serwil said, pacing in front of them. "Get your bows strung. You know the drill."

As one, the Seconds dropped to their knees, uncasing their bows and getting them strung. As soon as he was done, Cinder rose to his feet and rearranged the quiver full of arrows on his hip.

"We're doing something new," Master Serwil said. "A team competition, each one with two people. The pair of you will line up in front of one of the five stations. You'll face three targets, one far and two near. Both members get three arrows at them. Then you sprint to the next set. If a team catches you, you have to let them go ahead of you and wait for them to finish. The goal is to get two center-mass hits—the bullseye in this case—on all five farther targets and three bullseyes on the ten nearer ones." Master Serwil smiled sadistically. "The team that gets done first *won't* have to run a dozen laps around the range after class. Pair up. An elf and human. We get going in two minutes."

Cinder went to Mohal. They generally made a good team.

"You take the near shots, and I'll take the distant ones?" Cinder suggested.

Mohal's blue eyes flashed as he smiled. "There you go again, leaving me the more difficult shots."

Cinder grinned. "Feel free to go after the longer shots. I'm sure we'll enjoy running those laps."

Mohal chuckled. "Or maybe we'll stick with your plan."

"Good idea."

"Get on the shooting line!" Master Serwil shouted. "No one nock an arrow until I tell you to."

There was a mad dash as the Seconds hustled to get in position. Cinder and Mohal managed to claim a central station.

"Stances five feet apart," Cinder said to Mohal. "Shift around me to get your arrows in the nearer target."

"Yes, sir," Mohal said, sounding not the least bit ironic.

Cinder frowned in surprise. Since when had he become a *sir*?

He shrugged. They had a few more seconds before the competition started, and Cinder imagined his pool of *Jivatma*. He couldn't see it, but the attempted visualization still brought him calm.

He inhaled deeply and controlled his exhalation through his mouth. His attention narrowed on the distant targets. They were seventy-five yards away. Another deep inhalation, and he shook out the tension in his arms and shoulders. Relaxed focus was the key to archery.

"Get ready," Master Serwil shouted. "We start in five... four... three." He finished the countdown. "Go!"

Cinder nocked an arrow, drew and aimed it in a single motion. Countless hours had honed his movements. What had once been uncomfortable and awkward was now smooth and effortless. He locked onto the relatively large, red circle centered on the far target's torso. *The center-mass bullseye.* The place where he needed to land two arrows. The wind came left-to-right. Cinder made a slight adjustment and released.

The arrow whistled the downrange and quivered home an inch to the right of the central circle. Cinder nocked, drew, and aimed another arrow. He remained calm, steady in his breathing, his posture relaxed.

Release.

The arrow streaked, whistling until it slammed near the center of the circle. Cinder had a third arrow ready, and he loosed it while the second one was still quivering. This one barely made it into the circle, but anything inside counted.

"Done," Mohal said. He'd managed to land two arrows into one of the nearer targets.

"Move. Next target," Cinder ordered.

They shifted right, arriving at the next set of targets at the same time that Cariath and Ishmay were leaving. Those two had only landed one arrow each in the near and far bullseyes.

Cinder fell into the rhythm of the competition. A meditative flow of nock, draw, aim, and release. He never landed less than at least one arrow in the bullseye, and most times two. On one occasion, he even had time to aim at a nearer target and sent his arrow speeding into its center.

"Pathetic!" Master Serwil shouted in the midst of the competition. "Will any of you actually finish the course?"

Cinder ignored him.

He and Mohal finished several circuits, and the elf had come close to matching Cinder. They had the distant targets completed but still needed a third arrow in four of the nearer ones.

Cinder keyed on the final targets. He and Mohal got the first one out of the way. The second one, too. They caught Cariath and Ishmay.

Another near target down. One more to go. Cinder glanced across the line of archers. Three teams away, Riyne and Bones were on their last target. A far one. It was the same set that he and Mohal needed to complete their final near target.

"Go!" Cinder ordered Mohal, who sprinted away.

He wouldn't get there before Riyne loosed his next arrow. Which meant Cinder needed to get off his shot now. It wasn't against the rules, and who followed rules in battle anyway? He took aim at the near target. A difficult shot. An angled attempt from sixty yards.

Cinder breathed out, imagined the arrow striking the center of the bullseye. A flashing glint in the depths of his mind, like the embers of his *Jivatma*. He fired. Riyne had released his arrow an instant prior. The elf's shot landed just outside the red circle. Cinder's shot hammered home two inches from dead center, well inside the bullseye.

"Done!" Cinder shouted to Master Serwil.

"No, you're not," Riyne shouted. "You cheated. You took a shot from the wrong area."

Master Serwil laughed. "There's no such thing as cheating in battle. Cinder bent the rules, but he finished the task. Well done."

Cinder whooped, slapping hands with Mohal who had returned to his side.

Master Serwil's smile slipped, and he addressed the rest of the Seconds. "The rest of you owe me a dozen laps."

A collective groan met his words.

Cinder continued to grin in satisfaction, but he also couldn't tolerate the notion of standing around idly while the rest of the Seconds completed their laps. "I'm going to run with them," he told Mohal, who growled in annoyance but joined him anyway.

They raced to catch up with the others.

Riyne and Cariath viewed him in surprised speculation, while Estin scowled.

"Idiot," Bones muttered when Cinder reached his side. "I'd be camped out relaxing if I was in your shoes."

Cinder smiled. "I know, but you'll do what's right when the time comes."

Anya stood on the forecastle of *Raider*, the flagship of Yaksha Sithe's navy. In addition to patrolling the Sentient Sea, the powerful three-masted warship was also used to transport members of the imperial family or other important delegations. Right now, the vessel was a beehive of activity as the sailors got *Raider* ready to dock. They'd reached their destination: the city of Char.

A stiff breeze tugged ineffectually at Anya's heavy braid but managed to swirl her cloak like a crimson flag. Gulls cried as they winged across the sky. Gray waters washed against *Raider's* hull, and the typical port smells of brine and fish saturated the air.

Anya held her arms crossed over her chest and stared across the blue waves of Triad Bay on the shores of which sat Char, Apsara Sithe's port city on the Onus Sea. She had never been here before, and the place struck her as strange. Char was different from other elven cities, at least the ones of Yaksha Sithe. It didn't meld gracefully with the surrounding treed hills and offered no compromise to nature's green growth.

Instead, the city anchored next to the water like a crab, armored in gray stonework and with a pair of granite forts on either side of the harbor to act as pincers. Powerful. Forceful. This was a city meant to intimidate and overwhelm, to glower challenge at any visitors. Home to over a hundred thousand proud elves who shouted to the waters of their unyielding strength.

Could such a vulgar display of might have its roots in fear?

Her eyes went south. Several hundred miles in that direction lay Bharat, home to the rishis. The powerful human descendants of the Mythaspuris.

They were known to occasionally intrude into Apsara Sithe, giving no notice of their intentions and certainly never asking for permission to enter. The rishis simply sailed forth from Bharat, landed their forces, and went where they willed, apparently fearless in their disregard of opposition.

With good reason.

Rumor held that each rishi had opened four Chakras, and every one of them was guarded by one hundred rakishis, their powerful soldiers—each one equal to three elven warriors. It was a force to give pause to any army. In fact, one rishi alone might be enough to challenge all the warriors of any particular sithe or crèche. It was for this reason that entire nations trembled whenever a Bharatian cast a shadow on their shores. A rishi's four open Chakras would grant them unmatched power.

But only if it was true.

Anya privately doubted it. The rishis were powerful—she didn't deny it—but their puissance had to be an exaggeration, similar to their apparently ageless lives. After all, there were said to only be ten rishis on Bharat, and their names were unchanged for the past twenty-five hundred years. Ten humans who declared the achievement of immortality?

Ridiculous.

It was as patently absurd as their assertion to have opened four Chakras. An impossibility, not when only a handful of elves throughout history had ever managed even three Chakras. And those elves hadn't been immortal. Long-lived, yes, but in the end, they had all passed on, gracefully aged and gone.

But…

Anya considered the sea separating Apsara Sithe and distant Bharat. Only several hundred miles. Not a large distance to travel.

"What are you staring at?" her father asked. He'd climbed up to the forecastle, Lisandre trailing after him.

Initially, Anya had thought Lisandre's inclusion was for her supposed benefit; to place them in proximity so an affair could bloom between them and temporarily bind their families together.

She now realized there were other reasons. Lisandre was a skilled ranger, but he had little experience in diplomacy. This visit to Apsara would season him, possibly improve his future marriage prospects.

"I was thinking of Bharat," Anya said, answering her father's question.

He grunted. "It's too lovely a morning to waste on those sorcerers." He spat out the last word, as if it might clog his throat.

Sorcerers. A word of contempt, and the private name by which elves referred to the rishis.

Lisandre interrupted whatever Anya might have said in reply. "The members of the honor guard have gathered on the main deck," he said, pointing. "We'll be disembarking soon."

Anya glanced to where he indicated. The twenty members of the honor guard accompanying her and her father to Apsara were drawn up in a double-line, two rows deep, armed, armored, and heads held high.

"We've already collected your belongings," her father added.

Anya frowned. "You didn't have to do that. I could have managed it on my own."

"This is a diplomatic mission," Lisandre reminded her. "You are no longer the ranger, Anya Aruyen. You are the Princess Anya Aruyen of Yaksha Sithe."

Anya nodded understanding.

Her father cleared his throat. "Which means you can't wear your ranger's garb." He gestured to her current clothing, the pants, shirt, and jacket, all of them patterned in green and browns to camouflage with a forest. "The maids are waiting in your quarters. You have to change into something befitting a woman of your station."

Her father was telling her she had to wear a sari.

Anya grimaced.

"It's not that bad," her father said with a chuckle. "Lots of women wear saris and some even enjoy it."

Anya smiled. "It's not that. A sari means I can't ride a horse. I'll have to take a carriage." She gave a dramatic sigh. "Nothing is more boring than riding in a carriage."

"Well, I'll be joining you in the carriage," her father said, still smiling. "While we travel, we can review the trade issues we're trying to iron out with Apsara."

Anya had already studied the referenced documents in great detail. She had done so directly after being told of her inclusion in the delegation to Apsara. Some of it was simple. For instance, her mother wanted ongoing access to Apsara's *sathana* grass for the creation of *insufi* blades, the swords given during an *upanayana* ceremony.

It shouldn't be a problem. Yaksha and Apsara shared a long history of peace and good relations. In fact, it was Jenuwel Dhara, a duchess of Yaksha Sithe who had become the first empress of Apsara toward the end of the *NusraelShev*.

There were other issues related to commodities pricing, but a more important matter for Anya's mother was land. The area in the Dagger Mountains where the two sithes bordered one another had shifted southeast over the past seventy years. Anya's mother wanted the border shifted back north.

It made sense. The Apsaran elves were nomads. They loved their wide-open plains and riding their horses. They had no need for mountainous land but returning the border north would likely come at a cost, such as a guarantee of Redwinth's marriage to Enma.

Her mother also wanted a score of Apsaran horses for breeding stock to improve their own lines. It was an expensive purchase, and Yaksha would have to offer similar recompense, such as crafting only they could produce.

Anya smiled when she considered the Apsaran horses. They were fine animals. Fast, rugged, and able to run for miles. But they were not Yavanas, and it continued to stick in the craws of the Apsarans that Devesth's horses were forever finer than their own.

"Why are you smiling?" her father asked.

Anya explained.

He chuckled. "In the same breath, they both hate and love Devesth's steeds. Imagine if they ever saw a human in Yaksha's colors riding a Yavana."

"You mean like Cinder Shade?" Lisandre asked.

Her father nodded. "Anya thinks he might have it in him to be the first human ranger in Yaksha's history."

His tone was condescending, and Anya refused to be baited. She answered as if her father had made a serious observation. "He might have it within him," she said. "Master Absin thinks so as well. It's why he teaches all the Firster humans the means by which to cycle *prana*."

"I've read Prince Redwinth is also a ranger," Lisandre noted, thankfully shifting the conversation. "What I don't know is whether he plans on continuing his work in Apsara's army. If he insists on placing himself in danger, we should ask to pay a lower dowry."

"The same could be said of Anya," her father replied, his tone wry. "When you come of age to take a husband, the sithe in question will likely ask for a substantially higher dowry for whichever prince you end up marrying."

Anya hid a wince at her father's reply, mostly because it was true, and instead squared her shoulders. She was who she was, and she wouldn't apologize for it. "You're right, but I'm also worth it." She lifted a challenging brow toward her father, who laughed.

"You most certainly are."

Lisandre slapped the ship's rail, changing the conversation again. "This is a fine vessel, but it's not my favorite. For flagships, I preferred *Viper*."

"My favorite was *Falcon*," Anya said.

"That's not a flagship," Anya's father protested. "It's barely a *ship*. It's a piece of junk that should have been retired decades ago."

Anya shook her head, grinning. "I love *Falcon*. There's a certain roguish charm to her, a sense of fun and adventure. She and her twin, *Serenity*."

Sriovey collapsed onto the bench next to Derius and heaved a weary sigh. The two of them sat in the walled garden adjacent to Krathe House, the one favored by the princess. Even now in the early fall, flowers bloomed, and their pungent perfume filtered through the courtyard. Songbirds crooned somewhere close by, but Sriovey couldn't have named their species. He'd never placed much emphasis on the study of fauna or flora beyond what was edible or dangerous.

In fact, Sriovey didn't care much for the garden at all, and as if in proof of his antipathy, he sneezed.

He grimaced.

Flowers. The bane of his existence. So many of them caused his eyes to water, his sinuses to swell, and his ears to itch. He hated them.

Derius chuckled. "I'm sorry I asked you to meet me here. I forgot how much you loathe flowers."

Sriovey dismissed the words with a wave of his hand. "It doesn't matter," he said. "We need privacy to talk. This is as good a place as any." While waiting on Derius to explain the reason for their meeting, he massaged his aching calves, groaning in relief. It had been a long day, and the instructors had pushed them to their limits, expecting more than ever before. Master Jovick had been especially hard. All of it was in preparation for the upcoming Autumn Trial.

Sriovey wasn't looking forward to it. Not after the disaster of the Unitary Trial. The deaths of so many Firsters, especially Nathaz and Dorcer. It was unprecedented, and his throat still clenched with grief whenever he thought of his friends. In their chosen profession, there had always the threat of death, but did it have to destroy Nathaz and Dorcer when they were still so young? Why couldn't they have lived long, peaceful lives? Why did they have to die in the middle of the wilderness, slain by spiderkin.

But it was the way of the world. Seminal was a ruinous realm, one requiring dwarves to act in defiance of their natural state, their deep-seated desire to provide peace and comfort. It left them acting harshly, which was in utter opposition to their maker's intent.

Shokan.

Many woven had forgotten the Blessed One's importance and, even more, considered him a myth. But the dwarves hadn't forgotten. They knew the one who had created their people. How Shokan had shaped the dwarves from creatures he had brought to Seminal from his first world. Shokan had leached away the viciousness from a strange race of dog-like monsters, and with Sira's help, transformed them into dwarves, a people whose name had once been a byword for comfort and heartsease.

Look how far they'd fallen. It made Sriovey want to weep.

But now wasn't the time for tears, and he stifled his soft emotions. "What did you want to talk about?"

"Cinder Shade."

"What about him?"

"He isn't himself. You've seen him over the past few weeks. He's slower. Weaker. Less than he used to be, but still more than any human."

Sriovey grunted in reply.

Cinder was an enigma. Weeks ago, he had been swift and strong enough to give any dwarf, even Derius, the most powerful of them, everything he could handle. But something had changed. Cinder was no longer the force of nature he had once been. He still had incomparable skills for a human, but it was no longer matched to physical attributes to make even an elf envious. A skilled woven could and often did beat him nowadays, in both armed and unarmed combat.

Sriovey and Derius had already discussed the matter, just last week, in fact, but neither had an obvious explanation for Cinder's loss of ability. Unless Derius had one now? Sriovey waited for his fellow dwarf, the wisest and deepest thinker among them, to explain himself.

"He nearly defeated Jozep today in unarmed combat," Derius said.

Again, Sriovey had noticed, and again, he didn't know what it meant. He was tired, sore, and had no further patience for one of Derius' guessing games. "Just say what's on your mind," he snapped.

"I think Cinder came close to burning out his ability to source *lorethasra*," Derius replied, "but he's regaining it."

It was an unexpected answer, and Sriovey leaned back, hands behind his head. Could Derius' explanation be true? From what he knew of those who burned out their *lorethasra*, only a rare few ever regained it. He glanced at Derius and realized there was more to the explanation.

"I watched him closely when he sparred against Jozep," Derius said. "Cinder held him back until he couldn't. It was like his speed and strength came in starts and stops. It made it impossible for Jozep to commit to what should have been an easy win. There aren't many records available about woven who burned out their *lorethasra*, but the ones I've read state that they recovered it in fits and halts. Like what Cinder did today."

Sriovey could guess the rest. "But you also don't think he sources *lorethasra*. You think he conducts *Jivatma*. Like the Mythaspuris or Shokan." It was their greatest fear.

"Like the Mythaspuris or Shokan," Derius agreed. A second later. "Or Shokan's Fated Foe." He quoted the *Crèche Prani*, their holy text. "*The Fated Foe will know your powers better than you know them your-selves. He will pretend weakness, but mastery of all arts will come to him as easily as breath. He will wield* Jivatma *and proclaim affection and brotherhood, but behind his cunning smile watches the* Elonic Ciprion, *the Fated Foe.*"

Sriovey swore. The *Elonic Ciprion*. It was from *Shevasra* and rough-ly translated, it meant the Bringer of Destruction, although his peo-ple named him the Fated Foe. He was mentioned in the *Crèche Prani*, in the same portion prophesizing Shokan's return. The Blessed One would arrive on Seminal like the wind, unseen and unknown, but owning the power of a storm. No one would know of him prior, but all would recognize his enemy, the Fated Foe, the Son of Emptiness, who would blaze across the world in glory. No doubt, the *Elonic Ciprion* was Shet's heretofore unknown son.

"And Shokan is supposed to be the *Cipre Elonicon*," Derius said. "The Destroyer of Falsehood, the usurper of all power. It's strange how similar their names are. Only a single dot to the final syllable of *Elonic Ciprion* to transform it to *Cipre Elonicon*." He let loose a bitter chuckle. "We pray for Shokan to save us from the Son of Emptiness, and yet, both will destroy our way of life."

In the best of times, Sriovey hated discussing religion and prophecy, and now was no different. Devesh save him from priests and prophets.

Too many of them were false. "Or it could all be meaningless. All these fears are based on an old, discredited book."

"The *Crèche Prani* is old, but it isn't discredited. It has never led our people astray. The Fated Foe *will* come, and Cinder has some of the attributes of the enemy."

"It doesn't matter if he does. The *Crèche Prani* also instructs us to kill the Fated Foe as soon as he is identified," Sriovey said. "I can't kill Cinder. I love him like a brother." He glanced at Derius, understanding now why his fellow dwarf wanted to meet with him today. "You wanted to know how I feel about Cinder. Whether I can carry through what's needed if he really is the Fated Foe."

"Yes," Derius admitted with a sigh. "I love him, too."

Sriovey rubbed his face, hating this conversation. "Hotgate," he muttered. "I should have never given him a nickname. It makes him too real."

"He earned it, and how were we to know this might happen."

Sriovey had a thought. "What if he's Shokan?"

Derius laughed. "He can't be Shokan. Shokan will explode into our world out of a clear, blue sky. It's part of his prophecy. His is an unheralded return." He quoted again from the *Crèche Prani*. "*No one shall know of him before his arrival. He is as he will be; wielding Wild Lightning in one hand and Undefiled Locus, the Diamond Sword, in the other.*"

"I never understood that last part. Why is it so important for him to wield Shet's blade?" Sriovey asked.

"Undefiled Locus isn't Shet's blade. The sword was always meant for Shokan's hand. Shet killed the dwarven smith who crafted Undefiled Locus along with his entire crèche in order to steal it."

Shet. The Son of Emptiness. Shokan. Too many gods for a humble dwarf who longed for the soothing grace of peace.

Sriovey stared north, as if he could see past the hills of Yaksha proper, across the distant Sentient Sea, and all the way into the heart of the Dagger Mountains. Legend told of a mountain in those jagged peaks. A soaring spire from whence Shet had once commanded a land of ruin and death. Naraka had been the name of both his citadel and his empire, and it was in the bones of those lofty peaks that the Mythaspuris had chained the god for eternity.

But according to the *Crèche Prani*, eternity was not forever. Shet would rise again. The Fated Foe would free him, and Shokan would face the god and the Son of Emptiness.

Sriovey prayed none of it had anything to do with Cinder Shade, the young human for whom he had come to so deeply care. If it had to be anyone, let it be Genka Devesth, the barbarian warlord of the Sunset Kingdoms.

11

The week after his discussion with Master Absin, Cinder held fast to his optimism for the future. He refused to brood on the fact that his *Jivatma* remained lost to him, and nothing appeared able to change that fact. No matter the situation, it remained absent. Even in the Foe, the place where he had the greatest odds of finding it again, his *Jivatma* was simply gone. Rather than a still water of perfect purity, there existed only emptiness. Not even the lightning.

So what?

He still had his fellow cadets, classes, and research, and they all helped. In fact, it was because of the latter that he was on his way to the library right now, intent on investigating a few books. With any luck, the texts would answer some niggling questions. Specifically, questions related to the strange visions he often saw, such as the glorious city on the ocean, the sense of a forgotten family, and the beautiful woman with honey-blonde hair.

Initially, Cinder had reckoned the images were nothing more than simple imaginings, but their repetitive nature, the unchanging people within them, and their sense of authenticity had him considering

152

other possibilities. What if the dreams were real? What if they represented visions from a past life?

Reincarnation.

Many people believed in it. They maintained that upon death, some people were reborn. Cinder wondered if he was one such individual. What if the Cinder Shade of Swallow, the crippled young boy with a club foot and withered leg, had truly died when the *aether*-cursed cat had attacked him on that long-ago summer day? What if the person he was now was a poorly remembered past life version of someone else? A warrior from another time, an era possibly prior to the Mythaspuris and Shet. An age when humans could do wonderful things with their *Jivatma.*

It would account for so much. Cinder's explosive growth and mastery of his martial talents. His *Jivatma*. The flashes of insight and wisdom he had never been told or read. The haunting visions. Reincarnation would resolve so many of his questions.

And while there couldn't be true proof of reincarnation, he hoped there might be records of others who had experienced visions similar to his.

Cinder reached the library and smiled as he always did when he inhaled the musty aroma of old paper. He'd never get tired of the feeling of calm found here, the sense of bated breath and the excitement of learning. A few students, instructors, and warriors sat at the various tables, reading beneath the light of the *diptha* chandeliers.

Cinder glanced to Master Molni, who appeared to be in deep conversation with Master Absin.

He nodded acknowledgement to the two of them before heading upstairs to the second floor. The books he needed were shelved in the area related to religion. He soon reached the section, grabbed the books, and minutes later, he was seated at a corner table, a lit *diptha* lamp overhead.

The first book on reincarnation was actually focused on Shet and referred to certain prophecies, which foretold the rebirth of the slumbering god. It was unhelpful for the information Cinder wanted, but nevertheless, he found it fascinating. Who knew evil had its own set of prophecies?

Then again, on further consideration, maybe it wasn't so surprising. After all, in the dwarven holy book, *Crèche Prani*, entire stanzas were devoted to describing a being named the Fated Foe and also the omens which would warn of the rise of the Shackled God.

Cinder set the book on Shet aside but made a mental note to return to it at a later date. The next few texts he perused were more of what he had in mind, and he dug deeper into their pages.

Hours passed as he read accounts of people who claimed to know their past lives. Most had detailed but implausible remembrances. Terrifying descriptions of a battle. Cooking a type of dish foreign to their palate. Describing lands they'd never before visited. Hearing music and songs they'd never before encountered. However, a common theme in nearly all of the recollections was a connection to someone greater than who they were in their current lives.

It sounded like an understandable wish fulfillment, and it also wasn't too different from Cinder's own dreams.

He continued on until the dimming of the main lights heralded the closing of the library. Cinder sighed in disappointment. He could have read for far longer, but it was time to go. He re-shelved the books and headed downstairs, where Master Molni sat at his desk with no one else about in the library.

The old elf smiled as Cinder approached. "Did you find what you were looking for?"

"I found some interesting books," Cinder allowed, unwilling to divulge anything more than that. His research into reincarnation was a private matter, even more private than his belief in his *Jivatma*.

"Good," Master Molni said. "Was there anything else you wanted to discuss?

"Not right now."

Master Molni smiled. "Well if you do, you know where to find me."

"Yes, sir," Cinder replied.

He left the library, and as he walked back to Krathe House, he stumbled when a vision washed over him.

Clouds swirled in a gray sky, and high in those steely curtains, lightning forked. Mad voices gibbered, incomprehensible sounds. A hole formed, and through it, a black shape entered the world, plummeting to the ground and taking on definition. Legs. Arms. And wings, which snapped open with a thundercrack. Her descent—and the creature was a she—slowed, but she still hammered the ground when she hit. Her knees flexed, and she rose to her full height. Taller than a yakshin and armored in black chitin. Fires wreathed about her horns, smoke drifted from her nostrils, and a sense of evil billowed about her.

Her name was Salachar, and she was a Rakshasa. A demon of an ancient world.

The world snapped back into being, and Cinder found himself bent over at the knees and panting.

It had been another vision, another series of sights he was increasingly certain represented a true experience. And this time, the images weren't erasing. They remained with him and left him shaken. Such surpassing evil.

What kind of person must he have been to have witnessed such horrors?

The next evening, the Seconds were congregated in the commons of their dorm hall, discussing the day's events. Cinder sat alone, strumming his mandolin and playing notes rather than an actual song. His mind was on tomorrow's small unit drill. It would be the final training session involving all the Seconds before shipping out for the Autumn Trial.

"What's the name of the zahhack with the scorpion tail?" Bones asked the room at large. He and Ishmay sat at a table together, notes spread out in front of them. They appeared to be reviewing material related to the zahhacks and other information they'd covered in Tactics and Strategy as well as in history over the past few weeks.

"They're called ajakavas," Cinder said. He'd read all about the various species of zahhacks and memorized all the important details. Their strengths, weaknesses, and the easiest ways to kill them. "Their balance is poor, and they can't shift direction very easily."

"They're still scary bastards, though," Sriovey said.

Riyne snorted. "Ajakavas are nothing compared to the Rakshasas."

Upon hearing the word, Cinder hit a discordant tone on the mandolin. The sound rang jaggedly. *Rakshasas.* Demons. He felt certain he'd seen one yesterday. A black creature in his visions. Salachar had been her name. He shivered. Had it been real? In his past life, had he truly fought a Rakshasa?

"Rakshasas aren't zahhacks," Derius said. "They're not even from this world. They're from the Realms." A beat later. "If they're even real."

Estin, who was playing euchre with Mohal, Jozep, and Wark, spoke up. "Oh, they're real. I read about them in my mother's library. She has books there. Rare volumes no one else is allowed to read, except the empress and—"

"Then how did you get to read them?" Depth asked.

Estin shot him a glare. "I was about to add *and* the royal family. The Rakshasas fought for Shet against the Mythaspuris, and if half of what was written about them is true, they'd ravage the world if Shet ever lost control of them." Estin appeared to be warming up to the topic, and he set his cards down. "There was a lot of information like that in my mother's library along with more details about the zahhacks than we learned in class."

Cinder stopped strumming the mandolin and paid closer attention. He didn't like Estin, but the man had information they could all use. "What else can you tell us?"

For a wonder, Estin didn't sneer or snap at him. He merely answered the question, taking on a studious tone. "The echyneis, the crocodile-like zahhacks, and the erawans, the ones like elephants, hate each other. They kill one another on sight. The ghouls are small and cowardly, but they make up for their weakness through sheer numbers. They breed like rabbits."

Sriovey wore a scowl. "I hate ghouls. Those fuckers destroyed Elasmara Crèche and took over the Pischa Hills."

"But the gnarled-toothed little monsters didn't do it on their own," Estin said. "They had help; a leader when they took Elasmara, the Kenga Kain. He's the one who forged the Black Horde, the only army they ever managed to field. The ghouls think Kenga will come again, and their leaders are named "Kains" in his honor." The prince leaned forward, and his eyes twinkled. "Here's what the ghouls and everyone else don't know. Kenga was a goblin king."

"What!" Derius shouted, his surprise reflecting Cinder's. "Goblins don't have kings. They're like insects with queens, warriors, breeders, workers, and stuff."

"There are kings," Estin said, "but they're weak when they're young, but upon maturity, they're stronger than the queens and better at controlling the warriors. It's no wonder the queens fear them. The kings are killed upon their birth, but Kenga somehow lived and managed to escape his nest. He went to the ghouls, looked enough like a powerful ghoul warrior that they accepted him as one of their own, and he ended up taking over their entire race."

Sriovey and Derius shared a look of speculation.

"Is this true?" Derius eventually asked of Estin.

The prince held up a hand as if making promise. "It's as true as Devesh."

"Shit," Sriovey said softly. "We always figured Kenga was some freakishly strong ghoul, not a goblin king."

"What about the ketus? Anything we should know about them?" Depth asked. His mouth was turned down in distaste. Depth hated snakes, and the ketus looked a lot like disgusting snakes with legs.

"Cut their heads off, and they die," Bones said dismissively before Estin could answer. "I want to know about the unformed and the vampires."

Riyne scoffed. "Vampires are weak. Fire and steel will do them.

Lisandre killed a half-dozen of them and all their blood slaves last year in a raid. He didn't lose a single ranger. And the unformed are only as strong as whatever animal they can imitate. If they pretend to be a lion, they're as strong as a lion, but weak as one, too. No weapons or extra reach except teeth and claws."

Estin was nodding agreement. "The truth is, zahhacks are only dangerous because of their numbers, but we'll handle them in the Daggers."

"Damn straight," Riyne said.

The room fell quiet as the Seconds absorbed the information Estin and Riyne had provided.

"The necrosed," Cinder said into the contemplative silence. "They aren't weak. They—"

"Anya killed several of them last year," Estin interjected. "By herself."

"But Anya is also the best warrior and ranger in all of Yaksha. No one has her skill." Cinder glanced at Riyne and shrugged in apology. "No offense to your brother."

"None taken," Riyne said. "Anya *is* special, but if we have to, we can still kill a necrosed."

"But we can't battle them like Anya. We have to be cunning when we face them, or they'll murder us." Cinder didn't want the Seconds to get an over-inflated sense of confidence against the zahhacks.

Bones exhaled heavily. "You know, you're not the cheeriest fellow in the world?"

"About the least cheeriest," Ishmay agreed.

Cinder grinned. "Say that to me when a necrosed is about to eat your face, and I save your asses."

The next evening saw Fastness displeased, a reflection of Cinder's own state of mind. The white had gotten into a brawl with Byerley, Estin's high-strung Yavana stallion. It was all because of impatience on the prince's part. During the small unit drill, Estin had pushed forward when he should have hung back. He'd disobeyed his orders and heeled his black stallion to get into the fray. In so doing, Byerley had shoved into Fastness, nipping at the white.

Fastness hadn't taken the bite well. The white had lunged at Byerley, seeking the other horse's neck. The stallions had fought, rearing and steel-shod hooves lashing at one another. It had taken a hard jerk on Fastness' reins to get the white to back off, but by then Byerley was bleeding. Estin's horse had taken several strikes to his chest and a clipping blow to the forehead, which if it had landed flush, could have crushed the black's skull.

By the time Cinder and Estin had gotten their respective mounts under control, the drill was over. Their team had been summarily defeated, distracted as they'd been by the rumbling stallions. It was a ridiculous way to lose and all because one damn elf couldn't hold it together and follow orders.

Of course, Cinder's explanation didn't matter to Masters Absin and Halin. They'd been furious with him, and he had been unable to provide any excuses for his side's miserable showing. Ultimately, their poor performance was his responsibility since he had been the one in charge of the unit.

As punishment for his warriors' lack of discipline, the masters had set Cinder running laps for two hours, and the only consolation was that Estin had been forced to join him.

It was dark by the time they finished their penance and returned to the barn. Grooms had already seen to their mounts, including healing Byerley's injuries, but it went without saying that Cinder and Estin had to check on their horses anyway.

Currently, Cinder stood in Fastness' stall, brushing down the white. A single overhead *diptha* bulb shone down upon them, but otherwise the rest of the barn was dark. It was the end of a long week and a longer day, and no one else was about. The other horses were already bedded down for the night, occasionally snorting or whickering. No breeze moved the air, which was pungent with the smell of horse and hay and loud with the sounds of crickets chirping.

The white nickered, nosing into Cinder's jacket. He was likely seeking an apple, his favorite treat. He nosed more deeply, neighing in betrayed frustration.

Cinder laughed. "You're incorrigible."

Nevertheless, he fetched an apple from the one pocket Fastness had yet to sniff through. The stallion chomped down on the fruit, and while he chewed, Cinder ran his fingers against the horse's forelock, the place in between his eyes. Fastness liked it when he stroked him there, and Cinder found it soothing as well.

In the past few months, he and the white had thoroughly bonded and only rarely argued. They worked well together, and Cinder regretted the inevitable ending of their partnership. When he finished his studies at the Directorate, the stallion would either be put to stud or given as a mount to a royal guard.

Fastness rested his head on Cinder's shoulder. *"I'm sorry."*

Cinder stroked the white's forelock and forehead, smiling in affection. "Why are you sorry? You were only defending yourself."

"We lost the trial."

"It's fine. You have to put bullies in their place, and Byerley and his rider are bullies." He gave the stallion some sugar cubes he'd fetched from the kitchen and gave him a final pat. "I'll see you in the morning."

He stepped out of the stall and noticed Estin making his way to the barn's exit.

"Estin!" Cinder shouted. He had words to say to the prince, and he'd be burned by a Rakshasa if Estin didn't hear them. He cursed when the elf continued to march away from him, not bothering to slow down in the slightest. *Fragging jackhole.* He had to have heard him call out.

Cinder jogged to catch up with Estin, finally reaching the prince a few steps past the barn's exit. "Estin," he called again.

The elf continued walking.

Damn it! Cinder spun the elf around, immediately ducking a punch he knew was coming. A sound of rustling vines told him what to expect next. *A weave of Earth.* Sure enough, a rumble under his feet had him dancing aside. The damned elf was sourcing.

His anger distracted him, and he only noticed a hissing noise right before a blast of air shoved him off balance. He stumbled. Estin landed a punch flush to Cinder's chin, knocking him down.

Cinder tried to get back to his feet, but an unseen force shackled his torso to the ground.

"Don't you ever touch me again," Estin growled, standing directly over him.

Stupid jackhole. Cinder sent an upkick, hammering it into the elf's gut. Estin grunted as the breath exploded out of his lungs. He stumbled backward. Cinder was free, and he rose, stalking forward. Anger and outrage coursed through him. He'd only wanted to talk to the fragging elf!

Another hissing noise, but this time Cinder was ready. The same force that had pinned him to the ground tried to grip his entire body, but fury powered his movements. He pushed through Estin's attempt to trap him, reaching the elf in two strides.

The prince glared at him, managing a mocking smile. "Do your worst, human. It won't change the facts. You'll always be my lesser."

Cinder raised his fists. His heart pounded in time to his fury. He could barely think. All he knew was the desire to inflict pain. He wanted to wipe the arrogant smirk off the elf's face, beat him into the ground. Hurt Estin so bad, the prince would never consider challenging him again.

With a growl, he let his hands fall to his side. Estin wasn't worth it.

Estin's smirk widened. "I knew you didn't have the courage to do what is necessary. You're—"

The words were enough to rekindle Cinder's rage. His vision went red, and his hand whipped around. He backhanded Estin in the face, using every bit of force he could muster. The elf's head rocked, his eyes momentarily rolled, and he promptly fell on his ass, spitting blood from a split lip. He glared at Cinder, who squatted in front of the prince.

Coldness bled into his bones, doing nothing to quench his fury but allowing the clarity of icy thoughts. He hated this man. He hated what he represented. Arrogance, unearned confidence, and privilege. But he also had to get through to Estin. In two days, they were leaving for the Daggers. Estin had to get his head on straight. The rest of them couldn't afford his incompetence.

"What you do on your own time is none of my business," Cinder began, his voice chill as a winter wind. "You can throw your sword down and stomp out of a sparring circle like a toddler throwing a tantrum. You can pick your nose in public, pick your ass. I don't care. When we train as a unit, though, you do as you're told. Next time you disobey me, I'll beat you bloody." His voice filled with venom. "Then I'll really start hurting you."

A sneer lit the prince's handsome features, which were less handsome given his split lip and the ribbon of blood streaming down his chin. "Don't make threats you can't keep. I've seen you. You're not who you once were. You're weak. Like all your kind."

Cinder snorted in disgust. "Then why are you the one lying on the ground bleeding, you fucking idiot?" He didn't give Estin a chance to reply. Cinder leaned closer, hissing. "You're a prince of Yaksha. Try acting like one. Have you seen the faces of your countrymen? They're disgusted with you. You're supposed to lead them, but how can you if they hold you in contempt? They remember the Unitary Trial. The fight against the spiderkin. They know it was Depth who rallied the Firsters there. It was a human, not an elf. You're losing your warriors."

Awareness and possibly shame crawled across Estin's face followed by mulish stubbornness. "I don't need your advice."

Cinder was abruptly tired of dealing with the prince, of dealing with his Devesh-damned stupidity. "Do what you want, but in the Autumn Trial, if you put anyone else in danger, I'll cut you out and cut our losses. You won't be the reason one of us dies."

"You wouldn't dare," Estin sneered. "Kill a prince of the realm?"

"Who said anything about killing?" There were ways to remove a problem other than murder.

Estin stared up at him, puzzling over what he might mean, and the promise in his words must have finally penetrated the prince's thick head. His sneer transformed into fear.

12

Certitude, the city closest to the Third Directorate, had an undeniable elegance to it, one no human city could match. The ambling green spaces, the tree-lined, meandering roads, which felt more like winding woodland paths… the city was a merging of the artificial and natural; the subtle combining of stacked stones and straight-line construction mingled with the arterial aspect of trees and the organic nature of wildflowers, with neither holding power over the other. From Cinder's perspective, Certitude was a city masquerading as a park, or perhaps vice versa.

Bones and Mohal, who strode to Cinder's right didn't seem to notice, while Sriovey, marching to his left, had a scowl affixed to his face.

Apparently, the dwarf didn't find the city quite so lovely, which Cinder realized made a sort of sense. The dwarf's home was in the deep caverns of the Dagger Mountains, within dark fortresses where the sun never reached. As such, he probably found the green spaces of Certitude charmless. At least it seemed that way given Sriovey's stomping manner and frozen frown as they made their way through Certitude.

However, when Cinder peered more closely at Sriovey, he recognized an emotion underneath the scowl: envy. The understanding brought him an unexpected insight. Sriovey had once spoken of how his people used to live closer to the surface, in small villages with the sun streaming into their homes. Maybe he wished they still did. Maybe he wished dwarven villages and cities were more like those of the elves.

Bones muttered under his breath. "It's making me right uncomfortable. All these people staring at us."

He was right. People *were* staring. Cinder had first noticed their regard on Certitude's outskirts. Other travelers, farmers on wagons, or people whose tasks Cinder couldn't reckon had all paused their endeavors, falling quiet and watching the four of them with scrutinizing eyes. They didn't say anything, never even pointed, but they didn't have to.

Cinder had a notion as to why they were interested.

It was him. Their gazes didn't rest on Sriovey, Bones, or even their fellow elf, Mohal. It was Cinder. This was his first time to Certitude since he'd returned from the Unitary Trial, and until now, none of the elves outside the Directorate had really caught sight of him. But, apparently, they remembered him. They remembered his victory in the Grand Melee. He was the first human who had ever won the contest.

But their constant observing made traversing the streets of Certitude taxing. Not in the physical sense, but in the emotional one. It was a strain, having all the people pause and eye him in silent speculation.

Mohal must have noticed the same thing as Cinder. "It's not us," he said, jerking a thumb at Cinder. "It's him."

"I should have realized," Bones said, while Sriovey simply growled under his breath.

Cinder graced Bones with a smirk and couldn't help needling his friend. "I guess nothing gets past you."

"Of course not. My reflexes are too fast."

Their conversation—and more importantly, the staring—cut off when they reached their destination. *Silent Reverie*, the alehouse and restaurant the rest of the human and dwarven Seconds often frequented. Cinder, though, hadn't been here in months.

On entering, it seemed like nothing much had changed. Still facing the entry was a small bar and a door leading to the kitchen, while to the left stood a cold hearth, but in a few weeks a fire would likely burn inside of it. Heavy beams supported the ceiling, which gave way to warm, white-washed walls. Afternoon sunshine shone through floor-to-ceiling windows upon the side of the building facing the road, and a row of chandeliers provided further illumination. A handful of elves were already present and seated in the restaurant.

Cinder recognized a few of them, such as the owner, Quire Shoal, a middle-aged elf, handsome like all his kind, but thicker through the middle than was the norm. There was also the farmer, Heloin Sapnashen, also handsome but having a stolid presence like farmers everywhere. In addition, Heloin was their most reliable source about the world at large, especially the warlord, Genka Devesth, who was quickly consolidating the Sunset Kingdoms under his black horse banner.

Heloin smiled at them. "Afternoon, gents." He nodded at Cinder. "Haven't seen you in a while, champion. Congratulations on your victory."

Quire hustled over to shake Cinder's hand, a broad grin on his face. "I am so sorry for not congratulating you earlier on your win. Consider your meal and drinks today on the house."

Cinder wore a confused smile, not expecting his generosity. "Thank you, but you don't have to—"

Quire rapidly waved his hands. "I'll not have any arguments. I can't accept your payment. Your meal and drinks are free."

Bones scowled. "All this time I've been coming here, and you never offered me free drinks and a meal."

Quire sniffed. "Win a tournament, and I'll consider it."

"Any word on Genka?" Sriovey asked Heloin as they settled themselves at a nearby table.

Cinder glanced at Sriovey in question. For whatever reason, the dwarf had a fascination with Genka. So did Derius. At first, Cinder figured it was just the vicarious thrill of witnessing a bloody chapter in history, but now he wasn't so sure. There was an intensity to Sriovey's and Derius' interest in the Sunset Warlord. They seemed to fear him for reasons unrelated to the man's genius for war.

Weeks ago, Cinder thought he might have caught Sriovey viewing him in the same appalled fascination. A strangely contemplative aspect to his features, gone quicker than the blink of an eye. To this day, Cinder wasn't sure how to interpret the fleeting expression on Sriovey's face, or even if he'd actually seen anything at all.

Heloin twisted in his chair to face them. "None I've heard," he said in reply to Sriovey's question. "Things up north seem to have calmed down some."

"Let's hope they stay that way," Sriovey grumbled, a fervent tone in his voice.

Quire changed the subject. "Rumor says you achieved your skills in only two years," he said to Cinder, his tone not-quite disbelieving.

Cinder didn't have a chance to reply since Bones spoke first.

"It's true," Bones said. "I remember when he walked into *Steel-Graced Adepts*. He was a full foot shorter than he is now and dozens of pounds lighter. A scrawny little shit is what I thought. He didn't even know how to properly grip a sword back then."

"Amazing," Heloin said, his voice filled with admiration. "You must be a rare genius."

Cinder shrugged, not wanting to discuss his past. It made him uncomfortable. He was skilled and had achieved much, but he hated when anyone spoke about him with awe. He was only a man. "What's for supper?" he asked Quire, hoping to shift the topic of conversation.

"What's odder is Cinder doesn't remember the first sixteen years of his life," Bones said to the room at large.

Cinder groaned. Here it came. All the questions. Why did Bones have to bring this up now?

"Truly?" Quire asked. "How did this happen?"

"He likely mouthed off to someone and got conked in the head," Mohal said with a grin.

"It was an *aether*-cursed cat," Cinder corrected. "It killed my parents, and when it came after me, I tried to escape from it by hiding in a well, I nearly drowned, and when I woke up, I had no recollection of myself, my family, or my home."

"Someone actually had to tell him his name," Bones added.

Quire frowned in Heloin's direction. "Didn't something similar happen to Princess Anya?"

"So I've heard," Heloin answered. "Decades ago, she took ill, and they say she lingered on death's door for weeks. When she finally recovered, she woke up and had no knowledge of herself."

Cinder's gaze sharpened on Heloin. Anya had a similar history to his own? Given his life over the last two years, he doubted it was a coincidence. His incredible growth as a warrior. The name given to him by a yakshin. Conducting *Jivatma*. There were vast oddities to him, and it seemed Anya had similar ones: a princess who had lost her memory, the first female graduate of the Third Directorate, and the finest warrior of her nation.

"Well, Anya and Cinder may have some surface resemblances," Bones said, "but one of them is a princess and the other one is an ugly pug. They aren't so alike.

Duchess Marielle Cervine sat on the outdoor patio of a small café, sipping tea while gazing about her home, the lovely city of Certitude. The winding roads opening on unexpected vistas never ceased to charm her, nor did the live oaks draped in gray moss or the beautiful buildings designed to defer to the large copses of trees making up most of the city. She sighed in satisfaction when a pleasant breeze brought her the fragrance of rose and honeysuckle.

The duchess loved this city. Its peace and tranquility. The joy of her people. Their trust in her policies and positions. In other realms, a ruler couldn't relax in public like she could. In other places, rulers feared the ruled. They had to hide from them like turtles in their fortress-shells.

Not in Yaksha. This was an empire at peace, a stable nation without peer. There was little her fellow elves needed to fear other than the various monsters of the Dagger Mountains. And Certitude, which existed in the heart of Yaksha proper and was possibly the oldest city in all of Seminal, had even less to fear.

The duchess took another sip of tea, glad of her home while her companion and confidante, Karthalyn Shoma, filled her in on the latest happenings from the capital.

Karthalyn was an unremarkable man of middle years and average in all ways. There was nothing about him to cause anyone to look twice. The world thought Karthalyn a harmless, traveling merchant, and the most interesting thing about him was his decades-long friendship with the duchess. Otherwise, he was bland, boring, and utterly forgettable.

In truth, however, Karthalyn was Marielle's spymaster, and he had recently returned from Revelant with information to share.

Most of it pertained to Enma, the crown princess, and her possible engagement to Redwinth Wheat, a prince of Apsara Sithe. Hopefully, marriage would smooth some of the older princess' rougher edges. Enma was intelligent, but she was also immature and selfish.

There was also information regarding Anya, of whom the duchess was far more familiar. Over the past few decades, she'd gotten to know Sala's younger daughter and grown to approve of and respect Anya's fighting prowess, her success as a ranger. Achievements the duchess had never thought possible for an elven woman.

But was all her acclaim worth it?

Everyone who saw Anya proclaimed her a beautiful woman. Even the dwarves said so. Her heart-shaped face and utterly arresting green eyes. Unfortunately, those glorious features rested atop an unmistakably muscular build. It was a side effect of the princess' martial training, and the duchess thought it marred the younger princess' loveliness.

Then again, there were many who found Anya's combination of beauty and build even more alluring, so perhaps both features served her well enough.

Anya's greatest attributes, though, were her maturity, generosity, and willingness to listen before making a decision. She was remarkably wise for her age, and so different in that regard than Enma, who was rash and opinionated. In the privacy of her mind, Marielle believed Anya would likely make a better empress than her older sister.

Currently, Anya was visiting Apsara Sithe, part of a trade delegation which had a secondary and more important undertaking: to find out if Redwinth would make a suitable husband for Enma.

Thus far, everything Karthalyn had told her was already known to her since Marielle had her own sources.

She listened to Karthalyn's report with half an ear, fingering the signet ring on her left index finger. It was the one passed down from mother to daughter in the nine generations of her family since the birth of Yaksha. The ring represented the foundation of the *Lamarin Hosh*—the Saviors of Hope in old *Shevasra*—which stemmed from the work of Sarienne Cervine, the founder of Marielle's line.

Sarienne had been a powerful quelchon, and during the *NusraelShev*, she had been graced with a vision. In it, she had seen the rebirth of the Blessed Ones—Shokan and Sira—and the rise of their ancient enemy, Shet. She had seen the dead god's fortress empire of Naraka rebuilt and flames of war engulf the world. According to Sarienne's vision, no one alone could ride out the storm, and it would fall on others—the *Lamarin Hosh*—to rally the free peoples of the world on behalf of Shokan and Sira. Then would follow a final battle against Shet and his unknown master, the Fated Foe.

What remained a mystery was how Shokan and Sira would make themselves known. Sarienne's prophecy only indicated that dragons would play a role, drawn to the Blessed Ones in some inexplicable way. In many ways, it sounded like nonsense. Dragons were a myth, or at least none had been seen since the *NusraelShev*.

Nevertheless, despite the prophecy's lack of clarity, over time others had been inducted into the *Lamarin Hosh*, and although the cabal had slowly grown, it remained small and hidden. But it was also effective. Its members occasionally provided the duchess information well before Karthalyn could.

Surprisingly, Prince Estin was a devoted member. In fact, he was the first member of the imperial family ever inducted into the *Lamarin Hosh*, and Marielle wondered if his presence in the conspiracy indicated the empress' awareness of her organization.

Karthalyn broke into her ruminations. "My informants indicate the crown princess is pleased with the notion of finding a husband."

The duchess already knew this, too, but she nodded her head as if it were new information. "Good," she said. "It's time she married and produced an heir."

"Once she does—

"Then I will no longer be so high in the line of succession." Currently, the duchess stood third for the throne, after Enma and Anya.

It was because of a tradition dating back to the time of Swan Yaksha, when Swan had required the help of her sister, Sarienne, the duchess of Certitude, to secure the crown. It was in the chaotic last years of the *NusraelShev*, shortly after the death of their mother, Koran, the sithe's founder.

And as payment for receiving her help, a convention had been established, one in which the duchess of Certitude, no matter how distant a relation to the imperial family, was placed in the line of succession directly behind the empress' own daughters and granddaughters.

Of course, no duchess of Certitude had ever ascended the Sun Throne, but the possibility—remote as it was—always existed, and Marielle would prefer if it were made even more remote.

The duchess's considerations drifted again, and she nearly missed Karthalyn's final statement. A moment later, she blinked. Had she heard correctly? She replayed his words in her mind and frowned in consternation. "The empress wants a full report on a human?"

Karthalyn nodded. "She not only wants a report, she intends on having Quelchon Ginala recite him."

The duchess was missing something. "Why does she care so much about this human?"

For once, uncertainty disrupted Karthalyn's normally placid mien. "It is thought he might be able to source his *lorethasra*."

"So I've heard," the duchess replied. "But how true can it be since no human has been able to source *lorethasra* since the Mythaspuris."

Karthalyn shrugged. "I don't know, but what *is* true is that he moves like one of us. You weren't at the Grand Melee. He was every bit as fast and skilled as an elf. Sourcing *lorethasra* could explain his achievements."

Marielle nodded. She had heard similar accounts from many others, including one of the boy's martial masters. *Cinder Shade.* Who was this human to inspire such attention?

She had met him once, on the streets of Certitude, spoken to him, although he had no idea who she was. She had asked how he was finding his time amongst civilized people, and his answer had surprised her. He had said he found it enlightening and wished human cities were more like the ones of Yaksha Sithe.

"There is more," Karthalyn said. "I've learned the dwarven wisdoms have also developed an awareness of him."

The duchess frowned. Dwarven wisdoms interested in a human was never a good thing, not given their shared history. She unconsciously leaned forward, intent. "Do you know why?"

"I only know of their awareness. They are also paying close attention to the Sunset Warlord, Genka Devesth."

"I see." The duchess sipped her tea and considered the matter.

What was the reason for this dual interest? What linked Cinder and Genka? A moment later, clarity came to her. *The Fated Foe.* It had to be. The *Crèche Prani* spoke of this Son of Emptiness and the portents of his arrival. And every human generation saw the dwarves grow frantic with worry over some human possibly fulfilling their silly prophecies. Whether it was Mede, a ruler of Gandharva, a warrior from the Sunset Kingdom, or an accomplished king, it was always the same: terror followed by relief. This time, it seemed they were concerned the Fated Foe might be either Cinder Shade or Genka Devesth.

Likely rubbish, she thought.

But what if they were right this time?

Marielle eased back in her chair, pondering what next to do. After a few minutes, she made a decision. "Interview all of the boy's masters. Find out everything they think of him. Everything they've heard. I want a complete portrait of Cinder Shade."

Just in case.

Anya sat at a simple wooden table, sipping coffee on a balcony she had to herself. The world around her was quiet except for birdsong, the buzzing of insects, and the murmur of workers in the nearby garden. This was a private balcony, one jutting like the prow of a ship extending off the quarters she had been provided in *Kal Rone Novin*—the Field Palace in old *Shevasra*, and the home of Apsara Sithe's imperial family. A number of potted plants, flowering shrubs, and small fruit trees—orange and banana—broke the unnatural symmetry of the gray flagstones flooring the area, and they also provided shade, although none was needed now. The palace's bulk reared at Anya's back, keeping the balcony in shadow.

From here, Anya had a view of a private garden and the unimaginatively named capital of Apsara, which held her attention. The sinuous blue line of the Gideon River bisected the place, which was so different from Revelant, Certitude, or even the brutal coastal city of Char. The capital of Apsara was rustic, with farms and meadows separating a sparse grouping of buildings and broad oaks shading the streets in green-leafed serenity. Yet despite the sweetly bucolic nature, there was an undeniable energy and youthfulness to the place, an understated elegance. This in spite of its obvious lack of wealth.

Then again, wealth didn't necessarily equate to happiness, and no one here was truly poor.

This was still an elven city, and Apsara was lovely, bathing in the morning sunshine, which poured from a sky decorated with gauzy clouds and hawks soaring on the thermals.

Anya continued to watch the capital as she sipped her coffee, savoring the beverage's delicious aroma.

The beans for the beverage grew abundantly along the foothills to the east, and while in some parts of the world coffee was considered a delicacy, here it was simply what was served with breakfast or any meal. During Anya's weeks in Apsara, she'd had the beverage whenever she liked, even at supper, although she chose not to drink it then. She found having coffee late at night left her restless and unable to sleep.

Anya's expression grew pensive. *Her time here.* She and the rest of the delegation had spent several weeks in Apsara thus far, and she considered what she had learned.

There was the obvious information which could have been ascertained through reading rather than experience. For example, this was a sithe which prided itself on the providence of its farms. Not only the coffee beans, but also the cocoa beans for the world's finest chocolate, the *sathana* grass for *insufi* blades, and of course, their pride and joy, their horses.

Anya smiled.

She recalled the first time she rode into Kal Rone Novin on Silence, her pure-bred Yavana mare, and the reaction triggered by the horse's presence in the stables. Astonishment was too mild a word to describe their response. The obvious power and intelligence of Silence and her regal gait had left the Apsarans speechless, awe evident on the faces of the grooms and stable master. None of them had ever seen anything like Silence since it was a crime to import a Yavana into Apsara for breeding—the elves didn't want their horse lines polluted by an "inferior breed."

Awe had eventually transformed to affection, and over time, Anya caught the grooms talking to Silence, feeding her extra apples, delight on their faces with her every movement. They would be sad to see Silence leave, and it would be soon. Anya had accomplished all her mother and sister had required. She had learned enough about Redwinth to determine that he and Enma would make a good match.

As if cued by her thoughts, a voice cleared behind her. *Prince Redwinth.* "May I join you?"

Anya twisted about in her chair. The prince stood in the doorway leading into the public portion of her quarters, an eyebrow quirked, and his handsome features set in a questioning smile as his blue eyes sparkled with intelligence. Redwinth was tall like all elf nobles, peaked ears framing dark hair that was collected in a topknot before it cascaded down to the middle of his shoulders in a single length. Strongly built as well, although not in the same fashion as Lisandre. While Prince Redwinth was a ranger and could fight—Anya had sparred against him, and he'd done well enough—his true interests lay in music and art. He also had a sharp mind for economics. Not a surprise given Apsara Sithe's mercantile background.

"Of course. Please join me," Anya said to him, gesturing to a chair opposite her own. She'd expected his visit. The prince likely wanted to confirm his status as the most likely contender for Enma's hand in marriage. She could empathize with his worry. As a younger son, he had likely never expected such good fortune as to potentially marry Yaksha's future empress. "Would you like some coffee?"

Redwinth grinned winningly. "I'm Apsaran, aren't I? I would love some."

Anya poured him a cup while he seated himself. He took it from her and silently stirred in the cream and sugar, slowly and carefully, deliberating on the matter as if it was of the gravest importance.

Anya waited on him. He'd come to her. Let him speak first.

"You leave today," he said.

"I do." Anya said nothing more. This morning would be a final test. In her mind, the prince needed to gather himself and plainly state his wants and desires. Diffidence wouldn't serve him well as her sister's consort. Enma would chew him up and spit him out since she had little patience for fools and the frightened.

The prince met her gaze. "And you have found answers for all of your delegation's questions?"

"I have." While Anya had nominally headed the negotiations, she had leaned heavily on her father's wisdom and advice. Even Lisandre had helped. He had a surprisingly strong head for diplomacy and the art of politics, the art of the possible. Then again Lisandre appeared to be skilled in all matters. He was a warrior, a poet, and a diplomat.

It made her question again her reticence in not taking Lisandre as a lover. Choosing him for an affair made perfect sense. But her heart refused her mind's rationality. Rukh lingered in her thoughts, and she couldn't forget or set aside the love they had shared.

She often wished she could. Life would be so much easier then.

Redwinth carefully placed his cup of coffee on the table and leaned back into his chair. "And what about me? What will you tell your mother?"

At last, he'd asked the question he should have brought up last night during the farewell dinner.

"I will tell her the truth," Anya said. *Let him chew on that and decide how to respond.*

He impressed her by answering at once. "I hope that means you'll speak favorably on my behalf. In your estimation, have I proven myself worthy of your sister?"

Anya smiled, pleased with him. Mild hesitancy at the beginning, and now he was bold. *Excellent.* "Only my sister can measure the worth of her future husband," she replied, hedging what she could tell him. "But I am sure she and, more importantly, my mother will judge the delegation a success, including your mother's hospitality and the worthiness of her heirs."

The prince exhaled in clear relief, and a smile lit his features. "I am glad to hear it."

"Many issues are yet to be resolved," Anya warned.

"I'm sure your father can handle these small details." Redwinth said. "He does still plan on staying here after you return to Yaksha, does he not?"

Anya nodded. "He will."

"And you cannot stay?"

"I'm afraid not. Home calls me." A worry had sparked within Anya over the past few days, and she had long ago learned to trust her instincts. She needed to return to Revelant, and for some reason, she felt it best to go by way of the Dagger Mountains.

"Would it not be safer and swifter to return to your home by ship?"

"Safer and swifter, yes, but there are garrisons in the Daggers that require my attention. This delegation is only part of why I was sent west. There are other matters to which I need to attend." It wasn't the truth, but Anya had no interest in telling the prince of her true reasons for choosing the Daggers. Of the dangers she felt sure threatened from somewhere in those vast peaks. He wouldn't believe it. No one would, not even her father, who still pressed her to go home by the sea road.

But Anya could feel it. The world was changing. The reports received while at Taj Wada from other rangers in the Dagger Mountains. A shadow casting a pall, a whisper on the wind. Something deadly was stirring to life, and Anya needed to discover what it all meant. She and the bulk of the honor guard would leave tomorrow by horse, taking the long way back over the Daggers to hopefully learn the basis for those rumors.

"In that case, I leave you to your packing and your privacy." Redwinth stood, bowed, and left her balcony.

After his departure, Anya's gaze landed on the frozen form of Liline Salt, the silver-eyed, silver-armored Titan standing in the nearby courtyard. She was like Garad Lull, a living statue, and the ancients had called her the Water Death. Her undeniably beautiful features were twisted in a contemptuous smirk of casual arrogance and disregard, and Anya couldn't help but wonder about the stories claiming Liline and Shokan had been lovers before he met Sira.

How could the Blessed One lie with someone so wicked and cruel?

Then again, other stories claimed Shokan and Sira had traveled to Seminal from another world, husband and wife already.

Which myth was true? Or was it neither?

The library at the Third Directorate might hold the answer, and if so, Cinder would likely be the one to have found it. He read, studied, and fought to improve himself more than anyone she had ever met.

She smiled, finding herself wondering how the young human was doing. It startled her when she recognized that she missed him.

13

Cinder pressed his finger into the book he'd borrowed from the Directorate's library, *A Compilation of Aphorisms*, considering what he had just come across. He remained uncertain why he had taken this volume. He'd been wandering a dusty corner of the library, looking for something to read when he noticed the carnation-red volume bound amidst its imprisoning brethren. The bright color and interesting title were perhaps what had caught his attention, and Cinder had withdrawn the book. He'd briefly perused the contents, and ultimately decided to read the slim volume during the Autumn Trial.

He currently sat near the bow of *Sacred Spear*, the ship transporting him and his brothers to the mainland city of Agnisahar. Sailors moved around him, but this late in the evening—twilight—most were down below getting rest or eating a late supper. A single *diptha* lantern hung from a pole directly above where Cinder was seated, casting a halo of illumination by which to read.

But he paid the world around him little attention. His mind remained on the aphorisms within the book. He found most to be merely humorous, but others were thought provoking. There was also wisdom, and it was the latter type of aphorism that had caused Cinder to halt his reading and ponder.

There are many realms but only one God. Love Him well before all others.

God. Devesh. The True Lord. *Love Him well.* Why were Devesh's creatures expected to love Him to the exclusion of all else? It was what the prayers to the Lord often instructed. But what did it really mean? Above their own desires and needs? Above their own families and children? Their own lives?

Did Devesh truly require such selfish devotion?

Cinder wasn't sure, but he didn't think so. As far as he understood matters, the Lord was selfless in His love. He required nothing in return except for acceptance of that love.

But maybe those instructions ascribed a deeper truth. Everyone's lives and souls were blessings of the Lord, and while anyone could ignore the wonder of such a gift, was it wise to do so? Was it intelligent, much less moral, to disregard the Creator's instructions on how to live a happy life?

Cinder contemplated the matter while staring out at the waters of the Sentient Sea.

Ultimately, he decided that while Devesh loved him, His love didn't come without responsibility. However, it wasn't a price owed, but a choice every person had to accept on their own. Everyone had a responsibility to their brothers, sisters, and parents. Didn't they also have a responsibility to the Lord? One no different than the one a child had for the ones who raised him? Was there not honor, devotion, love, and most of all, respect for parents, grandparents, aunts, and uncles? Didn't Devesh's creations, his children, owe him the same?

While he continued to deliberate on the matter, he glanced at the spine again, as if he could find the answer to his question somewhere within that warped, frayed material.

Unsurprisingly, there were no answers to be had, and he shifted his gaze to the darkening waters where the falling sun peered beneath a blanket of clouds on the horizon and beamed down on the waves, causing them to glow golden.

Like Anya's hair.

He frowned. Where had that observation come from?

He shook off the strange simile and focused instead on the here and now, letting the calming motion of the ship's gentle rocking soothe away all worries.

While his mind relaxed, he vaguely noticed his breath pluming in the cold air. A little while ago a chill wind had kicked up, ruffling the waters but otherwise leaving the Sentient Sea quiet. Perhaps it would hasten their travel, but Cinder doubted it. They'd already made good time. Three days out of Revelant and they only had two more to go before they reached Agnisahar—the Place of Fire. It was a Yaksha city built upon the site of a heroic battle during the *NusraelShev*, a place where five hundred elves had held off two legions—fifty thousand warriors—of the Drakar, Shet's army.

The sun dipped behind the clouds, but it managed to pierce them with a single last lance. The beam speared down from the heavens, wrapping Cinder in unexpected warmth and battling the wind's chill. He imagined a song carried now on that same breeze, a majestic score of singing light. Cinder smiled, closed his eyes, and surrendered to the providence of the day's last brightness.

His grip on the girl loosened as he stared at her in puzzlement. She had the bearing of a warrior; was equipped like one, too, wearing camouflaged clothing, a short sword, and a brace of knives strapped to her waist. He looked closer, and his confusion deepened. She had the emerald eyes of a Muran, the honey-blonde hair of a Rahail, and the delicate features and red-golden skin of a Cherid. She was like no woman he had ever seen before.

A hand shook him. "Cinder. Wake up."

Cinder shuffled in his chair, disregarding the voice seeking to drag him out of his dreams. The woman… he could see her face this time, shadowed though it was by a dim firelight. She was beautiful, arrestingly so, and familiar. He sought to carve those features into his memories, to never forget them this time.

He was shaken harder. "Cinder."

Cinder desperately fought against wakening. The woman was already fading from view. Only the sense of who she was remained; someone he might have truly known. A deep longing filled him to recognize her She had been special to him. Had he loved her?

"Cinder."

A final shake, and the last fragments of the memories—and at this point, he was certain they were memories and not imaginings—left him as the dream dissipated like fog under warm sunshine.

Cinder sighed in disappointment. When would he learn who the woman was? Who he really was? Or was it all a figment of his imagination?

No. He couldn't believe such vivid visions could be the product of his own mind. They had to be real. They felt real. The feelings he had for the woman were real. Or so he thought and hoped. But when would the truth be known? He was frustrated by the lack of answers. The inability to even ask or discuss what he was experiencing with anyone else. They'd likely think him insane.

He grimaced at the notion and finally cracked open his eyes. Master Absin stood in front of him, blocking off the light from the *diptha* lantern. The swordmaster and a few other senior warriors at the Directorate had volunteered to accompany the Seconds to Agnisahar.

"It's time to turn in for the night," Master Absin said with a smile. "Some of the cadets were hoping to hear some music. Riyne has his fiddle and Jozep has his tabla."

Cinder levered himself upright with a groan, tried to shove down the last of his disappointment, and forced a chuckle. "And I'm sure Sriovey hasn't been cursing and demanding no one play some maudlin love song."

Master Absin affected a shocked expression. "Sriovey cursing? Not him."

Cinder affected a chuckle, still haunted by his recent dream. "Right.

I'm sure Sriovey and cursing are as unique as a horse with four legs. Or the sun rising in the east."

Master Absin laughed. "Impossibly rare."

Wind and rain were an inaccurate description of the blustery weather currently befouling the Seconds. The world had been drenched in misery ever since they had first sighted Agnisahar. Both at a distance and from within the city's stoutly walled borders, Agnisahar had been shrouded in a melancholy ceiling of clouds, mist, and rain. It seemed impossible that such a damp, dismal city was labeled the Place of Fire. How could anything catch flame in Agnisahar's depressing, wet gloom?

And while many other locales suffered under such dreary conditions, it was usually limited to a particular time of the year.

Not Agnisahar. According to the locals, the city was afflicted by miserable weather and endless rain in all seasons. Even in winter, Agnisahar received rain. Not snow, but cold, icy precipitation.

From Cinder's perspective, weather of this kind, no matter how lush it left the natural world, would have trapped him in a melancholic and near infinite sadness.

However, upon departing Agnisahar, Cinder had hoped the rest of their journey to Fort Shiva, their destination, would not be depressed by such dreary weather.

Those hopes had been quickly dashed. Their travel into the mountains did nothing to relieve the cheerless rain. Instead, the mountains magnified it, adding the dimension of an uncomfortable chill to the climate. Oddly enough, although it was often freezing cold at night, there was no snow; only patches of ice coating boulders on the surrounding heights or forming dripping icicles from overhangs like a curtain of stalactites.

According to a member of Jameken Battalion—the James—an experienced five-hundred-man unit and their assorted train of supplies to whom the Seconds were attached for the Autumn Trial, it was a geographic anomaly to this area, explicable by the tall mountains to their east and west, which gathered and funneled the warm winds blowing north from the temperate Sentient Sea.

In some ways, Cinder would have preferred snow. The constant bone-chilling, icy rain and the damp dreariness was soul wearying. Plus, snow would be less likely to penetrate his wax-covered clothing, unlike the lashing wind and precipitation.

Nevertheless, Cinder did his best to ignore the rain. It was futile to complain about the weather or wish it away. The world existed beyond anyone's wants or desires. Better to focus on his task, watching the rocky terrain and heights.

The battalion traversed a well-trod trail—three abreast—along a valley floor. To their left rose a scraggly evergreen forest while to his right coursed a stream, rushing downhill over boulders and stones. Beyond the water bulked a line of rugged foothills. Unfortunately, a morning mist fogged the valley, limiting visibility and dousing conversation.

It made for a relatively silent progression. Only the dull plodding of hooves, occasional equine snorts, and a few quiet comments from the warriors broke the silence. Otherwise, the James maintained a steady alertness and discipline.

It hadn't taken the Seconds long to mirror the attitude of their seniors. A few sharp words from the sergeants had sorted them out, and by now, almost three weeks out of Agnisahar, they were rarely, if ever, rebuked for not paying attention to their surroundings.

Currently, the human and elven members of the Seconds rode in the middle of the column while their dwarven brethren were further afield. Today was the dwarves' day to reconnoiter with the scouts of Jameken Battalion. They had left an hour ago, at first light, and not yet returned to make their initial report. It was like this for all the Seconds. Every day a different group was rotated into the scouts. Yesterday it had been the humans. Tomorrow, it would be the elves.

But no matter where he was stationed, Cinder had encountered much during the Autumn Trial. They had come across a few beds of young ajakavas, a tribe of unformed, and an isolated necrosed, but none had been a threat to the battalion. Cinder had watched as the James quickly dispatched the fell creatures, bringing overwhelming force to bear in a well-coordinated attack.

So far, the only problem the James hadn't been able to handle was a distant wraith who had mocked them before speeding off. The creature, a female, had leapt down a steeply sloping hillside like the nimblest of mountain goats. Her frayed clothing had whipped about her until she disappeared from sight.

Cinder shook off the recollections and resumed his attention on the terrain. He and the other Seconds rode in a tight cluster; Bones to his left and Wark to his right. Behind them were Ishmay and Depth while directly ahead of them were Riyne, Estin, Mohal, Cariath, and Loriam.

Bones appeared ready to crack a joke, but a swift headshake from Cinder persuaded him to keep his mouth shut.

He didn't know why, but for some reason, he didn't think it was a good time to be cutting up.

And it was a good thing he'd warned Bones to remain silent because just then Lieutenant Garelt Brick rode up alongside them. The lieutenant was the only human member of Jameken Battalion, a graduate of the Third Directorate who had stayed on in Yaksha's Imperial Army after his four-year enlistment period had ended. By now, he was a still young but grizzled veteran, and the elves clearly respected him.

"Stay sharp," the lieutenant said, his eyes surveying the nearby rugged foothills. "Something buggery is out there."

"Yes, sir," Cinder replied, followed a beat later by Bones and Depth.

"Thanks," Bone said to Cinder after the lieutenant rode off.

"The lieutenant would have hided your ass if he caught you trying to be funny," Wark added.

Bones rolled his eyes. "Thank you, Captain Obvious."

Wark made to reply, but Cinder spoke first. "Shut up and pay attention."

There *was* an unknown danger lurking in these hills. An inkling, a heightened sense of trouble brewing that had been rattling in the back of his mind all morning. Until this moment, he hadn't recognized what it was, mistaking it for a mild headache caused by the bad weather.

It was nothing of the sort, and if pressed to describe it, Cinder would have said the feeling reminded him of dimly remembered danger, like an ember struggling to flicker to life.

Something threatening lurked close by. Or maybe the danger was approaching their column, or they approached it. Whatever the case, Cinder's instincts blared warning, and he surveyed their environs in worry.

The forested foothills remained blanketed in a shroud of gray fog. The rushing stream sped along its bed in a bass rumble as the water smashed against stones and boulders, spraying high into the air. The steady hoofbeats carried the battalion forward, mingling with the creak of the wagons carrying their supplies. The world appeared peaceful.

But appearances could be deceiving. Cinder was sure of it. The harbinger of danger wasn't letting up.

By mid-morning, clouds gave way to piercing sunshine, and warmth spread across the mountains and valleys. The fog burned off, and the nearby trees came into sharper relief. They were mostly evergreen—fir, pine, and cedar, with an occasional aspen and maple. The stream continued to slam and shudder against encumbering boulders, but under the influence of the unexpected sunshine, rainbows coruscated above the waters.

Jameken Battalion had a hasty lunch, consumed while still mounted, but several hours later the formation clattered to a halt. A ripple of unease carried across the ranks, moving from front to back. Uncertain questions were voiced as warriors called out for information.

"Silence!" Lieutenant Garelt shouted. Upon hearing his growled order, everyone fell into an uneasy quiet.

"What do you think is going on?" Bones asked, nudging his horse alongside Cinder's. Wark, Depth, and Ishmay edged closer as well.

Cinder had no answer, but the warning note sounding all morning in the back of his mind, blasted like a trumpet now. "I don't know," he said, "but it's not good."

Jameken Battalion had ground to a standstill. Lieutenant Garelt rode ahead, reaching a group of warriors moving in the opposite direction. He spoke to them briefly before pressing on, apparently to reach the head of the column where Colonel Shaloce Astreas, the commander of the James, and the rest of his officers were likely discussing whatever had caused the battalion to halt.

A few moments later, Cinder saw to whom the lieutenant had been speaking. *The dwarves.* They traveled down the line, and when they reached their fellow Seconds, Cinder shot Sriovey a questioning look.

"You'll find out," Sriovey growled in reply.

The battalion settled down, and the air was filled with the noises of horses snorting, whickering, or shifting about, and whispered speculation.

A short time later, all questions were answered when Lieutenant Garelt rejoined them. "Gather round and pass the word," he called out. "The scouts have encountered a massive nest of spiderkin, over three thousand of the eight-legged fuckers. No more than a few hours ahead." The lieutenant's visage held unexpected sourness. "We'll be burning them out."

Brilliance crouched low on the lip of a ledge, her tail swishing in agitation. She narrowed her eyes to slits, guarding her vision against the steady rain lashing only this slender portion of the mountains. The precipitation had picked up a few minutes ago, following a brief spell of wonderful sunshine, and with the resumption of the wet weather, there rose a chill wind that blustered like a bull elk bugling his territory.

She wasn't impressed by either. Brilliance was a snowtiger. She was built for far harsher conditions than today's dismal weather. Bred for icy snows and winds that cut like claws. This mildly cold rain was nothing to her. And an elk was easy meat.

No. What had her bothered was the line of horses and riders traversing the sinuous valley below her perch. She couldn't count, but she knew the difference between a few and many, and this was definitely many. Many elves, humans, and dwarves, all trudging along on horses. Or as Brilliance reckoned them, four-legged treats.

The two-legged were also tasty, but around them Brilliance had to be very careful. Ever since the feast of humans from a few seasons ago, she had sought more of their delicious kind, and every time, she had been driven off. Her frustrations had started seasons ago—many sunrises after the deaths of the man and woman who had imbued her with such wondrous power and knowledge. It had begun when Brilliance had tried to kill a lone elf. She had stalked her prey, remaining downwind, moving ever closer, unseen and unknown, crouched low like she was now, ready to ambush the two-leg.

But it had been Brilliance who had been ambushed. Somehow the elf had become aware of her presence and nearly put an end to her. He had thrown a sharp, pointy stick in her direction, one which whistled like the wind through a narrow cleft and flew as swiftly as a striking falcon. Brilliance had barely dodged the stick. Or the next two that came right after the first one.

She'd been forced to flee, but the elf hadn't been content with defeating her. Rudely, he had given chase. It had taken all of Brilliance's speed, stamina, and intelligence to evade the discourteous elf. Even in the dark, he hadn't let her be. Seven days and nights of running and hiding until he finally ceased his pursuit.

And he hadn't been the only kind of two-legs to cause her such fright. A few months later—during which Brilliance had feasted on her usual prey of deer, wild goats, or foul-tasting, scorpion-like creatures—she had gathered her courage once again and went after a band of shorter two-legs. Dwarves she later learned they were named. She had believed them to be weak. They should have been. After all they were short, with short legs and were slow and thick like the tastiest types of prey.

However, when Brilliance had launched her attack against the short ones, the very ground had betrayed her, throwing her off balance, knocking her off her feet and onto her back where a dwarf almost crushed her head with a sharp, half-moon shaped piece of metal attached to a stout stick of wood.

Only frantic twisting, yowling, and wild swiping of her paws had saved Brilliance's life. Once righted, she had immediately fled, and thankfully, these two-legs weren't so rude as to give chase. And while she couldn't imagine how they could have caught her, she also hadn't imagined how easily they would overwhelm her.

It had taken two seasons more until Brilliance felt brave enough to attack the two-legs, this time the original village where she'd sacrificed the man and woman. Even there, in the heart of where she'd first gorged and grown powerful, treachery had found her. Another dwarf. He had seen her before she'd seen him. Brilliance had been so focused on the lush morsels working in the fields, she hadn't noticed the dwarf until nearly too late. He'd attacked, wielding one of those cursedly sharp, half-moon pieces of metal—, an axe it was called—and rode her down while riding a donkey.

A donkey!

The seconds of fleeing from the dwarf on his donkey had been simultaneously terrifying and humiliating. In the end, Brilliance counted herself lucky to have escaped the fiends. The dwarf had nearly sliced off a section of her ear before she could retreat, and she shivered at how much more he could have taken.

Her lips curled in anger. How could the two-legged creatures be so powerful? They only had two legs! They couldn't run. They had no claws or teeth to speak of. In all ways, they resembled prey.

And yet, somehow, impossibly, they were more dangerous than any predator Brilliance had ever met. She realized how lucky she had been to have sacrificed the man and the woman from that lone village. They must have been feeble for their kind, and it was well known that the old and weak were often driven away from the herds of prey animals by their younger, stronger members. Just like the boy she had nearly killed on the same day.

But the boy had never been old, and now he wasn't even weak. He was strong and fierce, and in her vision, he blazed with more power than anyone she had ever seen.

She eyed him as he rode along, in the midst of many two-legs. Her eyes narrowed. Where were they going? Didn't they know spiderkin commanded these parts of the mountains?

Brilliance's tail flickered.

It wasn't fair. The spiders couldn't take the boy from her. He was hers. Only she was allowed to feast upon him.

14

Cinder crawled forward, slow and sure up a rugged slope of boulders and stones. His footing was solid since the brief downpour from overnight had dried up. But the sunlight made evident the lack of cover. All the trees had been cut down—chewed down really—by the large nest of spiderkin up ahead.

In fact, the world was silent. The spiderkin had likely eaten all the local fauna. No birdsong was apparent. No sounds of any animals or insects.

Only quiet, except for the sandpaper scraping of fifty warriors crawling on their bellies as they moved cautiously across loose shale, stones, and dirt. They crept up the slope toward the spiderkin caverns. While Cinder couldn't yet see the opening, he knew it was there, somewhere past the crest of the hill, twenty feet ahead.

It would be visible soon enough, especially with sunshine brightening the mountains. However, at these heights and at this time of year, the brightness was weak and empty of heat, but Cinder still appreciated it anyway. As far as he was concerned, sun was better than rain. He was also glad for the lack of wind to further chill the air.

He chided himself to focus. They were closing in on the spiderkin, and his heart began pounding out a nervous rhythm, not for himself, but for the warriors entrusted to his command. He was in charge of this unit, and he didn't want to fail them. They certainly wouldn't fail him. These were veteran members of the James, and they seemed to know their business. Their demeanors thus far had been calm, collected, and serious.

As if in opposition to his calculation, a sharp rattle of stones caused him to jerk about. To his left, a member of the James had been careless. It didn't matter that all the elves and dwarves in their unit held tightly woven Blends, a braid of *lorethasra* that could camouflage sight, scent, sounds, and even emotions. The spiderkin might still hear the tumbling of the loose rocks, and the warrior should have known better.

Cinder glared at the elf. He wouldn't have their mission compromised by stupidity. "Keep it quiet," he hissed.

The elf glared in return. "Shut your mouth. I know my job, human."

"Then do it silently."

Cinder moved on before the man could respond.

Minutes later, any considerations about the elf left him. They had reached their destination: the crest of the hill where it transitioned to a broad, flat shelf. He signaled, and the warriors shuffled off the slope. They reached a large grouping of boulders, crouching behind them. Slightly to their left and downhill of where they huddled was the opening to the spiderkin caverns, about fifty yards away. It gaped like a blackened maw with stringy vines draping the entrance. No creatures were visible. This early in the morning, it stood to reason that only their guards were awake while the rest of them slept.

Cinder studied the tableau, eyes narrowed as he examined the details. Nothing stirred in the near distance, except the vines hanging across the cave's mouth. Those rustled now and then as a mild wind moaned across the cavern's entrance. There were occasional chittering sounds from deeper in the cave.

Cinder's brow knitted in consideration. If they were quick about it, the chittering might conceal the sounds of their approach. They could kill the guards and enter unimpeded.

Unless the scouts they'd killed downslope had been noticed, and this was a trap.

Bones, stooped at his right shoulder, leaned over and whispered in his ear. "You sure this is a good idea?"

Cinder most definitely didn't think it was a good idea. It was the farthest thing from a good idea.

Yesterday afternoon, the scouts had encountered warriors from this nest. Of course, all of them had been female since the spiderkin males were nothing more than breeders. Jameken Battalion had hunkered in a steep-shouldered hollow, waiting out the dark hours when the spiders were at their most deadly. During the night, the commanders had devised a plan of attack and decided to begin its execution a few hours ago. It started with splitting the James into three units of roughly one hundred seventy warriors each. Two groups would approach the spiderkin cavern from flanking positions, while the third would attack from straight ahead, which was the role of Cinder's group.

Surprise should be on their side since the James had killed any spiderkin scouts they had come across, preventing them from returning word to the nest. Cinder's warriors would enter the caverns and seek to draw out the spiderkin where they would be pincered by flanking warriors.

According to the colonel, the spiderkin would emerge enraged, unaware, and confused. Easy prey. The confused creatures would be killed en masse while they tried to sort themselves out.

Cinder thought him delusional.

Why battle the spiderkin in a place of their greatest strength? Near their caverns. They should have allowed a spiderkin scout to 'escape' and carry word of the battalion's location. The spiderkin would come at them, but they'd be forced to attack a position of the battalion's choosing, a hastily fortified position surrounded by a series of traps to kill the creatures. There could be kill zones where the archers could destroy the monsters at a distance, and armored cavalry could crush the creatures on an open field.

There were so many better options than this straight-ahead ambush, which was little more than an uphill charge. The senior officers saw it, too, but Colonel Shaloce refused to listen.

It wasn't a surprise. The colonel was the untried son of the duchess of Agnisahar, and he had apparently been granted his officer's commission at the insistence of his mother. According to rumors, she had placed him in command of the James because of the veteran officer corps. The thinking was that they could keep her son out of danger.

Unfortunately, the colonel had stocked the senior command with untested friends, those like him who had visions of glory dancing in their stupid heads. They had supported his moronic decisions, overruling any of the older officers' recommendations. As a group, they were either fools or foolhardy with the lives of the James, apparently believing that the elves would "fight with the strength of their righteous courage."

Warriors with courage were wonderful, but husbanding their lives was better.

Thankfully, Lieutenant Garelt and others weren't so foolish. They knew the colonel's plan was a bad one. There hadn't even been an accommodation for the supply train. As a result, Lieutenant Garelt had insisted on taking charge of the unit that would enter the caverns, and his fallback position *was* both fortified and able to defend the supply train.

His fortifications began with a series of trenches covered in a light layer of dirt and leaves and lined with sharpened stakes. From there, hunkered behind a wooden palisade set atop a solid, stone fence—a handy construction of the dwarves—the warriors under Lieutenant Garelt 's command would lay down a withering fire of arrows. And once it was close-in fighting, his warriors would be armed with pikes and proper shields. Plus, the lieutenant also had a mobile group of heavy cavalry armed with lances.

Even now, Lieutenant Garelt was further fortifying the fallback position, but he'd entrusted command of this portion of his unit to Cinder.

Why he had done so, Cinder didn't know. He only knew his duty. Right now, that meant enacting the colonel's plan but also making sure his men had a way out when it fell apart like he figured it would. His main goal was to get his men back to the fortification the lieutenant was readying.

"When do we enter?" Sriovey whispered.

Cinder didn't answer at once. He glanced to the east and the west, where he saw the tumbled curve of the stony hill's shoulders merging with boulders the size of houses. The flanking units were supposed to signal, and he waited for it, fretting. They should be in position by now, but they would be hidden behind their Blends.

A few minutes later, from both the right and left, there blinked flashes of light. The other two groups were in position.

"We enter now." Cinder eased out of his crouch. "Signal the other units."

He trusted Sriovey to do as he ordered.

Meanwhile, the other warriors of his command rose to their feet, stretching and loosening limbs grown stiff. They were safely concealed by the camouflage of their Blends, but nevertheless, they were quiet and restrained in their movements.

All the while, Cinder continued to stare at the cave's opening. A disquiet filled him. Everything was as it should be, but he didn't like it.

Cinder gestured for the Seconds—all of them were in his unit. He spoke to the elves and humans. "I want two dozen arrows fired into that cavern."

Estin scowled. "They'll know we're coming."

Daliwin Servius, one of the junior sergeants of Jameken Battalion, overheard and was far blunter. "If you don't have the courage to follow orders, then give over command to a true warrior." The other elves rustled about, some of them murmuring support for the sergeant.

Cinder paid them no mind. He continued to peer at the cave's opening. His disquiet had become a certainty. He was suddenly glad he'd insisted on bringing spears. "They already know we're here. It's a trap."

Sergeant Daliwin sneered at him in disgust. "Or maybe you're a coward."

Cinder held up a hand. "Listen to the cave. What do you hear?"

The elf continued to scowl. "Nothing but occasional chittering."

Cinder nodded. "But listen to the chittering. How regular it is. Every five seconds, one of them chitters and for exactly five seconds. That doesn't strike you as odd?"

The elf's scowl didn't initially diminish, but as the truth of Cinder's observation became evident, his expression settled into a thoughtful frown. "You might be right."

"I think a ton of spiderkin warriors are ready to come surging out at us." He pointed to several smaller openings, upslope and to the right and left of the main entrance. "I would bet they have a number of warriors stationed there, too. They'll flank us and cut us down."

"But they'll be fighting on two fronts," Sergeant Daliwin countered. "You forget we've got our own units ready to ambush them from both directions. They'll flank their flankers."

"Unless they've already placed warriors behind our own. Then it will be our warriors fighting two fronts."

"They'd only do so if they knew we were coming."

Cinder held back an eyeroll. "Which I already told you, they do. This is a trap. We're not going in that hole to die. We'll spring their trap, kill as many spiderkin as we can, and fall back to Lieutenant Garelt's fortification." He faced Sriovey. "Signal the other units. Tell them what we're doing. Have them look for spiderkin warriors hidden above their positions." He drew the human and elven Seconds and another twenty elves to him. "On my mark, I want at least three score flaming arrows in their main cavern inside of two seconds." Next, he addressed the dwarves. "Those loose stones on the slope above the cavern, can you touch them from here?"

Sriovey nodded. "We can reach them."

"Good. As soon as the arrows are fired, drop them. You'll know when."

Sriovey studied the area above the cavern's mouth. "Even if we drop everything on them, it's won't slow them down long."

"It only has to slow them down long enough for us to retreat. Drop them as soon as the spiderkin emerge." He hesitated. "Any chance you can drop an avalanche on them?"

Sriovey shot him a startled look. "Are you crazy! Sir."

"Can you do it?" Cinder pressed.

Sriovey shook his head. "We can't make an avalanche. None of us have the power for it, but we can maybe start a small rockslide."

Cinder grimaced. "I'll take anything at this point."

"You're sure they're in there waiting on us?" Sergeant Daliwin asked, no longer appearing so dismissive.

"Absolutely," Cinder said. He pointed to another set of boulders, ten feet to their rear. "Get another dozen archers over there. Have them fire free when the spiderkin emerge." He gestured to another sergeant. "Get your braided Shields and your wooden shields ready. Spears out." He continued calling out orders. There was a cluster of tall boulders twenty feet downslope of their position with a natural channel through the center. "We retreat through those stones. I want three lines. They'll try to overwhelm you. Those rocks should slow them down from flanking us."

"But they'll flank us anyway," Bones groused.

"I said slow them down. That's all we can hope for," Cinder said. "We're going to make them pay for charging straight ahead. *Lorethasra*, arrows, spears, swords, and shields, we'll use whatever we can to kill them while we retreat back to the fortification." He glanced at Sergeant Daliwin. "Any questions?"

"No, sir," the sergeant replied, chastened now.

"We're ready," Bones said, indicating a nearby row of archers.

Cinder waited for the rest of the unit to get themselves situated. Once they were in position, he evaluated their placement one final time. He set his shield on his left arm. They were ready. Automatically, he reached for *Jivatma*, unsurprised when he failed. Three weeks into the Autumn Trial, there remained nothing but the same emptiness he'd grown used to seeing.

This is a terrible idea, he thought, not for the first time, but there was no help for it now. He lifted his sword arm and dropped it. "Fire!"

Brilliance had grown in both stature and knowledge in the short time since she'd reached greater self-awareness. But there was one lesson she'd learned long ago as a young snowtiger leaving her mother's den for the first time: run from the spiders. It was instruction she'd acquired when she saw a large black bear overrun and killed by the creatures. He hadn't stood a chance. He'd managed to mangle one spider before he'd been overwhelmed by the rest of them.

The eight-legged fiends had then hustled the poor bear off—still alive—to wherever they made their homes.

Brilliance had watched from the boughs of a tree, hunkered low and fearful of making even the slightest sound. She had been close enough to see the whites of the bear's eyes as he'd been carried off, all the while terrified the spiders would notice and come after her, too.

From that point on, whenever she caught wind of a spider or noticed their spoor, she ran. The direction didn't matter. All she knew was that she had to evacuate the area as quickly as possible.

There had been only one occasion when she'd broken her rule. It had been when she had chased down a deer. She had dispatched her prey and was prepared to feast when the spiders had found her. She hadn't wanted to relinquish her kill, and she'd crouched over it, snarling at the spiders as they gathered about her. They'd encircled her then, and almost too late had Brilliance noticed the danger she was in. A webbing from one of the creatures had glued one of her paws to the ground, and only frantic tugging had freed it. Brilliance had managed to barrel through the grasping pincers of the spiders, barely escaping with her life.

From that moment on, she had always given a wide berth to the eight-legged creatures. Brilliance was a powerful predator, but even predators gave way to killers.

Which made her boy's maneuvers all the more worrisome.

Brilliance studied him. A number of two-legs accompanied the boy, but none of them realized she crouched upon a ledge fifty yards above their position. It was a perfect vantage point, one overlooking the spiderkin's cavern, although she didn't like being here. It hadn't been easy to get so close to the caves unseen, but she had forced herself to edge past her terror. The boy was hers. His death should be under her claws, his glorious *lorethasra* meant for her and only her. Not for spiders.

Her ears perked, and her eyes widened when fiery sticks flew from the strange devices held by the two-legs. The sticks whistled and hissed into the cavern, and an outraged chittering resulted.

The spiders were coming. Brilliance drew back from the edge of the shelf, tail tucking. The boy and his band needed to dash away to safety.

But the boy and his fellow two-legs didn't. They stood fast.

Brilliance found herself awed by their courage and idiocy. She crept closer to the ledge's lip in order to watch.

The scene below was chaos. She lacked the words to describe it. All she saw were fires erupting, the earth shaking, and spiders attacking.

But not immediately winning. The two-legs were fighting them to a standstill. They gave no ground.

Brilliance leaned over the edge of the shelf, weight forward. The boy needed protection. He was surrounded. Should she go down and defend him? But then the spiders would kill her. And if they didn't, the two-legs would.

She growled, low and frustrated.

Cinder concentrated on the spiderkin cavern while the archers let loose their fiery arrows. Their bolts whistled, crossing the short distance and speeding through the vines draped across the cavern's entrance, shredding them.

Immediate outraged chittering, chirping, and crackling echoed out of the cave. Despite the alien nature of the noises, the sounds held unmistakable notes of fury and bloodlust. More noises. Blaring from all directions, including the nearby heights.

Oh shit.

Cinder frantically searched out the source of the sound, his gaze darting about.

Shouts of surprise. Screams of outrage and pain. *The other units.* A mass of crawling spiderkin emptied out of barely seen holes, surging forward from above, below, and everywhere else. The other units of Jamekin Battalion were holding their own, but only barely.

Cinder had no more time to spare to see how they were doing. A black tide of pincers, legs, and fangs erupted out of the caverns toward his own men. Too many to hold here. They needed a controlled retreat to get back to Lieutenant Garelt's fortification.

A rumbling of stone and boulders fell upon the spiderkin, crushing scores of them. More fury-filled chirping arose.

"Arrows free!" Cinder shouted.

The spiderkin broke toward Cinder's unit like a black wave.

The archers fired at their foes, and scores more of the spiderkin crashed to the ground. Their tight packing ensured they tripped over several of their own.

The archers managed to get off two arrows each, but now it was time for shield, sword, and spear. Cinder barked orders. The archers rejoined the rest of the unit, buttressing the lines as they gathered their own spears and shields.

Cinder stood to the rear, overseeing the battle.

Despite some of the elves' initial reluctance to fight with shields, they clearly knew how to use them. They were also familiar with how to fight in formation, creating a hedgehog of bristling spears and stabbing swords. These men knew their business. *Thank, Devesh.*

Here came the spiderkin, and Cinder's world eroded into a fever of stabbing, whirling, and cutting. Training took over, and while he didn't have the sublime speed he once possessed, his instincts were up to the task. He slammed his shield into the maw of a spiderkin, stabbed another one in the thorax, ducked beneath a set of pincers. A warning in his mind screamed, and he parried a serrated leg. A horizontal slash cut his attacker in two.

A few seconds of respite gave him the chance to see how the lines were holding.

Good enough.

It was time to make their way back to the fallback position.

"Retreat at pace!" Cinder shouted. "Weapons forward. Don't show them your back!"

The warriors of his unit responded admirably. They managed ten steps backward from the spiderkin before they were forced to stand and defend. Unfortunately, they no longer had the wall of boulders to protect the sides of their formation. The spiderkin tried to take advantage of the change, but the dwarves made it difficult. They shifted whatever ground the flanking creatures stood upon or collapsed boulders upon them.

Cinder continued to fight from the rear of the formation, calling out orders. He noticed the spiderkin shift their movement, massing.

Three of the creatures attacked, distracting him. They were a danger, but his mind was focused on what he'd seen.

Cinder absently bashed a spiderkin out of position. Another rushed behind the first. Cinder slid aside. A vertical chop decapitated the creature. Spinning with his movement, he amputated three legs from the third spiderkin. She keened in pain.

The first spiderkin returned.

Cinder front kicked it, knocking it off balance. He finished by stabbing the creature through its head. A shift to the side, and he used the dying spiderkin as a temporary shield before re-engaging the third still-keening spiderkin. A straight stab through its maw killed the creature.

The fight had taken no more than a handful of seconds, but he worried what he might have missed during it. What were the rest of the spiderkin doing during his moment of inattention?

He immediately saw. The spiderkin had formed a pincer. His warriors were about to be overwhelmed. They were retreating downslope on an open field.

"Shift left. Fifty feet!" Cinder shouted.

"Do you want that rockslide now?" Sriovey shouted, sounding urgent.

"Patience, grasshopper," Cinder replied.

Sriovey gave him a double take. "What?" The dwarf looked confused and upset.

"Nevermind." Cinder returned his attention to the advancing spiderkin, judging the moment.

"Sriovey. Go! Do it now!"

The formation of warriors shuffled left, throwing off the pincer's aim. At the same time, boulders and stones up slope creaked into a slow-motion movement. They shifted ponderously. One rock at a time, sliding down the hill, rolling and picking up speed. They gathered more stones in their wake.

The small rockslide gained momentum. All told, it wasn't much, just like Sriovey said, but it was enough. The boulders and stones slammed into the spiderkin. Tens of them died. Many more were injured, and the pincer movement was shattered. The spiderkin halted, chittering in confusion.

It was the break Cinder was looking for.

"Retreat! Full speed!" he shouted.

They'd still have to halt and defend against the enemy, but Cinder had an idea of where to hold the line. A bottleneck a hundred yards downhill. It was a narrow passage, sheer-walled and topped with a long shelf, essentially a tunnel. The spiderkin would be forced to come at them in a line no more than ten wide.

And a quarter mile beyond that, where the slope rose again, there stood the fallback position.

Ghouls lull you to sleep.

It was the warning Anya had repeatedly given to the twenty men who had accompanied her home from Apsara. They were members of the Sun Guard, the warriors tasked with protecting the imperial family in Revelant. They were the best of Yaksha's army. To say they were elite was an understatement. Half were graduates of the Third Directorate, and all of them were skilled in the use of the sword, spear, bow, and dagger. Each one was the equal of two warriors from any other nation's army.

But a warrior wasn't necessarily a ranger, and in the badlands of the Dagger Mountains, awareness and stealth counted for more than proficiency with a blade.

In this, the Sun Guard actually slowed her down. Anya was generally the one who sighted zahhacks along their flanks or the rare *aether*-cursed beast trailing after them. Sometimes she simply killed whatever foe she encountered, not bothering with shouting for help. She didn't need it. These lands were most certainly wild and treacherous, but no worse than other places she had traveled. Those other treks had been months-long affairs and generally with only two other rangers for company.

Nevertheless, though the Suns might not be proficient in the field, it was nice to have more than just two taciturn companions on the road with her. Plus, Anya figured the journey was proving a learning experience for them.

The Sun Guard had known of Anya's skill. They knew about her history at the Third Directorate and the rumors of her ability in the wilderness.

But hearing wasn't the same as knowing. This journey had hopefully taught them much. The Suns had gone from mildly condescending in response to Anya's orders to deeply respectful when her decisions shaved time off their travel, protected them from unexpected snow, or kept them away from dangerous encounters with deadly zahhacks and even a pair of wraiths.

As a result, they now closely heeded her words whenever they made camp, wary for ghouls and staying alert and awake during their watches at night. Enough for Anya to feel comfortable to be taken off the watch schedule tonight. It would be her first full rest during the entirety of their journey through this section of Daggers.

They'd stopped for the evening along a flattened ridge, one wide enough to easily accommodate the warriors and all their horses and pack mules. On three sides, slopes made of loose stone and scree fell toward a river valley treed in hardwoods, and on the final side reared the granite bones of a mountain.

After helping set up camp, Anya had eaten supper and washed off the day's grime in the river. The honor guard had given her privacy while she cleaned up, and afterward, most had settled around the cookfire, joking and laughing with one another while five of them stood guard along the camp's perimeter.

Anya, however, sat by the fire and wrote in her journal. It was a habit that was decades old, one arising from shortly after she'd first awoken after the terrible illness that had nearly killed her. That same illness had left her bereft of all of her memories but those from her first life. It was a faithful ritual in which every evening Anya wrote down the day's events in a small leather-bound book. Simple scribblings, quick notations of events or interesting anecdotes. Over the years, she had filled over a dozen such red-leather books.

She sometimes questioned why she did it, and she had yet to arrive at a satisfactory answer. The best she could determine was that maybe her habit was driven by fear. What if she had another fever? Another bout of amnesia? The journals might help her recover her sense of self. Nevertheless, despite her faithful adherence to her nighttime observance, she hoped they'd never be put to the test.

Once she finished jotting down the day's relatively boring occurrences, Anya went to her tent, snuggled into her bedding, and quickly fell asleep.

She dreamed.

Her heart hit her throat, eyes widening in sudden panic. Creatures marched in her direction, massive brutes of a type she'd never before seen. Tall as a troll and possessing yard-wide horns like the famous Strata bulls of the Coalescent Desert. She prayed they would overlook her. Her heart threatened to beat out of her chest as they approached, resounding like a bass drum in time to the pulse of her fear. How did the monsters not hear it?

Baels. The name hit her like a smack to the face. It was the name of the species of creatures striding her way. And they commanded the Plagues of Chimeras who ruled the world under the brutal heel of their dread Goddess.

She bit down and tightened her Blend. Would it hold? Baels could sense emotions, and her emotions—her mind-numbing fear—were likely leaking through her otherwise perfect camouflage.

Suwraith's spit! They were still coming.

She sidled aside, further away from their predicted path. She kept her attention on the creatures, all the while whispering a prayer. "First Mother and First Father, grant me protection from these servants of evil."

She swallowed a bolus of terror, eyeing the line of Baels as more than two score of the red-eyed monsters passed by her position. They strode close enough for her to reach out and touch, but she didn't dare move even a single inch. She held as still as a bird before a cobra. Never before had she ever been in such a tenuous situation, and no amount of training could have prepared her for such danger.

She held her breath as they moved off, only letting it out after the last of them was dozens of yards away.

The general, though. For some reason, he had remained behind.

She frowned. Why was he still here? Did he have something more to do?

Her face cleared as a plan flashed into being. It was either inspired by lunacy or merely inspired. In either case, it was dangerous, but she also thought it worth the risk. With the general standing all alone, maybe she and her brothers could take him out.

Her vision shifted to a large mound of boulders near the Bael commander. All she had to do was reach them. From there, she could signal her brothers, who were Blended as well. They could flank the general and kill him.

She inched out of the hollow in which she'd hidden, crouching on the balls of her feet and edging her way toward the boulders. A slow, careful lifting and setting of her feet, one step at a time. On she went, smiling in relief as the boulders loomed closer. Only a few yards to go, and she could unBlend and signal her brothers.

She realized her mistake an instant too late.

Her eyes widened in shock as a Blend, deeper and richer than any she had ever encountered suddenly Linked with her own.

At the same time, a hand clamped across her mouth, muffling any noise she might have made. A voice whispered in her ear. "Be silent," it ordered. She was held in a grip of iron.

She twisted and saw him. He was Kumma, and he had three companions. Two other Kummas and a Rahail.

First Father! What had she fallen into?

Anya woke up with a start, her eyes wide in the darkness. Her throat clenched, and her heart pounded as hard as it had in the dream. What was that dream? Who were those monsters? Those men? What was that place?

A waterfall of questions cascaded through her mind. None of them could be answered, and in their path was left confusion and fear. Who was she? In truth, she wasn't simply Anya.

A stutter of unwanted laughter bubbled up her throat at the reminder of how Cinder jokingly referred to her.

She forced away the humor. Really. Who was she? She wasn't merely Anya Aruyen, not entirely, maybe not even mostly. Those images had been real, as real as the life she was living. Maybe more, as if her current life was the dream.

Anya grabbed hold of herself.

No. It was only a dream. A vivid one, but nothing more. It didn't matter where it came from. It changed nothing about herself. She *was* Anya Aruyen, a princess of Yaksha Sithe. A child of the elves. Her parents were Sateesh and Crena Grey.

Anya gasped. Those names. Those weren't the names of her parents. They weren't Avan Aruyen and Sala Yaksha.

Horns bugled, shattering the quiet and her concerns. The camp was under attack.

Anya shoved aside the dream and everything it might mean. Danger threatened, and her mind settled into familiar patterns of combat. She threw off the bedding, collected what was required, and stormed out of her tent.

She discovered the camp surrounded by hooting creatures with swords. *Ghouls.* But the stench of rot indicated something worse was also present.

15

The unit Cinder commanded had managed to reach the fallback position, the small fortification at the crest of a small rise. It had been a brutal retreat, but they'd made it, which was enough, at least for now. Cinder was proud of his men. They had never once panicked, not even the rawest recruit or any of the Seconds. Instead, they had fought, hammering the spiderkin, bloodying them enough to teach the creatures caution.

There had come a pause in the attack, though, and Cinder had used it to get his men inside the walls of the redoubt. The spiderkin, of course, had followed, but rather than a straight-ahead charge, they had opted for a slower approach. Despite carefully edging forward, many of the eight-legged horrors had died crossing stake-lined trenches. And during it all, they had been under constant attack from the warriors in the fortification. Sheets of arrows had bombarded the creatures, one flight after another.

But this, the spiderkin had learned to overcome. At first, the arrows had blasted through the creatures, but once the monsters were prepared, most of the bolts simply bounced off their reinforced chitin.

Spiderkin, like almost all intelligent life, could source and weave *lore-thasra*, at least to a certain extent. Even the lances of fire, coils of water, and arrows of air flung from the speartips and swords of the elves did little to thin the lines of the eight-legged monsters. They surged like a black wave.

Cinder grimaced in disgust as the spiderkin threw themselves at the square fortification. He studied the situation, standing behind the Seconds, providing support where needed, and offering guidance when required. Layers of spiderkin surrounded their position, writhing and smashing against the wooden walls. Even driven deep into stone and mortar, it would likely soon give way.

Then would come the end.

The small fortification was never meant to hold the creatures back for so long. It was simply a fallback point, a place to hold the attention of the spiderkin while the rest of Jameken Battalion rallied to their aid. Unfortunately, a rally didn't seem likely to happen. Hundreds of spiderkin had peeled off the main force and headed upslope where the other two units of the James were apparently still locked in fighting.

Lieutenant Garelt's plan wasn't going to work. The trenches around the fort had been hastily built, and despite the deaths they had inflicted, the spiderkin had too easily overcome them. Arrows were proving useless, and the cavalry had been driven off. According to their signaling horns, they were still minutes away from being able to provide support. Minutes where the fortification might be only seconds away from falling.

A change in plans was required, but what?

Even as Cinder observed the battle, an elf was pulled off the line, drawn into the mass of spiderkin. The creatures mobbed him, losing any pretense of discipline. But the elf didn't go down easy. He stabbed and thrust, and black ichor flew. The ground rumbled. Icy darts shot off the elf's hand in a metronomic, low-pitched rumble. His sword caught fire, and he sliced through the spiderkin. He killed half a dozen, but in the end it wasn't enough. Moments later, another elf was hauled into the midst of the spiderkin, and again they mobbed him, tearing him apart before he could do much damage.

Watching the brutality sparked an idea. Cinder grabbed the arm of a nearby sergeant. He had a reserve knot of warriors meant to plug any holes in the defense.

"Get to the wall," Cinder ordered, not caring the man was his senior. "I'm pulling the Seconds off."

The sergeant blinked in obvious confusion. "What? Why should I?"

Cinder gritted his teeth. He didn't have time for this. "There aren't as many spiderkin in the rear. We've got enough horses. I'm taking the Seconds and five other warriors out of the fort. We'll punch through and lead them away. Their bloodlust is up. They'll follow, and I bet while they're busy chasing us, they'll forget to strengthen their chitin. You can cut them down with arrows."

Lieutenant Garelt, standing nearby, heard the plan. "Even if you're mounted, they'll run you down. They have the advantage on this kind of terrain."

"They'll overrun us all if we don't."

The lieutenant stared at him. An instant later he gave a sharp nod. "Choose your five. We'll cover you." He addressed the sergeant. "Get your men in place. Do everything you can to support them. We won't let their courage go to waste."

The sergeant didn't hesitate. "Yes, sir." He spun about, shouting orders.

It was all Cinder needed to hear. He pointed out five nearby elves. "You men want to ride through hell and kick some ass?"

The elves offered him startled glances that became predatory smiles. They quickly joined his side.

Cinder called out again. "Seconds! On me!"

Bones was the first one to peel away from the wall. Next came Derius, Sriovey, Jozep, Mohal, and the rest of them. Other warriors took their place. Cinder faced the Seconds and the five elves of Jameken Battalion and explained his plan. "We're going to punch through their lines and draw them after us. The dwarves will hold the wall." He addressed Sriovey. "You have to keep them off us. Do whatever it takes.

Keep them occupied while we cut a hole in their lines and ride out."

"That's the dumbest plan I've ever heard," Estin said.

"The colonel's was dumber," Riyne muttered.

Estin shot him a look of betrayal.

"Then stay here," Cinder snapped at Estin. "The rest of us are leaving."

The Seconds joined him as they mounted the horses Lieutenant Garelt had already ordered saddled. Cinder patted the neck of his gelding. These weren't the heavy breed of horse with full barding used by the Gandharvans on the central plains of their nation. These were lightly armored mounts, nimble and meant for hard terrain. They were perfect for the Daggers. Even better, they could reach close to full speed in the small confines of the fort.

Bones shifted his horse closer to Cinder's. "Just so you know. Estin is right. This is a dumb plan."

Cinder chuckled, noticing then the mounted presence of Riyne and even Estin. Both had decided to join him after all. He gave them a brief nod of acknowledgment.

The Seconds made for the rear of the fortification. Lances were passed up to them along with exhortations and encouragement.

Cinder had a shield on his left arm and a lance clutched in the crook of his right. He made a final adjustment to his helmet.

Horns trumpeted from upslope and to the north. It was the cavalry. They must have finally managed to lose or destroy their pursuers. They sounded no more than a quarter mile away, and in the same general direction as the path Cinder's small band intended to follow.

Cinder adjusted his plan. "As soon as the gate is open, we ride flat out. We head uphill, toward where we just heard the cavalry bugles." Bones, Cariath, and Mohal had the signaling horns, and he spoke directly to them. "Once we're through, signal the cavalry. Let them know we're coming."

Murmurs of assent met his words.

Cinder patted his restless mount's neck and tried to push aside all notions of defeat. He knew what was required. *The mission.* There was nothing else.

He nodded to the elves manning the rough-hewn gate. Their timing would have to be impeccable.

One last settling breath. "Charge!" Cinder set his heels to his gelding, and the horse exploded forward.

The elves flung open the gate, and Cinder reached it an instant later.

A swarm of spiderkin tried to use the opening to batter their way inside, but Cinder and the Seconds were on them. They smashed into the creatures, spilling them about and out of the way. The Seconds stayed in tight formation, bunched close and riding hard.

Cinder held his lance steady. It shivered under the hard impact of slamming into a spiderkin. It battered another one, shattering into splinters this time. He drew his sword, cutting down another spiderkin. His gelding kicked out, crushing the skull of another creature. On they pushed. It felt like they were moving glacially slow, like moving through crystallized molasses.

Then, like a plug blown out of the way, they blasted through the spiderkin lines. Cinder led his men upslope, toward where the cavalry had last been heard.

A cacophony of high-pitched horns and wrenching screams rose in anarchic patterns. But the greater concern for Anya was the stink of a corpse wafting on the swirling breeze. She recognized the stench. *A necrosed.* A powerful one based on the fifty ghouls who had showed up at the monster's behest.

From the northern edge of the camp came the clash of swords and the wailing screams of the ghouls against the ringing cry of the Sun Guard. The ones who had been awake while everyone else slept were locked in a ferocious battle. Three of them were already down, pincushioned by arrows. The rest struggled to hold their positions.

Other members of the Suns tumbled out of their tents, hastily donning armor, weapons, and boots.

Anya directed them. "Get to the north. Shields up. Spears and swords. A double-line."

The remaining dozen warriors entered the fray. They rushed the ghouls, who tried to retreat, but the zahhacks were quickly entangled by their own brethren. A handful of the twisted creatures were killed. The guards who had been on watch were now able to step back into the midst of their brother warriors.

Anya's attention shifted east. The stench of the necrosed was stronger in that direction. It was also where more ghouls were clustered. Why had the necrosed, who were generally solitary creatures—often hating their own kind—gathered this small company of zahhacks? How had it done so?

Her jaw clenched. The necrosed was actually the greater danger, and it wouldn't be easy to kill. The easiest way to destroy one was with lightning. But such a power—the Wildness—was not one given to the elves. Only the holders possessed it. The other was to cut the necrosed apart. Separate arms and legs from the torso and remove the head from the body. And afterward, the parts of the necrosed could be burned to ash. Only then could the creature truly be confirmed to have been killed.

But it was easier said than done. A necrosed had skin like stone, and destroying one generally required at least five warriors working in concert. Otherwise, only the most skilled of elves could hope to defeat a necrosed on their own.

Fortunately, Anya had the necessary skills.

She opened both Chakras she controlled, *Muladhara* and *Manipura*, sourcing *lorethasra* into them. Her Chakras spread her life's energy as *prana* through her *nadis*. From *Muladhara*, her senses heightened, and the darkness brightened enough for her to make out the features of individual ghouls. The Chakra also caused her muscles to bunch and relax in the fast-twitch fashion of her dead husband's Caste. If needed, she could move much faster than any other elf. *Manipura*, on the other hand, granted her control of fire and the ability to strengthen her weapons. It was a power common to most elves, but not to the extent that Anya exerted. Her off hand flickered with flames. She stood balanced on the balls of her feet, watching for the enemy.

It soon became evident, a massive shape moving amongst the ghouls. Although the image was vague given the darkness and flickering flames of the campfire, the stink of a corpse drifted on the wind, telling her what she faced.

Anya's lips twisted. She hated the necrosed. They were an abomination against nature. Necrosed were creatures of perpetual decay and rot, and to survive, they had to regularly replace their limbs and organs. The source was whatever creatures they managed to murder, and their favored were either a woven or a human. But they weren't picky. They took whatever was available.

This one, a female, would have the same needs and desires. She stood a half a head taller than Anya, moving like a shark through minnows as she pushed aside the crowd of ghouls. When she stepped more fully into the firelight, Anya saw a discordant pair of eyes viewing her, one clearly from a wolf or dog and the other likely that of a dwarf. Stringy hair, greasy and limp, hung from her pale skull, framing a misshapen face. A smashed nose, a weak chin, and a mouth filled with an overgrowth of fangs filled out her features. Her skin was covered in pus-ridden ulcers from which a gangrenous stench emitted. Add in long arms—ending in fingers with the claws of a bear—which dragged past the creature's knees, while the monster's legs looked to have once belonged to a horse.

Anya noted five of her guards moving to protect her flanks. They'd hold off the ghouls while she dealt with the necrosed.

The corpse-like creature smiled at Anya, a grotesque, twisting expression. "Elf woman," the necrosed whispered, her voice hoarse and gravelly. "You will taste fine. I will—"

Anya didn't allow the creature to finish her threat. She attacked. The necrosed backpedaled, shock plain on her grotesque face. While the monster was off-balance, Anya lashed out with a whip of fire. It crackled, snapping on impact with the necrosed's chest.

The creature screamed. Fire normally fed a necrosed, but Anya's flames burned hotter than the monster could handle. In her previous life, she dimly recognized she could have done even more with the flames, but not in this one.

Still, causing pain and injury were better than nothing.

The necrosed batted at her chest, putting out the flames. She glared at Anya, snarling in outrage.

"Afraid of a little fire?" Anya mocked, wanting the creature's attention focused on her.

In the corner of her vision, her guards were mowing down the ghouls. It might have been a far different outcome if the necrosed could have taken part in the battle against them, and better for her men if they never found out.

"You fucking bitch!" the necrosed snarled.

Anya had her Shield in place and sword at the ready. She waited for what she knew would come. The necrosed's intentions were easy to decipher. Anya baited the monster, smirking and gesturing the creature forward.

The necrosed charged.

She might as well have moved through molasses.

Muladhara still fueled Anya's motions while *Manipura* strengthened the *isthrim* steel of her sword, granting her the ability to easily cut through the monster's stone-like skin. She blurred forward, making sure to step off the center-line. She dodged arms meant to decapitate. Her sword flashed, biting deep. The cut nearly severed the necrosed's left arm at the shoulder.

The creature grunted in pain, swearing at her. "Elven whore. I'll eat you alive."

Anya answered the pointless threat with a vertical slash. This one did sever the creature's left arm. Pus-like blood oozed like sap from the terrible wound.

The necrosed gaped.

Anya pumped more *lorethasra* into her Chakras, forcing most into *Muladhara*. Her speed quickened. Her strength was enhanced. She ducked low under a hooking slash. Her blade lashed out.

The necrosed lost a foot and crashed to the ground. She managed to catch herself on her knees and remaining hand. Fear filled her discordant eyes. "What are you?"

Anya didn't bother answering. There was a battle to win.

The ghouls were dying in droves. This necrosed would soon follow them.

But counting chickens before they hatched and all.

Anya gripped the hilt of her sword more tightly and dashed forward. She feinted toward the remaining arm. The necrosed fell over on her back, legs aimed at Anya. The creature thrust a heavy kick. Anya easily evaded and cut off the remaining foot. She amputated a leg below the knee. The other leg at mid-thigh. The final arm was severed an instant later.

Anya was surprised by the ease of her victory. She marched to the now-unmoving necrosed, readying the killing strike.

The creature glared hatred at her. "This isn't the end. You're already dead. Someone greater comes."

Anya might have paused to question the necrosed, but staring into the creature's eyes, she knew an answer wouldn't be forthcoming. She decapitated the necrosed in one swift strike.

Seconds later, the ghouls seeing their benefactor dead, howled their terror and fled.

One of the guards approached Anya. "What should we do about the bodies?" he asked.

"Burn them," she ordered, frowning at the necrosed, or the pieces of it. She remained troubled by the creature's final words. What had the creature meant? *Someone greater comes.*

Anya shuddered as a fearful certainty pressed on her mind like a weight. The world was changing. Some strange power, dark and deadly, was stirring the zahhacks. Her mother needed to know about this.

She swayed as a vision stole across her mind.

A winter-bare meadow. A single oak towering over the field. From its base, an albino necrosed, bald-headed sauntered forward, marching with all the pride of a king or a herd stallion. Despite his thin frame, she knew he would be fast and powerful. Dangerous.

He leered at her, his mouth full of mangled teeth. "Where are you, pretty?"

The vision popped like a soap bubble. The world returned, and Anya gasped. Her heart raced, but not with fear—she feared no necrosed. But rather with pity. She had known the leering monster, the strange albino necrosed, and a confused part of her believed she might have loved him once like a brother.

And just as confusing, why could she still recall the creature's image when family and loved ones faded from her mind like images drawn in water.

Brilliance viewed the boy from her high perch within the concealing boughs of an aspen, eyes wide and ears perked.

Where was he going? He'd left the safety of his walls, his open-aired house and taken the fight to the spiders.

Idiot!

The boy had to be insane. He rode a horse, leading many elves and humans. Dust trailed from where he and the others stormed up the hill and from where the spiders—a vast number, one greater than she could count—charged after them.

Brilliance growled in frustration. She might have to help the boy. Otherwise, the spiders might kill him before she could.

She leapt from her perch and raced after the boy, always alert for any skulking spiders. Thankfully, none were present, which made sense. They were all chasing after the stupid boy. Brilliance growled again in low-throated frustration.

She pondered the best way to approach the matter. Should she focus on saving the boy? Or would it make more sense to kill him if the opportunity allowed. She could rip him off his horse if he was ever separated from his group of humans and elves.

It might work.

She snarled a second later.

It wouldn't work. The spiderkin were everywhere. Even if the boy was away from his group of two-legs, the eight-legs would likely be there. She couldn't kill the boy today, which meant she would have to save him.

Her decision made, Brilliance raced along the forest floor. Her padded feet pounded the hard ground, the sound likely lost amidst the nearby tumult. The late afternoon sun dappled the ground, and she flashed through the patchwork of light and dark. The iron-rich stench of blood and ichor stained the air, filling it as if the world had become an abattoir. Screams of pain and agonized chittering carried on the wind. There was so much death.

Brilliance was a predator, but what was happening here spoke of an ugly, evil action. Murder and war. She wanted to hide from this horrible place, run far, far away, but she couldn't. She couldn't lose the stupid boy.

Didn't he realize he could die? And his death would be so meaningless then.

The fool. Didn't the boy know he was meant for her consumption? Not the inglorious death of being bound like an insect so the spiders could happily feed upon him for months on end. The stupid spiders probably didn't even know enough to devour the boy's *lorethasra*.

Cinder and his gelding blasted through the spiderkin's chitinous lines and out the other side. Worry filled him all the while, but it wasn't a personal fear. It was a fear for his fellow Seconds and the other elves of Jameken Battalion who had followed him out of the fortified position. They had done so on his command and were risking everything based on his word.

He had to believe it would be worth it. That their actions might save their brother warriors. Ride flat out and taunt the spiderkin into giving chase.

And they had. The creatures swarmed after them, at least half the monsters surrounding the fortified position had peeled off in pursuit. The spiderkin raced after Cinder and the others, faster and nimbler than the horses on this rocky, uphill terrain. A mighty dust plume marked the creatures' position. A far smaller one indicated Cinder's command. And the distance between the plumes was narrowing. Cinder risked a glance back. Less than seventy-five yards separated them.

He faced forward, searching for the cavalry. Where were they? He needed them. His men would be dead without them. Bones, Cariath, and Mohal continued to blare their horns, calling in the cavalry, but so far there had been no response.

On they ran, the gap between the two groups continued to shrink. Their horses desperately lunged up the slope, their eyes rolling in terror. Some straggling spiderkin took up the pursuit as well. By now, Cinder's unit had nearly five hundred spiderkin racing after them, only fifty yards distant.

Cinder's head jerked to the forest on his left. He caught movement. Horses. The cavalry. They were fifty yards upslope, veiled by a large cluster of evergreens, at a place where the hill flattened and near the opening of the spiderkin's cavern.

"Keep going," Cinder urged his men. "The cavalry is right ahead."

Some of the warriors saw the same thing he did. They cried encouragement, and all of them spurred their mounts onward.

The chirping, scrabbling horde of spiders crashed up the slope after them, continuing to gain ground.

Cinder's group reached the flattened area and cut left. The cavalry remained partially concealed by the copse of pine. The spiderkin were a dozen yards behind. Cinder's heart raced. What was the cavalry waiting for? They had to charge now, or he and his men would be over-run.

Seconds later, one hundred mounted elves cried in unison. The cavalry charged in a staggered line, fifty wide and two deep. Their horses pounded a staccato drum of retribution. The elves were Shielded, a green shimmer about them. Flames roiled on the tips of their leveled lances.

They crashed into the unsuspecting, unprepared spiderkin like a rockslide, smashing into the tightly packed creatures. A terrible din resounded. It was the low booming tone of Shields impacting chitin. The sound of wood splintering. The eggshell-sharp crack of carapaces breaking. Spiderkin screaming in pain. Horses neighing.

Cinder glanced back. The cavalry had cut off the spiderkin. None of the monsters were close at hand. He eased his mount to a halt and turned around to watch the cavalry work.

In the initial charge dozens of spiderkin—hundreds perhaps—had already died, and the cavalry wasn't done. The skilled elves quickly got their mounts ready for a second pass.

The surviving spiderkin stood upon the wide plateau, milling about in confusion. A good start, but not enough.

Cinder shouted orders. "Arrows! Loose at will. Keep their attention on us."

His warriors unstrapped bows, and seconds later, a dozen arrows, most of them alight, slammed into the mass of spiderkin. Another dozen were in the air before the first ones had landed. Another set.

The spiderkin chirped, fury evident. In slow clumps, they began charging toward his men. A dozen. A hundred. Most of them. *Perfect.*

"We ride!" Cinder swung about, heading his warriors on a course parallel to the copse of trees where the cavalry had been waiting. The spiderkin raced after them, but this time, they weren't able to gain any ground, not on the flat terrain. Cinder had his unit slow, taunting the spiderkin. Keeping their focus locked on his riders and no one else. Certainly not on the cavalry charging on them from the rear.

A few spiderkin managed to outpace their sisters, but Cinder's warriors quickly cut them down. More reached them, and they, too, were summarily killed. Cinder had his unit slow further, and in a single surge, the creatures rushed forward.

It was the sign Cinder had been looking for. He spurred his gelding. The others followed suit, and they darted away.

A dull roar echoed from the rear edges of the spiderkin. Similar to when the cavalry had first smashed into them. The dull sound of bodies colliding with Shields. Chittering screams, panicked now.

Cinder's unit reached the edge of the plateau, and he cut right, following the mountain's curve. They reached an incline and began climbing. The horses heaved, spent from all the running. Sweat poured down their flanks while thick strings of white spittle foamed at their mouths.

Cinder glanced back. The mass of spiderkin had been destroyed by the cavalry, but scores of them still lived. Most were scattered, but ten… twenty… fifty came for him and his men. They were rapidly gaining ground on Cinder's command.

He quickly reorganized his warriors. "Elves to the rear and on the wings. Humans centered. Shields up. We turn and charge on my signal." He waited for the warriors to get sorted out, and as soon as they were, he shouted. "About face!" He tugged on the reins, and got his gelding aimed downhill, toward the onrushing spiderkin.

He now rode at the rear of his warriors. The elves were up front and on the sides, Shields covering the unit.

"Charge!" Cinder shouted.

The unit dashed downhill, a rolling mass of horse and men. Swords were out and ready. They crashed into the spiderkin, blasting through them. Carapaces cracked in sharp retorts. More high-pitched chirps of pain. A few spiderkin managed to break aside from their charge, and Cinder found himself hard-pressed. He defended against pincers, serrated legs, and fangs. His well-trained gelding hammered his rear legs into a spiderkin behind them. Cinder slashed aside a creature, and they were through.

The copse of trees was directly ahead. Dozens of spiderkin streamed into them in a mad, chaotic dash.

A smile bloomed on Cinder's face. They'd won. He didn't have to know how the other units had done to know it. The bulk of the spiderkin nest had been crushed, and their corpses littered the plateau where the cavalry had ridden them down.

Celebration in mind, his warning instinct blared to life an instant too late.

A hard mass, a large spiderkin, rammed into him, and the world tumbled in a swirl of sky and stone. Cinder crashed into the ground. He rolled with the impact, sword still in hand, but his shield was ripped from his grip. The creature must have leapt off an overhanging boulder and unhorsed him. The rest of his unit were yards away. Too far to be of immediate help.

Cinder faced his attacker. It was a big monster, taller than Cinder, which meant she was older and more powerful than any spiderkin he had ever faced. Along one side of her thorax, the creature's chitin was webbed with scars, arguing for a near fatal encounter in her youth. The spiderkin reared, chittering in anger.

Cinder knew better than to attack, not without having any gauge of the monster's speed and power. Better to defend and evade, hold on long enough for his unit to get back to him.

She had no name but Big Mama. She had lived long, survived the terrors of the shadowed valleys where the centuries old, ancient crones lived in unchallenged rule. Big Mama had come to this faraway place to establish her own nest and her own power.

And she'd succeeded. For a time at least. But now? What of her nest? Her daughters? So many dying, slaughtered. Hundreds of them. Thousands.

She keened in rage and grief.

It was all the fault of the soft-shelled creatures on two legs. Elves, dwarves, and humans. Big Mama hissed. In all the world, few challenged the spiderkin but those three accursed races. Prey who used tricks and taunts to kill her children.

Big Mama chittered in fury.

Her daughters should not have fallen for such tricks and taunts. Big Mama had warned her brood to be wary, but they hadn't listened to her wisdom. Her daughters had charged after the riders and their horses. Bloodlust had filled their minds, shattering reasoning and causing them to give chase.

The decision had cost them. A cleverly hidden cavalry charge had destroyed many of her children. Worse, it had given the elves in their walled nest a chance to take the fight to the spiderkin surrounding them. They'd used the opportunity to crush many of Big Mama's kin.

With the scent of ichor flooding the air, Big Mama's remaining daughters, the ones who had managed to corral the elven forces in the heights, had streamed off to help their sisters. Another disastrous decision. Her daughters had streamed downhill, en masse and without a plan of defense, and the elves on the heights had made them pay. They had attacked from behind, mercilessly butchering hundreds of her children.

Big Mama understood. It was the way of the world. The elves and her kind were bitter foes, killing one another with every encounter. After all, the first spiders had been fathered by a Rakshasa and birthed within the wombs of twenty elven females. Their shared history ensured a shared racial hatred. The elves were the enduring enemy of all spiderkin. They deserved death or enslavement. Nothing more. Nothing less. And in the end, Big Mama treated the extermination of the elves as akin to simple labor, similar to weaving a web. A necessity of life.

But this human, the one she'd unhorsed. Big Mama glared at him. He had been the one to lead the others from the fort. He had been the one who had planned for the destruction of her children. He had been the one who had led her daughters to disaster.

She *hated* him. The human had to die. Slowly if possible, but dead quickly was also fine.

The spiderkin charged, a blur of flashing limbs and anger. Cinder bent his knees and readied his sword. At the last moment, he spun aside, thinking to escape her attack and gain distance. His eyes widened in shock. The creature was huge, but despite her bulk, she slammed to a halt and twisted about faster than he expected. Here she came again.

Cinder rolled beneath slashing pincers. When he rose to his feet, he discovered two more spiderkin flanking the larger one.

Fragging hells.

The warriors of his unit were only now turning around, finally noticing his absence. They were over a hundred yards distant, too far to be of aid. The three spiderkin would finish him by then. Right now, they were trying to box him in a triangle.

Cinder backed away, planning, judging. He edged closer to one of the spiderkin, the smaller of the three. He feinted a slash at the largest of the creatures, the one who had unhorsed him. She lunged, but he was gone. Cinder redirected his motion and attacked the smaller spiderkin. A diagonal blow nearly bisected a leg. He swayed away from a return slash. Shifted to place the spiderkin between himself and the other two. The creature was slow in turning. Cinder slashed hard, cutting through most of her thorax.

A deep-throated growl drew Cinder's attention and also that of the remaining two spiderkin.

The largest cat Cinder had ever seen in his life stood close at hand. *A snowtiger.* Her head rose as high as Cinder's chest, and she had a build every bit as impressive. Claws long enough to shear him in half flexed from her paws. The snowtiger glanced at Cinder, and her eyes flashed silver. *Aether*-cursed.

Fragging unholy hells.

The world seemed profoundly unfair in that moment, and any hope of surviving drained away. The snowtiger snarled at him once, mocking him with what might have been a sly smile. A furrow creased his brow. There was an odd familiarity to the cat.

Any further questions were discarded when the snowtiger attacked the larger spiderkin. The two monsters tore into one another, rolling about in a wild snarl of growls, yowls, and screaming chitters. Dust was thrown into the air, obscuring their battle, but within moments, the large spiderkin was retreating toward the nearby trees, the snowtiger giving chase.

Thankfully, Cinder's distraction during all this didn't cost him. The other spiderkin had been equally inattentive when the snowtiger had shown up. Cinder sized up the remaining creature. The spiderkin was smaller, of a size he was familiar with.

Feeling confident, he attacked the creature. A handful of flung dust distracted the spiderkin, who reared away from the dirt. It left her abdomen exposed. Cinder stabbed deep. The spiderkin keened and tried to slam claws and pincers into him, but he was already out of reach. Ichor flowed from the creature's wound, but the injury didn't seem to slow her down. The spiderkin charged.

Cinder met her. He blocked a wild slash from the spiderkin's forelegs. Slapped aside her pincers. He ended his movement by cutting deep into her head. The spiderkin chirruped, sounding confused. She took a halting stumble, tried to right herself, but collapsed. She shuddered once and lay still.

Cinder's unit finally arrived. They were a silver piece short and a day late, but they were here. He glanced at their numbers and realized three of the elves who had followed him out of the fort were gone. He stifled a rising regret. It wasn't yet time to grieve.

"What happened?" Bones asked, holding the reins to Cinder's gelding and guiding him over.

"A big spiderkin happened," Cinder said, mounting up. "Then some big fragging cat." Bones' face held a question, and Cinder shook his head. "Don't ask. Some other time. We still have a battle to fight."

"Not much of one left," Riyne stated, gesturing around them. "Look."

He was right. The warriors from the fortification were cresting the rise onto the plateau. They must have broken the spiderkin encirclement. At the same time, more warriors were streaming around the hillside. The other units. The spiderkin raced away, their numbers greatly diminished, hundreds where once there had been thousands.

16

It took several days for Jameken Battalion to gain full control of the hills surrounding the spiderkin nest. Days of burning out scatterings of the creatures wherever they went to ground or hid in the surrounding forest. Then it came time to enter the deeper caverns where were found the spiderkin nest's two hundred or so males. Weak, stupid, and expendable in comparison to the females, they'd been left behind. The fight against them had been brief. Afterward, the caves were set afire, destroying any remaining webbing so the nest couldn't so easily be rebuilt.

In the end, of the roughly three thousand spiderkin in the massive nest, roughly twenty-seven hundred were accounted for in the form of corpses. It was assumed the other three hundred, or however many survived, had managed to skulk away into the depths of the Daggers.

In some ways, it was a successful battle, but the cost had been steep. Cinder figured it was generally the case with battles. So much blood and carnage. The images felt like they'd been carved into his mind and memories. Sometimes when he closed his eyes, the graphic scenes of death would replay in his head.

224

The battle had reinforced a difficult lesson. A warrior's life was a hard one. It was where death would be a constant companion. It left him wondering if he would ever know a time of peace.

He also scowled whenever he considered how much lower might the price have been if Colonel Shaloce and his lickspittle sycophants had listened to Lieutenant Garelt and the veteran officers. If the battalion had formed a plan of attack to fully exploit their advantages in tactics and strategy. The straight-ahead charge had been a fool's decision, and Cinder seethed at the waste of lives the colonel's decision had caused. Over one-quarter of the James had been killed and another one hundred severely injured. Cinder was grateful none of the dead or injured included the Seconds.

Two days after the battle's finale and many miles travel later toward Fort Shiva, Cinder finally had a chance to discuss his troubles with Lieutenant Garelt. The two of them stood alone upon a low rise at the outskirts of the camp, near the line of surviving horses, many of whom had also been savaged.

The battalion had reached the outer aspects of the Dagger's foothills, a place where the forests were thicker and the evergreen trees gave way to hardwoods. The scent of burning wood mingled with that of the sizzling meat being prepared for the evening stew. The aromas carried on a chill breeze. It was dusk, and the sun lingered a finger's breadth above the horizon. The world was full of noises, the soft nickering of the horses, muted conversations from the battalion, and the rattle of branches and leaves stirred by the wind from the surrounding forest.

There was one other sound. The moans of the wounded. Below where Cinder and the lieutenant sat, the camp was spread out in a hollow, orderly and precise, and within it, the injured warriors were gathered in a central area. The healers were doing their best to keep them alive.

They would fail in far too many instances, but Cinder hoped actual physicians would arrive soon enough with the expected relief force. Early on after the battle, scouts had been sent to Fort Shiva to explain the battalion's dire situation and the need for more physicians, healers, and warriors to bolster their ranks and gain full control of this section of the Daggers. Their desperately sought arrival was expected in the next week or so.

Cinder gritted his teeth in anger, still furious at the colonel and his followers. Fragging incompetent bastards. The rage coursed through his mind, and he had to close his eyes and shut away the world, focus on his breathing until he could reassert control of his fury. He was only a Second, and it wasn't his place to publicly criticize a vastly more senior commander.

But if the decision *was* his to make, he would have broken the colonel for his lack of judgment.

"Why didn't the commander listen to your suggestions?" Cinder asked, once his emotions were reined in. He pitched his voice low so no one else could hear.

The lieutenant didn't answer at once. He stroked his chin, seemingly lost in thought as he gazed at the campfires. "It's the elven way," Lieutenant Garelt finally answered. "The younger ones can't help themselves, not until they've had some bloody learning. Probably the same with the dwarves."

"Sir?" Cinder asked in confusion, not comprehending what the sergeant was saying. Certainly not all elves could be as incompetent as the colonel. Could they? It didn't make sense. While the elven and dwarven Seconds had never demonstrated proficiency in Tactics and Strategy, they weren't stupid. They learned from their mistakes. They were improving, and Cinder reckoned any of them—even Estin— would have done better than Colonel Shaloce.

The lieutenant sighed. "You've spent a lot of time around young elves." His mouth formed a wry smirk. "You've likely noticed their view of themselves."

"Their superiority?"

"Yes, and I think it blinds them." He sighed. "I've been with Jameken Battalion for three years, and the colonel has been with us for six months. He's unseasoned, and what I've learned about him is this:

whenever we are in our normal routine, he's good enough. He's competent at planning our movements, assessing upcoming danger, and gathering our forces in a way to maximize the damage we can inflict and reduce the injuries we might receive. At least to a point. But like all unbloodied elves, if there's a real battle happening or it's about to get hot, he is as useful as a bucket of water in a thunderstorm. I always knew it."

The answer raised all sorts of questions, but Cinder didn't voice them. He merely viewed the lieutenant, hoping for a fuller explanation.

"For elves like the colonel—arrogant and prideful—planning goes out the window. Men like him want to attack everything head-on. Insist on it." He snorted in disgust. "Maybe it's because of all their talents. Their Shields, their ability to make themselves faster and stronger, all the other things they can do that we can't. I figure they think it makes them invincible, but it doesn't. It only makes them stupid."

Cinder considered the lieutenant's explanation. It was similar to his own experiences with the elves, especially in Tactics and Strategy. They were able to understand the coursework, but when it came to applying it during small unit drills, they usually flailed and failed. They were improving, but they still generally charged straight at defensive positions, unthinking and idiotic, especially Estin and Riyne. It was like once the battle began, their passions overcame their good sense. They had trouble holding back and waiting for support or following a plan that called for feints and deceit.

Cinder had always figured it was because the elven members of the Seconds could already overcome obstacles that would have defeated lesser fighters. They were too sure of their own abilities, and it made them rash. They pushed on when they should wait and fought single-handedly instead of as part of a group.

Same with the dwarves, although they at least listened when they were told to do something, or at least they did if it was Cinder or one of the other humans who did the telling. The dwarves tended not to listen to the elves.

The musings brought a realization. Elven armies, even veteran ones like the James, might often have warriors in command instead of soldiers. Men who thought of battle as a contest of individuals. In contrast, human armies were made of and commanded by soldiers, and soldiers fought with cohesion, planning, and as a single unit. The distinction was critical. Soldiers did everything they could to avoid fighting as individuals. For this reason, an army of soldiers could more readily set the tempo of war, enhance advantages and mitigate weaknesses, and bring overwhelming force to bear at a place of their choosing.

It was why human forces, despite being monumentally outclassed in terms of individual fighting capability, were able to overcome elven ones. It was why Mede had been able to forge an empire on the broken bodies of elven and dwarven armies. It was why Genka Devesth, the Sunset Warlord, would be such a challenge to Aurelian Crèche and possibly even Shima Sithe if he ever united the Sunset Kingdoms.

It was an instructive lesson.

"Why do you fight for them, sir?" Cinder asked.

Lieutenant Garelt considered the matter. He exhaled heavily. "Because their army is the only thing standing between the spiderkin and zahhacks and Rakesh. Any of Rakesh's forces would have been slaughtered by that nest of spiderkin we fought no matter how well led they were. And they're not. Our officers are incompetent in a completely different way from the Imperial Army's."

Cinder hadn't known. However, he had met some of the soldiers in Rakesh's High Army. They hadn't struck him as incompetent. He said as much.

"The soldiers and non-commissioned officers are good at their jobs, but the senior staff aren't. The generals are all sycophants, children or close kin to the shrews. They couldn't win a battle against boredom." Lieutenant Garelt picked a stone out of the ground and flung it in obvious disgust. "So I fight with the Imperial Army because despite the vast flaws of their leadership, they can win the battles against spiderkin and zahhacks that the High Army can't. They can protect Rakesh." He threw another stone. "Things might be different if the Errows were in charge."

"Sir?" Cinder asked in confusion.

"The only military group in Rakesh worthy of note is the Errow militia. Their soldiers are dedicated, but most importantly, the senior commanders earn their rank through merit. You know about them?"

Cinder nodded. He'd studied Errow history. His initial assessment of them, back when he'd been a broken boy living in an orphanage, had been ill-informed at best. He'd made his judgment about the Errows based on four bullies. It was a private shame.

The Errows were from the Sunset Kingdoms, fair-skinned and tall, and originally a religious sect. Some would call them a cult. They claimed to be the remnants of Mede's army and had been driven out of the Sunsets for what the majority believed heretical beliefs. Over the past one thousand years, they'd faced discrimination as they traveled ever southward, but in spite of it all, they had held onto their culture. Their religious devotion drove them, and their elders—men and women chosen at large—led them, interpreting their version of *The Medeian Scryings*. They had even managed to become wealthy, but that wealth didn't always lead to acceptance. It often led to envy, even in Rakesh where they'd made a home for themselves.

Cinder admired the Errows, and he regretted judging them so harshly. He'd thought that achieving wealth should have taught them to let go of the discrimination of the past. He was wrong. How could anyone simply accept their lot in life just because they had wealth when the animus of the past continued to crush them low?

"You don't want to be repeating what I told you," Lieutenant Garelt said, speaking into the silence which had fallen over their conversation. "I've brought up my concerns and observations enough times to be considered a troublemaker. And no matter how many times the commander has promised to listen next time, he never does. At least not enough. He'll give me full command of whatever unit I ask for, but otherwise, he goes on his merry way to charge straight at whatever enemy he sees." He peered sharply at Cinder. "Like I said. None of this goes past the two of us."

"None of what sir?" Cinder asked, taking on an innocent expression.

The lieutenant laughed. "Good man."

Two days after his discussion with the lieutenant, there was an unexpected tumult when the battalion came across what appeared to be an innocuous pond.

Cinder had been riding amidst the bulk of the warriors when excited cries had trickled down the column. He'd stood in his stirrups, trying to find out what was going on, but a shouted explanation made any questions unnecessary.

The pond was apparently fed by a leyline of *aether*, recognized by a strange pearlescent shimmer best seen at dusk. Colonel Shaloce had called for an immediate halt and began shouting orders. The battalion would halt early and camp here for the night.

"What's going on?" Depth asked, obviously confused as the sick and wounded streamed past them. "Where are they going?"

"Toward the pond," Bones answered.

Cinder had read about leylines. They were rivers of *aether* flowing through the bedrock of Seminal, and from them extended dendritic tendrils spread across the world. In the oceans and seas, the *aether* quickly dispersed, unable to concentrate, but on rare occasions, a leyline would rise to the world's surface and interact with a body of water or a stretch of land. It happened infrequently and didn't last for much longer than a day or so. The leyline would then subside, returning to the world's roots.

But during the time when the *aether* mixed with the water, it formed a unique liquid—*mana*—one with remarkable properties that allowed for miraculous healing. It was why the wounded were being sent to the pond. Regular consumption of the *aether*-mixed liquid over the next few hours would likely heal even the gravest of injuries. And it had to be over the next few hours, directly from the pond. The water's potency couldn't be carried off and stored in bottles or canteens.

The rest of the battalion would also partake of the *mana*. It would help all of them, allow them to grow, more fully open any Chakras to which they had access. For humans, unfortunately, the water provided little benefit. It healed them but did little else.

But little wasn't the same as nothing.

Cinder dismounted and helped arrange camp. He began by brushing his mount, making sure the gelding was fed and watered from a source other than the pond. Some speculated that *mana* was also how *aether*-cursed beasts came to be. Next, he pitched his tent, heaped his belongings inside it, and helped gather wood for the Seconds' campfire.

All the while, however, his mind was occupied by thoughts of the pond. Might it help restore some measure of his *Jivatma*?

Of course, he told no one about his hopes. He couldn't. First, who would believe him? Second, if they did believe him, what would they think? The only humans who claimed the use of *Jivatma* were the rishis, and everyone hated them. And finally, what difference did it make?

Based on his research, Cinder believed *Jivatma* might be specific to him alone. No one else other than the Mythaspuris, Shet, and the ancient *asrasins* were definitively known to have utilized it.

Bones must have noticed his distraction.

"You're wanting to drink some of that water, aren't you?" he guessed after they returned to camp.

Depth, Wark, and Ishmay lingered close at hand, taking care of their own tents. They were the only Seconds not at the pond. The dwarves and elves had long since departed, gone down at the pond, the entire perimeter of which was clogged. Not a single inch of space between those busily slurping the water directly. The James surrounded its entire perimeter.

"We should all go," Cinder said.

"What's the point?" Ishmay asked. "None of us are injured."

"But what if it helps us become better than we are," Cinder replied. "More like the elves and dwarves?"

"You think it could?" Wark asked.

"I don't know," Cinder said. "Maybe." He eyed the others, his brother warriors. They had fought and bled with them. They'd shared sacrifice and the agony of watching those they loved die. They needed all the advantages they could get.

"Did you drink *aether*-blessed water in the past?" Ishmay asked.

Depth grunted. "It would answer a lot of questions."

Cinder frowned at Depth. "What questions would it answer?" he asked, although he had a pretty good idea which ones they had in mind. His friends weren't stupid. They trained with him every day. They saw what he could do. How he beat elves and dwarves in nearly any kind of combat, or at least he used to. They recognized the oddities about him and probably wondered about it almost as much as he did.

"Your speed for one," Wark said. "You're as fast as an elf."

"And as strong as a dwarf," Ishmay added.

Yes. Their perceptions were accurate and expected.

Bones cracked a grin. "You didn't think we had noticed, did you?" He chuckled. "We've all seen what you can do and talked about it."

"Well, you used to be as fast as an elf and strong as a dwarf," Depth allowed. "You lost some of it when you came back from the wilderness drill. But we always figured you had *lorethasra* like the woven. Maybe you're part woven."

Cinder blinked in surprise. He had never considered the latter, and he narrowed his eyes in thought. After a moment, he shook his head. No. He didn't source *lorethasra* like a woven. He conducted *Jivatma* like a Mythaspuri. He also felt a sense of relief wash over him. If his friends already knew about his speed and strength but assumed it was due to *lorethasra*, maybe they could accept the rest. But there was a final question to ask. "And you don't think I'm going to turn into a wraith?"

His question elicited startlement.

Bones barked laughter. "The hell would we think that?" He asked. "Or have you been measuring our heads to see how much brain you might find inside them? You know, because you're figuring on feasting on them like a wraith."

Cinder grinned. "In your case, I don't need to do any measuring.

I'm pretty sure I know what I'd find."

"A brain as smooth as a coconut?" Depth asked.

"And as hollow," Wark added.

"And likely filled with as much milk," Ishmay said.

Bones scowled in outrage. "Why the hell are you mocking me? I didn't say anything the rest of you weren't thinking."

"And what were you thinking?" Cinder asked, wanting to make sure he understood what the others had already apparently discussed.

"That you have *lorethasra* and can source it like a woven," Ishmay answered, solemn for once.

Cinder shook his head. "I can't." He glanced around the circle of Seconds. "Have any of you heard of *Jivatma*?"

They hadn't, so Cinder explained what he had learned over the past year or so.

When he finished speaking, it was Wark who spoke, cursing like he rarely did. "What the fuck are you?"

"I'm the same person you've all known," Cinder said, injecting levity into his tone. "Now you just know a bit more." He explained his theories about what conducting *Jivatma* might mean for him and how he'd lost it.

When he finished, it was Bones who had the next question. "Who else knows about this?"

"Anya," Cinder said.

"Of course she does," Bones muttered.

Cinder overlooked the undertones to Bones' statement. "So do Masters Molni and Absin."

The Seconds viewed him in another round of restless silence.

Depth cleared his throat, breaking the quiet. "And you think if we drink the water, we can gain what you had?"

Cinder shrugged. "There's only one way to find out."

Ishmay was nodding his head even before he finished speaking. "If it means being able to beat the shit out of the elves, then I'm in."

"Fuck, yes," Bones agreed. "Now that's a plan."

As a group, they headed to the pond.

It was finally Cinder's turn to drink the *mana*. He knelt like a penitent, and on either side of him, Bones and Ishmay mimicked his posture. Same with Wark and Depth. Threads of silver light wove through bright colors that swirled in chaotic rainbow patterns. The pond shined and shimmered, and Cinder bent his head to the water.

Impressions rolled over him while his mouth was inches from the water. A fire snapping, a breeze whispering, ivy rustling, and water ebbing and flowing like the tide.

The sounds grew louder, deafening, and he wondered at them. They abruptly disappeared when Cinder took a sip of *mana*, and he no longer found himself concerned by the strange noises. Another sip. More. When he had drank his fill, he staggered away from the pond. The world of Seminal grew simultaneously more and less real. He seemed able to think with supreme clarity, but there also felt like a fog pressed on his thoughts. Mistakes of the past, a lack of judgment and empathy weighed on him, but so did a joyous singing light. It called out to him, and in the core of his being, there rang an answering hymn.

And where once his *Jivatma* had resided, a flicker of silver glow flashed and faded, extending past his being. Again, it flashed and faded, but this time there remained a small thimbleful of light. It grew steadily stronger, and after a while, it remained, a bare puddle of what had once been a pond of mirror-reflective water.

But it was there.

Cinder closed his eyes and prayed in gratitude.

In a distant part of the world, a solitary, rocky island reared out of the aquamarine waters of a deep bay. It was a stony place, broken-backed with tumbled boulders the size of cottages and devoid of any greenery and life other than lichen and wave-tossed seaweed. The island faced an area of the coast where a cliff-edged desert met the sea. From a distance, it appeared off-balance; a lumpy mass, much of it barely above water except for a single cliff, which thrust at the sky like an accusing finger. It was the only part of the island to rise high enough above the waves for the surf to never touch its top.

And high up on this cliff, a beetled ledge led into a broad, shadowed cave that peered out at the bay. From its entrance was a view of the mainland desert, a broken set of escarpments shaded in orange and brown that merged with a lifeless plain extending off to the horizon.

All told, this was a grim, inhospitable place, but it was where the Calico had decided to make her home. Here she waited, ever since the long-ago war against the false god, the ancient age when she had fought on behalf of her human's memory and his hopes. And here she slumbered in her cavern by the sea, this place where she had taken Indrun's assigned task and protected the Orb. She hadn't wanted to, but the Mythaspuri had been persistent. He had foreseen the possibility that everyone she had lost would be restored. A chance for joy in her life, and she trusted him.

She would be a fool not to since Antalagore also trusted Indrun, and Antalagore was a synonym for wise.

Her vow to Indrun given, she had waited here, slumbering and dreaming, content as the centuries unspooled. Quiet and largely forgotten by the world of Seminal.

But lately, recollections troubled her dreams. Remembrances of her past, of her family. This time, it was of Rukh, her human. She missed him, missed his fingers when they scratched her chin. Sometimes it felt as if he had finally returned to her, and she rustled her wings, considering whether to end her long sleep. She occasionally did so, testing the ties binding her and her human, but always it remained like a wispy fog, ethereal and impossible to measure.

Just then, the Calico's great wings involuntarily flared, extending wide enough to shade a farmhouse. In that moment, she had felt a familiar touch, the distant, fading call of someone closer than family.

But who? The memory was already dissipating into emptiness, and she growled in irritation, a rumble like an avalanche as the calico fur on her neck and back ruffled. Who had she felt?

She didn't know. She couldn't tell or recollect, and the annoyance of ignorance roused the Calico, not to full wakefulness, but enough that she felt the need to give her paws several quick licks. The soothing movements from another life calmed her, settled her mind enough for her to recognize what she really wanted. She wanted someone to scratch her chin.

It was her final thought as she shifted about, curling around her body as she recaptured her lost slumber.

17

For the human Seconds, the *aether*-blessed water proved true to its name. It blessed them with a heightened awareness of their bodies, along with increasing their speed and strength. They were graceful in ways they had never before known, quick and powerful. They could spar against an elf and be every bit as swift. They could wrestle a dwarf and hold their own or even overcome. Everyone noticed and commented on their gains.

But eventually the gains faded, and then the *mana* became a curse. The humans lost all they once had. Their wondrous physical attributes became like the recollections of an ancient warrior remembering his youthful glory. It left the humans bitter. Especially when the woven amongst them did maintain their advances, at least to some extent. After drinking the *mana*, all of them were just a bit quicker than before. Stronger, too.

And this didn't even touch upon the difficulty of making peace with the horrific nature of the Trial. The deaths weren't so easy to forget.

As a result, the Seconds who returned to the Third Directorate five weeks after the battle against the spiderkin came back with vastly different emotions. They arrived on a snowy day where a curtain of dreary clouds drifted across the sky. Some of them piled out of the blacked-out carriages in an abundance of energy while others stared about, appearing lost and troubled. The humans were certainly part of the latter group. To a man, they were quiet and deflated.

Mirk was waiting for them when they arrived, and he grinned widely when he caught sight of Cinder and Bones. "You two gits look like someone killed your dog."

Cinder didn't know how to reply. For him, the *aether*-blessed water had also proved a boon. He, too, had been graced with enhanced speed and strength, but unlike the others, his growth hadn't been temporary. His endured because his *Jivatma* was finally recovering. A part of him was as giddy and excited as the woven, but another part empathized all too well with his despondent brother warriors.

"It was a hard journey," Bones replied in answer to Mirk's statement, his voice uncharacteristically soft. He stared off into the distance, as if searching for meaning in the world at large. Of all of them, he had taken the deaths suffered by the James and the loss of his newfound strength and speed the hardest. "I'll see you upstairs," he said to Cinder. He nodded his goodbye to Mirk and joined the rest of the Seconds, who were trudging toward Krathe House, gear in hand.

"It was another fragging disaster in the Daggers," Cinder added, "or at least enough to not make much difference between winning or losing."

Mirk's welcoming grin twisted into a drooping expression of worry. "You fellows want to talk about it?"

"Not really," Cinder said, unwilling to relive the deaths and injuries he'd witnessed.

Mirk shifted on his feet, somberness stealing his usual chipper demeanor. "Well, I had some fun stories to tell you about the elves, but I guess they can wait."

Cinder managed a smile. "Funny stories are always welcome."

Mirk's grave air lightened somewhat. "Most of them have to do with how arrogant those pointy-eared prigs are."

Cinder's smile came more naturally, and he clapped Mirk on the shoulder. "Describing elves as arrogant is kind of like saying peacocks are proud."

"Yes, but what's funny is how afraid the ones in my class are of you."

Cinder's brow lifted in surprise. "Really?"

Mirk nodded. "They heard how you won the Grand Melee, but hearing isn't the same as seeing. And they've seen you train. Then you go and kill a monster of an *aether*-cursed bear. They think you're tougher than steel."

"I'm as human as everyone else," Cinder said, unable to keep the bitterness out of his voice. He recalled the recent battle against the spiderkin. The elves of Jameken Battalion. The ones who had died. It could have been him. Or one of his brothers. It all seemed so random and pointless.

"If you say so." Mirk didn't sound like he believed him.

Cinder glanced at him.

Mirk shook his head. "Forget I said anything. Go join the others. You look like you're on the ragged end."

"We'll catch up later?" Cinder asked.

"Count on it, mate."

Cinder left Mirk then and headed toward Krathe House. Upstairs, he found everyone in the midst of stowing away their gear. He joined them, shucking the clothes out of his rucksack. They needed washing, and he left them in a pile outside his door for the cleaning staff. Next, he tended to his weapons, cleaning them prior to storing them away.

While working, a vision stole over his mind, and he smiled. He hadn't had one in over a month, and he could use the distraction. His arms fell to his side, and he lost himself in the images.

He slumped to the ground, tired and dirty, sitting in a shaded alley. At the very edge of his hearing, the sounds of battle reached him. The curdling stench of buildings burning drifted on the air. High above, a lightning-laced, bruise-purple cloud battered the ground and sky. From it emanated mad shrieks. The cloud had a name. The Sorrow Bringer, and She occasionally moved against the wind, eclipsing the sun.

But for this one moment, he wouldn't allow the world's turmoils to touch him. Within the alley, he rested next to a woman he loved. She was his island of calm amidst madness, and she nestled against him, leaning her head on his shoulder.

He dipped his head and kissed her forehead. "I love you," he told her.

"I love you, too" she said in her confident contralto.

The world—the true one—snapped back into being with a harsh, disconcerting suddenness, and Cinder found himself on his knees, shaken and unable to move. His emotions roiled, and his shoulders lifted and fell in time to his heavy breathing. He closed his eyes, wanting to hold onto the dream's imagery.

This time it worked. He was able to recall the vision, more vividly than ever before. No longer was it the painful sensation of a dimly remembered, treasured memory. This time it was a crystal-clear recollection of the past.

He had known the woman. Everything about her was real. Everything about who they had once been had been real. He had truly known her in ways he doubted he'd ever know anyone ever again. He trusted and loved her as deeply as he could ever imagine trusting and loving someone. And he'd been blessed in that past life because she'd trusted and loved him just as deeply.

But he still didn't know her name or her face. Or maybe he did and simply couldn't remember it. He wanted to growl in frustration. He suspected many questions would be answered if he could recall her features, especially since her voice was hauntingly familiar, a teasing recognition on the distant shores of his knowledge.

"What do you think?" Bones' voice carried from the commons, interrupting his thoughts. "Eat first, bathe later? Or bathe first and eat later?"

Cinder listened in on the conversation, needing the diversion from the vision. It was too abrupt, too real, and in many ways, too painful. He needed privacy and the distance of time to allow the immediacy of the moment to dissipate so he could make peace with it.

Sriovey answered Bones. "If I was in your shoes—

"If you were in my shoes, you'd trip and fall on your face," Bones said. "You being so short and all."

"Shut up, asshole," Sriovey said. "Do you want my advice or not?"

Bones chuckled. "Fine," he said as if he was humoring the dwarf.

"If I was you, I'd definitely bathe first," Sriovey said. "You smell like you mated with a skunk." He said the last in a smug tone.

"No," Bones replied. "You've got me mixed up with your sister again."

Cinder's head shot up. The commons quieted.

It was Wark who said what they were all thinking. "Did Bones just make a sister joke?"

"Why yes. I believe he did," Mohal said, sounding equally stunned.

Cinder smiled. His past was a mystery. His present uncertain, and he worried about the Seconds. But if his friends could laugh with one another, he reckoned they'd be alright.

The long, cold millennia of his imprisonment had cast the being into a dream-filled slumber where he gave himself over to recollections of victory and glory, of dominion and rule. Those were the just rewards for a man become a god, and how the being ached for his stolen valor and might. Only in his dreams was he as he should be.

He knew none of this. In this way was his imprisonment kinder than he deserved, but even still, the being occasionally wandered to wakefulness. Rare moments filled with a restless hatred for those who had wronged him. Those times were achingly few, and he wished they could be otherwise.

But he dared not hope so. Never that. Hope was a siren song. She was the most terrible of angels, the worst of all things. In the being's view, only might and decisive domination should matter. Hope was for the weak.

Then again…

The being absently tugged at the smoke-like bindings securing him to the heart of a mountain. He stretched and rustled his chains, and echoes somberly rang out, sounding like the tolling of deep-throated bells. In those moments, trapped in his dark chamber, he would awaken and wonder. Might the imprisoning chains binding him be withering? Might his ageless incarceration finally be at an end? He *hoped* so.

Chink.

There it was. The faintest sound of his chains weakening, of one link breaking.

It disturbed the being's sleep, and he struggled to wakefulness, his eyes blazing with anger and knowledge. He grew aware. He recognized his situation, his imprisonment, and how he hated it. Hated those who had bound him here in this dead, lightless place.

However, he husbanded his energy. He remembered those other times of clarity and how minutes from now, sleep would reclaim him. Soon enough his anger and fury would drift away along with his consciousness, and his eyes would close—both his normal one and the one which had been burned out along with the right side of his face. Flames might have still lurked within the socket of his destroyed eye, but more likely it was rage at his fallen state.

He wanted vengeance even while recognizing his impotence at addressing his desires. The sleep would—

The being halted his mental diatribe, blinking in slowly gathering amazement. He hadn't yet fallen asleep. He was still awake. What did this mean?

The being stretched the chains tethering him to the mountain. He pulled them to their limits, tugging hard.

The activity of muscles long unused to use caused him to spasm in agony. The pain brought him low, but he smiled despite the anguish. His struggles had been worth it. He had heard what he had intended. A chinking sound had rung out, indicating the breakage of another link. Indicating a certainty: he would soon be free.

The being's smile became a grin of anticipation. Freedom would simply require the conduction of his *Jivatma*. He reached for the blackened pool of absence at the center of his mind, halting when he noticed the blue-and-green lightning shielding it.

He grimaced, recognizing what the lightning meant. Someone had ignited the Orbs of Peace. They would severely limit his power and make it ghastly to attempt the use of it. Such knowledge might have dismayed a lesser man, but the being was no man. He was Shet, and he would break the chains that imprisoned him.

18

Anya strode through her mother's palace of Taj Wada, headed to her rooms. Guards bowed as she marched past them, and she acknowledged their greetings with a simple dip of her head. She might have stopped longer to speak to them, but she didn't want to tarry. The stink and fatigue of the road clung to her, and she looked forward to a bath and rest.

She'd only just arrived, minutes before dusk as darkness prepared to settle across the city like the drawing of a curtain. She'd already seen to Silence, her pure-bred Yavana mare, and had her belongings delivered to her quarters, although her personal items she carried over a pair of saddlebags flung over her shoulder.

It had taken Anya the majority of two months to return home to Revelant. In fact, she had actually arrived a few days *after* her father and the trade delegation had returned.

Ironic. Had she waited for her father to finish hammering out the details of the remaining few items Yaksha required, she could have returned home with far greater comfort, safety, and swiftness than the mountain trek she had ended up taking.

She didn't regret her choice. She and the guards had destroyed a large swarm of ghouls along with an apparently charismatic necrosed. Her honor guard had suffered losses—three dead and five wounded—and that, Anya did regret. She mourned the death of her warriors, hated they had to place themselves in danger, but the work was necessary.

Still, Anya longed for a world and time in which she wouldn't have to order people into battle. She longed for peace.

The word whispered in her mind.

Peace. How she wished for it. But it was a state of being she no longer believed she'd ever know. She and Rukh had once thought they had achieved that blessed state in a different time. It had been after they'd defeated…

Who had they defeated?

Anya slowed her march through Taj Wada's halls, lost in her hazy memories. The details wouldn't come, and she irritably shook off her thoughts. The knowledge of who she had once been continued to evade her even while it harassed her. In essence, her past life remained a mystery, and it was one she was tired of trying to solve. She had spent decades wishing and hoping to know who she really was, but by now, she had long since grown weary of the chronic ignorance.

Her footsteps slowed again.

Then again, over the past few months, she had learned several key details: the names of her husband and some of her family. There were times when she could recollect snippets of her husband's voice, his laughter, the times he'd shown her Ashoka, his home city, and the sound of his mandolin while she sang accompaniment.

She even recollected a young woman, lovely with curly, dark hair and dark eyes. Serena Paradiso had been her name, and Anya had considered her a younger sister.

Again, she threw off her maudlin memories, quickening her stride. It was the past. Best to leave it there.

On she went, marching forcefully toward her rooms, as if the rhythmic clicking of her boots across the marble flooring could somehow erase her doubts and desires. She turned a final corner and discovered her sister exiting their mother's quarters.

The two of them stood in an arched hallway lined by white-washed shiplap and a ceiling painted in murals of pink magnolias. One of Anya's ancestors had fallen in love with magnolias and shiplap, and in the privacy of her mind, she could admit that she liked them, too.

"Your Highness has at last returned," Enma said, an indecipherable smile on her face.

Anya briefly closed her eyes and gathered her patience. Enma appeared to be in a playful mood, but playful for her sister could also easily be taunting and cruel. "Hello, Enma. How are you?"

"I'm fine. Father returned several days ago and had promising words about Prince Redwinth." Her smile grew sly. "Did you know your impatience ended up costing you? Had you waited a few more weeks—"

"I know," Anya interrupted. She'd been thinking those very thoughts only a few minutes before. "Is mother in her rooms?"

Enma's smile grew frosty. "She is, but given your"—she lifted her nose and pretended to inhale, her lips pursed—"fragrance, you should probably wash first. You stink of horse sweat. Did you bathe in it?"

Anya gritted her teeth, holding back a sharp retort. Her sister wanted to start an argument. It was childish, and Anya refused to give it to her. "You know me too well." She held out her arms and offered Enma an impish grin. "Now how about a hug for your favorite sister?"

Enma's eyes flashed in annoyance, and her pursed lips became a scowl.

She never had a chance to reply because their mother stepped out of her quarters. She wore a welcoming smile. "I thought I heard your voice," their mother said to Anya, stepping forward with arms wide for a welcoming embrace.

Anya shied away. "You really don't want to hug me. I'm fresh off the road."

"She stinks," Enma said with a sniff. "I'll see you both at supper," she added, sweeping down the hall.

Their mother watched Enma's departing figure. A crease furrowed her brow, and she shook her head. An instant later, she faced Anya. "I heard some of what Enma said. She is right. You would have been better served by waiting for your father." Her head tilted in question. "Why did you leave so early?"

"I felt a calling," Anya said. "It's an instinct I've learned to trust, and I was right to do so. On our way back, we came across a large swarm of ghouls."

Her mother's expression went sour with disapproval. "I assume they're all dead."

"They are."

Her mother remained unhappy. "Ghouls are like rats: impossible to entirely eradicate. They may have established their foul dead cities in our lands by now." Her gaze sharpened on Anya. "Perhaps it *was* a good thing you took the overland route home."

"They also had a necrosed leading them."

Her mother's gaze sharpened. "Truly?"

"I killed her, but she said something." Anya relayed the dying necrosed's final words.

Her mother crossed her arms, her gaze going distant as she frowned in displeasure. "I'll ask Ginala about it," she said after a moment of consideration.

"The quelchon." Anya didn't try to hide her distaste. She had never liked the deceitful old witch, and the feeling was mutual.

Quelchon Ginala had never trusted her, and there was always an undercurrent of sneering mockery beneath the woman's guise and words. Or at least Anya thought so. No one else seemed to notice but speaking to the quelchon always set Anya's teeth on edge.

Anya's mother smiled wryly. "Yes, Ginala. She's also heard more about the Sunset Warlord. He's captured most of the Sunset Kingdoms. She sees him attacking Aurelian Crèche next."

"He'd be a fool to do so. Those mountain passes aren't places where his cavalry will be of much use."

"Ginala thinks he might be the *Garnala lon Anarin*, the Sower of the Wind."

Anya's eyes narrowed. A powerful title. "I thought there was only ever one Sower of the Wind," she said. "Mede. Is she saying he is Mede Reborn, like the Medeian Scryings proclaim will happen?"

Her mother hesitated. "Ginala was unclear on the matter. I think her mind isn't as sharp as it once was."

Anya snorted derision. "Was it ever?" she muttered.

"Anya," her mother's tone was sharp.

"Sorry," she replied, her tone unrepentant. Thankfully, her mother chose to overlook her tone. A thought occurred to Anya. "If Genka Devesth is the Sower of the Wind, should there not be a *Zuthrum lon Varshin*, a Reaper of the Whirlwind? Who would that be? Shet?"

"There wasn't a Reaper of the Whirlwind in the time of Mede."

"Maybe he was never the true Sower."

"You may be right," her mother said, surprisingly accepting Anya's viewpoint. "Ginala says the true Reaper of the Whirlwind will also be the known as the *Elonicon Festh*, World Killer in *Shevasra*.

"*Elonimon Festh*, World Changer," Anya corrected. "The words are similar, but *Elonimon Festh* means World Changer. It was Shokan's title, bastardized by Shet into a curse, *Elonicon Festh*, and given to any who followed Shokan."

Her mother's eyes rose in surprise. "You certainly know a lot about mythology, and *Shevasra*. When did you learn all this?"

Anya quirked a smile. "The Third Directorate." It wasn't true, but no one need know it. It would raise too many questions. Anya had actually known how to speak *Shevasra* nearly upon first hearing the language, as if the knowledge had always been present.

"If you know *Shevasra* so well, do you also know who first held the title of *Zuthrum lon Varshin*?"

"No."

"It wasn't Mede like you thought. It was Shokan, the Lord of the Sword. He and Sira both. It was a title given to them and those who followed after, including the Mythaspuris."

Anya hadn't known of it, and she made a mental note to read more about it later. The thought made her smile. Cinder was always making mental notes to study certain topics.

Her mother noticed her smile. "What do you find so amusing?"

Anya thought fast. "I was wondering if Shokan and Sira had a last name," she said, hoping her lie would hold under her mother's scrutiny. She didn't feel like explaining how she had been thinking about a human man. Some things were simply not acceptable in elven society, and an elven woman smiling upon considering a human man was high on the list. "Did they? Have a last name, I mean?"

Her mother shrugged upon hearing Anya's reply. "Not that I know of." She seemed to gather herself. "You'll be returning to the Third Directorate soon?"

Anya nodded. "In a few weeks."

"Good. You can travel with Lisandre. I want both of you to study this Cinder Shade. He and his cohorts finished their Autumn Trial about a month ago."

"I thought Ginala was looking into Cinder," Anya said, not liking having to spy on the young man she considered a friend.

"She has other issues to attend, such as the Sunset Warlord."

"And you want me and Lisandre to study Cinder?" Anya said. There was more to her mother's request. Something must have happened, likely in the Autumn Trial.

Her mother confirmed it. "A little over a month ago, Jameken Battalion was almost destroyed. It would have been if not for the actions of a certain Second from the Third Directorate. You know who I mean?"

"Cinder."

"He led a charge out of a fortified position, and as result, the commander and his officers were able to rally their warriors and defeat three thousand spiderkin."

Anya's eyes boggled. "Three thousand?" She could already guess the elven tactics of 'swords unsheathed and charge'. It was a stupid way to fight, and the James should have been overwhelmed. She said as much.

"They got lucky. A human is attached to the unit. A Lieutenant Garelt. It was he and Cinder who turned the tide of battle." Her mother's gaze grew cold. "This is the third time Cinder Shade has earned acclaim. Once is luck. Twice is a coincidence. Thrice is a pattern. There is a strangeness about him and his history. Learn it. Report it. Ginala wants to know as well."

Anya nodded, managing to keep the frown of disapproval off her face. Her mother trusted Ginala too much. They all did, and if the quelchon wanted to know about Cinder, then Anya was certain it meant the old woman shouldn't learn it.

Though it went against her mother's commands, she would do her best to protect Cinder from Ginala's prying eyes.

Classes resumed shortly after the Seconds returned to the Third Directorate, and everyone settled into their usual routine. It seemed like the second year was passing too swiftly. Already more than half of it was gone. It was Winsath, the middle of winter, and there was still the Secondary Trial awaiting them several months hence. So far, the year had been difficult for all of them, but especially for Cinder, and he felt it as an indescribable aching in his bones, a tiredness of his spirit.

It wasn't simply holding Nathaz as he died or fighting an *aether*-cursed bear or Jozep almost dying. Nor was it losing his *Jivatma*. After all, he'd recovered a glimmer of it, a shining shard of water reflecting something unknowably vast and beautiful. It wasn't even the gory deaths experienced in the Autumn Trial, the stench of offal filling the air, or the squelching, slurping noise of his boots as he sank into blood-soaked mud.

No. What had Cinder feeling stretched and worn, like frayed clothes washed one too many times, was the entirety of his time at the Directorate. The mind-numbing, seemingly non-stop horror of it all. The violence, the fear for his brothers, the chronic sorrow of suffering. A part of him felt like he'd seen it all before, as if all of this death and dying had an awful, well-known ring to it. And his soul was tired of being burdened by toil and turmoil.

"What's wrong?" Jozep asked.

Cinder started out of his morose thoughts. He blinked when he realized Jozep, and even Riyne, were staring at him in concern. "I'm fine," he said, not wanting to burden them with his worries. "I was just thinking. It's nothing important."

"Are you sure?" Jozep asked. "It didn't look like it was nothing."

"You looked like you were about to cry," Riyne said, his voice surprisingly empathetic.

Cinder offered Riyne and Jozep a tight-lipped smile. "I'm fine. Really. Don't worry about it. Let's play."

The three of them formed a triangle, sitting close to one another; Jozep in a wooden chair, a tabla set between in his knees; Riyne on a high stool, fiddle in hand; and Cinder at his usual spot in a soft armchair, next to a closed window overlooking Anya's garden. She was expected to return to the Directorate soon, or so rumors stated. If true, Anya should arrive any day, and Cinder looked forward to seeing her again.

He distractedly strummed his mandolin while thinking about her.

The rest of the Seconds were spread throughout the room, some playing cards, others darts, and a few seated at the pair of couches placed near the roaring hearth. Their conversation bobbed and fell like the waves of some bizarre ocean. A few pointed comments sparked sudden laughter, serving as the taller swells of the water.

It was friendship and relaxation in one another's company.

Cinder wished he could achieve the same carefree manner as his brother warriors. *Maybe one day.*

He spoke to Jozep and Riyne. "What should we play?"

Riyne's voice went gravelly. "None of that romantic shit you're always playing."

It took Cinder a moment to realize the elf was mocking Sriovey, and he shared a look of startlement with Jozep. The two of them broke out in laughter.

"I do believe a miracle just occurred," Jozep said.

In some ways, his statement was the truth. Ever since the Autumn

Trial, and maybe even before, Riyne had become… friendly. It didn't mean Cinder and the noble elf were friends, but at least they weren't enemies. They were acquaintances, which was fine enough.

"You three dickheads going to play any music?" Bones shouted at them.

"Just make sure it's not any of that romantic shit," Sriovey added.

Cinder, Jozep, and Riyne broke out in fresh laughter.

"What?" Sriovey asked, sounding affronted.

"It's nothing," Cinder said. "Just a joke Riyne told us."

Sriovey eyed them in suspicion. "Oh, fuck off," he eventually declared.

Cinder chuckled at his response. "Why don't we play a lively tune for a whining dwarf?" he suggested, making sure Sriovey could hear him.

"I said fuck off," Sriovey repeated.

"I've got a song in mind," Riyne said. He began with a few simple chords, letting Cinder get a feel for the music.

"I know this one," Jozep said, sounding excited. He joined in a few bars later.

Their pace picked up, and they played harder.

Jozep began singing, belting out the tune, which was about a man encouraging a woman and speaking of the rolling changes of life.

Cinder's bleak mood lifted some as he listened to the lyrics. It felt like they spoke to him on a personal level.

Jozep continued to sing, the lyrics now about thunder bursting in a burning desert and the woman's love pouring on the man like a sweet sunshower.

"I said no fucking romantic songs!" Sriovey protested.

Cinder wasn't listening, and his heart lifted further. He wanted to laugh as the song's unexpected optimism carried him upward.

When the song finally ended, Cinder was grinning. "That was a great song," he said to Riyne.

"Glad you liked it," Riyne replied. "It's one of my favorites. And you looked like you needed something happy. You've been whining a lot."

"Like someone kicked your puppy," Jozep added.

"I wasn't that bad," Cinder protested. *Was I?*

"Yes, you were," Jozep said. "Speaking of whining, I know you're going to complain when you find out how much new clothes are going to cost."

Cinder frowned. "What new clothes?"

"The new clothes you'll need for the Duchess's Banquet."

"The what?" Cinder asked with a frown.

"The annual banquet the duchess holds for the Seconds," Jozep answered. "The Thirds have theirs in the fall, the Firsters in midwinter as the Winter Gala, and we have ours a month after theirs. It's a long ways away still. You didn't know about this?"

Cinder scowled. *No, I didn't know.* "Did you?"

"I just told you about it," Jozep replied as if speaking to a simpleton.

Cinder overlooked the tone, still upset at the notion of having to waste more money on new clothes. "Did they hold it last year?"

Riyne barked laughter at him. "Of course they did, you dumbass."

"If you weren't always busy sparring against Master Absin, you'd have heard about it, too," Jozep said.

Cinder grimaced. Fragging hells. A Duchess's Banquet, and he really would need new clothes? His happy mood threatened to crumble. Where was he going to get the money for new clothes? And why did he need new clothes anyway? Why couldn't he wear what he wore last year.

He opened his mouth to ask, but Jozep somehow guessed what he was about to say. "It's considered poor form if you wear last year's clothing to this year's banquet."

Cinder cursed under his breath. Wear clothes only once? Ridiculous. As if material possessions were more important than giving, friendship, experiences, and love.

"It's our way," Riyne said. "If you don't obtain new clothing, the choice reflects poorly on you, your school and masters, and ultimately on the Duchess."

Cinder cursed anew. He had earned extra coin by winning the

Grand Melee, but he had hoped to save the money, not spend it friv-
olously. And who knew how much the clothes would cost? It might
leave him with hardly any coin left to his name. Barely enough to send
a few letters to Riner, the masters and students at *Steel-Graced Adepts*,
and Coral… if she ever wanted to hear from him again.

"I can send you to my tailor," Riyne said. "I'm sure he could provide
some kind of discount."

The offer was kind, and Cinder viewed the noble in fresh surprise.
In the face of Riyne's openness, it was hard to remember how little he
had liked the elf in their first year, hated him really. Riyne was now
trying to make amends, and Cinder was glad for it.

"Thank you," Cinder said. "I appreciate it, but I'd probably be better
off staying with the tailor I have. He's been good to me."

"Of course," Riyne said with a smile. "Let me know if you change
your mind."

Anya's stay at Taj Wada proved short. Only a few days, just long enough
to spend some time with her family before she was ready to move on.
Once again, it was an instinct drawing her on, this time back to the
Directorate.

On the afternoon of her leavetaking, the empress' stables at Taj
Wada were quiet since everyone who worked there was out on their
own errands and tasks. As a result, Anya had the barn to herself, and
the peacefulness granted her a few minutes to reflect and think on
what she needed to do before leaving the palace.

Had she forgotten anything?

She didn't think so. She'd reviewed her positive impressions of
Apsara Sithe and Prince Redwinth with her mother. She had reported
about the necrosed and the ghouls and even mentioned her interest in
sponsoring a Directorate student during the Secondary Trial. The last
issue had elicited some raised eyebrows, but once her family learned
that she would also be asking Lisandre to sponsor Estin and have them

accompany her and her own student, their worries had faded. Her mother had even gone so far as to state how it would do Estin good to have Lisandre teach him.

Of course, Anya hadn't mentioned that it was Cinder she planned on sponsoring. She could only imagine her family's reaction if she had. *Monumental drama.* As she figured matters, it was better to ask them for forgiveness rather than permission.

Satisfied she had done all she needed during her brief stop in Revelant, she focused on readying the chestnut gelding she planned on taking to the Third Directorate. She would have taken her normal palomino, but he had been invested as part of Enma's own stable of horses. A part of Anya wondered if her sister had made the choice out of true desire for the horse or a petulant means to spite Anya.

Regardless, the palomino was no longer available, but the gelding should do. Barton was his name, and he had the bloodlines of a Yavana, stronger and faster than most any other horse, and with a sweet, steady demeanor.

She smiled at the gelding, stroking his long face. "You'll keep me safe, won't you friend?"

"Talking to the horses now?" a voice asked. *Her mother.*

Anya's attention snapped to the open doors of the barn where her mother stood, highlighted momentarily by the morning sun before she entered the stable. Several horses nickered as the empress passed them by.

"I speak to them as well," her mother said, stroking the nose of a filly who had pushed her head past her stall. "Don't I, sweet girl?"

The filly pawed the ground in seeming agreement.

"I'm surprised to see you here," Anya said. "I said my 'goodbyes' to you, father, and Enma at breakfast."

Her mother frowned, her mouth making a moue of feigned hurt. "Can't a mother just love her daughter and wish her safe travels?"

Anya didn't doubt her mother's love, but she had doubts about her desires to simply wish her safe travels. Her mother was here for some other reason, likely so no prying eyes or ears could listen to what she had to say.

"Safe travels?" Anya asked. "What would I need to fear in Yaksha Proper?"

"There was the incident with the *aether*-cursed bear," her mother reminded her. "Your favorite human barely survived the encounter."

Anya didn't hide her smile of amusement very well. There it was. Her mother was here because of Cinder. Last night over dinner, Anya had drank a bit too much wine and had rashly spoken of her admiration of Cinder's abilities.

"You find my concerns entertaining?" her mother asked, her tone frosty.

Anya schooled her face to stillness. The woman standing in front of her was no longer her mother. This was the empress. Anya bowed her head in respect. "Of course not, Your Majesty." She glanced past lowered brows and caught her mother viewing her with a flat look of disapproval, and she dropped her gaze once again.

"This Cinder Shade vexes me," the empress said after a few seconds. "He has achieved too much, especially for a mere human. And there are twisted whispers about him. About you. Any elven woman—much less the empress—shouldn't hear such rumors about her daughter."

Anya recognized the danger she was in. The empress had come here to privately interrogate her about the truth of those rumors. She had come to the stables, to a place where Anya would feel least threatened and most likely to be caught off guard. And if the empress was dissatisfied with Anya's answers, the many freedoms Anya enjoyed could be lost to her forever.

She thought quickly. "I understand your concerns, Your Majesty, but there is no substance to those grotesque rumors." Her tone was calm and measured, although she allowed her irritation to lace the edges of her words. "In addition, I believe I can allay your fears." She glanced at the empress, who gestured for her to speak. "I wasn't merely going to ask Lisandre to accompany me and my student on the Secondary Trial for propriety's sake. I was also going to ask him to—" She inhaled heavily "—court me."

"Court you? Truly? Why didn't you make mention of it until now?" The empress sounded surprised, which was much better than sounding shocked. Shocked would almost surely mean disbelief whereas surprise meant Anya still had a chance to convince the empress of the truth of her intentions.

"I didn't mention it because I didn't want you and father to make a fuss about it. It would have been embarrassing, especially given Enma's likely reaction."

The empress smiled warmly, Anya's mother once more. "I suppose we would have made a fuss," she agreed. "And Enma would have been insufferable with her snide comments." She nodded. "I can see why you would have wanted to keep this matter to yourself. Carry on."

Anya did her best to shove down any sense of relief she might have felt as she bowed again to the empress. "Yes, Your Majesty."

19

Cinder strode along Whileaway Path, the road which led from the Third Directorate to Certitude. With him were Bones, Wark, Depth, and Ishmay, and their boots crunched upon the road's stone pavers. Since it was a rest day, the four of them were on their way to see Brance Reaville, the tailor they'd befriended last year. Hopefully, Cinder would be able to afford his prices for the new clothes he needed for the Duchess's Banquet.

In addition, it was a perfect time to head down to Certitude. The day was warm and sunny, sending runnels of melting snow streaming down the Whileaway. A mild breeze blew, warm and fine, and the bright sunshine reflected off melting snow. In all ways, it was a welcome break from winter's coldness.

Cinder turned his face to the late morning sky. He loved the feel of the warm sunshine on his face and how heavy the air smelled. A trace of humidity had replaced winter's brittle dryness, and there was also the mossy, wet scent of the Pantheon Forest, which surrounded him. From within its evergreen depths could be heard the scramble of small creatures in the undergrowth.

258

"Cinder looks like he's praying to the sun," Ishmay scoffed.

Cinder opened his eyes, peering aside at the other man. "No. I was actually praying for you."

"Really?"

"Yes. I was praying you wouldn't always be a lackwit."

"A lackwit?" Ishmay shook his head. "You and your stupidly big words."

Cinder grinned in anticipation, thinking Ishmay had stepped directly into his verbal trap. "Or you and your small ones? Which can be regarded on several levels. See, I could also be referencing your—"

"I get it," Ishmay cut in.

Bones shook his head in pity at Cinder. "If you have to explain a joke, it's no good."

Cinder glanced to the others, disheartened when they nodded agreement. "You really didn't think it was funny?"

"Hell no," Ishmay said. "It was terrible."

"Terrible?"

"Terrible," Ishmay confirmed. "And I wouldn't shit you about things like that. You're my favorite turd."

"Gross," Cinder said with a short chuckle. "Maybe I should just stick with jokes involving your mother or sister."

"Sisters are off-limits," Depth said automatically, nudging Bones, who grimaced.

"I don't have to worry none about my sister anymore," Bones replied, affecting a nonplussed attitude. "She got married last month."

"Who did she marry?" Ishmay asked. "Your other brother?"

Bones rolled his eyes. "You're getting your family mixed up with mine."

Ishmay had a rejoinder at the ready, but Cinder wasn't paying them much attention. He was too busy being glad. After the music from nearly a week ago, his emotional weariness had lifted, and the day's uplifting air only enhanced his recovery. Maybe it had to do with the glorious weather or the wonder of being here with good friends. Whatever the case, the joy of the moment filled Cinder, and he threw his arms around Ishmay's and Bones' shoulders. "It's a good day to be alive, don't you think?"

"Something odd is going on with Cinder," Depth noted, sounding troubled. "He's smiling."

"It's scary," Wark said, nodding sagely. He faced Cinder. "Please stop doing it."

Cinder chuckled in reply, and they continued on their way to Certitude. They passed a number of farms, and every once in a while, Cinder recognized odd sensations: the sulfurous crackling of fire, the clean whispering of wind, the loamy rustling of ivy, and the fresh wash of the waves.

He'd experienced them before, the sounds and smells. The battle against the *aether*-cursed bear might have been the first time he had noticed them, and ever since then, he had begun to perceive them more and more regularly. The sensations had grown stronger after he drank the *mana*, and shortly after returning to the Directorate, he had looked into the matter.

He now knew what the sounds and aromas were.

They were the Elements of a woven's *lorethasra*. Fire crackled. Air hissed. Earth rustled. And Water susurrated. Cinder shouldn't have it in him to sense them, but he did. It aided him. Whenever he sparred against an elf or a dwarf, he now knew what Element and likely weave they employed and could thus plan for it.

And with his speed and strength also recovering, he was re-establishing himself in the hierarchy of the Seconds. He was no longer an easy out for the woven.

Cinder's calculations of his martial prowess disintegrated when a few blocks into the city, he caught the barest hint of cinnamon. She was here.

A moment later, he saw her. *Anya*. She sat alone at a small outdoor café, a cup of tea close at hand. She didn't notice him at first. Her head was bent as she read a book. Cinder's breath caught as her honey-gold hair gleamed in a ray of sunshine. It haloed her features, casting them in an ethereal glow. She took a delicate sip of tea while turning the book's page, holding an expectant expression and the tip of tongue upon her upper lip. An instant later, she smiled in delight.

"Don't let an elf catch you staring at her like that," Bones warned.

Cinder recognized the truth of the admonishment, and he was about to break his gaze, but Anya glanced up from her book. She noticed him then, and her face brightened with warmth.

"Or let any elf catch *her* looking at you like that," Ishmay muttered.

Cinder barely heard. He was caught anew in the warmth of Anya's emerald gaze and her lovely features.

Bones frowned, his gaze shifting back and forth from him to Anya. "Be careful. We're off to see Master Brance. Find us when you're done talking to the princess."

Cinder broke off from staring at Anya, finally recognizing the stupidity of his actions. He tried not to redden with humiliation and embarrassment. How stupid of him. Bones was right. He couldn't stare at Anya like that, with such obvious admiration and in public no less. He was about to simply wave a greeting to the princess, but she called him over.

"Cadets," she said, still smiling. "It's good to see all of you again."

The others spoke their greetings to the princess, but they clearly had no plans of lingering. They murmured a couple more acknowledgements to Anya before moving on.

"I'll see you soon," Cinder said to them as they departed.

A few elves—men and women—glanced between Cinder and the princess, suspicion writ large on their faces. Their uncertainty appeared to ease once they noticed the eagle emblem on Cinder's lapel, his status as a member of the Directorate.

Cinder drifted closer to where Anya sat. She closed her book, turning it face side down so he couldn't see the title, still smiling at him.

"I heard you returned to the academy a few days ago," Cinder said.

She nodded. "I'm sorry I couldn't find time to meet you any earlier."

Cinder blinked in surprise. "You don't have to apologize to me."

"I suppose not, but it's the polite thing to do between friends."

Cinder didn't have a ready response, and he shifted the topic to the book Anya held in her hand. "What are you reading?" he asked, auto-matically reaching for it.

"Wait!" She darted her hands to intercept him, but he was too fast.

He held the novel and read the cover. "*Dawn's Light. A Forbidden Romance.*" His mouth twitched, and he kept from grinning by the bar-est of margins. She'd probably punch him if he did. "A romance?"

Anya seemed to collapse on herself, and her shoulders hunched. "Yes."

Cinder couldn't explain why he found the notion of Anya reading romances so amusing, but he did. He also knew Anya would not appre-ciate his laughter. "What's it about?" he asked, trying to sound curious.

"It's about a young human woman and an undying Mythaspuri. They live in the mountains of Yakshima Sithe. He's lived all this time since the *NusraelShev*, pretending to be a noble elf from the mountains where the weather is always cloudy."

"Why cloudy?"

"Sunlight makes him glitter."

Glitter? What kind of…

This time, Cinder couldn't hold it in. He barked laughter, quickly suppressing it when Anya glared at him.

She grabbed the book from him. "You idiot. It's not funny."

Cinder still grinned. Who would have guessed the fearsome elven princess liked romances?

He noticed them then, the people staring at him in dawning indig-nation. He immediately schooled his features to stillness. It was time to leave before any further misgivings were raised. Cinder bowed low to the princess. "It was good seeing you again, Your Highness. I look forward to our next sparring match."

"Oh, I think you've sparred against me well enough today," Anya replied, her tone curt.

"I have no idea what you mean, Simply Anya," Cinder said, for some reason teasing her one final time.

Anya rolled her eyes. "There it is. I was wondering if you could go the entire conversation without slipping in the only joke you know."

Cinder stared at Anya aghast. *The only joke I know?* First the Seconds and now Anya. Why did everyone suddenly seem to think his witticisms were boring?

She chuckled. "Now, I'm the one who's teasing."

Cinder wasn't sure she was, and he viewed her askance. "If you say so." He bowed again to her. "I'll see you at the academy."

"Of course. And Cinder," she called as he was about to leave. "If you ever tell anyone of my reading proclivities, I promise you won't enjoy our next sparring match."

Cinder grimaced. "Yes, Your Highness."

For the benefit of the other patrons, Anya continued to glare at Cinder even while he departed. She had made a mistake with him just now. It wasn't necessarily calling him over, but rather her behavior afterward. The way she'd smiled at him, welcomed him, and spoke to him with such clear fondness. Her reaction had skirted the bounds of elven propriety.

Worse, several of the customers and staff at the outdoor café had noticed, and Anya had been blissfully unaware of their interest until too late, until after the damage might have already been done. She had laughed at Cinder's words, and only in that white-hot moment of self-realization had she perceived the stares of the hard-faced strangers seated around her. She hadn't missed their expressions. Nor those of several passersby on this quiet street in Certitude.

Anya had done her best to salvage the situation. While she wouldn't pay much of a price for smiling and laughing with Cinder, he would. It was the reason for her frosty expression when he'd left. She only hoped her pose of annoyance would soothe the wagging tongues of those seated here. Hoped they wouldn't speak about Cinder's conversation with her or spread rumors about them and cause him grief.

Cinder's future was too important to risk on frivolity. She had to be careful with him. No harm had come about from her questionable actions thus far, and she had to keep it that way. Cinder deserved better, and she vowed to treat him in a completely professional manner from now on.

She frowned.

If only Cinder didn't make it so hard to hold onto rational thought. Around him, she was able to relax in ways she rarely could with anyone else. She found it safe to lower her defenses and the walls around her emotions. Cinder made her laugh and forced her not to take herself so seriously, and she liked their playful repartees.

An alarming realization swept over her, and Anya's smile fled. Her eyes widened. Her heart pounded the rhythm of her shock and fear, and the center of her stomach hollowed.

For Cinder's sake, she had to do better, especially if she intended on sponsoring him for his Secondary Trial. No one could believe anything but the most decorous of relationships existed between the two of them. In fact, it might make sense to sponsor another Second for their upcoming Trial, someone in addition to Cinder. She briefly considered not choosing Cinder at all, but the notion of not seeing him for more months on end sat poorly with her.

She was denied further opportunity to contemplate her relationship with Cinder when she found herself cast in shadow. Someone stood next to her table, and she glanced upward.

Lisandre's smiling visage met her gaze. "Your Highness," he said. "Thank you for meeting me."

Anya leaned away from him, blinking in confusion. What was Lisandre doing here?

A second later, her mind started working again.

Oh, yes. Lisandre had asked to meet her here, and she could guess why. This was one of the most romantic streets in Certitude. It was a secluded space, one consisting of a wide footpath floored in flagstones and macadam and lawns of grass fronting the surrounding brick buildings. The structures stood three and four stories tall and cupped the space, leaving it often cast in shade. A fountain gurgled within the center of a small roundabout, and along the pathway's length, through its center, ran a row of dwarf oaks. From their limbs, bare this time of year, were hung small *diphtha*-lanterns.

Anya knew how lovely this quiet neighborhood could be at night, especially in the spring when the lavender and rose bushes bloomed and the moons shone down, golden and ivory and haunting. Or when the *diptha* lanterns set amidst the trees beamed soft illumination and music played from within the café.

She only wished she had someone she truly loved to share in the neighborhood's beauty. Always before when she had come here, she had felt like an intruder, someone unable to partake in the romanticism of the place.

Which brought her to Lisandre. He wanted to court her. It was possibly one of the worst kept secrets in all of Yaksha, and she had promised her mother she would seek it as well. And why not sooner rather than later?

She had no reason not to, no true ones. Her husband was dead. Rukh was gone, and she had to accept his passing. No matter how much she longed for him, he would never return to her side.

Plus, formally attaching herself to Lisandre might help Cinder since the gossips who might have whispered deceit about him would have a lush, new topic to discuss. Rather than an arrogant human seeking that which was forbidden, they could focus their attention on her burgeoning relationship with Lisandre.

Just as important, maybe a romance would provide her a much-needed distraction from her fears about the changing world in the Dagger Mountains. Something she sorely needed. She still recalled the grating promise from the dying necrosed, and whenever she did, a tingle of fear trickled down her spine.

Anya set aside all grim tidings and graced Lisandre with a brilliant smile. He looked taken aback, and she almost chuckled. "What did you want to talk about?"

He gathered himself with admirable aplomb and offered her a smile in return, one charged with veiled hope. "Do I really have to play this game, or will you give me a definitive answer?"

Anya smiled wider. Yes. Spending time with Lisandre might be exactly what she needed. "You need not play any games. And my definitive answer is yes."

20

The next day, there was no sunlight to brighten the room where the Seconds sat for their class on Tactics and Strategy. It was mid-Karnasth, the transition between fall and winter, and the skies outside were shrouded in a curtain of thick, gray clouds. A misty rain fell, and the day veered toward the dismal and depressing appearance.

But the weather had no effect on Cinder.

He was happy. He smiled more readily and laughed more easily, particularly following yesterday's quick trip into Certitude. Any lingering nuggets of melancholy from the Autumn Trial had melted under the contentment and burgeoning camaraderie of the Seconds. As time passed, friendships were deepening between the members of the different races. Sriovey teasing Mohal and being teased in return. Bones and Ishmay studying alongside Cariath. Even playing music with Riyne. All of it brought him joy for reasons he couldn't rightly name.

And maybe some of his gladness was also from seeing Anya again.

He remembered how she'd appeared when he'd seen her at the outdoor café, and he smiled wistfully at the recollection. She wasn't for him, but it didn't mean he couldn't appreciate her beauty, honor who she was as a person, or admire her wisdom. Her cool attitude at the end of their brief conversation had been an intentional, yet kind, reminder of the vast gulf in their stations, and he had needed it.

He had chosen a martial life, and if he wished to achieve his goal—defending the righteous and protecting those who required it—he had to re-dedicate himself to learning and mastering everything the Third Directorate could teach him.

Such as the current lecture from Master Nuhlin—disheveled as usual—who was reviewing a famous battle from the life of Mede's father, Fileep of Parn. "Two thousand years ago, in the year 1012 Sapro Yan, Mede's father, Fileep, had conquered all the fractious principalities that currently make up the nation of Parn. However, many parts of his kingdom didn't appreciate being conquered, particularly the city of Brone. That city along with its allied principalities of Bha Fong and Bha Singsay raised an army of twenty-five thousand. Against those, Fileep had only fourteen thousand. Can anyone explain why the outcome was a foregone conclusion when the two armies met?" Master Nuhlin glanced around the room, a sly smile on his face, like he knew a secret no one else did.

Estin sighed dramatically. "Why do we always have to learn about human wars? Wouldn't it make more sense to study battles fought by elves?"

Cinder sighed just as dramatically. As sure as a rooster at dawn stealing a person's sleep, the one person who could steal away his joy was Estin. So damn stupid and opinionated. The prince regularly demonstrated how false the old adage was about how there was no such thing as a stupid question. He proved it was wrong every time he opened his mouth. Plus, despite the hardships they'd endured, the terrible carnage they'd survived, they were not yet brothers in battle, and Cinder doubted they ever would be, which was fine. It just made it so he would feel no guilt when he mocked the prince.

"What can we learn from battles fought by elves?" Cinder asked Estin. "What not to do?"

Estin bristled, and Cinder rolled his eyes. The prince always bristled. But this time, Cinder didn't let Estin express his idiocy. He wasn't in the mood to listen to his nonsense. "We all just survived a near-catastrophe. The Autumn Trial. Colonel Shaloce's decision to straight-ahead attack a defended position. If it hadn't been for Lieutenant Garelt's alteration of that stupid plan, we'd all be dead."

"He's right," Cariath said.

"Colonel Shaloce is one elf" Estin began. "I've already written my mother about him. He's—"

"Too often typical for our kind," Master Nuhlin said. "Cinder is correct. All we can learn from elven battles is what *not* to do. For whatever reason, we usually lack the necessary guile, planning, and cunning once battle is joined. The typical elven response to a battle is to tackle the problem head-on. Don't ask me why, but it is a limitation of our kind, just like humans are limited in being unable to access their *lorethasra*."

"What about the dwarves?" Jozep asked. "Are our commanders as incompetent?"

Master Nuhlin nodded. "In general. Mistakes are also about the entirety of what your people can teach us." He tilted his head as if in consideration. "Mistakes do offer their own set of lessons, and perhaps in some later classes, we'll cover them." He rapped his lectern. "Back to my original question. Why was the battle between the forces of Brone's and Fileep's a foregone conclusion?"

Cinder knew the answer, but he kept his mouth shut. It shouldn't be his place to supply all the solutions. The other Seconds needed to be able to think through these questions and learn the heart of the lessons. It couldn't always fall on his shoulders to explain it to them. At one time, it hadn't, but the others who understood battle like he did—Rorian and Joria—were dead.

He pursed his mouth when silence persisted in the room. Either no one knew the answer, or no one was willing to venture a guess. Maybe a small clue would stir their thinking. "Because Fileep's soldiers were never outnumbered," Cinder said.

"His forces were outnumbered fourteen thousand to twenty-five thousand," Estin sneered. "Try to pay attention."

"Pay attention yourself, dumbass," Bones muttered.

"What did you say?" Estin demanded.

"I said, pay attention yourself, dumbass," Bones replied, his voice louder. "Cinder didn't say Fileep's *forces* were never outnumbered. He said his *soldiers* were never outnumbered." He seemed to gain confidence as he continued speaking. "Brone's army likely consisted of untrained conscripts; angry peasants, merchants, and farmers fighting for their home. The romantics like to talk about how an inspired will can overcome any odds, but they're wrong. Dead wrong. Desire alone won't win against a professional military. Not like Fileep's army. Brone's army probably only had five thousand true soldiers. So, yes, while Fileep was nominally outnumbered, the quality of his personnel was vastly superior to that of Brone's."

Cinder dipped his head in approval at Bones. He was glad someone had caught his hint.

Master Nuhlin was nodding excitedly. "Exactly. Fileep *was* outnumbered, but he knew his men were professional soldiers, and they faced men who had never before held a spear, shield, or sword; men who didn't know how to ride a horse as part of a cavalry. A few members of Brone's army had experience with the bow as hunters, but none were the equal of Fileep's companies of dedicated archers. His *soldiers* vastly outnumbered those of Brone, whose one advantage was that they held the high ground. Fileep could have attacked them in a direct assault, and he likely would have won. We elves would have appreciated that. Fileep, though, was too cagy. He didn't charge." Master Nuhlin grinned, leaning forward as if anticipating the revelation of a great secret. "Instead, he retreated."

Cinder could guess what was coming next. If he had been in Fileep's position, he would have somehow encouraged the Bronian army to come to him, to fight on a place of his choosing.

Master Nuhlin continued. "Fileep initially launched a lazy attack, but his orders were for his men to immediately disengage and withdraw.

He tricked the opposing army of farmers and merchants into believing his army consisted of cowards. The Bronians should have known better, but they couldn't help themselves. They chased Fileep's forces onto the Plains of Aether, where his waiting cavalry destroyed half the Bronian army in a series of brutal charges. In the end, Fileep lost less than three hundred soldiers while the Bronian's were utterly crushed. Only two thousand of them may have survived the battle."

The carnage must have been terrible, and Cinder shuddered involuntarily. Killing spiderkin and zahhacks was one thing, but killing a person? He grimaced in disgust. The notion of people warring against one another didn't sit well with him. It never had, and he hoped it never would.

Master Nuhlin glanced around the room. "What lesson can we take from this?"

Cinder, disturbed still by the awful imagery of people hacking down one another, recollected a funny quote he once heard. It brought a smile to his face, and given the somber expressions of everyone else in the room, perhaps they needed to hear it too. "Never get involved in a land war in Parn?" Cinder said.

Everyone chuckled, including Master Nuhlin. "Close enough," he said.

Weeks passed, and the days settled. On one evening, the Seconds, having finished all their classes for the day, were seated at the cafeteria, all of them sharing a single, long table. Large wagon-wheel-shaped chandeliers ringed with *diptha* bulbs hung from the broad beams holding up the ceiling, and the generous glow from the lights illuminated the room. The delicious aroma of tonight's supper—chicken masala, spiced potatoes, and curried carrots—suffused the air.

Sharing the mess hall with the Seconds were others, such as Masters Absin and Jovick. They were seated alongside several of their aides and a trio of elves staying at the Directorate for specialized training. Their voices were generally muted, although knowing chuckles occasionally rolled out from their table.

Anya was also having her supper at the same time as the Seconds. She sat at a private corner table, alone with Lisandre. Her lustrous hair was arranged in a simple weave, and the tips of her peaked ears were barely visible beyond the bounds of her braid. Her gaze never broke from Lisandre's visage, and her lively, emerald eyes seemed to sparkle as she smiled at something he said.

Cinder had heard she and Lisandre were seeing one another, which apparently everyone had expected them to do a long time ago. While he eyed them, he refused to admit or acknowledge the empty feeling in the pit of his stomach at seeing Anya in the company of another man. She wasn't for him, and he had no business staring at her. Besides, it was a good thing that she had found happiness with Lisandre.

He forced himself to believe his musings and turn away from the happy couple, concentrating instead on the people at his table. *The Seconds.* All of them seated together, the humans, dwarves, and elves intermixed. It was a good thing to see, and Cinder smiled, watching as they swapped stories, told jokes, and stole one another's food. Bones casually reached over to Riyne's plate and swiped a spoonful of potatoes. The elf merely grunted and reached across the table to Sriovey's plate and took most of his potatoes in exchange.

"Dammit! Stop stealing my food," Sriovey exclaimed, glaring at the table in general.

While he was distracted, Cinder, seated next to the dwarf, smoothly and without the slightest hint of shame, snagged a slice of naan from Sriovey.

"Damn it! I said stop stealing my fucking food. Not steal more of it."

Cinder wagged the naan at Sriovey. "Then you should have paid better attention. You know the rule: if you don't watch your food, your friends"—he gestured to the table at large, glad beyond measure to be able to indicate nearly all the Seconds—"will steal it."

"Well, it's still an asshole thing to do," Sriovey protested. While he continued to glare at Cinder, Depth, seated on the other side of the dwarf, took a large spoonful of carrots, and Riyne took most of his chicken.

Sriovey turned about just in time to see the thievery. "You dickheads!" He stood. "Now I have to get another plate."

Derius tossed Sriovey a piece of naan. "Here. You can have my bread."

Sriovey tossed it back. "I'll get my own." He stomped off to get another plate of food, and while he was gone, the last of his chicken was consumed, his few remaining carrots eaten, and Cinder stole his brownie. Anything made with chocolate was just fine by him.

"Split it?" Bones asked.

Cinder shrugged and gave him half the dessert.

Sriovey eventually returned, muttering still about asshole friends. He sat down, crouched like a gargoyle over his plate, one arm hovering protectively over it, and began shoveling the food into his mouth.

While he ate, Mohal and Cariath were entranced by Wark, who was relaying the story of his first encounter with Cinder. It had been in Swift Sword at the Lonely Donkey. The two elves glanced over at Cinder.

"Is this true?" Mohal asked, wide-eyed. "The first time you met Wark, you hit him in the head with a mug?"

"Hotgate, aren't you the one always going on about fraternity?" Riyne asked, a note of challenge in his voice.

"I am," Cinder confirmed, shifting about in embarrassment. Smacking Wark with a mug wasn't one of his prouder moments. "But in my defense, I was only trying to protect Wark. He was itching to start a fight with Bones."

Jozep chuckled, clapping Wark on the shoulder. "That wouldn't have gone well for you."

Wark grinned. "No, it wouldn't," he replied. "Looking back, I guess a hit on the head was a lot less than what Bones could have done to me."

Ishmay, who had been absent until now—he'd been held back after their last class of the day—arrived in a fume. He slammed his tray full of food on the table. "Fucking vampires," he cursed. He squeezed in next to Cinder. "I hate those fuckity fucking fuckwad fuckers."

Cinder glanced over at him in amusement. "Are you going for a record?"

"Oh, fuck off," Ishmay complained. "You know what I mean about vampires. They're more arrogant than the elves." He shot a glance at the elven Seconds. "No offense."

"What's got your undergarments all twisted?" Cariath asked from down the table.

"Lieutenant Capshin had me stay around after class. I got fussed *and* cussed."

"We know," Cinder said. "We were there."

"Yes, well, Lieutenant Capshin didn't like my last paper on vampires. He wants me to rewrite it. It's going to take all night, and I wanted to get in some extra training with Master Absin."

Cinder pursed his lips in commiseration. "Is there anything I can do to help?"

Ishmay shook his head, shoveling food into his mouth. "No offense, but you're…" He frowned as if searching for the right word.

"Pedantic?" Bones suggested.

"Self-righteous?" Sriovey added.

"Pretentious?" Mohal offered.

Cinder did a double take. *What the hell?* He stared about in shock, unable to figure who to address. Did the others really think of him in that way?

His discomfort caused the others to laugh.

"We're joking," Sriovey said to him.

"Speak for yourself," Bones countered, grinning at Cinder.

"It's none of that," Ishmay said before Cinder could reply. "It's because you're long-winded. You always take twenty words to say three. I want a quick, dirty paper, not some chapter length dissertation."

Cinder leaned away from the table, staring at Ishmay as if in shock. "Does anyone know what happened to Ishmay? I swear he just used a word with four syllables."

"See," Ishmay said, holding his fork like it was a baton. "Syllables. A big word."

"You're the one who used dissertation," Cinder reminded him.

Derius, seated across the table, interrupted their conversation. "I can help you with the paper," he offered. "What do you need to know?"

"Everything," Ishmay said, sounding desperate.

Derius shrugged. "Let's start with the basics. All vampires are pretty similar in appearance. They're pale monsters, usually slim and have gray eyes and long, dark hair. Some of them go for brash clothing— bright colors, like reds, blues, and yellows—and it's always perfectly tailored to their bodies. Their biggest advantage is the power of flight, but thankfully they're slow in the air."

"I read something about their screams scaring a person to death," Ishmay said.

Derius laughed, and Cinder shared his humor. Scaring a person to death with a scream? How silly. However, he clamped down on his amusement. He didn't want to embarrass Ishmay.

Bones had no such compunction. "You dumbass. Where did you read that?"

Ishmay hunched his shoulders. He tended to be sensitive about his lack of acumen in their more scholarly classes.

Cinder took pity on him. "They freeze their prey with their screams," he said. "Then they attack. Usually no weapons. They prefer using their teeth and claws. They're supposed to be able to unhinge their jaws like a snake and have a shark's mouth full of teeth."

"What can kill them?" Ishmay asked. "I heard it takes fire or some special type of sword."

"A special metal. Not a special sword," Estin surprisingly supplied. "That or lightning or something really hot."

Cinder wouldn't have thought the prince was listening or cared enough to help if he had been.

"The metal, though, is *aether*-infused steel," Sriovey said, taking up the explanation. "*Isthrim*. My people forge it, but it's not easy to work."

"*Isthrim* destroys vampires," Derius said. "Tears them apart." He gestured to Cinder. "Your sword has *isthrim*. Your master gifted you a finer blade than you know."

Cinder's eyes widened in surprise. He had no idea Master Lerid had given him an *isthrim*-steel sword.

"If they're so hard to kill, what keeps them from taking over the world?" Ishmay asked.

"Because they're weak and lazy," Riyne said.

"Plus, the rangers," Estin said, jutting his jaw, his tone both proud and firm. "Those like my sister and Lisandre."

Cinder glanced again to where Anya and Lisandre were having their supper. Anya's smile had left her, and she was shaking her head. She caught his glance, and her jaw firmed. She returned her attention to Lisandre, shook her head one last time, and left him alone at the table, gaping in shock.

"Looks like a lover's quarrel," Bones murmured.

Cinder agreed, and he hated how happy it made him.

21

Duchess Cervine had a communiqué in hand and mulled what to do about it. It pertained to the Seconds, who had returned to the Third Directorate over a month ago from their Autumn Trial. She had been having lunch with Karthalyn at an outdoor café when their blacked-out carriages had rumbled through Certitude. But even prior to their return, rumors had reached her about the difficult Autumn Trial the Seconds had survived. Apparently, they were lucky to be alive, and given all the privations they'd endured, many were starting to believe them a cursed class.

She tapped the missive against the arm of her chair, lost in thought as she sat in her study. It was a sumptuous room on the highest floor of the main building, several doors down from her personal quarters. At her back, a pair of windowed doors opened onto a broad balcony overlooking her private gardens. Late-afternoon sunlight beamed inside, while on the other side of the study, a fire crackled in the hearth.

The flames brought cheery warmth to the space, and centered before the fireplace were a pair of armchairs, facing one another across a large coffee table while a comfortable, cream-colored leather sofa completed the seating arrangement. Floor-to-ceiling bookshelves marched along the study's perimeter and were burdened by a plethora of scrolls and texts, neatly organized by topic. The shelves also held mementos from the Duchess's journeys: graceful carvings, small paintings, and jewel-crusted daggers.

But her most prized possession was a simple stone, perfectly round and shining with an inner luster. It had been given to one of the Duchess's ancestors, generations ago, by a traveling yakshin, one who had also been a quelchon.

However, it wasn't a stone. It was a rare seed, the Mananut of an Ashoka tree. The yakshin had apparently claimed the nut would eventually find a gardener, someone to restore a lost forest and a lost realm. The yakshin's only cryptic hint had been this person would wield the Crystal Lightning.

No one in the duchess's lineage had managed to decipher who or what that might mean, but the seed had remained a treasured possession passed down from one generation to the next.

But thoughts of the seed weren't pertinent. Instead, it was the letter the duchess held in her hands. It was from the First Directorate, the shadowy group of spies run through the office of the Empress. Or at least that's what the First Directorate wanted the world at large to think, especially the nobles of Yaksha Sithe.

The Duchess knew the truth. Ever since the First Directorate's founding during the reign of Koran Yaksha, the quelchons had commanded it, and they answered to no one but their leader. Currently, the titular head the First Directorate was Shamira Quill, but the true commander was Ginala Suranom, who was supposedly the only living elven quelchon.

Or so the world believed, especially the nobles of Yaksha Sithe. But once again, the duchess knew the truth. In fact, there were *two* quelchons. There always had been, throughout the entirety of Yaksha's history, an unbroken chain, always women and an elder who trained an heir. A secret history unknown to even the empress.

And Ginala, through her mouthpiece, Shamira, had sent a

communiqué. The old bat wanted to learn more about Cinder Shade while pretending concern for all the Seconds. The missive raised a whole host of questions. What was there about Cinder Shade that so many important folk were focused upon him? Could he truly be so relevant?

She had seen Cinder a few weeks ago. He had been in Certitude for some reason, and the one thing that had struck her was the grace with which he moved. He walked like a stalking leopard. However, beyond that, his height, and warrior build, he seemed rather unremarkable. True, he was handsome. The duchess could appreciate that about him.

She stood then, hands clasped behind her back as she paced her study, reconsidering her prior assumptions about the young man. Thick rugs softened the stone floor and muffled her footsteps while she walked the room, organizing what she knew about Cinder Shade.

Fact one. The empress knew of the cadet, which was unsurprising. After all, the boy *had* won the Grand Melee, which should have been impossible given his human lineage.

Fact two. Anya Aruyen was said to spend time with the boy. Nothing untoward, but they often trained together, and he offered the princess a challenge during their sparring, something few elves could claim. And it was Anya who had found Cinder, mortally wounded by a spiderkin during the Unitary Trial. She had followed a clear trail of conflict leading away from the battle's site, but why had she chosen that particular trail? Was there something else to her decision, and if so, what might it be?

Fact three, the dwarves were concerned about Cinder. They feared he was the *Fated Foe* and were so worried that they had sent Shadion Carrend, a spy, to the boy's home village of Swallow. He'd spent a few weeks there, and whatever he'd discovered had apparently set his crèche to rumbling. Certainly, based on the frequency of the dual missives sent to Derius—the duchess knew all about their coded letters— his father was very worried about Cinder Shade. And his father was an important figure in crèche politics. He was the strong arm of the wisdoms, the matriarchal holders of dwarven history.

And fact four, Quelchon Ginala herself was demonstrating an interest in Cinder Shade. That last was the most worrisome, and once again, the duchess pondered why. What was the old bat thinking?

The duchess halted her pacing, and her lips pursed. Seminal spun, forever changing. Nothing ever stayed the same. But there were some winds that began from nowhere, and when they gusted, they heralded a far greater alteration. They were heralds of chaos, casting down all prior orders and unions. The last such gale had blown three thousand years ago when Shet had arrived on Seminal.

What was coming now?

And how did Cinder Shade figure into it?

The duchess didn't have enough information, but it was time to learn it. She rang a bell, and the sentry standing outside her study entered the room.

She recognized him, Prash Holivine, although he was new to her service. He was young, his face unlined, and his eyes retaining a certain innocence. However, despite his lack of seasoning, the guard had already proven his competence, possessing a keen wit and subtle sense of humor. The duchess had her eye on him. If he proved trustworthy enough, she might even induct him into the *Lamarin Hosh.*

"You know Lisandre Coushinre?" she asked.

Prash nodded. "I know of him, my lady." He quirked a smile. "It's hard not to have heard of the one everyone says will earn the title of *Sai* faster than any elf in history."

The duchess smiled with him. Lisandre was said to be a superlative warrior, but she also suspected his reign as the youngest warrior titled *Sai* would be shattered by Anya. "Send him a message. I'd like to meet him for afternoon tea tomorrow."

"Should I explain the nature of the meeting?"

"A business proposition."

"I'll see to it." Prash ducked out of the room.

The duchess crossed her arms. There were others she needed to speak to. Master Absin for one. She'd invite him to dinner. A few days from now. The swordmaster was also said to be close to Cinder Shade.

Same with the Directorate's head librarian, Master Molni.

And with the upcoming banquet in a few months, it would be the perfect time to personally speak to the boy and gain his measure. Her aunt could talk to him, too. She would enjoy the challenge. The duchess had never known someone so skilled at ferreting out an individual's secrets as her aunt. Not even Karthalyn could compare.

Absin sat alone in the Cauldron. His breath plumed in the cold air, visible in the ghostly light of *diptha* lamps, and he gazed about, clutching his shoke. It was night. The sun had set a half-hour ago, and the evening was quiet, except for the pleasant harmonies of a pair of songbirds wintering at the Directorate. The comforting smell of smoke from fires in hearths drifted like a recollection of better days.

He wondered if anyone would show up tonight. He doubted it. The usual warriors weren't in attendance. The senior elves who were usually at the Directorate for specialized training had matriculated out of the school a few weeks ago, and their replacements were days away from arrival. Meanwhile, the Firsters were involved in their first wilderness drill, and Cinder had indicated he had some reading to do.

It was why Absin was out here by himself. With no one to bother him, this was a good place to think. His musings circled back to Cinder.

The young human.

Day by day, the boy was recovering his speed and strength, just as he seemed to have recovered his good humor. He'd been despondent after returning from the Autumn Trial, and while he'd never spoken to Absin about the carnage he'd witnessed, he didn't have to.

Absin understood. He certainly still remembered all his battles. Those terrible screams of mortal pain, good friends dying, the smell of blood. The dead scattered like broken dolls on a blood-soaked ground. There were some nightmares that still lingered in the back of his mind, waking him at times in the middle of the night, drenched in sweat and trembling in terror.

Thankfully, those episodes had grown rarer over the decades, but now he had a new fear: worry for the young men of the Seconds. They'd witnessed so much tragedy and heartbreak, so much death and desolation, at an age no one should have to experience. First, the catastrophe of the Unitary Trial and then the Autumn Trial.

Now a new surprise: the duchess had invited him to dinner, and during the meal, she had suggested the Seconds were a cursed class. They had suffered through more deaths and hardships than any group of cadets in the long history of the Third Directorate. *Cursed.*

Absin felt the opposite. He thought the Seconds were blessed. After all, they had Cinder Shade. The young cadet was proving a savior of sorts. In fact, if not for his leadership, all the Seconds—along with the entirety of Jameken Battalion—might have died during their Autumn Trial.

Other classes would have, but this year's Seconds were a tight-knit bunch. Absin had seen them at dinner several nights ago, their camaraderie, and it all started and revolved around Cinder.

Blessed.

As if thinking about the boy had summoned him, here he strode toward the Cauldron. He was still at a distance, but his leopard-like grace was unmistakable, one any elf would envy. As Absin watched him approach, he wondered what to do with the young man. Many elves of stature had developed a keen interest in Cinder. This now included Duchess Cervine, which apparently had been the reason for tonight's dinner meeting. It was one Absin couldn't turn down. As a member of the *Lamarin Hosh*, he owed the duchess greater allegiance than anyone save Empress Sala.

The duchess had explained to him that the dwarves were worried that Cinder might be the fulfillment of a prophecy proclaimed in their holy book, the *Crèche Prani*. A deadly entity called the Fated Foe, the *Elonic Ciprion*. And reading between the lines, the dwarves were also trying to figure out if they should kill Cinder. They were considering whether to assassinate him so he could never rise to his full power as this Fated Foe.

The duchess obviously wanted him to know about the dwarves, but he doubted she expected him to notice a small detail she'd let slip at the end of their conversation.

Apparently, Quelchon Ginala had also taken note of Cinder, which was both interesting and dangerous. Absin didn't know the quelchon very well, by reputation mostly. In fact, he'd only met her once, and the meeting had left him shaken. It was her eyes, vibrant and powerful and constantly shifting colors. Her eyes seemed able to peer into his mind and sift through the deepest recesses of his thoughts to elucidate his darkest secrets. It was said Quelchon Ginala could read a person's soul, and Absin didn't doubt it.

So why did she also have an apparent interest in Cinder Shade?

He continued to ponder the matter, and at the same time, he also contemplated his own relationship with the boy. He liked Cinder, and in the past few years, he had likely spent more time with him than any other cadet at the Directorate, possibly anyone period. It was all the work he'd put in with the boy, his training, his teaching, his instruction, which was the largest part of his improvement as a warrior. In many ways, he had grown to consider Cinder a son of sorts.

He inhaled sharply at the realization, struggling to control his emotions and expression before Cinder reached him.

The boy had a shoke in hand and grinned at him. "Ready to spar?"

Absin held in an exasperated sigh. He should have known. Cinder must have finished his reading early, and like clockwork, here he was, ready to practice again.

"We don't have to if you're too tired," Cinder said with an irrepressible grin. "Or if you're feeling your age."

This time Absin let out the exasperated sigh. The boy could be as charming as a puppy when he wanted something, and he laughed at the comparison.

"What's so funny?" Cinder asked.

"Nothing," Absin said, still chuckling at the notion of Cinder as a puppy. The boy was a dangerous warrior, nothing at all like a cute, cuddly puppy. "Are you sure you're not too tired to spar? It's late. You've worked hard today."

Cinder shrugged. "I want to test myself tonight."

There was a note of excitement in his voice, and Absin scrutinized him, wondering what had him so happy. "What's changed?" he eventually asked.

"Since my *Jivatma* is recovering, I want to see if I can conduct it. The few times I've seen it, I've noticed the lightning isn't as prominent, which means it won't hurt as much to reach through it."

Absin forced a smile, hoping to hide his troubles. *Jivatma.* He'd studied the concept after Cinder had made his fantastical claim, and everything he'd read correlated with what the boy had told him. *Jivatma* was the soul, or at least the Mythaspuris believed it to be the case. In all of Seminal's history, they were the only ones who could source it, although their supposed descendants, the rishis of Bharat, also made the assertion.

Absin doubted it. The rishis were liars and braggarts. Powerful, true, but deceitful. He trusted nothing they said about anything.

However, there was one other race who was also said to have the ability to source *Jivatma.* The wraiths. It was a troubling idea. What did it mean for Cinder if he could source the same substance as some of the most dangerous, evil creatures on Seminal?

Absin realized he'd been too long in responding to Cinder's statement.

"You're troubled," Cinder said, eyeing him in concern.

Absin decided to tell the boy what had him worried. He spoke about the wraiths.

Cinder's expression grew grim. "I've read the same, but I don't think I'll end up like one of them. Emotional pain is supposed to be the stimulus for their creation. I'm not in emotional pain."

The explanation was the same as what Master Absin had learned, but it didn't settle his mind. He still worried for Cinder. Worried for all of them if worse came to worst. He only hoped none of it would come to pass. "Why don't you show me what you can do."

22

A month after being fitted for his new garments, it was time for Cinder to pick them up. He made the short walk to Certitude by himself, late in the afternoon on a rest day. The other Seconds had long since departed for the city or had other work to do while Cinder had spent the morning training with Master Absin and reading anything else he could find about *Jivatma*.

Only the Mythaspuris could teach him what he hoped to learn, but they had left behind precious little information on the topic. As a result, on most days, the research on *Jivatma* had Cinder feeling like a man blindfolded, trying to scry the shape of a room through uncertain steps and outstretched hands. It made for frustratingly slow progress, and he often didn't know if he was actually moving forward or ignorantly circling the same details over and over again.

His attention snapped back to the walk when an icy gust of wind blustered, causing him to shiver. Earlier, the weather had been overcast, but the clouds had given way to sunshine as the day progressed. However, the biting breeze left no room for warmth. The drafts rattled the winter-bare branches of the trees, sending cold fingers questing across the long grass and knifing through his clothes. The breeze gained sudden strength, pushing against him, and he leaned forward against its resistance, tugging his coat closer about him and stuffing his hands into his pockets.

Cinder glanced at the surrounding trees of Pantheon Forest and didn't spy any young buds on their branches. It didn't surprise him. Spring was months away, but he still found himself disappointed. He preferred summer's warmth to winter's chill.

Then again, the changing of the seasons would bring its own set of problems. Spring would herald the beginning of the Secondary Trial, and Cinder had far less surety of what it meant for him.

Originally, he thought Anya would sponsor him, but since her return to the Directorate, he had rarely spoken to her. There had been the one conversation at the café a month ago when he'd gone for his clothes fitting, and a few other pleasantries shared in passing at the academy, but otherwise, their interactions had been minimal. Never enough to have a proper discussion or even spar.

He didn't know if Anya still intended on sponsoring him for his Secondary Trial, and he also didn't know how to ask her. She was clearly busy, either training some of the older elves or spending time with Lisandre. These days those two were together more often than not, and he didn't want to intrude on their privacy.

He only hoped Anya *would* let him know if she couldn't sponsor him for his Secondary Trial. It wouldn't surprise him if it were the case. When they had spoken at the café an awareness had stolen across Anya's features, a sense of guilt. Maybe she had come to recognize the danger she risked to her reputation by spending time with him, much less choosing him for the Secondary Trial. It would be the two of them alone in the wilderness, and many ugly rumors would likely spark over what that might mean.

If that is what she was thinking, then Cinder understood. Anya needed to protect herself, and if she couldn't carry through with her offer, it was fine. He had already made arrangements to join the Rakesh High Army as a scout in one of their frontier units.

In due course, his thoughts eventually drifted away from Anya. He had no influence on what she made of her future, and unfortunately, the same held true about Fastness. Cinder still rode the Yavana stallion, and it was an absolute pleasure and joy, especially since the white continued to surprise him. Still playful and teasing, over the past month, the horse had taken to his training with a steely determination. In fact, despite Cinder's own relative lack of skill as a horseman, as a *team*, they could now cover any course or obstacle far more swiftly than any of the other riders and mounts.

Fastness was a treasure and too important to permanently hand over to a human. But still, fantasies were fun.

The gust he'd been pressing against finally fell off, and Cinder relaxed his hunched posture. He stared about, happily realizing that his deliberations on Anya and Fastness had provided him a side benefit. It had distracted his mind, and he'd already covered most of the distance to Certitude with only a few final farms to pass.

Minutes later, Cinder was amidst the city proper, heading for *Elegant Weaves*, Master Brance's tailor shop. He had spent much of his remaining money on his new clothes, and he already wondered how he would be able to afford the garments for next year. He might have to beg funds from his friends, and the idea made him nauseous.

He had his pride, after all.

Setting aside his concerns as a worry for another day, he took a short-cut toward Master Brance's shop, and it drew him into a private neighborhood where dwarf oaks bifurcated a narrow footpath paved in flagstones. *Diptha* lanterns hung from the bare branches of the trees. It would likely be a romantic place in the evening, but for Cinder, the best part was that the surrounding buildings cut off the wind. Add in the westering sun beaming along the length of the footpath, and the area here was much warmer than the trek along Whileaway Path.

There were other pedestrians about, and Cinder stepped aside for them. They viewed him with a mix of confusion followed by recognition. He was sure they didn't see many humans in their part of Certitude, but given Cinder's status as the winner of the Grand Melee, they probably knew who he was.

Up ahead—centered in a small roundabout—was a statue of an elven woman gently pouring water upon copper roses and peonies. His destination wasn't too far from there.

"Cinder," a man's voice called to him.

Cinder glanced about, and it didn't take him long to locate the person trying to get his attention.

Lisandre.

He sat opposite Anya, at the same café where Cinder had last spoken to the princess. They wore thick coats, and Anya's golden hair shimmered in the sunshine. Her emerald eyes were cool and assessing as he approached their table.

"I'm surprised you're not back at the school training with Master Absin," Lisandre said with an easy grin. "My brother says you do nothing but train."

Cinder liked Riyne's older brother, who had always been friendly and fair with him. He smiled in reply. "Some of us aren't gifted with sublime talents. Some of us have to work for what we have."

Anya arched an eyebrow. "And you don't think elves work hard?" The question had a teasing element, and she smiled, taking the sting out of it.

Cinder chuckled. "I'm sure your people work hard, but the only way I can match you is to…" He paused, searching for the right words.

"Work harder?" Lisandre supplied.

Cinder smiled. "I suppose so."

"So where are you headed?" Lisandre asked.

"I'm collecting my clothes for the Duchess's Banquet."

Lisandre laughed. "You say it like you're approaching a funeral."

Cinder shrugged, not wanting to share the truth about his financial situation with them, especially Anya. "I've never been comfortable in fine clothes. It makes me…" Again, he ran out of the right words.

"Uncomfortable?" Anya filled in, smiling at him.

"Have you decided what you'll do for your Secondary Trial?" Lisandre asked.

Cinder briefly glanced at Anya, who lifted a brow in either challenge or question. He couldn't tell, and it seemed like her offer should remain a secret between the two of them. "I'll likely join the High Army of Rakesh as a scout."

"A pity," Anya said. "If you really could match our people, you'd make a fine ranger. Or maybe you already can match our people. When is the Unchained Trial?"

"Five weeks." It was the final assessment of standing for the second-year cadets, similar to the Grand Melee, except the Unchained Trial was a single elimination weapons sparring event. And with the slow but deliberate recovery of his *Jivatma*, he liked his chances to win the tournament.

"Five weeks," Anya mused. "And the woven will be allowed to use all their skills, including their *lorethasra*. Do you think you can win?"

Lisandre's mouth thinned, and his gaze went to Anya, a disappointed expression on his face. "Dreams of the impossible have never helped a warrior. You know this."

Anya viewed Lisandre in return, not dropping her eyes or evincing any sense of regret. "Cinder has the requisite skills with sword, bow, and horse to become an elven ranger."

"But he lacks *lorethasra*. Without it, he would be a hindrance to himself and others in the field."

"He has some kind of ability," Anya replied. "You've seen it. He doesn't rightly know, and neither does anyone else, but it's undeniable. You've seen how he moves."

Cinder watched their interaction in confused irritation. They talked about him as if he wasn't standing directly in front of them.

"How he *used* to move," Lisandre was saying. "He isn't as fast as he once was. We've all noticed."

Lisandre was wrong. In the past several months, Cinder had regained most of what he had lost. However, since he and Lisandre rarely sparred, the elf just didn't know it yet.

Anya's attention was on him now, her head tilted to the side as if in question. A strange intensity filled her eyes. "Is this true?"

Cinder nodded. "I was injured during a wilderness drill. I'm still recovering." He smiled in certainty. "But I'm regaining what I lost."

The intensity left Anya's features, replaced by relief. "Then consider this a promise. If you win the Unchained Trial, I'll sponsor you."

Lisandre hissed in outrage and shock. "Anya? Don't offer the boy false hope. Without *lorethasra*, he can never hope to best one of us."

Cinder continued to stare at Anya, surprised she'd made her offer so publicly.

Her attention remained on him. "It's not false hope. I believe in Cinder."

"Then think of the scandal," Lisandre urged. "You and a human man alone in the wilderness for months on end."

Anya faced him again. "I won't be alone. You're sponsoring Estin. They can share their Secondary Trial."

Cinder wanted to groan. Months on end with Estin. The High Army was suddenly sounding like a much better choice. "I appreciate the offer," he said, addressing Anya. "But I doubt your brother would care to spend so much time with me." *And I sure as hell don't want to spend months with him.*

Anya smiled, dazzling and bright. "Which is the advantage of being an older sister. He won't have any choice."

After ensuring his new clothes fit and taking final possession of them—Cinder still winced at the cost—he had returned straightaway to the academy. He hadn't been in the mood to stop in for a drink at *Silent Reverie*, and it wasn't because Cinder didn't want to share fellowship with the Seconds. He had no doubt they were at the alehouse, even the elves, most of whom had started spending their free days with the humans and dwarves.

It was because Cinder didn't want any company tonight. He had more research to do. Always more work. Plus, his mood wasn't improved at the notion of sharing his Secondary Trial with Estin.

Enduring the hardships of the dangers of the Dagger Mountains was bad enough, but doing so while in the company of Estin?

Cinder shuddered.

At least Anya hadn't forgotten about her sponsorship, which was a relief. But was her instruction worth the cost of dealing with Estin?

Probably. Anya could teach him in ways no one else could, and they got along well. He liked her—and not just as a friend—even as he recognized that she was well beyond his station.

During the hike home, he decided to stop thinking about it, and once back to the academy, he hung up his new clothes and headed over to the library. In the evening, the library was generally quiet, and tonight was no different.

Cinder entered the library, and his troubles melted.

As always, the magical fragrance of old paper captured him in its weave, and he closed his eyes, breathing deep its enticement. The scent clung to the air, and by now the smell had likely seeped into the wood of the bookcases and the plaster of the walls. His mind soothed under the calming aroma, which hearkened to wisdom and patience.

Cinder opened his eyes and took in his surroundings. There were a few elves here tonight, students and librarians both. They sat at the various tables in the main area, stacks of books scattered about them. A few lifted their heads from whatever they were studying, acknowledging him before resuming their studies.

The library was otherwise unchanged from the norm.

Except for the presence of Anya. She stood next to Master Molni, chatting quietly with the old elf. The princess could occasionally be found at the library, but this was the first time Cinder had seen her here since she'd returned to the Directorate. She and Master Molni turned to the front entrance upon Cinder's arrival, and the old librarian smiled welcome at him, while Anya offered a cool tilt of her head.

"What brings you here tonight?" Master Molni asked when Cinder reached them.

"The same as always," Cinder said. "Information on my *Jivatma*."

Master Molni shot him a worried frown, glancing askance at Anya.

"I see."

"She knows what I can do," Cinder said, hoping to set the librarian's mind at ease.

"I was likely the first to learn," Anya added.

Master Molni's visage relaxed with relief. "Thank Devesh," he said with a chuckle. "For a moment, I thought you had taken leave of your senses."

"Have you read Manifold Fulsom's autobiography?" Anya asked.

"Which one?" Cinder asked. "There are at least three I've come across so far."

"The one titled *A Conspiracy to Live*?"

Cinder hadn't heard of it, and he said so.

Anya smiled at him, and Cinder felt like the room had lightened.

"Then allow me to show you the location," Anya said. "Come. Master Molni has work to do."

Master Molni appeared grateful. "I do have some work I'd like to finish before closing the library tonight."

Cinder caught Anya quirking a brow at him in challenge. "Or do you think such a task too simple for me?"

Cinder couldn't help but chuckle, and he gestured her to lead on. "After you."

She went to the stairs and began climbing with Cinder following. As he ascended the stairs, he glanced up toward Anya only for a single instant before quickly averting his gaze.

For once, the princess wasn't in her martial ranger's garb. Instead, she appeared relaxed and comfortable, wearing a pair of sandals laced around her ankles and a sleeveless, lemon-yellow dress. It ended at her knees, swirling about her legs, but with every step she took, her red-golden calves and lower thighs flashed into view. It wasn't a sight Cinder felt was his place to appreciate, but he did appreciate it nonetheless. Anya was a lovely woman, and her legs matched the rest of her.

He hummed, not realizing he was doing so until Anya paused, staring down at him.

"What song is that?" she asked, appearing both curious and

uncertain.

Cinder shrugged, unsure as to the cause of her reaction. He didn't know the song's name. "Just a tune from home, I guess."

"Am I right that this is the home you can't remember?"

"You heard about that?"

Anya nodded. "Someday I'd like to hear the story of how you lost your memories. I had a similar situation."

"I heard that, too," Cinder said. "Maybe we can share stories."

Anya's lips briefly tightened, an expression of what might have been pain flitting across her features. "Perhaps," she said, speaking as if the word had been chosen with great care. She ascended the stairs again.

Cinder watched her, still bewildered by her reaction and response. A moment later, he shook off his reveries. He was staring upward, to where he once again saw Anya's red-golden calves and thighs flashed into view.

An instant later, he realized what he was doing, and turned aside his gaze. He trotted after Anya, hoping she hadn't caught him staring. In times past, she often had.

They went to the topmost floor of the library, a part Cinder had yet to explore.

"Here we are," Anya halted in front of a bookshelf, lifted to her tip-toes, and withdrew a book. It was a plain, leather volume with nothing to mark it as being special other than the title, which was lettered in gold foil. "*A Conspiracy to Live*," she said, handing him the book.

Cinder perused a few pages. It was as she said, a supposed autobiography of Manifold Fulsom, but from his early years, a time spent on a different world, a place called 'Earth'. Odd claims, but nothing he hadn't come across before. More surprising to him, though, was that Anya had known the exact location of the book. There hadn't been the slightest hint of indecision.

She must have noticed his surprise. "I'm not Simply Anya," she said, teasing him with his own joke. "I do enjoy reading."

Cinder smiled. "I don't know if romances count."

The tips of Anya's ears briefly reddened, but an instant later, she controlled her reaction and chuckled, low, throaty, and warm. "They count, and I'm sure you remember what will happen if you tell anyone about our little secret."

"Oh? We have secrets now?"

Cinder had unconsciously eased forward, and he realized he now stood within inches of Anya. If anyone came upon them, there would serious questions as to what they were doing. She must have had the same awareness. As one, they both stepped back a pace.

"Thank you for the book," Cinder said.

"You're welcome," Anya said, her voice cool now. "If there's nothing else, I should go."

"Of course," Cinder said, stepping aside so she could leave.

She stepped past him but paused a few feet away, twisting to look back. "I really would like to hear your story. The one where you lost your memory."

"I'd be happy to," Cinder said with a smile. "It's the least I can do after your help tonight." He held up the book she'd found for him. "Maybe we can talk about them at the Duchess's Banquet. I can tell you while we dance." The words sprung from Cinder without conscious thought, and the moment they exited his mouth, he mentally cursed himself. *Idiot!*

She glanced at him over her shoulder, lips quirked in a faint smile, eyes twinkling. "I'll see what I can do."

Sriovey grunted as he sought to grab hold of Cinder. He dove for a single leg, but Cinder shifted aside. No matter. Sriovey didn't let up. So far, Cinder and his slippery-fast quickness had kept him out of danger. Not anymore. Sriovey followed the human, driving forward until they were locked up. He held onto the Cinder's wrists, risking a grin, knowing victory was seconds away. He dropped low for an ankle pick. Cinder shucked his leg out of the way.

He sourced his *lorethasra*, creating a braid of water to soften the ground beneath Cinder's feet, slow him down, and then—

Sriovey's face slammed into the ground.

What the…

Before Sriovey could figure out what had happened, he discovered his arms pinioned to his side by Cinder's long legs and a rear-naked chokehold applied around his thick neck. The human began to squeeze. Sriovey tried to free his arms, yanking hard, but to no avail. His vision grayed, and he was forced to verbally tap.

Cinder let off, and Sriovey gasped for blessed air, a state of disbelief settling over him. He had just lost to a human in wrestling. It shouldn't be possible. He was a dwarf, stronger than any human. Faster, too. He also had *lorethasra*.

Sriovey shook his head, yet unable to reconcile what had just happened. Had Cinder really beaten him in wrestling? How? Again, he ran through the litany of reasons it shouldn't have occurred.

Worst of all, Cinder didn't even have the decency to shout his victory. He merely stood off to the side, waiting for Sriovey to recover.

Sriovey glared, and the shame of his defeat burned. He flushed with both fury and humiliation, but Cinder didn't pay his anger any mind. The little fucker even had the gall to hold out a hand to help him rise. Sriovey scowled. He wanted to do nothing more than slap away the hand.

"Give me your hand, brother," Cinder said.

The words calmed Sriovey's irritation. He exhaled heavily, his raw emotions easing. "Thanks," he grunted.

Cinder quirked a small smile. "You're welcome."

They went to the stone bleachers, collapsing upon them. Cinder appeared worn out. Perspiration dripped off his brow, down his nose. It soaked his shirt, and he breathed heavily.

Sriovey wasn't in much better shape. His heart raced, but he controlled his breathing by taking slow, deep inhalations. All evening, his wrestling matches against Cinder had proven a challenge, and his only blessing was that no one else was present today to witness his defeat.

Since it was the hour after supper, the time when reasonable folk

rested and relaxed prior to training again, the Cauldron was unoc-
cupied. For now, this place where warriors were forged was peaceful.
The sun hung a few fingers above the horizon, and a gentle wind blew.
It carried the faint hint of water and minerals from the rugged hills
surrounding the academy and a slight chill. Spring would arrive in
another month or so. Sriovey could feel it in his bones.

While recovering, Sriovey further mulled the evening's events. Even
while sourcing *lorethasra*, he wasn't able to easily break Cinder's hold.
The man was an eel, twisty fast and having an unsuspected strength.
Whatever speed and physical attributes he had lost during the wilderness drill, he'd more than regained them. In armed combat, none of the
Seconds could offer him a challenge. These days, only those elves who
had earned an *insufi* blade could hope to contest him.

But still, this had been unarmed combat, and Cinder was only a
human. He shouldn't have won.

Unless he wasn't merely human.

The idea had Sriovey shifting about on the bleacher, disturbed.
What if Cinder was truly the Fated Foe, the terrible evil the *Crèche
Prani* warned against. Wasn't it Sriovey's duty to see him dead? To save
the world from his tyranny and malevolence.

But looking at Cinder, all Sriovey saw was someone he loved. He
saw his brother.

He cursed under his breath. Cinder even had him thinking like he
did. *Brother.*

"What's wrong?" Cinder asked, staring at him in worry.

How could any man hate someone who looked at them with such
concern? "Just angry I lost," Sriovey lied. "Looks like you have the
Unchained Trial locked up. You ready for it? It's in a couple of weeks."

Cinder grunted, shrugging noncommittally. "I got lucky tonight."

"I doubt it. What did you do?"

Cinder merely shrugged in answer.

Sriovey grunted again. It wasn't luck. He was sure of it. It was *lorethasra*. It had to be. A human who could wield what should have
been forever denied them. The reason for the penance placed upon

humanity was lost in the mists of time, but the *Crèche Prani* explained the reason. Humans had caused the *NusraelShev*, and for this, humans had been punished. The Mythaspuris had stripped themselves and all who followed of their glory. Only the Fated Foe, the *Elonic Ciprion*, would prove immune to the holy punishment. He would come, the Bringer of Destruction, the Harbinger of Calamity.

Unless it was as Derius seemed to believe. The prophecies were mistaken and contained some strange amalgamation of misstated translations from *Shevasra*.

Sriovey discovered Cinder grinning his way.

"Don't worry," Cinder said. "No one saw me win."

A small blessing, but it didn't matter. Sriovey knew what had occurred. Derius needed to learn of it as well. He remembered their last conversation about Cinder.

"We couldn't stop the elves from learning of our interest in Cinder," Derius had stated.

"Our people are a sieve," Sriovey had complained.

"But we only told them what they already suspected. His awakening in a well and having no memory. We didn't tell them about the aether-cursed cat and what followed after, his likely death."

"They'll find out anyway," Sriovey had groused.

And, worse, they probably had, but it didn't matter. Cinder had more secrets, and whatever they were, Sriovey was determined to learn them first and keep it secret from the damn elves. No one else could know until those much wiser than him could decide the human's fate.

He slapped Cinder's shoulder. "I'm off," he said. "Your next set of sparring partners should arrive soon."

Cinder grinned at him. "Same time tomorrow?"

"Only if you tell me how you won tonight."

Cinder's gaze went hard, and Sriovey tried not to shuffle like a disobedient child beneath the judging stare.

"You don't have to tell me if you don't want to," Sriovey mumbled, kicking at a loose piece of dirt.

Cinder's features cleared, and he nodded as if in agreement. "It's fine. The humans know the truth. I guess you should, too. I could tell you were sourcing *lorethasra*. I could tell you were using Water."

"Because you can use *lorethasra* yourself."

Cinder started. "Of course not."

"Then how?" Sriovey demanded, not sure he wanted to know the answer. The truth might push him into making a decision about Cinder, and the idea of seeing his friend killed terrified him.

Cinder hesitated. "It's a skill I've learned over the past few years."

There was more to the man's story, and while Sriovey was tempted to let the matter lie, he knew he had to press the issue. "Is this a skill you lost when you fought against the *aether*-cursed bear?"

Cinder snorted, and he wore a wry smile as he shook his head. "Everyone noticed, didn't they?"

"Of course. We weren't blind then, and we're not blind now. You're getting back to who you once were. What's changed."

"*Jivatma*," Cinder said. "I had it. I lost it, and now, I think I've recovered it. I hope I have anyway."

Jivatma. Sriovey recognized the word, but it wasn't a concept with which he was familiar. Wasn't it something to do with the rishis?

His confusion must have shown because Cinder chuckled. "It's too hard to explain, so consider this your reading assignment for tonight."

Sriovey sighed. "Unholy hells—"

Cinder broke out in fresh laughter.

"The hell's so funny?" Sriovey realized the answer a moment later. *Unholy hells.* One of Cinder's stupid, made-up curse words. He glared at Cinder. "Never mind what I just said. What I want to know is why are you so Devesh-damned bent on sparring against me?"

"Because I want to become the best I can possibly be. I want to go against you while you're sourcing *lorethasra* and properly test myself. I want to win."

Sriovey shook his head in seeming pity, but it was merely a ruse to hide his shock. The man was serious. He truly believed himself capable of standing against a woven who was sourcing *lorethasra*. Which made him ever more certain that Cinder could do the same.

He coughed into his fist, dissembling as he tried to mask his disquiet. He had remembered a prophetic sutra from the *Crèche Prani.*

He will comprehend your powers
In ways you can't hope to emulate.
And you will unwittingly aide him
On his vast and terrible road to mastery.

23

Days and weeks of study and training sped by, and Cinder continued to advance his awareness of when the woven sourced *lorethasra* and how to counter it. At the same time, he continued his own studies about *Jivatma*, and how to conduct it.

But on the evening prior to a rest day, Cinder entered the Foe in order to test his *Jivatma*. As he reckoned matters, the half-world on the other side of Misery Gate was the best place to do so. In the reality of Seminal, he only caught faint glimmers of the mirror-like water, but he wanted a better appraisal of how much he had truly recuperated.

At least Cinder assumed his *Jivatma* had recuperated. He hoped so, but at this point, assumptions were no longer good enough. Next week was the Unchained Trial, and he had to be ready. For the Seconds, their standing wasn't determined by a Grand Melee. There were no tests on horsemanship, military strategy, history, or archery.

All those aspects of training were already considered throughout the year, the instructors having judged the abilities of the cadets during their classes and the Autumn Trial. Based on those aspects alone, Cinder felt pretty sure he could hold onto his position as Prime.

However, he wasn't interested in only maintaining his status. He wanted to win the Unchained Trial, the one and only weapons tournament of the second year. Cinder had to win, possibly just a single match against a warrior wielding *lorethasra* would do. A single match, and Anya's offer for the Secondary Trial would be available to him.

He hadn't yet decided if he should accept. Her people's probable reaction still bothered him.

Nevertheless, the Unchained Trial was important. No matter what else, Cinder wanted to win. But in order to know if he stood an actual chance at victory, first he needed a definitive answer of what he could truly do as a warrior. The Foe could tell him.

Cinder approached Misery Gate, ready to face the truth. He squared his shoulders, stepped forward, and activated the chevrons in the proper sequence.

Moments later, the black gate opened with a snarling whoosh, a shimmering film covering its opening. Cinder stepped through the oily substance, and the moment he came in contact with it, ice filled his veins and poured into his bones. He accepted the brutal cold, gritted his teeth as his body seemed to stretch to the breaking point. A raucous wail filled his hearing, and a tunnel traced with chaotic smears of light curved and tumbled.

With a snap, he stepped into the Foe, and the cold abated, replaced now by nausea. The discomfort didn't bother Cinder, though. He had long since learned to overcome the sensations, and within seconds his stomach was settled.

He breathed deep the dry air of the Foe, and the smell of the surrounding woods, the detritus of fallen leaves, moss, and decay, filled his nostrils. The sky held a smooth layer of evenly distributed golden light from whatever sun illuminated this odd half-realm. The forest held quiet, no sounds of spiderkin rampaging forth. No birdsong either.

Cinder had wanted a quiet place of contemplation tonight. He sat upon the ground, one foot resting atop the opposite knee. Eyes closed, he focused inward, upon the place hidden in the caverns of his mind where the liquid pool of his *Jivatma* should reside as it peacefully reflected some faraway light.

Minutes passed with nothing to show for his work, but Cinder didn't give up. Although his *Jivatma* had definitely recovered after he drank the *mana*, it still wasn't as easy to visualize as it had once been prior to the battle against the *aether*-cursed bear.

Cinder persisted in the meditative pose. His heart slowed, and he imagined every beat as a sonorous, plodding echo rippling into the depths of his mind. It allowed him to relax his desires and wants, and his breathing slowed, grew deeper. His muscles went fully loose.

Within the depths of his mind's eye, a hazy light flickered. The flicker brightened, grew richer. *His Jivatma.* The mirrored water was half the size it had once been, but it was progress.

A vision swept over him.

He huddled in a small meadow in the wilds of a strange place alongside three men he loved. They'd suffered great tribulations together, and two of them looked close enough like him to be his brothers. In his hands, he tightly gripped a woman. She was an impossibility.

"What in the unholy hells," one of the men whispered. "Where did she come from?"

"And what is she?" someone else whispered. "She looks like…"

"Let me go," the woman whispered furiously after working his hand off her mouth. "I've done nothing to you."

A shock, like lightning, raced through him, and his blood ran cold. He knew what she was.

Red-gold skin, honey-blonde hair, and emerald green eyes.

He struggled to hold back his sudden disgust and anger. She was a ghrina, a child of two Castes, an unholy abomination. Her kind was warned against by the First Mother and First Father. She was evil incarnate. She should immediately be killed.

The revulsion crested.

"Cinder." A voice spoke his name, calling him home as if from some great distance.

Cinder might have answered, but the dream held him rapt. He couldn't exit it even if he wanted to.

He assessed the woman, measured her life's worth, all the while trying to determine Dharma's proper judgment. His hand went to the hilt of his sword, and he readied the killing blow.

"Cinder," the voice repeated. It sounded like an evocation, a lure set in his mind, reeling him in from the waters of the dream.

He frowned in irritation.

A third time the voice spoke. "Cinder."

This time the spell of his dream shattered like a broken mirror, the shards melting like wax over a flame until they spread out and smeared. Any trace of the imagery or memory was removed. The vision of the men, those brothers-in-arms he'd so deeply loved, seeped out of his mind like water poured onto a desert until only the barest knowledge of their existence remained. And the woman…

"Cinder."

He opened his eyes on the fourth call and gazed at whoever had disturbed him. A woman stood in front of him, peering down, a gentle smile of amusement on her features. Another tremor jolted through Cinder. Anya stood over him. Anya with her red-gold skin, honey-blonde hair, and emerald-green eyes.

Just like the woman in his dreams, and he stared at her in shock and fear.

She must have seen something in his visage because the warm smile fled her face. "What's wrong?"

Cinder didn't know how to answer. He was struck silent as a question raged through his mind. Was the woman in his visions Anya? He had always wondered. The two women shared so many similarities. Another question, one hitting with the force of an epiphany, rippled across his awareness. Did he love Anya? Is that why he kept dreaming of a woman with the honey-blonde hair? Imagined walking with her through an enchanting city? Played the mandolin while she sang?

What then did tonight's dream mean? The vision in which he might have murdered the woman with honey-blonde hair or at least had been on the cusp of doing so? What did the violence represent? Was it real? Had it happened?

Devesh help him, but he had no idea.

His confused thoughts slowly congealed on another explanation, the one he was starting to fear might represent the truth. The visions were images from a past life, and in this past life, had he known two women with honey-blonde hair? One he had loved, and the other he had killed? And if true, what did that say about the kind of person he had been? He had viscerally hated the woman he'd seen tonight, and for no other reason than because of her ancestry. What evil teachings could inspire a person to hate another for such a reason? And what kind of person would unthinkingly accept such an evil instruction?

Apparently, he had been exactly that kind of person.

His gorge rose. The truth ate into his mind like acid. In the past, he hadn't been a hero. He had been a villain.

He noticed Anya frowning in concern. "Are you well?"

Cinder gathered the dregs of his discordant thoughts. "I'm fine," he managed. "You surprised me is all. It was the shock of waking up from a dream." He forced himself to meet her gaze.

"I see," Anya said, eyeing him uncertainly. "Well, if you don't mind, I'd like to do some training tonight."

Cinder scrambled to his feet. "Of course. I'll leave you to it." Without another word, he moved to the Foe's exit, the dark doorway like a hole in creation. He had to get away from Anya. He couldn't face her right now. The woman with the honey-blonde hair and Anya... he kept twisting them in his mind. It left him feeling like he really had murdered her in the past.

The next morning, the urgency of discovery had faded. When Cinder awakened, the dawn's light was only a sliver on the horizon, and he found that the bizarre dream from the Foe had flown apart like a dandelion blown by a child. There was nothing left behind but a bewildering mix of emotions and nebulous possibilities.

He sat in his room for a few minutes, pondering the remnants of his dissolved vision. Whatever he had seen, he could no longer recall it. Only the vaguest of sensations remained. It was always the same with these dreams. Once the immediacy of the moment was past, every aspect of them dissipated except for hazy impressions.

It left him in a state of uncertainty, and he often wondered if the visions weren't so much memories of a past life, but manifestations of some unfulfilled desire. Certain books interpreted dreams in such a way. For instance, he recalled anger and loathing from last night's vision, and what if it meant the woman he saw last night represented repressed feelings of antipathy toward the princess?

It was one potential explanation, although he didn't believe in it. He liked Anya and couldn't imagine even subconsciously feeling such loathing for her.

The other possibility was that the visions *were* memories of his past life. And in the past, he might have killed a woman whose only sin was her appearance and lineage.

The knowledge left him distracted, and he spent the rest of the morning having difficulty focusing on training or his classes. He decided to end his day early and go to the library, where he hoped to find some measure of solace from last night's dream.

Cinder entered the library, which was quiet and empty this early in the afternoon. Sunlight beamed through the tall windows running along one wall, brightening the space, burnishing the tables, bookcases, and a large globe set next to the stairs.

How odd.

He had been here almost daily for most of two years and spent hours on the various floors reading, but never once had he paid any notice to the globe. He made a note to study it in the future.

Master Molni was manning the front desk, and Cinder nodded

acknowledgment to him before sweeping on upstairs. He wasn't ready to speak to the discerning old librarian. Master Molni would likely see the upset on his face and ask him the reason for it. Cinder wouldn't tell him, and he didn't think he could lie to the librarian either.

Cinder wandered up to the top floor, perusing titles at random and eventually came across the autobiography of Manifold Fulsom, the one Anya had pointed out a couple weeks ago. Since she had shown it to him, training for the Unchained Trial had taken over the majority of his time, and he had yet to fully read the book. He pulled it off the shelf, eyed it for a moment, and with a mental shrug, decided to take a longer look at it. He went to a table set in an alcove and cracked the book open.

The first few chapters were disappointing, nothing but a recitation of Manifold's apparently charmed childhood and his eventual transformation into an *asrasin* of renown. Sometime in his twenties, Manifold had caught the attention of Shokan. The book spoke of their fateful meeting and Manifold's feelings toward the Lord of the Sword.

"I loved him like a father. Like a brother. He wasn't the holy figure so many others saw. He was my friend, and I betrayed him."

Cinder halted. *Wait.* What was that? It couldn't be right. Had Manifold just admitted to betraying Shokan? Impossible. He re-read the passage. No. He'd read it correctly. Cinder sat back in consideration.

Along with Sapient Dormant, Manifold Fulsom was the greatest of the Mythaspuris. How could he have betrayed Shokan? Or perhaps it represented some artistic flair, one meant to trick a reader into thinking one thing when really the author meant something else. Another notion. What if this book wasn't an autobiography at all? It made more sense that it was a tract written by a jealous rival, one designed to wreck Manifold's reputation.

Then again, Cinder recalled a supposed biography of Sapient Dormant which made a similar ludicrous claim. But it went further. It claimed that Sapient had gone from one of Shokan's dearest friends to one of his greatest enemies, that he'd become a necrosed.

Bizarre.

Cinder shook his head and decided to keep reading.

Despite the book's bland beginning, he quickly grew engrossed by the autobiography. It described Manifold's growth, the war in this other world—Earth—against Shet and his children, and the escape of the so-called god's eldest daughter across an anchor line—the book unhelpfully didn't explain what this term meant—to another realm.

And there it was: Manifold's fall.

The Mythaspuri had become a necrosed, an undead horror, serving under none other than Sapient Dormant, the so-called Overward of the Necrosed. Together, the two of them had been curses against creation, monsters who reveled in the torture they inflicted. Manifold in particular had gloried in his fallen state as he feasted upon the lives of the innocent, basking in the sacrilege of murder.

Even after Shet's defeat on Earth, and his escape to Seminal, Manifold had continued his perversion. Millennia of horror visited on the innocent. And in all those long centuries, the essence of his past life as an *asrasin*, a healer, was long forgotten, gone as if it had never existed.

Again, Cinder sat back in his chair. He couldn't believe this was the same Manifold Fulsom the world held in such high honor. The claims in the biography couldn't be true. They were too fantastical. After all, how could someone so supposedly wicked and cruel ever find absolution? What grace had allowed Manifold to transform from utter evil into a figure of holy myth?

In that moment of consideration, Cinder recognized the harmony between Manifold's story and his own. He might very well have been a murderer in a past life.

He stared at the book for a moment, wondering if there would be any answers to his questions and needs.

Pages later, Manifold's fall only ended when he learned that Shokan still lived. For millennia he had thought the Lord of the Sword dead, but it wasn't true. Shokan lived. So did Sira. Neither of them had died as Shet had stated. They were very much alive.

Cinder's heart quickened. If Shokan hadn't truly died, could he still be alive even now?

A few paragraphs later, his brow knitted with confusion. This couldn't be right. When were the events in the book taking place? The past? The present?

He stared at the book, disappointed. It was a fabrication. It had to be. According to the so-called autobiography, Manifold had begun his long struggle to regain his humanity during a time when Shet was alive and active in the world, his empire of Naraka rebuilt, which was patently absurd. Shet was gone, and he showed no signs of reviving, and his empire was nothing but tumbled stones and long-dead malice.

Cinder shook his head. What a waste of time. He was nearly at the end of the book, and he thumbed through the rest of it desultorily, accidentally happening across an interesting passage.

"William Wilde. The boy was more powerful than he knew. When he ran me down on Sinskrill, he could have killed me. His brother stood with him in support, but William held his hand. I like to believe it was due to mercy, and in this, I see the guiding hand of Devesh."

The passage sounded familiar. Intrigued, Cinder read to the end, although there wasn't much more to the book.

Manifold and Sapient—he had also been in this place called Sinskrill—had fought alongside Shokan and Sira against Shet, and the two necrosed had somehow ended up in the Realms of the Rakshasas. There, in a place of bleakness, chaos, and emptiness, they had somehow rediscovered a path back to the Singing Light and were graced with forgiveness.

Words nearly forgotten, ones spoken by the gleeman, Tomas Linimer, in Swift Sword, resounded in Cinder's mind. *"...consider the place from which Sapient and Manifold set sail. Dark kingdoms. Pallid realms. Think of how they must have ended up in such a place for they had prior been boon companions to the Blessed Ones."* The story seemed an echo of this supposed autobiography's message.

Cinder read on.

In the darkness of the Realms, the now-former necrosed re-ignited the love of Devesh, teaching those who could learn. Strangely, Manifold claimed their greatest student was the near-forgotten Mythaspuri, Indrun Agni. In the Realms, Indrun had apparently been a young Rakshasa, thrown out of his home for failing at a task well above his station: the seduction of a carpenter's son.

On that odd note, the book ended, and Cinder closed it, staring at it thoughtfully. He wasn't sure whether to believe anything within the autobiography, but in the most personal part of his heart, he hoped it was true. He hoped there truly was a means to save even the worst of people.

A person like the villain he might have once been. Perhaps that was the entire purpose of the story. Through Devesh and true repentance, forgiveness and a second chance was possible.

The knotted tension stirred by the unsettling dream from last night slowly eased. Muscles he hadn't even realized were tight—at his neck, brow, and shoulders—loosened.

Forgiveness. The word resonated in Cinder's mind like soft footsteps of someone carrying him during the hour of his greatest need. He knew he didn't deserve such grace, but he hoped it truly was being offered.

24

While Cinder held pride of place amongst the Seconds, today might see his reign end. Today was the Unchained Trial. It was to be held at the Cauldron, and Master Absin, the presiding judge over the event, reviewed the rules one last time. He paced in front of the Seconds, who were lined up according to their rank, from first to last. The instructions were the same as usual: two points for a kill shot, one for a disabling blow, and four points for the win.

Cinder imagined how the tournament might play out. He'd likely face Cariath, second in rank, and if he lost, it would give the opportunity for whichever cadet was in third place to challenge him. Any subsequent loss could lead to another match against the next lower ranked student, and so on.

But it wouldn't happen. Cinder would face Cariath, and he'd beat Cariath. Cinder refused to allow fear of losing—even the notion of losing—to enter his mind. He'd finish this tournament in the same position where he started it: as Prime.

He braced himself, focused on victory.

It was a cold winter day, but at least the heavy padding he and all

310

the Seconds wore as protection during their sparring matches provided some warmth. A band of tattered clouds tried to hide the sun, but every so often a sunbeam broke through their ragged trails. Sunshine poured through the gloom then, illuminating portions of the Cauldron and the surrounding woods where a number of dogwoods and rhododendrons would display their spring flowers in the upcoming months. To the west, more clouds piled up, promising to deliver rain in a few hours. Hopefully, the Seconds would be done by then.

They should be, and if they weren't, so be it. Cinder was ready to fight in the rain and cold. He was relaxed and ready to get this competition done. Sure, the odds might seem stacked against him—the woven would be allowed to use their *lorethasra*—but all it would mean is that his victory would be all the sweeter.

Especially since Anya was watching. She sat upon one of the bleachers, Lisandre next to her, and a number of other warriors and instructors also in attendance. Word had gotten out about Anya's offer to sponsor him, and some had taken it as a joke. They didn't think he had a chance and were sure this was simply the princess' way of humiliating a human who thought too much of himself. They were easy to spot, seated at the bleachers and laughing like fragging donkeys.

Cinder didn't pay them any mind. They weren't worth his attention.

Others, though, had taken the information with outrage instead of jocularity. Be they servants, librarians, members of the administration, even citizens of Certitude, most of them disapproved of Anya's proposition, and they didn't hide their antipathy. Cinder caught them sneering at him, smirking in mockery. Estin—of course, Estin—had been much more vocal in his displeasure. He had barely been able to contain his outrage when he'd learned what his sister had offered. He had stormed into the commons, demanding Cinder refuse Anya's proposal.

Jackhole.

Cinder had never listened to Estin's ravings in the past, and he hadn't done so then. Anya was her own woman. If she wanted to train Cinder in his Secondary Trial, then it was her decision to make, not

Estin's.

Plus, there was a deeper reality to the situation. All those disrespecting him were also disrespecting the princess. They disrespected her judgment. It wasn't a secret that many elves didn't approve of Anya's behavior. They considered her conduct a failing, especially her friendship with humans, and as Cinder reckoned matters, if he failed today, he wouldn't merely fail himself. He'd fail her.

He wouldn't let that happen.

As if in echo of his thoughts, a rent in the clouds allowed the sun to pour down its light.

Life can be strange, Cinder thought, smiling at the harmony of thought and reality.

Once Master Absin finished speaking, the line of Seconds broke apart and settled on the bleachers surrounding the main sparring circle. Cinder took a seat between Bones and Ishmay. As the top ranked humans other than Cinder, the two of them would be sparring soon.

"Good luck defending your spot," Ishmay said.

"Same to you," Cinder said. He didn't much feel like talking, and his terse response must have been noted because no one spoke to him afterward.

The Unchained Trial began. First to face off were Depth and Wark. Cinder leaned forward. He'd been looking forward to their bout. Those two were closely matched, and both warriors had grown so much during their time at the Directorate.

The match began, and it proved every bit as exciting as Cinder had imagined. It was a grueling fight, a proof of both warriors' mettle. Neither of them gave an inch. They evaded killing blows, defended against disabling attacks, and ranged across the sparring circle. They pushed into the heart of exhaustion. Both of them sweat soaked and panting, but their shokes never dipped. They continued to fight, and in the end, Depth managed to eke out a hard-won victory. However, he had little energy left to face Ishmay—next up in the rankings—who bested him quickly.

The matches proceeded from there. Ishmay against Bones, Bones against Riyne.

Cinder perked up, paying closer attention. Although Riyne was far down the list in terms of ranking, it wasn't due to lack of skill. It was because of Riyne's repugnant actions during the Grand Melee. In truth, the elf was easily one of the most skilled of all of the Seconds. Unsurprisingly, he made short work of Bones, but then he had to face Jozep.

Here the matches grew more interesting.

This was the Unchained Trial, and the woven could utilize whatever skills they possessed, including *lorethasra*.

Cinder watched as Riyne fought Jozep, entranced by the skill of both warriors and their use of *lorethasra*. The ground trembled, the air shimmered, and tongues of fire snapped like whips from the end of Riyne's shoke, only to immediately be doused by a wash of water extending off of Jozep's warhammer. Steamed hissed. A cloud of vapor veiled the two warriors. When it cleared, Jozep lay on his back, Riyne's shoke at his neck.

"Yield," Jozep croaked. His beard appeared noticeably shorter, likely singed by Riyne's fire.

They sparred again, and the outcome was no different: Riyne quickly victorious.

Bones could have challenged Jozep at that point, but he decided against it.

Next up was Derius, and he wasn't so easily defeated. There was then a break in Riyne's progression when Jozep decided to challenge Derius. The younger dwarf fought valiantly, but in the end, he didn't succeed.

Afterward, Riyne continued his progression up the ranks when he faced Sriovey. He struggled against the dwarven leader, but in the end, he proved victorious. Then it was time for him to face Loriam, whom he defeated soundly. Mohal next, and another win.

By now, Riyne had fought six matches, and the effort was starting to show. He hunched over at the knees, gasping for breath, sweat pouring in runnels down his face and neck while waiting on Estin, his next opponent.

Luckily, Riyne had a chance to recover some in between his matches. There was a pause in his ascent as lower ranked cadets he had defeated jockeyed for position.

During the last of those matches, Cinder caught Riyne glance at Lisandre, who nodded to him in approval. Riyne must have taken heart from his brother's show of support because he straightened, throwing his shoulders back and evincing courage and determination. His breathing recovered, and he took deep, controlled breaths.

Then came the fight between Riyne and Estin.

Riyne pulled out the victory, two 'kills' to one, but by then, he had nothing left for Cariath, who easily bested him.

Regardless, it had been a tremendous run. Riyne might have regained some of the honor he'd lost last year, and Cinder was happy for him. The two of them had made peace with one other, possibly even becoming friends, and Cinder was glad for it. How had he come to like Riyne so well?

He shook off his musings then.

Now wasn't the time for such considerations. Now was the time to defend his rank. He stepped off the bleachers and entered the sparring ring. Once inside, he shook out his legs and arms and inhaled deeply, urging his aggression to awaken. He blew out a hard breath and clenched his jaw. He wasn't going to lose today. He was the Prime, and he would remain the Prime.

Cariath smirked at him from the opposite side of the sparring circle, where he had waited after defeating Riyne. He aimed his shoke like a spear. "Cinder Shade. You're mine. Step on in or stay on out. It doesn't matter. You're going down. I'm going to get what you got."

Cinder grinned back at Cariath, fixing his eyes on the smirking elf. "Big talk, but all you're getting is an asskicking."

His response stoked a murmur of excitement, but he hardly noticed it. He had his gaze locked on Cariath. He hadn't been lying or boasting. Cariath was going to get an asskicking.

Master Absin stood a few feet away and reviewed the instructions one last time.

Cinder continued to stare down his opponent, forcing himself to think of him as an enemy. Cariath's *lorethasra* and abilities wouldn't be enough to save him. Not anymore. Cinder's Second year had been rough, but in some ways, losing his *Jivatma* had been a blessing. He had been forced to rededicate himself to his training, to enhance his predictive ability to the utmost, and perfect his form as much as possible.

Cariath had no chance to take what was his. He pitied the elf, but pity transitioned to anger. No one would steal his opportunities. He glared at Cariath now. A flicker of worry slipped across the elf's otherwise impassive face.

Good. Worry led to distraction.

All the while, Cinder reached for his *Jivatma*, which day-by-day, continued to refill. Less welcome was the resumed presence of the blue-and-green lightning. Still, simply having his *Jivatma* available was enough.

A final pregnant moment, and Cinder gauged Cariath's stance, his balance, the clenching of his fists.

He understood.

Master Absin shouted, "Fight!"

Cinder shot to the side. The ground trembled in a line leading from Cariath straight to where he'd been standing. The elf wasn't done. Cinder scented sulfur. He rolled under a blade of flame and launched over a hissing discus of air.

He landed a few feet away from Cariath, too close for Elements. Cinder stabbed forward with a thrust. Cariath batted aside his strike and landed a heavy elbow to Cinder's mouth.

His lip split, and he rocked on his feet. His vision momentarily blanked, and he automatically lurched away from Cariath, needing distance. His vision finally restored, possibly only seconds later. Cinder discovered Cariath approaching. Cinder tried to gain more distance, but his legs were gelatin. They barely supported him. He wobbled, nearly falling. Cariath walked him down. Cinder saw the attack coming, but he was slow to react. A shoke slammed into the meat of his thigh. Cinder tumbled to the ground. He clutched his leg, biting back a shriek of pain.

He barely heard it when Master Absin called out Cariath's two points. Nor did he care. All he understood was agony. His leg felt like it had been amputated. Cinder gritted his teeth, focusing on his breathing, imagining the torment leaving his leg. It must have worked because the pain exited his leg seconds later, but the limb felt dead afterward. There was no strength in it. Cariath hadn't pulled the blow, and Cinder glared at the elf.

But most of his anger was self-directed. He'd taken Cariath too lightly.

Cinder hobbled to his feet, cursing himself. He reclaimed his position on the opposite side of the sparring circle.

"Can you continue?" Master Absin asked, his face filled with concern.

Cinder spit out a wad of blood. "I'm good," he answered, although he still needed more time to recover. He glowered at Cariath. "You finally done playing?"

"I never play," Cariath said flatly.

Cinder grinned at him, teeth blood-stained, refusing to show his opponent even the slightest hint of weakness. "Not from where I'm standing. You think swords are toys. You play like every other elf I've known."

Irritated grumbles from the watching crowd reached him, but he didn't care. Every second prior to the match's resumption was time for him to recover, time for him to restore some measure of his balance.

"You think I'm playing, but I'm still kicking your ass," Cariath replied. "How's the leg?"

"Leg's just fine. Show me what you got."

Cariath grinned. "I'll show you the sky when I lay you out again."

"Bring it."

Cariath didn't reply this time, but it didn't matter. Cinder was finally ready. He shook out the last of the deadness in his leg. Just as importantly, he could also visualize his *Jivatma*. It glistened behind the wall of lightning, but the tiniest bit ebbed into him, empowering his body. His vision cleared. He stared at Cariath, his posture and set of his shoke. He instantly understood what the elf intended.

Master Absin shouted. "Fight!"

The earth rumbled. Cinder rolled with the motion, and when he rose, Cariath was coming. Cinder's instincts took over. He parried a horizontal strike. Blocked a thrust. Cariath's eyes flashed blue. *Here came water.*

Cinder jumped backward, easily evading grasping fingers of muddy water rising from the ground.

The elf's eyes glowed yellow.

Fire to flash the water. Just like when Riyne fought Jozep.

A tongue of flame snapped out from Cariath's shoke. Where it touched the water, steam and vapor billowed. The elf likely expected Cinder to lose track of him, but Cinder never did. A shadowy shape rushed at him through the mist.

Cinder shifted minutely, presenting a smaller target. Cariath punched through the steam, shoke ready to deliver a vertical strike. Cinder twisted and in the same motion, he slashed, slamming his shoke into Cariath's abdomen.

The elf screamed in agony. He probably felt like he'd been bisected.

Cinder winced in sympathy. He hadn't pulled the blow either, and it had to have hurt, padding or no.

"Two points to Cinder. We're even," Master Absin stated. Next, he addressed Cariath. "Can you continue?"

The elf grimaced, slowly clambering to his feet. "I can go," he said, still clutching a hand to his stomach.

Cinder wiped his still bleeding mouth and took his place opposite the elf on the other side of the sparring circle. He studied Cariath for any signs of weakness. The elf hunched over to his place in the sparring circle, pulling a face as if still in pain. But the firmness of his stance, his untroubled breathing, his overly expressive grimace… He didn't think Cariath was quite as injured as he was making it seem.

Master Absin shouted again. "Fight!"

Cinder held off from engaging. He'd seen a green flash in Cariath's eyes, and he wasn't sure what it meant. The answer came a second later as vines surged out of the ground, seeking to trap his legs. Cariath rushed at him during his distraction.

A surge of strength allowed Cinder to rip himself free of the entrapping vines. Just in time. Cariath was on him. The elf swung what would have been a decapitating strike. Cinder dropped low, parried a diagonal follow-up. He stood upright, leaned away from a thrust. He followed up by stepping forward and frontkicking Cariath.

The elf launched backward; his eyes widened comically. He landed on his back, flipped ass over end and came to a stop lying prone.

Cinder reached Cariath before he could rise and placed his shoke to the elf's neck.

"Yield," Cariath said with a groan. He rolled over, face tight with pain. "You sneaky fucker. That hurt."

Cinder knelt next to him. The kick had probably broken some of Cariath's ribs. "Sorry about that," he said, helping the elf sit up.

Thankfully, an attending physician was also at Cariath's side in seconds. She placed her hands on the elf, and Cariath sighed in relief, his clenched-jaw anguish fading some.

The physician reached for him as well. "I can heal your lip," she said. She was slim and slight, coming no higher than Cinder's collarbones and had brown hair and hazel-green eyes. She was beautiful like all elves, and there was a playful youthfulness to her gentle smile.

"Thank you," Cinder said. The truth was that his entire face ached. "What's your name?"

"Estefania Lynsee." She quirked a grin. "You're lucky, both of you. Most of my training is in the healing of children, but I think I can fix your injuries. They aren't so bad." She placed her hands on his shoulders, and Cinder sighed when she was finished, testing his lip for any lingering soreness and his teeth for any that might be loose.

Once satisfied, he rejoined Cariath. They arranged themselves so they stood on either side of Master Absin, who lifted Cinder's arm, presenting him to all those present. "I present your winner, and still the Prime amongst the Seconds, Cinder Shade!"

Cinder grinned. He'd done it. It wasn't as surreal as prior victories, but it still felt damn good. He noticed Anya smiling broadly and applauding his victory.

25

Over the next few days, Cinder remained caught up in the joy and brilliance of winning the Unchained Trial. He had been confident going into the tournament, but actually succeeding still left him with a heady sense of accomplishment.

Shortly afterward, it was time to get back to work, and on the next rest day, he stood in the basement of Firemirror Hall, staring at the chevrons on Misery Gate. By now, there was a familiarity to them, odd in some ways, and he felt like if he stared at them long enough, he might be able to translate the meaning of the symbols.

A faint hint of cinnamon broke Cinder out of his reflections. *Anya.*

She spoke an instant later. "Why am I not surprised to find you here?"

Cinder turned about and watched as the princess descended the stairs. She wore her camouflage ranger's gear, a shoke at her hip, and a bow and quiver of arrows in one hand. Obviously, she meant to enter the Foe and train against the spiderkin.

He hadn't seen or spoken to her since the Unchained Trial, and he wondered if she would want any company when she entered the Foe.

As she continued her descent, Cinder frowned, perturbed by her for some inexplicable reason.

Seconds later, he figured it out. It was her clothes. While Cinder had a similar outfit—all the Seconds had been given a set—Anya wore hers with an unmatched aplomb. Hers were loose enough to provide proper range of motion, but they also accented her curves in a way his never would or probably should.

She continued down the stairs, her movements graceful as a dancer's.

An imagining surfaced in his mind, one in which he danced with Anya at the Duchess's Banquet. It was next week, and in the vision, she wore a lemon-yellow dress, one ending a few inches above her knees.

"I have to admit" she said, "I was impressed by your performance during the Unchained Trial. Did you learn to overcome our *lorethasra* through your training here?"

Cinder smirked. His win had surprised everyone. The woven had bet on the outcome, and all of them, dwarves included, had lost a lot of money wagering against him. Only the humans had believed in him, and as a result they had made out like bandits. Cinder was grateful he had been smart enough to bet on himself, too. He needed the extra money.

"You didn't think I could do it?" he asked.

"I wasn't sure. I hoped you could. I felt like you could." Anya grinned, reaching his side. "And you proved me correct."

Cinder chuckled. "I don't think I overcame Cariath, so much as lucked into a win."

Anya shook her head. "It wasn't luck. You defeated Cariath. You overcame him and his skills."

Cinder wanted to reply, but Anya stood too close, inside the boundary of his personal space. A warning bell clanged in his mind. His breathing hitched. He shouldn't stand so near to her... and she shouldn't place herself in such close proximity to him. He shifted away from Anya, gaining distance and, hopefully, perspective. His breathing eased. "It wasn't studying and training here that allowed me to best Cariath," he said, drifting closer to Misery Gate and away from the princess. "I learned by training against the dwarves. I can see the Elements they plan on using."

Anya's interest sharpened. "How so? Did you open *Muladhara*?"

"No. It's their eyes. There's a flash of color, and it tells me what Element they're going to use. I don't know what they'll do with it, but it's enough to evade their attacks." He gave her a crooked, half-smile. "Like I said before, I didn't really overcome Cariath. I just dodged most of whatever he threw at me."

Anya's mouth pursed, and she appeared pensive. "I've never heard of such a skill. All woven can feel when Elements are about to be unleashed. They each have a distinct sound, appearance, or smell. But a flash of color in the eyes is…" She frowned.

"Unusual?"

"Very unusual," Anya said. "Do you suppose it's because of your—" She gestured vaguely.

"Because of my *Jivatma*," Cinder asked, guessing her meaning.

"Yes. Your *Jivatma*." She shook her head. "I still have trouble accepting that's actually what you're seeing."

"Masters Absin also thinks it might be my *Jivatma*," he said by way of a counter.

"You spoke to him?" Anya sounded surprised.

"I had to speak to someone," Cinder said. "After the battle with the *aether*-cursed bear—"

"I heard about that, too," Anya interrupted. During their conversation, she'd somehow drifted back into his personal space. She peered at him intently, eyes going to his, concern on her features. "What exactly happened?"

Cinder shrugged. He was pressed close to Misery Gate, and there was no easy way to move away from Anya. "During the battle, I burned out my *Jivatma*," Cinder said, going on to explain what had occurred.

"But now you can sense it again?" Anya still peered intently at him from a distance of less than a foot.

Cinder prayed for strength. His hands twitched, a betrayal of his thoughts. He wanted to run his fingers through Anya's lustrous hair. It was held in a ponytail by a simple clasp. Her eyes remained on his, and Cinder tried to speak, but his mouth was dry. He cleared his throat and exhaled in relief when Anya took a step back.

"My *Jivatma* isn't what it once was, but it's recovering. I can conduct it again."

Anya tilted her head and smiled, amused and warm. "You insist on using those archaic terms, don't you?"

He smiled back. "They fit." He changed their conversation. "From what I read and what Master Molni and a few of the dwarves mention, each of the Elements has its own sounds."

"Their own smells, too." Her lips twitched into a grin. "Fire is the worst."

"It stinks like sulfur and crackles like wood burning."

Anya nodded. "Weaves made of Water sound like waves breaking. For Air, it's a hiss and a pulse of distortion; Earth"—she seemed to search for the correct word—"rustles or grinds like crushed stones or vines dragged along the ground."

"But once your Chakra is opened, you don't need to focus on the direct weaves anymore. You simply think what you wish to do?" He sighed. "I've been practicing at opening *Muladhara*, but so far, no luck."

"Keep working at it. And you're right about not needing weaves, at least to a certain extent. It's based on which Chakra you use, and it's also based on your affinity." She waved aside his follow-up questions. "There's a lot more we could cover, but I came here tonight to train. Not lecture."

Cinder couldn't resist asking a final question. "What does your *lorethasra* smell like?" He had read about the unique nature aroma to every woven's *lorethasra*.

Anya chuckled, low and throaty. "Learn to source your own, and you'll find out."

"Or you could simply tell me."

"Now where would be the fun in that?"

"Knowledge is its own reward?"

Anya laughed again. "Mine smells like a mountain stream."

A lovely scent for a lovely person.

"I wonder what mine smells like."

"You don't have one," Anya said. "You have *Jivatma*, not *lorethasra*."

"But if I did have *lorethasra*."

"Iron," Anya said without hesitation.

"Iron?" Cinder made a moue of disgust. "Then mine would smell like blood. That's awful."

Anya stood too close to him again. Why was it he never noticed when she entered his personal space? "Enough talk. I came to spar deadly spiderkin." She patted him on the cheek. "But you will do. What do you say?"

Cinder answered by pressing the appropriate chevrons. Misery Gate whined to life. An explosion of a watery-looking substance collapsed to form a silver shimmering film. He gestured to Anya. "After you."

"Age before beauty, is it?" Anya asked, a twinkle in her eyes.

Cinder grinned. "I wouldn't call you aged, and I wouldn't call myself beautiful."

Anya lifted a single brow. "You're wise in one direction and blind in the other."

Cinder didn't have a chance to ask her what she meant. Anya stepped through Misery Gate and was gone.

Anya stepped through Misery Gate, aghast at her flirtatious replies to Cinder's comments. *Age before beauty? Blind in the other?* She had no further opportunity for recriminations as the cold of transitioning to the Foe stole her thoughts. A step later, it was nausea curdling her stomach then, but it too passed quickly. She moved to the side so Cinder could enter, glancing about.

The clearing was brightly lit and quiet. So was the surrounding forest. Cinder had set the world to be absent of spiderkin and to contain the full light of noon, although as usual, the source of the illumination remained indeterminate. The entire cloudless, blue sky was lit.

While waiting for him—and Anya was grateful he didn't immediately follow on her footsteps—she had time now to reconsider her actions.

Would she forever be foolish in Cinder's presence? What had she been thinking? Standing so close to him? Pleased when he made her laugh? Those weren't the actions of a proper elven woman, much less a proper elven princess.

Then again, she wasn't exactly a proper elven woman, much less a proper elven princess. She had once been human, and her past life clearly influenced her current one, persuading her to conduct herself in a manner most elves would deem inappropriate.

What was it about Cinder that caused her to utterly forget herself, to behave so rashly?

She had thought of him during her visit to Apsara Sithe, but at the time, she had been able explain it away as simply being worried for him. After all, he'd battled a powerful *aether*-cursed bear. She'd known of it. This, after all the injuries he'd suffered in the Unitary Trial.

The truth, though, was far simpler and more frightening. She liked Cinder. She liked him in a way she didn't want to admit, not even in the privacy of her thoughts. It was the way he spoke to her, listened to her, appreciated her advice. The way he made her laugh.

She had already known all this prior to this evening's meeting. She had known of it when she caught herself enjoying his company in the café a few months ago. In hindsight, she had known of it even from last year when she'd forced him to dance with her.

Thank Devesh she had sought out a relationship with Lisandre. Doing so had alleviated those treasonous emotions, and while she had behaved poorly tonight, all it meant was that she had to redouble her efforts. No matter the source of her odd feelings toward Cinder, there could be nothing but friendship for him in her heart.

Cinder stepped into the Foe, a brief grimace to indicate he felt the nausea, and then it was gone from his features when he faced her. "I meant to ask, are you still willing to sponsor me for my Secondary

Trial?"

In hindsight, Anya realized she should have never made him the promise, but she wouldn't ever think of taking it back now. She had made a public declaration that she would sponsor Cinder, and she would hold to her vow. Thankfully, Lisandre and Estin—he still planned on sponsoring her brother for his Secondary Trial—would be accompanying them, and her reputation wouldn't suffer.

"Of course," she said. "I promised I would. You defeated an elf utilizing his *lorethasra*."

Cinder's response surprised her. "Are you sure it's wise?" he asked, appearing to struggle with his words. "I don't want to sound ungrateful, but how will your people react? What will they think? You'll be alone in the wilds with me. I worry about what it might mean for you."

She found his concern for her endearing. It was sweet of him to think of her. She stepped closer to him, her arm twitching toward his hand. She wanted to take it in her own, but she held off. "I appreciate your concern," Anya said, "but remember, Lisandre and Estin will be with us. There will be no rumors spread about me."

Cinder's smile was like a sunrise. "Then I accept, even if it means I have to put up with your brother for however many months we're on the road."

It was sad how much Estin had managed to offend Cinder, a man who didn't truly hate or want to hate anyone. Or at least so she reckoned. She'd seen how he'd forgiven Riyne, the elf who had put Cinder in the infirmary twice last year. Meanwhile, Estin was nowhere near to earning that grace. Cinder continued to detest her brother, and based on his behavior, her brother deserved it. "You really don't like him, do you?"

Cinder shook his head. "He's a—" He halted.

"A jackhole?" Anya suggested.

Cinder laughed. "That's my word."

"It's not your own personal curse word," Anya chided. "I like to use it, too."

"Well, I'm sorry to say, but Estin is a jackhole, but if putting up with him means I get to train with you and Lisandre, I'll still accept your offer. I can't imagine anyone finer to teach me."

"Then as your teacher, get your shoke ready, it's time for some schooling."

Cinder offered Anya a crooked grin. "It's been months since you sparred against me," he said. "I've learned a lot since then. You sure you want to have a go against me?"

"I'll take my chances." Anya gestured him forward.

Cinder obliged, reaching for his *Jivatma*. It came more easily than ever before. More vivid and fuller, too, even compared to a few days earlier when he'd defeated Cariath. He conducted it, and his senses heightened. The Foe was brighter, sounds crisper, the caress of a soft breeze more defined, the scent of detritus and moss from the forest clearer. More importantly, his muscles twitched, ready to burst into blurring motion.

Anya became all seriousness, her brow furrowing. "Come get some learning." Her eyes flashed white.

Cinder recognized she was sourcing *lorethasra*, but he had no idea what she meant to do with it. He'd never seen a woven's eyes go white before. No helping it now. He attacked, surprising himself with how quickly he covered ground. He sent a thrust which transitioned into a knee aimed at her midsection and ended with a vertical chop.

Anya kept up with him, defending, controlled and with no unnecessary extra movement. She parried his thrust, slipped his knee, blocked his vertical strike and launched a knee of her own.

Cinder drifted right. The knee glanced off his left hip. He parried with a follow up diagonal slash. They separated.

"Is that your best?" Anya challenged, a glint in her eyes. "A Firster could do better."

Cinder took up the gauntlet. She wanted better from him? She'd have it. He swirled his shoke, reset, and feinted right. Her balance shifted. He had gotten her moving the way he wanted, and he took advantage, committing to an attack. A horizontal slash was parried. He pressed down, and her shoke dipped. It was now aimed at the ground. He twisted, coming over the top of his shoke with an elbow.

It would have cracked her jaw, but she leaned away from the blow. Her shoke slithered out from under his. Quicker than a snake, she aimed a thrust at his lead knee. He saw it coming and pulled away.

She lunged, and again, he hammered her shoke, punching it at the ground.

Cinder might have ended the maneuver by sliding his shoke against hers and slashing her fingers, but he held off. A vague disquiet alerted him. Anya's eyes went yellow, and he withdrew. Flames burst off her shoke. A whip of fire. It snapped at him.

Anya wasn't wearing a governor. Cinder had a moment of worry, but he squashed it. He trusted Anya. She'd never truly hurt him.

His belief was immediately put to the test. The whip snapped several inches from his cheek. If he hadn't moved aside, he'd have been burned.

The grass and dirt moved like a million worms sliding through the ground beneath Cinder's feet. Panic didn't set in. He simply leapt to a more settled part of the meadow. He backflipped another whip of fire, landed on his feet, and reset himself. Anya stood twenty feet away, advancing slowly.

The momentary break allowed Cinder to experience elation. Anya hadn't been able to defeat him with her skills alone. She had to resort to *lorethasra*, which meant he really had progressed far in his abilities.

"Don't be so proud of yourself," Anya chided. From one step to the next, she blurred forward, faster than his eyes could follow. Her shoke slammed at him.

From a buried part of his mind came knowledge and an instinctual response to her attack. He conducted *Jivatma*, managing to block her blow. A straight-ahead surge, and he shoulder-blocked her off-balance. At the same time, he snuck a leg behind her knee.

She tripped, losing her balance and falling. Cinder had his shoke aimed at her heart. He had the finishing blow ready. The ground trembled. He fell, losing connection with his *Jivatma* at the same time.

Get up, he urged himself.

He went to rise, but Anya got to her feet first. Her shoke rested against his neck.

Cinder dropped his head against the ground and closed his eyes. "Yield," he said with a stifled groan. The shoke was gone from his neck, but the disappointment bubbled like a pot overflowing, and it wasn't so easily reduced. He'd been so close to defeating her.

He exhaled heavily, trying to find some solace in his defeat. Yes, he'd lost, but he had done better than any other time he'd faced Anya. And next time he'd do even better. Next time he *would* win.

He opened his eyes, finding Anya grinning broadly at him, her shoke sheathed. "You have come far. Only a few elves could have matched me the way you did. Well done." She helped him rise to his feet.

He slipped his shoke into a loop in his belt, more to distract himself than any real need to do so.

Anya grinned at him, and he smiled at her in return, unable to hold onto his disappointment. Her joy was infectious, and he traced the lines of her features, finding an odd kind of comfort in their loveliness. He didn't know what it was. Maybe it had to do with the woman in his dream. The woman with whom he played music and with whom he took romantic strolls through a park. The woman who reminded him of Anya.

But so did the woman he might have murdered.

His pleasure dropped away.

Concern took over Anya's features. "What's wrong?" she asked, taking both his hands in hers.

It was an oddly intimate moment, and Cinder's heart skipped. "Nothing," he replied. "I was only wishing I had *lorethasra*. If I did, I might have won."

Anya shrugged. "I don't know. Your *Jivatma* seemed to serve you well enough. You moved faster than most elves."

"You kept up with me," Cinder reminded her. He continued to hold

Anya's hands, finding it natural to do so.

"So, it *was* your *Jivatma*." Anya sounded excited.

Cinder nodded in reply. "But like I said, it wasn't enough. You kept up with me."

"That's because I'm special," Anya said, her self-deprecating tone removing any sense of arrogance from her words.

Cinder grinned. She'd provided the perfect setup. "Special in what way? There are many ways in which you might carry such an appellation."

Anya slowly blinked in surprise before throwing her head back and laughing. When she finished, she gazed at Cinder, eyes still crinkled in amusement. "Oh, my. Someone has been studying a dictionary. I guess you think you're pretty smart."

"I don't think I'm—"

Anya cut him off. "Good. Because you're not." She shook her head in mock pity. "Asking if I'm special. I'm sure you weren't implying I'm simple."

Cinder's smile returned. "I would never do that, Simply Anya."

Anya chuckled. "That's going to cost you. Ready your shoke. Prove what you just did wasn't a fluke."

Cinder drew his weapon. "As you wish."

26

"Hurry up, Cinder," Derius shouted from the commons. "The rest of us are ready to go."

It was the evening of the Duchess's Banquet, and Cinder was nearly done getting dressed. He adjusted his collar one last time before stepping back from the full-length mirror in the hallway and studying the fit of his new clothes. As a Second, he didn't have to wear the school's uniform, and tonight he wore polished black shoes, sky-blue trousers with a matching jacket and vest, and a subtle gray shirt. A ruby-red pocket square with tracings of paisley and a cravat of similar hue and design finished off the outfit. It was a simple, yet elegant outfit, which was his best option since he couldn't afford the fancy garb the elves were sure to wear, at least he assumed they would, based on what he'd seen at last year's Winter's Gala.

"Come on, you fucking slow poke," Sriovey shouted.

"Give me a second," Cinder shouted back.

"We've given you a thousand seconds," Sriovey replied.

Cinder rolled his eyes. He was almost done. All he needed was a few final items. He pinned the ruby-eyed eagle brooch—the Directorate's symbol with precious, red gems indicating his status as the Prime—on his left chest, adjusted his sword sheathed at his waist, and gave himself a final assessment. He normally didn't preen or care about clothes, but he couldn't help it. He looked good, and he grinned at his reflection. A giggle escaped his lips, and he instantly clamped a hand over his mouth. What had gotten in him tonight? He unsealed his mouth, still grinning.

One last look in the mirror, and he went to the commons where all the Seconds were gathered. Even Wark, who was usually the slowest. They stood around, impatient expressions on all their faces.

"What took you so long?" Bones asked.

"Your mother probably wanted a goodbye kiss," Ishmay said.

Bones glared at the Gandharvan. "Shut up, asshole. It was your sister."

Ishmay laughed. "Look who's not afraid of making fun of sisters."

"Your sister is also your mother." Bones glanced at the room full of suddenly poleaxed cadets. "What? I figured if I can't beat you assholes, I might as well join you."

Cinder chuckled along with everyone else.

"Yes. Fine," Ishmay said to Bones. "But saying my sister is my mother doesn't make any sense."

"Your sister doesn't make any sense."

Ishmay groaned. "We've created a monster."

"Happy with your clothes?" Mohal asked Cinder.

"They fit," Cinder said, trying to sound modest. He dropped into a full squat, demonstrating his ease of movement.

"I don't care about your stupid clothes," Sriovey said. He and the dwarves were outfitted in their typical, high-fashion garb of a brightly colored achkan, matching trousers, and braided beards and hair. "Let's go eat."

A ludicrous idea formed in Cinder's mind, one so out of character for him that he had to go with it. "You worried the food might jump up and run away?" he asked Sriovey.

"Of course, I don't think—"

"Silence! It doesn't matter what you think!"

The room held quiet for a single moment before everyone burst into laughter. Cinder laughed the hardest, especially on catching Sriovey open-mouthed expression of disbelief.

"Asshole," the dwarf finally said. "Now if you ladies are done screwing around, there's food waiting to be eaten."

They left the commons as a unit, heading for the duchess's palace— Granthim Hill. They met a few other travelers along the way—carriages only—and the Seconds stepped to the side when one of them appeared. Eventually, they reached a winding road edged by large, mature cedars leading to a long lawn of grass that was overseen by topiary in the form of dragons, unicorns, and other mythical creatures. From there, the pathway ended at a semi-circular drive where carriages disgorged the high society of Certitude. From the sedate, black vehicles emerged elves dressed in garments more akin to plumage than clothes.

"I think we're under-dressed," Bones whispered to Cinder as they approached the palace.

"It's not any different than last year," Cinder replied. "Besides, we're only here as a courtesy. We're not here to actually see or be seen."

"You're right," Estin interrupted. "You are here as a courtesy. So be courteous. Eat the food provided. Stay out of the way, and for Devesh's sake, do not dance with my sister. She is meant for a prince of the blood."

"Now hold on. First of all, she asked me to dance last year, not the other way around. What was I supposed to do, tell the princess no?" Cinder scoffed. "How stupid do you think I am?"

"You don't want to know."

Cinder shook his head when Estin moved off. Of course Anya was meant for an elven prince? Who else could she possibly marry? And why in Devesh's name was Estin idiotic enough to think he needed the reminder.

Bones chuckled. "I think the prince has a problem with sisters, too."

"So, you admit you have a problem," Ishmay asked, standing close by.

"Yes. Your sister gets lonely without me."

"You jackhole," Ishmay muttered.

"Now don't go using those made-up curse words," Sriovey said.

"It fits," Ishmay said to him.

"Fits like my boot up your ass," Sriovey said.

"Shut it," Cinder told them. "We're here. No more cursing." He caught Estin listening in and shot the elf a wry smile. "We wouldn't want to be discourteous."

Estin muttered something coarse under his breath, but the rest of the Seconds quieted. They climbed a set of wide, semicircular stairs that ended at a pair of open double doors large enough to allow in a herd of horses. At the top of the steps waited an elf wearing black pants, a black coat, white shirt, white gloves, and a self-important air. He glanced them over, clearly recognized Estin, and his stiff demeanor softened somewhat.

They were quickly ushered inside and joined a line of other attendees waiting to enter the ballroom. The women wore colorful saris and necklaces and earrings of heavy gold and precious gems along with jasmine garlands braided into their hair. The men were outfitted in garments every bit as bright. They had tiny mirrors sewn as part of the piping along the sides of their pants and coats, and they, too, wore expensive jewelry. And like last year, they also wore sharply pointed shoes that appeared very uncomfortable.

It was a vast flashing of plumage, bright and vivid enough to put an ostentation of peacocks to shame.

They continued on, following a sinuous line of elves who traced a path through halls floored in white marble tiles and softened by costly rugs. The ceiling soared several dozen feet overhead and bore a plethora of lit chandeliers. A final left-hand turn, and they reached the ballroom where another self-important elf loudly announced their presence.

"He's the one in the sky-blue colored suit," Duchess Cervine noted to the elf standing next to her.

"I see him," said the other elf, a much older woman but still spry based on the clarity and sharpness of her eyes.

"Find out all you can."

The older elf gazed at the duchess in exasperation. "I know what you need," she said, clearly annoyed. "Or would you rather do this yourself?"

For a wonder, the duchess bent her head, a subtle bow. "My apologies, auntie."

The old elf's irritation wiped away, and she patted the duchess's cheek. "You're sweet, Marielle, but you worry too much."

A half-dozen steps extended from the ballroom's entrance and ended at the floor of the cavernous space where hundreds of people talked, mingled, laughed, or danced. Since this was one of the grand galas of the year, of course the cream of elven society in Certitude and its environs would be here. How else would they be noticed by their lessers and peers, but most especially their betters.

Cinder gazed about, taking in other details. The ballroom appeared unchanged from when he had been here at last year's Winter Gala. Gold filigree decorated every nook and cranny in the area, a display he found tasteless. The coffered ceiling, however, he found lovely. It soared over fifty feet above them and contained vast murals depicting scenes from nature: a desert transitioning into the sea, which then ended on a rugged, forested shore. On the right, there were also the regularly spaced arched doorways bracketed by classically grooved columns and entablatures decorated with images of animals. The openings led to various parts of the palace, such as large alcoves or small rooms. In those spaces, business was done by serious seeming elves locked in deep discussions.

Cinder paid them no mind. Their business ventures held no interest for him, and he doubted his martial prowess held any interest for them.

He continued his study. On the far end of the space was a bank of tall windows and glass doors. However, with darkness falling, and the ballroom lit so brightly, they became mirrors, and nothing could be seen of the world beyond them. Cinder remembered there was a wide, deep balcony outside the banquet hall.

His perusal continued, and he noticed one difference from last year. It involved the large fireplaces lining the left-hand wall. They were tall enough for Cinder to easily step into them, and during the Winter Gala, they had blazed with logs the size of small trees. Currently, with spring nearly upon them, the fireplaces were dormant.

"Food," Bones moaned, gesturing to a laden table.

Cinder's mouth thinned. Bones' single declaration triggered a sad state of déjà vu. Last year, Rorian had been the first to notice the food, and he'd reacted in the exact same way.

"Remember what I said," Estin said. "Behave yourself and don't dance with anyone."

"We know what to do," Cinder said, irritated with the prince. He shooed Estin away. "Now run along. Some of us want to eat."

"Damn straight," Sriovey muttered.

"Just don't be an ass," the prince hissed.

Cinder nodded. "Got it. Don't behave like you."

Estin reddened. "You're hopeless," he finally said, spinning about and leaving them.

The elven Seconds, all dressed as gaudily as the rest of their kind, moved off to join him, although Mohal and Cariath gave Cinder a sad smile and a shrug of their shoulders. Riyne appeared on the verge of saying something, but instead, he muttered to himself and trailed after the prince.

Derius quietly chuckled next to Cinder. "You weren't very kind to him just then."

"Does he deserve my kindness?" Cinder asked, unable to feel guilty for how he'd spoken to Estin.

"Aren't you the one always talking to us about fraternity?" Sriovey asked.

"In battle, all men are brothers," Cinder agreed. "But this isn't a battle, and even brothers argue."

"Still," Derius pressed. "I think you could have been nicer to him."

Cinder's annoyance flared. "I'll be kinder when he apologizes for what he did to me last year. Until then, I'll be *exactly* what he thinks I am."

"But a warrior worthy of the name wouldn't treat their brothers with such contempt," an old elf said, sidling up to their group. She smiled at Cinder. "I didn't mean to interrupt, but I couldn't help but overhear your conversation."

Cinder had never met the old woman before. She was elderly, likely in her fifth or sixth century, with cheeks standing prominent amidst a face holding a riot of wrinkles. Her hair was white and collected in an imposing bun. But despite her fragile build, her blue eyes were bright and clear as she gazed at Cinder, viewing him frankly.

Before he could say anything to her, the old woman turned away from him and addressed the rest of the Seconds. "It's good to see you gentlemen. I'm glad you were able to attend my niece's little gathering."

Cinder inhaled sharply. He knew who she was now. Duchess Simone Trementh. The dowager duchess of Arraya. Duchess Cervine's aunt.

The elderly elf pointed to the table piled high with food. "There are some truly delicious strawberries for those interested."

"Go on. I'll catch up later," Cinder said to his fellow Seconds. The old elf obviously wanted to talk to him alone. After they left, he addressed her. "It's a pleasure meeting you, Your Grace."

"Please call me Simone," the dowager duchess said, smiling warmly at him. "You're surprisingly well informed. I didn't expect that."

Cinder shrugged, not knowing how to reply. He caught the faint fragrance of her lavender-scented perfume when she leaned closer.

Her voice fell into a stage whisper. "Tell no one you've discovered my identity. I'm on a secret mission."

Cinder smiled, charmed by the duchess. "What kind of secret mission?"

"To learn all I can about you," Simone declared.

Cinder viewed her in surprise. "You know who I am?"

Simone chuckled. "False modesty becomes no one. Every elf in Certitude knows who you are. You are Cinder Shade, the first human to ever win the Grand Melee, and now confirmed as the Prime of the Seconds."

Cinder nodded. "Guilty as charged."

Simone smiled at him again, as if he was a long-lost friend. "I like you, Cinder Shade. You have a pretty name. It fits you. Now go take out the garbage."

She tittered, and Cinder couldn't help but laugh along with her. The request was patently absurd, and he could tell she didn't mean it.

Anya stood in an island of calm in the banquet hall, a glass of red wine in hand. The quality of the drink surprised her, containing an excellent blend of honey, citrus, and earthy oak notes under the bitterness of the tannin. Some might have guessed the wine came from the famed vineyards of Sern, long the seat of the world's finest wineries, but it wasn't the case. This vintage came from Rakesh, in a small vineyard north of Swift Sword, grown in a valley situated in some strangely perfect locale of mountains, wind, and rain, where the climate and soil supported the proper kind of grapes.

Anya took another sip of her wine, watching as the attendees swirled around her. For now, she had a small cone of quiet, but it would shatter soon enough. There were always people who would need her aid on some matter or another, and she was happy enough to help them.

It was the sycophants she detested. Men and women who only desired her company for the fame it might bring them. She had little patience for them, although she'd grown accustomed to their fawning presence. Over the years, she'd learned to respond to their ingratiating attitudes with bland phrases of possible agreement.

For now, they had yet to discover her presence, and she had a moment of privacy. She watched as Lisandre, her escort for the ball, danced with a local noble, Aowhin Rohal, a lovely young woman. Anya had only spoken to her on a few occasions, but she was clearly intelligent, and there was also a kindness to her. Aowhin loved small cats, and in Anya's estimation, anyone who liked cats had to have a sweet disposition. She might also make a good match for Lisandre as an actual wife if he only had the wit to notice the young woman's charms and talents.

She watched the pair swirl about the dance floor, seeming to be enjoying themselves. *Good.* She made a mental note to learn more about Aowhin. She only had a vague sense of her ancestry, parentage, and wealth, and the information was necessary to determine if Lisandre was worthy of the young woman.

Anya's gaze drifted about the room, and she noticed Simone speaking to Cinder. Her eyes narrowed. Simone was a grandmotherly appearing woman with a grandmother's warmth and love. She had always been kind to Anya, even approving of her attendance at the Directorate when many others wanted to see her gone. That first year at the academy hadn't been a good one. Harsh and cold were how her fellow cadets had treated her, but she'd persevered, and in large part due to the support of Simone.

Anya frowned as she watched the old dowager shuffle alongside Cinder, clutching his arm as she laughed at something he said. Her frame was frail, but the centuries hadn't diminished Simone's sharp mind and keen insight. Her blue eyes remained bright and curious, and right now, they were locked on Cinder, appearing as if she was trying to decipher him, just like she had so many others over the years.

People were a puzzle for Simone. She enjoyed understanding who they were, learning their past, their truths, even the ones they didn't like to tell anyone. In her many, many decades of life, Simone had become quite adept at ferreting out those secrets.

In fact, the dowager was the only person who knew of Anya's dreams of a previous life.

Anya started. She had nearly forgotten about that decades-ago conversation with Simone. It had been shortly after her arrival at the academy. Anya had been lonely. As the first and only woman to matriculate into the Third Directorate, she had known the path she had chosen was a solitary one, but knowing wasn't the same as experiencing it. And she'd learned quickly enough, especially when her fellow cadets jeered at her every mistake and refused any attempt to bond with her.

The stinging rebuke of isolation had been a knife, and it was Simone who had somehow drawn out a younger Anya's pain, listening patiently as she spoke of the hardships she endured. The dowager's mere presence had been a balm, and in the course of their conversations, for reasons Anya still couldn't explain, she'd told Simone of her dreams.

Later on, a more mature Anya regretted revealing those visions to the dowager, but at least her younger self hadn't foolishly explained her certainty that the dreams were actually memories from a past life.

And now the dowager stalked Cinder. He didn't know it yet, but it was the truth. Before the evening was through, Simone would learn all of Cinder's secrets.

Anya smiled in pity for him.

"Something amuses you?" Lisandre asked. He and Aowhin had rejoined her side.

Anya didn't feel like explaining, and she merely shook her head. "Just a stray thought."

She shot another glance at Cinder and Simone. Poor Cinder. He really had no idea what was happening. When Simone had her prey in sight, she was impossible to dislodge. She became a hunting cat, a Kesarin.

Anya's brow furrowed at the odd word choice.

Cinder caught the Seconds staring at him in consternation and confusion as he gently guided Simone through the crowd of people at the gala.

He understood the reason for their incredulity. This was his second grand ball at the duchess's palace, and his second time spent in the company of a female member of Yaksha Sithe's high nobility. Last year, it had been Anya. This year, it was Simone, the dowager duchess of Arraya.

It gave him pause, the inordinate interest others had in him. Made him wary, actually, since it wasn't only the elves who had an inordinate interest. He hadn't missed the various times Sriovey and Derius had stared at him, their faces pensive and considering when they had no reason to be. Nor had he forgotten his meeting with the yakshin in Swift Sword when the tree maiden had named him Maynalor—*someone of interest with a secret*. Or Maize, the troll last year who had recognized him. Many of the woven seemed to see something in him, something he himself didn't know.

But he had his suspicions.

They sensed a difference about him, and possibly an aspect beyond merely a notion that he could source his *lorethasra*. Thankfully, none of them knew about his dreams of a past life, and he planned on keeping it that way.

"You seem distracted, dear," Simone said.

Cinder smiled at her. "I was thinking how lucky I am to be here."

The dowager laughed softly. "Really? Most humans find my kind supercilious and overbearing."

Cinder chuckled in reply. "Are you trying to imply elves are arrogant?"

Simone grinned and poked him gently in the side with her elbow. "I'm fairly certain I said *exactly* that." As if in demonstration of her observation, she gestured to a pair of elves—two men—holding a loud conversation, one they clearly meant to have overheard by those standing close at hand. The elves spoke of a business venture and the money needed to fund it. The cost was jaw-dropping, but the breezy manner in which they discussed the price, as if it was of no account, told Cinder all he needed to know about their quality: gauche and narcissistic.

"Two of our finest," Simone said, her voice carrying and her expression contemptuous.

The two men in question glanced their way. They reddened in either embarrassment, anger or both, before bowing to the dowager and swiftly departing.

On watching them leave, Cinder's misgivings at Simone's motives faded some. He couldn't entirely mistrust someone who had such little patience for fools. And at her age, she no longer had to maintain the fiction of requiring society's approval. Which was probably why she had sought him out tonight. She was curious about him. Many elves were, and he hoped that was the extent of her interest as well.

Cinder couldn't entirely tell.

"What did you think of those two?" Simone asked, returning his attention to the departed businessmen. "And be honest." Her eyes twinkled with suppressed mirth, as if she already could guess how Cinder would answer.

Cinder chose his words carefully. In the presence of unknown elves, he wasn't rash enough to speak too harshly of their people, no matter how kindly they seemed. "I think they enjoy the fame of their wealth."

"A kind way of saying you think them vain."

Cinder grinned, not taking the bait. "I said no such thing."

Again came the poke in his side. "You were *thinking* it but clever enough not to voice it. Don't be afraid to speak the truth to me." She pointed to a woman in her middle years. "What of her?"

Cinder viewed the woman in question. She was stately and grand in the way she carried herself, but he noted a tightening at the corners of the woman's eyes. Sadness maybe. He was about to speak his impressions, but he hesitated in doing so. What did the dowager really want with him? "Why do you care what I think of any elf?"

"Humor me," Simone said, still smiling. "I'm old and tired, and I like to hear the thinking of the young."

Cinder considered her answer. It was a possible explanation, but he doubted it covered the extent of her curiosity about him. But what harm was there in doing as she asked? He more closely studied the woman Simone had pointed out, scrutinizing the manner in which she walked and stood, looking past the surface. The woman was lovely like all elves. Elegant in her carriage, gentle in her smiles, but tension ridged her back and shoulders. And there was the previously noticed unhappiness lurking in her eyes.

"She is beautiful, but she doesn't want to be here. Despises it."

"You are correct. She doesn't want to be here," Simone said in soft agreement. "Her father was a blacksmith. Her mother a maid at the Directorate. She married her father's apprentice, who has a cunning wisdom when it comes to investing. They are wealthy now, but newly rich, which means they remain on the fringes of high society. Banished for not being of nobler lineage. However, because of their wealth, they are also expected to attend these types of functions, no matter how poorly they are treated."

"It's sad. They're trapped by their money."

"It is sad, but there is hope." Simone pointed to Lisandre who danced with a lovely young woman. "Their daughter will find herself in a bidding war. Young men from all over Yaksha will offer themselves as her husband. Her parents' cruel dismissal from high society will shortly end."

They continued their meandering path, Simone greeting well-wishers now and then, and Cinder noted the speculative glances imperceptibly aimed at him, a mix of curiosity, deliberation, and annoyance.

"You don't miss much, do you?" the dowager asked after one such greeting.

Cinder eyed her sidelong. "You don't miss much either."

She chuckled. "I'm old. I've learned some tricks over the centuries." She halted and gazed up at him. "But what about you? You're an enigma. Tell me something about yourself."

Cinder mentally shrugged, seeing little harm in telling her about his past. "I was born in a village called Swallow."

Simone nodded. "I know, but I was hoping for something more personal."

Cinder smiled. "Is there anything more personal than where I come from?"

"Your past is merely biography. As soon as you won the Grand Melee, agents of the crown verified every aspect of your history." The dowager peered at him intently. "We may know more about your past than you know yourself."

Cinder tried not to show his shock. He had no idea the empress might have sent people to delve into his past. Had they actually visited Swallow? Did they know about his clubfoot? That he'd died? His loss of memories?

"So, what did you learn?" he asked after a moment.

Simone ticked off the items she apparently knew on her fingers. "Clubfoot. You died. You don't remember your past. Your martial prowess is extraordinary and only matched by how extraordinarily fast you mastered them."

Cinder's distrust about her motives surged. "If you know all that, then you know everything," he said, unwilling to reveal anything else about himself.

The dowager's lips pursed in a moue of annoyance. "We know nothing. How your past impacts you as a person is the personal, and in this, you are an enigma."

Cinder wasn't sure what the purpose of tonight's conversation was, but he was tired of the dancing about. "Why did you really want to speak to me tonight?"

"Such suspicion," the dowager tutted with a shake of her head. "As I said, you're an enigma, and no one likes puzzles like an old person." She grinned at him. "But the true reason I wanted to speak to you tonight was to provide you an honest means to talk to your mentor."

They approached a group of people crowded around someone. A trace of cinnamon alerted Cinder who he would see when the crowd opened.

"Hello, Anya," Simone said. "I believe you know Cinder Shade."

27

Kesarin. It had been a long time since she'd heard the word. It indicated a species of cat, a gigantic species if the myths were to be believed. Shokan and Sira were each known to have such an animal as a companion, although Anya could never recall their names. While she tried to remember, in her mind rose the image of a giant cat, one whose head overtopped her own. This one was tawny in color and enjoyed being scratched at the base of his ears.

"Does something trouble you, Your Highness?" Aowhin asked.

The image popped like a soap bubble, and Anya forged a smile. "Nothing of importance. Why don't you and Lisandre share another dance."

"Are you sure?" Aowhin asked.

She noticed Lisandre also viewing her skeptically. "I'm sure," Anya said, maintaining her bright smile. She needed a few moments to gather her thoughts, to understand why she had thought of the word *Kesarin*, and why when doing so, she had pictured the massive, tawny cat. "Go and enjoy yourselves. I'll be along shortly." She gestured to a group of elves heading her way—sycophants. She hid a grimace upon seeing them. "Besides, it looks like some people would like a word with me."

Lisandre and Aowhin smiled in wry sympathy before returning to the dance floor.

After they left, Anya cut a diagonal path away from the approaching sycophants. She wanted a few seconds of quiet, but it was not to be.

"Your Highness," a voice intruded. "It's so good to see you again."

Anya grimaced, but schooled her features into a pleasant smile as she rounded upon a middle-aged elf, a supposed diplomat. Trailing him like a rafter of turkeys bobbed a group of businessmen.

The sycophants had arrived.

On entering the hall, Cinder had noticed Anya straightaway. She was hard to miss, taller than any other woman here, but that wasn't the reason his eyes had gone to her. It was who she was as a person, including her beauty, and her outfit only enhanced that loveliness. She wore a green, silk sari edged in silver gulabi and a matching choli. The sari's end piece transitioned to a honey-gold that matched the luster of Anya's hair, the mass of which was piled atop her head and cascaded like a waterfall to her shoulders. A silver tikka with a diamond and emerald setting and matching earrings and necklace completed her outfit.

A pack of elves had been gathered around her when Simone greeted her, and afterward, they quickly dispersed, some muttering in disappointment. Cinder caught a few of them complaining about how they had been denied a chance to speak to the princess. They shot him annoyed glances. Same with Simone, but they only did so to her when her back was to them.

Anya smiled at them after the crowd left. "Hello, to you as well, grandmother," she said to the dowager. "And you also," she added to Cinder.

"I've hardly seen you at all since your return to Certitude," Simone said.

"I know, and I apologize. I've been busy."

Simone's eyes went to Lisandre. He had been dancing with Aowhin Rohal, but now he stood at a distance, in the midst of a conversation with a group of warriors, evident by the swords belted at their waist. Among them were Riyne and Estin. A knowing smirk formed on Simone's lips. "Is that what they call it these days?"

The words triggered a flash of jealousy, and Cinder beat it back. It wasn't his place to be jealous of Anya and Lisandre. While forcing his emotions under control, he made sure to display no more than a mild smirk. Allowing anyone to know he might have felt even the tiniest smidgeon of jealousy for the princess could prove catastrophic.

Anya laughed at the dowager duchess's comment. "You can't make me feel embarrassment like you once did. I am busy, but it isn't only to do with Lisandre." She abruptly shifted the conversation. "How is your hip?"

Simone grimaced. "At my age, the hip always bothers me. Hips, knees, shoulders, hands… They all ache. Which is as good a segue as any." She faced Cinder. "It was a pleasure speaking to you, young man, but I think I need to rest my feet." Cinder made to help her, but she waved him off. "I can make it across a hall on my own."

Cinder remained concerned for the elderly woman. He had felt the thinness of her skin and bones, her frailty. One fall could be dangerous. "Are you sure?"

Simone graced him with a smile and patted his hand. "I'm fine. Enjoy the princess' company." She hobbled off before he could say another word.

Cinder watched her go, wanting to make sure she arrived at her destination without any difficulty.

"She's not made of crystal," Anya said, although she was also closely watching Simone. "In fact, she'll likely outlive both of us and any children we have."

Cinder's head to riveted around to her. *Children we have.* It took him a bit to understand her meaning.

Anya laughed at his response. "Clearly you've been drinking too much if you thought I meant *our* children together."

"I wish I could blame it on drink," Cinder replied, morosely. "This time, it was just me being stupid."

Anya continued to grin, amused by him. "Admitting you're stupid? Are you sure you want to do that, especially to someone you tease as being simple?"

Cinder grinned back at her. "You wouldn't tease me back, would you?"

"Oh. Now you think I should let your years-long teasing go unanswered? Is that how it works?"

"Two years. We've only been together for two years."

"We're not together," Anya said pointedly.

Cinder rolled his eyes. "You know what I mean. We've only known each other for two years."

Anya took a sip of wine and smiled at him over the lip of her glass. "Our children?" She chuckled softly.

Cinder groaned. "You're going to remind me of that for years to come, aren't you?"

Anya grinned. "Not years. Decades. In the decades and even centuries to come, whenever we're still together, I'll remind you."

She realized what she'd said an instant after the statements left her lips. *Still together.*

Thankfully, Cinder didn't seem to notice her slip. "We're not together," he said, using her own words against her.

Anya rolled her eyes. "You know what I meant." She peered at him intently. "You did know what I meant, right?" she said, as if he were a simpleton. "Because sometimes—"

"I got it," Cinder growled.

"—you make the wrong assumption."

"I said I got it."

Anya chuckled. She was enjoying herself. Whenever she and Cinder had a conversation, only rarely did she have an opportunity to poke fun at him.

A wistful longing settled over Cinder's features. "We won't know each other for centuries. I won't live that long."

Anya had forgotten, and an emptiness filled her. Cinder was human. He had perhaps another dozen years before age would start wearing away at his body. Another twenty, and he'd slow down. Fifty, and he'd be considered an old man.

She hated the notion of seeing Cinder broken-bodied and elderly. It didn't sit right with her. In her mind, Cinder would always be young, should always be young, or at least the same age as her.

A melancholy silence fell over their conversation, and Anya tried to lighten the mood. "Then in the years to come, I'll tease you."

"Didn't we agree you wouldn't tease me?"

Anya arched an eyebrow. "We did no such thing."

"We should. You're much older than me. Ancient almost."

"Careful now."

"And with age comes wisdom, right?" Cinder's eyes twinkled.

"Your point?" Anya asked, glad to see Cinder's brief bout of ennui dissipate.

"It's said that the elderly overlook the foibles of the youth."

Anya sighed as if praying for patience. "First, I'm not elderly, and second, no one says that."

"Your Highness," a voice intruded on their conversation. It belonged to an elegantly dressed man. He wore a gray suit, a black vest, and a white shirt. A red tie was his only capitulation to a bright color. In a blustering gathering of those dressed in the visual equivalent of a cacophony, the man was a calm harbor.

Anya could tell Cinder approved of the man's modest attire. Then again, he didn't know Bardon Dumbes like she did. Pompous, egotistical, and stupid were the kindest words to describe him.

"Bardon Dumbes," Anya said, plastering a patently false smile on her face. "What a joy to see you again. I thought you were still in Revelant."

Somehow, Bardon missed the lack of cheer in her voice or the lack of sincerity in her smile. Instead, he grinned at her—leered really— leaning forward as if to release a great secret.

"How could I miss the Duchess's Banquet?" he asked. "Especially when I learned you would be in attendance. I dropped all my business matters forthwith and rushed back to Certitude."

Anya made a vague noise of agreement. "Have you met Cinder Shade?" she asked by way of introduction.

Cinder held out his hand in greeting.

Bardon flicked the proffered hand a disgusted glance and promptly ignored Cinder, speaking directly to Anya. "They should know their place and cease their noisome and vulgar bothering of their betters."

Anya closed her eyes, and this time she truly did pray for peace. She hoped Cinder wouldn't take offense from this fool's words.

She opened her eyes and found Cinder staring at Bardon; not in anger, but rather in astonishment. Cinder surprised her by laughing at Bardon. "Please tell me that's not your best insult."

Bardon rounded on Cinder in a flash. "If I wanted to insult you, boy, you'd know it. I'd have you whipped from one end of Certitude to the other."

Anya saw Cinder's eyes flick to the sword sheathed at Bardon's hip. A more useless weapon, she could have never imagined. The scabbard and hilt more than made up for the man's sedate outfit. They were crusted in gems and fanciful touches of gold. Add in the round handle and use of the weapon would be perilous.

"You actually know how to use your pigsticker?" Cinder asked.

Bardon drew himself up, outraged. "How dare you," he hissed. "I will have satisfaction."

Again, Anya prayed for patience. Why did Bardon have to seek her out right now, in this very hour, when she was talking to Cinder and enjoying herself?

Satisfaction was a byword for a duel, and as much as she would enjoy seeing Bardon receive his comeuppance—for a shining moment, she imagined Cinder beating Bardon senseless—she couldn't allow it.

Bardon was a fool, but he was a rich and noble fool. A man of importance. He had a strong voice at her amma's—*Wait. What's an amma?*
Anya shook off the stray thought. At her *mother's* court.

"Cinder won the Grand Melee last year," Anya said to Bardon, her
voice quiet. "He recently defended his position as Prime."

Bardon's gaze shot to her. "Truly? This is the human?"

"I mentioned his name when I introduced him to you."

Bardon paled, staring at Anya as if to catch her in a lie. "I see." He
faced Cinder and bowed. "I am most sorry if you were offended by
whatever words I used."

As an apology, it was sorely lacking, but Cinder seemed to allow it.
Apparently, he felt arguing with the pompous man wasn't worth his
trouble. "I'm sure you were thinking of someone else when you said
what you did."

As an acceptance of an apology, it was also lacking.

Anya shrugged. So be it. As long as no further trouble resulted from
the conversation.

Bardon bowed again, this time to Anya, mumbling something under his breath about thirst, and wandered off.

"What did you say his name was?" Cinder asked.

"Bardon Dumbes."

Cinder stroked his chin as if lost in thought. "I think he was named
correctly. "Dumb, dumber, dumbes."

Anya laughed, delighted by Cinder's made-up declension. "I always
went for the more obvious insult myself. Dumbass."

Duchess Cervine searched out the ballroom, and discovered her aunt
seated in an alcove, a drink in hand and her cane leaned against the
wall. There was a matching chair placed diagonal to the dowager and a
small table set between them.

The duchess took the other chair. "What did you learn?" she asked
without preamble.

"I learned some interesting tidbits," Simone said, "but not enough, not as much as I expected."

The duchess waited on a further explanation, and when one wasn't forthcoming, she scowled in annoyance. "Am I supposed to guess?"

Her aunt shot her a sharp glance. "No. But you are supposed to know how to be patient. There is more to Cinder Shade than I reckoned. I am still formulating my views about him."

The duchess leaned back into her chair, pensive and surprised by the unexpected answer. "In what way?"

"He is smart. Much brighter than I expected. Intelligent enough to pay heed to his cautions. Cunning. He isn't one to charge blindly into a situation."

The duchess frowned. Her own intelligence about Cinder indicated he was a dedicated warrior, studious as well, given the amount of time he spent in the library. But cunning? This was new. "What makes you say so?"

"He verified the history we have on him and was upset that we knew so much about his past. But a second later, he had his emotions under control. He didn't bother trying to explain away matters. He simply accepted my knowledge and moved on. It was a mature handling of the situation." Simone grimaced. "There is more. I sourced *lorethasra*, used it to make him believe me nothing more than a fragile, old woman—"

"You are a fragile old woman." The duchess smiled when the dowager scowled at her.

"Thank you for the helpful reminder," her aunt said, her voice sour, "I wanted Cinder's trust, and I never fully captured it."

The duchess raised her brow in surprise. "Few elves can overcome your *lorethasra*. Few even know when you're sourcing it." She waved a hand about in a vague indication of the soft lavender-scent in the air around her aunt, the aroma most accepted as the dowager's perfume. "No human should be able to either."

"And he didn't, but he also didn't fall sway to it. It seems General Arwan's warnings about Cinder Shade may be true."

"You think he can source *lorethasra*?" The duchess found her heart pounding. Very few humans had been able to do so since the *NusraelShev*, and only then on rare occasions and never willfully. Of course, there were the cursed rishis of Bharat, who claimed to wield *Jivatma*, but the duchess and the *Lamarin Hosh* knew the truth. The Bharatians weren't entirely human, and it was *lorethasra* they sourced. Could Cinder be of their breed?

"He's not a rishi, a sorcerer," Simone said, as if she could read the duchess's mind. "His skin—"

"Is odd. The hue. It's not the same as what's found in Rakesh. Nor is it from any part of Gandharva. Maybe the Savage Kingdoms," the duchess mused. "Along the borders of the WraithLands. There are some there who are said to share Cinder's coloration."

"Yes," Simone agreed, "but what I was going to say about Cinder's skin is that it doesn't contain the telltale blue undertone of a rishi."

"Then what is he?"

"A mysterious man who can partially defy my *lorethasra*, and I never scented his own."

The duchess exhaled slowly. Her aunt's information changed matters considerably. "We need to learn all we can about him."

"I spoke to Bardon. He confronted Cinder, just as I requested."

"Bardon." The duchess knew she spoke the man's name like it was a mild curse.

"He's good at his job."

"To act the fool?"

"To go unnoticed," the dowager corrected. "He did what I asked, learned what I wanted."

"Which is?" the duchess asked, annoyed afresh having to beg for answers.

"He approached Anya while she was engaged in conversation with Cinder. He believes the princess feels protective toward the human."

"And Anya truly plans on taking him with her on his Secondary Trial?"

"So, I've been told," her aunt replied.

A plan formed, and the duchess smiled. "Then we can still learn what we must. We'll have someone keep an eye on him."

"Who did you have in mind?'

"Someone loyal to *the Lamarin Hosh*. Someone loyal since child-hood. Someone who'll be close to Cinder Shade for months on end as a member of his Secondary Trial. Someone whose greatest dream is to serve Shokan."

Simone harrumphed in annoyance. "I know you mean to sound mysterious, but we both know who you are talking about, and he will hate it."

"Yes, he will." The duchess nodded, her gaze going to Estin. The prince was in the midst of dancing with the daughter of the mayor of Certitude, laughing in the carefree fashion of the young.

"Tell him after the Firmament Hour," Simone advised. "Let him have some joy."

"He'll have his joy," the duchess agreed. "Just as he has a duty to the *Lamarin Hosh*."

28

"Today's the day," Estin said, sounding as excited and bubbly as a little schoolboy. It was a few mornings after the Duchess's Banquet, and the prince was grinning broadly, all but bouncing in his seat. "The sun is shining, the cafeteria is clean, and we'll soon find out where we're heading for our Secondary Trials."

Upon hearing the prince's comments, Cinder did a double take. *Who is Estin addressing? Me?* It looked like he was, and Cinder nearly fell out of his chair in shock. Since when did Estin Aruyen ever start a conversation with him? He peered at the prince in suspicion.

The two of them sat at a table with the rest of the Seconds, all of them sharing a late-morning breakfast in the cafeteria since classes were cancelled for the day. No one else was about, except for a few servers sweeping and cleaning the room. Otherwise, this was a private meal, one consisting of some of Cinder's favorites, such as idli with sambar, spiced egg casserole, and masala dosa.

The food smelled divine and Cinder had been about to tuck into his heaping plateful when Estin had spoken to him.

It was as the prince said. Today was Firmament Hour, the morning when the Seconds would have confirmation of who had sponsored them for their Secondary Trial. In a short time, General Arwan and his staff would arrive to provide the official paperwork.

Of course, little of what would happen today was a mystery. The morning ceremony was essentially perfunctory. Everyone knew where they were going.

The Directorate had strong, longstanding relations with the various armies and nations along their borders, and agreements were etched in stone for members of the academy to train alongside those forces. And while rarely a human might join Surent Crèche's War Collegium, or a dwarf the High Army of Rakesh, in general during the Secondary Trial all the races trained alongside their own kind.

And this year was generally no different.

All of Cinder's fellow humans had already applied for and been accepted as scouts with the High Army of Rakesh where they would train under the tutelage of seasoned veterans. The dwarves had a similar arrangement with the grizzled commanders of their War Collegium. And, of course, the elves would all be paired with rangers—the elite members of the Imperial Army—those agreements having been hammered out over the past few months.

All of them had spoken about it, everyone sharing their plans, and Cinder had never lied about his own intentions. How could he when everyone knew of Anya's proposition? It had led to several interesting discussions in the commons room.

The elves had been tactful in their response, but it was clear they disapproved. Despite how they viewed Cinder as a brother warrior, most—if not all—considered it repugnant for an elven woman to spend months alone in the wilderness with a human man. The dwarves, on the other hand, were less vocal in their concerns. In fact, they didn't seem to care one way or another. As for the humans, they had listened in silence during most of the conversation, appearing unsure what to make of it, although Cinder saw them shoot him looks of apprehension.

Estin had remained incensed throughout the entire matter, which wasn't a surprise. He'd complained bitterly about the shame Anya was incurring, the ruin to her reputation. But when reminded that he and Cinder would be sharing their Secondary Trials to prevent such a ruin, his anger went combustible. Estin had raged about the unfairness of it, how it was demeaning to train alongside a "crippled human."

It had taken an immense amount of self-control for Cinder not to punch Estin in the mouth when he had said the last.

For this reason, upon hearing the prince's question, Cinder had flicked him an uncertain glance. Had something changed? Did Estin know something different? Had Anya changed her mind? Was that the reason for Estin's good mood?

Cinder had trouble believing it. Anya had confirmed her decision to him, spoken of it directly, and she wasn't the type of person who would break a promise. Only if her family or Lisandre demanded it could he imagine her not keeping her vow. And if she had, wouldn't she have told Cinder first?

Unless her hand had been forced by her imperial mother, and she wasn't allowed to. Cinder could imagine such a scenario.

He swallowed heavily. His nerves had sweat beading on his brow and his heart racing. There was nothing he could do about it now. He stared at the closed doors through which General Arwan and his staff should soon arrive, hoping to see them show up more quickly.

Derius provided a distraction when he addressed the room at large. "We'll learn about our future, but I can't say I'm excited."

"Why not?" Riyne asked, appearing genuinely curious.

It was Jozep who answered. "Because we'll be sent out into the world, and given how tough the Unitary and Autumn Trials have been, who knows how many of us might return."

"Well, I plan on making it home," Estin said, sounding certain of himself.

Cinder mentally cursed. The fragging prince definitely knew something. That confident grin wasn't because Estin's sponsor was Lisandre, one of the very best of the rangers. His cockiness had to be because of some other reason.

But what?

Cinder didn't know. He had spent the time after the Unchained Trial striving to make peace with the notion of spending months on end with Estin. He wondered now if it had all been a waste of time.

He mentally cursed again.

This might be the most embarrassing Firmament Hour in the history of the Directorate.

He was drawn out of his morose thinking when he noticed Bones scowling at Estin.

"You'll make it home," Bones said to the prince. "But some of us might not. It's a reason not to celebrate. This might be the last meal we share together."

Riyne seemed to agree with Bones, and his improved attitude no longer surprised Cinder. "Our last certain meal as one brotherhood." He met Cinder's gaze, a hopeful glint in his eyes.

Cinder pushed through his looming worry, nodding in agreement toward the elf. He lifted his glass of juice, tapping Riyne's. "To brotherhood."

Everyone clinked glasses, even Estin. All the while, Cinder studied the prince, searching for an anticipatory smirk or sign the other man might know a humiliating secret about him.

He saw nothing.

After finishing their breakfasts, the Seconds put away their trays and waited for the general and his staff to arrive. The servers were gone. So was all the food and dishes, and all doors leading into the cafeteria were closed. The wagon-wheel chandeliers were lit to brightness, and late-winter sunshine beamed through the tall, mullioned windows making up the east wall.

The Seconds stood about in a softly murmuring cluster, a nervous tinge to their gathering. Of them all, Cinder probably felt it most.

Minutes later General Sylve Arwan, Lieutenant Capshin, and a number of elves, including Anya, Lisandre, and others who had been at the Directorate for specialized training, filed into the cafeteria.

A buzz of excitement rose from the Seconds upon their arrival. Anya briefly inclined her head to Cinder, and when she did, his fears unclenched. He should have never doubted her. She meant to keep her vow, and he smiled her way. Their expression of familiarity earned him a scowl from Estin.

"You're asking for trouble going out on your Secondary Trial with her," Ishmay whispered out of the corner of his mouth. "You sure it's worth it?"

Cinder was about to reply but had no chance to do so.

"Form up," General Arwan said.

The Seconds quickly got themselves organized into a straight line based on their class rank, shoulders braced and at attention. As the Prime, Cinder stood to the far right, Cariath to his left.

"At ease," General Arwan said, viewing them in silence for a few seconds. "The Firmament Hour is a tradition dating back to over two thousand years. It's true; you all know who has agreed to sponsor you for your Secondary Trial, but today, this morning, you find out for certain. It won't be a long, laborious process. This is meant to be a private day of learning, reflection, and acceptance. I'll simply call out your name, you'll step forward, and I'll let you know by whom you're to be sponsored. We'll continue on until I reach the Prime, and once we're finished and you've had a chance to meet privately with your sponsor, you'll be expected to maintain a vow of silence until tomorrow morning. As for the Secondary Trial itself, it is meant to test your every skill as a warrior. It is your greatest task. Complete it, and you'll gather at the end with your fellow Seconds at Fort Carnate and share what you've learned before returning to the Directorate." He clapped his hands. "Let's get started."

He called for Wark, who stepped forward.

"Wark Nil, you have been accepted by Lieutenant Blate Parm of the High Army of Rakesh as a member of the Red Rider Scouts. Lieutenant Capshin has your papers. It has all the information you'll need on joining your new unit. All the materials required, weapons, and when they expect your arrival in Swift Sword."

"Yes, sir," Wark replied. He stepped over to Lieutenant Capshin, who handed him a leather folio.

It was Depth's turn next, and the general gave him his instructions. Then it was Ishmay, Bones, Jozep, and the rest of the Seconds.

When it came time for Estin, the prince could barely manage to control his smug smile of satisfaction.

"Your sponsor is well known to everyone here. Lisandre Coushinre," the general said. "You can speak to him after the completion of Firmament's Hour about his expectations for you."

"I'll speak to you in my quarters," Lisandre said to Estin.

"Yes, sir," Estin said, this time unable to hold back his grin.

Then it was Riyne's turn, and he shifted about in apparent unease. After his disastrous Firster year, there had been a real chance that he wouldn't earn patronage from any ranger. He might have been forced to join the general army, a terrible humiliation and setback for Riyne. Thankfully, his changed attitude, behavior, and performance in his Second year had allowed him to overcome most of the issues from his Firster year.

He and Cariath had both earned patrons amongst the elves who had come to the Directorate for specialized training, some of whom had been asked to assess the elven Seconds and decide amongst themselves who was worth sponsoring.

The ones who had agreed to sponsor Riyne and Cariath had sterling reputations, and both wielded *insufi* blades.

After Riyne, it was Cariath's turn, and then finally, Cinder.

The commandant called his name, and Cinder stepped two paces forward. His heart beat faster. This was it. For reasons he couldn't fathom, a trickle of tingling nervousness rippled down his spine.

Before declaring Cinder's sponsor, the general shot Anya a glance, as if to ask if she was sure about this.

She dipped her head to him in confirmation.

The general shook his head and possibly muttered under his

breath before making his announcement. "Cinder Shade, Prime of the Seconds. Your sponsor is none other than the finest of all rangers. Our princess, Anya Aruyen."

Cinder exhaled in relief, while behind him rose a tumult of victory, hisses of disbelief, and a single shout of outrage.

"Anya! No!" Estin cried out.

Cinder didn't need to turn around to know the prince wore an apoplectic expression.

"Silence!" General Arwan roared. The excited conversations shut off like a spigot. The commandant glared about the room. Once certain no one would speak up again, he continued. "Cinder Shade, the princess will speak to you as soon as we are finished with today's ceremony."

"Meet me tonight at sunset at Breachwood Café," Anya said. "You know the one I mean."

It was the café in the quiet neighborhood of Certitude where Cinder had first seen Anya months ago following her return to the Directorate. "Yes, ma'am," Cinder replied.

"You can resume your place, cadet," the general said.

"Yes, sir." Cinder stepped back to his fellow Seconds.

"And now, we come to the conclusion of Firmament Hour," the commandant said. "From this point until sunrise tomorrow, you will speak to no one else except your sponsor." He glared at the Seconds, particularly Estin. "Any concerns you might have on *any* matter can wait until then. Dismissed."

The general and the rest of the senior elves departed the cafeteria, leaving behind a quiet group of Seconds. But while they weren't allowed to speak, it didn't mean the others couldn't offer wide-eyed expressions to Cinder, some in support, others in disappointment, and others in disgust. The prince, meanwhile, simply glared murder at him.

Cinder ignored Estin and silently exited the cafeteria.

"Are you sure this is the right approach?" Lisandre asked Anya after the conclusion of Firmament Hour.

Since they were to share duties during their combined Secondary Trial, they had decided to meet for lunch in the academy's cafeteria in order to more clearly delineate their chain of command. While Anya was the finer ranger, Lisandre was the better instructor. They needed to understand one another's roles and intentions.

A few other tables were occupied, mostly by the Firsters, who sat in two distinct and separate groups. There were the elves at one table and the humans and dwarves at another. In this, they were typical of most classes, and utterly unlike the current Seconds, who behaved like a brotherhood. Nearly every member of that class was clearly fond of one another in a way never before seen at the Directorate.

General Arwan had noticed it, too, and he, along with the rest of the administration, wanted to see such unity fostered. The Seconds were exemplary. Thus far as a group, they had easily outfought and outperformed any other class in the long memories of any graduate or instructor at the Directorate.

But the reason for their exceptional showing was simple, or at least Anya imagined it was. In this, she agreed with Masters Absin, Serwil, and Jovick. It was because of the leadership of Cinder Shade. He drove the Seconds. He pushed them to better themselves and never let them rest on their laurels or accept anything less than their best. It was this combination of his inspiring hard work, forceful exhortation, and un-stinting faith that had encouraged the Seconds to see one another as brothers. That had led to this spectacular class of students.

Anya didn't think it could be replicated. Not easily at least. Not without a student in each class like Cinder and a change of attitude on the part of her people.

"I know Cinder defeated Cariath," Lisandre continued, "but we both know it was more by luck than skill alone."

"Have you noticed how much luck seems to follow Cinder?" Anya asked Lisandre in return.

"Luck, no matter how frequent, is still luck."

"Then have you noticed how he continually rises to whatever

challenge he faces?" Anya asked.

"Maybe so, but I'm still not convinced he is the best use of our time. Cariath would have been a better choice for you. At least he and Estin don't hate one another."

Estin. Her brother was young, immature, and had many improper beliefs hindering his progress. She worried for him. His self-confidence reminded her too much of their brilliant but truculent sister. Overconfidence, though, was no different than arrogance in that both were unflattering, unbecoming traits. One which could all-too-easily lead to disaster. Witness what had nearly happened to Jameken Battalion. Elven conceit would have led to catastrophe if not for a pair of competent humans who had kept their wits about them. But what if in some future engagement it was Estin who had command of the unit and chose the path of hubris?

She could easily imagine it, and she hoped seasoning and experience, especially the months spent with someone he detested and considered his natural inferior, would soften some of Estin's hard edges. In many ways, this Secondary Trial might be more beneficial to him than even Cinder.

"Cariath isn't the Prime," Anya said to Lisandre, "and I never offered to sponsor him. Nor will I go back on my word to Cinder. I promised him. If he defeated a woven utilizing *lorethasra*, I would take him on his Secondary Trial. He did so. I chose him during the Firmament Hour. The discussion is ended."

Lisandre grunted again. "What about when he arrives at Revelant. Where will you house him?"

This, too Anya had already considered. "Taj Wada. The palace."

While only humans or dwarves who served in the Imperial Army or were members of a trade or diplomatic delegation were allowed to see Revelant, an exception could be made if they had a minder, someone to take responsibility for the individual. As Cinder's sponsor, it only made sense for Anya to also act as his minder.

Lisandre frowned. "To act as Cinder's minder means he'll be housed in your own guest quarters. It is…" He trailed off, clearly not wanting to say what was foremost on his mind.

An elf woman and a human man, essentially sharing the same quarters. It was beyond unseemly. It was scandalous.

"I won't be alone with him," Anya replied. "I'll have several of the married maids and their spouses with me at all times. There will be no stain on my honor or that of my house."

Lisandre seemed to relax, exhaling in relief. He chuckled. "I'm glad to hear of it. You disregard so much of what others consider proper behavior and comportment."

"You mean like when I begged and pleaded with my mother to allow me to try for the Third Directorate?"

"Coming here was the least of your lapses in judgment," Lisandre said gruffly.

Despite his surly sounding tone, Anya could tell he was only joking. His reminder wasn't meant to snipe or hurt. It was the teasing truth relayed by one friend to another.

Anya's heart warmed at the notion. For years, Lisandre had been persistent in wooing her, but his actions had done little more than turn her stomach. But in this season, in the months since she had accepted Lisandre's courtship, she found herself enjoying his company and liking him enough to consider him a friend.

"What is it?" Lisandre asked.

Anya smiled. "I'm just glad you're here to tell me what to do, to keep me from making too much of a spectacle of myself."

"If there is one thing I've learned in our time together, it's that no one tells you what to do. The best anyone can hope is to advise."

Anya's smile widened. "You've grown wise."

"Well, you have kept me on my toes," Lisandre said with a chuckle. After a short time, the smile left his face, and a serious mien came over him.

Anya caught him staring at her, his eyes wide with uncertainty. He inhaled deeply, seemingly gathering his courage. She sat up straight. Lisandre had something important to relate.

"I need to tell you something," he began. "First of all, I have enjoyed our months together."

Anya's stomach dropped. She had read enough romances to recognize where this conversation was going. "You no longer wish to court me."

Lisandre halted in the middle of whatever he meant to say, his mouth hanging open in stunned disbelief. "How did—" He collected himself an instant later. "I'm afraid so."

While Anya recognized she hadn't been truly committed to their relationship—the most she had allowed was for Lisandre to kiss her on the cheek—nevertheless, the sting of rejection hurt. "Why?"

"Because you don't want to be courted," Lisandre said. "I don't know if you're waiting for someone special—"

Rukh.

"—or if you simply don't like men, but you're happiest alone."

"That's not true," Anya said. "I enjoy your company. I enjoy being around people. And I like men."

"I know you do," Lisandre allowed, "but you don't enjoy my company in the same way I enjoy yours. In the same way others do. You are a very private person."

"I see." Anya couldn't meet his gaze, and she stared at the table. He was right. She was a private person, and when it came to love, she *had* chosen loneliness.

But if she didn't like being alone, why did she continually choose it? She wanted to share her life with another, but somehow she never could manage that trick. It was as if the memory of her dead husband persisted in holding her back from forming a connection with someone else. And during the months spent with Lisandre, she had hoped the barriers of the past would eventually break.

Apparently not.

"I'm sorry, Anya," Lisandre said.

Anya's lips thinned. "You don't need to apologize. It's my fault." She met his gaze. "Will you be well?"

"Do you mean will I be heartbroken?" Lisandre shook his head. "It's hard to lose what was never mine."

Anya exhaled in relief, smiling faintly. She liked Lisandre, respected him tremendously, and the last thing she wanted was to see him hurt. "I'm glad to hear it," she said. "The only other question I have is why tell me about this today? On the eve of the Secondary Trial?"

"Because we need to be clear-eyed in where we stand with one another during the Trial. The *bishans* deserve nothing less."

Bishans. Their sponsored students. to whom they would serve as *Ishas*, their instructors and masters.

"There is one other issue we should discuss," Lisandre said.

"Oh?"

"Your family. If we break off our courtship now, what will the empress say?"

Anya hadn't considered it, but now that she did, she realized the likely outcome. Her mother would deny her a chance to sponsor Cinder. She might go so far as to pull her from the rangers altogether.

"As I thought," Lisandre said, apparently reading the future based on her expression. "We won't tell the empress or anyone in your family. Until the Secondary Trial is completed, we'll let them go on believing we're courting."

"Thank you," Anya said, taking Lisandre's hands in hers. "You're a good man. This means more than you know. I won't forget it."

"And you're a good woman. You deserve happiness. You deserve a person with whom to share your life."

Anya smiled faintly in agreement, even while her attention flitted elsewhere. *Someone with whom to share her life.* When would that ever happen? When would she escape the shadow of loss? The death of her husband?

"You'll find someone," Lisandre said.

Anya smirked, wanting to roll her eyes at the ghastly phrase. It was so superficial and worthless.

"Besides," Lisandre continued, "I learned long ago that you march to the beat of your own drummer."

Anya's smirk slipped. An indistinct melody flitted through the recesses of her mind. The vague notes vanished, and when they were gone, she could recall no trace of what the strains might have sounded like. It was often the way with her possible past-life memories, but in this instance, she remembered the instrument used in the music. "A mandolin," she said, remembering her husband and how much he loved playing for her. "I like to march to the strumming of a mandolin."

The area around the outdoor café where Anya had asked to meet was quiet today. Perhaps it was the time, the early evening. The sky was burnished a vivid orange-red from a late-day sun. The only sounds came from the gurgling of a nearby fountain and the muted conversations of the few folk walking the narrow footpath traversing the neighborhood. It was warmer than usual as well, but an outdoor fireplace was still required to ward off the evening's chill. In addition, at this time of year, since the sun still set early, the strings of *diptha* lanterns traversing the lane were already lit. They hung like streamers from the brick buildings to the bare branches of the dwarf oaks bifurcating the footpath.

Cinder had arrived early, shortly after mailing off letters to Riner and Master Lerid at *Steel-Graced Adepts*. His Secondary Trial would take him to Swift Sword, and he knew his likely arrival date based on what Anya had told him shortly after the Firmament Hour. He hoped to visit his friends during his time there.

He had also mailed a letter to his brother, Pitch, in Swallow. It wasn't his first. He'd sent many such missives over the past several years, but writing them had never grown easier. Pitch, no matter their familial ties, was essentially a stranger, and Cinder felt disconnected from the man. Nevertheless, he owed him. If nothing else, Pitch had saved his life, and Cinder could spare a few minutes and a few copper coins to write to him now and again.

Those were his thoughts when he took a seat at the café and gazed about. He had always loved this neighborhood. It was beautiful, and in a few weeks, with spring erupting across the land, the lavender and roses blooming and the moons shining overhead, it would likely be romantic as well.

He smiled when he saw Anya approaching the café. He had only been waiting a few minutes, not even long enough to order a drink. Once again, his hand automatically went to his money purse, making sure he'd brought it. He would have been mortified if Anya had to buy his meal for him tonight.

The princess drew the glances and bows of her fellow travelers as she made her way closer, and she angled her head to some of them in acknowledgment, offering others a smile. Her golden hair and golden skin seemed to glow in the warm light of the *diptha* lanterns. Cinder noticed the gaze of some of the men linger on her, and he knew why.

Anya was beautiful.

Even a human could notice a self-evident truth.

He stood when the princess reached his table.

"You don't need to stand on my account," Anya said, smiling at him. "Please. Sit."

Cinder took his seat, and as if he had been waiting just for that moment, a young elf boy, likely the café owner's son, dashed over to their table to take their orders, and once he knew what they wanted, he departed just as swiftly.

"Your brother isn't happy having to travel with me," Cinder said.

Anya's cheerful demeanor darkened some. "My brother has a good heart, but he has much to learn about life."

Cinder privately doubted the former. He had seen no evidence of Estin's good heart, but of the latter he was certain.

"More importantly, my brother will have to accept matters as they stand. He has no other option."

Cinder narrowed his eyes, a suspicion forming. He wasn't willing to voice it, but some aspect of his thinking must have given him away.

"And, no," Anya said. "I didn't sponsor you out of some misbegotten hope that you might aid my brother in some way."

Cinder's suspicion faded, and he relaxed.

Anya's smile returned. "Is that why you seemed nervous this

morning?" she asked. "You thought I was only choosing you to help my brother."

Cinder blinked, surprised by her insight.

His reaction elected a warm chuckle. "Sometimes you are as inscrutable as stone, and other times your features shout out your intentions."

Cinder smiled in wry amusement. "I see it now. You asked me to dinner tonight so you could mock me."

"Not entirely," Anya said. "I asked you to join me for dinner so we can discuss how we'll approach the Secondary Trial." She grinned, her teeth flashing. "The teasing is only a secondary benefit." Anya held up cautioning finger. "And if you answer even once with 'Simply Anya,' I'll know you're a simpleton. I expect more original jokes from you."

"I'll do my best not to disappoint," Cinder said.

"Good," Anya replied, still smiling. A moment later, she took on a serious air. "Now, for the real reason you're here tonight. What I want from you during the Secondary Trial, you likely already know, but it's good to review it anyway. For this Trial I want your best. I want you alert at all times. Learn everything you can. Be curious. Ask questions. Push me to teach, and I'll share everything I know. I want you to excel. In addition, you'll take watch alongside me. You'll scout alongside me. You'll do exactly as I tell you to do at all times, but in the event you see danger that I haven't yet noticed, tell me. Don't be afraid to speak your mind. Do you have any questions so far?"

Cinder shook his head. Nothing she had told him so far surprised him.

"Excellent. Now finally, as your sponsor, I need to provide for any requirements you might have. I know you have all the necessary weapons, and the Directorate has provided your field clothing. What else do you need?"

"Can I bring my mandolin?" Cinder asked. "I left it behind in the other two Trials. I want to take with it me this time."

Anya frowned. "Why?"

Cinder shrugged, not sure how to explain his desire for the mandolin. "I like to play. It's soothing."

"There was a time in my life when I liked to sing. It was usually to the accompaniment of a mandolin, and normally I would allow it, but this is the Daggers. I don't want you distracted, or worse, providing distraction during our time there." Her lips thinned. "I'm afraid the answer is no."

Cinder wasn't surprised. He had expected the response. "I understand," he said, thinking about what else she had told him just now. "You really sing?" He'd never expected the princess to be a singer. Intelligent, wise, and a gifted warrior, but also a musician?

Unbidden, into his mind rose the vague image of the woman of whom he had occasionally dreamed, the woman whose face he could never recall, only her hair. He stared at Anya, wondering why the woman he had imagined had so many features similar to those of the princess.

"What is it?" Anya asked, evidently noticing something in his expression.

"It's nothing," Cinder replied. "Just a stray thought." He wasn't willing to share what most would think lunacy. *I remember my past life.* If he spoke of it, he would be lucky if they only decided to throw him out of the Directorate.

"Are you sure?" Anya asked. "You appeared… troubled."

"I'm sure," Cinder said, hoping she'd drop the matter.

Anya let it go. "In that case, what else do you require?"

"What about Fastness?" Cinder asked jokingly.

"If you need him, you'll have him," Anya replied without the slightest hesitation.

Cinder stiffened, shocked by her answer. When he'd spoken the request, he'd never actually expected her to say yes. "Really?"

Anya chuckled. "You forget. I'm a princess. I can do a lot of things most sponsors can't. As I said, if you need Fastness for the Trial, then you'll have Fastness."

Cinder slowly smiled, imagining the stallion's joy at finally getting to use all his skills. Of late, Fastness had complained of boredom. Having mastered all the courses at the academy, he found the practice

rides repetitive and tedious. Cinder did, too, but in the wilds, challenges abounded.

"You're pleased," Anya noted.

"Absolutely."

"Is there anything else?"

Cinder shook his head. "I think that covers it."

Anya grinned at him then, as if she had a secret she knew he
wouldn't like.

Cinder's felt a tremble of nervousness. "What is it?"

"There may be times during the Secondary Trial when you'll
be required to attend formal events. We leave for Revelant in two
mornings—"

"Oh, no." Cinder had an inkling as to what Anya was going to say,
and she confirmed his suspicions an instant later.

"—and when we arrive, we'll have a formal meal with my family."

Cinder sighed, disheartened. "I need new clothes."

Anya nodded, her smile brightening. "You get to go shopping."

Cinder's heart sank. There was no way he could afford another set
of clothes. He'd have to borrow the money from his friends.

Anya's bright smile faltered. "It won't be that bad," she said. "If you
like, I can go with you."

"It's not that," Cinder replied. "It's…" He trailed off, not wanting to
explain his financial straits.

Anya's humor fell away. "It really isn't a problem," she said.
"Remember, as your sponsor, I'm required to see to your needs. New
clothes are a need. I'll pay for them."

"You don't have to," Cinder said, not wanting her charity. The charity of a woman felt wrong.

"It's not charity," Anya said, somehow guessing his thoughts. "I
know about your pride, but in this matter, I insist. I'll pay for your new
clothes. Nor will I allow you to borrow money from your friends. This
is ultimately my responsibility. You are my *bishan*."

"How do you know about my pride?" Cinder asked, some of his
antipathy melting away and curiosity taking its place.

"You're a man."

"And you're a woman." Cinder lifted his brows, asking for further explanation.

Anya rolled her eyes. "I'm glad you noticed."

"It's hard to overlook."

Anya's face reddened, and he wasn't sure if it was from anger or embarrassment. Regardless, it took her a couple of seconds to compose herself. "Which is why you don't want my help. Because I'm a woman. It's foolish, doubly so for this most vacuous of reasons."

The last of Cinder's aversion to accepting Anya's offer left. A smile lurked at the corners of his mouth. "It will be as you say, my beautiful and far older *Isha*." He mentally groaned. Had he just called Anya beautiful? *Idiot.* Even if she wasn't an unapproachable elf, she was in a relationship with someone else. He had no business saying such things to her.

Luck must have been with him, though, because Anya only smiled in return. "Just for that, your outfit will include those lovely, pointy shoes I saw you scowling at during the Duchess's Banquet." She reached into a bag he hadn't noticed at her side and withdrew a long tube. "I also bought you this. Consider it my first gift to you, *bishan*. It's a spyglass. Bring it with you on the Trial. I've found them to be quite handy."

29

Cinder exited the blacked-out carriage which had carried him from the Third Directorate to Revelant. He and Anya had arrived at their destination—Taj Wada—and he stepped forth, arching his back and reaching for the sky as he stretched out the kinks in his legs, arms, chest, shoulders, and torso. As always during his travels, he hadn't been allowed to see any other aspect of the city or the rest of Yaksha proper, but at least this time, he might have a chance to explore the royal palace.

It had surprised him when Anya said he'd be staying here since he'd assumed he would board at the same villa where he'd been housed during the other times he'd traversed Revelant. Apparently not.

He gazed around, taking in his surroundings. It was early afternoon, and the sun beamed down from a spring sky the color of a robin's egg. Dense flocks of small birds flittered about, darting and weaving in mad patterns, somehow avoiding crashing into one another. Cinder inhaled deeply, appreciating the air's moisture and warmth. In the hill country of the Third Directorate, the days remained cool and dry or even chilly, and he looked forward to summer. Ponderous clouds crowded the west, promising an evening rain as they slowly crossed the sky.

More impressions.

He stood in a large courtyard, one paved with weathered flag-stones. On all sides rose buildings made of white granite veined in black. There was a stout stable, barracks, a wing of the palace, and a tall gatehouse, the iron-sheathed doors thrown open. Flags and pennons, most of them containing Yaksha's symbol—a fiery crown on a red field—snapped from atop the towers soaring along the courtyard's perimeter. A dozen sentries faced outward as they marched along a walkway protected by crenellated battlements. Closer at hand, grooms and other servants rushed to and fro, completing whatever tasks were set to them. But they studiously avoided a corner of the courtyard where guards trained under the watchful eye of a foul-mouthed sergeant. Cinder smiled. The sergeant could have given Nathaz advice on how to curse.

Any further inspection had to be postponed, however. The grooms were unhitching the horses from their traces, and Cinder knew they'd have trouble with Fastness. The white had been harnessed to the back of the carriage, and he was not happy.

"I'll handle him," Cinder told a wide-eyed youth who gazed at the huge, white Yavana stallion in a mix of fear and fascination.

Fastness tugged on his halter rope, kicked backwards, and attempted to rear. His mane seemed to stand on end, he was so angry.

Cinder inched toward the white, speaking quietly and reassuringly. "Easy, old son. We're here. These kind folk only want to brush you down and give you food and water."

Fastness whinnied a strident challenge. He attempted to rear again.

Cinder approached closer. "You're fine. We're done traveling."

The white cocked an ear, and his gaze went to Cinder. He hoofed the flagstones, which Cinder took as a good sign. At least the stallion wasn't snorting anymore.

"You said you wanted to run wild and fight," Cinder reminded Fastness. "This is what we have to do to get there. Sometimes we have to make ourselves uncomfortable in order to improve."

Fastness whickered *"I don't want to be uncomfortable. I want to be brushed and fed oats and a lot of apples. Get them. Now."*

Cinder chuckled. "Yes, my Lord Brat."

"I'm not a brat. I'm a horse."

Cinder continued to chuckle. Fastness was fine. He untied the halter rope attaching the horse's bridle to the carriage. The groom had remained close at hand, and Cinder addressed him. "Where do I stable him?"

"Does he really speak to you?" the boy asked.

Cinder eyed the groom in surprise. He hadn't expected the boy's reaction. Most every other elf he'd met had been filled with an innate sense of superiority and arrogance. This boy was filled with nothing but curiosity. "He speaks," Cinder confirmed. "The challenge is getting him to shut up."

As if in proof of his observation, Fastness whickered.

The young groom laughed nervously, his gaze going to the stallion. "I see what you mean."

Despite Fastness' initial complaints, it didn't take long to get him settled into his stall. The stallion was true to his word, only requiring a quick brushing, a bucket of oats, and a handful of green apples until he was happy. Only then did Cinder deem it safe to leave the stallion in the hands of the young groom. However, he made sure to extract a promise from the white to behave himself.

In answer to this, Fastness snorted derisively as if to say it was silly for Cinder to have to even ask.

Outside the stable, Cinder found Anya waiting for him. He glanced around, searching for his belongings.

"I've already had your bags sent to the guest quarters," Anya said.

Cinder lifted his brow in surprise, not expecting her to know what he'd been thinking about. She apparently had keen insight.

"Come. You'll want to get cleaned and changed. It's been a long road."

"And you're sure it's fine for me to stay in your quarters?" Cinder asked. She had mentioned it to him prior to their departure from the

Directorate, but it still sounded like a terrible idea. He figured her people, especially her family, would have a fit over the sleeping arrangements. At a minimum, they'd be scandalized.

"I'm sure," Anya replied. "It's the guest portion of my suite, and we'll never be alone. We'll be chaperoned the entire time. I've made sure several of the servants and their spouses will also be staying in my rooms."

The small knot of worry in Cinder's chest loosened, but he wasn't completely satisfied with her reasoning. He still thought it was a bad idea. He simply wasn't sure how to tell her. "If you say so, but I still think…" He trailed off.

"Stop worrying about it," Anya snapped, a distinctly frosty edge to her voice. "I can take care of myself."

"Yes, ma'am." Cinder knew when to step away from an annoyed Anya. She clearly didn't appreciate his concern on her behalf, and in immediate hindsight, he could understand why. He wasn't her father, and it wasn't his place to be so concerned about her honor. "And you're right. It's not my place to be worried for you. I'm sorry."

She inhaled deeply and gave him a brief dip of acceptance. Her tone was softer this time. "I appreciate your concern, Cinder, but your protectivity isn't required. It's actually an irritant."

Cinder observed the annoyance fade from her face, and he ventured a wary chuckle, hoping to make light of the situation and lighten the mood. "Protectivity? That's a weird word."

Anya shrugged. "It fits." They held silent for a moment before a measuring expression filled her features. "You really were worried, weren't you?" she said as if she'd discovered an unforeseen gem or jewel. "I wonder what else makes you nervous. I'll have to find out." A forgiving smile flitted across her face. "As your *Isha* it's my duty to learn these things. I need to help you overcome your limitations."

Cinder eyed her askance, not bothering to reply. He doubted charity was the reason she wanted to learn about his fears.

"You were anxious during the Firmament Hour," Anya said, changing the topic. "Why?"

Cinder hedged, not wanting to explain the source of his disquiet. "I had a strange notion you weren't going to accept me for my Secondary Trial," he said after a few moments of deliberation. "I know it makes no sense, but there you have it. And the strangest thing is I'm never nervous."

Anya's brow creased in confusion. "What do you mean?"

"I mean exactly that. I'm never nervous. Ever since I woke up in the well, I've been afraid for others, but not for myself."

Anya's gaze grew thoughtful. "You and I really need to have that discussion about your amnesia. It's long overdue."

Cinder might have replied, but the moment they entered the palace, he crashed to a halt. The sheer beauty of Taj Wada overwhelmed his senses. "Oh, my."

Anya grinned. "I'm glad you appreciate my mother's home."

The utilitarian courtyard outside had given no hint of the beauty to be found within, and Cinder gaped like a bumpkin from the back end of nowhere as Anya led him through the main palace. There was so much to see. The palace's wide corridors were paved with white marble, but the floors were cushioned by plush runners, rugs, and carpets from the faraway, exotic places, likely the cities of Toil and Fare. Beautiful paintings—some of them taller than Cinder—graced the white-washed walls and were lit by cleverly placed *diptha* lamps. Then there were the vibrant murals that stretched from one groined vault ceiling to the next and the glorious sculptures of famous empresses staring about in stern judgment.

Taj Wada was a treasure house, and it contained a priceless collection of artwork and history.

Anya didn't give Cinder much time to view any of it, though. She led him at a martial clip as they passed through an endless maze of wide hallways, long corridors, and the occasional immaculate garden where retainers prepared spring plantings. The servants all paused in their duties when Anya stepped into their midst, acknowledging her with a quick bow.

All the while, Cinder kept close track on their progress, doing his best to memorize every passage and turn they took. It wasn't mistrust that fueled his obsession, but rather his pragmatic nature. He hated being lost, and he also hated how much the palace intimidated him.

Oddly enough, the more time he spent traversing Taj Wada, the more he grew to resent it. It was too big, too vast, too much for one person to need or want. Cinder didn't like it, and it didn't matter how enchanting he found the brilliant artwork. His hand clenched, wanting to flex around the hilt of his sword.

Eventually, they entered a modest hallway of normal dimensions. It was wainscoted in mahogany with a chair rail embossed in a leaf-and-vine pattern and walls painted a warm yellow color.

"Here we are," Anya announced, halting at a pair of white doors paneled in gold-leaf. She let them in.

Cinder paused at the entrance. These were Anya's guest quarters? They were every bit as beautiful and ostentatious as the rest of the palace. He studied the rooms where he would be staying.

Directly ahead was a sitting area larger than the common room at the Directorate. All the Seconds could have fit comfortably within it and had plenty of room to spare. The walls were an emerald green like Anya's eyes. Inside, Cinder discovered a round dining table to the left with seating for eight, while to the right rested a large, upholstered couch and a granite-topped coffee table flanked by a pair of high-backed chairs. The entire arrangement was clustered in front of a crackling fireplace and near a stocked bar, which the Seconds would have appreciated. Leather chairs, highlighted by pools of light from overhead *diptha* lanterns, were nestled in several of the room's corners. Finishing the seating at the far end of the room was another couch and matching chairs, but these faced floor-to-ceiling windows and doors exiting to a broad balcony outside.

"Your room is over here," Anya said, pointing out a door near the bar.

Cinder nodded in response, but his attention was now given over to examining the handful of paintings on the walls. Some captured the majesty of nature, others the glory of imperial Revelant as seen from the harbor. There was also a small painting atop a chest of drawers. It was of Anya. She wore a long, tan tunic belted at the waist and sandals laced at her ankles. Cinder felt drawn to the painting, and he lifted it off the chest of drawers, staring at it. Anya sat amidst a field of flowers, legs tucked underneath her. Her hair was braided, and she was smiling in a way he couldn't interpret. Was it wistful longing or warm welcoming? He didn't know, but to have her smile at him like that… His mouth went dry.

"I sat for it a few years ago," Anya said, standing at his shoulder. "I'd just returned to Revelant by way of Swift Sword."

Cinder had to work moisture into his throat. "Why were you smiling?" he asked, unable to take his eyes off the painting.

"I don't know," Anya said. "There was a moment on my journey home where I felt like I'd found something I'd been missing all my life."

"What did you find?"

Anya shook her head, and Cinder breathed in her cinnamon scent. It reminded him of his feelings for her. He liked Anya, but it wasn't simple lust, but rather…

He gritted his teeth, unwilling to even think the word.

But he couldn't avoid the truth, which had been hiding in plain sight for many months, from the first time he'd seen Anya. The feelings had crept over him, and in many ways, he had allowed it, welcomed it.

He wanted to smack himself.

All this time, he had thought himself utterly focused and dedicated on the mastering of the martial strategies, and yet in the midst of his endeavors, this awful flaw had occurred.

"I don't know," Anya said in answer to his question. "I was walking through Swift Sword, and somewhere along my journey through the city, I realized a hollow place inside me was filled." She lifted the painting out of his hands, staring at the image herself and standing close, her shoulder brushing against his.

Cinder couldn't have moved even if the room was on fire. He didn't want to alter that mild physical connection with Anya, although he recognized he should. His heart felt like it was pounding as loudly as a bass drum. How could Anya not hear it? He stared at her, unable to look away. "Are you still empty?"

She stared back at him, smiling slightly, just like in the painting. "Not for a long time," she whispered.

Her eyes rested on his. Her breathing deepened. He wanted to brush his fingers through the glory of her hair, to truly know her, to taste her lips. It would only require the slightest bend of his head to kiss her.

She is meant for a prince of the blood. Estin's words echoed in Cinder's mind, reminding him of the impossibility of kissing Anya, even if she allowed it. She was an elven princess, and no matter his feelings for her, there were some differences of station that could never be overcome. Cinder mastered his treasonous emotions, tied them off, and shoved them down in the innermost sanctums of his heart.

He forced himself into motion, putting distance between himself and the princess. "You grew up in this luxury," he said, knowing his statement was inane even as he spoke it. It didn't matter, though. He was grasping for straws, anything to take his mind off of Anya's closeness and his feelings for her.

"I did," Anya said, her voice might have quavered for an instant, but more likely it was Cinder's imagination. "But don't forget, most of the time I sleep under the stars."

Her tone sounded defensive, and Cinder pointed it out. "You don't have to apologize for growing up wealthy."

Anya nodded. "Sometimes I feel like I have to." She pointed to the door on the right once again. "Your bedroom is in there. Your belongings should have been delivered by now. The servant and her husband I mentioned will be sleeping in the other bedroom. There will also be another servant sleeping in the sitting room."

"Plenty of chaperones," Cinder said, privately praising Anya for her forethought. The more chaperones the better, especially with his vivid thoughts and forbidden feelings toward her.

He couldn't help but speculate on how it would be in the wilderness, months on end in Anya's company. How difficult would it be to keep his emotions in check? Then again, what choice did he have? The Secondary Trial wasn't a time to moon like a Devesh-damned jackhole over what could never be.

He and Anya faced a brutal, dangerous excursion into the Dagger Mountains, one where distractions could kill. Every ounce of his dedication, concentration, and will would be required to survive, and he refused to fail himself or Anya.

He would barricade his emotions for her, one brick in the wall at a time.

For the first time ever, Cinder was glad for Estin's generally stupid statements. In this instance what the prince had said had actually been useful. It had held Cinder back from making a colossal error in judgment.

One brick at a time.

"Will I see you at dinner?" Cinder asked, moving their conversation to safer topics.

Anya shook her head. "I'm afraid not. The meal tonight is for family only. You'll dine here. Or you can join Riyne and Mohal. They should have arrived yesterday."

"We could have arrived yesterday if I was allowed to ride Fastness," Cinder groused.

Anya laughed. "My poor *bishan*. You know why you couldn't."

"Because of your people's demented decision to let no one see their precious city?"

"Exactly," Anya replied. "And now that you know you're still unworthy—"

"I didn't say I was unworthy," Cinder interrupted, glad for the trivial nature of their talk since it helped him shape more bricks for his wall.

Anya waved away his argument. "Get some rest. You need it. Sitting for hours on end is more tiring than it should be." With that, she left him alone in the suite of rooms, but afterward, Cinder discovered she was right.

He was tired, and he chose to take a quick nap.

Later in the day, with the sun barely visible over the horizon, Cinder stood alone on the balcony. He stared at the portions   of the palace complex he could still see in the fading evening light. Anya had departed, off to share a private dinner with her family, while Cinder had decided to remain in the spacious guest quarters. He could have left the rooms, but he wasn't sure where to go. Perhaps the library, but where exactly was it? For all he knew it was on the other side of Taj Wada's grounds. This wasn't simply a single building like the duchess's palace in Certitude. This was a veritable city within a city where a person could easily get turned around and become lost.

In the distance, he spied a soaring granite wall, thirty feet in height or higher. It supported a wide walkway guarded by scores of soldiers. To both the right and left, the wall extended beyond the limits of Cinder's view, but within its bounds were green spaces, meadows, and rectangular fields wide enough to ride horses twenty abreast. There were also copses of various trees, including a few maples pressing against the edges of a large pond. An arching bridge led to a gazebo centered within the water.

Closer at hand—directly off the balcony, in fact—was another wall, this one much smaller than the massive fortifications marking Taj Wada's boundaries. It cupped a lovely garden and courtyard where a swinging bench overlooked a gentle stream gurgling within the center of the plot. A playful breeze rustled through dogwoods already in bloom in Revelant's lower elevation. There were also azaleas, bright with pink, purple, and white flowers. Low bushes wrapped around a sitting area where a wrought-iron table and chairs hunched on a bed of white gravel.

This was where Anya had grown up. This was the view greeting her at the beginning of every day and at end of every evening. Cinder wondered if she ever tired of it.

He doubted it. After all, it was her garden that was behind Krathe House, and it was similar to the one he saw below. She had probably tried to recreate a portion of her home at the Third Directorate.

While he stood outside, an interruption came when the three servants meant to act as his chaperones arrived. Two were a middle-aged couple, a husband and wife, and the other was an older gentleman who, among his other duties, apparently helped keep the small garden in the courtyard overlooked by the balcony.

They bowed their way inside, and an uncomfortable silence fell over the four of them. Cinder could tell the servants didn't know how to behave around him, and he knew it wasn't because he was merely a human. Nor was it because he was a guest of their princess. Mostly, Cinder reckoned, it was because the servants had never been tasked with acting as chaperones. They weren't sure how they were supposed to treat him. Was it with familiarity since they were going to share his quarters? Or formality since they were also supposed to see to his needs?

It left them in a bind, and rather than have them struggle with their discomfort, Cinder decided to head off in search of Mohal and Riyne. He could have dinner with them.

He left the balcony and was readying to head out, but his fellow Seconds and Lisandre arrived at his quarters just as he was lacing his boots.

Mohal grinned at him as he and the others filed inside. "We figured you'd get lost wandering around the palace looking for something to eat, so we came to you instead."

The three of them carried large trenchers, and Cinder lifted his nose in appreciation of the wonderful aromas drifting off the platters. He helped out by fetching plates from the bar along with a bottle of rose wine. He doubted Anya would mind. While he gathered the dishes and goblets, Lisandre, Riyne, and Mohal arranged the meal on the dining table, and supper turned out to consist of roast chicken, chana masala, potato curry, and mango lassi.

Before they settled in to have their meal, the servants granted the four of them privacy, departing the guest quarters and promising to return later in the evening.

Only then did Cinder settle into the serious business of eating. He took his first bite, and his eyes involuntarily closed. He groaned in appreciation. The supper was every bit as delicious as it smelled.

Mohal snickered. "I think you need a pipe."

Cinder opened his eyes, frowning in confusion. "What do you mean?"

Mohal shoved a bite of food into his mouth and pulled a face. He made noises like he was either in pain or in the midst of exquisite intimacy.

The others laughed, and so did Cinder even though he was aghast at Mohal's imitation. "Was that really what I looked like?"

Riyne nodded. "If anything, Mohal wasn't giving it his all. It was more like this." His face contorted and gruesome sounds issued from his mouth.

"I wasn't being tortured," Cinder said with a chuckle. "I was just enjoying the meal."

Lisandre smiled indulgently. "You were definitely enjoying something." He shifted the conversation. "What do you think of Revelant?"

"Not much," Cinder said. "I haven't seen enough of the city to form any kind of an opinion."

"You need a minder," Riyne said around a mouthful of food. "Mohal wouldn't *mind*." He nudged his fellow Second, grinning. "Get it?"

Mohal rolled his eyes.

"Mohal is a cadet," Lisandre said. "He doesn't have the standing. I'd act as your minder, but I have other duties to attend. Besides, how much can you really see in one day? We sail for Swift Sword morning after next."

"I'll manage," Cinder said, sipping at his wine, which was excellent.

"Manage what?" Mohal asked.

"Manage not to be bored being cooped up in these rooms."

"You could visit the library," Riyne reminded him. "It's where you're most at home, all hunched over a book like an old man."

Cinder grinned. How was it this most detestable of elves had earned his begrudging respect and even more begrudging friendship? "Do you think the empress will mind if I borrow a few of her books?"

"I'm sure Estin will mind if his mother does not," Lisandre said.

Estin. Cinder's stomach soured. The prince had been surprisingly cordial in the days prior to leaving for Revelant. In fact, for once, there hadn't been any snarky comments or references to elven superiority.

Cinder pushed aside thoughts about the prince. He'd have all of him he'd ever want in the coming months. "Let's talk about something else," he suggested.

"Like what?" Mohal asked.

"As long as it's not philosophy," Riyne said with a shudder.

"You mean like the large question of where everything comes from? Is it all chance?" Cinder asked, knowing his question would annoy Riyne. "Did reality expand from emptiness?"

Like clockwork, Riyne complained. "I said no philosophy."

"It's not philosophy," Cinder said, "so much as an exploration of the natural world."

"Fine. Natural world," Riyne scoffed. "Dress it however you wish. It's still boring."

"Then how about this," Cinder asked. "How did something come from nothing?"

"Or the converse?" Lisandre grinned, joining in the teasing of his younger brother. "Can nothing come from something?"

Riyne groaned. "Shut up. Shut up. Shut up. I hate philosophy, and I hate 'exploring the natural world.' I'd rather face a thousand spiderkin."

"You already did," Mohal reminded him.

"Oh, right," Riyne replied, his mien somber. "I'm going to miss you two."

"We'll see each other at Fort Carnate," Lisandre said. "When your Secondary Trials are over. It's tradition, and you know how we elves don't like to muck with tradition."

"We don't like to fuck with it, either," Riyne said with a grin.

Cinder laughed, raising his goblet. "Twice we've faced annihilation, and both times we've endured. We fought over a thousand spiderkin, and now the world has a thousand less of those fragging monsters to worry about. It'll be the same with the Secondary Trial. We won't just survive it, we'll crush our enemies. They'll die on the sharp edges of our swords."

"Yes!" Riyne shouted.

"Kill them all!" Mohal said on top of him.

"To fraternity!" Cinder called.

"To fraternity!"

30

Cinder kept himself from nervously shifting in his chair, but he couldn't stop from picking at his fanciful coat. He felt awkward and self-conscious, although his anxiety wasn't because of the stiff, elven clothing Anya had somehow managed to procure during their short time at the palace. He wore a long, overly decorated coat—dark red with silver buttons and thread-of-gold embroidery—over white, silk trousers and the stupid pointy shoes elves seemed to love. Nor did his discomfort stem from the fact that everyone here was an elf and he was the only human.

Rather, it was because everyone in the large room where the imperial family had their meals shared a clear familiarity and friendship with one another. Their conversation and laughter simply confirmed Cinder's status as an outsider.

He glanced around the room, listening in on the various discussions while doing his best to remain quiet and unobtrusive.

Quiet and unobtrusive. Those were the bywords by which he would endure tonight's dinner. He would speak only if directly addressed, provide the most banal of observations if asked to proffer an opinion, and otherwise remain utterly silent and dull. His views here were as clearly unwanted as his presence, at least judging by the attitudes of the empress and her eldest daughter. Their disdain for Cinder during his brief introduction to them had been as palpable as a skunk's stench.

Elven arrogance at its finest.

But these elves were members of the imperial family. They were people of supreme importance, and beyond their exalted status, they were also Anya's family, his *Isha's* family. Cinder would best show her respect by demonstrating the proper courtesy and politeness that her mother and sister refused to show him.

While listening in on the various conversations, Cinder unconsciously ran his fingers across the dining table's smooth, teak wood, noticing the furniture's fine quality, its subtle details and curves, the inlay of curly maple in the shape of a seven-limbed golden tree with leaves veined in purple heart. A pair of posts, thick and carved like fluted columns, supported the structure and eighteen matching leather chairs marched along its length.

The entire dining room suite was a masterwork, and that same dedication to excellence extended to the place settings: the fine earthenware dishes, the shining silverware with handles shaped like blades of grass—Cinder could make out tiny tracings of veins—and the water-filled goblets made of the clearest crystal.

Cinder shrugged off his appreciation of the quality of the furniture and place settings and resumed his attention on the people in the room.

The empress held pride of place at the head of the rectangular table, while to her left sat the prince-consort, Avan—Anya's father—a man in his middle years and someone difficult to read. His expression indicated either boredom, annoyance, or possibly both. Next to him sat his son, Estin, followed by Lisandre, Mohal, and finally, Cinder.

The seating arrangement was no accident. It was obvious that those seated closest to the empress were considered of greater importance, while those seated further were lesser.

For example, on the other side of the table and to the empress' right sat Enma, the haughty daughter-heir. She was someone Cinder didn't care for in the slightest. Upon their introduction to one another, Enma had sneered at him and said, "So you are Anya's pet?" She had then snorted in disgust and turned aside.

Bitch.

Next to Enma sat Anya. So far, they had only spoken a few words today since she had been busy with other commitments, a matter Cinder reckoned a good thing. He admired Anya, and being alone with her made him uncomfortable, at least here in Taj Wada.

He snorted.

Admiration wasn't what he felt for her.

He chided himself an instant later.

Anya was a lovely person, and Cinder would have been infatuated with her even if he were blind. And it was only an infatuation he felt. Nothing more. He couldn't allow it to *be* anything more. It wasn't what he'd thought it might be yesterday afternoon when she'd stood so close. No. He'd merely mistaken his infatuation for something deeper, and he just had to harden his heart against it.

That commitment had been sorely tested early on in the evening when he'd first caught a glimpse of Anya. She had appeared in front of him, a vision of loveliness wearing a shimmering, golden sari decorated with emblems made of ruby-red thread. It had taken an uncomfortable amount of effort to remain impassive when she had made her presence known in the dining room, but he'd succeeded in giving her no more than a friendly nod.

Cinder forced his attention away from Anya and onto the elderly elf interposed between the princess and Riyne. *Quelchon Ginala.* Her chalk-white hair and wizened face marked her as a true ancient, and in fact, she might even be older than Master Molni or the dowager duchess, Simone Trementh. But more impressive than her age was Quelchon Ginala's rare talent, the ability to recite a person, a power supposedly akin to prophecy. For this reason and others, Ginala was said to be the most highly respected member of the court outside the royal family.

Cinder had taken an instant dislike to her. He couldn't say why, but to him it seemed like a strange hunger lurked in the quelchon's eyes, a predator's gaze hiding behind the kindly face of a tender grandmother.

In this, she was vastly different from the dowager duchess, who was similarly elderly and hard-nosed but who was honest instead of false. Simone didn't try to hide her blunt persona behind a lying, sweet smile. She faced the world with a truthful demeanor, and everyone knew where they stood with her. Plus, Cinder had seen the warm way the dowager treated those she loved. He recollected how Simone lacked the hungry eyes of a beast, which was the first comparison he envisaged when first introduced to the quelchon.

Then again, perhaps his disquiet with the quelchon actually had nothing to do with her. Perhaps he was conflating his general unhappiness with being here tonight—the dismissive manner in which the empress and Enma had spoken to him—onto Ginala's otherwise bony, innocent shoulders.

After all, Quelchon Ginala's smile was soft and her demeanor gentle, and everyone greeted her with warmth and affection. The one noticeable exception was Anya, who spoke to the quelchon in a voice full of constrained politeness.

The princess didn't like Ginala either.

Quelchon Ginala made a regular habit of studying the imperial young, their intellect, their capacity to reason, the issues driving their passions, and the bridges beyond which they would never cross. She had to. The youthful members of the imperial family were the ones who would one day lead Yaksha Sithe, and she needed to know as much about them as possible.

How else could she guide them?

She pondered if tonight would require a greater expenditure of her wisdom. She wasn't sure.

Her gaze went about the room in subtle calculation. It was certainly an odd gathering in which she found herself, a private dinner, held in the small dining hall where the imperial family generally had their meals. Plum-colored wallpaper with platinum embroidery covered the walls, and along one length, a fire crackled within the hearth. But the quelchon's focus quickly passed over such prosaic features and went instead—like it most often did—to the large painting hanging on the wall behind the empress. It was a portrait of Koran Yaksha, the founder of the empire. In it, Koran was depicted atop a mountain's peak, urging warriors to attack Shet's bleak palace at Naraka.

There was other artwork scattered about the room as well. The corners held decorative statues, mostly famous people from the sithe's past, but included amongst their number was one figurine that never failed to cause Ginala's figurative lips to curl into a disgusted snarl. It was of Sachi Mithara, a Mythaspuri, a woman far more famous during the *NusraelShev*. She stood proud, her infamous mace slung casually over her shoulder, a mischievous twinkle in her eyes, and a careless grin on her face. The world had largely forgotten about Sachi, but Ginala hadn't. She knew Sachi's history, and she hated her for it.

Traitor.

The statue of Sachi wasn't the only artwork which annoyed the quelchon to no end. The worst was the large painting hung between the pair of pocket doors leading into the room. It featured Shokan and Sira, the so-called Blessed Ones. They were caught in profile, their faces obscured as they held hands and stared longingly at some distant place of salvation that only they could see.

Ginala hated the painting. She hated the failure it represented. Throughout her many centuries of life, she had sought to erase, or at least diminish the influence of Shokan and Sira, but thus far, her efforts were for naught. No matter their human ancestry, the people of Yaksha loved those two imbeciles. The quelchon tossed a final glare at the painting. At least the artist had given the couple the hint of proper elven ears. It was artistic license, but Ginala approved. In her considerable estimation, humans were, at best, filthy beasts.

Irritation at Shokan and Sira's ongoing influence caused Ginala to perspire, and she fanned herself. The room was too hot. The fire was too high. In fact, with the warm night, why was the hearth even in use?

Ginala wanted to snarl in unaccustomed anger, wanted to smash the dishes on the floor, and…

She realized the trend of her emotions, and she closed her eyes. A series of calming breaths settled her mind, and she gathered and snipped the threads of her rage.

It was odd. Generally, she had exquisite control of her passions, but not tonight for some reason. Tonight, her mood was foul, and Ginala found herself silently berating the empress for even hosting this farcical meal.

What was the point? Ginala knew everyone present. They were understood commodities. There was the empress and her husband, the arrogant Enma, the mulish Anya, the dullard Estin, and the various guests: Lisandre and Riyne Coushinre and Mohal Holwarein. She had measured every last one of them, tallied their worth, and through painstaking analysis, figured how best they might wittingly or unwittingly aid her schemes.

Her eyes then went to the human, Cinder Shade, and she halted her private diatribe. Only he was unique. Only he represented a possible unknown.

The quelchon had heard much about this boy, knew all about his absurd past. How he supposedly hailed from some no-account village in Rakesh, deep in the Daggers. How he had been born with a club foot and a withered right leg, and how he had been miraculously healed following the death of his parents at the hands of an *aether*-cursed snowtiger.

Ginala scoffed. She had witnessed much in her long life and never once had she witnessed a miracle, and she didn't believe in them either.

Which meant Cinder Shade's story was a preposterous fabrication. He hadn't been miraculously cured of his ailments, nor was he the callow, yet competent, youth he pretended to be. He was something else. Not an enigma, but rather the kind of person Ginala had encountered far too many times in the past, someone coarse and venal.

A parvenu, a worthless sot. See how he attached himself to Princess Anya, and she fool enough to allow it. Then again, the younger princess had always been rebellious, and her rebellious nature made her stupid in a predictable fashion. Always she chose the path of humiliation. Did she not comprehend the rumors whispered about her and this Cinder Shade? Or maybe she heard them and didn't care? Or worse, what if the rumors were true?

Ginala's eyes narrowed as she scrutinized the two of them. Anya and Cinder sat on opposite sides of the table, the princess adjacent to the quelchon and the human seated to the right of Mohal, the point farthest from the empress. The foolish boy likely didn't even understand the meaning of his placement.

The quelchon continued to watch the two of them, silently scrutinizing their interactions. Anya's gaze occasionally went to the boy, and his to her, but no more than they did to anyone else at the table. They smiled at those who spoke to them, and sometimes to one another.

After a few minutes of study, Ginala finally felt certain she had their measure. Anya and Cinder liked one another. It was as clear as the glass goblet holding her water. But it was a liking based on friendship and trust only. In their voices, visages, and demeanors, there was none of the undercurrent of passion that lovers held for one another.

Good.

With her plans nearing fruition, Ginala didn't need any sort of complication to mar her path to redemption. She had matters well in hand for Yaksha. Hers had been the work of centuries, forging this sithe and these elves into a proper empire built of might and steel.

"Quelchon Ginala," the empress said, interrupting her contemplations. "Would you grace us with the use of your talents? I don't think I've ever seen you recite a human, and here we have one who is quite accomplished."

Ginala bowed her ancient head. "As you wish, Your Majesty." In truth, she had meant to recite Cinder Shade anyway. The empress' request simply gave her an easier opportunity to carry out her design.

"What do you require of me?" the boy dared ask her.

Ginala wanted to slap him. He should know better than to address his superiors without their prior consent. She opened her mouth, ready to lash out and school the simpering idiot on his expected decorum. She...

No. Ginala clenched her jaw, collecting herself. In deference to Empress Sala and her dramatic daughter, Princess Anya, she would swallow her angry words. "I only require that you allow me to place my hands on your head," she said, her voice quavering. "The reciting will happen, or it will not." The boy made to rise, but Ginala waved him back to his seat. "I will stand behind you, learn what I can, and speak the words to the empress only."

She stood, shuffling and limping her way to where the boy sat, pretending a weakness that wasn't actually present. In her long life, Ginala had learned to manipulate the feelings and emotions of the young and hale. What better way to earn their empathy than to have them judge her old and frail?

But while she was old, she was far from frail.

As she hobbled to the boy, she saw the concern for her bloom on his face, and she smothered a smile. *So easy to read and so easy to manipulate.* She reached him and placed her hands on his head without asking permission.

Cinder's concern about Quelchon Ginala and his disquiet in her presence only heightened the closer she approached. He suppressed a flinch when she touched his head. There was a feeling about her hands. They reminded him of lumpy flesh constraining bony claws.

Quelchon Ginala exhaled, and he smelled rain.

Ginala closed her eyes, breathed deep, and sourced her *lorethasra*, creating the necessary braid. She sent it rippling through two of her four open Chakras—Vishuddi and Ajna—and her *nadis*. Next, she conducted her *Jivatma* and devoted the appropriate application of will, Talent as Shokan might have described it. Her power flowed, and she waited to see what it would show her.

Seconds passed, and Ginala noted nothing unusual about the boy. He was as plain as a blank sheet of paper and as simple as an illiterate shepherd. He was as void of future greatness as anyone she had ever encountered. But the quelchon remained patient. Sometimes a recitation took time.

She waited, a full minute longer to confirm her initial suppositions.

The minute dragged, but in the end, there was nothing. Cinder Shade was utterly bland, a person unreservedly empty of future glory. There was no chance he would ever achieve anything of note.

Ginala held back a triumphant smile. It was perfect. Her plans were finely balanced—they had to be given the opposition of her sisters—and she would allow no upstart human *vermin* to erase her hard work. And based on her recitation, it seemed she wouldn't have to worry about this particular pest.

Nevertheless, although she had her answers about Cinder Shade, when it came to reciting, a certain spectacle was required. Ginala kept her eyes closed, feeling and reading the currents in the room, planning what to tell the empress. Sometimes it depended on her audience. Right now, Lisandre, Riyne, and Mohal emoted excitement. The same with the empress and her husband-consort. Anya was merely curious while Enma seethed contempt. From Estin, she noticed…

Here, the quelchon paused. What was it the prince felt? Fear? Fear of what? Fear of what Ginala might say about the human?

She restrained a scowl. Time was slipping away, and she didn't have enough of it to properly meditate upon the matter. The empress required an answer.

Choices flitted through Ginala's mind. Should she tell the truth, some version of it, or an outright lie? What would be the best method to see her plans come to fruition? For so long, she had striven to remake the Yaksha elves, to force them into frames where they were more… human. Base, coarse, and easily swayed to violence.

And it was working. The elves in Yaksha were her clay, and she was slowly shaping them into a people who were shedding their love of nature and rather seeking to dominate it. To believe the weak deserved their fate, where the poor were no longer tolerated or coddled. It meant the sithe would wither and die, but such had always been its fate.

Now how best to aid her mission?

In the end, Ginala decided upon a forceful falsehood, an obfuscating statement meant to trouble Sala and her husband. Yes. That would do best. It would also answer the questions about Cinder's supposed abilities, such as sourcing *lorethasra*.

Ginala tottered down the length of the table, imagining the correct phrasing for what she had in mind, the vacuous meanderings which would send Sala chasing off in the wrong direction.

She reached the empress' side, and by tradition, bent to whisper directly in the sovereign's ear, ensuring no one else could hear her words. However, Ginala trusted Sala to share her recitation with her family. She always did. She stupidly believed her children should be trusted with state secrets.

"A nameless curse threatens," Ginala whispered. "An ancient shadow looms. The world's hour is late. Death and destruction come for Seminal. The *Elonic Festh*, the World-Killer comes." She made sure to flick her gaze at Cinder. "And this man wields a white blade."

Despite the fearful portents, the empress held her face impressively still, displaying no inkling of how deeply the words had affected her. She kept her eyes facing forward, her features impassive, proud, and steady as a flagship on an even sea.

But the quelchon could tell the empress was shaken, possibly fearful. *Good.* Tonight, tomorrow, or a few days hence, Sala would seek Ginala's counsel, and she would have it. The quelchon had provided such guidance to every unsuspecting, unknowing empress since the *NusraelShev*, and she would continue to do so until the time came when she could finally reclaim her true name: Jesherol, a name even the mighty Indrun had respected and dreaded.

"Thank you," the empress said.

"You're welcome, Your Majesty," said Quelchon Ginala as she hobbled back to her seat.

31

Sala Yaksha stood braced in front of the large window in her study, staring out at the night-darkened garden. The lights in the room were turned down, and she could barely make out a few flowering shrubs, a couple of large, potted plants, and several gently swaying trees. Mostly though, she saw her reflection, and right now she was scowling.

The delicious meal served at the recently completed dinner sat like a ball of lead in her stomach. But it wasn't the food that had her unsettled. The source of her ire was Quelchon Ginala's recitation of that… *boy*.

The empress' scowl became a grimace of disgust.

Cinder Shade. She had reports on his early life in Swallow, his apparent physical disability and resuscitation following the attack by the *aether*-cursed snowtiger. His complete amnesia followed by the miraculous healing of his clubfoot. Oh, yes. She knew all about him, all about his supposed mysteries. She likely knew more about him than he knew himself.

And she didn't believe any of it. She had no reason to. Everything

398

about Cinder Shade's early life screamed falsehood. None of it made sense, unless a person trusted in miracles. Which Sala most definitely did not. Miracles had died with the passing of the Mythaspuris.

Ginala felt the same way, and in this, the two shared a common belief, the elder having taught the younger.

And they also shared a similar assessment about Cinder Shade himself, mistrusting him. He was no hidden prince. He wasn't some boy from the back end of nowhere destined for greatness. He was something else, something vulgar. He was someone who used tricks, skill, and the oh-so noble language of fraternity to earn the trust of his betters, worming his way into their hearts.

Cinder Shade was nothing but a confidence man. A very *good* confidence man, but nothing more and nothing else. Witness how he had somehow earned the respect of two noble elves, Mohal and Riyne, such that they deferred to him. Outrageous! Especially from Riyne, the cadet who was said to hate Cinder with a fierce fire.

Clearly not. In this, the younger Coushinre was a disappointment, an assessment causing Sala to scowl once again.

While she didn't share Estin's and Enma's extreme animus toward humans, she had a certainty about where her people stood in relation to other races. And all elves stood above any human. None of them should ever defer to a human. Not in any matter.

Which led her back to Cinder Shade. What should she do with him? A human pretending to have the skills of an elven ranger. Ridiculous.

Of course, she couldn't completely dismiss the boy's abilities. General Arwan and many masters at the Directorate believed he actually did have the warrior attributes of an elven ranger. They went so far as to claim Cinder Shade might be able to source his *lorethasra*.

Sala hoped not. What a disaster if it were true. Her people would face a terrifying future if humans regained even the slightest aspect of their historical power. And if it were true, it meant Sala had to prepare for the worst. It was the duty of an empress.

She considered what next to do. Should she allow her daughter to go through with her silly sponsorship of the boy's Secondary Trial? A large part of her argued she should disallow it.

Sala's scowl transitioned into a contemplative frown. Then again, it was likely too late to make such a demand. Anya was stubborn. She could give stones lessons in mule-headedness. Tell her to do something, and she would do the opposite. She had to be led to a correct decision, not forced. More importantly, Anya had promised the boy her patronage, and no force on Seminal could make her break her given word.

Unless the boy died before departing Revelant. It was a possibility, but one Sala dismissed. She wasn't afraid to get her hands dirty, but Ginala's words, while fearsome, weren't enough to cause her to stoop to such a level. Wielding the white blade didn't have any known relation to the *Elonic Festh*. She had no idea what the quelchon meant by the recitation, and she'd have to ask her about it tomorrow. Only holders wielded white blades.

"You're unhappy," Avan said. He sat on the couch before the banked fireplace, watching her and wise enough to wait a few minutes for her mind to reach an equilibrium.

The two of them were alone in her study, and Sala had asked him here so they could discuss their impressions from tonight's dinner, but especially Ginala's recitation. The empress might have invited Enma, but her oldest daughter wouldn't be of any use. She too richly despised Cinder, and therefore lacked the necessary emotional detachment to offer any kind of sound advice. The same held true for Anya, although in her case, the situation was opposite. She truly liked the boy. Estin wouldn't do either. He shared Enma's dislike for Cinder.

Sala's brow creased.

Or did he?

Estin had been oddly cordial to Cinder tonight. More well-mannered than she expected. Had something changed between him and the boy?

"What did Ginala tell you?" Avan asked, intruding on her suppositions.

Sala glanced at him. She recalled Ginala's recitation in exquisite detail, every last word, and those dense phrases weighed upon her mind. She repeated them to Avan, needing his advice on how best to proceed. *"And this man wields the white blade,"* she ended, wanting to see her husband's reaction to her final statement.

Avan's brow furrowed. "Only holders can wield the white blade, the wildness. But if Ginala's recitation is true, and Cinder can as well, then doesn't this change everything? All along we thought Cinder was a grifter, but if he is a wielder of the wildness, we have to re-examine everything we think we know about him. He may actually be a holder, lost to his tribe or people."

"Holders serve the yakshins and the trolls. They have no lost members."

"Unless Cinder is the first," Avan argued. "Think about it."

Sala was thinking about it—had thought about it—and reluctantly, she had to agree with her husband's supposition. Cinder as a holder would explain much. It would explain everything. "What if all those ridiculous stories about him and his past are true? The healing, the *aether*-cursed snowtiger, all of it?"

Avan sat upright, surprised awareness etched on his face. "Wasn't there some account about an *aether*-cursed snowtiger seen during the Autumn Trial? During the battle between Jameken Battalion and the spiderkin?"

Sala's eyes widened. Avan was right. There had been mention of an *aether*-cursed snowtiger. And it couldn't be a coincidence. A boy orphaned by an *aether*-cursed snowtiger, and another *aether*-cursed snowtiger saving him during a battle?

But what did it mean? *Aether*-cursed animals killed woven and human alike whenever they had the chance. They never acted as protectors. So why had this creature reacted differently?

"Anya," Avan said, an alarmed ringing in his voice.

"What about her?"

"Her past is similar to the boy's. When she was a child—eight decades ago—she nearly died, and when she awoke, she had no recollection of the first twenty years of her life."

Sala's features slackened. Avan was right. Anya's past was similar. The empress recalled those terrible weeks when her youngest daughter, always sickly and frail in her earliest years, had caught a terrible illness. She had lingered between the lands of the living and those of the dead for weeks without end. At one point, the physicians had even felt sure she *had* died. They'd been unable to find either breath or pulse within Anya, but suddenly, she had gasped as if surfacing from some great depth of water.

She had lived.

A miracle, the physicians had stated, which was utter folly. Anya had simply defeated whatever illness had nearly killed her. There was no need to bring in Devesh or express gratitude in His benevolence for saving Anya. He hadn't done so. Her child had fought for life and survived of her own will and volition.

The only aspect to Anya's recovery that thereafter bothered Sala was when Ginala had recited the girl. *"Your daughter's spirit is changed, and she is no longer entirely yours. She will betray you."*

Upon hearing the slanderous recitation, Sala had grown apoplectic. She had commanded the quelchon to silence, to never again speak the recitation.

But even an empress couldn't rearrange the tides of life, for Anya *was* changed. Her prior feebleness was gone, and over the years to follow, she had transformed into a strong, tall, powerful woman. And she didn't recall anything of the first twenty years of her life.

Two youths with similar stories. Two youths who shared a similar set of skills in the martial world. Two youths who had found one another. Could there be a larger connection between them? And if so, what was it?

"Who are they?" Sala whispered aloud.

"Anya is our daughter," Avan replied. "She always will be. But Cinder is a cipher."

Sala smiled at the alliteration. "He is a cipher, and we need to solve his riddle."

Avan stood to join her in front of the windows. "There's an aspect to this that troubles me."

Sala smirked. "Beyond what troubles we already have?"

Avan nodded. "Ginala felt certain Cinder was a social climber of the worst sort. But then she recites what can only be viewed as a disaster for Yaksha. The *Elonic Festh*, and then this inclusion of a lost holder. Have you ever known her to err so grievously in her judgment?"

Sala hadn't. As far as she knew, Ginala rarely erred in anything, and her apparent incorrect assumptions about the boy added another layer of mystery to the entire matter. And in Sala's experience, mysteries had a way of spawning ever more questions, ones that she didn't need right now. Right now, she needed answers.

Avan wrapped her in his arms, and she relaxed in his embrace. "You'll have my support and help in whatever you need," he said. "But we have to keep a close eye on Cinder."

Sala nodded, and a bitter truth surfaced. "And our youngest daughter as well."

At this late hour, the night was quiet and peaceful. Cinder stood alone on the balcony beyond his rooms, staring at the darkened lands of Taj Wada. In the distance, from atop tall posts and towers, brightly lit *diptha* lanterns illuminated parts of the environs while closer at hand, dimmer lights were looped through ropes of wrought-iron chains, tracing the various paths and sinuous roads through the vast grounds of the royal palace. A wind susurrated like whispers through the branches and leaves of the garden down below, and the sound reminded Cinder of waves ebbing and flowing against a far, distant shore.

He missed the ocean. He'd always loved it as a child.

He smirked as soon as the notion crossed his mind. How could he have loved the ocean as a child? He'd grown up in Swallow, deep in Rakesh's interior, amongst soaring mountains and lofty evergreen forests. He would have never seen the ocean.

The soft creaking of the door opening from Anya's bedroom told him the princess had stepped out onto the balcony. But even if he hadn't heard the noise, her cinnamon scent would have told him of her presence.

"Hello, princess" Cinder said, not bothering to turn around.

"How did you know it was me?"

Cinder smiled faintly. "Who else would it be coming out of your bedroom. And there's also your cinnamon scent."

"Of course." Anya moved to stand next to him, smiling in return. "You can smell what no one but my family can. And they only do so rarely."

Cinder glanced at her. She wore a simple shift that hung to her mid-thigh and a pair of pajama pants. Dormant's ivory light highlighted the glory of her honey-blonde hair until it shone liquid. She shifted, and he was aware of how close she stood. He inched away, changing the conversation to a safer topic. "Why don't you like Quelchon Ginala?"

"I noticed you didn't like her either," Anya replied.

"I'm sure it's a failing on my part. Everyone else thinks she's wonderful."

Anya didn't respond. Instead, she stared into the night. "We need to talk," she said at last. "And not about Ginala. We need to talk about your past."

Cinder sighed. He hadn't been looking forward to this conversation, but Anya was right. They *did* need to talk about his past and about his dreams. They should have discussed them weeks ago, maybe months. Too much was happening to them. Too many similarities. Too many questions that had no answers.

"I know all about how you grew up in Swallow," Anya continued. "The clubfoot. The *aether*-cursed cat. Everything." She angled her head to peer at him. "Is it true?"

Cinder nodded. "As far as I know. I woke up in a well and was told by the man who saved me—my brother, Pitch—that our parents had been killed by an *aether*-cursed snowtiger. But I don't remember any of it. Mostly what I remember is about the clubfoot and the withered leg and how both were healed by the time I reached Swift Sword."

"And what about your dreams?" Anya asked, an odd hitch in her voice.

Cinder eyed her with a frown. There was a strange undercurrent in how she had asked the question. An unspoken sentiment to which she was afraid to give voice. "What about them?" he asked.

A wry smile lit Anya's face. "I think it's time you heard about *my* past," she said. She spent the next few minutes telling him about her early years, about how she used to be small and frail. About how she used to easily sicken, catching a terrible illness when she was in her childhood, in her early twenties and nearly dying. And afterward, like him, she had awoken with no memories of her past, and her weak body had transformed to one full of strength.

Cinder inhaled sharply when Anya finished speaking. Her story was nearly identical to his, and he studied her, worrying and wondering if there was a deeper link between the two of them. *Hoping.* Or if Anya was the woman in his dreams, a vague possibility in the past but in light of this new information… His heart thudded in his chest, and his breathing quickened. What did it mean if she was?

In that moment, he noticed Anya's tension, visible in the tightening at the corners of her lips, the narrowing of her eyes, the stiffening of her shoulders, and her clenched jaw. It was like she was terrified of speaking what was on her mind.

"What's wrong?" he asked.

She stared into the distance, not immediately answering. "Do you ever have visions so real that you aren't sure if they're dreams or memories?"

Cinder faced outward as well, heart racing even faster. Could it be? Did Anya also have dreams she thought were memories of a past life?

He needed to know for certain, and the only way to learn was for him to speak plainly, to let her know his judgments and beliefs, and maybe she would share her own.

"I don't remember the details," Cinder began, unsure how to express himself. He didn't want her to consider him a lunatic.

Anya surprised him then by placing her hand atop his and giving him a reassuring squeeze. "It's alright. I don't remember the details of mine either."

Her support helped, and Cinder was finally able to say what was on his mind. "I think my dreams are memories of a past life."

Anya closed her eyes, and the tension drained out of her. "Thank you," she said, her voice soft yet throbbing with emotion. "Thank you for being brave enough to say what I couldn't."

"Then..." Cinder had to hear her say it.

Anya nodded. "I feel the same way about my dreams."

He exhaled in relief. Their shared history and dreams, there had to be correlation. "Do you ever see a city by the sea and a park?" he asked in sudden eagerness.

Anya shook her head, and his excitement crashed. "No. My dreams are of a mountain fortress, a city deep in its heart. My home." She paused. "And I also see my husband, but I can never see his face. I have no idea what he looks like."

It had been a forlorn hope, to imagine their dreams might be the same, and Cinder worked to contain his disappointment. A second later, he latched onto the end of what she'd said. *Her husband?*

Like a funeral cloak, Anya wore an air of grief and longing. She might not have remembered her husband's face, but she evidently remembered her love for him.

"His name was Rukh," Anya said, her hand still atop his. "Does that name mean anything to you?"

Cinder shook his head, still shocked by her revelation. A husband? "No. I've never heard it before tonight. All I remember is fragments about the city by the sea. A lovely park. I walk through it with a woman. She has hair like yours. The same shade of gold." His hand twitched underneath the warmth of her own, an unconscious reflection of a known desire. He wanted to run his fingers through the Anya's hair, to feel the shimmering strands, and...

No. He constrained himself from making an idiot of himself, reciting his private mantra. *One brick at a time.*

His comment, though, had elicited a smile from Anya. "My people would deem it unseemly for you to have dreams about me."

"I don't care what your people think. The dreams of my past won't change because of their disapproval." He shrugged. "Besides, I've never seen her face, either." This time, it was he who paused.

She noticed his hesitation, and he found himself frozen by her emerald-eyes. "What aren't you saying?"

Cinder stared at the ground, unable to meet her gaze. "I might have murdered her," he whispered, going on to explain the vision he'd had, vaguely recalled but ending with a killing blow aimed at a woman with honey-blonde hair.

Anya shook her head. "I don't see you as a murderer, not in this life or in whichever one your dreams mean."

Cinder didn't think so either, but to hear someone else say so was a comfort. "Do you think we knew one another?" he asked. "I mean, the woman I see has your hair and height."

"I suppose anything is possible," Anya said, offering an empathetic smile. "We both had near-death experiences. We both recovered, were stronger afterward, and we both have had visions of a possible past life. But it's late. I don't think we're going to find any answers tonight."

Cinder recognized she was likely correct, and he wished her goodnight, watching her walk back into her quarters. Afterward, he remained outside, preoccupied by their conversation, and a large part of him hoped—

He knew what he hoped, but he refused to give it expression. Not yet anyway. Maybe not ever. Not until he knew more about himself and his dreams, and he knew for certain who he was.

In that moment, he made a vow. He would apply the same dedication to learning his personal truth as he did the mastery of the sword.

Estin Aruyen sat in the quiet of his night-darkened chambers, staring at a blank wall while considering his people's past and his own future. It was strange for him to think on such matters. He generally eschewed worrying overmuch about what was or what would be. He preferred to exist in the present, or so he liked to tell himself.

Tonight, though, he was starting to understand: the past forged the present, and the present contained the future. And he needed to consider how his past would shape his future.

Estin was proud of who he was and especially where he came from, the resplendent ancestry of his people. He was a royal elf, a member of the greatest nation on Seminal, Yaksha Sithe.

But Yaksha hadn't always been able to make such a bold proclamation. Once they had been far less. Once they had been a backward province in a far grander world than currently existed, and it was the tragedy of the *NusraelShev* that had fueled their ascension. Few knew the ways of the elves prior to that horrific war, but Estin did. There were accounts in ancient tomes in his mother's library, histories discussing the nature of the war itself as well as a few key phrases and statements to reveal the truth to the discerning reader.

In the ancient past, the elves of Yaksha Sithe—all elves, actually— had not been rulers, but stewards and servants, caretakers of the natural realm, entrusted with maintaining the world's balance and harmony. It was a holy yet gentle task, a tranquil burden granted them by their creators, the ancient *asrasins*. Humans, possibly Shokan and Sira themselves. The elves of the times had been content and at peace. Granted a glad existence because of the enduring sacrifice of the Blessed Ones when they had delivered a shattering defeat upon Shet and his forces and lost their own lives in the process, in the mythical millennia before the *NusraelShev.*

Shokan and Sira; surely every bit as powerful as the legends and stories proclaimed. They had battled against Shet and his Titans, alone and unsupported. Two versus eight, but in the end, the Blessed Ones, had smote their enemy's ruin.

And what difference did it make that Shokan and Sira were human?

None as far as Estin was concerned. The Blessed Ones were the standard by which every warrior and all right-living folk measured themselves. Against those facts, nothing else mattered.

But when Shet returned to Seminal, the serene pattern of elven culture had been destroyed. The dread god's black legions had heralded forth from his capital of Naraka, unopposed and conquering territory after territory. Nation after nation, woven after woven.

And Shokan and Sira were nowhere to be found.

It was then, in the time of the world's greatest need, that the elves had risen to the call. Estin's ancient ancestors, Koran and Swan, had accepted the mantle of leadership and fought for decades against Shet's forces, unsupported and unaided.

Estin had imbibed those histories, and pride filled him to overflowing at his people's accomplishments.

Singlehandedly, his forebears had fought a grueling war of attrition against the dark god, holding the line until the Mythaspuris exploded into the world in a flash of singing light. They had relieved the pressure in just the nick of time, but even after their arrival, it had taken many years to fully defeat Shet. Many years to send him and his black legions scurrying back to their fortresses at Naraka, to burn his capital to ash and leave it forgotten for all time so peace could reign.

But the secret histories left by the Mythaspuris indicated they had only been able to shackle Shet and his Titans. They lacked the power to kill him entirely. They could only imprison the ancient god, bind him in bands of stone and steel in the abysmal center of a mountain's heart.

Those same histories also contained a prophecy, one Estin had discovered only a few months prior to the beginning of his Firster year at the Third Directorate. It foretold Shet's resurrection. Of how he would arise one last time and revive his Titans and armies and rebuild Naraka. Of how he would wage war and subjugate the timid nations of the world who would seek to ride out the storm through abasement and flattery.

And as before, it would remain for the elves to oppose Shet, to battle against unending odds until Shokan and Sira strode forth once more. The Blessed Ones would arrive like a rainbow, unforeseen and unknown until the sunlight revealed their glory.

Estin had all-but memorized the prophecies indicating Shokan's and Sira's return, read them in detail, each one further firing a blazing call to glory. If the Blessed Ones arrived in his lifetime, he would serve them to the last of his strength and will.

It was a passion Estin felt deep in his bones, the desire to aid Shokan and Sira and fight alongside them, to battle evil and live up to the standards of his mighty ancestors, like the empresses Koran and Swan. Or have his name spoken in the same breath as the great warriors of history: Gode Halewin, Taprick Mahomine, and Mote Bradwing.

Visions of valor had filled Estin's mind, and several weeks prior to matriculating into the Third Directorate, he had fully committed himself to the cause of the Blessed Ones. He had joined the *Lamarin Hosh*, and although he never expected to actually serve Shokan and Sira, if chance and fate allowed for it, then his place in history as a warrior of legend was assured.

It was odd then, how a simple human, a member of a fallen race, was the one who impeded Estin's calling. A simple boy from a place of no renown who had halted a prince's progression into a warrior of legend.

Cinder Shade.

Estin had despised Cinder from their first meeting, hated watching him grow taller, stronger, and ever more skilled. It was an affront to everything the prince believed true about his kind. The elves were the Blessed Race. They were the best of all woven. They were the finest of all people and all warriors.

And yet, at the Directorate, the elves *and* dwarves lost again and again to a *naaja*, a tainted bastard. It helped some that Cinder, skilled like no human in the Directorate's long history, had saved their entire class on two separate occasions.

But to require salvation from a human was still humiliating, and Estin's dislike for Cinder had waxed, never waning.

Until the meeting with Karthalyn Shoma, Estin's *Isha* in the *Lamarin Hosh*. The prince recalled the meeting with perfect clarity. It had been held the morning after the Firmament Hour, and words and instructions had been spoken, and while it hadn't been spelled out, enough had been said to shake him to his core.

The *Lamarin Hosh* was concerned about Cinder Shade, worried he might be a child of destiny, a *thoraython*, someone around whom history would be written and who changed and shaped the world by his very existence. One conceivable fear was that Cinder might be the Fated Foe, the vessel of utmost evil spoken of in the dwarven prophecies. It was unlikely, but there was another possibility: Cinder might be Shokan reborn.

Karthalyn expected Estin to determine which, if any, of those fears might be true, to study Cinder during their shared Secondary Trial and determine if he truly was a *thoraython*.

It was a ridiculous task, a foolish waste of his time. In fact, upon first hearing of the fears of his *Isha*, Estin had openly scoffed. Cinder Shade a *thoraython*? Impossible.

But then had come a recent conversation with his parents. Just a few minutes ago, in fact. Estin had been asked to attend them in his mother's study. There, he had learned of Ginala's recitation of Cinder.

It had been one harrowing declaration after another.

Estin worried now for his people in ways he had never imagined, and he was slowly coming to realize it would be best if Cinder Shade was neither the Fated Foe *nor* Shokan reborn. It would be best if Cinder was merely a superlative warrior like Anya. By now, Estin could admit that much about the man, and hopefully, the human would accrue no further glory.

For if he was Shokan reborn—Devesh let him not be Shokan—it left Estin in an appalling position, forced to bow to the person he disliked above all others, and who disliked him in equal measure. How could Estin ever serve such an individual? And how could Cinder ever accept his service? The prince's dreams of battlefield fame would be finished, destroyed during his time at the Third Directorate when he'd earned the Blessed One's ire.

Unless Estin somehow got back in Cinder's good graces. He pondered how that might be possible, and whether it was even worth the effort. After a moment of consideration, he realized it might be necessary. What if Cinder *was* Shokan reborn? Stranger things had happened.

And if Cinder was the Fated Foe? Estin shuddered. It didn't bear consideration. The Fated Foe was the harbinger of calamity. He would bring about the end of all things.

32

The morning following their private dinner with the empress and her family saw Cinder, Anya, Lisandre, and Estin board a ship headed for Swift Sword.

With them went Fastness, who had loudly bugled his unhappiness at being stuffed down below. Eventually, the white had quieted down, but only after he saw Anya's and Lisandre's steady geldings, Barton and Slew, and Estin's own high-strung Yavana stallion, Byerley, march down the ramp without the slightest hesitation.

Fastness had snorted in obvious embarrassment, seemingly glancing around to see if anyone had noticed his temperamental display, before quickly following the other horses. Cinder, though, could tell the white was still upset about being locked in the hold, so he made sure the stallion had plenty of hay and even snuck him a couple of apples.

A half-hour later, it was time to set sail.

Cinder hung in the background while the sailors readied their vessel, *Defiant*—a short, stubby naval ship in the Yaksha fleet—for the open water. Sails were unfurled, orders shouted, and lines coiled. Minutes later, on a sunny day with a warm wind to speed their journey,

413

they exited Revelant's harbor and entered the Sentient Sea, heading toward Swift Sword.

Cinder watched the sailors a little while longer before deciding to get to work himself. He'd been sitting around doing nothing for almost half a week, and he could feel himself losing his sharp edge. It wouldn't do. He needed to train, and he searched about for one of the others in his party to act as a sparring partner.

Anya was busy with other matters, and Cinder didn't want to ask Estin. Thankfully, Lisandre was available.

They met in an area near the ship's bow, each carrying a shoke.

Tattered clouds drifted across an open sky, allowing warm sunshine to pour down. However, the earlier warm wind had turned cold, and Cinder was glad for the padded shirt and trousers he'd brought with him from the academy.

While limbering up, Cinder noticed the sailors continuing with their varied tasks, but they also made sure to give him and Lisandre plenty of room to maneuver. They were also clearly curious, and they paused every now and then to see what would happen. No doubt, they figured the famous elven ranger, Lisandre Coushinre, a warrior who wielded an *insufi* blade and might soon earn the label *Sai,* would demolish the upstart human.

"What do you want to do?" Lisandre asked once they were finished stretching. He wore a padded shirt and trousers that were identical to the ones Cinder had on. "Spar? Practice your forms? Grapple?"

"A bit of all three," Cinder replied. "Maybe start with forms, do some sparring, and finish with grappling."

Lisandre nodded agreement. "It's good to see you taking your training so seriously. Where we're going, you'll need to be at your best."

"Should I find Estin?" Cinder asked. The prince could use the training, too.

"No need. I'll see to him myself," Lisandre said in a tone of finality. "We begin."

They started with forms, moving at half-speed and working on technique and balance. Cinder hadn't trained much with Lisandre, only on a handful of occasions. This was the first time he had taken actual instruction from him, and he found himself shocked by Lisandre's insight into weapons training.

"When you lunge, you extend your shoulders more than is needed," Lisandre had taught early on. "It gives you an incrementally better range, but you pay for it with a fractional loss in recovery. Do you think those extra two inches of reach are worth it?"

Cinder repeated the maneuver, his way first, and Lisandre's way next. One more repetition. A third time, and then a fourth. Lisandre's way did allow for a substantially quicker recovery, which was probably going to be of greater benefit than the extra inch or two of reach.

"I see what you mean," Cinder said.

They continued practicing their forms, and Lisandre continued giving out helpful pieces of advice. By the time they finished, Cinder felt like he'd enrolled in a master class on the art of the sword. Lisandre understood balance, extension, feints, and attacks better than anyone he had ever met, and that included Master Absin.

Cinder wanted to smack himself for not taking greater advantage of Lisandre's expertise. All those hours in the Cauldron, and most of the time, he had done his best to avoid the man. And why? Not because of anything Lisandre had done, but because of who he was related to. He was Riyne's older brother. He had allowed his dislike for the younger Coushinre to shade his judgment of the older.

He was wrong to have done so. In effect, he had robbed himself of an excellent instructor, but of greater and uglier import, it was deeply unfair to Lisandre. A man should be evaluated based on their own individual identity; not based on their ancestry.

Cinder vowed to never again make such an error in judgment. Dharma demanded better behavior.

It was another in the list of promises he made to himself.

The steady breeze which had filled *Defiant*'s sails from the moment they left Revelant's harbor stayed with them throughout the rest of their journey. As a result, their travel proved swift and uneventful. In a word, boring, which was a good thing. Cinder figured they'd have all the excitement they could handle once they entered the Daggers.

Several days later, they reached their destination, and Cinder stood at the bow as they entered Swift Sword's harbor. During his very first voyage, he'd suffered seasickness, but afterward, he found his legs. Nowadays, he loved standing at the bow, feeling the ship rise and fall, the wind rushing through his hair. Some proclaimed they felt like a king when standing on the ship's prow, but for Cinder it reminded him of riding Fastness, of letting the stallion run flat out and free. A far better way to live.

His only displeasure on the afternoon of their arrival to Swift Sword was Estin's presence by his side. For some reason, the prince, who had steadfastly ignored him throughout their journey thus far, had decided to come and stand next to him as *Defiant* pulled into the harbor.

Cinder viewed Estin askance, hard-eyed and suspicious as to what purpose the other man might have in being here.

After a moment of consideration, he shrugged off Estin's motivations as unimportant. So long as he kept his mouth shut, there was room enough for both of them.

Right on cue, Estin chose to address him, and Cinder exhaled in annoyance. Unholy hells! It was like the prince could read his mind. However, his disgust turned to surprise when he actually listened to what Estin was saying.

"May the seas lie smooth before you," the prince started. "May a gentle breeze forever fill your sails, may sunshine warm your face, and may kindness warm your soul." He faced Cinder. "It's an old Rakeshian blessing. There are other versions for those traveling through the mountains. Do you know them?"

Cinder didn't. He knew little of Rakesh's culture, only the nation's history, and all of that had come through his reading. "No," he replied. "I don't know much about my nation. I still don't remember my past."

Estin nodded, his face serene rather than gripped by its typical arrogance. "Then let me offer one such blessing since we're heading into the Daggers." He drew himself up, standing tall. "May the road rise up to meet you, may the sun shine upon your face, and may Devesh hold you in His hands during all your travels."

Without another word, he departed, leaving a shocked and bewildered Cinder in his wake. *What the hell had just happened?*

Estin's odd blessing continued to echo in Cinder's mind when they disembarked the ship. He still couldn't figure out what had gotten into the prince. For a few minutes, he'd sounded—not exactly friendly or even cordial—but apologetic, which was both bizarre and impossible. There were two certainties about Estin Aruyen. First, his arrogance refuted any semblance at humility. And second, he detested humans, especially Cinder, which is why his bizarre half-apology struck such a jarring note.

Cinder cut off his examination of Estin's odd behavior when their ship pulled into port. He had more important matters to attend. He grabbed his belongings, and once everyone had disembarked, primary among these was checking on Fastness. He'd made sure to spend time with the bored Yavana during the voyage, inspecting his legs and joints for swelling and ensuring the stallion came through the sea-borne journey without any injuries. He did so again.

"*I'm fine,*" Fastness said, dancing about and moving out of Cinder's reach. "*But I smell apples. Fetch me some.*"

Cinder chuckled. He'd noticed the aroma as well. Somehow the mouthwatering smell of stewing apples was carrying over the stench of fish drying in the sun and reaching them on the pier. "I'll get you some as soon as we get everything squared away."

He gave the stallion a pat on the side of his neck before joining the others in getting their bags settled on the packhorses.

After they finished, Lisandre, the senior-most member of their party and titular leader, although Anya had the higher rank, reviewed their plans. "We head out of Fort Carmine in two days." He shifted to address Cinder. "Which means you have today and tomorrow to visit your friends."

"I have some business in the city as well," Anya said.

Lisandre nodded. "We'll see you tomorrow then." He faced Estin. "Let's go, *bishan*."

"Yes, *Isha*."

Now that the Secondary Trial had officially begun, formality was apparently expected. Cinder had jokingly referred to Anya as his *Isha* when they were still at the Directorate, but to his ears, it had never sounded right. Anya was his friend, not his master. He hoped she would understand.

"Do I have to address you as *Isha*?" he asked her once Estin and Lisandre had headed out.

She smirked, her crooked grin unreadable. "What do you think?"

Cinder stared at her for a moment before sighing. "I think you're going to enjoy having me at your beck and call."

"I've always had you had at my beck and call. I've just rarely exercised my authority to make it so."

"You did during the Unitary Trial," Cinder reminded her.

"Which means you shouldn't have any trouble taking orders. Now, let's roll. The day won't get any longer. What do you have on your agenda?"

"Well, first, I have to feed the pest," Cinder said, nudging Fastness. "Lord Brat demands some apples."

"I'm not a pest or a brat. I'm a stallion." As if in demonstration, Fastness bugled a neigh.

Cinder chuckled. "I know, old son. You're the best stallion in the world."

His words mollified the white, who lifted his head proudly. *"Now you're learning."*

At the end of the dock, they came across the stand selling the warm, stewed apples they smelled, and bought some for Fastness and the other horses. Once their purchase was complete, they mounted up.

"You never answered," Anya said as they made their way toward the wharf's exit. "What are you doing today?"

"I'll start with Riner. He should be at the library. I'll visit him first," Cinder said. He'd told the princess about his friendship with the one-time kitchen boy who was now an apprentice librarian. "It should be a surprise since we arrived a day early."

"Do you mind if I join you?" Anya asked. "I'd like to meet this young boy you've spoken so highly about. Besides, I've got hours to kill before my meetings tonight."

Cinder forced a smile. Being alone with Anya didn't strike him as a good idea, but he also couldn't tell her no. He had no reason to deny her request, and he certainly couldn't explain the reason for his antipathy. Better to simply grin and bear the discomfort. "Of course."

One brick at a time.

"You like her," Fastness chuckled. *"You want her as a filly to mount and—"*

Cinder clapped the stallion's neck. "That's enough of that," he warned in a soft whisper so Anya couldn't hear.

Fastness whickered laughter but at least he offered no further comment.

A sudden notion came to Cinder. "Wouldn't your meetings have been for tomorrow night?" he asked Anya.

She nodded. "They are, but I'll send word to everyone so they'll know to expect me tonight."

They headed out then, exiting the wharf and entering the congested, cobblestone streets of the city proper. However, while Cinder expected their travel to slow to a crawl, they turned out to have no trouble navigating the roads since the crowds moved aside for them.

It was probably because of Anya. She was an elf, and the people of Rakesh understood their status as essentially a vassal state of Yaksha.

However, Cinder noticed how Fastness was garnering nearly as many approving glances as the princess. He was a powerful animal, perfectly proportioned, and graceful beyond what would be expected for any normal horse. Those with knowledge of the equine likely recognized Fastness' status as a Yavana, and their gazes were often hungry.

Cinder tightened his grips on the reins.

"They won't steal me away," Fastness said, whinnying in amusement. *"If they tried, I would stomp them to bloody paste."*

Cinder shuddered at the vivid image. "Remind me to never make you angry."

"Feed me warm apples, and you'll have no worries."

"Of course," Cinder said with a smile.

"Talking to Fastness again?" Anya asked.

Cinder nodded. "He was asking for more warm apples."

Anya shook her head in exasperation. "I don't think I've ever met a more spoiled Yavana."

Fastness huffed. *"She's pretty, but she's annoying."*

Cinder laughed.

"What did he say?"

Cinder told her.

Anya laughed as well. "He's the one who's pretty. It lets him get away with all sorts of silliness."

They rode on, and the crowds thinned the further they got from the docks. The buildings changed as well, transitioning from the wide, windowless warehouses by the piers to tall, narrow structures where folk lived cheek-to-jowl in their flats. The cries of vendors selling grilled meat, pastries, or sugared confections mixed with the cacophony from the many wagons, drovers, and merchants hauling their belongings. And then there were the poor, sitting in clusters upon porches, doorsteps, and dank alleys, desultorily watching the world and their lives waste away.

Cinder glanced about, jaw clenching in disappointment and sorrow. In Certitude, he had never seen the truly destitute, but here they were everywhere. He was left fuming in anger at his own people. How could so many wealthy folk do so little for the poor?

They soon left the impoverished areas behind, but their haunted eyes stayed with Cinder. "Have you had any more dreams?" Cinder asked once they reached an area of relative quiet. He spoke to distract himself from the images of the poor more than anything else.

Anya shook her head in response to Cinder's question. "You?"

"Same."

Anya sighed. "It's strange how much our histories are alike, but how different our past lives seem to be."

"I wish I knew if our dreams are only coincidence or if they actually mean anything."

"I would bet on coincidence," Anya said. "We can't be the only people who almost died and recovered. I think we're just a rare two who happened to discover someone else with similar dreams."

Cinder grunted agreement. She was probably right, although privately he wished she wasn't, for a host of reasons he didn't want to acknowledge or admit. He snuck a glance at Anya, wishing once again he didn't like her so well.

One brick at a time.

They traveled on, entering a wealthier neighborhood. There, they encountered one of Swift Sword's parks. It was a square, green oasis set amidst the gray stone and red brick buildings, which were similar in size and shape to those in the poorer section—long, narrow, and three or four stories tall—but the quality here was vastly improved. The people in this area also carried themselves in a different manner. They walked with a purpose, none of them appearing beaten down by life's toil—or maybe lack thereof since some folk were poor because there simply wasn't enough good paying work to go around.

A few miles later, they arrived at their destination, a large, red-brick building rising out of the center of a park. *The library.* It soared above the surrounding trees and shrubs and resembled a castle with towers on all four corners and balconies at the heights. Wide, stone stairs wrapped the building on three sides, drawing visitors toward fluted columns that supported an arcade and a pair of bronze doors half again Cinder's height.

Anya gestured. "I know of a nearby stable where we can board the horses."

Once their mounts and packhorses were seen to, they entered the library, discovering a vast atrium. A dank odor permeated the air, mixing with the more pleasant aroma of old paper. The smells reminded Cinder of the library at the Directorate, but what completely captured his attention was the vast array of books. Soaring above him and Anya were four floors of stacked shelves, all of them filled to capacity with books and scrolls.

He nearly salivated at all the knowledge the library contained. How many forgotten secrets and lost truths? How much unknown wisdom to make the world a better place?

Cinder took in more details.

Large chandeliers, hung from on high and containing a plethora of *diptha* lamps, did their best to illuminate the massive space. However, the oppressive, gray stone and the reams of stacked bookcases sucked in the lights and returned dimness. In addition, the rows of windows lining the upper gallery of the entrance hall had seemingly not been cleaned in years. The bright sunshine penetrated them as little more than a wan light, leaving the room with the appearance and atmosphere of a large underground cavern.

The dark ambiance didn't hinder those visiting the library, however. There were many people here this afternoon. Quite a few were seated at the square tables spaced about the ground floor while others strolled about, speaking to one another in hushed tones, but their gazes often flicked to Anya—and then to him.

Cinder disregarded their attention when he noticed the unwavering approach of a smiling young man in black robes. Cinder frowned. A librarian, perhaps? Initially, he didn't recognize the man, but an instant later, a broad grin spread across his face and joy bubbled in his throat when he realized who it was.

Riner.

The last time he had seen him, Riner had been a boy, rotund, softly spoken, and lacking self-confidence. Look at him now. Riner walked with assurance, his head held high and his stride poised. His round face had finally settled into a young man's handsome features.

Riner reached them, and Cinder pulled his friend into a crushing hug. "It's good to see you," he said, pulling back slightly and still grinning. "How have you been?"

"I'm doing well," Riner said, still smiling broadly. "But I didn't expect you until tomorrow."

"We had good weather and made better time than expected," Cinder explained. He remembered Anya standing patiently next to him, and he moved aside to introduce her. "This is Princess Anya Aruyen of Yaksha Sithe."

"I know who she is. I've read all about the imperial family," Riner said, bowing to Anya. "Plus, you've written to me about her."

Anya quirked a single eyebrow upon hearing this. "Written about me? How interesting," she said, smiling enigmatically. Or was it knowingly? It couldn't be pleased... could it?

Cinder turned aside when he realized he was blushing.

"He only spoke of you in the very fondest of terms," Riner said, smiling earnestly. He sounded and looked like he thought he was being helpful.

Anya chuckled in response, low and throaty. "I'm sure he did."

Cinder cleared his throat and shot Riner a pointed look.

"As a friend," Riner hastily added before mercifully changing the conversation. Cinder could have kissed him. "You arrived at the perfect time. I have a few hours off, and there is a wonderful restaurant close by. We can talk while we walk there."

Cinder stared longingly at the books rising all around him. He wanted to wander the stacks.

Anya chuckled at him. "Come along." She tugged on his hand. "You can wander the stacks some other day."

Cinder caught Riner glance in confusion at Anya clasping his hand, and he quickly disengaged from the princess.

He cleared his throat. "How is Coral?" Cinder asked, hoping to distract Riner even as he fought to control another embarrassed flush on his face.

"She is doing well," Riner said, his voice neutral, indicating an unwillingness to speak further on the topic of his sister.

Cinder didn't bother pressing the matter. It wasn't his place. It had been he who had ended their relationship, and while he might still consider Coral a friend, he doubted she viewed him in the same light. It was a sad truth, but her well-being could no longer be his business.

Riner flicked a guarded glance at Cinder. "She's seeing someone."

Cinder smiled, seeking to set Riner's mind at ease. He wasn't angry or even unhappy to learn Coral was seeing someone new. He only wanted the best for her. "Is he worthy?" Cinder asked.

"You probably know better than I," Riner answered. "It's your friend, Dorr Corn, from *Steel-Graced Adepts.*"

"Is this the same Dorr Corn you've spoken to me about?" Anya asked. "The one who trained you even though you replaced him in the Maker's Tournament?"

Cinder nodded. "Dorr was the best of us, maybe not with the sword, but definitely as a person," he answered, his mind going elsewhere.

Dorr Corn. The eldest of the apprentices during Cinder's time at *Steel-Graced.* The person Cinder had asked to drop in and make sure Coral and Riner were doing well. A good man. A trusted friend and brother. Cinder prayed Dorr would treasure Coral the way she deserved.

"Is she happy?" Cinder asked.

Riner smiled, his face joyful. "Happier than I've ever seen."

A lurking twinge of guilt that Cinder hadn't realized was present, relaxed. Coral had found someone worthy of her, and she was happy. It was a good thing.

Cinder and Anya shared a wonderful lunch with Riner, and the fare was every bit as good as he claimed.

However, it wasn't the food that made the meal so fulfilling. It was the company and conversation. Cinder relayed some of his various experiences, briefly touching on the the *aether*-cursed bear and the near disaster of the Autumn Trial. But most of what he told Riner had to do with slice-of-life occurrences, such as a funny joke one of the dwarves might have said, a humorous event, something foolish Estin might have done—which was the same as a humorous event.

"Careful," Anya warned. "That's my brother you're disparaging."

Cinder didn't need the reminder. The woman he… liked was the sister to a man he hated, or at least, for whom he held minimal respect. She knew it, and he'd spoken to her about it in private, but this was a public setting, and she couldn't allow him to speak ill of her brother, a prince of Yaksha Sithe. "Yes, *Isha*," he said respectfully, bowing to her. Cinder moved off the topic of Estin and described playing music with Jozep and eventually even Riyne.

"Riyne!" Riner exclaimed on hearing this. "I thought the two of you hated one another."

Cinder shrugged. "Don't ask me how, but it seems like we fell into a friendship."

The conversation then shifted to Riner. There were many changes in his life. For example, *Our Lady of Fire*, the orphanage where he and Cinder had first met, had undergone drastic changes. Apparently, Master Choff had found a woman brave enough to take him on as a husband. She was a schoolteacher by the name of Marya, and at her insistence, the orphans were now given regular schooling, including reading and writing, arithmetic, and history. It was welcome news.

Less welcome was the information about the zahhacks. This past winter, the monsters had been more active than usual. There were reports of massacres at isolated farms and hamlets throughout Rakesh. A few of the attacks were even within a day's march of Swift Sword. The army had been dispatched, and everyone hoped they'd destroyed the marauding monsters.

Riner also shared stories about Jarde Linger and Stard Lener, the Errow bullies who had made Riner's time at *Our Lady* a living torment. Cinder recalled his own run-ins with them, and the last time had ended with Jarde and Stard bloodied and beaten. The Errows had eventually been drafted into the army, and the last time Cinder had encountered them, they had seemed surprisingly repentant of how they had treated Riner.

"They apologized?" Cinder asked Riner, unable to believe it.

"People can change," Anya murmured.

"I guess," Riner said. "But I never thought Jarde and Stard would. They were horrible, awful bullies, but yes, in the end, they apologized. They went to Coral first, and she was about to throw them out on their ears, but they said you told them to go see her."

Cinder remembered his last conversation with the Errows, when he had advised them to apologize to Riner and Coral. He just never expected them to carry through and do it. "I wonder why they listened to me," he mused.

"I don't know if they did," Riner said. "There was one time when they stopped by to apologize to Coral, and they let it slip that their elders were making them."

"*One* time when they apologized?" Cinder's eyes narrowed. "Just how many times did they apologize?"

"I lost track after five."

Cinder chuckled.

There was more conversation, talks about Cook Nestle from *Our Lady of Fire*, discussions about Riner's work, such as when he would become a journeyman librarian, or possibly even a master, and information about some of the other orphans they knew.

Afterward, Cinder and Anya walked Riner back to the library and said their goodbyes, promising to see him again if they had the chance.

As they readied to depart, Riner blurted, "You should see Coral, I think she'd like it."

Cinder offered a thin smile but not agreement. He had survived nearly drowning in a well, battled *aether*-cursed beasts, and defeated monstrous spiderkin, but he doubted he'd ever have the courage to visit Coral Strain again. And, honestly, he doubted she would want him to, either. It sounded like she was happy, and as he reckoned matters, it might be best to just leave it like that, unless he received a message from her otherwise.

He gave Riner a final hug before he and Anya exited the library. As they were departing, he shot the stacks of books one last longing look.

"I know what you're thinking," Anya said.

"There's so much to learn?" Cinder said, hating the whining note that had crept into his voice.

"Yes, there is. I've spent years here and only scratched the surface of what this library contains."

"You've spent time here?" It shouldn't have surprised him, but for some reason it did.

"Of course. I do enjoy reading."

Cinder grinned. "The library's romance section must be well-stocked."

Anya chuckled. "Well played."

33

"Where to now?" Anya asked after they had left the library and collected their horses.

"*Steel-Graced Adepts*," Cinder said, his breath frosting in front of him. Despite the lingering sunshine of the late afternoon, the day had grown cold. "I want to see my old masters and friends."

While she'd been there on a prior occasion, Anya also wanted to visit Cinder's original martial academy. "Mind if I join you there also? I can't stay long, but I'd like to pay my respects again to your first swordmasters."

Cinder smiled. "I think they'd like that."

They mounted up and headed into the busy, sun-burnished streets of Swift Sword. Folk bustled about in their various labors, merchants hawked their wares from outside their stores, and farmers passed by with wagons groaning under loads of a late winter harvest of wheat, edamame, and chickpeas.

The congested roads slowed their travels, but with Anya's gelding, Barton, ambling alongside Fastness, the two horses were able to cut through the bustle, and only rarely did they have to force open a

428

passage.

Whenever Anya visited Swift Sword, the crowds generally swayed out of her way before closing behind her like the wake of a boat. They did so for most of her kind, especially those on horseback. It was part and parcel of the respect the humans of Rakesh displayed toward the elves of Yaksha Sithe, although Anya was conflicted by the honor shown to her.

The people of Rakesh were proud folk, and if they were deferential to her, it should be as a matter of courtesy, not because they considered her, and her kind, their betters. They should bend knee to no one.

Anya glanced at Cinder, wondering if he noticed how the crowds moved aside for them.

It didn't seem so, or at least it wasn't of his highest concern. Right now, Cinder's features bore an odd mixture of sadness and defeat. They had just entered an especially poverty-stricken area of the city, the buildings dilapidated and the macadam streets in poor repair.

Anya had a sense of what was bothering Cinder, and he confirmed her guess a second later.

"I never saw the poverty before," he said, his voice was filled with a combination of disbelief and self-directed disgust. "Not like this. Not until this visit." He jutted his chin at a man and his family of three young children—two boys and a girl—their clothes little more than rags. "How could I have been so blind?"

"Because you were trying to survive?" Anya suggested.

Cinder grimaced. "It's not much of an excuse. The poor deserve to be known. They deserve an opportunity to thrive, to find a worthy purpose, to create beauty, stories, music, or art. They deserve a chance."

It was a warm-hearted sentiment, and one Anya shared. In truth, traveling through Swift Sword always posed a challenge for her. Many elves who frequented human cities and towns reacted to the impoverishment with either contempt for humanity as a whole or a forceful refusal to see what was directly in front of their eyes. Anya found the former attitude repugnant and refused the deceitful solace of the latter.

Bearing witness to the hardships of the destitute was a burden she gladly shouldered. She *saw* the poor. She witnessed their struggles, and her heart broke every time she saw a hungry child, hence her meeting this evening. It was with the board of directors of her charity, *Sira's Heart*, through which Anya did her best to provide shelter for the homeless, care for the sick, and food for the hungry. Some of the money even went to *Our Lady of Fire*, Cinder's orphanage.

But somehow the work was never enough. Swift Sword never seemed to suffer from an abatement of the needy.

Cinder's jaw clenched, his features frozen in discontent as he stared resolutely ahead. He heeled Fastness ahead of her.

He didn't want to talk about the poor anymore. That much was obvious, and Anya let him be. He was finally seeing the hard lives of those in need, and he would have to find his own path to peace with his newfound awareness. Not only that, but he'd have to discover how little his otherwise laudable martial skills would help him with such a weighty duty.

They rode on in silence, finally leaving the poorer area and entering a somewhat finer one where the homes and buildings were cleaner and the streets were no longer pitted with potholes like festering ulcers. A few blocks later, the neighborhood transitioned into a wealthy quarter.

They were nearing *Steel-Graced Adepts*, and during the final few minutes prior to their arrival, Anya considered the masters at the school.

They had done a surpassingly fine job training Cinder. He had already been a talent when he'd arrived at the Third Directorate. He already had his preternatural ability to predict an opponent's movements, as well as a fine foundation of skills. Early on, Anya had noticed how smoothly Cinder transitioned from one motion to the next, recognizing his outstanding balance and the precision of his swordwork. Master Absin had taken a buffing cloth to those excellent abilities and skills, scraping and polishing off the rough edges until Cinder glowed like a polished diamond.

But the masters at *Steel-Graced* deserved a proper acknowledgment for their superlative training. She had done so before, during her first visit to the school, but it never hurt to tell them a second time. She would only stay long enough to pay them her regards, and then she'd leave, just as she'd told Cinder.

He probably wanted time alone with his friends, and just as importantly, she had her own matters to attend: her meeting with the board and another with some merchants important to Yaksha. Afterward, she would settle in for the evening at her favorite inn within Swift Sword and relax. It would start with a much-needed shower, which would also be the last one afforded her given the months she expected to be in the field.

Tomorrow, she and Cinder would reconnect with Lisandre and Estin and head into the Daggers.

Anya blinked.

Where was Cinder going to sleep tonight? Somehow, she had never thought to ask him. She asked now.

"I'll stay at *Steel-Graced*," Cinder said, flashing a charming grin. "I'm used to sleeping in the closet under the stairs. It's like a home away from home."

Anya smiled. When he grinned at her like that, she couldn't help but reply in kind. A thick strand of hair had fallen over his head like a forelock, and she wanted to sweep it aside. She wanted to step closer to him, cup his face and kiss him.

Her eyes widened as she nearly committed herself to what would have been a terrible mistake. Her stomach hollowed. Her gorge rose. *Oh, Devesh. What am I doing? What am I thinking?* Anya closed her eyes, working to control her emotions.

"What's wrong?" Cinder asked.

Anya opened her eyes. Cinder was staring at her, concern writ on his features.

"Nothing," she said, forcing the dismay to the back of her mind. "I was thinking on what we might face in the Daggers."

Cinder had a doubtful air, but he gave her a slow nod of agreement. "I'm sure whatever it is, we'll face it together."

"Of course." Anya slowed her gelding, allowing Cinder to press ahead of her. She watched and studied him, filled with fear and self-loathing. How could this have happened?

She couldn't allow it. She had to harden her heart against Cinder, and she imagined herself laying a barrier of bricks around her emotions. She had to wall them off so they didn't betray her.

Thoughts about the poor continued to crowd Cinder's mind during the rest of the ride to *Steel-Graced Adepts*. Their need was obvious, and it sickened him that he had never before paid them any mind. And he had even once been counted amongst their number.

"Cities bind us in obligations," Fastness said, apparently picking up on his ruminations. *"They are cages."*

"They can seem that way," Cinder agreed.

"People should run free."

Cinder had no response to the stallion's declaration. It didn't really help him much with answering his unawareness for Swift Sword's poverty.

But whatever the case, his eyes were now wide open. He couldn't forget the impoverished ever again. He only wished there was a way to help them, and he made a note to ask Anya her opinion when he had a chance.

For now, other considerations took precedence. They had reached the neighborhood containing *Steel-Graced*, and he gazed ahead, imagining the quiet avenue where the martial school sat. The white-washed building, its terra-cotta roof, blacked out windows, and the grassy sward planted across the street. He remembered the blacksmith and the baker on either side of the school and the one thousand and one lessons he'd learned at *Steel-Graced*. But mostly his deliberations focused on memories of his martial masters and his once-fellow students, Gorant Sin Peace and Sash Slice. Anticipation at seeing them had him smiling.

A nearby inn had room in the stable for Fastness and Barton, and after ensuring the horses had fresh water and hay, he and Anya went to the martial school. The front door was unlocked, and Cinder let himself in. He led Anya to the courtyard at the back of the building where they discovered Masters Lerid File and Jine Kole along with Journeyman Faine Kole training the two senior-most students, Sash and Gorant.

They were working in the brick-walled courtyard that contained a million fond memories. The space was floored in broad flagstones and perimetered by a narrow strip of grass. *Diptha* lanterns, mounted atop the wall and strung from thin ropes stretching across the space, provided illumination for sparring at night.

Cinder stood next to Anya, indicating for her to remain silent. The two of them waited to be noticed, standing in the breezeway running the building's length while watching the instructors and students go through their forms and limber up for the sparring to come.

Master Lerid appeared little changed from when Cinder had first met him. His bowl-cut hair might have a trace more salt, but he remained lean and fit, clothed in half-boots and tough, tan clothes—a hemp shirt and trousers.

Master Jine, the older of the two masters, possibly had a bit more stoop to his back, but otherwise he remained tall and unsmiling with a close-cropped white beard and white hair. His blue eyes were a reflection of his Errow heritage and rounder than the norm for Rakesh. It was he who called out the cadence to the stretching, his voice holding a raspy edge that Cinder hadn't heard last year.

Journeyman Faine, Master Jine's son, was in his thirties, shorter than his father but thicker of build and possessing the dark, almond eyes and dark hair of a typical Rakeshian. He also had two stripes on his tan shirt, lacking only a third one to indicate his status as a master. Faine smiled more easily than his taciturn father, but a steely determination filled his eyes.

Cinder's study finally went to the two students, both of whom he knew quite well, and both of whom were a year younger than him. Sash Slice no longer resembled a whip—he had gained much-needed muscle—but based on his kicks and punches, retained his customary grace and lethal speed. And Gorant Sin Peace, his build was similar to Faine's, but he was also every bit as quick as Sash, possibly even more explosive. In the past, the only thing holding him back was his timidity, his unwillingness to demand victory.

Cinder grinned when Master Jine finally noticed him and Anya. The old master smiled, his seamed face cracking into a web of welcoming wrinkles. "Halt," he called to the others, who turned to see what had captured Master Jine's attention. They immediately shouted their happy greetings, and it took many shouts, hugs, and laughs before Cinder was able to re-introduce them to Anya. Sash and Gorant obviously hadn't forgotten the princess, and the two of them nearly fell over themselves in their efforts to be the first to welcome her.

"We received your letter," Master Lerid said after the greetings were complete. "But you said you'd arrive tomorrow, and you never mentioned the princess would be accompanying you." His voice held a chiding tone.

"It wasn't his fault," Anya said, coming to Cinder's defense. "We had good weather and made excellent time, and I joined Cinder on a whim. I wanted to once again congratulate and commend you and the other masters on the excellent training you provided Cinder and Bones. They have been exceptional cadets."

"Thank you," Master Lerid said, bowing slightly, his eyes lit with pleasure. "Training the two of them has been one of the great honors in life. They arc an instructor's fondest dream."

"I've never known anyone like them, especially Cinder," Master Jine agreed. "I thought Lerid was joking when he said we were taking Cinder on as a student. So small when he first walked through the doors. I didn't think he'd last a day." The old master shook his head. "The boy proved my judgment wrong within the very first week. I was cold to him, and he used it as motivation to push himself harder. Harder than anyone I've ever met. It was a blessing to educate him."

Cinder blushed in embarrassment. He had never known Master Jine to speak so warmly to anyone.

"Well, he has been a blessing to the Directorate as well," Anya said. "Ask him about the Unitary and Autumn Trials. He saved a lot of lives." She cleared her throat and smiled. It was like sunlight breaching a wall of gray clouds. "And now, gentleman, I'm afraid I have other business to attend." She glanced at Cinder. "I'll see you tomorrow morning. Be ready."

"Yes, *Isha*," Cinder replied.

Anya shared a few more words with the masters before sweeping out of the school.

Sash whistled in appreciation. "That is some woman."

Gorant nodded agreement.

Faine fingered Cinder's eagle brooch. "It still has ruby eyes," he noted in wonder.

"I defended my position as Prime." Cinder smiled, unable to hide his pride at the accomplishment. Defeating woven sourcing their *lorethasra* was the stuff of fantasy.

Laughter and congratulatory shoulder slaps met his statement, but shortly afterward, Master Lerid asked about the Unitary Trial, and Cinder was caught up in re-telling of the events that had transpired in both it and the Autumn Trial.

Faine eyed him in sympathy. "You've been through some rough times."

"I guess I have," Cinder said softly. It wasn't something he wanted to discuss, and he gazed about the school. "Where is everyone else?"

"It's a rest day," Master Lerid explained.

"Then why are you two here?" Cinder asked Gorant and Sash.

"Because of your bad influence," Gorant answered. "We want to win the Maker's Tournament. We figured the best way would be to work as hard as you did."

Cinder nodded. Hard work was good, but it had to be the correct kind of hard work. "Are you making yourselves uncomfortable?" he asked Sash and Gorant.

"What do you mean?" Sash asked.

"Exactly what I said. Study yourself. Learn your weaknesses. Shore them up. Better yet, make your weaknesses a strength. Don't just focus on your strengths."

Master Jine slapped the back of Sash's head. "See? What have I been preaching for the past six months?"

"Yes, sir," Sash said, appearing abashed. "We'll work harder."

"But you'll work correctly this time," Master Jine added.

Sash grimaced. "The work never ends."

"It might end this year," Faine muttered sourly.

"What might end?" Cinder asked.

"Not now," Master Lerid said to Faine, a stern warning in his tone.

Cinder's confusion deepened. "What's going on?"

"You might as well tell him," Master Jine said to Master Lerid. "He deserves to know."

Master Lerid sighed as if he bore the weight of the world. "I suppose he does," he said, facing Sash and Gorant. "Get back to work. Faine will oversee."

Sash opened his mouth to argue, clearly wanting to know what was going on. "But—"

"Now," Master Lerid's tone brooked no dissent. Once the three of them were gone, he addressed Cinder. "When I purchased *Steel-Graced Adepts* from Master Sharn, I had to take a loan from one of the banks. There was a fire five years ago. The building burned, and I had to take another loan to repair the school. The terms offered were difficult."

"You should have never accepted them," Master Jine said with a scowl.

"It's done," Master Lerid snapped. "The school needed rebuilding, and I had no other options." He sighed, the anger abruptly leaving him. "The rebuilding loan was coming due, and when I sought to combine it with the other loan, I found out the bank had sold both notes. The individual who bought them…" He grimaced in disgust. "He asks for immediate repayment or he will take possession of the building."

"What happens to the school if he does that?" Cinder asked.

"This new person will own the building, the school, its name and history. *Steel-Graced Adepts* will be under his ownership. We'll have to re-establish ourselves somewhere else and with a new name."

Cinder rocked on his feet. It wasn't the worst news, but it certainly wasn't good. "Is there nothing you can do?"

Masters Lerid and Jine shared a speculative glance.

"Tell him," Master Jine said.

"This individual, Ald Prince, is also a promoter. He promotes fights. If we allow one of our former students, a Maker's Tournament finalist, to fight in the gladiatorial games next season, he'll offer fair terms on the refinancing. If our student wins, he'll give us the building and name free and clear."

It wasn't even a choice. "I'll do it," Cinder said.

"No, you won't," Master Lerid said. "We are a martial academy. We don't train gladiators to entertain the coarse masses. We train warriors who protect those coarse masses."

"It'll stain your reputation amongst the true warriors of Rakesh if you take part," Master Jine added.

Cinder loved *Steel-Graced Adepts.* He loved this school, its history, and its people. And he wouldn't stand idly by while this Ald Prince stole it out from underneath Master Lerid, especially since it sounded like the man merely considered it a business transaction.

At the same time, he was also angry with Masters Lerid and Jine. Not for allowing themselves to get into this situation. Sometimes when dealing with those who loved money above all else, these types of situations arose.

No. What had him upset was that the masters had told him the easiest way out of their dilemma, but when Cinder offered his help, they tried to stride the high road and warn him off. If they truly felt such disgust about one of their students taking part in a gladiatorial exhibition, they should have never mentioned it. It felt like they were simultaneously asking for Cinder's help but also wanting to wash their hands of accepting it.

"I know what it means to my reputation," Cinder said, doing his best to curb his irritation. "But you knew this would be my reaction. You knew I'd fight. I'll do whatever is required to save the school. But you should have never told me about it if you were that worried for me."

Master Lerid stared at him, not answering at first, his face filled with guilt and grief. "You're right. I'm sorry. I should have never told you, and I won't let you do this." His voice was a ragged whisper.

"We'd rather lose the school than to see our finest student lose honor," Master Jine stated.

Cinder's anger with the masters dimmed. They both appeared conflicted, clearly hating the notion of Cinder taking part in a gladiatorial competition.

"I know you don't want it, but it will happen," Cinder said. "What are the terms?"

Master Lerid held mute.

It was Master Jine who answered. "Ald Prince thinks it would be best to take part after the finals of the Maker's Tournament. He thinks the promotion for such a competition will sell itself." He hesitated. "It'll also be our warrior against two gladiators."

Cinder's mouth pursed. Two-against-one wasn't so bad. In fact, compared to fighting against elves and dwarves, two human gladiators were unlikely to pose much of a challenge. He'd defeat them, and the school would be saved. "Let Ald know I accept on behalf of *Steel-Graced*."

Master Lerid shook his head. "I won't do it. I was serious when I said I'd rather lose the school than see any of mine choose dishonor."

"I know, but see it done anyway." Cinder's only concern at keeping his promise was surviving the Secondary Trial. Otherwise, the timing should be fine. He was to have a month of rest after the Secondary Trial anyway, which should be completed several weeks prior to the Maker's Tournament.

The rest of Cinder's time at *Steel-Graced Adepts* went far better than the initial hour, a fact for which he was grateful. He spent the remainder of the afternoon sparring against Faine, Sash, and Gorant. For the latter, he halted now and again to correct their form and technique and provide guidance on how to read their opponents to create openings by setting up proper feints. Afterward everyone had a supper full of merriment and joy as they reminisced about the past, laughed over shared follies, and spoke of what each person had been doing since they'd last shared a meal.

Shortly after breakfast the next morning, Anya arrived, and Cinder said his goodbyes to his first instructors and his first warrior-brothers. He was sad to leave; the visit to Swift Sword was too short. He could have spent days longer here. Riner and the folk at *Steel-Graced* were part of his first found family, and he was going to miss them.

But before leaving, Cinder made sure he had the correct date and time of the Maker's Tournament.

"What was that about?" Anya asked, having overheard the last snippets of the conversation.

Cinder explained while they were on their way fetch Fastness from the stables.

"Bankers and financiers." Anya grimaced, appearing disgusted. "So many of them are nothing but scum. I hate them. They only see a coin instead of a person. Force you to do their bidding just because they have the money and power, and you don't."

Cinder largely agreed with Anya but hearing her express such a sentiment still caused him to do a double take. He stared at her, trying to hold back a smirk. "Wait a second. Aren't you a princess? You're the definition of someone with more money and power than someone else."

"I realize the irony," Anya said. "I have the money and power to force people to do what I want, and maybe I even use it sometimes, but the difference is that I don't do it for my own personal gain. Not like that promoter."

"But you could."

"I could," she allowed. "But I don't. I never have, and I never will. That isn't the kind of person I would ever want to be." She glanced at him askance. "There are other royals and nobles, I'm sure you've run into them, who behave otherwise."

Estin and Riyne. Or at least how Riyne used to be.

They reached the stables, and after ensuring Fastness had no complaints, Cinder saddled the stallion, and they headed out of Swift Sword, journeying in companionable quiet.

The crowds were thin this early, only a few other travelers. All of them quickly making their way to whatever destination they had in mind. There were also a handful of wagons trundling along with their covered goods. Compared to yesterday's bustle, the streets at this hour were serene, and the roads a mix of light and shadow with the sun peeking above the eastern facing buildings.

Anya broke the silence between them. "I have the money to pay off the debt," she said, her breath pluming in the cold air, surrounding her like a tarnished halo. "If you think Master Lerid will allow it."

It was a generous offer, and Cinder considered how Master Lerid would receive it. Would his pride allow him to accept the money? Agree to charity rather than see one of his own assume possible dishonor?

The answer seemed obvious. "He'll allow it," Cinder said, "but from what he told me, it also sounds like this Ald Prince fellow won't care. He has no reason to accept your payment. He wants to see his gladiators battle someone trained at the Third Directorate. He'll earn three or four times as much money promoting a match like that compared to how much he'd make if someone paid off the debt."

Anya didn't have an answer to his statement, and they traveled on in companionable silence once again.

A few hours later, they caught sight of Fort Carmine, which guarded the northern approach to Swift Sword. There, they regrouped with Estin and Lisandre, who waited directly outside the fortress' open front gate, mounted and ready to go.

Estin's stallion, Byerley, briefly exposed his teeth at Fastness, but as soon as the big white bared his own and took a threatening step forward, the black Yavana backed off.

The four of them exited Swift Sword without further ado, but Cinder glanced back one last time at Fort Carmine and Swift Sword, praying they'd all make it back here safe and secure.

They headed north then, traveling steadily and without pause, except for a light lunch. It was late in the afternoon before they were finally rid of the last of the city's traffic, and where they journeyed now, the road was no longer paved. It was little more than a hard-packed gravel lane, wide enough for a wagon, but nothing larger.

At least it was well-maintained. There were no weeds or grass to choke it out.

They followed the road, climbing and descending foothills that grew steadily rougher, their steep shoulders forested in bare hardwoods yet to bloom. The land was wild in these parts with thick brambles and hardy brush filling the undergrowth, except for the cleared farmlands surrounding the single village they came across.

By now, their small group had settled into a comfortable pace with Cinder and Estin trailing after Lisandre and Anya, who rode a few yards ahead.

Lisandre was speaking to Anya. "If your visit went so well, then why do you appear so troubled?"

Anya momentarily glanced back at Cinder. "My *bishan* finds himself in a bit of a conundrum," she replied, going on to explain the troubles between Master Lerid and Ald Prince.

Cinder's mouth twisted. He would have preferred if she had kept his problems private, but there was no helping it now.

Lisandre scowled. "It is disgusting to use one's power so. Preying upon the weakness of another."

"Humans," Estin cursed, as if the word was a synonym for contemptible.

Cinder was doing his best to forgive or forget Estin's prior actions, but the man was making it nearly impossible. Every other word out of his mouth only confirmed his bigotry.

"It's why humans lost their *lorethasra*," Estin said. "They can't be trusted with power."

Cinder had heard enough. "Right. I guess you must have forgotten the times you did me harm when I was helpless," he snapped, shaking his head in disgust. He heeled Fastness ahead before the prince could reply, not having the patience to listen to whatever Estin might have to say.

34

From atop the tallest tower in the Unconquered Fort, Genka Devesth stared at his latest conquest, the mountain city of Quoresth and its surrounding environs. All of it was spread out before him like a chessboard, and all of it was his now. All he surveyed, he ruled. For as far as his eyes could see.

As it should be.

Quoresth had been a difficult prize to secure. The city had been built upon a steep-walled mesa, massively walled and savagely protected, and beyond her fortifications extended the ancient Trendil mountains. This was an older range, one worn down by time, wind, and weather, but the area was still harsh and difficult to access. Cliffs of gray granite occasionally punctured the hardwood forest carpeting the slopes, and a perpetual fog-like smoke hugged the surrounding peaks and valleys.

Getting his soldiers here hadn't been easy, but by doing so, Genka had achieved the improbable, some would say the impossible. He'd conquered the unconquerable Quoresth.

His finest generals had warned him against attacking this place. They had been certain the narrow mountain passes, rugged any time of year, would have made such an assault unwinnable. How could any invading force position enough soldiers to take the impregnable fortress? Or just as importantly, protect the supply line, which all considered tenuous and easily broken in the mountains.

Genka had answered the first through deception, and the second through a mad gamble.

From the stairway behind him came the scramble of a missed step and a resounding curse. Genka faced about, watching as Vel Parnesth, possibly his most trusted advisor, certainly his oldest, trudged up the final flight of stairs and joined him atop the tower. The old man gasped; the climb was apparently hard on him.

"We did it," Vel croaked after taking a moment to catch his breath. "By Holy Mede's balls, we fucking did it. We kicked the shit out of that arrogant fuck, Gin." He pointed to a portion of the wall against which the nobles of Quoresth had been crucified. "If you squint your eyes, you can see him yonder."

Gin had been arrogant, and his arrogance had led him to this demise, a fitting fate for the obese fucker. "The crows will grow too fat to fly after eating such a corpulent corpse."

He grinned at his clever alliteration while Vel barked laughter, his thin shoulders shaking and his round belly bobbing. The old man was no longer the warrior he had once been. Bald but for a ring of hair, stoop-shouldered, and his breathing ruined by too many cigars, he wheezed with every exhalation, and the tips of his fingers too often contained a blue hue.

But what of it? Vel's mind remained knife sharp. He had been among the first to recognize Genka's glory. Vel had cranked open the gates to his home city of Parnesth and bent low to Genka, acceding to his title as Mede's Heir, as the *Garnala lon Anarin*, Sower of the Wind.

And Genka *was* the *Garnala lon Anarin*. He'd known it since he'd first had the dream of his coming glory, a dozen years ago now. And wasn't it said that Holy Mede had similar dreams of his greatness? Visions of conquering the entire world, controlling everything from the Savage Kingdoms all the way west to the Shakaran Ocean? And was it not also said in the Medeian Scryings when describing Mede's return: *One who dreams shall see his past and his future. He will overcome the world's evil.*

Genka didn't know about the past, but he'd dreamed of the future, and his future was writ large in unrestrained exultation.

Vel was chuckling. "I still can't believe your plan worked."

"Our plan," Genka corrected, willing to be magnanimous in this time of victory, especially with the best of his advisors.

While Genka accepted subjugation as his due, he was wise enough to realize his men needed to feel like they had played a great role in the conquering as well, and they *had* played a great role. It was Genka's steel will which forged and inspired his warriors to great deeds, but it was his men who had to follow where he led and share his passion.

And his men were passionate. Their fervor would now reach a fever pitch following the conquest of Quoresth.

"It was your plan. I advised against it," Vel said, waving aside Genka's sharing of the glory. He grinned, displaying yellowed teeth. "I'm just glad you were lucky enough to prove me wrong."

"It wasn't luck," Genka said. As the *Garnala lon Anarin*, luck accounted for little in his destiny. His future was certain glory.

Vel grunted. "I suppose not. You used the Quoresthians' sense of superiority against them. They thought we were just another dirty army of Sunset Kingdom barbarians."

"They thought we were an undisciplined mob," Genka corrected. "It's why I wanted the rumors spread about our men, their supposed cowardice. Why the cookfires we lit were fewer and fewer every night we closed on the city. They never bothered with disrupting our supply train because they thought our army had fallen apart long before we reached their gates."

"And they were arrogant and foolish enough to open those gates and meet us on the field."

Genka snorted in derision. "The Quoresthians are as haughty as any elf and as easily destroyed. Mede never had trouble with those pointy-eared shits." He recognized the same flaw of hubris could be said about him, but it was untrue. Genka was the *Garnala lon Anarin*, the chosen of Devesh, the one tasked with setting the world to right. He couldn't be arrogant, merely sure of himself.

"On their own, the men are calling you *Garnala lon Anarin*," Vel said. "So are the people of Quoresth. We only whispered the title to them before, but now every tongue wags it on their own. Plainly and loudly. Shouting from the heights." He pounded the railing in excitement. "It is happening!"

Genka grinned. "And you thought I was being superstitious in riding my Yavana across the waters of Barnesth Bay. The Scryings speak of the *Garnala lon Anarin* riding his steed across the city's bay and never touching water." He chuckled. "Which I fulfilled."

Vel snorted in wry amusement. "By tying all the ships together and riding your stallion across the connected decks."

"It worked," Genka said with a shrug. "Deeds trump words, and the men needed to see me fulfill prophecy. They have their superstitions, but it turns out *my* 'stitions are super."

Vel laughed. "That, my *Garnala lon Anarin*, is one of the most idiotic things I've ever heard you or anyone say. Your stitions are super?" He guffawed.

Genka chuckled with him. He *was* the *Garnala lon Anarin*, but it didn't mean he couldn't laugh at himself.

Vel's laughter died away, and his amusement was replaced by a scowl. "There is one other matter we need to discuss. I was speaking to Chancellor Brel, Gin's spymaster."

"Speaking or torturing?"

"Chancellor Brel is a wise man. No torturing was required. Brel can feel the direction of the wind as well as any man, and he was quite willing to bend to it and talk. He had this on his person." From within a bag hanging at his side, Vel withdrew a round crystal the size of a fist. It glowed with its own light, a wash of blue-and-green lightning. "I pried it off his staff."

Genka gasped in awe. "Mede's Orb," he breathed. "The crystal he used to create the Immortals."

"So the legends say."

"So it will be again in truth," Genka replied, his vision filled with the glory of the Orb. If Mede had used this crystal to create the Immortals, then he, the *Garnala lon Anarin*, would do the same. After a moment, Genka reluctantly handed the Orb back to Vel. "Secure it with my personal belongings. No one is to touch it but me."

"Of course, my Lord," Vel replied, bowing low. After placing the crystal in his leather satchel, he cleared his throat and appeared discomfited. "There is one other matter Brel brought to my attention. There is a warrior of Rakesh that the Errows—"

"Apostate bastards," Genka fumed. "They should have been gutted for their treason."

"Apostates and traitors, they most certainly are," Vel agreed, "but they read the portents the same as we."

"And ran away from their duty like bitches in heat," Genka said in bitterness. The Errows had once been the lowest of all servants in the Sunsets, but a thousand years ago, over a period of decades, they'd migrated south, the entire caste. As a result, the unsavory work of cleaning latrines and sewers, of preparing the dead for their funerals, and the butchering of animals was now a foul task shared by the other castes.

"The Errow elders have their eyes on a young warrior. They say he is of surpassing skill, a student at the Third Directorate, and able to defeat an elf in single combat."

Genka grimaced. He sensed where this story was going. "And let me guess, he rides like one born to the saddle."

"He rides a pale, full-blooded Yavana, one no other could tame."

"Sunbane?"

"Sunbane," Vel confirmed, the elder brother to Genka's own stallion, Midnight's Silence.

The people of Devesth kept careful track of the Yavanas. They could recount the pure bloodlines all the way back to the time of Mede. And every year, a few Yavanas—the stupidest and weakest of their breed, or in Sunbane's case, the most irredeemable and untamable—were traded away from the Cord Valley, but their ultimate fate was still recorded in the Great Annals.

And this warrior identified by the Errow elders rode a famed Yavana, one who had by himself killed an *aether*-cursed wolf.

Shit.

"What are the Errows saying about him?"

Vel shrugged. "All this is rumor and fifth-hand information, but several things are clear."

"They think he is the *Garnala lon Anarin*?" Genka guessed.

"No." Vel paused theatrically, causing Genka to grind his teeth with impatience. "They say he supposedly speaks to his Yavana, and the stallion has taken the name Fastness. And that he might be the *Cipre Elonicon*. The Destroyer of Falsehood."

Shokan Reborn. *Shit, indeed.* The Errows were apostates and traitors, but strangely, they had their admirers amongst certain castes in the Sunsets. And admirers equaled influence. As for whether this warrior was Shokan Reborn… Genka smirked. Steel would tell, and if this so-called *Cipre Elonicon* was unable to bear the pressure, he would break.

"You know what needs to be done?" Vel asked.

Genka nodded. They had to clip the wings of this potential rival by killing him. He considered the best way to handle the situation. "What is this warrior's name?"

"Cinder Shade."

"Cinder Shade," Genka said, tasting the name. "A strong name." If this man was a student at the Third Directorate, it meant he possessed a warrior's skill. "Learn what you can about him, his appearance, home, everything. As soon as we know enough, send a dozen *hashains* south. As soon as Cinder Shade noses out of the Directorate, they are to kill him. Have them leave now."

"With winter approaching? Impossible. It'll take them half a year."

Genka grinned. "You forget. We control the docks of Barnesth. Send them by ship. They should arrive in Rakesh inside of three months."

35

Residar Charvin struggled to rise from the muck of old leaves and dirt covering him like a filthy cloak. Confusion filled his mind, dousing his thoughts. *Where am I?*

Like slithering snakes, his most recent memories were the first ones to return. They crept across his mind, the dried-leaf sound, bringing with them the recovery of horror.

Residar touched his stomach, felt for the lacerations which had spilled his guts and innards. He remembered dying at the hands of an ajakava. And yet, he lived. *How?* He should be dead.

More memories swirled, coalescing like ash in his hands.

His wife, Marin, and his children, Sep, Tola, and the newborn Jape. If he was alive, then maybe his family... He knew it was impossible, but he had to find them.

Residar pushed himself upright, gaining his feet and instantly swaying. The room spun, and his gorge rose. But he wouldn't let his lack of balance slow him. He took a single step forward but immediately crashed to the floor. He hooked an arm on the back of a broken chair, sweat beading on his head. For a second, his vision grayed, recovered,

449

and he knew enough then to halt and take stock of his situation.

His vacant gaze, lost in the fog of his memories, cleared and he finally recognized where he stood. The shattered remnants of his home, the log cabin he and Marin had built together. Of it, nothing remained but burnt timbers, cinders, and ruin. The rest was destruction, the furniture a wreckage of shattered wood. Only the river-rock fireplace remained whole, and an afternoon rain poured through the collapsed roof.

Shet's creatures, zahhacks—a bed of ajakavas and a nest of ketus—had come upon his homestead farm, which was situated several miles from the closest village, Core's Knoll. It was only a week's ride from Swift Sword. It should have been safe here.

Residar stared about, unable to make his mind work.

A strange image. Marin's stockinged leg poking out from beneath a heavy timber. The rest of her was buried in burned thatch and broken spans of wood and debris. The sight drew him out of his stupor.

Residar stumbled to Marin's side, grunting as he tossed aside the heavy lumber like they were twigs. His strength should have surprised him, but he was lost in a sea of terrified hope.

Hope that was instantly crushed to grief.

Marin was dead. Her eyes stared sightlessly at the sky. Clutched in her dead arms were their children. Sep, his strong boy, who tried so hard to please. Tola, his middle child, who took after her mother. And baby Jape, who had yet to sprout his first teeth.

Gone. Their bodies savaged. Residar clutched their broken forms to his chest, screaming his grief that knew no bounds.

More memories.

Residar remembered the ajakavas more clearly now. They had come at twilight, battering through the door. Residar had faced them with nothing more than a fire poker and his courage. And in the moment when one of the fell creatures had ripped its claws through his stomach, he recalled pain. He recalled his guts oozing through his wounds like coils of gray worms. He recalled when Tola was speared, and a greater pain than any he had every known savaged him.

And he also recalled a pond of the purest water, restful and perfect. Blue-and-green lightning had surrounded it, warning him away. But Residar had reached for the water anyway, drawn to the shimmer, the reflected light of something vast and unknowable.

Fierce agony, enough to make his rent stomach seem a mild scratch, had ripped through every facet of his being.

And a terrible voice, a rasping, sawn-wood sound belonging to neither a man nor a woman, had whispered in his mind, a promise to ease and end his suffering. *"I can ease the pain,"* the voice had vowed. *"Suffer my touch, heed my will, and vengeance shall be yours."*

Like a drowning man seeking any lifeline, unthinking and uncaring, a fog of the deepest pain scouring all considerations, Residar had accepted the voice's pledge.

"Do you agree to serve me? From now until death claims you?" the voice had demanded.

"I will," Residar had cried.

As soon as the words escaped his mouth, the lightning around the water had died away, but the pond of purity became black and oily.

It didn't matter. Power had flooded Residar's body. It healed all his wounds, filled him with righteous fury. He'd risen, crackling with the need for revenge. He had—

Residar blinked. What had he done? He couldn't remember.

But he could guess. He rose to his feet, the bodies of his children slipping from his grasp, slipping to the ground in loud, neglected thumps. He saw parts of the ajakavas scattered around his farmhouse, a leg here, an arm there, a stinger. Same with the snake-like ketus. Some force had torn them apart.

He had torn them apart.

"You will serve me," the voice from last night whispered in his mind once again.

Residar spun about, searching for the speaker. "Show yourself. Where are you?" he demanded. Instinctively, he reached for the blackened water in his mind's eye. Power surged into him like a river in flood.

"*I am everywhere, child,*" the voice answered. "*You accepted my power. But all power comes with a cost. You will serve me, or torture will be your boon companion.*"

Residar screamed. The blackened water in his mind's eye disappeared behind a wall of red noise. If murder had a voice, it would be that sound. Residar felt as if his body were being flayed.

"*But if you serve me, you shall never again know pain. You shall administer it.*"

The anguish tormenting him lifted like a blanket whipped away from his crumpled form. Residar took a shuddering breath, gasping in relief, grateful for the absence of agony. He slowly crawled back to his feet. He wouldn't face whoever this voice was like an insect on its back. He would face it like a man standing on two sturdy legs. "You say I will administer pain," Residar said, his voice firming as his eyes settled on his murdered family. He wanted revenge. And the handful of zahhacks he'd apparently killed last night weren't enough. Not even close. An ocean of them wouldn't be enough. "I want to kill zahhacks."

The voice chuckled. "*Of course. You will kill legions of so-called zahhacks.*" There had been contempt in the voice upon speaking of Shet's monsters. "*This, I promise. You will kill any who threaten us.*"

"Who are you?" Residar asked, mistrusting the voice.

"*I have many names. The Hungering Heart is the one I was blessed to take upon my creation, but you can call me Master.*"

Residar might have argued, but the red noise welled, only for a split second. The black water disappeared, and pain took its place. He crashed to his knees. "What is thy bidding, my Master?" he asked, the formality sounding correct in the face of this invisible, terrifying being.

But in the recesses of his thinking, there was anger. Anger which flooded his being. He would bend knee to this voice, this creature, but not forever. He'd kill it, too. He'd kill everything standing between him and vengeance for his family.

"*There is another of my servants close at hand.*"

In Residar's mind, a steady, red flame lit to life. It seemed to urge him west.

"Follow the fire, and you will meet her. I have a simple assignment for the two of you. There is small group entering the Daggers, three elves and a human. Kill them."

Following her battle against the monstrous mother spiderkin, Brilliance had followed after her boy as best she could, but she had been slowed by her injuries—wounds earned defending him. Nevertheless, she persisted in trailing after him, following ever southward. He had ridden amidst a large band of elves, and she took to skulking along the edges of their column, seeking a moment when her boy was alone and unprotected.

But it had never happened. Always he was in the company of others—humans, elves, and even dwarves, all of them close at hand. For miles and miles she had followed him, past the point where the Dagger Mountains ended and the foothills began, into tamed places of docile forests and farms. She had watched as her boy entered into a vast crowded place—a city it was called—and disappeared across the sea. Too far away for her to truly sense.

She had stared across the waters for hours after her boy's departure, worrying for when he would return.

And he had to return. He owed her his *lorethasra*, and she intended to collect.

Brilliance had lingered near the swarming area of stink and refuse where her boy had left her, hoping he would come back to the same place. For months she'd stayed, hunting and killing as needed, but she was never foolish enough to take a human. Other humans would have then hunted *her*, driven her away from the smelly hovels they called their homes.

But in the end, her vigilance had been rewarded. Brilliance had sensed her boy. He had come back to her!

Eager to see him again, she had watched from a distance as he exited the wretched city, riding a powerful, white stallion, who shone like the sun at noon. Her eyes had narrowed when she had seen the pair, and she had panted softly in desire.

Brilliance wanted the boy *and* his horse. The four-legged grass-eater had something of the boy's power to him. So, too, did the elves, and at least one other of their mounts. Brilliance wanted to consume all of them, but she wasn't greedy. The boy and his horse would be enough for her needs. The others could live.

For the past few weeks, she had stalked the small group, her boy and the elves, keeping out of sight. She hid amongst the snow-covered copses dotting the hillsides and valleys, scampered along ice crusted brooks, and rushed across rocky hills slick with snowmelt. Always trailing her prey, always planning how to make the kill. Perhaps when they settled in for the night, during the dark when her senses were keen, and those of the two-legs were not. When the boy would be alone. Easy meat for her claws and teeth. Kill him and finally claim what was rightfully hers.

Or maybe she should start with the horse. She had seen how the elves and humans hobbled their mounts at night. The stallion wouldn't be able to run from her then, and she could easily evade his powerful hooves.

Brilliance nodded to herself, growling softly. *Yes.* The stallion would be the easier prey. She'd begin with him.

She watched her boy from amidst the branches of a massive cedar in a natural blind. He and his companions slowly made their way through a ravine cut through by a frozen stream. They would halt soon, not much farther than a few miles, since the day would end in a couple of hours. She would stalk them, find where they planned on camping, and finalize her arrangements while they slept.

Brilliance slipped down through the branches of the tree, barely disturbing the snow-heavy limbs of the cedar on her way to the ground. She made to follow the boy, but the stench of old meat, cold and murderous, caused her to snap to a halt. Her head lifted in worry. This reek was different from the rot of a necrosed—Brilliance had learned the names of the corrupted creatures who shared the Daggers. They were dangerous predators, the ajakavas, ketus, goblins, and others like them.

She inhaled deeply, and worry became fear. This stink belonged to a wraith. Two of them.

Brilliance crouched lower. Even more than spiderkin, she feared wraiths. They were deadlier than any elf or dwarf. Faster, stronger, and utterly implacable. She had seen a wraith tear through a trio of elves with nothing but its bare hands, killing them in the span of seconds.

And now two of those gray-skinned monsters might be stalking her boy. Two, which were a danger to any predator and likely more than her boy and his companions could handle.

Brilliance wanted to scream in fury. Why was it every time she was intent on killing her boy, some other predator wanted to do the same? And why did *she* then have to then save the boy so another couldn't steal what was rightfully hers? It wasn't fair! She would have laughed at the irony if it wasn't so maddening.

Another smell drifted to Brilliance, and she lifted her head in surprise. This aroma contained the scent of bark, dark soil, and leaves. Similar to, but not the same as the cluster of trees in which Brilliance crouched. Something else, something Brilliance had never before encountered. Only ever seen from a distance. Living trees. *Yakshin.*

They, too, followed her boy but were apparently unaware of the wraiths.

Fragging unholy hells.

Brilliance had no idea what the words meant, but they sounded right in this situation. If her stupid boy had any idea of the trouble he was causing her... She mentally sighed. Of course, he didn't, and he never would. After all, Brilliance planned on killing him.

She slowly rose to her feet and growled in irritation. Time to go save her boy.

As she raced off to intercept the wraiths and the yakshin, she had a flittering thought. When had she started thinking of him as *her boy*?

36

Weeks of hard travel saw Cinder, Anya, Lisandre, and Estin enter the depths of the Daggers as they journeyed northeast, pushing toward the edge of Rakesh's borders. They followed a frost-covered animal trail that wended amongst the foothills as they transitioned into striking mountains and valleys. Snow blanketed much of the land since spring's call had yet to be heard. A damp chill permeated the air, becoming uncomfortably cold at night, and they made sure to keep the campfire burning.

They needed the flames, not just for the warmth it provided, but also to ward against wolves. The animals—likely winter lean and hungry—could be heard howling from among the surrounding peaks and valleys, but it was impossible to discern their location. Sounds echoed oddly in the Daggers, and the wolves might have been miles distant or within the very same valley in which they trekked.

The lupine predators didn't cause them to halt their journey, however, and onward they went, journeying ever closer to the heart of the Daggers where the spiderkin would become their primary concern. So far, they'd seen little evidence of the eight-legged monsters, possibly due to the fact that the creatures tended to hibernate from late autumn through the middle of spring.

Still, some of them might be awake and alert, and only seventy miles northeast began the unofficial borders of the Webbed Kingdom, the land ruled by the spiderkin monarchs. They would go no closer to that benighted realm. It was said that any who entered the Webbed Kingdom, never exited the place. The spiderkin queens killed all who entered their territory.

By contrast, another fifty miles west was said to exist the mythical Shalla Valley, home to the yakshins. But there, they also couldn't go. Shalla Valley was denied to all but the most penitent and holy or those who the yakshins had directly invited. As a result, vanishingly few folk had ever seen its mystical slopes and forests, which ranged from the boreal to the tropical—a quirk of either Seminal's weather in the valley or a miracle of the yakshin's magic.

Cinder tossed aside his meanderings about the fables of Shalla Valley.

The terrain here was treacherous. Icy and slick. Anya had the lead, and they rode single file down a rocky trail, along the side of rock-strewn hill, and toward a slender valley. The path was slippery with hard snow and black ice, shadowed in areas where the sunshine rarely touched the ground. Directly to their left gurgled the watery thread of a nearly frozen stream, and other than a large thicket of trees a dozen yards to their right, the rest of the vegetation close at hand was low-lying shrubs or tall grass.

Fastness carefully picked his way down the narrow track, one cautious step at a time, slipping now and then. All of them took the trail slowly, but once they reached the valley floor, Cinder was able to relax enough to glance about.

In every direction, snow-covered peaks glinted in the late afternoon sunshine. A cold breeze gusted now and then, carrying the scent of pine, cedar, and aspen from the evergreen forest carpeting the base of the slopes. A quarrel of sparrows chirruped as they flitted about in the cloudless, blue sky, flying above trees bowed beneath the weight of snow.

The setting was serene, but a warning siren slowly built in the back of Cinder's mind. Anya might have noticed something as well because she came to halt. Cinder edged Fastness forward, reaching her side. The world was silent. The sparrows, seen flitting about only seconds earlier, were gone. No animal sounds filled the air. Even the wind had died. Danger lurked.

The tingling heightened, and Cinder stared about, searching for the source of peril. He couldn't locate it, but he knew it was out there, studying them. He spoke to Anya, his voice hushed. "We're being watched."

"Yes, we are," she replied, never taking her eyes off the hills closest at hand.

It was the only confirmation Cinder needed. He withdrew his bow and strung it. Anya did the same.

"What is it?" Lisandre asked, riding up to them.

"There's danger around us," Anya said. "Watching. Get ready."

Lisandre didn't bother arguing with her. He merely pulled out his bow.

Cinder continued studying the land. His gaze settled on the slope of a nearby hill. It was covered in evergreen trees. Directly ahead of them, several hundred yards away. His heart began to race. A menace emanated from the woods. It pricked his nerves. Something wicked was coming their way.

A strange, ringing cry shattered the quiet.

Ululating screams were their only warning.

Estin spun about, searching for the source of the cries. His heart clenched. He'd been trained to identify the sound. It came from wraiths. *Two of them.*

Cinder had already reacted. Same with Anya and Lisandre. They had their bows out, an arrow on the rests.

A pair of gray-skinned terrors streaked down a hill, a couple hundred yards away and closing quickly. Clothed in rags, they moved like sharks surging for the kill, and it would be a kill. Estin didn't favor their chances against one wraith, much less two.

Cinder loosed his arrow. It whistled like wind through a ravine, slamming into one of the wraiths—a female—hitting her in the chest. She didn't slow. Neither did the other one, a tall, thickly built male. An arrow sprouted from his abdomen. *Anya's.* The larger wraith evaded Lisandre's shot. Cinder and Anya simultaneously released a final arrow each, their motions oddly coordinated. Both bolts struck the male wraith in his chest. He never stumbled, simply snapping off the arrows.

Fastness, Cinder's powerful white stallion, had his teeth bared. The big Yavana seemed to welcome the onrushing attack.

"Swords and shields," Lisandre shouted.

Estin realized he had been doing nothing but watching. He hastily prepared, unsheathing his sword, slinging his shield on his off-arm, and sourcing his *lorethasra*. Weaves might slow the wraiths. He urged his stallion into place, next to Lisandre, making sure both of them had room to swing swords. He was ready.

And not a second too soon.

The female darted at him. Her claws extended, six inches and glowing blood red. They dripped red globs of acidic toxin that hissed when they hit the ground.

Estin swung his sword at her. She twisted aside, effortlessly evading. She blocked Lisandre's slash with her long claws. The impact had the dull tone of steel striking soft stone and did the wraith no harm. Estin attacked again, followed by Lisandre. She dodged or pushed away both their swords with shocking grace. Estin was still trying to track her when she spun about, raking his stallion's flank.

Byerley screamed in pain, kicking backward.

Again, the wraith avoided the attack.

Estin got Byerley facing the right direction.

"You're all going to die," the wraith pronounced, her pleasant voice and pretty features at odds with corpse-like skin and white, irisless eyes glowing like lanterns.

A guttural shout of pain drew Estin's attention to the other fight, the one between his sister, Cinder, and the male wraith.

Estin's eyes widened. Cinder's blade moved in a blur, never slowing. Same with Anya. She took the fight to the wraith, weaves of fire crackling and lancing at the creature. Earth trembling beneath the creature's feet. Braids of Water and Air spearing at the monster. She and Cinder fought together like they had born to it, perfectly synchronized and always covering one another.

The wraith clutched his chest from where a slash had gotten through his defenses. He snarled and came at them again. This time neither Anya nor Cinder could touch him. The creature slipped or blocked every one of their slashes, thrusts, and cuts.

But he didn't evade the massive snowtiger which attacked from his blindside. *Aether*-cursed. With those glowing white eyes, she had to be. She locked onto the wraith's calf, eliciting another guttural cry of pain. The wraith blocked Cinder's slash, but Anya's thrust buried in his abdomen, painful, apparently, in a way the arrows hadn't been.

The wraith screamed again, falling back. In the same motion, he kicked aside the snowtiger, tossing her away like she was a kitten. With distance gained, he hobbled away from Cinder and Anya, glaring, white eyes leaking red tears.

Estin's seconds-long distraction could have proved fatal, but he was lucky. The female he was fighting had also momentarily glanced over when the male wraith had screamed.

But Lisandre hadn't been distracted. He attacked, aiming a sword thrust straight at the female wraith's heart. Somehow, she sensed her danger. The wraith twisted aside, taking a long cut along her ribs, hissing in pain.

Good.

The wind, quiet until now, rustled through the trees like a hurricane. Estin, about to attack, started. No. It wasn't the wind. A massive form pushed through the nearby trees, twenty feet tall. *A yakshin.* She was flanked by a human.

This time Estin's inattention did cost him. Blazing pain tore across his abdomen. The female had raked him across the stomach. He slumped, staring into the wraith's white eyes. Blood dripped from her claws. His blood. She smirked.

Estin grabbed her arm.

She ripped it free, but this time it was *her* distraction which proved her undoing.

Lisandre slammed a sword through her back, the tip protruded through her abdomen.

The wraith howled.

Estin slipped off Byerley, crashing to the ground. He clutched at the agony burning in his stomach. The wraith yanked herself off Lisandre's sword and sprinted back in the direction from which she had emerged.

Estin groaned, letting his head fall back. He wanted to rest here a while.

Anya's thrust to his abdomen caused the wraith to cry out. The creature kicked away the *aether*-cursed snowtiger, who had her teeth securely lodged in the calf of the wraith.

Until she didn't.

Cinder blinked in shock when she yowled, flying past him. *Shit*. He had known wraiths were strong—they were certainly fast—but tossing the massive snowtiger like she was a pillow?

The cat—probably the same snowtiger from the battle with the spiderkin—wailed during the entirety of her flight. She slammed into the turf and snow, sliding face-first to a stop. She didn't rise.

I guess not all cats land on their feet.

"Pay attention," Fastness snapped at him.

Cinder hastily threw off his consideration of the snowtiger. The wraith was glaring at them, his white-hot gaze going from Cinder to Anya, as if weighing who to attack.

Cinder made the creature's decision for him. He spurred Fastness forward, swung the stallion to the right when the wraith slashed at them, and blocked a backhand blow. Fingers of Earth sought to trap the monster's legs. *Anya.* The creature quickly freed itself, but Cinder used the distraction to aim an attack at the monster. His slash struck true, cutting deep into a shoulder and drawing blood.

The wraith growled in anger or pain, darting to the side. Anya shouted, but Cinder couldn't tell what she was saying. He spun Fastness to where he'd last seen the wraith, thrusting his sword.

He caught nothing but air.

Pain exploded into Cinder's torso. The world swirled, and he slammed into the ground, staring at the sky.

Why was he lying down? He blinked, trying to get his mind to work. Iron-tanged wetness seeped down his chest and ribs.

A creature howled, shrieking like a fiend. *The wraith.* He sailed across Cinder's darkening vision, arms and legs flapping wildly.

Cinder knew no more.

37

Anya's heart went to her throat when Cinder was thrown from Fastness. His fall was uncontrolled, and he slammed into the ground with a jarring impact. Estin was down as well, and for a moment Anya was conflicted over who to see to first.

"He's injured, but I can handle it," Lisandre shouted to her. "See to Cinder."

It was all the information Anya needed. She rushed to Cinder's side.

He'd been gored, his intestines threatening to press past the five deep gouges rending his abdomen. Blood poured, pulsing in time to his beating heart. An artery had been cut. Cinder's life hung by a thread.

Anya knew what to do. It didn't matter that she had little skill with *Anahata*, the Heart Chakra. She opened it anyway, sourcing every last bit of *lorethasra* she could manage. She was Cinder's only hope. There was no room for even the slightest shred of doubt.

She worked quickly, pouring *lorethasra* into *Anahata*. It transformed into *prana*, scintillating along the web of her *nadis*. A stabbing pain formed in Anya's chest, but she kept at it. More *lorethasra*. She focused on her intent, what she wished of her *prana*. This was different than weaving her *lorethasra*, both harder and easier in some ways. A glow built in the back of her vision. Tiny lightning rippled across her knuckles.

Devesh let this work.

She ripped open Cinder's shirt and placed her hands upon Cinder's chest. The moment her skin came into contact with his, she released her *prana* and her intent. The lightning sparked, buzzing and roaring like a breaking wave, straight into Cinder. He jerked, his entire torso coming off the ground. When he settled on the tall grass, Anya unstoppered her canteen and liberally poured water over Cinder's wounds, washing away the blood.

She stared intently, praying and hoping. Seconds later, blood filled his wounds, a seepage rather than a pumping or spurting. The arteries were likely—hopefully—closed, and she breathed a sigh of relief. There was hope for him.

"Cinder," she whispered, briefly cupping his face. He couldn't die. She couldn't imagine—

She cut off her fears. She still had work to do. While the most dangerous of his wounds were healed, the wounds could still fester.

"Do you require help?" a melodic voice asked.

Anya started. *Who else was here?* She glanced at the speaker but saw nothing but a pair of bark-covered ankles. She then glanced up. And up and up. A yakshin towered over her. Anya had forgotten about the tree maiden. The battle against the wraiths had occupied the totality of her attention, then saving Cinder.

"Do you require help?" the tree maiden repeated, her soft voice at odds to her rough appearance. Twenty feet tall, she wore a simple shift that was large enough for many boats to have used as a sail. Her skin was like bark and her hair like gray moss. It was held away from her eyes by a circlet woven from green, scalloped leaves and tiny, purple flowers like the petals of a hyacinth, fresh and floral.

No. The circlet wasn't woven. It was a living vine, extending out of the center of the yakshin's forehead, a part of her body. Her large, hazelnut eyes seemed to view the scene below her in concern.

Anya could only gape.

"He needs the healing fruit of an Ashoka tree, an Aushadha," declared a man standing next to the yakshin. A holder. Like most of his kind, he was of an indeterminate age, anywhere between twenty-five to over one hundred. While not as long-lived as many other woven, holders ceased aging from the time of their maturity to the times of their deaths, generally in their mid-one hundreds. "The wraith's claws penetrated deep. He likely stole a good portion of the boy's *lorethasra*. It will be impossible for him to heal no matter how much *prana* is poured into him."

Anya feared the holder was correct. Cinder's pallor and blue lips indicated the severity of his blood loss. Worse, his gray skin proclaimed the truth about the holder's assessment. Cinder needed an abundance of *mana*, and the most reliable such source was the Aushadha fruit of an Ashoka tree. Unfortunately, the yakshins were loath to hand them out to just anyone.

Tears trembled at the corners of Anya's eyes, and a terrible fear filled her. Cinder was dying, and she couldn't imagine anything worse. The very thought devastated her. Her composure faltered, nearly failing, but she collected herself. She mastered her terror, focusing on the present, on Cinder's need. He had met a yakshin once before, and the tree maiden had named him.

"Maynalor," she said to the yakshin. "One of your kind named him Maynalor."

"Maynalor," the yakshin repeated, lifting her nose and seemingly tasting the word. "Yes. I know of who you mean and the sister who named him." Her eyes settled on Cinder, her features intent. "This is he? Maynalor? *Someone of interest with a secret.*"

"Can you save him?" Anya asked, praying silently on the answer.

The yakshin nodded. "He is Maynalor. If it is in my power to see him saved, then he will be saved. We will take him to Shalla Valley."

Anya closed her eyes and breathed out gratitude. *Thank you, Devesh.* Shalla Valley was the most sacred place on Seminal, the place where the purest of Ashoka trees grew. Maybe this yakshin meant to offer Cinder an Aushadha fruit. The *mana* contained within it could heal him.

"He hasn't been purified," the holder complained. "He has the wretchedness of a wraith coursing through him."

Anya glared at the holder, red hot with rage.

Her anger, however, proved unnecessary.

The yakshin denied her holder. "He is Maynalor. Our sister sensed him. She tasted his spirit. She named him. And Mahamatha and the Shriven have deemed he must live. Thus, if it is in our power to save him, we must. It is our obligation."

The holder bowed his head to the yakshin. "As you will, so it shall be." He faced Anya. "If you allow, the tree maiden can see to your human. She can hold him on this side of life, possibly long enough for us to reach the valley."

Anya shuffled aside, unwilling to fully leave Cinder's side. "Whatever you can do," she said to the yakshin.

The tree maiden didn't reply. She knelt in a creaking of wood and spread her branchlike hands and fingers across Cinder's body, her eyes closed, clearly determining his health. After a few moments, she sat back on her haunches and spoke. "He cannot travel in his current state. He will have to be seeded."

Anya had heard of seeding, but she didn't know what it meant. No one did. It was part of the murkiness of yakshin life and culture. Nevertheless, she trusted the tree maiden. Yakshin had well-earned reputations for patience and kindness. She crept closer to watch.

The yakshin's fingers played above Cinder, moving as if she worked an invisible loom. The dirt and turf shifted, punching through the ice and snow. It lifted from beneath Cinder, the clay slowly extruding until all that was left was black soil. The rich dirt wrapped Cinder in dark bands, encasing him, starting at his feet. It coiled around his form, up his legs and abdomen, covering his wounds. On it went, all the way to his shoulders and neck, forming a cowl and mask about his head, leaving only his nose and mouth exposed.

From the yakshin's hands, a flash of gold poured forth like a shower of water, moistening the soil. Another flash, this one the red of sunset, and the soil hardened.

"It is done," the yakshin pronounced.

Anya leaned in, rapping the shell enclosing Cinder. It was hard as a nut, but flexible enough to allow Cinder's regular breathing.

She breathed another sigh of relief. Cinder had a chance to live. She wouldn't let herself think about the months of labor he'd have ahead of him to recover, if he ever did. Those worries were for another day. As far as she was concerned, having him alive with a chance to heal was enough.

Anya glanced to where Lisandre was wrapping Estin's chest in fresh bandages. Her brother's face was pale, but his eyes were open and clouded in pain. At least he was alert enough to wince when Lisandre tightened the bandages.

"Estin will be fine, but he needs further treatment," Lisandre said. "I gave him a field healing, but it won't be enough. He needs a proper physician."

"Fort Ermine is only a few days ride southwest," Anya said. "They have physicians. You can take him there."

Lisandre's gaze sharpened. "You aren't coming with us?"

Anya shook her head. "I can't. Cinder was badly injured."

Lisandre finally seemed to notice Cinder, wrapped as he was in the nut-like seeding. He frowned. "What happened to him?"

Anya relayed the events of the past few minutes. "They seeded him. The yakshin says it should keep him alive long enough to reach Shalla Valley."

Again, came the sharpened gaze. "They're willing to give him an Aushadha fruit?"

Anya nodded. "So she says."

"And must you accompany them?" Lisandre asked. "There is no one else?"

"Only she can come with us," the yakshin interrupted. "He requires her if he wishes to gain the entire benefit of the Aushadha. He'll need the help of someone close to him to fully accept it."

"I understand," Anya said. She had planned on staying with Cinder regardless.

Lisandre appeared unhappy. "What about the wraiths? They won't attack a yakshin and a holder, but what about me and Estin? What if they attack us on our way to the fort? Should we come to the valley, too?"

"We can't let so many unwashed into the valley," the holder growled.

The yakshin creaked to her full height. "And regardless, you need not fear them. They are powerful, but they don't deal well with damage. It will take them weeks to heal. You will be safe pressing on to your fort." Decisiveness settled across her features. "It is time to go. Every second we delay may alter Maynalor's fate."

Lisandre approached Anya. "I know you share a bond with Cinder," he whispered, leaning close as they quickly got their gear sorted out. "I don't know if you know why, but you have to be careful. For both your sakes."

His advice was unnecessary, but Anya nodded anyway. And while her emotions had been whipsawing like a storm, she was finally drawing them under control. When Cinder had fallen, his stomach ripped open and bleeding, her heart had taken a shock. She knew her feelings for him, and she knew what his death would do to her. But now wasn't the time to delve into her emotions, no matter how treacherous.

Beyond that, Lisandre's statement required a response. "I'll be careful," Anya said. "I promise. We'll meet you and the other Seconds at Fort Carnate, just like we planned." The whole while, she maintained a firm grip on her voice, letting no hint of her terror shine through, and once she had her gear organized, she checked on her brother, kissing him on the cheek. "Stay alive," she said to him. "Don't do anything foolish."

"Wouldn't even if I could," Estin said, managing a self-deprecating smile. "Keep yourself safe, too. Same with Cinder." A tentative, unreadable expression flitted across his face. "You're both important."

His last statement caused Anya to frown in surprise. Since when did

Estin think of Cinder with anything other than scorn and contempt?

Again, it wasn't the time to delve into it. "We'll be fine," she said, kissing her brother's cheek once more.

She prayed then for Estin's and Lisandre's safety, trusting in the words of the yakshin. The wraiths *were* badly injured, and the *aether*-cursed snowtiger was gone. A blood trail led away from where the massive cat had landed and apparently limped away from the battle. The snowtiger wouldn't be a problem for Estin and Lisandre. They should be able to reach Fort Ermine without any difficulty. *She hoped.*

Anya noticed then the yakshin standing off to the side, and if a tree could be said to be impatient, it was reflected in the tree maiden's posture.

"I have to go," Anya said to Lisandre and Estin before joining the yakshin and the holder.

Without any further words, they got underway, the tree maiden holding Cinder as if he was a babe.

"I never learned your name," Anya said to the yakshin.

"You can call me Sepia," the tree maiden said, gesturing to the holder. "This one is Banner Chai."

Anya trailed after Sepia and Banner as they headed west toward Shalla Valley. They were entering higher elevations, the heart of the range. This was a place of rugged peaks thrusting into the pale blue heavens and where the evergreen forests thinned until the slopes were only covered by various grasses—mountain brome, wild rye, and clumps of fescue poking through a heavy coat of snow.

In these heights, the party often stood above the clouds. The sky was clear, and the sun reflected blindingly off the snow but brought no warmth. The day was frigid, and their breaths billowed like smoke. Anya wore a double layer of clothes under her coat and heavy gloves to ward off the freezing temperatures, and she might have worried for Cinder, but his seeding felt warm to the touch. He was safe from the elements.

But what about the animals? They felt the cold, shivering at times despite the blankets thrown across their shoulders. Even Fastness struggled with the frigid temperature. Rather than his usual alert posture, his head hung low, his energy given way to simply dealing with the weather.

As for Sepia and Banner, if they noticed the knifing chill, they made no mention of it. The yakshin and holder doggedly pressed onward, never slowing their pace. They didn't even don any further garb, and they might have been automatons for how much the icy-cold and hard terrain affected them. In this, they were as unyielding as the mountains around them.

Their small party currently followed a narrow trail, which draped along the snow- and ice-laden shoulders of a cliff overlooking a valley split by a frozen stream. Oddly, the path they took seemed to flow about them, as if they were a ship sailing across quiet waters. The trail opened up several yards ahead of them, the snow crunching aside to form a tunnel walled in white and the ground bare. It closed directly behind their footsteps, leaving a line of broken snow and ice in their wake.

Early on, Anya had noticed it, wondering what it meant and how it was possible. Sepia explained it was part of her magic. The means by which a tree maiden was of the world but didn't unnecessarily harm it. Regardless, it was an amazing use of *lorethasra*. It was certainly easier than the trudging progress she and the others had made before their encounter with the wraiths. This way was much faster, but like all things familiar, by now—four days into their journey—Sepia's magic had become mundane.

But what wasn't mundane was the excellent time they were making. Last night, Sepia had promised they would reach Shalla Valley by mid-morning. It certainly helped that they started out every day when the first rays of the sun were just cresting the mountains and long shadows still draped the ground, and they didn't stop until late in the evening when twilight darkened the land like a cloak. But the true reason for their swift pace was Sepia's magic. She had reduced what might have taken several weeks of a hard slog into just a few days.

Hopefully the time saved would be enough to save Cinder. He had yet to awaken, and Anya worried. Sepia carried him, clutched protectively to her chest, and his seeding remained warm and his breathing regular, but without seeing his features, she couldn't tell how he was doing. He was so quiet, and she didn't know if it was because he was growing weaker or if it was due to some other aspect of the seeding.

At least he breathed. It was enough for now, enough to give her hope, enough to give her the strength to push aside any imaginings of him dead and gone from her world.

But during the heaviness of the night, when she was alone with her thoughts or amidst the drudgery of their travel—the trail stretching endlessly ahead of them—she lingered on her reaction to Cinder's injury, of why the notion of his passing caused her such pain and panic.

The life of a ranger was a dangerous one, and Anya wasn't a stranger to death. She had witnessed the death of several close friends, even a cousin. It didn't take great insight to recognize why her emotions roiled so much at the thought of Cinder dying.

But she hated having to confess it. In Revelant, and even prior, she had recognized the danger of her feelings for Cinder, but unfortunately, recognition did not equal prevention. She was tied to Cinder, in ways well beyond their shared history of near-death experiences, complete amnesia, and moth-eaten memories seen only in their dreams. Her past might be tied to his and so might her future.

And in the privacy of her mind, Anya admitted to perhaps not wanting it any other way.

"We are almost home," Sepia said, interrupting Anya's musings.

Anya breathed out a prayer of gratitude. *Blessed be Devesh.*

"Pay attention and stay close," the holder cautioned.

Anya straightened in the saddle. They had entered the mouth of a narrow ravine, one formed by a pair of blunt-nosed cliffs. Scree littered the floor, and ice-covered walls rose around them. The stony soil didn't allow for the growth of any vegetation. The air became cold as a frozen razor, and the slope grew steeper. Higher up the trail, fog enclosed an area where the cliffs seemed to lean against one another, but Anya spied a possible opening—a shadowed area through which the wind moaned like a low-pitched promise of loss.

They slogged into a soup-like fog that covered the ground. Visibility shortened to mere yards. The horses, even Fastness, struggled. Anya dismounted, trusting her own feet over the hooves of her gelding. She clung to the hill, inching forward, and when she glanced up, she caught the briefest image of Sepia already cresting the rise. Same with Banner.

Cinder! She wouldn't be separated from him.

Anya hastened forward, spurred by the notion of being left behind. She gasped, breath fogging, struggling to draw in the thin mountain air. Her legs burned. Her heart pounded, but she never slowed. She continued to scramble and claw her way upward, tugging and guiding Barton, Fastness, and the packhorses until she finally reached the summit.

There she saw nothing but the unbroken face of a cliff shadowed within an overhang. Her heart leapt. *Cinder.* She pressed trembling fingers toward the ice-slick stone and encountered the mountain's obdurate granite. She moved more quickly, pushing her hands against the stone, desperate to find a way through. This was where Sepia and Banner had entered the valley. She was sure of it.

A gnarled arm, like a branch, reached through the rock, and Sepia's face pushed past the stone's surface as well. The yakshin smiled. "You can only enter Shalla if someone of the valley or someone previously welcomed into it guides you." She reached for Anya's hand and drew her forth.

Anya winced as she passed through the stone, a tingle on her skin followed by darkness all around. She started in fear. A bridge made of all the colors of the rainbow extended in front of her, the only light in the blackness. It had to be the magic of the yakshins.

A second later, she was through. She stumbled but quickly regained her balance.

On this side of the steep trail, the thick fog was dispersed, wafted apart in eddies, and she paused to catch her breath and capture her first view of Shalla Valley.

She gasped. Her people prized nature's beauty above all else. It was why they built their cities, their farms, and all aspects of their lives in the way they did. And if Yaksha Sithe was a lyric to nature's glory, then Shalla Valley was a clarion-filled song. Majestic didn't begin to do the place justice.

Before her stretched a long valley, miles wide and surrounded by vertiginous, serrated mountains. Their gray shoulders lifted through tangles of lush, green growth. Meanwhile, closer at hand, a hundred yards from where she stood grew an evergreen forest of cedar, juniper, spruce, and pine. Mountain laurel and blossoming rhododendrons sat sentinel upon lonely outcroppings or formed their own private thickets amidst their taller brethren. Further down the steep hills, the trees transitioned into a hardwood forest of oak, ash, hickory, and golden maple. All of them were leafed in green, and not a trace of snow dotted the land despite the winter-cold weather on the other side of the ridge.

At the floor of the valley, the hardwoods eventually gave way to a broad field of golden grass waving tall and sedate in a steady breeze. Then came banana, coconut, and palm trees growing along the shores of a long lake, the waters of which were mist-shrouded and ghostly, sending lustrous blue fingers questing into the hidden reaches of the valley. And barely visible through the fog were several small islands protruding through the lake.

Anya forced aside her awe of Shalla Valley's grandeur. Sepia had already led the horses through, and she and Banner were striding down the hill. Anya quickly remounted Barton, hurrying to catch up. She reached them minutes later.

Banner dipped his head in brief acknowledgement of Anya's presence, but neither he nor the yakshin ever slackened their gait. They pressed onward, the trail opening and closing with their passage, but it still took them several hours to reach the valley floor. They passed through the forest of hardwoods, including teak and mahogany, which had no business growing alongside northern maples and oak.

But Anya had no chance or desire to ask about the composition of the forest. Sepia had glanced at Cinder, frowned once, and increased her pace.

Anya swallowed a bolus of fear. In their nearly five days of travel, the tree maiden had never shown the slightest sign of concern toward Cinder.

"He will be fine," Banner said to Anya, apparently catching sight of her concern. "We will reach the Shriven, the Holy Grove of Ashokas, in only a couple of hours. Late afternoon, for sure."

Anya nodded thanks to the holder's words, but they didn't entirely comfort her. Her eyes kept going to Cinder's unmoving form. *He has to live.*

They entered the broad flats at the valley's base, a savanna, one dotted with stands of trees and populated by a wide variety of animals. Lions lounged on lumpy hillocks. A score of elephants moved ponderously about, occasionally trumpeting to one another, and a herd of wildebeests cropped grass. Anya also caught sight of an orangutan annoying a pair of young leopards. The primate would reach down to tug on the cats' tails whenever they had their backs turned before leaping back to the safety of the branches when the felines would swipe at their tormenter.

The antics would have amused her on any other day, but not now. Anya continued to flick worried glances at Cinder.

An hour or so later, Sepia shifted their route east, toward a distant stand of trees, each one massive and towering. The yakshin exhaled in relief when she caught sight of the grove. "We've arrived in time," she said. "My sisters wait at Mahamatha, Mother Ashoka. We will see if Maynalor will receive an Aushadha."

Her statement had Anya casting a sharp glance in her direction. "I thought the fruit was a foregone conclusion."

The yakshin glanced down at her, pity on her face. "I know and respect your feelings for Maynalor, but only Mahamatha and Sadana, the wisest of my sisters, can determine if an Aushadha shall be given. Come. Let us learn of Maynalor's fate."

There was nothing to say in reply to such a proclamation, and Anya followed silently alongside the tree maiden, hoping Mahamatha—Mother Ashoka—whatever she was, would heal Cinder.

As they approached the large grove, Anya realized, her earlier assessment of the size of the trees undersold their true girth. Each one soared hundreds of feet in the air, as tall as the famed redwood cedars that grew along the coast of Mahadev Bay near the Savage Kingdoms, but these also had the expansive sweep of a pin oak. As a result, none of them grew close to one another. Each one was an island unto itself, separated by several hundred yards. In addition, their first branches started fifty feet off the ground, spreading out to shade an acre of land. Their broad leaves were shaped like a heart, wide in the belly and narrowing to a sharp point.

There was one, however, which stole Anya's breath. Centered in the grove, the tree thrust into the sky, rising above the rest like a protective mother over her children, half again as tall and broad. From her—and Anya knew without being told that this was Mahamatha—there emanated a whimsical serenity, a calm regard seen in those grown wise in their age where nothing was new and yet everything was still a wonderful mystery.

Upon seeing Mother Ashoka, some of Anya's worries for Cinder faded, and she found herself smiling.

They soon reached the grove, an open field where a dozen yakshins waited along with over thirty holders, men and women both. The tree maidens viewed their approach with unwavering calm, while their protectors watched with caution. Some rested hands on the pommels of their swords.

Anya dismounted, distantly noting how all the horses, even Fastness, urgently bent their heads and began grazing. They apparently loved the grass of Shalla Valley.

The tallest of the tree maidens, possibly older than the others also, stepped forward. She emanated a calmness similar to that of Mahamatha. Her dark, barklike skin creaked with her every movement, and white mold grew in some of her cervices. The moss of her hair was thin, and her face was long and pitted. She came to a halt, her air subdued as she addressed Sepia and Banner. "It is good to see you, daughter," she said, her voice breathy and weak, confirming her age. "You as well, my son."

"Thank you, Sadana," Sepia said. "It is good to be home."

Banner bowed low. "Thank you, Sadana," he murmured.

Sadana's expression grew grave, inspiring a knot of trepidation within Anya. It seemed like the elderly yakshin's unhappiness might be related to her and Cinder's presence.

A second later, her guess was shown to be correct.

"I see you've brought an unpenitent, unwashed elf and human to the Shriven," Sadana said, addressing Sepia. "Their presence erodes the sanctity of our borders. Our enemies might take advantage of our weakness. I hope you have a good reason to bring them here."

"I do," Sepia said, lowering Cinder to the ground. "I bring to the Shriven and Mahamatha a mystery, someone of interest housing a secret. Come and see."

Sadana stepped forward, leaning down to view Cinder. She appeared to sniff him, straightening abruptly. "Nut and root! Is this Maynalor?"

"He is," Sepia confirmed, sounding pleased with herself. "Banner and I discovered him and his companions under attack by a pair of wraiths. Maynalor was injured. You can see his *lorethasra* was ripped apart. Without it—"

"He cannot heal," Sadana finished with a sigh. "Tell me what occurred."

It was Banner who answered. "Five days southeast, we sensed two wraiths, one newly fallen, not yet entirely depraved, and the other one older and driven by malice alone. We sought to run them off." He went on to explain of his and Sepia's arrival toward the battle's end and what they had seen.

Anya discovered Sadana staring at her. It felt like her hazelnut eyes could peer into her soul, and she shrank back a bit. With a breath, she straightened, settling steel in her spine. She bowed to no one. And she most certainly wouldn't show fear when Cinder's survival might depend on her courage.

Thankfully, her bravery proved unnecessary.

Sadana was smiling lightly at her, bending low at the knees to meet Anya's gaze. "And what of you, child of violence? What words can you add to Banner's account?"

Anya might have pondered Sadana's address of her. A child of violence? It had the ring of a title rather than a mere adjective. However, she didn't have long to consider the elderly tree maiden's statement. She reviewed her part in the battle against the wraiths.

At the arrival of the *aether*-cursed cat, Sadana interrupted her retelling. "An *aether*-cursed beast aided you?" she asked, shock tinging her words.

Anya smiled wryly. "Believe me. No one was more surprised than me. But, yes, an *aether*-cursed snowtiger helped us. She attacked the male wraith, who did this while retreating." She gestured to Cinder. "Then Sepia threw the wraith into a hill. It looked like he broke some bones."

Sadana rose again to her full height, silent as she stared at Mahamatha, seemingly sharing a silent conversation with the vast tree.

Anya tried to hold back her impatience. Cinder needed healing, and she wanted to see it done.

"A strange story, but it explains much," Sadana said after a while. "Two days ago, Mother Ashoka ripened a fruit, an Aushadha."

Sepia gasped. "She has already bloomed four times in her life, and the last one was but a century ago."

Five? Anya frowned. "I thought an Ashoka tree could only produce two fruits in their lifetimes."

Sadana shook her head and smiled. "A common misconception, one we long ago ceased trying to correct." From a sack slung across her back, one Anya had overlooked, she withdrew an object, an Aushadha, the white fruit of an Ashoka tree.

Anya had never before seen one. She didn't know anyone who had. The fruit was the size of her fist, shaped like a pomegranate, white as bone and smooth and shiny as a polished gem. Upon its surface and within its depths, there swirled spirals of light, moving in strange motions, as if they formed a grand tapestry of hidden truths or meanings.

Anya instinctively reached for the fruit, but at the last instant, she yanked her hand back to her side. The fruit was not meant for her.

"You can hold it if you like," Sadana said, offering the fruit.

Anya took the Aushadha in hand, surprised by its dense weight. It was easily as heavy as a bucket of steel filings. She cupped both hands under the fruit, raising it to her eyes, staring at the whirling patterns. Her gaze focused on a single mote of light. It expanded, rushing to fill her vision. She saw white clouds and blue oceans. Two continents. The place seemed oddly familiar.

Sadana snatched the fruit out of her hands. "Some can lose their mind if they stare too deeply into the fruit," she said. "Let us see to your friend."

Cinder remained unconscious, and Anya glanced at him, fear rising again. He lay on the ground, unmoving. How would they feed him while he was encased in a seeding?

"Worry not," Sadana said. "The fruit for your intended is not meant to be eaten. It is meant to be absorbed. Observe."

She squatted down next to Cinder. A touch, and the nut-like seeding around him fell away in large chunks, drifting apart in a whirl of fine dirt. Sadana opened Cinder's shirt, exposing his wounds. They remained ragged and raw, but thankfully they didn't bleed and showed no signs of infection. Still, Anya swallowed heavily. He looked so weak, his skin pale and bloodless, cheeks sunken.

Sadana cautioned Anya. "He will jerk about. Hold tight to him. Show him peace. Don't allow him to hurt himself. We would hold him if we could, but as you can see, our skin is like bark. It would tear his open."

Anya nodded understanding. She rested Cinder's head on her lap, hugging him to her. It felt so natural and right, and part of her struggled with accepting why it was so easy for her to hold him close and with so little shame—an elven woman fully embracing a human man. But mostly she didn't care. Cinder was her only concern. "I'm ready."

Sadana placed the fruit on Cinder's chest. "He must choose to live. Encourage him."

Upon her words, the world seemed to halt. Birdsong quieted. The wind no longer shivered through the trees. Even the clouds might have paused in their movements.

The fruit brightened, pulsed once. Cinder twitched in Anya's arms. "Come back to me," she whispered.

A deep bell tone rang through the grove, a ponderous note of the seasons turning, steady and forceful as time's wheel. The scent of sandalwood and lavender filled the air. The swirling in the fruit increased in intensity. Cinder's skin warmed, and he shifted in her lap.

She held him closer. "Be at peace," she whispered in his ear.

He might have exhaled softly.

The whirling lights in the Aushadha increased further. The bell rang again. The scent of sandalwood and lavender grew stronger. Cinder twitched again, harder this time, but she didn't—wouldn't—let him go. His skin burned, but she ignored the discomfort.

A third time the bell rang. The swirling became a white blur. The rich scent of sandalwood and lavender was now potent enough to seem visible, and Anya choked on the overwhelming aroma.

Cinder spasmed harder.

Anya clutched him tight. "You're safe." She pressed her forehead against his. "It will be over soon."

Cinder's skin was a furnace. Her senses overloaded, and she clenched shut her eyes, praying for him to be well.

With a sudden absence of sensation, she realized the ringing had ended. The scent had faded away, and Cinder's skin no longer felt like an open forge. Anya opened her eyes.

The glade was unchanged. A breeze fingered through her hair. The leaves rustled, and the yakshins and their holders had gathered around her, watching, standing still as statues.

She glanced at Cinder's chest. The fruit was gone, but he was changed. His face was no longer pale, and he breathed easily. Most of the hollowness in his cheeks had even filled out. But most amazing were the patterns of light shifting across his skin, which was smooth and hard as stone. Just like the fruit.

She was about to ask Sadana if it was over, but Cinder convulsed in a wracking shaking. His heels drummed against the ground, and Anya gripped him about the torso, as hard as she could, pressing his head to her chest. "I've got you, Cinder. You're safe."

"Do not let go of him," Sadana warned.

Her advice was unnecessary. Anya intended on doing nothing else.

38

Cinder's last recollection during his fight against the male wraith had been of soul-gripping pain. The creature had eviscerated him. Then had followed shock and agony as his writhing intestines threatened to spill past the walls of his shredded abdomen. His awareness of the world had narrowed to his terrible hurt, fading until blackness consumed his consciousness.

An indeterminate time later, he realized his awareness had sluggishly returned, imperceptibly perhaps, but he was awake now. He opened his eyes and discovered himself somewhere else. This wasn't Seminal. This was a strange locale of timelessness and waiting. He floated in darkness, absent of any feeling, not just of pain but all sensations.

In his vision slowly formed a flat landscape, an endless plain of motionless red dust. Nothing moved upon it, and the world it inhabited appeared barren of life. An understanding came to him. This empty existence lived in the dark recesses of his mind where hatred and rage held sway, and from this lifeless place emanated the lure of selfish power. It promised him. He would never again be responsible for anyone else. Only himself. He would be made great and fearsome, and the

481

only payment needed for this gift would be his essence along with a never-ending need for domination.

Cinder instinctively shied away from the offer. He could never see himself willingly accepting such a terrible fate.

A metaphorical blink, and he was elsewhere.

This time, his vision latched upon the glorious, mirrored water in the center of his mind's eye. His *Jivatma*.

It's another option.

No lightning laced the water's surface or barred its soothing embrace. It was smooth and calm, reflecting a light that Cinder could now tell existed outside of him. A whisper floated on a mild breeze. It made no assurances, but it provided the possibility of glory or a content life if he was willing to listen and learn. Pain would undoubtedly occur if he decided to live for others, but so would growth and the delivery of aid for those in need.

Another blink, and a third choice was made manifest. Dissolution. Acceptance of a grand song in the form of light where all burdens were lifted, and the gentle yoke of harmony placed on his soul. No worries or fears. Only love.

Cinder considered his options. The singing light strongly called to him, and he edged toward it. He had spent countless years in struggle and conflict, and he was ready to lay aside his wearying toils.

But then, in the vision of the mirrored water, he saw a woman, and he halted his motion. He knew her, knew the softness of her golden hair and golden skin, knew the warmth of her lovely smile. She sang, and his heart lifted. Her voice wasn't of surpassing quality, but it didn't have to be. It fit who she was and what he needed. Her strength matched his flaws, and she was willing to accept his help to support her weaknesses. There was more, a lifetime of love.

But the singing light also offered love.

For an endless moment, Cinder couldn't decide what to do until the woman opened her lips and spoke as if from an incomprehensible distance. "Come back to me," she said.

Cinder's decision was made. He couldn't imagine existing without the woman. Didn't want to imagine it.

He chose the second option, and a bell rang in the vaults of his mind. The sweet scent of sandalwood and lavender wafted. A flashing of light revealed unknowable truths. He grew warm, fevered. Again came the bell, the smells, light, and heat. A third cycle, and this time, he burned. He ached for a bath of ice, but there was no solace for him.

The pain built, becoming a torment of fire, and he bucked, unable to control himself. He grew aware of the tearing of his wounds. At the same time, faint tracings were etched into his mind, the impression of a white-hot knife carving into soft wood. Into these etchings were poured what might have been molten metal, silver and shimmering with heat. Cinder imagined a sizzling sound, and his mouth opened in a soundless scream. The silver stream cooled. The anguish abated, and in his sacrum, a red flower opened. *Muladhara.* The wounds on his abdomen knitted shut, his intestines wriggling back into place. It was a strange sensation, but when it ended, so did the last of his pain.

He exhaled in relief. His racing heart slowed. The memory of what he had endured faded, and when he tried to view the silver stream, it was gone like it had never existed. Same with *Muladhara.* But his *Jivatma* remained in place, full like it had been prior to the long-ago battle with the *aether*-cursed bear. The blue-and-green lightning was recovered as well, but it was thinner than before, faint lines rather than thick bolts.

Cinder opened his eyes. His first view was of Anya clutching him protectively. He was cradled in her arms, and she peered at him, terror and hope writ large on her face.

"Cinder?" she asked, her voice trembling.

He couldn't stop his reaction and wouldn't have even if he could. He reached up and pressed a hand against Anya's face. He felt her warm tears and a soft kiss on his palm.

During the first few days after his healing, Cinder learned much, such as the names of those who had come to his rescue: the yakshin, Sepia, and her holder, Banner. He learned also of his seeding—a feat he found difficult to comprehend—the challenging journey to Shalla Valley, and his acceptance by the Shriven Grove because of who he was, or rather who he had been named: Maynalor. And finally, he learned of the generosity of Mahamatha, Mother Ashoka, who had granted him the Aushadha, which had healed him.

To all of them, Cinder's gratitude knew no bounds, and he wished he had a means to properly express it. Perhaps he could do so when he had more energy. Right now, just talking could be exhausting.

He spent much of his time resting, often lying against the massive trunk of Mother Ashoka. It was comforting.

Mother Ashoka. Ashoka. The name rippled in his memory, a recognition of his past in ways he didn't know but felt he should.

Regardless, there was a welcoming peace to Mother Ashoka, to Mahamatha, a tranquility he never wanted to abandon. A large part of him would have been happy to simply sit here in peace, forever maybe, and watch the world unfold as it willed.

Cinder gazed into the distance, at the wide-open spaces of the savanna, the area just past the Shriven Grove and watched Anya train against the holders. She was doing poorly. The protectors of the yakshins and trolls had a reputation as the finest warriors in all of Seminal, and it seemed their fame was well-earned. Anya was unmatched in Yaksha Sithe, but against the holders, she struggled. More often than not, she lost her matches, barely able to land a touch or even defend adequately.

Cinder wished he could join her, but he was as weak as a newborn kitten. Merely standing upright and unsupported was a challenge while walking was an embarrassing exercise in drunken stumbling. As for sparring, he chuckled. For now it was impossible, a distant dream, and until it wasn't, he would use his hours appreciating Shalla Valley's beauty.

This was a special place. The weather in Shalla Valley was kinder than elsewhere, full of soft breezes, gentle rain, and comfortable weather of all sorts, nothing too extreme. In addition, this was one of the few places where the yakshins could obtain the kind of sustenance needed to support their kind. As if in proof, close at hand, a tree maiden stood rooted, her legs pressed together and forming a trunk, her toes extending roots into the lush soil, and her arms and hands raised high as if to greet the sun. Patches of leaves covered her torso and arms, rustling under the influence of a quiet wind.

A pair of yakshins approached him, and Cinder pushed aside his observations. He levered himself upright and faced the tree maidens. He recognized them. The shorter of the two was Sepia, the yakshin who had saved him, and the taller was Turquoise, the one who had named him Maynalor. Early in his convalescence, he had briefly been introduced to them.

They halted in front of him, and Cinder noted the fresh aroma of spring-fragrant moss and leaves washed in a rain. The tree maidens' joints creaked as they folded into a kneeling position. Even then, Cinder's head rose no higher than their waists.

"I am Turquoise," the yakshin who had named him Maynalor said. "Do you remember me?"

Cinder smiled. "Of course. You're the reason I was allowed into Shalla Valley." He faced the other yakshin. "And you're the reason why I'm still alive. Thank you both. I don't know why you named me or saved me, but thank you."

Sepia smiled, a lattice of wrinkles crinkling her face. "There is no need to thank either of us," she said. "I'm sure the princess would have insisted I bring you here even if I hadn't already planned on doing so."

Cinder's gaze went to Anya, who was taking instruction from one of the holders. She was mimicking his motions, moving at a deliberate pace to shadow his forms. She appeared calm, but Cinder could tell she was frustrated. It was the barest hint of a frown marring her features, and the slight tightening of her jaw. No doubt, she intended on learning everything the holders could teach her because it was her way. Anya accepted nothing less than perfection, and failure was never a consideration.

"Yes," Cinder said to Sepia, still gazing at the princess. "She has a forceful nature."

Sepia chuckled. "Yes, she does."

"Do you ever wonder why I named you Maynalor?" Turquoise asked.

Cinder grinned her way. "All the time," he replied, "especially after the troll recognized me."

"A troll?" Turquoise asked, sounding surprised. "How did this happen?"

Sepia laughed. "You sang his name on the wind, sister. Of course, the trolls would hear of it."

"It was at the Third Directorate," Cinder said. "It's a martial—"

"We know of the Directorate," Sepia interrupted.

Cinder smiled in chagrin. He should have known the long-lived, widely traveled yakshins would know of the Third Directorate. "Anyway, the troll and his holders came to the academy. They wanted to check on Garad Lull. I was there, and the troll, Maize, said they had come to the Directorate because of the Titan, but then he recognized me and called me Maynalor."

"And Maynalor you remain," Sepia said. "Turquoise was correct to call you such. We still don't know who you are. And neither do you, not your centermost truth."

They were more correct than they realized. Cinder didn't know who he was, at least not his true self, and he found himself wondering if the yakshins might. He stared at the tree maidens, trying to decide if he should tell them about his dreams and what he believed they meant. He had only confided his secrets to a few people he trusted, but he realized he could also trust the yakshins. It was an instinctual awareness, and he followed where it led. "What do you know of dreams?"

Turquoise tilted her head to the side, gazing at him curiously. "An odd question," she noted. "Why do you ask."

Cinder told them, relating his first memories, of awakening in the well, the dreams he felt certain were recollections of a past life. Everything. The woman who always showed up in his visions, walking with her through a park at night, her singing while he played a mandolin, and the dream in which he might have murdered her.

During it all, he made sure not to glance at Anya. Nor did he speak of her own similar dreams. She hadn't given him leave to tell of her past, and he would honor her privacy.

Sepia frowned. "Interesting. And you can never recall these dreams?"

Cinder shook his head. "I can remember the impressions of what I dream, but most times I can't even remember that much." He also suspected there were a great many dreams he didn't recall whatsoever, and that they were every bit as important as the ones he did.

"You truly are Maynalor," Sepia said. "*Someone of interest with a secret.* A secret even from yourself. But I am afraid we don't know how to help you search through these entangling dreams for your roots." She sighed, sounding dejected. "It seems your quest must remain a private matter."

Cinder had expected the answer, but it still left him disappointed. He had hoped the yakshins might know the means to unlock the mysteries of his vacant memories.

"I am sorry," Turquoise said, also despondent. "We can ask the others and find out if they know more."

Cinder forced a smile. There were no reasons for the tree maidens to feel bad on his behalf. "I appreciate it, but even if they don't know anything, it's all right. I'm alive, which is enough." He gently patted the massive tree trunk against which he rested, and his smile came easier. "I'm alive because of you and Mother Ashoka, and I'm grateful for everything you've already done. Anything more is being greedy."

Anya knelt next to the stream that wended through the Shriven Grove. She washed her face before lifting it to the dying light of the setting sun. Her eyes were closed, and her wet hair glistened, the tips of her ears poking above the splendid mass. Droplets of water sparkled on her forehead and tracked down her neck.

Cinder watched her from the nearby bank, leaning on a stout staff. He rarely needed it during the day, but by the end of the evening, his legs could sometimes give way without warning. However, every day, he was growing stronger, and maybe soon, he would be recovered enough to take part in the sparring and really work at rebuilding his strength and endurance.

"Why are you staring?" Anya asked, face still lifted to the sky.

It was a good question, but one without a good answer. At least not an answer she would appreciate.

Ever since Cinder's healing, a week ago now, he often caught himself searching for Anya. There was a connection between them. Of this, he was sure. He had awoken in her arms, and she had been relieved. The fear on her face had been real, and so had her tears when he had cupped her face, and the soft kiss she'd placed on his palm.

But if there was a connection, what was it? Cinder knew what he wished it might be, but he also knew better than to name it. Acknowledging his feelings for her carried danger for both of them. Better to continually add bricks to the wall around his heart.

"You didn't answer my question," Anya said.

"Did you know you're controlled in your every movement?" Cinder replied. "Even when you wash your face. You're so precise."

Anya smirked at him. "I don't think the precision of my movements was at the forefront of your mind."

Cinder's mouth involuntarily tightened. Anya obviously knew the pattern of what he had been thinking, but he wasn't ready to confirm her guess. "Then what reason is there?"

Anya rose to her feet and paced toward him. "You are an uncommonly brave man," she said, halting a few inches inside his personal space. "Do you really wish to play coy?"

So, she's not willing to let it go. "You kissed my hand," Cinder said, hating how his tone made the words sound accusatory.

Anya nodded. "I did, and it was a mistake. The emotion of the moment overcame my good sense, and now you wonder if there might be something more to our relationship than that of an *Isha* and her *bishan*."

"We are who we are," Cinder said, the enigmatic statement the best answer he could give her without lying.

Anya stared at him for a period of time, as if testing the truth of his words. In the end, she nodded as if satisfied with what she had seen. "So you say."

Now it was she who was being enigmatic, and Cinder tilted his head in consideration. What was she hiding? Could she possibly feel the same way for him as he did for her? And was she equally unwilling to state the truth? And for the same reasons as his own?

He found her gazing at him, standing too close, and this time he didn't step away. Her people wouldn't allow any kind of relationship between them, but he no longer cared. Not anymore. Not after nearly dying. "You were right before. I wasn't only noticing the precision of your movements. I was also noticing your beauty."

"You shouldn't say such things," Anya said in a half-hearted way, easing away from him and swallowing heavily. "If my people heard what you just said, in the way you said it—" She shuddered, straightening. "I am a princess of the blood. They would kill you for it."

Cinder blinked in shock. *Death?* He had never figured they would go so far.

Anya nodded as if she could read his thoughts. "They would kill you Cinder. I could never allow it to happen. You can never repeat those words. You must be strong. We both must be."

Cinder understood, and he crushed any sense of disappointment. He had always known she wasn't for him, but in the moment, he had thought to be courageous. Instead, he was being foolish.

Anya was right. They had to be strong for one another or pain would be the only ending either of them would experience. He pointed to the horizon, shifting the conversation. "It's a lovely sunset tonight, is it not?"

Anya glanced to where he indicated. A wedge of swans flew highlighted against the lustrous, western sky. The sun lingered a finger above the hills, sending a last set of golden rays lancing through the clouds and burnishing Shalla Valley. To the east, the sky edged toward darkness, and in a short time the stars would come to life, lighting the firmament in a broad spread of glory. It was like this most nights in Shalla Valley.

"It is beautiful," Anya agreed, her voice hushed and full of awe as the arc of her gaze gathered their surroundings.

"And I don't lust for it. But I appreciate it."

Anya quirked a grin, still staring at the sky. "It would be odd if you did. Lust for it, I mean." But while she smiled in wry amusement, there was an undertone of longing and regret to her expression. She pointed to his walking staff. "How are you coming along?"

"I should be ready to spar within a few days. Maybe another week-and-a-half for traveling."

Anya nodded. "Good. We need to leave as quickly as possible."

"I know. Our being here weakens the valley's defenses." Early on in his convalescence, Sadana had explained to him how his and Anya's presence in the valley placed the yakshins in danger. It allowed a flaw in their otherwise impregnable aura, which flowed from the Ashokas, especially Mahamatha.

Cinder wouldn't allow it. He owed the yakshins and Mahamatha too much to put them at risk.

"I've heard a gathering of wraiths is testing the borders," Anya said. "If they breach the valley's aura, the holders are certain they can handle them, but…" She trailed off, apparently wanting him to intuit the rest of her meaning.

"It would be best if they never managed to penetrate the aura in the first place."

"That's right. The Shriven isn't the only grove. It's the oldest, but there are at least a dozen more scattered throughout Shalla Valley. Defending all of them would be a challenge if wraiths invaded this place."

Cinder nodded, considering the various entrances into Shalla Valley. There were only three, but given the relatively small numbers of holders, three was two more than they could easily defend. "I'll heal faster," he said, recognizing the absurdity of his promise even as he made it. He couldn't control the speed of his recovery.

"Just do your best," Anya said, patting him companionably on the shoulder before heading toward the grove.

Cinder watched her depart and had an odd notion spring to the forefront of his mind. Had there been a choice of some sort to make during his healing? And why did it seem like Anya had played a significant role in whatever decision he had made?

Fastness was ready to bed down for the evening, and he yawned mightily. It had been a good day. In fact, he'd never before had so much fun. Shalla Valley was a wondrous place, and he loved it here.

He'd spent the day playing. He had nipped a water buffalo in the butt, darting out of danger when the creature had charged after him. Time and time again, he'd done so, leaving the poor buffalo roaring in impotent frustration.

Then there had been the encounter with the trio of male lions. He'd barreled into one, kicked another in the chest, and chased off the third. They'd all scattered before him, the expressions on their furry cat faces a mix of utter confusion and humiliation. *Priceless.* The lions hadn't been able to understand how they, the lords of the savanna, were being run off by a mere horse.

Even the chimpanzees had been fun playfellows. Fastness had seen them clustered near a copse of acacias, and he had snuck up on them. And during a moment of distraction on their part, he had dashed into their midst, bugling a neigh as he roared past and nearly scaring the life out of the little primates. Their screams of terror had been wonderful, and while they had tried to retaliate by flinging their poop at him, they had been unsuccessful. He was too swift for the feces-flingers.

Fastness whickered in satisfaction and humor. Yes, it had been a good day. He settled down, content and happy while glancing about at this magical place one last time before closing his eyes.

Night had fallen, and in the darkness, he thought the Shriven Grove had the appearance of a long cavern with the low-hanging arms of the trees forming the walls and ceiling. The space beneath the branches was lit by fireflies flitting about like a flock of flashing jewels. Otherwise, the savanna was dark since a cloudbank shrouded the stars and moons.

However, it didn't mean the savanna was quiet. Even at night, life made its presence known. A long-legged, pink bird—in the morning Fastness would ask Cinder for the creature's name—honked from the shallows of the massive, nearby lake. It sounded mournful, a counterpoint to the crickets and insects singing happily in the savanna's tall grass. A calling bird chirped, a set of high-pitched cries, and further away, the rumbling groan of a crocodile echoed over the grasslands.

Fastness found the sounds fascinating and soothing. He loved the vibrancy of the savanna, even the savagery. He also enjoyed the weather, such as the gentle winds that blew across the waters of the nearby lake. The breezes were cool and refreshing and carried the clean fragrance of high mountain moisture. Such a wind flitted about Fastness even now, curling through his mane.

He sighed in contentment and had just closed his eyes when a silvery moonbeam pierced a tattered rent in the cloudbank. It was like a blade of light, illuminating a narrow part of the savanna.

Fastness started, instantly awake and alert, distantly noting a polecat racing for cover under the brilliance of the silvery beam. However, the feline didn't hold his attention. Instead, his gaze went to the moon itself, to the silvery orb which hung like a pearl in the night sky. It gleamed like something ethereal and lovely, and Fastness stared. He remembered the name of the moon. *Dormant.*

He nickered then, shifting in nervousness. *Dormant.* The name was known to him for reasons he couldn't express, and it inspired visions of an abnormally tall man, thin, hairless, and skin pale as bone.

Or as pale as Fastness himself.

39

Cinder stood next to Anya, the two of them facing Banner from a distance of twenty feet. They shared a ring of stones, a sparring circle near the Shriven Grove. No one else was about. The rest of the holders were with their tree maidens in various parts of the valley, including Sepia, who could barely be seen walking the length of the distant lakeshore, caring for the palm and coconut trees.

It was morning, and the grass was slick with dew. A convoy of heavy, white clouds paraded across the sky, and the possibility of rain carried on a warm, wet wind. The breeze also brought the fragrances of the savanna: wet grass, dirt, and the musk of the many animals which made the place their home.

"Are you ready?" Banner asked.

Cinder didn't answer at first. He wasn't sure. Was he ready? It had been most of a week since he had finally discarded his walking staff, and so far, the only person he had trained against was Anya. They had sparred, and while in the past he'd never done well against the princess, currently it was much worse than the norm. Cinder still struggled with his timing, reaction speed, and coordination.

493

He knew his poor form, stamina, and quickness would show up even worse against a holder, but those weren't the causes for his indecision. It was because of the manner of instruction the holders demanded.

When sparring, they used wooden staves over shokes, allowed no protective gear other than a leather helmet, and seemed to believe that pain and injury were the best means of teaching technique and tactics. Sometimes the instruction was brutal. Broken bones weren't uncommon, and Cinder didn't know if such learning would be useful for him at this early stage of his recovery. Even with the healing abilities of the yakshins—which were above and beyond anything elven physicians could manage—he worried a serious injury this soon after his near fatal one might cause a significant setback.

Cinder glanced at Anya, who viewed him in return, a questioning lift to a single brow. "What do you think?" he asked her. "Am I ready?"

"You've seen how easily they handle me," she replied. "What do you think?"

Cinder released a heavy sigh. "I think I'm in for an asskicking."

Anya gave him a slight smile. "You probably are, but I still think you should do it. It'll be a valuable learning experience, especially if you face another wraith. Holders and wraiths. Other than the rishis, there are none deadlier."

"I'll be gentle," Banner called out across the sparring circle. His vow was ruined by a sharklike grin.

Cinder narrowed his eyes at the holder. "Promise?"

Banner held up a hand. "I promise not to hurt you." He paused a beat. "At least, not too much."

Cinder grumbled under his breath, recognizing it was the best he could expect. He twirled his practice sword, getting used to the heft and weight. It was shorter and lighter than his normal sword and shoke, but it would do. "Let's get it done."

Without another word, Banner edged forward, his wooden sword tilted downward and to the side at a shallow angle. Cinder tried to make sense of what the holder intended, studying his poise, his balance, the way he placed his feet.

He determined nothing. Banner was an enigma, utterly indecipherable even in comparison to Anya.

The holder darted forward, too fast for Cinder to make an adjustment. He was caught flat-footed, barely able to get his sword around in time to bat away a thrust aimed at his chest. He clumsily fell away from a follow-up slash that could have cracked ribs.

Fragging hells!

Cinder barely checked a sidekick aimed at his calf, but even then, it felt like he'd been hit with a club.

The holders were fast and strong. Cinder had seen it, recognized it, believed it, but feeling and knowing it were altogether different things.

Banner feinted a thrust, but this time his positioning exposed his true intent. *A vertical chop.* Cinder parried, pulled away from a crackback elbow, and blocked a downward slash.

Cinder launched an attack of his own. A straight thrust, but Banner didn't bite. It didn't matter. The thrust was a feint, meant to distract and disrupt the holder's view of a coming headkick.

The holder never hesitated. He somehow saw the kick coming and stepped into it. Cinder drew his leg back, desperate to reset. He was off balance, and Banner was too close. The holder rammed his shoulder into Cinder's chest. A rhino might have hit as hard. Cinder flew back five feet, landed on his backside, and slid a few feet.

He groaned. His chest was sure to be bruised. He patted it carefully, wincing when he found some tender places.

Anya appeared in his vision, kneeling at his side and blotting out the sun and sky. She appeared concerned. "Can you stand?"

"I think so," Cinder said, struggling to lever himself upright.

She helped him, gripping him around the back, supporting him. "You can't land a kick against a holder," she said. "They're too fast, and you're too slow. You're best sticking with short, crisp attacks."

"Thanks for the advice," Cinder said with a wry grin, although he had already come to the same realization.

He caught Banner stalking toward him. The holder appeared angry.

"Next time you face me, do me the courtesy of sourcing your *lorethasra*," Banner said.

"I'm human. I don't have *lorethasra*."

Banner blinked. "But when I saw your fight against the wraith, you moved far more swiftly than you did just now. Was it not your *lorethasra*?"

Cinder shrugged, unwilling to explain about *Jivatma*.

"Is it your injury then?"

Cinder shook his head. "My injuries are fine. I'm just slow." He clambered to his feet. "Let's go again." He wanted to try himself against Banner at least one more time. Despite the holder's blistering speed and balance, he'd actually managed to grasp his intent, at least in part.

"It's a waste of time. Your skill might be exceptional for a human, but it's less than marginal for a holder. It's like you said. You're too slow to offer me a challenge, and I'm too fast for you to really learn anything sparring against me."

"I can move faster."

"I thought you said you couldn't source *lorethasra*."

Cinder grimaced. "I can't, but I think I have a way." He had conducted his *Jivatma* on only a few occasions since his injury because each time it had been exhausting. He had needed a long nap afterward.

But conducting *Jivatma* would be worth the cost of any resultant fatigue if he could truly test himself against the holder.

Banner canted his head. "If it's not *lorethasra*, the only other thing would be *Jivatma*. You're not a hidden rishi, are you?" He smirked, clearly joking.

Cinder chuckled, but even to his ears it sounded strained.

Banner picked up on his tentative expression, and the holder's smile became a suspicious frown.

"I'm not a rishi," Cinder said quickly.

Banner peered at him, seemingly deliberating on the matter. In the end, he nodded acceptance. "I believe you," he said, "but you're also not just a human who happens to be superlatively skilled. How can you make yourself faster?"

Anya muttered under her breath, while Cinder stared at the holder, trying to figure out what to tell him. If not for Banner and Sepia, he would have died. And since he already trusted the yakshin with some of his secrets, why not her holder, too? "I'm not a rishi," he said at last, "but I do have *Jivatma*. It all began when I awoke in the bottom of a well. I don't remember anything else before—"

Banner held up a hand, urging Cinder to silence. "This has the makings of a long story, and it also sounds like something the tree maidens should hear. I will fetch Sepia. She will judge."

He spun about and left without another word, headed for his yakshin.

Anya sauntered to Cinder's side after Banner's departure, a teasing grin on her face. "He knew you were hiding something the moment you started talking about getting faster," she said with a chuckle. "You never could hide your emotions. You'll want to work on that."

Cinder grunted agreement, recognizing she was right, at least in part.

"Come on. Let's spar," Anya said, giving him a playful shove.

Cinder responded by leaning his shoulder into Anya's, knocking her off-balance. But he also grasped her hand to keep her from falling over. She likely didn't need his aid, but it was the thought that counted. "Whenever you're ready," he said, still holding her hand. It never occurred to him that he shouldn't be touching her.

"I'm ready now," Anya said, withdrawing her hand and striding to the opposite side of the sparring circle. "Begin."

It turned out Cinder wasn't allowed to tell his tale about conducting *Jivatma* to Sepia alone.

As soon as she heard the beginnings of what he had to say, she held up a branchlike hand and had him halt his account. "My sisters will want to hear of this."

She knelt, eyes closed and facing Mahamatha as she sank her hands into the dirt, which parted like it was a fluid. A green glow, the rich hue of an Ashoka's leaves, enveloped her body, and the verdant shining collected, forming thick threads which sounded like rustling ivy as they wove across her torso. In a rush, the glow flowed down her arms like streamers of water. It emptied into the rich soil, flashing outward in a circular wave of green light that extended out to the limits of Cinder's vision and bent the sturdy turf as if placing it under the influence of an expanding wave.

There was silence afterward, and several seconds passed before the noise of the world, the call of birds, the cries of animals, and the wild hunt of lions on the prowl, resumed.

When Sepia finished whatever she had done, she admonished Cinder to remain close by for when her sisters returned to the Grove. He did as she instructed, sparring against Anya until he couldn't go any longer.

Hours later in the early afternoon, the rest of the tree maidens and holders returned to the Shriven Grove and collected near Mahamatha, Cinder and Anya centered in their grouping. The score or so of yakshins sat in semi-circle, their features patient as an old-growth forest while their thirty holders waited outside their gathering, watchfully guarding their wards. As soon as the group settled, Cinder repeated what he had started to tell Sepia.

And when he completed his narration, the yakshins wore quizzical expressions while the holders held skeptical ambivalence, their muscled arms folded across broad chests.

"You are certain of this?" Turquoise asked, referring to his claim of being able to see his *Jivatma*.

"I'm sure," Cinder said. "The mirrored water I see matches the few surviving accounts of how the Mythaspuris describe *Jivatma*."

"Describe it again," Sepia ordered.

Cinder did so. "But for some reason, the lightning is thinner now," he added, not knowing if the detail was important.

"And how do you conduct *Jivatma*?" Sadana asked.

Cinder struggled to answer. Whenever he conducted *Jivatma*, it was instinctual. He simply reached for it, and it filled him. He was one with the force of it, and it was one with him. "I don't know what to tell you," he said in the end, frustrated by his inability to explain how he conducted *Jivatma*. "I just do it, and then everything is clearer. All my senses are heightened. Time flows more slowly. I'm faster and stronger."

This time his explanation was met by a wary assessing quiet.

Sadana eventually ended the silence when she creaked to her feet, her demeanor flat and inscrutable. "Do you know why we honor Mother Ashoka?"

Cinder's brow creased. It was an odd question. What did Mother Ashoka have to do with what he had just told the gathering? He eventually shook his head. "I assumed it was because she is the oldest of all the Ashokas."

"Not just the oldest, but the first. She was seeded at the end of the *NusraelShev*. Our kind, the yakshins, are unique amongst the woven. We were not directly created by humans, but by Mother Ashoka."

Cinder's jaw dropped, surprise nearly flooring him, and based on Anya's gasp of shocked disbelief, her as well. There were stories, myths really, stating what Sadana had confirmed. Cinder had read many of them, but he'd never given those tales much credence. The accounts claimed that the races of woven were created by humans. It sounded impossible given the history of the world. After all, if humans had created the woven, then what sin had caused their fall? What had stolen their grandeur and glory? Their power?

"You claim humans created the woven?" Anya demanded, her face alight with a skepticism Cinder shared.

"I claim nothing," Sadana responded. "It is the truth. And it is why we tree maidens honor humanity in the manner we do. Our groves are planted entirely in human nations. We never plant them in places where other woven hold authority."

"Why did Mother Ashoka only create tree maidens?" Cinder asked. "Why didn't she make any tree men?"

"She did," Sadana replied, appearing sorrowful. "They held a meeting of some sort, a moot they called it and wandered off into another Realm, lost in a forest full of fangs."

Anya was shaking her head. "That can't be right," she said, apparently still upset about what Sadana had said about humans and the woven. "I know of the Mythaspuris, but our stories state—"

"Your stories are fables," Sadana sternly interrupted. "Fables meant to proclaim elven glory. Fables where your kind singlehandedly held the line against the forces of Shet until the coming of the Mythaspuris. Fables including your poorly remembered prophecies about the rebirth of Naraka, Shet's citadel of power. But even in this matter, your people have twisted the truth so all your foretellings state that elven greatness will save the world once again. It is false."

Anya's eyes glittered in response to the tree maiden's statements, in either anger, sorrow, or denial. Cinder couldn't rightly tell.

Sadana must have noticed Anya's unhappiness because her voice gentled. "You do not have to believe me, child, but you will believe Mother Ashoka. She knows the truth. I will ask if she is willing to tell it to you. You must hear her." She faced Cinder. "Both of you. It is your duty."

A spark of misgiving lit inside Cinder. There was more going on here than met the eye. There was also some secret Sadana wasn't telling, and he was deathly tired of secrets. His entire life seemed a secret, mysteries he wasn't ever allowed to know. "Why is this so important to you?" he asked Sadana, managing a manner just short of a demand. "What aren't you saying?"

Sadana vacillated. "I wish I could tell you, but it is not my place. Your question is one only Mother Ashoka can answer." She bent her head in apology. "I am sorry. But know this: your story of *Jivatma* may relate to a prophecy first spoken by Indrun. It relates to a time when Mahamatha will return to her heavenly realm."

Sadana's words set off a chain reaction. The yakshins transitioned from dumbfounded to appalled, but it was the reaction of the holders that raised Cinder's hackles. They wore the demeanors of those expecting to kill, tightly gripping their sword hilts, tense and poised.

Cinder took a step back. His hand went to the shoke at his waist, even though he knew it was a useless weapon against the holders and their steel. He scanned the small clearing in front of Mother Ashoka.

Anya shifted to stand directly at his side. "Relax," she whispered to him in a soothing tone. He noticed she kept her hands at her side, pointedly not touching her own shoke. "They are scared, but they won't hurt us."

Cinder wasn't so sure, but he decided to follow her lead. He didn't know why the holders were fingering their swords, or why they seemed on the precipice of violence, but he also knew that he and Anya had no chance against them all. Maybe one, but not a score.

"What's going on?" Cinder asked Sadana, never taking his eyes off the yakshin's guardians.

Sadana swept her gaze over the holders. "They are not our foes," she said to them. "Release your fears."

The holders didn't immediately do as she instructed. Rather, they stared at one another in uncertainty, and it took time for them to calm down enough to remove their hands from the hilts of their swords.

"Mother Ashoka will explain if there is anything to explain," Sadana said to Cinder and Anya. "Come with me." She strode to Mother Ashoka, and there, she bowed low to the great tree. Next, she placed her forehead against the trunk, closing her eyes and appearing to commune with Mahamatha.

Cinder and Anya shared a confused glance before joining Sadana at the base of Mother Ashoka.

"Do you know what's going on?" Cinder asked Anya.

"No idea," Anya answered.

Sadana addressed them. "Place your palms upon her trunk and rest your head against it. Close your eyes. She will speak to you if you are worthy."

"And if she doesn't want to talk?" Cinder asked.

Sadana expression grew more severe. "Then you and I will have a very different conversation."

Again, Cinder threw a questioning glance at Anya, and she shrugged minutely in reply. Neither of them knew what was happening. Why did the tree maidens appear horrified? And the holders, too? And why did Mother Ashoka have to converse with them?

"Please do as I ask," Sadana said, her voice carrying an unexpected edge, like a sword unsheathed.

Seeing no other choice, Cinder did as instructed. He placed his palms upon Mother Ashoka and rested his head against her trunk. Anya did the same.

The tree maidens chanted as one:

> *Goddess of the wild forest,*
> *Who vanishes from our sight.*
> *Seeming to sound like dancing bells,*
> *The Lady of the Wood exults.*
> *The Forest Queen frees our wains.*

Cinder closed his eyes, and the sound of tinkling bells rang in his mind.

40

Cinder's world narrowed to the sound of tinkling bells.

He opened his eyes and discovered himself standing on the edge of a sun-dappled wildflower meadow. Fat bumblebees flitted across the air and around the blossoms, and a warm breeze played with his hair, carrying the scent of fresh flowers, dirt, and moss.

But what held the entirety of his attention was the woman dancing in the center of the field, swaying, darting, and twirling. She had skin pale as snow and hair so blonde it reflected white in the sunshine. A dress made from roses of various colors—red, yellow, pink, and white—trailed to her ankles and wreathed her form. A circlet of purple jasmine graced her fine brow, and woven into the long, braided locks of her hair and wrapped in circlets around her ankles were tiny, silver bells. They tinkled with every spin and step she took.

The woman smiled in Cinder's direction, locking him in place with her arresting blue eyes. They were simultaneously inquisitive and innocent as an infant's, yet ancient and powerful as a monarch on her throne. It was a strange dichotomy.

She indicated for him to enter the glade, and as if he was in a trance,

Cinder complied. He had no notion to fear the woman, to question this strange place, or to wonder if he was dreaming. The woman was gentle, and she belonged here. And this place—no matter where it might be located—was real. He was certain of it. Just as he was certain that he knew this woman. She was Mahamatha. Mother Ashoka. And her presence was every bit as soothing as her namesake tree, especially when the leaves of the trees swayed under the song of a warm wind, a gentle reminder of summer's idyllic, never-ending joy.

The woman stilled her dance. "Come closer, Cinder Shade," she said, her voice echoing like the open notes of a guitar and deep like a surging surf. "You know who I am?"

"Mahamatha," Cinder said without hesitation. "Mother Ashoka."

The woman's smile widened, revealing pearlescent teeth. "Those are the names my children have granted me, but in a truer Realm, I am known as Aranya. We have never before met, but the prophecies granted me by Indrun promised one such as you might aid me."

Indrun? A Mythaspuri. She had known him?

As if Indrun's name broke a spell, the trance of Aranya's powerful presence lessened some, and the veil over Cinder's mind lifted. He found himself able to think again, and his eyes darted about the glade in confusion. *Where am I?*

"You need not fear this place," Aranya said, her voice soft and lilting. "Just as I was born from a wish and a dream, so too, are the outlines of my world. This place is a wish and a dream. You are safer here than anywhere on Seminal."

Cinder's eyes had yet to settle. "I don't understand," he said after a moment, his eyes finally focusing on the woman. "Who are you?"

She smiled faintly. "I told you. I am Aranya. Mother Ashoka. Mahamatha." Her smile fled. "We don't have much time. Listen close. There is knowledge of your future that you require."

Cinder didn't need the recitation of a quelchon or Mahamatha to know his future. It would be filled with danger. It was as obvious as snow in winter, and it also wasn't of significant interest to him right now. Of greater importance was his past, or rather, his strange imaginings of a past life. "Can you tell me what my dreams mean?"

Aranya shook her head, her air one of regret. "Your past you must learn on your own. It is not my tale to tell."

Cinder frowned in annoyance. "But you know it," he demanded.

Aranya's countenance hardened at his effrontery, and clouds shrouded the sun. Thunder rumbled. "Part of it. But as I said, it is not my tale to tell."

Cinder bent his head, shuffling in embarrassment at his brashness and discourtesy. "I'm sorry," he said in profound grief. His emotions seemed to whipsaw in this place, spiraling past his control, and he chided himself to take greater care of his speech and attitude.

Aranya smiled again, and the clouds broke apart, the sky brightening. "You don't need to apologize. Sit, and I'll tell you what I can of *lorethasra* and *Jivatma*. Then we will speak of your future."

Cinder sat on the ground, eager to hear what Aranya had to say. He had studied all he could about *lorethasra* and *Jivatma*, but no matter how much he read, always there was a missing element, an unknown aspect he had yet to hear properly explained. Not from old Deepak, Master Lerid, or any of his instructors at the Third Directorate. And no book had the correct answers either.

Aranya began dancing again, the circlets at her ankles and the bells in her hair tinkling like windchimes. The perfumed fragrance of her rose dress and jasmine circlet drifted in the wake of her movements as her path took her in a circuit about him. She spoke. "*Jivatma* is the soul. You know this. It is a grace granted to us by Devesh, and on our deaths, our Singing Lord of Light gives us a choice."

She paused her speech, granting Cinder time to consider her words. *Singing Lord of Light*. He'd never heard Devesh described as such, but it struck him as correct. And he also reflected on what she'd just confirmed. Jivatma *was the soul*. So, why could he see his? At least he assumed he could. But what if he was wrong? He had to know.

"Can I see my *Jivatma*?"

"You can."

Cinder rocked backward a bit. He hadn't expected such a firm reply.

"Then why can't the woven? Why can't anyone else?"

Aranya continued to dance. "Because the conduction of *Jivatma* is an instructed skill. It must be taught and learned early, and the woven were never taught so they never learned. And like any aspect of living, if a skill is never used or never taught, it will wither and die or become forgotten."

"And I was taught?" Cinder asked, edging toward querying about his past. "By whom?"

"You know I won't answer your question," Aranya answered, laughter in her voice. "Your memories are clouded, and you must be the one to clear them. No one else. But I can tell you this: the woven had no need to learn how to conduct *Jivatma*. They had *lorethasra*, an easier power to master since it is of the physical world, of the mind and body."

Aranya's explanation filled in a couple of the gaps in Cinder's knowledge, but there remained many missing pieces. "Can I teach others to conduct their *Jivatma*?"

"You can, but only if they first forgo the use of *lorethasra*. The easier path stunts conduction of *Jivatma*." A hard edge entered her voice. "We have no more time for simple lessons. Listen closely. War comes. Go to the northernmost border of my vale. I can deposit you in close approximation to where you need to be. A day's ride from Darand's Gap. You'll learn what you must when you reach it and Mount Kirindor, the Piercing Heart. It is the tallest peak in the Daggers. But be cautious. You will skirt the edges of the Webbed Kingdom, a dread place haunted by both the creatures of Shet and the spiderkin, the children of Sheoboth."

Cinder frowned, not liking what he was hearing. Aranya expected him to trek into the depths of the Daggers and approach the boundaries of the Webbed Kingdom where no one had ventured in centuries? He hoped the unusual woman had a good reason to require such a risk. "Why do you want me to go there?"

"It is necessary," Aranya said. "A storm approaches, and you must discover what the world faces. There are long-sought answers there as well, and after you learn them, do not linger. Return straightaway to the valley. I'll have the border interposed where you need it." She raised a hand, denying Cinder from asking any follow-up queries. "Our time grows short. We are nearly done here."

"Wait!" Cinder said in a near panic. "I have so many questions."

Aranya halted her dance. "And I wish I could answer them, child, but it is forbidden. Unlike the rishis, I take my vows seriously." She held up a cautionary finger. "But there is a place where you can learn the entirety of what you seek."

Cinder's anticipation rose. "Where?"

"Mahadev."

Cinder's burgeoning excitement crashed into the shoals of reality. Mahadev? The city of ghosts? The place into which any who ever entered, never exited.

His antipathy must have been evident on his face. "If you truly wish to be complete and know yourself, there is nowhere else you can find the instruction you lack," Aranya said. "But you must be cautious. An enemy has touched you and seeks you there. He thinks I don't know this. He is like smoke, and you must avoid him at all costs. In addition, once you are safe, you will face a terrible dilemma. It will not be easy, but you must choose wisely and use faith as your guide."

An enemy like smoke and a terrible dilemma? Cinder had no idea what she was talking about. As far as he was concerned, a terrible dilemma was even having to go to Mahadev. And as for enemies, it seemed like he had plenty of those already.

He exhaled heavily. Nevertheless, he would do as she advised. "Yes, Amma." The title slipped onto his tongue, sounding and feeling right even as he spoke it.

Aranya smiled gently. "No one has named me such in millennia. Thank you." She was suddenly standing before Cinder, slightly taller than him. "There is much I can't *tell, but I* am allowed to provide you one small gift." She pressed her lips to his brow, which tingled when she released him. "You will know it when you recall what you have forgotten. Go now. Safe travels, child."

The world of the glade seemed to pull away from Cinder's sight, becoming ever smaller and distant.

A trailing admonishment reached his ears before the meadow was entirely erased from his vision. "Go north quickly. To Darand's Gap and Mount Kirindor. And afterward, Mahadev."

Aranya's glade became a distant pinpoint of light, and the rest of Cinder's vision was filled by a formless emptiness.

An instant later, a soundless hastening of light and energy heralded the return of the real world. Shalla Valley resumed, quivering as every form flexed and warped like fluid. Reality wrapped around Cinder, pressing into him like a weighted blanket. Time resumed when a ponderous bass note sounded.

Distant voices met Cinder's emergence, but he was unable to focus upon them. Nausea gripped his stomach. His balance was gone, and he stumbled away from Mother Ashoka, hunched over at the waist with hands on his knees. *His gorge.* It felt like he'd stepped into the world of the Foe, except this was a hundred-fold worse.

Anya seemed to be having the same trouble. She took a knee, head bent and eyes closed as she inhaled and exhaled, slow, even, and steady. She must have also traveled into Aranya's world, although Cinder hadn't seen her there.

It was several minutes longer until Cinder's stomach settled enough for him to stand. His vision swam momentarily, but after a bit, he was fine.

He glanced about the Shriven Grove. The holders remained tense, but at least their hands no longer hovered over their sword hilts. As for the tree maidens, they appeared enraptured, silent and waiting.

Sadana, her long, rugged face calm and expectant, addressed them. "What did you see?"

Anya answered. "A dancer."

Cinder glanced at her in surprise. "You saw her, too?"

"Blonde and pale?" Anya asked.

Cinder nodded. "She was in a wildflower glade."

Anya smiled. "Purple coneflowers, orange poppies, asters, daisies, blanket flowers, and coreopsis. Those were the flowers."

Cinder shrugged. Trust Anya to actually identify the plants. She loved horticulture in a way he never would. "I didn't see you there."

"I didn't see you either," Anya replied.

Sadana chuckled. "It is Mother Ashoka's magic. You only saw what she allowed and what your minds could tolerate."

The statement birthed a messy knot of questions, which had Cinder frowning in frustration. So far this morning, all he had were ever-increasing questions but far fewer answers. Beyond what he wished to know about his past, about *Jivatma* and *lorethasra*, there was now Mother Ashoka. What was she? Who was she?

"She told me her true name," Cinder said to Sadana. "The dancer, I mean."

The yakshin's laughter cut off. "Do not speak it. Her enemies might hear."

Cinder shot her a look. Aranya could create entire worlds, ones eerily similar to the Foe, and her tree form soared as high as the clouds and was as wide as a village. She was powerful in ways he couldn't begin to fathom. What enemies could cause her even the tiniest ounce of fear?

"What did she tell you?" Sadana asked, interrupting his reflections.

Cinder flicked his eyes toward Anya, silently urging her to answer before him. He was still trying to process what Aranya had said.

Anya took the hint and spoke first. "She warned me there will come a time when I must choose between what I have always believed and what might be the truth. She also advised me to cling to my better nature and to never forgo my love." The princess seemed both disturbed and frustrated. "I don't know what she meant."

"Memories are often forgotten or distorted, and so are writings and prophecies. You would be wise to remember her advice." Sadana nodded slowly, deliberately, as if she were offering wisdom, but to Cinder her statements sounded apropos of nothing.

Anya must have felt the same way. "What advice?" she said, anger lacing her voice. "She didn't give me anything. What she said made no sense."

Cinder privately agreed. Whatever Aranya had meant to convey to Anya didn't sound like much. Either that or the significance was lost in the vast gap between thoughts and words.

"Not now, it doesn't," Sadana said to Anya, "but it will in a time to come. It always does." She faced Cinder. "And what did she say to you?"

"She told me a little bit about *Jivatma* and *lorethasra*," Cinder replied, "but she also said she couldn't explain the full truth."

"Interesting," Sadana mused, not pushing for details on what for Cinder had been of utmost importance.

Maybe it was because she already knew everything there was to know about *Jivatma* and *lorethasra*. Or maybe it was because it didn't matter to her. Maybe Sadana was already powerful enough with whatever abilities or talents she possessed.

"Was there anything else?" Sadana asked.

"She said I needed to go to the northern borders of Shalla Valley," Cinder answered. "She said she could place me in close approximation to where I need to be." He frowned. "I'm not sure how she can do that."

"This valley is not entirely a part of the world," Sadana explained. "The entrances and exits can change depending on Mother Ashoka's desires. She has the ability to bend them to a certain extent. If she promised to deliver you where you need to go, she will see it done."

"How far does this ability extend?" Anya asked, stating the very same question Cinder had.

"Far enough," Sadana replied, her blunt answer simultaneously unenlightening and indicating she would say no more on the topic.

"She also told me to travel northeast to the tallest peak," Cinder added. "That war comes, and I should go quickly."

This time, the tree maidens stirred. They rustled about, murmuring to one another in alarm while the holders scowled, more upset than before.

"It is the words of *Revelatory Dreams* come true," Sepia said, sounding certain.

"Silence," Sadana's voice cut off the muttering like a knife. "We are yakshins. We do not engage in speculation." Her gaze focused on Cinder. "Did she name you the *Cipre Elonicon*?"

Anya's gaze shot toward him even as Cinder started. Why in the unholy hells would Sadana think Aranya might have named him that? He knew his past was odd, and his powers strange, but the *Cipre Elonicon*? Madness.

He'd run across the phrase during his reading of Indrun's biography, and it had left an impression, especially after he learned the proper translation. The name carried a dangerous heft. *Cipre Elonicon*. The Destroyer of Falsehood. Shokan Reborn.

He was unworthy of such a title, and Devesh save them all if Shokan returned in their lifetimes. It would mean Shet had as well.

Cinder shook his head. "She never called me the *Cipre Elonicon*."

Sadana peered at him. "You're certain?"

"I'm sure of it."

Sadana didn't seem relieved by his statement. If anything, she seemed more upset.

"The *Cipre Elonicon* is the Destroyer of Falsehood," Anya said, appearing pensive. "But in *Shevasra*, a slight alteration yields *Elonic Ciprion*. The Bringer of Destruction. The Fated Foe. A very different meaning. Someone the dwarves and some elves greatly feared ever seeing come to life. How was it they believed in a different, yet closely related prophesied figure?"

"Memories, writings, and beliefs can change with the seasons," Sadana said. "It is what Mother Ashoka was telling you. The truth isn't always what we believe."

The answer elicited a sour grimace from Anya.

Cinder had a similar unhappy knot in his stomach. His questions hadn't decreased in the slightest. If anything, they had increased, and he was also coming to realize that he wouldn't find what he was looking for here. He would have to do as Aranya said, travel to Darand's Gap and Mount Kirindor, and later, to Mahadev. "I still have to go north," he told Sadana.

"And so you shall," Sadana said with a nod. "Your journey will start tomorrow since Mother Ashoka says time is pressing. We will provide what you need."

41

Sadana was true to her word. Within an hour of their meeting with Aranya, Cinder, and Anya were kitted out with all the supplies they would need—extra provisions mostly. In addition, Cinder was the recipient of further yakshin healing, easing the bruising he'd received at the hands of Banner.

By the time everything was ready, the day was late, and they decided to settle in for the evening, sharing a quiet farewell meal with the yakshins and holders, none of whom would be accompanying them on their travel north through the valley.

According to Sadana, given Mother Ashoka's intention to deliver Cinder and Anya close to a very specific place in the Daggers, they would have to make the journey alone. She didn't elaborate on why this was the case, and Cinder didn't bother asking about her reasons. He chalked it up to another mystery of Aranya, the yakshins, and Shalla Valley.

The next morning, Cinder and Anya awoke early, prepared to get started with the day's travel. The sun had yet to crest the surrounding peaks, but its light could be seen warming the sky to the east, coloring it a lovely shade of rose and pushing back the midnight blue. The slowly brightening world also heralded the slumbering animals to rise, and a distant elephant answered the call with a grumpy-sounding trumpet. A flock of flamingos took flight, racing across the sky in a brilliant display of flamboyant pink plumage. Dew beaded upon the savanna's long grass, and Cinder inhaled the scent of wet vegetation and moist earth.

He and Anya had a quick breakfast of eggs and dried fruit, and in the midst of their meal, Sadana, Sepia, and Turquoise—arising early as was their wont—came to offer their quiet goodbyes. Cinder hugged the yakshins, grateful beyond measure for everything they had done on his behalf.

"Do not linger long near Mount Kirindor," Sepia advised. "It is a place of the utmost danger."

"We won't," Cinder said, quirking a smile at the unnecessary warning.

"Be quick about your task and return back to the valley as swiftly as possible," Sadana added. "The entire journey shouldn't take more than a week. We'll see to your pack animals while you're gone."

Given the short nature of the travel and the need for swiftness, Cinder and Anya would only journey with Fastness and Barton. They had all the food and blankets they might require packed away on the two horses.

Their advice given, the tree maidens strode off, and he and Anya made their final preparations. Fastness was especially frisky, dancing about as Cinder got him saddled.

"I think Fastness wants to run," Cinder said to Anya. He pushed aside the big Yavana's questing nose. The pest probably wanted a sugar cube or an apple. "If you don't mind, we'll ride on ahead, but we won't go any farther than what you and Barton can manage in a day."

"Riding across the savanna on Fastness," Anya said, envy clearly etched across her face. "I wish I could join you."

Cinder grinned. "No worries. At least we'll have the camp arranged for you when you get there."

"*We?*" Fastness whickered. "*I will do nothing of the sort. I will be brushed, given water and food, then left alone.* You *will set up camp.*"

Cinder laughed. "Of course, Lord Brat." He addressed Anya. "Fastness wanted to make sure you understood he doesn't do menial labor."

Anya chuckled. "So he's like every Yavana?" Her smile slid away, replaced a second later by a look of worry. "Just remember. Today's not a race, and as weak as you've been, you should probably take it easy—"

Cinder cut her off by vaulting into Fastness' saddle just to prove to himself—and her—that he could. Nevertheless, he was surprised by how strong his legs felt. There hadn't been the slightest wet-noodle sensation to them, which was shocking. They actually felt *good.*

Fastness whickered. *"Are you feeling better?"*

Cinder paused, considering Fastness' question. Despite the bruising Banner had inflicted during yesterday's sparring, the miracle of the tree maiden's food and their restorative braids of *lorethasra* had healed his injuries, and possibly even more. His breathing was better, and judging by the ease with which he'd vaulted into Fastness' saddle, so was his strength. Better than any day since the battle with the wraiths, in fact. "You know. I'm actually feeling almost normal."

Fastness tossed his head. *"Good. We should run. There is so much to show you. This valley is splendid."*

The big Yavana had spent the weeks of Cinder's convalescence ranging around the savanna. He had charged lions and hyenas, teased antelopes, and chased cheetahs. Cinder had heard of his antics and had initially worried for the stallion, but his concern had dissipated when he learned how Fastness had fought off three male lions, the leaders of a pride.

According to Banner, the fight hadn't even been close.

The big Yavana whickered. *"Do you want to run?"*

Cinder didn't need to reflect on the question. He knew the answer, and he slowly smiled in reply. His heart quickened. *Yes.* Let the adrenaline burn through him again and feel alive and vital. His heart quickened. "Let's do it." Cinder braced himself, legs gripping tight.

Fastness exploded forward, hitting a full gallop inside of ten strides.

Cinder bent low, moving in tune to the rhythm of his stallion's motions. Fastness' strides chewed up the ground. Great clods of dirt flew backward as he tore across the savanna. The world blurred, and Cinder squinted his eyes against the whipping wind and Fastness' lashing mane.

He whooped in delight.

Ahead, a lone hyena saw them coming, and she quickly hustled out of the way, seemingly grinning as they surged past her. A hundred yards further, a pair of gazelles glanced up, startled, from where they had been grazing. A cheetah stalking the ungulates launched out of the undergrowth, and the trio shot forth in a burst of sudden speed. The three animals seemed to consider the white's charge as a kind of challenge since they raced ahead of Fastness, paralleling his course.

Cinder whooped again. "Let's get them!" he shouted to the stallion.

Fastness answered by gathering himself and bursting forward. His stride lengthened, covering a dozen yards on each extension. The wind roared in the speed of his passage.

They caught the cheetah first, pulling abreast of him. Fastness snorted at the feline, as if to tell him he was too slow, before surging ahead. The stallion caught the gazelles next, but he never acknowledged his victory over them. He simply roared past and kept on going.

Cinder shouted their triumph.

They ran on, covering miles across rolling, grassy hills until even Fastness' great stamina began to flag. His lungs pulled air like bellows, and Cinder could feel the stallion's heart pounding like a drum.

"Ease off, old son," Cinder said, grinning wide and patting the white's sweat-coated shoulder. He hadn't had that much fun in months. "You were awesome."

Fastness nickered understanding. He coasted to a trot and finally to a walk. White foam flecked at the corners of his mouth. *"I was magnificent."*

"Yes, you were," Cinder said, patting Fastness' shoulder again and laughing. Today's morning run had been too long delayed.

For three weeks, Cinder had been laid up with his injuries. And prior to that, he and Fastness had been caught in the tension of traversing the Daggers in a slow, halting progress where danger continually threatened.

But riding flat out like this? No worries or troubles. He and Fastness doing nothing but outrunning everyone and everything causing them concerns.

Racing across the savanna had been a balm for his soul. Cinder grinned wider. It had been a balm for his *Jivatma.*

"Do you want to go again?"

"I'd love to," Cinder said, "but I think you should take a break."

"I'm fine."

Cinder trusted Fastness, but he also knew the great Yavana wanted to please him. He had to look after the stallion's welfare. "Catch your breath, old son." Fastness' lungs were still blowing hard. "We can run after you get some rest and some water."

Fastness snorted disagreement, but in the end, he accepted Cinder's advice. *"Fine. There's a pond up ahead. I'll drink some water, get some rest, and we can go again?"*

"Sounds like a plan."

Cinder kept his promise to Anya. Before she arrived, he had the camp ready for her, arranging it within the shelter of a ring of boulders hunkered next to a burbling stream. In addition, he caught a couple of trout and slowly grilled them on a skillet next to a simmering pot of chopped potatoes and wild beets. Perfect for a fish stew.

Once Cinder had everything well in hand, he relaxed, leaning up against a boulder and deciding whether to take a nap.

The last rays of the sun had bent to twilight, and wispy clouds spread like tattered flags across a sky turned ruby and purple. The smell of grilled trout steeped the air like a strange kind of tea. Closer at hand, a gentle breeze rippled through Fastness' mane as he contentedly cropped grass, having not a care in the world. Cinder smiled. The white deserved it. He'd run hard today.

It was a peaceful setting, and Cinder sighed in satisfaction.

"Smells good," Anya said when she rode in a half-hour or so later. She dismounted her gelding with a grateful groan and a long stretch. She held the position, arms above her head and back arched, backlit by the day's remaining light. Her golden hair seemed to glow in the firelight.

Cinder couldn't stop himself from staring at Anya. He admired her resolve, her intelligence and compassion, her generosity of spirit. Yes, she possessed an effortless beauty, but her true splendor was in who she was as a person.

He made himself turn away. He knew what he felt for her, and he also recalled the brief conversation they had about the impossibility of those feelings. He shuffled over to check the stew and review the day's travel. The weather had been fine, and they had covered many leagues. An easy journey so far, and according to Sadana, the remainder of their travel should be equally undemanding. They could likely get to the valley's northern border in another three or four days.

"How much longer until the stew is ready?" Anya asked, squatting at his side, a few inches closer than he might have preferred. Their elbows nearly touched.

Cinder made sure they didn't. He poked at a beet, testing its softness. *Not quite.* "Another half-hour should do it," he answered. "You have time to get washed up if you want."

She shook her head. "No need to get clean since we'll be sparring after supper. I'll see to the horses, though."

"It's going to be too dark to spar by then," Cinder told her.

Anya glanced at the dying sunlight. "I guess you're right. Looks like I'll be seeing to the horses *and* getting cleaned." She grinned at him. "Save me some food." She rested a hand on his shoulder, using it to help her rise to her feet before she marched off.

Cinder watched her for a few seconds. She had an elegance even when marching. He shook his head, scoffing under his breath at himself. "Idiot."

A short time later, Anya returned, her hair damp, and they settled in for supper, discussing the coming days. Primarily, they planned on how to reach their destination.

"If Mother Ashoka really does place us a day's ride from Darand's Gap," Anya said, "we should have a chance to get there and back without anyone the wiser." She stared into the fire, frowning. "It still won't be easy."

His alarm pricked. "Why is that?"

"No one has been to the Piercing Heart in generations," she replied. "Not in centuries or longer. The valleys around it are a battlefield, especially Darand's Gap. It's overrun by powerful spiderkin nests and hordes of zahhacks. They continually battle against one another."

"Should we even go?" Cinder asked. Given Anya's clear reluctance, it was a question that needed asking.

"I don't want to, but if Mother Ashoka says we must, then I think we should."

Cinder found himself surprised by her response. They were relying on the good will and advice of someone about whom they—and everyone else—had no prior knowledge. Yes, she was an ancient, powerful being, and yes, the yakshins trusted her—worshipped her really—but in the end, she was still a mystery. "You trust her that much?"

"I trust the yakshins," Anya said. "Throughout all of history, they and the trolls have ever been the wisest of the woven. Their judgment is beyond reproach and a byword for upright." She sighed. "If only we had their holders to help us. I wouldn't be so worried then." She shook her head in disappointment. "I wish I was half as good as the least of them."

After their brief discussion, the stew was done, and they shared a quiet supper, recollecting next to the fire once they had the dishes and utensils cleaned and put away. At that point, Anya was ready to call it a day, but she could tell Cinder had another matter on his mind.

"What is it?" she asked.

"I don't think you give yourself enough credit about how you did against the holders. I was watching you."

"Is watching a euphemism for staring?" Anya asked. She immediately wanted to bite her tongue. What Rakshasa had inspired her to say such a thing? It was too soon to joke about Cinder's emotions for her, or hers for him. "I'm sorry," she said. And if she was being honest with herself, her own feelings for him ran far too deep and true for either of their sakes.

Cinder waved vaguely in her direction, in either acceptance of her apology or telling her it was unnecessary. She couldn't tell, but she could see the tightness in his eyes, the lingering hurt in them. She felt terrible about it, and her hand twitched of its own accord. She leaned toward him, wanting to console him—

Thankfully, he interrupted the route her thoughts were taking. "You have nothing to apologize for," he said. "But what I wanted to tell you is that when I was watching you spar against the holders, you were getting the best of them every now and again."

Anya sat back, mulling over his observation. "Every now and again isn't something I'm used to," she said after a moment. "I'm used to success, usually immediate."

"There will always be someone better."

His statement sparked a flash of memory. It was of Rukh battling a score of unnamed monsters, facing them fearlessly. Her past self had been certain he would die, but instead, he'd killed the creatures with a casual grace, as if he were simply strolling through the park. It was a shocking display of martial abilities but also unsurprising. After all, no one could approach Rukh's level of skill or his Talents. He had been incomparable.

She started when she finally registered Cinder calling her name. He held her shoulders.

"What's wrong?" he asked, peering at her. "You're crying."

Anya touched her face and realized he was correct. He already knew most of her secrets about her past life, and she told him what she had seen. "I remembered something… My husband involved in a battle. He defeated his enemies effortlessly."

Cinder appeared puzzled. "The few times you've told me about your husband, you always talk about him as this amazing warrior, but was there anything else to him beyond his skill with a blade? I mean, *why* did you love him? What kind of person was he?"

Anya frowned, wanting to answer but finding herself unable. Cinder was right. Who was Rukh? All these decades she knew of her love for him, and she thought she knew of her husband's kindness, his generosity, and his implacable will to win, but was any of it true? Doubt crept in. How could she know for certain about Rukh when she could barely recall any of their moments together?

"You honestly don't know?" Cinder said, sounding bemused, letting go of her shoulders as he sat back.

Anya shook her head.

"So really, your husband could have been anyone." Silence fell between them, but after a few seconds, he spoke again. "Are you sure you were even married?"

Anya stood abruptly. She was tired and didn't have the energy or desire to defend herself against Cinder's insinuation, which felt self-motivated. Yes, she had been married. Yes, Rukh had been real. And yes, she had loved him. Those were her realities, and she wouldn't have anyone suggest otherwise. "I need to take a walk."

She tramped out of the firelight, angry for reasons she couldn't rightly explain. She clutched her arms around her chest, perseverating on Cinder's question. He was wrong. She knew Rukh. She just couldn't remember every detail. He had made her laugh, though. Of this, she was certain. And he was tall. He had dark hair and eyes and played the mandolin.

Her angry march came to an uncertain stop. *Played the mandolin.* Cinder played the mandolin, too. And he was tall and had dark hair and eyes. She found herself wondering if he might possibly be her lost love. It wasn't the first time, but it was the first time she had allowed herself to believe it.

It sounded utterly implausible, but it was no longer impossible. Even if it wasn't true, she couldn't deny her feelings for Cinder anymore.

She sighed.

No. She couldn't deny them, and she didn't want to. So what could she do about them?

Brilliance hunkered in the protection of a shallow cave, gnawing on the haunch of a strange beast that had the stinger of a scorpion. She had encountered the creature when he had been injured and alone, separated from others of his kind who had been busily battling spiderkin.

She had watched the fight from an overlooking ledge and caught sight of the beast. It had limped away from the battle, in pain and not paying attention to its surroundings. Its lack of awareness had cost it. Brilliance had stalked the creature and put it down.

An easy kill, but one tasting foul, like rancid meat. In fact, Brilliance wouldn't have consumed the creature at all, except for one thing: it had a depth of *lorethasra* unlike any creature other than the two-legs. She had hauled the beast's carcass miles from the site of the battle, to a place of safety where she could feast at her leisure.

All the while, she sensed her boy moving steadily north.

Her boy.

It had been weeks since she'd last seen him. Weeks since the wraith had tossed Brilliance aside like she was a kitten. The blow had launched her through the air, and she'd landed awkwardly, injuring a paw and straining her ribs. She had limped away once the tree woman and her warrior arrived to drive off the wraiths. There had been no reason for Brilliance to stay behind, especially since her boy had been dying.

She had seen him take a mortal blow and recognized that all her hard work and the injuries she had suffered on his behalf had been for naught.

Brilliance growled softly at the memory.

At the time, she had been outraged at the unfairness of it all. The boy should have been hers to consume. Not the wraith. What did he do to deserve the boy's precious essence?

Nothing. He had merely been lucky enough to be in the right place at the right time.

Brilliance smirked.

Over time, she learned that it was she who was lucky and so was her boy. The wraith had failed. Her boy had survived multiple battles and injuries against the spiderkin, and he'd also survived the wraith. What should have been a fatal wound wasn't, and somehow, he yet lived. Brilliance had seen the boy carried off by the tree woman and accompanied by her warrior and the elf maiden, disappearing from sight when they crested a ridge.

There, Brilliance had been stymied. She had intended on following the boy, but something about the surrounding steep hills had confused her senses. She often found herself traveling in circles, tracing winding, looping paths to nowhere, and discovering herself miles distant from where she intended to go. She eventually determined her problem: journeying directly toward where she sensed the boy caused her to lose track of time and location. It didn't matter how she focused on the matter, always she strayed from the proper path.

It had been infuriating, but Brilliance had recognized the futility of going against whatever strange influence denied her movement forward. So she chose to flank her boy, paralleling his course while hunting and killing as needed. All the while she had longed for a better meal. A meal of the boy and his precious essence.

When will he be mine? she wondered as she contemplated the events of the past few weeks.

She trekked onward, and a week ago, she had come across a stunted tree. It grew near the floor of a rocky ravine, barely seeing sunshine. Nevertheless, it persisted, clinging to life just as it clung to the side of the steep cliff. Brilliance had halted near the tree, staring at it.

She had never before seen its like, never before felt the sweet serenity emanating from it. The peacefulness called to her, and Brilliance had heeded its missive. She had quickly clambered up the side of the cliff, leaping from one boulder to another until she had stood at base of the tree. An instinct induced her to place her paws on the trunk, and when she did, she heard a whisper.

Brilliance had experienced many things in the world, many things no other snowtiger had known, but the whisper was special. A single word—one she couldn't have repeated even if she had a two-leg tongue—echoed in her mind. It had spoken of cool stillness and calm rather than storming anger and desire.

The voice had whispered again, causing Brilliance to glance to a nearby boulder. In the shadow of the stone rested a small nut or fruit the size of an acorn. But like the tree, this fruit was different than any Brilliance had ever before seen. It was white as bone and smooth as a polished rock. Without thinking, Brilliance had swallowed the fruit.

And her vistas had expanded. All her injuries had healed, and upon a single inhalation, she'd grown, expanded. She was now the size of a bear, long, powerful, and swift. More importantly, her hunger for *lorethasra* had largely faded. Not entirely, but enough for her to consider whether she really needed to kill the boy. What purpose would it serve? Was her appetite not satiated by a normal kill?

She might not have even killed the strange scorpion creature whose haunch she was gnawing upon, but she was still, first and foremost, a predator. And predators killed their prey.

But what about the boy? Was he her prey? Should she kill him if she had the opportunity? A week ago, the answer would have been an incontrovertible *yes*, but now?

Now, Brilliance didn't know. In one paw, there was the peace inspired by the strange tree. In the other, the boy had a wealth of *lorethasra*. So why not have one last feast?

Brilliance ripped the final piece of meat from the scorpion-creature and pushed the bones away. She was done eating. She would settle in and continue shadowing her boy. And when she next encountered him, she would then have a choice to make: kill him or allow him to live. His fate would be decided then.

42

He straddled a long, wooden board in the middle of aquamarine bay, thoughts going nowhere. He gazed into the distance, staring at the hamlet he now called home, Lilith, on the mystical island of Arylyn. How he had ended up in this place was an oddity of fate. Stranger still was how this small village recalled to him the majestic city of Ashoka, the home of his heart, which had also stood looking out over the sea.

But Ashoka did not have Arylyn's massive escarpment of five cliffs, which soared hundreds of feet above Lilith Bay. Nor did it have the swift-flowing waters running through the center of the village. River Namaste, which dove down from the heights as a sinuous waterfall cascading past ethereal bridges linking the various cliffs, fanning spray, and birthing dozens of glorious waterfalls during its descent.

Behind him, he felt a rising power. A wave was coming, and it was the right one.

He flattened prone on his board, rowing hard with his arms and hands.

The wave reached him, and he surged to his feet, balancing and gathering himself as he rode the long, wooden board across the waters. In

525

his long life, he had never expected to ride the ocean's might in such a fashion.

A kind of meditation swept away all worries and concerns, just as the wind whipped away the briny scent of the ocean and left the air fresh. Warm sunshine poured through a blue sky dotted with ponderous white clouds. Tiny rainbows sparkled in the wake of his passage.

The world was right and fine. He lost himself in the timeless moment of peace, became one with this fragile part of existence: his body, the board, and the unrelenting, untamable power of the wave.

The breaker curled over him, and he torqued his legs and torso in opposite directions. His board swung about, and he now raced parallel to the swell.

His balance kept him upright, the most fundamental lesson imparted to him by his good friend, William. It had been William and his wife, Serena—mostly Serena—who had taught him to surf. His close friends, and his eyes went to them. They rode their own boards, grinning with joy. William, a young man, lean, handsome. And Serena, a beautiful woman, with dusky skin of similar hue to William's and her dark hair slicked back.

He recalled their joy when they dragged him to the beach and taught him this wonderful exercise in excitement and meditation, and the means to achieve this perfection of form: balance.

Cinder's dream flickered, taking him elsewhere, to his life as a boy on the cusp of manhood.

He sat alongside his cousin Farn, and his family friend, Keemo. The three of them were new inductees into the House of Fire and Mirrors, one of the two Kumma military schools in Ashoka.

But the House of Fire and Mirrors was the finer of the two academies, and today was their first class. Seventeen young men in total shared the room, a long space paneled in teak with a long chalkboard up front and a bank of windows to their left. The sun poured inside, highlighting their instructor, Master Sinngin, the school's dean. He was a stern warrior originally from Kush and had survived eight Trials. He was a warrior of repute.

Master Sinngin spoke to them. "Will, desire, but above all, balance. Those are the pillars that form a warrior's skill." His voice still deep and resonant despite the weakness of his frame. "Remember this lesson. It will carry you far in this world and in your Trials."

His dream shuddered again, and he was sometime else. A toddler barely able to speak.

Nanna held him on his knee, smiling warmly.

He smiled back.

This was their special time, later in the evening when Nanna returned from wherever he went. His favorite part of the day, the hour before nightfall. He snuggled into Nanna's side, content in his father's love and protection.

"Close your eyes," Nanna instructed. "Listen to my voice. I will guide you. Hear me, and I'll describe the world. Incense burns. Sandalwood mingles with the perfume of jasmine filtering in from the garden. The wind whispers. A busker sings. A rickshaw driver shouts."

For days or weeks, his nanna had recited the same litany, and the boy knew what would come next.

"The world without isn't important. Only the darkness behind your closed eyes matters. See it. Breathe it in. Hear it. Feel it. Smell it. Taste it. Accept it. And once you have your senses and mind in balance, you will see a shining pool of water. I will guide you when you allow it."

The boy did as he was instructed, just as he had all the other times. And just like all the other times, he knew he would fail. He wouldn't see the shining pool of water.

He wondered if he should tell Nanna he did see the water. It would only be a small lie, but maybe that way he and Nanna could go back to doing fun things again, like reading stories or playing games.

He thought about it, but in the end, he knew it was wrong. He shouldn't lie to Nanna.

Rather, he tried again to do as he was told. He kept his eyes shut and stared at the dark. Hear it. *Listening for it only brought the rushing noise of his blood pulsing in his ears.* Smell it. *All he could smell were the floral scents of the garden.* Taste it. *Trying to taste it had him recalling the delicious potato curry and chicken biryani Cook Heltin had served at lunch.* Feel it. *He was aware of his body and Nanna's warmth, but not the darkness.*

A gentle touch reached his mind. It reminded him of Nanna's hand holding his when they walked along a busy street. Comforting and safe, guiding.

His mind drifted, and an unexpected glimmer, distant in his mind's eye, caused him to startle. The comforting touch left him, but he hardly noticed. His attention was on the distant pinpoint that was steadily growing larger. The darkness became a winter-cold moutainscape, and within it was centered a mirrored pool of water.

Just as Nanna had said would be there.

It called to him, and when he dipped his fingers into it, the water flowed into him. Everything in the world seemed better.

"You see it," Nanna said, pride and joy in his voice. "Remember to balance your senses, and you'll eventually be able to see your Jivatma whenever you wish."

Again the dream shook, and he went elsewhere and elsewhen. Again and again.

He was a boy, taking his first step on a warrior's path as he learned to create a Fireball. He was a young man, mastering his first Shield. The aftermath of a terrible battle gave him the stolen gift of Blending. A giant cat stalked out of the darkness and taught him to Heal.

And balance was the lesson of each dream.

Cinder shot awake, mouth dry and heart pounding. He didn't see the embers from the firelight or Anya pacing beyond the ring of boulders, nor did he see the surrounding savanna or hear the noises of nature. All he knew and wanted to know were the dreams.

They were already fraying, and he desperately fought against their dissolution. He tried to lock them in place before they fled his waking mind. He repeated the names of his loved ones and kept their visages in the forefront of his thoughts.

But as always, it was all for naught.

It only took seconds for the remembered images to fragment and tear apart into tattered remnants that amounted to emptiness.

Cinder slumped, the barrenness of loss making him want to howl in anger. For a short time, he had remembered being loved, remembered family and devotion. But it was gone now. Always gone. *When will I know who I once was?*

In the depths of his disappointment, a word echoed in his mind: *balance.*

Cinder's eyes widened in shock. Not everything was gone. Some of the memories remained. The faces of two people, a young couple—a man and a woman, clearly in love—stirred in his mind. Although, he couldn't name them, he recalled what they looked like. Excitement shivered. The faces of those two people didn't drift away. He could still see them, see them as they joyfully rode the waves on slender, wooden boards.

More images.

A Fireball, Shield, and a Blend. Some were braids created by elves and dwarves, but he knew them as something else. He knew how to form them from his *Jivatma* rather than *lorethasra*. He *remembered* how to reach his *Jivatma* more easily. He recalled the lessons from Nanna, his true father.

Eagerness and exhilaration welled within him, and Cinder did his best to tamp his rising hope.

He closed his eyes, reaching out as his Nanna had taught.

His *Jivatma* swiftly came into being, more rapidly than ever before. A simple thought, and there it was shimmering in his mind's eye. And as always, the blue-and-green lines of lightning denied any further progress. They weren't quite as thin as they had been when his *Jivatma* had started to refill, or even after he'd eaten the Aushadha.

The barrier was reforming.

"I am allowed to provide you a small gift. You will know it when you recall what you have forgotten."

The words were from Aranya, Mahamatha, and knowledge crashed through him. It left him vertiginous, and he had to brace himself from falling over. Once the dizziness passed, he had new understanding. Whenever he conducted his *Jivatma*, each time would still be painful, but each time would also thin the lightning and make the *next* time that much easier.

Cinder smiled and accepted the pain.

"You seem pleased with yourself," Anya noted the next morning.

"I am," Cinder said with a grin. He still recalled the images from last night's dream as well as the instruction on *Jivatma*.

He remembered it all. Aranya had given him a gift. The kiss to his forehead, either granting him access to his knowledge or allowing him to retain it. And he hadn't wasted the information. All evening, during the hours when he had been charged with watching over their camp, he had practiced visualizing his *Jivatma*. By now, he could do so as easily as breathing, and while the blue-and-green lightning still stymied his efforts at conducting, he didn't think it would do so for much longer. Pushing his will through those ragged bolts was still sheer agony, like being stabbed through the chest with a thousand needles, but the pain was worth it. The spears of lightning would eventually thin and no longer cause so much anguish.

Just as important, the lessons on creating Fireballs, Shielding, and Blending, of increasing his speed even beyond what he could now… All of it remained with him, and he couldn't wait to test them out.

"Feel like sparring?" Cinder asked, knowing his out-of-the-blue question was unexpected.

Anya viewed him in suspicion. "What's going on? You have something else in mind."

"Nothing," Cinder said, trying to maintain an innocent façade.

After a moment, Anya shrugged minutely and offered him a faint smile. "You can have your secrets for now, and you can also have your sparring."

They fetched their shokes and went to a relatively flat area that was free of rocks.

Cinder breathed deep. This was a moment pregnant with possibility. It had been nearly two years since he'd entered the Third Directorate. Two years, and he'd come so far in that time. He paused then, taking a moment to breathe in the world. The sun hid behind a line of gray clouds drifting slowly across the sky. A spring shower threatened, and it wouldn't be long before summer graced the world. In the distance, a cackle of hyenas watched them, mouths gaping in grins. They didn't come closer, though, apparently content to simply observe. A herd of elephants meandered toward the nearby brook from several hundred yards downstream. Other animals—wildebeest, leopards, and lions— were awake as well.

"Let's see what you can do," Anya said.

Cinder reached for his *Jivatma*, punching through the pain of the blue-and-green lightning. He grimaced when it flashed into him, stabbing him with frozen daggers. Then it was done, and he could breathe again. It had only taken a split second, and when it was over, the world was brighter and sounds carried a greater weight. He could feel the stiff wind buffet every inch of his exposed skin. The fecund scent of the savanna, a mix of dewy grass and ordure was more obvious.

"I'm ready," he said, using the lessons from last night to make himself faster than ever, to blur forward faster than any elf or holder.

Anya was on him, moving as quickly as he'd ever seen her. But not quickly enough. He smoothly defended, parrying a slash, blocking a vertical chop, and withdrawing from a frontkick. She kept coming. He backed off studying her balance and posture.

"You can't win by running away."

"I won't win by falling into your traps, either." Cinder continued to study Anya, and perhaps it was because he was conducting *Jivatma*, but he had greater awareness than before. He recognized what she intended. He simply knew it.

Cinder smiled to himself and set his own trap.

As expected, Anya came at him in a rush of diagonal slashes, ending on a thrust.

Cinder defended every attack. He slipped the thrust and angled off to deliver the perfect counter.

Before he could execute his plan, his legs slid out from under him. He slammed to the ground, landing on his butt. He was too shocked to defend himself when Anya squatted and tapped him gently on the head with her shoke.

"You're dead." She stood, offering him a hand. "Now. Why don't you tell me what has you so giddy."

Cinder took her hand with a grimace. He thought for sure he had her. Once he was upright again, he explained about the dreams from last night and his remembrance of how to conduct and use *Jivatma*.

"And you think Mother Ashoka gave you this educational gift?" Anya asked.

"Yes. I mean, she said she could give me a gift," Cinder replied. "So, if not her, then who?"

Anya shrugged. "I don't know, and it also doesn't matter. What's more important is you need to master them. The reason you fell just now is because your mind hasn't yet accounted for your increased speed and strength. You have to relearn your balance when you're moving so swiftly. We'll make sure it happens during our sparring sessions." She cleared her throat. "Now. Let's see what these skills—

"Talents," Cinder corrected. "In my memories, they aren't skills. They're Talents."

Anya tried and failed not to roll her eyes. "Let's see what these *Talents* can do. Start with the Fireball. I've never heard of it."

Cinder nodded agreement. He was curious, too. The woven could use Blends and Shields to varying degrees, but he'd never heard of a Fireball like this before last night either. Elves could weave something similar, but not one of this potency, and if his memories were to be believed, he should be able to fling one a hundred yards and have it impact with devastating effect.

He sourced his *Jivatma* and formed a Fireball in his right hand, or at least he tried to. A light formed in his palm, but immediately fizzled out. He tried again, staring at his hand, frowning in concentration.

Again it fizzled, and Cinder halted, annoyed with himself. What was going on? He knew how to create a Fireball. He'd known since the late childhood of his first life. A third time he tried, and on this occasion, he held tight to his concentration, never shifting his gaze from the nascent glow in his hand. The Fireball brightened, slowly, flickered a time or two, but in the end, it held steady.

He smiled in triumph.

In his hand, the Fireball glowed, a bright, yellow ball of flame, crackling with licks of fire. It was also strangely cool to touch.

Let's see what it can do.

Cinder cocked his arm, and toward an empty spot on the savanna, he flung the Fireball. It howled through the air, a high-pitched scream like a saw cutting wood.

While it fell well short of any animals—landing near none of them—where it hit, dirt was thrown half-a-dozen feet into the air. A boom like thunder pounded outward, and the shockwave flattened the savanna for ten feet in all directions from the point of impact. Embers drifted across the plain from where grass burned.

The cackle of hyenas took all this in, startling for a second before tearing off, yipping in panic. Same with the pride of lions and a small herd of wildebeest. Even the elephants were running, trumpeting terror.

Cinder blinked in shock.

"Fragging unholy hells," Anya said. "How did you do that?"

"*Jivatma*," Cinder said, trying not to sound smug, but failing miserably. This changed everything. He had a weapon that could never be taken from him, one he could use to keep his enemies at a distance and destroy them at his leisure. And that didn't even account for his Shield and Blend, which, if his memories were to be believed, were far superior to what the woven could manage.

"Yes, I get that part," Anya said in response to his answer, "but do you realize what this means?" She answered her own question, sounding excited. "It means your memories are exactly what we always suspected. Remembrances of a past life."

Cinder had already made the same realization. His retained memories were confirmation of their hypothesis. It also meant the woman with the honey-blonde hair was real.

"Let's break camp," Anya said, interrupting his thoughts. "We can talk on the road. We have a lot to discuss."

They broke camp and quickly donned their coats. Although the morning clouds looked like they might break apart, a stiff wind had kicked up. It contained a chill, a memory of the mountain heights toward which they traveled. The hills up ahead were taller and steeper, and some were gnarly peaks, wearing ragged clothing of moss and evergreens that weren't able to completely shroud their granite hearts.

However, despite the tough terrain they faced, right now their path remained smooth, an animal track through tall grass.

While they rode, Cinder told Anya what he remembered of last night's dreams, including the Talents he could now use with *Jivatma*.

Anya reined in her horse, and Cinder followed suit. "You remember the way to weave your Talents?" she asked. "You're sure of this?"

So far, they had gone over every aspect of his dreams in excruciating detail, and Cinder was doing his best to hold onto his patience. He was tired of repeating himself. "It's not weaving," he said. "Weaving is what you do with the Elements of *lorethasra*. *Jivatma* is conducted and imbued with will. Recognizing and enforcing what you want to do through focus and concentration."

"And you can do this?"

"A bit," Cinder said, "but I don't have the control I need."

"How long will it take to learn?"

Cinder shrugged. "Maybe a week. I don't know. This is all new to me."

Anya exhaled heavily, sounding disappointed. "Where we're going, we don't have a week. Was there anything else?"

Cinder nodded. "Two things. I remember a man and a woman. And before you ask, no I don't know their names. The man looks like me. Similarly colored skin and features, possibly a little lighter in both."

Anya appeared surprised. "You think you might have had a son in your past life?" She chuckled an instant later. "I can't believe what we're talking about. *A son in your past life*. It should sound ridiculous, but it doesn't."

Cinder smiled, joining in her amusement. "I didn't get the sense of him being a son. More like a good friend. And the woman was tall, but not as tall as you. She had dark hair and dark eyes, pretty. She and the man loved one another."

"A man and a woman. And some Talents you'll be a week or longer learning how to use," Anya said, sounding skeptical. "That's not much to go on."

"It's a hell of a lot more than we ever had before."

"Did you know I'm the black sheep of my family?" Anya asked.

Cinder glanced her way. After the morning's discussion, they had traveled the rest of the day in silence. He had spent most of the time conducting *Jivatma* and practicing his newfound Talents. He wanted to bring them to life as quickly as possible, but so far, re-mastering them was proving a far greater challenge than he initially imagined. It wasn't as simple as he thought it would be. It was like his muscles and mind knew the motions to make, but after years of disuse, they had lost the fluid certainty in how to do so.

His earlier estimate of a week to relearn the use of his Talents was going to be vastly optimistic. He reckoned it was more likely to require at least a month or two.

Anya's question, however, interrupted Cinder's reflections about his past and his future, and he found himself thinking about what her life must be like.

Anya pushed the normal bounds of what other elves considered appropriate, and he had always understood that she risked some degree of stigma by offering him friendship. As a princess, he also figured she was protected, but until now, he'd never considered how her own family might treat her.

Did they really think of her as shameful? As a black sheep?

It didn't seem like it based on what he saw in Revelant, but then again, who was he to say? Anya certainly felt otherwise, or she wouldn't have made the claim, which meant hers wasn't an easy position. She walked a narrow path between following her conscience and honoring her parents and past.

And who was to say what was actually correct in her decision-making? Cinder thought she was right in her choices, but the question remained: what if she was wrong? What if they were both wrong? They were both young, and some might say they lacked the wisdom that came with age to see it.

Cinder doubted it, though. He wasn't sure how elves or others in power should behave, but he didn't think they were meant to lord over others. He didn't think they were meant to believe themselves superior or sneer at those less fortunate.

"Why do they think of you as the black sheep," he asked at last.

Anya chuckled. "You got distracted there, didn't you?" She continued before he could reply. "I'm the black sheep because I consider myself a servant of those in need. My family thinks it makes me weak."

Servants of those in need. It sounded right, and if that's how Anya saw herself and it was the reason for her friendship with him, then he was glad.

"You're not weak," he said.

She didn't respond at first, and they rode on in quiet. The animal trail they followed was bringing them into hilly heights. In a matter of days, they'd reach the edge of Shalla Valley and enter the Daggers. Then their travel wouldn't be as easy. For now, the early afternoon sun warmed the rolling hills through which they traveled, and they were able to set aside their coats.

Cinder continued to think about Anya's situation. "I'm sorry you risked so much for me. You didn't have to."

"You have no reason to apologize. I chose the path of my dharma, and so far, it's been worth it," Anya said, offering a faint smile. "Besides, how I'm treated has little to do with you. The truth is, even if I didn't think differently than the rest of my family and kind, I'd still be an outcast. I'm taller and bigger than any elven woman. I decided on a warrior's life. I was considered eccentric even before I chose to sponsor you."

"Do you regret it?"

"Absolutely not."

She said the words quickly, but Cinder noticed her unspoken pain. Her lips had thinned, and a flash of hurt had flitted across her face. There was more to her situation than she was telling. "Then what do you regret?" he gently asked.

They'd talked of many things during their travels together, but very little of it had touched on the princess' personal matters. Nor had she revealed much about herself at the Directorate. He hoped she would be willing to talk about it now.

"I don't know if I have regrets," Anya said. "I have wishes. I wish to know about my past, my true past. About my husband." Her eyes flicked toward his. "And whether what you and I share is merely co-incidence or something truer. But if I did regret anything, it's how little time we have to train before we reach the Daggers." She gave him a crooked grin, and he knew she was done sharing thoughts about herself.

He mentally shrugged. If she wanted to talk, he would listen. If not, he wouldn't press. "Why don't we stop early tonight so we can practice?"

"Good idea. Why don't you and Fastness ride ahead and set up camp?"

Cinder smirked. "I think you just want me to make supper for you."

"Of course," Anya said. "Now off you go, *bishan*."

Cinder chuckled. He patted Fastness' shoulder. "What do you say, old son? Want to run for bit."

Fastness, quiet until now, snorted. *"I always want to run."*

Anya watched as Cinder struggled to control his frustration. In the four days since he'd relearned the Talents associated with *Jivatma*, he had yet to even come close to fully mastering them. She doubted he would anytime soon, either. Eventually, he would be able wield Fireballs, make himself stronger and faster than a holder, Blend more deeply than any elf, and Shield himself against seemingly any blow.

She amused herself by pondering if he could survive an avalanche. His power was that vast.

Unfortunately, it wasn't a controlled power. Cinder could conduct his *Jivatma* in the blink of an eye—forcing his way through the pain of his self-reported blue-and-green lightning—and he could manifest his Talents as needed. However, without the utmost concentration, they quickly disintegrated, and just as importantly, he couldn't move at speed in a balanced, consistent fashion. At this point, he was faster than she—faster than a holder—but his lack of coordination threw him off his stride, leaving him constantly defending against a misplaced foot or an over-extended thrust.

In many ways, he also had to defend against his own rising tide of frustration. His new Talents were fantastic, but in truth, they actually hindered him. Right now, he was *less* of a warrior than he had been. Sure, he had the promise of vastly improved power, but it was coming at the cost of a current sacrifice in skill and ability.

At least he was no longer slowed by injuries. Those had largely healed during their last night at the Shriven Grove and the days of traveling since. In fact, she would have considered him at his peak if not for his dream from several nights ago.

Anya watched Cinder brood, thinking on how to help him. They sat huddled next to a fire in the heights of the Daggers. Ahead of them, the trail penciled its way through a narrow mountain passage shaped like a corridor. Through it, the wind moaned like a broken man. Hard-packed snow and gray stone filled the limits of her vision, and around her and Cinder rose ice-covered boulders and jagged, rocky shoulders. The warmth of the savanna was now a distant memory, but at least the magic of Shalla Valley still somewhat calmed the harsh climate.

Tomorrow, however, would be a different story. Tomorrow they would exit Shalla Valley and re-enter the world with all its dangers. And if Aranya was to be believed, they would be a day's ride from Darand's Gap and Mount Kirindor, the Piercing Heart. Cinder was worried he wouldn't be ready, and he was right to feel that way. He wouldn't be ready.

A notion on how to help him came to Anya. "You have your *Muladhara* opened, do you not?" A tiny part of her resented the quickness with which he had managed to do so, but the larger part— Aushadha fruit or no—was entranced and glad for him. She was also amazed and fearful of how her people would react—if they learned.

And they wouldn't, at least not from her.

While her ranger's status clearly spelled out her duties, clearly spoke of her obligation to tell her mother about Cinder's ability with *Muladhara*, her heart told otherwise. She glanced at Cinder, wishing she could smooth away his frown with a simple kiss.

Anya swallowed heavily. A simple kiss between her and Cinder would quickly become something more complicated, and a large part of her welcomed the complexity. Lurid visions threatened, and she did her best to corral her wild thoughts.

A week ago, she had impressed upon Cinder the importance of never speaking to her in an overly familiar fashion, of the danger of doing so. And just now, she had thought of kissing Cinder and doing so much else with him, of ruining his future.

No wonder she found herself conflicted and unsure where her loyalties lay.

"What do you think I should do?" Cinder asked, lifting his gaze from the fire.

She was grateful for the distraction and took a few seconds to compose herself. "When was the last time you attempted to visualize *Muladhara*?"

Cinder frowned. "Never," he answered. "I never had a reason to."

Never? Why not? Did he not understand what a miracle it was for him to have opened his *Muladhara* in such a rapid fashion?

Anya wanted to shake him. "Well, you have a reason to now. It's time you practiced using it."

"Why?" Cinder asked. "I have *Jivatma*, and since it's my soul, it doesn't need to go through any Chakras or get sent through my *nadis*."

"Humor me," Anya said. "Right now, the largest part of your problem is how much you have to concentrate in order to shape your *Jivatma*. It's similar to what we woven face when we have to focus on the individual threads that make up *lorethasra* to create our weaves. At first, it's a slow process, but as we open our Chakras and advance, that effort is no longer so challenging. The Chakras help us manifest our desires without the messy interference of actual conscious effort. It becomes a natural aspect of our abilities then. No different than lifting a hand or walking. What if it's the same with *Jivatma*? What if sending it through your *Muladhara* will allow you greater control without such dedicated attention."

Cinder grunted, sounding thoughtful. "I guess I've got nothing to lose, do I?"

Anya smiled at his response. "No, you don't."

Cinder could be obstinate about his belief in fraternity, infuriating in his disregard for his own safety, and thin-skinned in how he refused to overlook a slight, but in regard to her counsel, he was always conscientious. Even better, he generally accepted her advice, which made training him a joy.

"What should I do?"

"Sit like me," Anya instructed, taking the simple cross-legged position of *padmasana*. "Close your eyes. Center yourself. Breathe as you were taught by Master Absin. She demonstrated by closing her left nostril with her left thumb. Her other fingers stood straight out, and with her other hand, she formed a circle with her right thumb and first finger, resting her hand on her right knee. Breathe like this."

Cinder did as she instructed, and his breathing grew steady, but his posture appeared tense and forced.

Anya studied his features. She sometimes felt like if she stared at him long enough, she would be able to unlock some unknown mystery about him. It often left her wondering what it was about this man that caused her so much turmoil?

She mentally smirked.

The reason for her turmoil wasn't such a mystery. Had she not just been imaging her and Cinder in all sorts of compromising positions?

"You're staring," Cinder said without opening his eyes.

Anya gathered her thoughts. "Because you're frowning. You can't force *Muladhara*. It should be no different than how you reach your *Jivatma*. You allow it, beckon it, ask for it. You don't demand it."

Cinder sighed, but his posture and features relaxed. His breathing smoothed, and the tension left him. He almost appeared to be sleeping.

Anya didn't interrupt his progress. She doubted he would connect with his *Muladhara* this evening, but the practice and meditation was still a good thing. And sending his *Jivatma* through his Chakra might truly help in the way she had suggested.

An hour later, the fire had burned down. Anya was in the process of gently adding more logs, not wanting to disturb a still-meditating Cinder when he opened his eyes.

He smiled. "Watch." He held open his hand, and in it, he cupped a Fireball. It didn't flicker and fade like the others he'd made.

Anya grinned at him. "Do it again."

He did so, but an instant later, his smile faltered. "I can't meditate for an hour or longer to connect with *Muladhara*," he said. "I have to be faster than this."

"And you will," Anya promised. "The first time is the hardest. Keep practicing, every chance you get, and it'll become as easy as breathing."

"How long will it take?" Cinder asked.

Anya waffled, not wanting to ruin his happiness. In the end, she knew honesty was best. "I don't know, but after opening my *Muladhara*, it took me months longer to be able to regularly use it."

"Then it doesn't help me much in this situation, does it?"

"Possibly, but your situation is unique, and we won't know if using *Muladhara* will help you master your Talents more quickly until you try."

Cinder's reaction to her statement surprised her. Rather than despondent, he became thoughtful. "I suppose you're right." He grunted. "I'll keep working at it."

43

Cinder reined in Fastness, halting next to Anya and Barton. The path before them was covered in hard-packed snow, and it cut through the ice-crusted mountains rising around them like jagged knives of stone. A gusting wind swirled, knifing through Cinder's clothes despite their heft, and he huddled within their protective layers. His hood was thrown forward to protect his face from the snow, which whipped like stinging crystals. Before them lay a slight opening in the mountains, the pass leading out of the valley.

Cinder gazed longingly in the direction from which they'd come, unable to see the savanna due to the thick foliage treeing the mountain's shoulders and the tangle of forested foothills marching off in the distance. However, he knew it was there, verdant and warm.

"Get ready," Anya said. "It'll be cold on the other side of the pass."

Cinder grimaced. "You mean this isn't cold?" His breath plumed as if in proof of his question.

"This is nothing," Anya said. "The magic of the valley keeps it warmer here than any other part of the Daggers. The cold will bite your nose off if you're not careful. Be ready for it."

She edged Barton forward, and Cinder followed, the snow crunching with every step their horses took. Slowly, they ascended the mountain's peak. A heavy mist soon shrouded the trail, and if the early morning sun still shone overhead, they couldn't see it through the thick fog. An icy finger of wind slithered through Cinder's clothing, and he prepared himself for the promised frigidness. They crested the final rise, and—

Cinder inhaled involuntarily, eyes widening in shock. There was no further cold or wind or even mountains. Instead, the world blinked away in a rush, replaced by a dark tunnel where a shimmering rainbow bridge extended in front of them through a vast blackness. The anchor line Sadana had mentioned.

Fastness took another step, and the strange vision disintegrated as Seminal's reality reasserted itself—and so did the frigid weather. It hit him like a hammer, leaving Cinder with no opportunity to wonder at the tunnel and rainbow bridge he'd seen. Instead, his attention was consumed by a freezing wind. It threatened to rip through him, a brood of vipers, twisting and turning into any opening, biting and unrelenting, and he clutched his coat tightly about his body

Fastness whinnied a protest. *"Why did we leave the valley? It was warm. This is not."*

"I know," Cinder said, gloved hand patting the stallion's neck. He glanced around, searching for some kind of marker to help him find this place again. He'd studied maps of the area, but he wanted to make sure in case the maps were wrong. "Can you get us back here?" he asked Anya.

She nodded. "Once I knew where we would be exiting Shalla Valley, I made sure to study the landmarks and how to find them again." She pointed to a cliff rearing to their left and shaped like a broken tooth. On its surface, red stone twisted downward like the scales of a snake. "I know that landmark. Bloody Snake is its name. Once we see it, it'll be no trouble getting back to this pass."

She heeled Barton forward, and they descended a steep decline, reaching a flatter portion of the trail before descending again. Several hundred yards later, their path reached a relatively flat plateau, a place of packed snow hard as stone and ice-crusted boulders thrusting through the whiteness.

Anya's vision snapped skyward, staring at the gray ceiling of gloomy clouds. "Eyes up. I heard something."

Cinder followed the path of her sight, looking to the heavy clouds. He had heard a distant cry, too.

Seconds later, he saw them. A dozen men and women, pale and bloodless, floating on the winds with wings like torn shadows. Cinder had never before seen their like, but he knew what they were. *Vampires.* He had read everything he could about them, and he imagined how they must be surveying the scene below, their gray eyes, dead like a shark's.

"You see them?" Anya demanded, drawing her sword.

"I see them," Cinder replied, drawing his sword as well. The only thing he and Anya wielded that could hurt the creatures was the *isthrim* steel of their blades. Arrows would be of no use.

"They'll sweep down on us. Get your shield in hand."

Cinder did as she advised, but he also conducted *Jivatma*, ignoring the searing pain of the blue-and-green lightning. Calmness soothed his mind, and he willed enhancement into his senses. He could make out more details now.

The vampires circled. Their ears were pointed like an elf's, but that was where the similarity ended. No warmth filled their features, and gold circlets secured dark hair and gray, lamellar armor perfectly fit their lean, elegant frames. They carried no weapons since they preferred fangs and talons. It was stupid on their part, but Cinder wouldn't overlook any advantage given.

As one, the vampires unhinged their mouths, displaying lines of dagger-like teeth and screamed. The sound, high-pitched and piercing, was meant to paralyze their prey with fear.

Cinder's lip curled. He was no one's prey. He was a predator, and he knew what was needed. He resettled his shield on his back

"What are you doing?" Anya asked, sounding curious rather than annoyed.

Cinder didn't answer. Instead, he conducted *Jivatma*, focusing until a Fireball filled his off hand. It didn't happen as quickly as he wanted, but it was quick enough. Once the Fireball was ready, he didn't throw it so much as will it straight off his palm. It screamed heavenward like a shrieking raptor, aimed at a cluster of vampires. The Fireball blasted through one of the foul creatures, incinerated another, and caught a third one on fire. The bodies of the first two plummeted soundlessly to the ground while the burning one screamed in pain, swerving into a fourth vampire. They entangled, their shadowed wings unraveling.

By then, Cinder already had another Fireball in hand. It wasn't as potent as the first, barely holding together, but with a further focusing of his will, it was enough. He fired it at the two entangled vampires. The Fireball exploded into them, separating torsos from legs.

The other vampires had sighted upon him, and they howled outrage. Six came at him and two at Anya. There was no time left for more Fireballs, and Cinder reset his shield on his arm. Three vampires streaked toward him like a trio of hawks. The others glided low, coming from all directions.

"I can handle the one straight ahead. Don't get overconfident. Remember your training."

Cinder patted Fastness in acknowledgement, setting aside the stallion's unexpectedly mature advice. He conducted *Jivatma* and increased his speed, calculating movements, planning how to handle the onrushing vampires.

Fastness bunched his muscles. It was an unspoken signal, and Cinder gripped the stallion tightly with his legs. The white surged forward. The stallion rammed a heavy shoulder into one vampire. The blow sent the creature sprawling. Fastness reared and proceeded to stomp the vampire's head to a pulp.

A vampire blazed downward, directly vertical. Cinder impaled him through the chest. He withdrew his blade. A blind slash slammed through the chest of the vampire lunging in from his right. Another vampire was behind him. Two were on his left.

Fastness knew what was needed. He spun about, stomping the creature coming up on their blind side. Another surge, and they threw off the aim of the vampires who were now on their right. One of the monsters swept past, while the other one winged to a halt, behind them now.

Fastness reared, hammering at the vampire, a female, in front of them. The monster became mist, and the stallion's steel shod hooves passed through the creature.

The vampire coalesced above them, grinning malice. "You may have killed many in my brood, but your power will be mine," she declared. "You will be my bloodslave. I will—"

Cinder ignored the creature's monologue. He rose in the saddle and launched like a lance at the suddenly fearful vampire. Cinder's sword took the zahhack in the mouth.

Another vampire was rising up to meet him. Cinder aimed a vertical chop. The creature spun away from it. Cinder leaned aside from slashing claws and landed. He countered, a straight thrust, and the attack found a home in the vampire's gut. The zahhack shrieked, clutching his torn abdomen. Cinder watched as the vampire attempted to fly away, but the creature's shadowed wings became ash. He fell to the ground, dead.

Cinder's gaze immediately went to Anya, and he found her killing an injured vampire. Blood splattered her camouflage clothing, but otherwise she was unharmed. He next glanced for more foes, but only the dead met his searching gaze.

He grinned and shouted in triumph. They'd destroyed a dozen vampires in a span of seconds and taken no wounds.

His joy faded when he noticed Anya's worry.

"We need to leave," she said. "One brood of vampires means other zahhacks are sure to be close at hand."

Cinder wordlessly cleaned his sword on the cloak of a dead vampire, and they were soon remounted and heading away from the site of the battle.

A few minutes later. "Next time let me know your plans," Anya said in obvious irritation. "The Fireballs. You're not invincible, and I can help."

Fastness whickered softly in agreement with her. *"She's right."*

Cinder nodded, accepting the rebuke. "I'm sorry. I'll tell you next time."

Anya wasn't done scolding him. "Only an idiot charges off without a plan of attack."

"Maybe so," Cinder replied, "but I did have a plan. I attacked."

Anya rolled her eyes, trying to appear annoyed, but Cinder could see a smile lurking at the corner of her lips.

Cinder flattened himself next to Anya on a ridge overlooking a rocky valley. They had ridden for hours following the battle against the brood of vampires, eventually descending down the mountain pass on the other side of Shalla Valley. It was evening now, and despite the lower elevation, the weather remained brutally cold. It was typical weather, according to Anya, for the heart of the Daggers even in the late spring. The wind bit hard, and while the fog atop the mountain had broken apart, the late evening sun slanting across the valley provided little warmth.

However, the light did enough. It illuminated the disorganized groups of zahhacks stomping across the valley floor far below them. Every species was represented, hundreds of them. Broods of vampires floated on the air. Tribes of unformed streamed about, constantly shifting shape, one minute wolves, the next eagles, the following tigers. Nests of snake-like ketus, iridescent scales shimmering in the light of the late day sun, slithered along, their short, thin arms clutching short swords and shields. Swarms of goblins—each the size of a dwarf—limbs serrated and carapaced like an insect's, paced alongside what appeared to be a horde of ghouls. The two species of zahhacks marched shoulder-to-shoulder, neither causing trouble for the other. There were also beds of ajakavas, their scorpion tails held high and threatening. And lording over them were necrosed, who apparently were in charge of this horde. They rode the dumb, buffalo-sized erawans.

The stench lifting off the monsters caused Cinder's stomach to roil and his eyes to burn. Did all zahhacks stink so bad?

He shook off the question, concentrating on his Blend. He knew Anya was doing the same. In fact, without her help, his flickering Blend would have likely left him visible to the zahhacks marching below. She was also the one Linking their Blends so they wouldn't disappear from one another's sight, as well as protecting the horses, who they had left a dozen feet downhill. Fastness and Barton should be safe unless there were other zahhacks combing the shoulders of the mountains.

Anya gestured for them to inch away from the precipice, and Cinder silently followed after her. He knew not to speak until they were far from the ridge's crest.

"I've never seen so many zahhacks in one place," she whispered directly in Cinder's ear, apparently wanting no chance for her words to be overheard by one of the creatures.

Cinder might have considered her close-in whisper unnecessary, but at least her warm cinnamon scent masked the wafting stink of the zahhacks. "It looks like an army," he whispered back.

"They might be headed toward Mount Kirindor." She pointed to the peak looming in the distance like a colossus amongst pygmies, massive, brooding, and exuding an ill-defined menace. Something waited for them there. Something deadly and powerful.

"Mahamatha only said to get to Darand's Gap," Cinder reminded Anya. "It's on the western face of Kirindor. What if we stay off the mountain itself and observe from a distance? Maybe that will be enough to find whatever she wants us to see."

Anya appeared to consider the matter. "Perhaps," she eventually allowed. "It'll certainly be safer than trying to cross Darand's Gap, especially with all the spiderkin nesting there."

"The children of Sheoboth," Cinder said, recalling another name. "That's what Mother Ashoka called the spiderkin."

Anya frowned. "Sheoboth? I've never heard of her." She shook her head a second later. "And it doesn't matter. We'll wait for the zahhacks to leave this area and cut north." She pointed. "Along that slope, there should be a ravine running east-west. It abuts Darand's Gap."

Cinder eyed the incline she indicated. It was rough terrain. The horses would have trouble with their footing, but there was no chance of leaving them behind. They would be naked to the storm if they were found by the zahhacks. "We'll have to Blend the entire way, and it'll likely add most of a day to our travel."

"The Blending isn't a problem. As long as you can continue to conduct *Jivatma* and take off some of the load, I can manage. And the extra day of travel is better than an early death." She indicated the valley behind them. "I want nothing to do with those zahhacks."

"If they're headed for Mount Kirindor, they'll probably battle the spiderkin."

"Not our problem."

"Fragging unholy hells," Anya breathed, sounding simultaneously dismayed and exasperated. "I've never seen so many necrosed in my life."

She and Cinder crouched within the embrace of a deep cave they had stumbled upon. They held their Blends as tight as they could manage.

Below, striding across the canyon floor like a gangrenous tide, were a hundred necrosed. In the darkness of falling night, it was hard to make out their individual members, but their rotting stench easily carried up the fifty feet to their cave's mouth.

Anya stared at the massive zahhacks, each one the size of a troll, as they rumbled past. Like vampires, they eschewed weapons, but then again, why would they need one? Their bodies were their weapon. Their powerful jaws could break boulders, and their long arms, dragging below their knees, ended in claws that could slice a bull in half. Add in their skin—nearly impenetrable to anything other than the Wildness, the battering power of a yakshin or troll, *isthrim*, or a blade strengthened in the way Anya could manage—and it was easy to understand why these were the deadliest of all zahhacks. She had no desire to tangle with five, much less five score.

Anya glanced at Cinder, who hadn't responded to her. Instead, he was frowning, silently scrutinizing the necrosed, and while she couldn't decipher his thinking, if she had to hazard a guess, she'd say he was apprising the necrosed, memorizing the way they walked, their speed and coordination, the best ways to defeat one.

"Why are they here?" Cinder asked, his question rhetorical since she didn't have the faintest clue.

First, the army of zahhacks marching in the direction of Darand's Gap, and now this company of necrosed. Whatever the reason, it had her troubled.

The last of the necrosed disappeared from view around the bend of the rock-strewn canyon floor.

Cinder groaned softly, straightening and relaxing his posture. "What do we do now?" he asked. "Should we still head toward the Gap?"

Anya wasn't so sure any longer. She glanced toward the back of the cave and considered what to do. Her eyes settled on Fastness and Barton. The horses waited quietly, both apparently understanding the necessity for silence given the terrible danger lurking outside. It was good luck they had found this cave since it allowed them to bring in their mounts and extend their Blends to cover the animals.

She wished they could simply slip away from here, flee back to Shalla Valley or anywhere else. It would certainly be safer.

But safety wasn't what a ranger sought. A ranger sought to learn the best means to protect Yaksha Sithe and her allied nations, which meant they had to learn all they could about this dangerous confluence of zahhacks.

She exhaled in regret.

"We're still heading to the Gap, aren't we?" Cinder guessed.

She nodded. "We have to."

"I'll take first watch," Cinder said without preamble.

"Get some food. It'll have to be cold rations," Anya said. "No fire.

The necrosed might not be the only zahhacks out there tonight."

"Understood," Cinder said. "And don't worry. I should be able to maintain my Blend."

His response didn't surprise her. He'd grown in his technique and Talent. In fact, prior to leaving Shalla Valley, he could barely create a Blend, and even earlier in the afternoon, he'd struggled at it. But throughout the day, his ability had improved, and here he was now, easily holding on to a Blend for over an hour. And it wasn't the wispingly faint Blend from the afternoon. This one was as firm and impenetrable as any elf's.

It seemed her gauge of months for Cinder to master his Talents was overly pessimistic. Anya hoped he would become equally as proficient with the rest of his skills and equally quickly.

Brilliance had tracked the boy as best she could, following his movements while he traversed through a place she could neither see nor sense. She had raced alongside his path, wanting to meet him when and where he exited.

It hadn't been easy. At their summits, the Daggers were bitingly cold, but with her thick coat, a blend of gray, white, and black colors, she barely felt it. Harder to overcome was the path she had been forced to take. She had to track across snow as hard as rock, inch across icy ridges where a single slip would spell doom, and bypass multiple deadends, but she had never slowed or given up. Brilliance had raced after the boy, and in the end, she missed his exit from wherever he had been hiding by only an hour.

The boy and his elf had been busy upon leaving the valley, halting to hack apart a dozen monsters. Brilliance had never encountered the creatures before, and she'd nosed their corpses, trying to gain an understanding of how they might have fought. They had long claws and teeth, but their slender frames didn't indicate great strength. No wonder the boy and the elf had been able to kill so many.

Further perusal had to wait when she sensed more such creatures closing in on her position. Or maybe they were closing in on the dead creatures. Whatever the reason, Brilliance knew well enough to dash away from the site, chasing after the boy once again.

Soon, she came upon another distressing scene: a many of zahhacks haunting this part of her mountains.

Brilliance's coat protected her again, providing the perfect camouflage from the marauding monsters. She hid from them, skulking along the steep shoulders of the mountains, unwilling to risk easier terrain closer to where the zahhacks marched. It slowed her pace, but better to be slow and safe than swift and dead.

All day, she had trailed the boy, and late that evening, she had finally caught up with him. She might have even attacked him then. She watched as he huddled in a cave, on the other side of a narrow canyon. She could see him, and she had inched forward, unsure what she would do with him. Kill him or let him live?

Just then, a large troop of necrosed had arrived out of the murk and clawed apart any notions of approaching the boy. Brilliance had hid again, and for the first time, she wondered at this plan of hers.

She wanted her boy's *lorethasra*. She had fought and bled for it, but did she really need it so badly that she was willing to risk her life? Given the dangers in this part of the Daggers, it seemed foolhardy. She could easily die if the monsters lurking in these mountains found her.

Brilliance didn't know what to do. If her boy insisted on placing himself in danger, might it be better to aid him directly? If she protected him with her teeth and claws, would he not do the same and protect her with his sword?

The idea of cooperation was foreign to Brilliance. She was a fierce predator, proud and indomitable. She needed and desired no one's help.

But as she watched the necrosed, she realized that if she wanted to survive this place, she might need to revisit her aversion toward cooperation. She might need the boy's help if she wanted to escape this part of the Daggers. The large numbers of zahhacks and spiderkin—she'd caught their unmistakable spoor—made the area dangerous for even her.

Brilliance settled in for the night, still unclear on what to do next. She huddled in a cluster of boulders where she would hopefully remain unnoticed from the view of any leering monsters.

Tomorrow, however, she'd have a decision to make.

Cinder lay next to Anya, the two of them quiet and prone on the hard-packed snow, witnessing what was happening a hundred yards ahead and a dozen below. On the rocky spit of relatively flat land, a fierce battle raged. The dawn light displayed the sheer fury as two companies of bitter enemies battered one another. Zahhacks fighting spiderkin. It was ghouls and goblins against eight-legged horrors. High-pitched keening cries filled the morning air. Blood collected in shallow pools. Limbs littered the ground. And the stench of offal drifted as no quarter was asked and none was given.

The zahhacks outnumbered the spiderkin two-to-one, but they had been losing the battle until the entrance of a troop of ajakavas and ketus under the command of five necrosed. The new arrivals swung the battle in favor of the goblins and ghouls, who tore into the spiderkin. Minutes later, the last of the eight-limbed horrors was put down.

The zahhacks milled about until the necrosed barked commands, and the creatures exited the ravine. The world was still for a few seconds until the harsh caws of vultures cracked the silence. The carrion eaters landed, and the wake began feasting.

Cinder and Anya turned away and headed back to the horses, who waited close at hand, near a snow-and-ice crusted overhang where icicles the size of timbers stabbed the ground. Their mounts had remained quiet throughout the entire battle.

"Barton is terrified. We should leave this place," Fastness said. *"He'll break if we don't."*

Cinder patted the white's snout. "We'll get going soon, old son."

"*Why not leave now?*"

"Because we need to know what's happening here. That many zah-hacks gathering in one place isn't natural. Something is drawing them here."

Cinder couldn't say anything else. The world receded from him in a rush. It collapsed into a pinpoint of darkness before surging back, but when it returned, he was elsewhere.

The world was dark. A rainbow bridge stretched into infinity, and the darkness around him was filled with uncountable pinpoints of light, falling, drifting, and swirling—shards of other worlds and times, other realms perhaps.

None of it mattered.

In front of him stood a man, tall as a troll, powerfully built, and handsome beyond measure. Behind him waited four others of equal stature and impressive in their own way. Two women and two men.

He hated all of them.

"*Your wife is lost,*" *the handsome man said.* "*Your cause is lost. Everything you love is dust, and I will rebuild Naraka on the slopes of Kirindor and on the bones of your dead hope.*" *He shook his proud head in pretend sympathy, his demeanor that of a wise elder ruing the follies of the young.* "*You cannot stop me. I am a god.*"

"*You are no god.*" *He attacked, vowing to see this man burned to ash.*

Again, the world receded to a barely visible spot before reality rushed back into place. Cinder stumbled. Once again, he stood next to Fastness. He clutched the saddle horn to steady himself.

Anya was peering at him in concern. "What happened? You went blank for a second."

Cinder shook his head, still confused by the vision, especially since he could remember every aspect of it. He described what he had seen.

Anya's face went white. "Shet. You saw Shet."

Fastness nickered warning. "*Spiderkin are coming.*"

44

Cinder bit back an oath and told Anya what Fastness had said.

"Mount up," she ordered. "How far away are they, and where are they coming from?"

"Close. Coming from behind and headed straight for us," Fastness replied. The stallion's tone was no-nonsense and steady. His usual jocularity hadn't been in evidence during their time in the Daggers, and Cinder truly missed it. When the stallion was being roguish and playful, it meant life was safe enough to have fun. As far as Cinder was concerned, fun was better than tense.

Anya merely nodded when Cinder relayed the message. "Then we'll either ride them down or ride away from them."

Cinder scowled. His Blend was in place, and his physical abilities, such as his senses and strength, were heightened. It wasn't enough. He had no Shield. As of yet, he could only wield two Talents at the same time. *No help for it now.*

He mounted the white, got his shield out, and unwrapped his bow. He set an arrow on the rest and peered back in the direction from which they'd come. Sunlight glinted off the snow, and he had to shade

556

his eyes. The hoofprints of their horses were clearly visible in the powdery whiteness.

Anya had her sword out, and it flickered with fire from whatever weave she was using.

Until this moment, Cinder hadn't paid much attention to her when she fought. He'd been too caught up in his own survival to see her use her skills, but he wished he could. He wanted to see her unleashed and study how she approached a battle.

"Hold onto your Blend," Anya advised. "It might be a hunting party returning to the nest. If we're lucky, they'll just pass us by."

Cinder hoped she was right.

A moment later, noises carried to him. It was a scrambling of claws, a frustrated growl, and ragged breathing. He frowned. The sounds were familiar.

Another second passed and a massive snowtiger burst around the bend, several hundred yards away. She was the size of bear and fleet as a deer, but right now, she wore fear like a cloak. The panic was evident in her wide-open eyes.

Cinder's jaw gaped. He knew this beast. She was the *aether*-cursed creature who had killed his parents in Swallow and aided him during the Autumn Trial and against the wraiths. How did she grow so massive? "Don't shoot the cat," he warned Anya, who nodded minutely, her aim shifting off the snowtiger.

Cinder watched as the massive *aether*-cursed beast slipped on the icy snow. She fell, sliding a dozen feet before regaining her balance, and rushed unerringly toward them. He wondered if she could somehow see him and Anya through their Linked Blends. He also wasn't sure why he was willing to protect her. Perhaps it was because they had a history together? And, nonsensically, with her current size, she reminded him of a cat he felt like he had once known and loved.

From behind the snowtiger came the sound of rustling, of scuttling legs, and raspy hisses. *Spiderkin.*

"They're after her," Anya said.

As soon as the words left her mouth, a swarm of spiderkin, each one the size of a pony, streaked around the same bend the snowtiger had recently taken.

The *aether*-cursed cat reached close enough for them to bring her into their Blends, skidding and clattering her way to a halt. She spun about, seemingly shocked upon seeing them and panting, which was unusual to see in a cat.

Fastness whickered at her, and the cat glanced at the stallion. The snowtiger seemed to duck her head at something that might have been shared between the two, but there was no time to investigate what it might have been. The spiderkin were in bow range.

Brilliance shuddered. She hated having to run from a fight, but she also knew when she was outclassed. And at fourteen spiderkin to her one snowtiger, she was definitely outclassed. They had caught her scent fifteen minutes ago, when she'd sought a way to track the boy while still unnoticed and unseen. She had been so intent on hunting him that she never noticed that she herself had become the prey.

Once over her initial shock, she had sprinted for safety, the only thought in her mind was to reach the boy's side. She hadn't been able to see him at first, but she could still sense him. Then he had flashed into view, and she trusted he would protect her. She had that belief about him. He and his elf and their strange weapons might keep her alive.

If the stallion didn't kill her first. He had flashed her a look, a promise to kill her if she snarled wrong, and she believed he could. He had a power unlike any she had ever encountered. Not the sweet *lorethasra*, which had fueled her transformation, but something else.

At least she had succeeded in reaching the boy. He and his elf had their bows out, but as of yet, they hadn't fired any arrows.

Brilliance couldn't understand why.

Her answer came when she gazed from them to the spiderkin. The creatures milled about in uncertainty, as if they could no longer see or scent her. One of the monsters had raised herself on her hindmost legs, feelers and antennae quivering. The rest chirped in seeming puzzlement.

Brilliance tilted her head in confusion. She was standing directly in front of the hairy eight-legs. Why were they acting like they couldn't see her? She glanced at the boy. Could he be the reason the spiderkin were behaving so bizarrely? She hadn't seen him at first, either.

The boy and the elf continued to hold tension on the bows, but they didn't release the strings. The two of them exchanged words, but Brilliance didn't know what it was. She didn't understand their language, only a few repeated words here and there, but in the end, the boy nodded.

One of the spiders screamed, waving her legs in the general direction of the boy and the elf. Brilliance hissed when the creatures charged.

A whistling sound, and the arrows were in flight. They speared a pair of spiderkin, who didn't slow. More whistling. More spiderkin struck. Another round of arrows. Two spiderkin were down. Another dozen kept on coming.

Brilliance was ready to run away again, but the boy and the elf had a different plan in mind. They charged the spiderkin. Brilliance growled in frustration. She was prepared to leave them to their fates, but an unfamiliar tugging locked her in place.

She had to help the boy.

Brilliance raced after him and the massive stallion, who had cowed her. The boy fought with a sword and shield. The elf held a sword only, but a green webbing—barely visible—crackled about her form. The boy, the elf, and their two horses crashed into the spiderkin.

So did Brilliance. She shredded the stunned eight-legs who hadn't expected such opposition. She ripped into two of the monsters, tearing off limbs, glad to hear them keen. The boy and the elf killed three more in the span of seconds.

Brilliance caused further chaos. She clawed and bit anything she could until she reached the boy's side. His horse reared and plunged, hammering the spiderkin out of the way. Brilliance bore the injured creatures to the ground, biting off their heads, tearing open their carapaces.

She was having a grand time, killing the spiderkin who had chased after her. Stupid eight-legs. She'd slay them all, destroy any who threatened her or her boy.

Her pleasure ended when a spiderkin crashed into her. She was knocked off her feet, the breath blasted from her lungs. Brilliance yowled in fear. She couldn't afford to lie on her back, her vulnerable abdomen exposed. Her limbs flailed as she frantically struggled to free herself of the spiderkin lying on top of her. A second later the truth of the situation penetrated. The creature was dead. Its head had a hoof-sized dent in it.

It didn't matter. Brilliance couldn't remain in such a helpless position. She exploded out from beneath the spiderkin and took stock of her situation, only then noticing the quiet.

The rest of the spiderkin were also dead. During the time she had been trapped underneath the carcass of the dead monster, the boy and the elf woman had killed the rest of the eight-legs.

Brilliance blinked in shock. The boy and the elf were dangerous. She wanted to scuttle off and hide, but she held still when she caught the massive white horse, the creature she had once dismissed as prey, glaring at her. His gaze had an oppressiveness, like he was trying to figure out whether to kill her now or not. And she didn't doubt he could, or that he could outrun her. She had seen him fight. The pale horse wasn't prey. He was death.

"She's *aether*-cursed," the elf said. "You know what that means."

Brilliance tilted her head in shock. She could understand the elf's hisses and yowls. She never had before. Had the recent battle against the spiderkin caused her to advance in some way?

The white stallion snorted derision. *"Stupid cat. You understand because of me and the gift I granted you. Don't move."*

Brilliance's eyes widened, stunned with every word spoken in her mind. It was the stallion. He was the one who was speaking to her. She had been inching away from him, but with his final statement, she immediately halted her retreat.

"Wait," the elf continued. "Didn't you say your parents were slaughtered by an *aether*-cursed snowtiger?"

The boy nodded, jutting his chin in her direction. "This is the same cat who killed them, but then she saved my life during the Autumn Trial and helped us against the wraiths."

"And she helped us now," the elf noted. "What do you want to do?"

Brilliance's tail went between her legs, and she started backing away again. She believed she could handle either the boy or the elf on her own, but not together, and definitely not with the stallion. He might be the most dangerous threat of them all, and she had no desire to test herself against him.

"Hold still," a menacing voice spoke in her mind.

Brilliance caught the white horse eyeing her in contempt, and she snapped to a stop.

The boy was peering at her through narrowed eyes. "No. We'll let her live. She and I are connected. I think we can trust her. At least for now."

"You think she'll stay with us? Should we let her?"

The boy continued to stare her way. "I think so," he said at last. "And I think we should let her. I have a feeling about this cat. I'm not sure why."

"Can we trust her not to attack us when our backs are turned?"

"Fastness says we can."

"Fastness says so?" the elf sounded surprised.

Fastness. The name of the pale horse.

"She's afraid of him," the boy continued. "She should be. Fastness wants to kill her, but he says…" The boy frowned. "He won't say why he won't kill her, but he says we can trust her enough not to stab us in the back."

Stab them in the back? Brilliance drew herself up in affront. Cowards stabbed others in the back. She had never done so, not to anything other than prey of course, but that didn't count, did it?

The stallion rumbled what sounded like laughter, the kind young cats gave mice they intended to murder, but only after playing with them for awhile and tormenting them. *"You will stay close, or I will end you."*

Brilliance shivered, but she did as she was told.

They left behind the blood-stained field of battle, and it was a half mile to their rear now, but the call of feasting vultures still reached them. The distant cacophony of their gorging was the only sound stirring the land. That and a moaning wind, dry and brittle as the last gasps of a dying man.

Cinder didn't like their current location. It was too open. Too easy for an ambushing party to attack from the heights and seal off any retreat. They rode along the shoulder of a mountain, a sloping trail that was ten feet wide and covered in packed snow as hard as the occasionally seen boulders and massive stones littering their way. To their left, an ice-covered cliff led to a steep, quarter-mile drop-off, while to their right, spiked ridges cast a shadow across their path.

The snowtiger was still with them as well. Surprisingly, she had decided to stay by their side, keeping pace next to Fastness. It was then that her massive size could truly be appreciated since her head rose to the level of the white's withers.

Currently, the cat was in the process of carefully edging away from their group, possibly in preparation to run off, but a hard glare from the Yavana cowed the animal. She meekly returned to the stallion's side.

"What was that about?" Cinder asked the white.

"Her name is Brilliance," Fastness replied in answer to Cinder's question. *"She has a chance to grow past the limitations of her inheritance and birth, to become a worthy creation."* He shot the cat another glare. *"But not if she acts like a coward."*

Cinder jerked his head back in shock. Fastness' voice—the cold, clipped nature of his speech, the word choice, and especially the un-mistakable promised threat aimed at the snowtiger—none of it was in any way similar to the Yavana's typical light-hearted demeanor. It was as if the white had become someone else, someone Cinder had never before met. He stared at the stallion in worry, unsure what was going on.

Fastness tossed his head. *"I am still your stallion."* He nipped at Cinder's feet as if in playful proof, leaving off when Cinder shoved aside the white's snout. *"I just don't like the cat."*

Cinder wasn't entirely mollified. The white's behavior still struck him as strange. Something was off about Fastness, ever since they had left Shalla Valley and possibly prior. Cinder hadn't noticed it at first. Fastness still raced around like a fool, but his formality, his stiffness and anger, or... Cinder frowned, finally recognizing what was bother-ing him. "You sound like a warrior wanting to destroy your enemies," he said to the stallion.

Fastness snorted, sounding proud. *"I am a warrior. I am a Yavana. We are swift and strong, and we fight. We were born and bred for battle."*

Further conversation between them was cut short when the snow-tiger—Brilliance—growled softly. She blinked at Cinder. Her ears were flat, her eyes narrowed, and her head tilted. It seemed like she was trying to communicate information to him.

"She says there is a zahhack just past the bend up ahead."

Cinder picked up on the stench a split second later. "I smell it."

Fastness whickered softly, sounding surprised at his declaration.

Cinder inhaled deeply, drawing in more of the scent. It was pungent and musky, the stink of an unclean animal. *An elewan.* The bull-sized creature used by some of the necrosed, which meant a necrosed might be monitoring this trail.

Cinder hissed softly to Anya, gathering her attention and indicating for her to stop. She did so, brows raised in question.

"Zahhack," Cinder whispered. "Up past the bend. An elewan. I can smell it."

"Truly?" she asked, sounding as surprised as Fastness. "I smell nothing."

Cinder shrugged. His senses were currently enhanced by his *Jivatma*. It stood to reason they were sharper than hers. "So can the cat and Fastness," he added.

The princess didn't reply. She stared up the path, and her lips pursed in thought. "We're Blended, and I don't smell the rotting-corpse stench of a necrosed…" Her jaw firmed. "We have to continue. Darand's Gap is only a mile ahead. We'll kill whatever's ahead of us."

The decision made, they pushed forward. Their horses' hooves crunched across the snow as they ascended the trail. No other sounds. They drew closer to the bend. Cinder's vision narrowed. His heart thumped, and his adrenaline spiked. He readied himself, loosening his sword, but more importantly, reaching into himself, conducting more deeply from his *Jivatma*.

He was already using it to elevate his senses and maintain a Blend, but for each Talent, he had to push harder through the by-now-familiar pain of the blue-and-green lightning. As soon as he did, he gritted his teeth, holding back a groan of anguish.

An instant later, the pain was done, and he conducted more *Jivatma*. In fits and starts, a Fireball sizzled and sparked in his hand. Seconds passed until it steadied, glowing golden and burning too brightly to view for very long.

Brilliance made a noise that sounded like a whimper.

Cinder glanced at the cat in question.

Fastness answered for the snowtiger. *"She doesn't like the Fireball. It frightens her."* The stallion sounded pleased and smug for an inexplicable reason.

"You have it under control?" Anya asked, glancing his way.

"I've got it."

"Good. We'll try to sneak in close. Stay Blended. If it's just one elewan, we kill it. Anything more, and we pull back and plan."

Cinder nodded understanding.

"Be ready." Anya had her sword unsheathed. A soundless fire wreathed it.

The bend loomed. The stink of the elewan drifted, heavy enough now for Anya to notice. She wrinkled her nose in distaste. Cinder settled his round buckler on his off arm.

They were readying to dismount when Brilliance sprinted past all of them. *Shit!* The cat stumbled to a halt on the other side of the bend.

An elewan roared, a bass rumble of fury. Brilliance's legs made scrambling motions as she attempted to backtrack.

Cinder raced past her.

On the other side of the bend, an elewan, riderless and alone, charged at them.

Cinder didn't think. He simply launched the Fireball.

The creature had no chance. The Fireball blasted the elewan off its feet. It barked once in pain as it slid backward a half dozen yards. It came to a stop, its chest nothing but a gaping wound.

Cinder had his sword out, and he cast his sight about. The trail widened to a snow-covered plateau dotted by large boulders. The wind shifted and swirled. A hawk cried. Nothing else. There had only been the one elewan. No other enemies.

The excitement of the moment dissipated, and Cinder's heart slowed. He dismounted, sword still in his hand as he peered more closely at the elewan. Eyes red as a furnace, six-inch talons at the end of its limbs, and tail thick as a tree trunk. It was ridged like a crocodile, and standing on its powerful legs, it would have overtopped Fastness. Its gaping mouth was filled with long, jagged teeth.

"The Fireball made it easy," Anya said, standing alongside.

"I suppose so," Cinder said, taking a deep, settling breath and finally sheathing his sword. The adrenaline dump had him feeling light-headed. "The stupid cat almost got us killed." He glared at Brilliance, who was nosing the elewan.

Anya grinned at him. "The life of a ranger, right? Days of danger and excitement and incompetent *aether*-cursed snowtigers."

Cinder chuckled weakly, doing his best to gather himself. He knew Anya was trying to calm him down with her feigned good cheer, but he didn't want it. The fight against the elewan had been brief, but the tension of their situation pressed on him, an ever-growing weight. Humor felt out of place. He wanted to learn what awaited them at Darand's Gap. He wanted to leave these cursed mountains. And he wanted this Trial done.

Anya must have noticed his grim mood because her features grew solemn and stern. "Saddle up," she ordered. "Keep your Blend tight. I think we're riding toward more danger than any ranger in decades."

Her sober air helped settle his own roiling emotions. "Yes, ma'am."

45

The last leg of the journey to Darand's Gap proved a relatively easy trek. It was a mild, uphill slope, wending along the lip of a gorge and with no zahhacks or spiderkin to challenge their travel. Nevertheless, they approached the trail cautiously. Every so often, they caught sight of dark openings, which no doubt led deeper into the mountain's heart. Those places they skirted, reckoning they might represent entrances into the caverns of spiderkin or ghouls.

They shortly reached a shallow but narrow ravine. Snow and ice ringed them on all sides. Their breath frosted, and Cinder blew warmth into his gloved hands. At least the cold wasn't worsened by a frigid wind. In fact, the day actually seemed to be warming. The afternoon sun glistened on the ice-crusted snow, and it might have made for a pleasant day of travel—at least for the Daggers—but a dull roar filled the air. Possibly a massive waterfall, but there were no nearby rivers—frozen or otherwise—to account for such a sound. The noise filled Cinder with disquiet, and a short time later, he recognized what he was hearing: the clamor of a large-scale battle.

He deepened his Blend and sensed Anya do the same.

On they went, and the sound intensified. It was now a clangor of roars, screams, and keening cries.

The tumult lofted from the very depths of Darand's Gap, cresting to the cliff on which they traveled, hundreds of feet above a long, broad canyon. They were yet unable to witness the battle, but they could see their destination.

Ahead of them brooded Mount Kirindor. The Piercing Heart was a titan amongst pygmies. It towered over the rest of the Daggers. Dull of color, made of black stone, and crowned by perpetual snow, the mountain reminded Cinder of a knife, one meant to rend hope.

A clamminess broke on his brow. His breathing quickened. His heart raced, and anger flourished within him.

There was a malice to this mountain, a dark-hearted presence which stole courage and inspired terror. And while he didn't fear for himself—his worry was for Anya and Fastness—the danger pulsing from the mountain made him want to collect them and run away.

Brilliance whimpered, and he glanced at the snowtiger. Her tail was tucked between her legs, and every now and then, she shivered.

Unexpected pity for the cat rose, and he leaned out to her, scratching her forehead. Her eyes snapped open in either alarm or shock, and she faced him, head tilted in consideration.

"She isn't certain why you did that, but she liked it," Fastness informed him.

Cinder grunted in reply. He didn't like Brilliance, but for whatever reason, she had chosen to ride at his side as a member of their small unit. He would defend and help her in whatever small way he could.

They neared the cliff's edge, and Cinder drew deeper from his *Jivatma*. He formed a Shield, striving to control it as it flickered and faded. Anya must have sensed his troubles. She waited silently on him, and many seconds later, he was able to form and maintain the Shield. But it remained difficult, especially with the added burden of holding his Blend and his heightened senses.

"You have your Talents activated?" Anya asked.

Cinder nodded. "Best that I can."

"Hold onto them."

She said no more, and they dismounted, leaving the horses and Brilliance behind as they crept toward the precipice. They hunkered behind a hulking boulder, shuffling forward on their stomachs until they could peer down.

Below them, a sea of zahhacks and spiderkin writhed in battle. It was a slaughter, and Cinder couldn't tell who was winning. The spiderkin had the greater numbers, and they swarmed masses of ajakavas, unformed, echyneis, ghouls, goblins, and ketus. But the zahhacks didn't give up. Necrosed commanded the battle, occasionally tearing the spiderkin limb from limb. Unformed changed shape, becoming water buffalos or elephants as they charged pockets of the eight-legged monsters. And vampires shrieked through the air, causing chaos when they alighted. Thousands of corpses lay on the ravine's floor, and hundreds more joined them every minute. The stench of blood and offal suffused the air, lifting to where Cinder and Anya huddled, causing them to gag.

"What do we do?" Cinder asked.

"I don't know," Anya said. "We were supposed to come here, but did Mahamatha tell you anything else?"

Cinder shook his head.

"Then we watch, and we wait. If nothing changes, we leave."

They observed the battle for an hour when a sudden roar ceased all struggles. It was the guttural basso thunder of a forest on fire. It echoed on and on, resounding, drawing closer, heralding from the north. The battle halted, and every eye went to the skies.

Cinder stared as well, searching for the source of that massive roar. He quickly spotted it, and his mouth dropped.

Streaking south, glistening in the sunlight, on blood red wings flew a creature out of myth. It banked and dipped, hurtling into the long ravine of Darand's Gap.

Cinder's mouth continued to gape. He had read accounts of these creatures. He knew what he was seeing, but he still grappled with the reality of the situation.

A dragon, a being not seen in millennia. Said to be extinct, but here one was, alive, vibrant, and even from miles off, the creature's deadly fury emanated like a promise of death.

Cinder had trouble making sense of the dragon's size, but it was large, taller than a yakshin and with wings as wide as a river. Its mouth yawned, exposing ivory teeth as long as an elephant's tusks. Fire rumbled in the back of the dragon's throat, and with a great roar, it let loose. Flames exploded forth, a narrow stream, white hot. The dragon passed over the site of the battle, sweeping its great head side-to-side, catching spiderkin and zahhacks alike, incinerating them to ash.

"Devesh save us," Cinder whispered. His eyes were glued to the dragon, much like Anya's, whose expression was one of confusion rather than awe or horror.

The dragon roared again, its great wings beating as it soared out of Darand's Gap. It circled the Piercing Heart, becoming a small speck as it disappeared behind the mountain's bulk and left behind a burned battlefield. Where once thousands had been engaged in battle, now it was only hundreds, and they immediately set about to kill one another.

Cinder and Anya continued to watch the struggle. The dragon was awe-inspiring, but he didn't think Aranya had sent them to Mount Kirindor for the mythic beast alone.

Shortly after, another noise filled the heavens, this one the delicate sound of thunder. Cinder's eyes went to the sky. There were no clouds up there for a storm. Was it the dragon again? He gave Anya a questioning look, but she shrugged, not having an answer.

What now?

The Calico struggled against sleep's soft hold. She had sensed her brother come back to her. Her brother who had fallen from the rainbow bridge and died, she'd been sure, but Indrun had promised he wasn't lost. Promised that her brother yet lived. Promised that he was merely adrift in the Web of Worlds, and that one day, he would find his way back to her.

The Calico stretched out her senses, seeking her brother's mind, but she couldn't latch onto it. His thoughts were clouded and confused. Angry. Her brother raged. She could feel his blood-red wings sweep through the sky and his fury burn.

He was a dragon, just like her.

In the same moment, the binding connecting her and her human tugged at her mind as well, and the Calico rumbled in excitement. Her human was finally here, and he was finally awakening!

The Calico opened her eyes for the first time in millennia. A dark cavern met her gaze, and her body was stiff. She had been asleep for untold centuries, and it would be months yet for her to fully rouse.

But she didn't mind. There were worse things than stiffness. At least she knew her true name and her past.

Her true name was Aia, and in the past, she had been a hunter, and hunters were patient. Once fully awake, she would search out her human, Rukh, and together they would find Shon, her brother. They were helpless without her, and just as importantly, her human needed to scratch her chin.

A single stroke of thunder cracked across Darand's Gap, and the sound rumbled through Cinder, the pressure momentarily making it hard to breathe. Snow shivered beneath the weight of the thunder's rolling echo, and icicles jangled to the ground.

Cinder distantly noted how the spiderkin and zahhacks continued their ferocious slaughter of one another, but his vision went to the sky south of Mount Kirindor. He scanned for where the thunder had originated, latching onto a small area where distortion shimmered the air. The rolling thunder now became a pealing gong as a tall, black line split the sky. It pulsed, expanding and contracting, rotating and extending, widening to form a tall doorway. Within it was framed a rainbow bridge stretching into the infinite distance, and in the darkness around the glowing span drifted pinpoints of light, swirling and falling.

A woman exited the doorway. Cinder couldn't make her out, but she held her position for a moment, seemingly gazing about. He drew out the spyglass Anya had given him and sighted her.

His mouth gaped in stunned amazement.

On a day of implausibilities—an *aether*-cursed snowtiger seeking his protection and a dragon bursting forth from myth—this woman was perhaps the greatest of them. Cinder recognized her, although he'd never before met her in this life. Memory surfaced, and with it came her name.

"Serena Paradiso."

Cinder didn't realize he'd spoken aloud until Anya gave him a sharp stare. "What did you say?" she asked.

"Serena Paradiso. The woman. I've seen her before. In my dream from the Shalla Valley."

"I've seen her, too," Anya breathed, appearing awed. "I know her. I know her name." Her eyes widened in shock. "If we both knew her, then we—"

Cinder nodded. "We knew each other."

Anya shuddered, seemingly gathering hold of herself. "We'll talk about it later. There is more going on we need to learn."

Cinder agreed with her, and he put the spyglass back to his eye, watching what was happening in the skies above Darand's Gap. A million questions poured through his mind. How was Serena here? She was from a past life? Shouldn't she be dead? Or were there others he'd once known who had been reborn in this time? And what was that doorway through which Serena had stepped? Why did it seem so familiar?

His questions stilled when he noticed Serena drift lower. She entered the shadow of Mount Kirindor, and halfway down the slope, Cinder saw it.

A cavern, a black pit, consuming all light. A fathomless space of emptiness and hunger. It might have led to the very heart of the mountain. But it was the titanic figure waiting near the entrance which caught Cinder's attention. The right side of the figure's face was consumed by a horrible burn, a weeping wound which would never heal. He struggled against his restraints, black chains made of smoke binding him to the depths of the mountain. But when he saw Serena, he halted his exertions.

Cinder's mouth went dry. He knew this being, too. He remembered battling him.

He looked to Anya, who stared back at him in dismay. "It's Shet," she whispered. "Devesh save us, the false god is alive."

"I don't think he ever died," Cinder whispered. He recalled the many texts promising the return of the so-called god, all of them pointing to some distant time in the future, which was apparently today.

Fragging hells, why did it have to be today?

Fastness arrived at the cliff's edge, and he stared at the god as well, clearly enraged. *"Wretched demon. Death is too kind for him. Eternal suffering would be a just punishment."*

Cinder did a double take at hearing Fastness' fury. What was going on with the stallion?

"They're talking," Anya said. She had her own spyglass pressed to her eye, and Cinder followed suit.

Whether it was a trick of acoustics, or an unknown use of *lorethasra* or *Jivatma*, the conversation between Shet and Serena was as clear as if they stood no more than ten feet away. In addition, the world had grown silent. The battle between the zahhacks and the spiderkin had ceased once again as the monsters stared at the so-called god.

"I see you, child," Shet said to Serena. "I have already greeted your sister, and now I greet you. I will greet you both in the flesh soon enough."

Serena appeared to shake like a leaf on the wind, the fear evident on her features.

"You have many questions," Shet said, "I will answer them anon. For now, understand that I am your lord, and I will rule you with a firm but gentle hand when I resume my rightful place."

"Who are you?" Serena asked, her voice cracking in obvious terror.

Shet sneered in disgust, a revolting twisting of his face given the burned right side. "You don't know me? Truly? Then know that I am Lord Shet, and this world is Seminal."

Serena screamed and fled.

"Five years, child," Shet called at her retreating back. "Five years, and these chains break. A half a decade, as you measure time, and I travel back to the world where I was birthed."

Serena hurtled through the doorway in the sky. It engulfed her and began to narrow.

But Shet shouted after her. "Mark my coming, for on that occasion there will be no Befouler and His Bride to save the world!"

The doorway spun about, and a black line remained where it had once existed. The heat shimmer formed again, and another peal of thunder cracked the world.

And at the end of its echo, the only sound left was Shet's laughter.

46

Cinder stared at the titanic figure across Darand's Gap, the figure who struggled once more against his chains. The figure, who by all that was good and holy, should be dead, but instead was very much alive and would soon escape his imprisonment. *Shet*. The god of the zahhacks, trapped still in Mount Kirindor, but destined to break free.

He edged away from the cliff overlooking Darand's Gap and the battle between the zahhacks and the spiderkin, a battle the eight-legged horrors were now losing. They had to get out of here. They had to take word of what they'd seen to the rest of the world.

"We're leaving," Anya said, as she and Fastness joined him in moving off the precipice. "There's nothing more to see. We have to get back to Shalla Valley. My mother needs to learn what we witnessed. The world does."

Cinder's reply was shut off by the ground rumbling, shifting, and shaking. Stones broke loose from the surrounding heights, and snow crashed in pounding hammerblows. The air filled with light drifts of thick, white flakes agitated loose from the slopes. *An earthquake.* Fastness whinnied alarm, and Brilliance yowled in fear as the world

575

quivered. The earthquake lasted for less than a minute, but it felt far longer, and when it ended, a few final temblors shook around them.

Those, too, eventually stopped, but then arose a new noise. A clattering of shrieks and keening cries.

"Ghouls and spiderkin," Anya said. "That earthquake probably collapsed a number of their tunnels. They'll be trying to exit wherever they can. Mount up and ride. We have to clear this area as quickly as possible."

Cinder immediately comprehended what Anya was telling him. The spiderkin and ghouls of this area constantly fought one another for supremacy in the burrows and mountains around Durand's Gap, but in this case, they wouldn't be fighting. They would have a temporary truce as they sought the same intention: escaping from the collapsed tunnels. Any who still lived would be exiting wherever they could—such as the entrance holes lining the trail bringing them here.

He and Anya had to ride flat out in order to get free of this place.

Cinder mounted up. "Tell the cat to run," he told Fastness. "We won't be stopping for any reason."

Anya's gelding took the lead, although Fastness could easily outpace Barton.

"Hold onto your Blend," Anya needlessly reminded Cinder, shouting over her shoulder.

Cinder was already doing so. He also kept hold of his Shield—barely—even as he rested his buckler on his left arm. Then they were thundering at a gallop across hardened snow, which might as well have been bricks for how deeply the horses' hooves sank into the crystallized powder. Luckily, the hardened whiteness wasn't slick, and they could let the horses run flat out. Cinder leaned low, urging Fastness on.

They exited the shallow ravine overlooking Darand's Gap and burst onto the trail sloping downward. A mile ahead, they'd reach the site of this morning's battle.

But first they had to get there.

Right now, a hundred yards distant, the ground appeared to bubble as black-carapaced spiderkin burst out of a dark hole and into the bright sunlight. Anya didn't slow, and Cinder drew alongside her. He hoped the bulk of two powerful, Shielded horses would give them a chance at punching through the spiderkin.

They plowed into the eight-legged monsters, scattering them. Keening screams rose as a number of the creatures were crunched under the steel-shod hooves of the horses. Most of the spiderkin were smaller members of their kind. Weaker. Probably males. Brilliance followed in the passage they formed, barreling past any spiderkin who remained upright.

They were through and thundered on. Anya rode to his right, and Brilliance ran to his left. A few spiderkin gave desultory chase but quickly gave up the pursuit. With the Blends, the creatures couldn't easily locate who they were chasing.

The trail swung left. Fastness dug in his hooves, keeping his speed while racing around the corner. A year ago, Cinder couldn't have managed such a turn. Then came a straightaway. Another opening. From it disgorged more spiderkin. For now, there were only a few, but given enough time, there would soon be many others.

Anya heeled Barton to greater speed. Fastness didn't need instruction. He quickly chased down the gelding. Brilliance drifted behind, likely not appreciating the shards of snow flung in her face.

Tough luck.

They reached the newest opening, and these spiderkin slowed them less than the last bunch. The horses simply crushed their way past the creatures.

Another empty straightaway and a half-mile to reach a sweeping right-hand turn that would deposit them at the site of this morning's earlier battle.

But Cinder didn't relax. Even afterward, they would still have miles to cover before reaching Shalla Valley's entrance. As far as he was concerned, they wouldn't be out of danger until then. He only hoped Mahamatha would have the borders of the valley close at hand like she had promised. Otherwise, they'd be weeks getting back to any semblance of safety.

To their left was another opening into the mountain, and the ledge in front of it bubbled with spiderkin, dozens of them. This time, they couldn't simply plunge their way through. This time weapons would be required. Cinder managed to bring a Fireball to stuttering life. It flared and flickered, orange instead of burning yellow or white. It wasn't as potent as he wished, but it was the best he could do.

From a hundred yards out, he fired off the Fireball.

It screamed through the air, whining and wailing like sawn wood. And while it wasn't as potent as a typical Fireball, in this situation, it proved more effective. It blasted into a tight cluster of the creatures, but the discharge didn't punch through one spiderkin only. This one detonated, scattering the monsters, stunning them. But at least they were out of the way.

Cinder might have been proud of his handiwork, but as soon as he'd launched the Fireball, he'd lost control of his Blend and Shield.

Anya rode straight for the rapidly closing gap he had opened. She pointed her sword, and a line of flames roared forward. A flick of her wrist, and the fire swung side-to-side. Spiderkin caught fire, screaming in pain. Black smoke and the stench of burning chitin polluted the air for the second it took to cut through the cluster of the creatures.

They punched through and faced the broad right-hand turn that should lead them past the site of the morning's battle.

Brilliance growled.

"She smells ghouls ahead of us."

"How far?"

"She isn't sure. Distant. Maybe a mile."

Cinder passed on the message.

Anya grimaced but nodded understanding. The gelding was beginning to tire, and she slowed Barton. Better to let him rest now and have him fresh for a hopefully final push past the ghouls than to flag when she most needed his energy. Fastness, of course, was good to go, for miles longer if necessary.

They let the horses walk for a short time, just enough for Barton to catch his breath. While he did so, Cinder fought and struggled to get his Blend and Shield back in place. It only took most of five minutes, but he managed it.

He scowled in disgust at the difficulty and the length of time.

"Does the cat…" Anya shook her head. "I still can't believe we have an *aether*-cursed snowtiger with us."

Cinder managed a faint smile. "Imagine how I feel. She's the one who probably killed my parents."

"I'd rather not imagine," Anya said with a scowl, staring at Brilliance. "Can she tell us how many ghouls are ahead of us?"

Fastness was the one who asked the cat. *"She doesn't know how to count, but she says it smells like many, many. A lot more than the number of spiderkin we've fought so far."*

"Fragging hells," Anya said in response to the stallion's answer.

From behind them, a portion of the mountain exploded. Black boulders and rocks shot outward and upward. The debris landed with a series of booms, and the din pounded out toward where they watched. Worst of all, from the resultant hole erupted a swarm of spiderkin.

"Ride," Anya ordered, making to heel her gelding into a gallop.

"Wait!" Cinder shouted. "I have a plan." The spiderkin continued to surge onto the trail, but with their Blends, the creatures couldn't see them. "What if we let go of our Blends and let the spiderkin see us. They'll follow us—"

Anya instantly picked up on the thread of his thoughts. "—and when they see the ghouls, they fight them on our behalf while we Blend again and slink away." She smiled. "It's a good idea. Let's do it."

Cinder let go of his Blend, and he sensed Anya do the same. Less than a second later, the spiderkin boiled in agitation. They set off a chorus of shrieks.

Anya didn't wait for the spiderkin to charge after them. "Now, we ride." She got Barton into a gallop, and they were off.

Fastness easily kept up with the gelding, and once again, Brilliance ran at the rear. They stayed just ahead of the spiderkin, teasing them onward, and soon, hundreds of the eight-legged horrors were trailing after them on the sweeping turn.

A quarter mile later, the stink of ghouls—a rotten meat odor of decay similar to that of a necrosed—became evident to all of them. A shallow downward slope, and there was the valley, the morning's battlefield. Little remained of those who had died, and their bodies appeared to have been picked over by vultures and possibly other zah-hacks. Their corpses lay like refuse on the valley floor, ignored by a mass of ghouls.

Each creature was no taller than a young child, but every one of them had the bulk of a dwarf. The ghouls fought with rusted weap-ons—mostly daggers and short swords—and a few held battered shields, but their claws and fangs could also serve as weapons if they had nothing else in place.

As soon as the ghouls spotted them, the creatures started jumping up and down in excitement, hooting and hollering like monkeys. But when they sighted the spiderkin, their excitement became rage. They beat at their chests and rushed toward the slope, which widened as it reached the base of the valley.

The spiderkin chittered and screamed their own anger. Both sets of monsters surged at one another like twin tides. Cinder didn't need Anya to tell him to Blend. He did so at the same time that she did, making them effectively invisible to the spiderkin and ghouls.

But they still had to get out of the way.

Cinder spied a sharp rising trail to the left at the same time as Anya. She had them take it. It was narrow—they had to ascend it single file— and they circled the valley, which was already consumed by fighting between the spiderkin and the ghouls. Cinder didn't care who won, so long as none of the monsters saw them leave.

Traversing the narrow trail proved slow going given the hidden rocks and unexpected icy patches, but in the end, they made it to the valley floor on the other side. The bulk of the fighting was behind them, and they pushed on. They still had a long day's journey ahead of them.

It took them hours longer to completely exit the site of the various battles. Hours of painstakingly making their way through rubble and rough terrain; of flattening themselves and hiding whenever they came across zahhacks or spiderkin; of taking long, circuitous passages that were untended and unused rather than gamble on the comparatively short, straight routes that were often occupied by the various monsters.

Brilliance helped. Her nose for zahhacks and spiderkin allowed them to stay safe and out of sight. Enough for them to eventually arrive at the same cave where they had huddled just the night before.

By the time they arrived, even Fastness was feeling the fatigue. His mouth was caked with foam, and his body steamed with sweat. Cinder empathized with the great horse. Since he and Anya had barely gotten any sleep the last several nights, they were both drooping with tiredness as well, and tonight would be no better. It was going to be another freezing evening without the warmth of a fire. Another night where they'd have to hope to avoid any and all prying eyes.

Cinder hoped they'd reach the entrance to Shalla Valley tomorrow. It didn't matter that they'd still have to camp in the mountainous heights because at least in the Shalla Valley they would be safe enough to start a fire and actually sleep without fear.

Cinder considered their situation while brushing Fastness and setting out his oats and water—melted snow thanks to a weave of Anya's—while she did the same for Barton. Brilliance hunkered by the entrance to the cave.

Fastness nuzzled Cinder's hair, and he pushed the horse's mouth away.

"Your hair tastes better than those old oats."

Cinder laughed, glad to see the stallion's playfulness, although he remained concerned by the stern attitude that Fastness had displayed earlier today and for the past few weeks even. It was as if the Yavana had developed a completely different personality, a fearsome one, unforgiving and hardnosed. Cinder had yet to determine what it meant, and it bothered him.

A somber note entered the stallion's voice. *"Brilliance is hungry. She wants to know if she can hunt."*

"If she leaves the cave, there's a good chance she'll be seen," Cinder said. "If she's seen, she can't come back. If she tries and the zahhacks track her, we'll kill her first so they don't find us."

Fastness must have told the snowtiger her options because she growled softly and collapsed in a graceless huff. Cinder felt somewhat bad for the cat, and he set a bowl full of melted snow in front of her, reckoning she was likely thirsty after their long day of travel. Brilliance sniffed the water before lapping it up.

Once he'd finished seeing to the snowtiger, Cinder sat next to Anya near the entrance to the cave. The sun had set, and the world was steadily darkening. Both moons were out—silver Dormant and golden Fulsom—lighting the world in a soft, ethereal illumination. Cinder wondered if they should travel on tonight. They were tired but getting out of this section of the mountains would be worth it if they could have the safety of Shalla Valley by tomorrow's late morning.

Anya must have been thinking along the same lines. "We'll rest here most of the night, but if the moons are still out, we'll leave before sunrise." She hesitated, like she had more to tell but didn't want to say it.

Cinder caught her eyeing him sidelong. "What is it?"

"You and Fastness could set out on your own and get to Shalla Valley before us. No zahhack could catch you. You'd be safe."

"No."

"Think about it," she persisted, fully facing him. "The world needs to know about Shet. Every nation does. They need to prepare for him. If both of us die out here, they'll lose that advantage."

The idea of leaving Anya was repulsive in a way Cinder could never put into words. The very notion made his stomach turn. He could never leave Anya. He never would. They were connected, shared a bond, and something more: they had known one another in their past lives.

"You knew Serena," he said.

Anya sighed. "Now isn't the time. We'll discuss it in Shalla Valley."

Cinder acquiesced to her desire. He wasn't ready to consider all the implications of what his dreams might mean. Some of his dimly recalled memories raised troubling possibilities, arrogant ones. "What about Shet?" Cinder asked. "How do we stop him? There aren't any Mythaspuris to fight him this time."

"Unless whatever bonds limiting the rest of humanity limit him, too. After all, he was once human."

"He isn't anymore. You saw him. He's a titan, at least as tall as Garad Lull. And you saw those black chains holding him back, how thick they were."

"Weaves of *lorethasra*," Anya replied. "They're of a fabrication I've never before seen or heard mentioned. I doubt anyone could recreate them."

"Then you know what I mean. Even if Shet was once human, he isn't now. We still don't have a way of stopping him without the Mythaspuris."

"It doesn't matter," Anya said. "We have to find a way. Every race has to work together. Humans will have to find their lost power."

Her answer surprised him. "You don't fear what that might mean to the woven, to the elves, if that happens?"

Anya wore a self-mocking smile. "You mean how elves have kept humans down for so long and should fear the revenge of your kind?"

"I hope that isn't the outcome," Cinder said. "If we're lucky, Devesh will see us, touch our hearts, and we'll seek justice instead of vengeance."

"If Devesh actually sees us," Anya said, sounding bitter.

"You don't believe in Devesh?"

"I don't know. I want to. Do you?"

"Sometimes, but if He's real, the world doesn't seem to care for His teachings."

"Or we're too stupid to learn," Anya said with a chuckle.

Cinder laughed with her.

Anya sobered a moment later. "Regardless of what happens, I have to believe that if humans truly have the same Talents that you do, it would be better to live under their rule than that of Shet's. Anything would be better than that."

They fell into an introspective silence. The moons rose higher, and

the world brightened in fragile colors of silver and gold. A wind kicked
to life, whistling among the boulders and stones, and penetrated the
first few feet of the cave's entrance. No foul odors drifted on the breeze,
which meant no zahhacks were close.

Minutes later, Anya ended the quiet. "Can you teach others to do
what you can? With *Jivatma*? The Mythaspuris were said to wield it."

"I don't know. Mahamatha said it's a skill that needs to be learned
young."

Anya grunted in reply. "She also told you to go to Mahadev, to learn
who you really are."

"And there is supposed to be an enemy and dilemma waiting there."

Anya wavered for a moment, seemingly unsure whether to speak
what was clearly on her mind. She eventually settled on an air of acceptance. "She told me much the same. She said I'd learn my truths, and
that I'd also have to make a terrible decision."

Now it was Cinder's turn to hesitate. Anya had said she didn't want
to talk about it yet.

She noticed his waffling. "Tell me what you're thinking."

"What if our truths are the means by which Shet is defeated? What
if what we learn in Mahadev gives us a chance to stop him again."

"Again?"

"I remember fighting him. I battled him and his Titans, and I was
with a woman with honey-blonde hair."

Anya's hand went to her braid, and she laughed softly. "And you
believe I'm this woman of your dreams?"

Cinder chuckled. "Well, when you put it like that..." A moment
later, his humor fell away. "The woman of my dreams. I loved her, and
she loved me."

Anya's humor left her, and she raised a cautioning hand. "You know
those feelings can never be reciprocated."

She was lying. "They already are. You can't deny it."

Anya stared at him, her expression inscrutable. In the end, she
sighed in annoyance. "I cannot, but I also can't speak what you want
to hear."

Cinder smiled. He hadn't actually expected her to do so. "It doesn't matter if you can or will or won't. Not now. Not with Shet. And the reason I brought up the dream of us fighting Shet is because in it, we fought him by ourselves."

Anya frowned in confusion. "You think our truths are that we were Mythaspuris in our prior lives?"

"No. We fought Shet alone. No one else. There are no such accounts in any histories of the Mythaspuris. No two of them were ever said to have battled Shet unsupported. And there are no accounts of a Mythaspuri with hair like yours. All of them were said to be dark-haired, except for Sapient Dormant, who had white hair."

Anya continued to frown in confusion. "Then if not a Mythaspuri, then who—" Her eyes widened in shock, and she gasped. "You think we were Sira and Shokan?"

"I honestly don't know," Cinder said, "but it sort of makes sense."

"It doesn't make any kind of sense. Sira and Shokan are myths."

"Myths we still honor. Your family honors them. They don't think they were myths."

"Sira and Shokan." Anya gave a disbelieving shake of her head. "It's too much to accept."

"Impossible," Cinder said in agreement.

Anya exhaled heavily. "It's also a problem for tomorrow. Right now, we need to rest and get out of these fragging mountains."

"I'll take first watch," Cinder volunteered.

Anya nodded acceptance and went to her bedroll. She was asleep in seconds.

Cinder blew on his hands, trying to work some warmth into them. He shook out his fingers, pacing along the entrance to the cave. As the night deepened, the temperature plunged. His breath frosted with every exhalation, and the cold burrowed through his coat and clothes. His nose and ears burned, but at least the wind had died down.

Brilliance padded to his side, and his eyes widened in surprise as he viewed the cat. What had her staring so intently out of the cave? Cinder followed her gaze, noticing when her ears flattened, and she growled softly.

He went alert, and an instant later, he recognized what had the snowtiger agitated. The stench of a rotting corpse flitted past his nose. *Necrosed.*

He went to Anya, shaking her softly. She came awake at once, an expectant expression on her face.

He mouthed the cause of the danger, gesturing toward the mouth of the cave where Brilliance hunkered.

Fastness also roused. *"What is it?"*

"Necrosed," Cinder whispered. The stench had grown stronger, and he formed a Shield. He didn't bother with a Fireball. As soon as he fired it, he'd likely lose his hold on his other Talents.

"Bring the cat back from the entrance," Anya said. She had her bow out, and Brilliance's bulk blocked her aim.

Fastness must have passed on the message because the snowtiger glanced to Cinder and Anya, then to the stallion, and silently retreated. The cat stood tense at Cinder's side, shivering with fear.

Anxiety, however, didn't touch Cinder. He worried for Anya, Fastness, and oddly enough, for Brilliance, but not for himself. Again, just like he had earlier in the day, he patted the snowtiger on the head, running his fingers across her forehead. "Easy," he whispered.

The cat stiffened at first, but shortly quieted—she even stopped growling.

Through it all, Cinder had his eyes locked on the entrance. The moons were still out, and the valley beyond the cave was bathed in soft light. It meant whatever was out there would be nicely backlit. Still, it would be best if the necrosed simply passed them by. He hoped they would.

A scrabbling of claws and a deep, raspy voice reached him, ending his hopes. "Stop bitching. I'm telling you I smelled fear."

"This better be the truth," another voice muttered. "I'm tired of spider. I want a real meal."

"I heard a growl," a third voice said. "It's probably a cat, maybe a snowtiger."

"Snowtiger's better than spider or ghoul," the first voice said. "Only thing better is a woven or a human."

"Humans are delicious," the third voice declared.

"Your mother was delicious," the second voice tittered. "She was sweet."

"Fuck you."

"Quiet," the first voice said. "The smell and sound came from the cave. We don't want to scare away our dinner and have to chase it."

"Who cares?" the second voice said. "It's a fucking cat. It's trapped in the cave. It can't go anywhere. We can even play with it."

"Your mother never told you not to play with your food?" The third voice chuckled, a horrific sound.

"No, but *your* mother did. Right before she grabbed hold of me and sucked my—"

A muffled smack, followed by a grunt and another smack and grunt, and the first voice spoke again. "Shut the fuck up. Both of you."

"We're only having fun," the second voice whined, an odd tone given how deep and threatening his voice otherwise was. "There's one cat and three of us. It can't get away."

Cinder flashed a smile, silently thanking the dumbass necrosed for giving them numbers on their enemies.

Anya leaned toward him. "I'll put an arrow in one," she whispered directly in his ear. "It might slow it down. Go after the one I injure. I'll take the other two."

Cinder knew better than to ask if she could handle two necrosed. If she said she could, then she likely could.

"Sure, but do you smell it now?" the first necrosed challenged. "Do you hear it? I can't, which means something is off about all this. Stay alert and shut it."

There was no more conversation from the necrosed as they crept closer.

Seconds passed, and a massive figure slipped in front of the cave's entrance, blocking the exterior light. It was a long-armed monstrosity, with the claws of a bear that nearly dragged on the ground. The figure lifted his head, inhaling deeply. "I smell horse." It was the second necrosed. He inhaled again, peering into the cave. "But there's nothing—"

Barton whinnied in terror at the same time Anya let loose with her bow. The arrowhead, glowing green, slammed into the necrosed, taking the monster in the chest.

The creature stumbled away from the entrance, cursing floridly. "There's a fucking elf in there," he complained. "The bastard stuck me good. Got me in the chest."

"You good to go?" the first necrosed asked.

"I'm good enough to eat elf if that's what you're asking," the second said. "No way I don't get to feast after taking a fucking arrow in the chest."

"Should we tell the captain?" the third necrosed asked, sounding uncertain.

"And have to split fresh elf and horse with five other bastards?" the first necrosed scoffed. "No chance. We do this. Go in hard and fast. Kill the elf and start feasting while he's still kicking."

Cinder shuffled forward. As soon as any of the necrosed tried again for the cave, he planned on cutting the creature down. Anya followed at his side.

A necrosed suddenly lunged into the cavern, fist moving in a blur. Its punch knocked Cinder back three steps despite his Shield.

"I can smell you, little elf," said the first necrosed. "I know *exactly* where you are. Your Shield won't save you." The necrosed was abruptly clutching his arm. Anya had cut off his hand. "Shet damn it! He cut off my good hand."

"I'm going back for help," the third necrosed declared, sounding fearful.

No. There was no way they could let any necrosed learn their location. Cinder raced out of the cave. He rolled under a vicious swipe from one necrosed. In the same motion, instinct had him conducting

Jivatma, strengthening his sword. He got to his feet and slashed a necrosed across the back of his knees. The creature grunted, collapsing as his legs couldn't bear his weight.

Cinder dashed past him, but as he ran, he felt himself losing control of his Talents. He held onto his Shield, poured strength into his sword, and let go of the Blend. It wasn't helping. The necrosed could apparently smell him in spite of it.

Twenty feet ahead, he saw the third necrosed sprinting away. The creature scrabbled up the trail, and Cinder feared he wouldn't catch him, until the monster slipped on the ice. He fell back, only a dozen feet ahead now. The necrosed got to his feet and spun around, his arms spread wide as if to embrace Cinder.

Cinder shifted to the side, letting a slash slide off his Shield. His follow-up chop cut inches into the necrosed's upper arm. The monster didn't react or even slow. He hammered down at Cinder, catching his Shield directly.

Cinder was slammed into the ground. His head rang, and if not for his Shield, he'd have been pulverized. He rolled away from twin hammerfists, which would likely have crushed his chest. One still managed to clip him in the leg. Pain flared, but he ignored it.

He couldn't stay on the ground. *Get up.* He got to his feet, and scrambled away, trying to get his wits about him. The necrosed walked him down, grinning now, certain of his victory. "A human?" He scoffed. "You are the reason for our fear? I'm going to eat your eyes and bite the tongue straight from your mouth."

His foolish monologue gave Cinder the time to get his mind working again. He shook off the last of his disorientation. The necrosed paced forward, slow and steady. Cinder's back was pressed against the mountain. He feinted with a thrust.

The necrosed didn't bother moving, and Cinder's sword stabbed into the meat of the monster's thigh. The necrosed made no noise of pain. He pounced, arms wide. Cinder ducked low and got away from the mountain. He spun about, facing the creature, who was still in the midst of turning. A vertical chop cut into the creature's shoulder. This elicited a hiss of outrage.

The necrosed twisted, but Cinder was already moving. He had the measure of this creature now. He understood the monster's speed and reach. The necrosed swung his arms, swiping at Cinder, seeking to eviscerate him.

Cinder wasn't there. He slipped aside, ducked low. A third swing he redirected. A fourth was sloppy. Cinder got behind the necrosed, cutting across both ankles. The monster crashed to his knees. A straight thrust punched through the back of the necrosed's neck and six inches of blade extended through the monster's mouth.

The necrosed slowly slumped to the ground, hitting face first and lying unmoving.

Cinder stared at the creature for a second before recollecting the other two necrosed. He rushed back to the cave, arriving just in time to see Brilliance gripping a necrosed by the leg while Fastness pounded the monster's head to a pulp.

The third one was also down. Anya stood up from where she'd been crouched next to it. She noticed him. "Are you hurt? Did you get the third necrosed?"

"Just a few bruises, and the third necrosed is dead," Cinder answered, rubbing out his leg. "How about you?"

"I'm fine," she replied.

"We're fine, too. The cat wasn't entirely useless."

Cinder looked to Fastness who faced him proudly, ears perked. Brilliance, on the other hand, was frantically chewing on ice.

Fastness whickered laughter. *"She says the necrosed taste terrible."*

Cinder relayed to Anya what he'd heard from the Yavana.

She chuckled. "Good. Then we're done here. Those three might represent a patrol. When they don't report in... We need to get out of here."

47

Cinder breathed out a sigh of relief when a twist of the trail brought the Bloody Snake into view. After the skirmish against the necrosed, they had pushed on through the night, making their way through darkened ravines and valleys and along rugged passes and narrow trails, always alert for danger. It was a journey filled with bone-numbing chill and adrenaline-fueled fear, but then again, what other option was there?

Luck must have been with them because they encountered no more zahhacks on their trek to hopeful safety. And with dawn's early light, they discovered they'd come much further than expected. Only a few hours longer to reach Shalla Valley's entrance. They pressed on, not halting as fresh energy filled them. Even their mounts seemed to catch the mood, managing a swift walk with the lightening of the sky.

And here was the Bloody Snake, rearing to their right. Cinder smiled. His hands were numb as stone, and every breath seared his lungs with freezing cold, but he didn't care. They only had to cover a couple of miles to reach safety and eventual warmth.

Minutes later, his optimism was shattered. From the southern heights rose an ululating cry. The hunting call of a wraith.

Cinder cursed floridly. He knew he should never have spoken or thought of safety while still in the wilds.

Another cry echoed. This one from the direction of the Bloody Snake. Cinder spied a figure racing along the cliff's crest, disappearing from view an instant later as it leapt downward.

Anya didn't hesitate. "Come on. We can still make it."

She spurred her mount, and Fastness followed, not requiring any instruction. The Yavana charged after Barton, and although he could have easily raced ahead of the gelding, the white reined himself in.

The horses thundered along the track, taking the snowy path at speed, not bothering with caution. The trail was slick in places, and one slip could doom them, but so would going too slow. They had to throw caution to the freezing wind and pile on the speed.

Brilliance kept up also, running to Cinder's right, her tail streaming and muscles bunching.

Fastness snorted, sounding derisive. *The cat is complaining. She doesn't like being hunted. She finds it humiliating.*

"Tell her she can go her own way if she wants," Cinder snapped, not having the patience to deal with the whining snowtiger. He didn't much like her anyway.

They raced on, and Anya caught his attention. "Don't wait on me and Barton. Ride Fastness. Get to safety."

Cinder held her gaze. "We can both get to safety. If Barton can't make it, you can transfer to Fastness. He can carry both of us."

"It's a risk."

"I'm not going to leave you."

The ululating cry came again, trailing them this time, well back. Cinder's heart eased the tiniest amount, but he wouldn't allow himself to dwell on any positive expectations. He still remembered the lesson from a few minutes ago, the old truism of not hoping for something good when something terrible could still occur.

The path they followed grew wider, flattening somewhat. It deposited them on the plateau where they'd battled the vampires only a few days ago. A half-mile ahead the trail ascended, and several hundred yards farther upslope would be the crest of the mountain pass and the entrance to Shalla Valley and safety.

They were so close, but he wasn't sure if Barton could make it. The gelding was blowing hard, and despite the cold, sweat poured down his neck and flanks. Thick foam collected at the corners of his mouth, but for now, he ran steady and strong. Fastness, on the other hand, ran as smooth as a mechanical time piece, breathing deep and easy, looking like he had miles more inside him.

Another cry rose, still far back.

Cinder glanced behind them. A wraith—a big male—chased them. He was several hundred yards in the rear, not yet onto the plateau, but once on the flat area, he'd probably start closing the gap. Another wraith—a female—agile as a mountain goat, jumped down a set of boulders from the heights of a nearby ridge. She slammed into the ground next to the male, and the pair of them hurtled forward.

Cinder distantly wondered if these were the same two wraiths who had attacked them weeks ago.

He immediately threw off the useless consideration.

They had reached the end of the plateau and plowed up the slope. The snow flew in flurries behind them with every stride the horses took. Another hundred yards and the trail flattened before beginning a final steep ascent.

Cinder silently urged Barton to greater speed even though it looked like he was already giving it his all. The gelding was taking great gulps of breath, lunging up the trail, but clearly flagging.

Cinder glanced backward again and wished he hadn't. The wraiths had reached the trailhead. They rambled upward, gaining yards with every breath.

It was going to be close.

Several dozen yards ahead loomed the massive stones demarcating the passage into Shalla Valley.

Just a little farther.

Barton stumbled, plowing face first into the ground.

Cinder brought Fastness to a dancing halt.

Anya had already smoothly dismounted, and she raced to where Cinder waited on her, vaulting behind him onto Fastness. They left the struggling gelding behind, but while Barton wasn't a purebred Yavana, he had an indomitable will. He shuddered once, as if gathering the last of his strength, before surging to his feet and pushing up the slope again.

Cinder put Barton out of his mind. The wraiths were closing quickly, but they weren't going to catch them.

Fastness carried them through the crest of the pass. Once again there was the strange sensation of striding across a rainbow bridge. It lasted less than a second, could still have been a figment of his imagination, and Cinder didn't care anyway. The weather on this side of the pass was noticeably warmer, which meant they were in the protection of Shalla Valley.

They'd made it!

Even Barton managed to eke his way across the finish line of their terrible race.

Cinder faced back in the direction from which they had come, laughter bubbling in his throat.

His humor died.

Brilliance, the great, stupid cat was still on the other side of the pass. She growled at the onrushing wraiths, but Cinder could tell it was terror inspiring her snarling. He didn't know why the snowtiger didn't cross the rise and retreat into the Valley's protection. She paced back and forth from one side of the opening to the other, frantically pawing at the heavy stones and the air.

"She can't cross," Anya said. "Only those who have been purified or are being actively aided by those already welcomed into the Valley can get in."

"Shit." Cinder didn't know what he felt about the snowtiger. She had inserted herself into their group only yesterday. She had joined them when no one had asked for her presence. But she was still a companion, and he couldn't simply stand idle and watch her die.

He dismounted Fastness and stepped across the protection of the borderline, taking little note of the rainbow bridge.

"Cinder!"

He barely heard Anya shout to him. His attention was on the snow-tiger, and he spoke to her. "I can push you across, but you have to trust me. Don't fight me, and you better not claw me, either."

Brilliance stared at him, panic in her eyes. Not knowing what else to do, he grabbed the snowtiger about the neck.

"Come on," he shouted, dragging her toward the top of the pass.

She yowled, but at least she didn't rake him. He pulled her forward, and she let him drag her along.

The wraiths were closing fast, eyes glowing white, mouths hanging open, their long teeth covered in drool.

Cinder ignored them.

He kept tugging Brilliance. "The fragging hells do you have to be so damn big!"

Anya sprinted to his side, pushing the cat's hindquarters.

Cinder's heart raced. *Just a few more feet.*

The wraiths cried out in triumph. Cinder could feel their pounding feet as they surged forward.

They weren't going to make it!

Fastness arrived. He shoved Brilliance hard in the rear. The wraiths' cries of triumph turned to rage. Cinder, Anya, Brilliance, and Fastness rolled through the tall stones marking the entrance to Shalla Valley. The rainbow bridge flashed past, and then they were through.

They lay on the unyielding snow, panting and sprawled out mere feet from death.

Cinder shoved Brilliance's head off his stomach. "You fragging idi-ot!" he shouted, angry with the stupid snowtiger.

Brilliance replied by ramming her forehead forcefully into his be-fore licking his eyebrows. She rose and made her halting way to Barton, who had crumpled to the ground as soon as he was safe and remained there.

Cinder lifted himself onto his elbows and watched the wraiths pound against an unseen barrier. One of them held a tuft of hair, ripped from Fastness' tail.

The white gathering himself and rose to his feet. *"Let's not do that again."*

Cinder laughed. "Never," he promised.

Brilliance had lived much longer than any member of her kind, three times more than the usual fifteen or so years. She had decades of experience, and in all her lengthy life she had seen every type of prey, witnessed every type of reaction from the creatures she hunted. Most simply ran from her. Others turned, fought, and lost. But a rare few risked their lives on behalf of those they loved, defending against her hunting prowess.

She had observed it all, and from her perspective there was nothing new under the sun.

Nothing new, until this morning, when Cinder had risked his life for her. So had Anya and the terrifying Fastness. All of them had nearly sacrificed themselves to bring her to safety, and she couldn't get the notion out of her head.

The question of why they would do something so foolish ringed endlessly in her thoughts. Did they not understand the circle of life? Lives were organized between predator and prey. The hunter and the hunted. In the circle, there was no room for kindness or empathy. There was kill or be killed and nothing else.

But what if she was wrong? It was possible.

After all, there had been a time when Brilliance had fought on behalf of others. The litters she'd had birthed in her early years, prior to when she had drunk from the shimmering water and grown into a being capable of greater thought. In those younger spans, she had born cubs, and she remembered loving them, feeding them, rearing them, and even battling for them.

She had once fought a bear on their behalf, run off a male of her kind who had wanted to kill her cubs, and savaged a pack of wolves who had considered her kittens an easy meal. She had the scars from those encounters, the wounds which had nearly killed her, and in hindsight, she wouldn't have changed a thing. She had gladly accepted every injury.

Which led her back to her boy. His behavior troubled her. Had he protected her because he considered her his cub? Loved her?

Brilliance huffed in disgust. Impossible. Cinder had been a spindly youth, meek and frightened when she had first met him, while she had been, and still was, a wise old killer.

And yet…

There was an aspect to the boy that made it seem like he was older than she. When he rubbed her head, soothing her fears. When he shouted at her, forcing her to make a choice rather than dither and complain. Like yesterday, when he had told her to go away if she didn't like the path they were taking. Her mother had once done the same. She had run Brilliance off so she could find her own direction. Just like Brilliance had done for her own cubs. Like any parent should.

Brilliance shook off her considerations when their small streak—their small pack—reached the base of the mountain pass, another ascent and descent, and they would enter the foothills.

She halted then, inhaling deeply.

Further ahead was burgeoning life, with many different types of prey, some of which she had never encountered. And also warmth. There wasn't a trace of snow, which she didn't care for. She was built for the cold, not heat and humidity.

She caught Fastness glaring at her. *"Hurry up. Or do you need us to push you the rest of the way like we did earlier?"* He neighed disgust. *"Worthless beast."*

Brilliance bared her fangs at Fastness, a low growl emanating from her throat. She didn't enjoy how contemptuously the stallion treated her. It was maddening. Fastness was a horse. She was a snowtiger. He should be afraid of her, not the other way around.

And yet, it was true. Brilliance feared Fastness, and her anger was all for show. She knew better than to test the white stallion.

Sometimes he was playful, lovingly coltish toward Cinder, but when faced with danger, especially the kind that might harm the boy, he was fierce and unrelenting. It was as if Fastness, a prey animal, had somehow been blessed with the heart of a killer. Fastness was fearsome.

"Ask her if she's coming," Cinder said to Fastness.

The stallion relayed the question, although Brilliance could understand the boy's words—she had since Fastness had gifted her somehow. Over the past few days, Cinder's language had winked in and out of her mind like a firefly, eventually trickling down into certainty. She knew what he was saying, and truthfully, she enjoyed the way he could describe so many things.

She only wished she could speak to him in the same way, but she lacked the tongue and the teeth, and she couldn't do as Fastness did. The stallion spoke directly in her mind. The first time he had done so, she had nearly bolted in alarm, terrified someone had slipped upon her unnoticed.

"Come on, Brilliance," Cinder called out to her, as if he could tell she knew what he was saying.

She noted his pleased expression of surprise when she did as he asked and trotted up to where he sat atop Fastness.

He reached out and rubbed her head.

And like a cub, she arched her neck, pushing into his hand, preening.

Fastness nickered mocking laughter. *"An* aether-*cursed snowtiger pretending she's a tame kitten."* His pretend amusement cut off, and he faced her. She tried not to shiver when she noticed the deadly seriousness in the stallion's eyes. *"I am not fooled by your silly actions. You are a killer. You see the world in the black-and-white shades of a killer, and if you dare make a move to kill Cinder—and do not think I won't see it coming—I will end you."*

It was a flat threat, and Brilliance couldn't help it this time. She shivered.

The journey through Shalla Valley was remarkably peaceful, but given the stress and tension of the past few days, it took Cinder a while to fully relax. He and Anya had so much to discuss: Shet, their past lives, and Serena, but neither much felt like talking. As a result, their journey was a rather quiet procession through the serenity of Shalla Valley.

They made good time, although they mostly spoke of nothing beyond the mundane, such as when to stop for the evening, who would prepare the meals, or whether they should spar.

Of the latter, they did little. They were too exhausted.

However, three days after their mad dash back into the valley, they had an evening where they were fully relaxed and at ease.

Cinder lay on his back, head propped on a portion of his rolled-up bedding. He stared at the starlit heavens, grateful to be alive and able to enjoy the peaceful night. He breathed deep, enjoying the musk and fragrance of the savanna, the evening's warmth. He glanced at Anya, who was also lying on her back, staring skyward. She was lovely in the firelight, and he spent a moment appreciating her beauty.

"You're staring," she said, rolling over onto her side and facing him with a smile.

"I loved you in my past life." The words were the simple truth, and they slipped out without hesitation.

"Didn't you once think you killed me?"

Cinder smiled. "So, you admit it was you in my dreams?"

Anya chuckled. "I admit nothing. I'm just asking who you think I really was? The woman you loved? Or the woman you murdered?"

Cinder's smile fled. The stark terms forced him to consider Anya's questions in relation to his own fragmented memories. "It was the same woman," he began, "but I never hurt her. I'm sure of it. The vision I had—it didn't end with the woman's death. She lived, and I loved her. She loved me."

"And now?"

"I still love her. I love you." He surprised himself by saying the words, but it no longer bothered him to care what society might think about his feelings for Anya. There were far greater concerns facing them, and if he didn't tell her now, then when?

Besides, it was so easy to say. His heart didn't pound, anxious sweat didn't bead on his forehead, and his breathing didn't grow tight with fear. Telling Anya the truth about his feelings carried the simplicity of stating an incontrovertible fact.

"I only ever loved Rukh," Anya said, her voice soft, her features pained.

Cinder smiled. "Was that my name?"

Anya smiled back at him. "Maybe." A beat later. "Probably."

Cinder grinned more broadly. "What are you saying?"

Anya's smile left her, and she shuddered slightly, inhaling heavily as if preparing herself for a difficult task. "There are words I have long been terrified of telling you. Terrified of admitting. Terrified of what it might mean for our futures. It shouldn't have taken me so long to say it, but this is my truth. I don't know or care if you are or were Rukh, but I love you."

Cinder's mouth dropped. He hadn't expected such an unfettered declaration.

Anya's features took on an expression of discomfort. "Do you mind if we talk about something else?"

He quickly acquiesced. "Of course. What do you want to talk about?"

"Mahadev."

The evening's peace crumpled.

"Mahadev," Cinder said, rolling the syllables over his tongue. "We have to go there right after we tell your mother about Shet."

Anya nodded. "Shet is real," she said, an air of disbelief filling her voice. "And if he's real, that means the stories about him are also real. The world itself is in danger."

It wasn't anything they hadn't already discussed. "We have to find a way to stop him," Cinder said. "Maybe we'll find out in Mahadev. And if you and I knew each other, if we're who I think we might have been—"

"It's too much to hope for," Anya said, dashing his rising hopes.

Cinder shrugged. Maybe she was right. To believe themselves Shokan and Sira reborn? *Hubris. Foolish. Idiotic. Arrogant. All of the above.* "At least the dragons have returned," he said. "They were supposed to have been Shet's greatest foes, other than the Mythaspuris."

Anya shook her head, her face filled with awe and wonder. "I can't believe we actually saw one. He was terrifying and beautiful at the same time."

"But locating where that red one went is going to have to be someone else's task," Cinder said. "We have to go to Mahadev."

"The journey would be quicker and safer if we had passage through the underground thoroughfares of Surent Crèche."

"Let's take it one step at a time," Cinder said. "We'll speak to Sadana tomorrow. She can spread the word to the trolls and other yakshins. Then we have to go to Fort Carnate and meet with the rest of the Seconds. From there we go to Revelant, and you can tell your mother." He pursed his lips. "There won't be time to keep my promise to Master Lerid and fight on his behalf and that of *Steel-Graced Adepts* at the Maker's Tournament. He'll lose the school."

"I'm sorry," Anya replied, squeezing his hand in support. "I can have the word out to Ald Prince that *Steel-Graced* is important to Yaksha Sithe. That should get the message across."

Cinder smiled grateful acknowledgment. Having her use her influence would solve all of Master Lerid's problems. "That would definitely get the message across."

Anya was shaking her head now, frowning. "Also. I don't think we have to go to Revelant. We'll tell the Seconds at Fort Carnate. Estin and Riyne can tell my mother. We'll go straight on to Mahadev."

Cinder eyed her in uncertainty. "Are you sure?"

Anya nodded, breaking into a smile. "You look like you're afraid."

"Well, you're not exactly the easiest traveling companion," Cinder explained. "You're always snoring and belching, and I swear, sometimes when you think no one's looking, you pick your no—"

Anya threw a pillow at him, shutting him off with a squawk. "Shut up, *bishan*," she lent his title as her apprentice extra weight. "Just for that, you can have first *and* second watch."

Cinder chuckled. "First and second watch? How generous."

Anya grinned at him. "Up you go, *bishan*. We don't want any wild animals attacking our camp while you're lazing away in your bedroll."

"Any wild animal approaching our camp would be a fool with Fastness and Brilliance watching over us."

"You would really trust your safety to the *aether*-cursed animal who likely killed your parents?"

His gaze went to Brilliance, who was grooming herself, looking every inch a massive, overgrown housecat. But the snowtiger was anything but tamed. She was deadly, a pitiless killer. It made no sense to trust her, but for some reason he did. Or at least he trusted her not to try and harm him so long as Fastness was present. Brilliance was terrified of the Yavana. It was as obvious as her glowing, white eyes.

As if she could read his mind, the snowtiger's gaze turned to him. She blinked once before resuming her grooming.

"They weren't my real parents," Cinder said in reply to Anya's question. "I mourn their deaths, but I don't remember them at all. Whoever I once was—I need to learn the truth. Mahamatha thinks it's important, and I trust her."

"If she's truly as old as Sadana said—alive during the *NusraelShev*— she must have fought against Shet. She would have known where he was imprisoned."

Cinder rose to his feet, not wanting to discuss Shet any longer. "Get some rest," he said to Anya. "I'll take first watch."

Cinder and Anya arrived at the Shriven Grove early the next day. A pleasant breeze, redolent with the smell of wet grass and life, flitted about the savanna and the Ashoka trees. A golden eagle soared on the thermals of the bright, blue sky, while a pair of giraffes cropped the leaves of a nearby acacia tree. The world was calm, and Cinder was enjoying the normalcy.

His relief proved short-lived when their party found itself confronted by a large group of holders. Their dagger-sharp glares were aimed at Brilliance. The cat scuttled behind Fastness, as if he could shield her bulk, her ears low and tail tucked. The snowtiger clearly sensed the hostility of the holders, who recognized what she was and had no intention of allowing her near their wards.

"What is the meaning of this?" Banner demanded, his deep-set eyes gone cold. "What is this… *thing* doing in Shalla Valley?"

Anya replied to his obvious anger with equanimity. "We didn't expect or want her company, but she joined our group several days ago. She has helped with certain matters."

"An *aether*-cursed animal is a member of your party?" Banner asked, doubt evident in his voice. "How? They are killers, every one of them."

"And so is this one," Cinder spoke. He might have added his near-certainty that Brilliance had murdered his parents, but what would have been the point. "But she decided to cast her lot with us, and we haven't yet decided to end that relationship."

"It ends now," Banner said, his tone unyielding as his drew his sword. The other holders followed his lead and unsheathed their weapons as well. "No *aether*-cursed has ever breached the walls of Shalla Valley. This one might have managed it, but her victory is over. Step aside."

Cinder had no desire to fight the holders on Brilliance's behalf, but he also didn't want to see her put down for no good reason. "She aided us," he said, speaking quickly. "She aided the world. You'll know what I mean once you learn what we've discovered at Mount Kirindor."

Banner's gaze went to him. "And what did you discover?"

"Perhaps I should hear this first," Sadana said. She had somehow snuck up on their group, the creaks of her knobby joints silent for once.

Banner spun about to face the yakshin, while the rest of the holders continued to watch the snowtiger, swords leveled. "Sadana," Banner said. "You shouldn't be here. The *aether*-cursed could strike at you."

"She might, and she would die," Sadana replied, her voice unhurried and unworried as she faced Brilliance from her towering height.

"Isn't that right, cat? You have a certain cunning, and you fancy yourself a great predator, but you know when to give way to those with greater ferocity than your own."

For her part, Brilliance blinked once before scuttling backward.

Sadana stepped toward the snowtiger, covering a dozen feet. "If you run away now, cat, the holders will track you down and kill you. Come forward. I know you understand my voice. They will gather around you, but you won't be harmed. You have my word."

Brilliance didn't move, and Cinder empathized with her aversion. Though Sadana's words might have been meant to be soothing, there was a rough undercurrent to them. In fact, right now, the yakshin sounded less like a maiden of trees and more like an arrogant monarch.

Sadana's long jaw tightened when Brilliance didn't come forward. "I am a yakshin, and I have great patience, but do not mistake my forbearance for weakness, cat. Step forward now, or you won't live past the next fifteen minutes."

Although Cinder couldn't say he knew Sadana well, he recognized this much: she didn't make empty threats or promises. "I think you should do what she says," he told Brilliance.

The snowtiger eyed him, her cat's face inscrutable. She blinked at him before facing Sadana. Cinder breathed a bit easier when Brilliance took one cautious step forward. Another. She kept going, a single testing paw at a time until she reached the yakshin elder. The cat craned her neck, gazing at the tree maiden while the holders quickly ringed her, swords at the ready and Shields woven.

Cinder was surprised to note that his own was likely stronger than theirs. At least the webs of his Shield were brighter than the ones formed by the holders.

Sadana smiled cheerlessly at Brilliance. "You show wisdom, cat." She next faced Cinder and Anya, viewing them with disdain. "Let your horses rest. You've abused them enough. Dismount and follow. It is time to unburden yourself and tell those with greater wisdom what you learned." Her statements delivered, Sadana strode back toward the Grove.

Her abrupt departure, and the entire contemptuous welcome he and Anya had received, had Cinder scowling. He had known Brilliance's presence would cause trouble, but the antipathy the snowtiger inspired had apparently also transferred over to them.

"Come on," Anya said. "I don't like it any more than you do, but we came here to tell the yakshins what we learned. We spend the night at the Grove, and then we leave."

Cinder nodded, still perplexed and troubled. Their last time here, the tree maidens, especially Sadana, had been wise and patient, not rude and dismissive. What had changed?

Without another word, he and Anya followed after the leader of the yakshins, where she had rejoined her sisters at the Shriven Grove. The tree maidens clustered in a rough semi-circle, appearing grave while they waited.

With uncertainty and worry in their hearts, Cinder and Anya reached the tree maidens. When they did, Sadana cracked a smile, and her reaction was a spark. The other yakshins broke out in a slow chuckle that soon became uproarious laughter.

Cinder's eyes went to Anya. She shrugged minutely, as confused as he.

"You should have seen your faces," Sepia wheezed, her joints creaking as she hunched over clutching her thighs. "You looked like you were walking to your executions."

Cinder still didn't know what was going on, but he had a sneaking suspicion, and he glared at Sadana. "You were just pretending to be angry and arrogant, weren't you?"

Sadana nodded. "We knew of your coming days ago," she said. "The Ashokas told us. They said you appeared despondent." She flashed a grin. "We thought a bit of humor was in order." She bent down, peering at them. "Did it work? Did you find humor in our joke?"

"You—I can't believe—" Cinder couldn't get the words out, and he found himself smiling reluctantly. A few seconds later, the smile came easier and transitioned into a grin, then an appreciative chuckle.

Anya was laughing, too. "It was a good joke," she agreed. "I never knew yakshins had a sense of humor."

Sadana smiled. "Of course we do." Her humor faded. "The Ashokas heard snatches of your conversation. It carried on the wind. But we need to hear. Tell us true with your own lips and heart. What happened?"

Anya was the one who explained what they'd witnessed in the Daggers.

"A red dragon?" Turquoise asked, sounding stunned. "I thought all the dragons had died during the *NusraelShev*." Her eyes went to Mother Ashoka as if in confirmation.

"But if one lives, then we have a mighty ally in the troubles to come," Sepia said.

"At least one still lives," Anya confirmed. "He laid waste to a horde of spiderkin battling an army of zahhacks. Then we saw something worse." She went on to explain about Shet, leaving out any mention of Serena or Cinder's dream and slowly recovering Talents.

"Shet," Sadana said, sounding as the name itself curdled her tongue. "So the crippled god has at last returned, just as Mahamatha always said he would." She closed her eyes. "We must prepare."

"Should we tell Mahamatha?" Cinder asked, speaking at last.

Sadana opened her eyes and shook her head, her expression sad. "We will do so on your behalf, child. Mahamatha said you would arrive on this day, and she told us what you might encounter. She also said you have a long journey ahead of you. The day is young, and you need to leave. You cannot tarry. You must spread the word to every land and nation that strives to live in freedom and responsibility."

Cinder stared at Sadana. As supposedly abrupt and distasteful as her greeting had been, her farewell was equally troubling. Why the rush to get them to leave? Why not give them a chance to collect themselves and rest?

Anya must have thinking the same thing. "We had thought we could spend the day here and rest."

"I wish you could," Sadana said with a sad tightening of her lips. "But it cannot be. You left two wraiths on the doorstep of Shalla Valley and brought an *aether*-cursed cat with you. Every member of your party is unwashed. It is too great a strain. You weaken our barriers and protections too much. The two of you cannot stay."

"You also have a task you cannot set aside," Turquoise said. "After you speak to your peoples, a city to the north waits for you. It would be better if you didn't delay your departure."

Mahadev.

Anya bent her head to Sadana. "As you say. We'll leave now."

Something Sadana had said clicked in Cinder's mind. "You said '*the two of you cannot stay.*' What about Brilliance? What happens to her?"

Sadana's sad expression grew grim. "She must speak to Mahamatha." Cinder was ready to argue, but she held up her hands to forestall his protest. "It is no longer your concern. This has to happen. Brilliance must prove she is worthy of having entered our sacred valley."

Cinder viewed her in appraisal before nodding acquiescence. Still, he wasn't happy over the situation. Forcing the snowtiger to speak to Mahamatha seemed like a veiled threat.

Then again, why did he care? She wasn't a true companion.

Or so he tried to tell himself.

He and Anya retrieved their packhorses, and prior to their departure, they said a brief farewell to Brilliance with Fastness explaining what was happening. For her part, the cat merely stared their way, somehow knowing she couldn't accompany them and remaining calm anyway.

"*She says she hopes to see you again,*" Fastness relayed.

The holders had already started herding Brilliance toward the Shriven Grove.

"Tell her I hope to see her, too," Cinder said, the trite words slipping out and surprising him when he realized he actually meant them.

48

Cinder viewed Fort Carnate with a frown. It overlooked the blue waters of the Sentient Sea, squatting like a massive toad on an escarpment of red cliffs. Surrounding the fortress was a walled city of the same name.

It was strange.

With its generous greenery and small forests merged among low-lying buildings, the city reminded Cinder of Certitude, but Fort Carnate could never be said to be a part of nature. It was a hunkering fortress, thick shouldered with a forty-foot outer wall, soaring towers, and crenellated battlements to command the sea and the land. This was a fortress meant to dominate the surrounding countryside, not meld with it.

"We're here," Anya said, interrupting his contemplation. "Let's get this done." She sounded impatient.

Cinder shared her desire to finish the journey. It had taken them three weeks to reach the end of this road. Three weeks of hard travel from Shalla Valley to this place. Three weeks of worry.

"Come on," Anya urged. "This is only the end of one path. A harder one awaits."

Cinder briefly clenched his jaw. Between everything he had endured and seen in his Secondary Trial, he could have used a few weeks of rest. Unfortunately, it seemed he was wicked because there was no rest for him. He and Anya still had to get to Mahadev.

"Should we tell the commander what we saw?" Cinder asked. "Before messaging your mother, I mean."

"I think so. Same with any Seconds who have already arrived."

She heeled Barton forward, and Cinder followed. The warriors of Fort Carnate, alert and wary, took note of their approach toward the main gate. The guards shifted to block their passage but swiftly moved aside when they recognized the princess. The two of them were then escorted inside, and there they separated, Anya to greet the commander and Cinder shown to his quarters.

It turned out to be a small room in the barracks, a single space, walled in stone and possessing a large window that peered out into the bailey. A number of cots lined the room, and a wagon-wheel chandelier hung from the beamed ceiling.

Of greater import, though, was what else the room contained: Sriovey, Derius, Jozep, Bones, Ishmay, Estin, and Riyne.

Cinder's heart eased. There was a magic in meeting long-lost friends. It was like all the hardships from his months on the road dropped away and a more innocent time was recaptured. Glad shouts of surprise and joy welcomed Cinder as he was embraced by the fraternity of his brothers. They congregated, hugging him and slapping him on the shoulders, all of them, even Estin, wearing relieved and happy smiles.

"You had us worried," Bones said. "After we heard how a wraith ripped you apart, we didn't know what to think."

"How did you survive?" Riyne asked. "Estin said the wraith nearly tore you in half."

Cinder's smile of joy evaporated. He had grim news for his friends. "There's a lot to cover. Why don't you fellows sit down. I've got a story to tell." Concerned expressions met his words, and he waited until everyone was seated. He proceeded to explain everything he'd experienced.

When he reached the portion about the Aushadha, his account was interrupted by whistles of disbelief and envy.

"An Aushadha? For real?" Derius asked. "What was it like?"

"Painful." Cinder shook his head. "I don't want to talk about it. Plus, there's more important things to tell." He went on to explain about meeting with Mahamatha.

"You spoke with Mother Ashoka?" Sriovey whispered, his features intense. "She is the holiest of all beings."

"There's more," Cinder said.

"More?" Derius demanded in disbelief. "How can there be more?"

Cinder shrugged. "Because there is." Next, he mentioned Mahamatha's orders for him and Anya to journey to Darand's Gap and Mount Kirindor.

Sriovey whistled. "Mount Kirindor? Please tell me you didn't actually go."

"What's so bad about Mount Kirindor?" Ishmay asked.

"The Piercing Heart is the heart of evil in this world," Sriovey explained. "Or at least that's what my people believe. We don't venture there or go anywhere close to those parts."

"The elves feel the same way," Riyne said. "The area around it is a perpetual battlefield between massive spiderkin nests and armies of zahhacks. No one has been there in centuries."

"We went," Cinder said. "And we discovered something worse than spiderkin or zahhacks." He took up his account again, getting to the point of the story where Brilliance arrived.

"Wait a moment," Bones said holding up his hands. "Is this the same *aether*-cursed snowtiger we saw during the Autumn Trial?"

Cinder nodded. "I think she's also the same *aether*-cursed beast who killed my parents." He waved aside the questions several of the Seconds wanted to ask. "Her past isn't important. You'll know what I mean in a second. We reached Mount Kirindor, and we saw a dragon." Again, he waved off any questions. "Even that isn't important."

"A dragon isn't important?" Sriovey demanded. "I'm starting to think you're pulling our fucking legs."

"There was a cave halfway down Mount Kirindor," Cinder said. "In its shadows, a figure fought against chains that looked like they were made of smoke. He was massive, the size of Garad Lull. And the right side of his face was burned."

Silence gripped the room. They knew who he meant.

Bones had grown pale. "Tell me this is a joke."

Cinder hated this. It felt like he was stealing the innocence of his friends, but he had no choice. They had to learn the truth. "Do I look like I'm joking?"

"Shet," Estin whispered, every bit as pale as Bones. "You saw Shet."

Cinder nodded. "We saw him. Right after the dragon. We saw him talk to a woman."

"What woman?" Sriovey asked.

"I'm not sure," Cinder said, hedging his words. "But he told her he'd break free and attack her world in five years of her time. I don't know if her world is our world, but the way he spoke, it didn't sound like it. I don't know how much time that gives us."

"You're sure of this?" Estin asked. "Anya will verify your account?"

"She will. She's doing so even now, speaking to Fort Carnate's commander. We saw Shet, and he's going to break free."

"Shet," Ishmay whispered, the word a curse in his mouth.

"Fuck," Bones growled, collapsing onto a cot. He held his face in trembling hands. "We're fucked."

"What about the dragon?" Ishmay asked, trying to sound hopeful. "Can he help us?"

"A dragon is no match for Shet," Sriovey said. His tone was grave and appearing like he had witnessed his own funeral. He collapsed on a cot as well. "Bones is right. We're fucked."

"This really isn't some kind of terrible joke?" Riyne asked, his voice hopeful.

"I'm not the joking type," Cinder said, "and every word I said is true."

Riyne stared at him a moment longer, probably hoping to catch him in a lie. He apparently didn't find it because he flopped down next to

Bones a moment later, muttering, "Shit. Shit. Shit."

Cinder glanced around the room. Everyone—elves, dwarves, and humans alike— stared off in the distance, rightfully stunned and afraid.

"There is more," Cinder told them.

"Fuck," Sriovey growled. "How much bad news do you plan on dropping on us today?"

"This isn't bad news," Cinder said. He'd spoken of *Jivatma* and his abilities to some of the Seconds, but it was time the rest of his brothers learned about them, too. He told everyone of his Talents, only leaving out any mention of his past life and association with Anya. He also told them of Mahamatha's advice for him to go to Mahadev.

A deeper quiet filled the room when he finished, and the Seconds viewed him in a kind of disbelief, blank-faced and slack-jawed, as if he'd told them too many impossibilities and their minds simply couldn't accept the entirety of it.

Sriovey snorted in derision. "You don't think having to go to Mahadev is bad news? Dumbass."

Estin laughed harshly. "What you've just said explains so much. All those sparring matches when you moved as swiftly as an elf and had the strength of a dwarf. Every bit of it makes sense now." He shook his head, his features bitter. "I only wish you'd arrived two days sooner to tell us all this."

Cinder frowned at the prince, not sure what he was getting at.

Estin cleared his throat, and every eye in the room was on him. "Ever since Quelchon Ginala's recitation—you didn't hear it, but my mother did, and she has learned to fear you. She sent orders to have you arrested and taken to Revelant. They reached Fort Carnate two days ago."

Sriovey blazed to his feet. "He can't be arrested. If what he says is true about Shet, his abilities, *Jivatma*, then—"

He had no chance to say anything else. The door to their quarters was thrown open, and in rushed ten heavily armed and armored elves, warriors of Fort Carnate. The Seconds surged to their feet with alarmed shouts.

But they were unarmed, and the guards bore swords, shields, and armor. They spread out across the room, warning off the Seconds, who eyed them in a mixture of wariness and challenge. Cinder was sure if his brother warriors had their weapons at hand, they would have drawn them. Blood would have been spilled, and it still might be. The barracks was on the edge of violence.

Cinder couldn't allow it. The world needed every able-bodied warrior to fight Shet.

The leader of the guards, a dark-haired elf with flat eyes, confronted Cinder. "You will come with us. Do so quietly." His hard gaze flicked about the room, taking in the Seconds. "And there will be no trouble."

Cinder kept his hands well-clear of his weapons. "Step back," he ordered the Seconds. "We don't fight our own."

The Seconds stared at him, some of them looking mulish, like they were going to fight the guards no matter what he said. Thankfully, they eventually calmed.

"I'll be fine," Cinder said to the Seconds, not knowing if it was true. He didn't know what Quelchon Ginala had recited about him—either Anya hadn't learned the information, or she had been unwilling to tell him—but it also didn't matter. Mahamatha had told him to make haste and go to Mahadev. An arrest and a voyage back to Revelant to face charges he didn't know was the opposite of haste.

He'd have to break free of wherever they imprisoned him in the fort and make his way to Mahadev. But would he go alone? For Anya to accompany him, it would mean going against the express orders of her mother.

Cinder didn't doubt she would. It made no sense, but for whatever reason, he knew she would go with him to Mahadev.

Anya should have realized that something was wrong the moment she stepped into Fort Carnate. There had been plenty of hints, starting with the close-lipped guards, who were normally cheerful and ebullient when they greeted her; the formal manner in which Marshal Filionath had spoken to her in the bailey when he had met her near the main gates; and the lack of information the marshal had provided until she was well inside the fortress.

Only then did she understand the warning tingling in the back of her mind: this was an ambush. But it wasn't aimed at her.

Cinder!

She spun about on her heels, ignoring Marshal Filionath's squawk of surprise. She headed back to the entrance.

"You can't help him," Marshal Filionath announced, pulling her up short. She faced the commander. "You can't help him," he announced again. "Word came from your mother. Orders to arrest him. I don't know why, but it's already been carried out."

Anya's rising fury made it difficult to think. Her vision went red, and she struggled to contain her rage. She had never learned the contents of Cinder's recitation, and she berated herself for not finding out. It had to have been terrifying for her mother to have reacted in this way.

And Quelchon Ginala—that bitch had to be the hand behind Cinder's arrest. She had likely worked on the empress all winter and spring, feeding on her fears. The old puppeteer was cunning and unrelenting, but no one saw it, especially when the quelchon's desires matched their own. Most elves wanted Cinder brought low. He was a human who dared rise too high, an equal to any woven, and they hated him for it. People like her sister and brother and mother. It would have taken little to convince any of them to act on their fears and racial animus.

For the first time in her life, Anya found herself despising her people. They were so short-sighted and confident in their unearned arrogance.

But now wasn't the time for unthinking fury. She needed to free Cinder, and that would require clarity of thought.

She collected her anger, imagining it like a ball of paper that she squashed. Only then did she face the marshal. "As you say. The empress' will must be done." Her tone was clipped and flat, giving no hint of her emotions. "But the road here has been long. I will retire to my quarters. I know the way."

Marshal Filionath's features relaxed into the expression of someone who had been spared a death sentence. "I'm glad you're seeing reason. And I'm sure the human is merely wanted for questioning. It's doubtful the empress has anything more severe in mind."

Anya lifted a single brow in question.

The marshal hastily continued. "He is to be given the full rights and measure of a student of the Directorate. We'll hold him in the jail here, but your mother didn't demand he be brought back to Revelant in chains."

A little of Anya's anger released. It was good that Cinder's life might not be in jeopardy, but traveling to Revelant and defending himself would slow them down. Mahadev awaited, and they couldn't tarry to answer the stupid fears of her people.

Anya nodded to the commander. "Good to know. I won't linger long at your fort. I'll depart tonight."

"You don't want to accompany your *bishan* to Revelant?"

"He ceased being my *bishan* when my mother decided to arrest him. I see no reason to humor her reasoning or beg on his behalf, if that's what she expects. She can make a carnival of her so-called questioning without my presence."

The marshal viewed her with confusion and concern. "You must be tired. Are you sure you should—"

"I'm absolutely certain," Anya said, not giving the marshal a chance to say anything else to her. She set off for her quarters, immediately planning how to free Cinder from his imprisonment. Not once did she consider otherwise. She entered the rooms set aside for her at Fort Carnate and didn't bother to unpack. There was no point in doing so. She and Cinder would be on the road before the morning.

She paced her quarters, lost in thinking and planning. A half hour later, a knock on the door revealed a harried-looking Estin standing at her doorway.

"Can I come in?" her brother asked, appearing unaccountably nervous.

Anya opened the door and gestured for her brother to enter, closing it behind him.

"I think I can help Cinder," Estin began without preamble.

Anya's brows lifted in surprise, and she silently scrutinized her brother. Estin hated Cinder. He had from their first interaction. That spite might have faded some during their second year, especially during their shared portion of the Secondary Trial, but not enough to convince her that her little brother would go against their mother's wishes.

"Help him how?" she asked.

"Break him free of the jail so he can get on with whatever he has planned. He told us about Shet and Mahadev."

Anya didn't reply. She merely studied her brother, wondering if she could trust him. Why was Estin so willing to help the one person he hated above all others? What had changed for him? Or was this some devious plan to see Cinder captured in the midst of escape? If that happened, it would likely mean the end for him. The empress would have him executed.

"I don't believe you," Anya said at last.

Estin rubbed his hands together, clearly agitated. "I know I haven't treated Cinder well, but I have my reasons for wanting to help. You have to trust me."

"But I don't."

Her response agitated Estin further. "You have to. Please. He cannot stay imprisoned, and he cannot waste his time in Revelant."

Anya wanted to trust him. She didn't like disbelieving her brother, but she couldn't risk it. Cinder was too important. Too much depended on him. "Everything you say is true, but you have to tell me why I should believe you. Why do you want to help him?"

Estin grimaced. "I can't say."

Anya sighed. It wasn't an answer, and she was about to tell Estin to get out, when he held up his hands, forestalling her.

"Wait. I can't say because I've taken a vow of silence. There is a society in Yaksha. Maybe all sithes. I cannot reveal it."

Anya stared at Estin. When had he become so untrustworthy in her eyes? The knowledge made her sad.

"If you can't trust me, then you can at least trust the dwarves," Estin said. "They're willing to help me, too."

"The dwarves?" This Anya hadn't expected. "If they're caught, they won't be allowed to return to the Directorate."

"They don't intend on returning. After what Cinder told us about Shet, they plan on going home to Surent Crèche and warning their wisdoms about Shet's return."

"Mount Kirindor *is* only a couple hundred miles from their capital," Anya mused. She stared at the ground, lost in consideration. Foremost in her thinking, she wondered if she could believe Estin. Her gaze shot to him. "And their reasons to help Cinder?"

Her brother's features became knowing. "You know their reasons. They have suspicions about who Cinder truly is. It's the same one I share. The same one, I think, you do."

Shokan. An impossibility when Cinder had first broached the topic, but during the weeks of their travel, it more and more struck her as true. And if she trusted he was Shokan, did she dare believe she was Sira? It sounded utterly ridiculous even as simple speculation.

What would her brother say to that?

Anya threw off her meandering thoughts. There was planning to do. "What do you intend?"

Estin smiled in relief. "Something simple and direct."

As a rule, elves rarely caused enough trouble to require anything but a few prison cells in their cities, even ones the size of Revelant. Rape, murder, and thievery—crimes too commonly seen in human nations—were a rarity in the sithes. More often than not, the only real use for the prisons was to give passed-out drunks a place to sleep it off.

The one in Fort Carnate was no different. There were only four cells here, and the prison was a clean, well-kept, and well-lit space, requiring only two guards to stand sentry. Currently, they were both seated at a square table in a small room outside the cells, having dinner—braised chicken in a spiced, roasted red-pepper soup.

They snapped to attention when Estin entered.

"I'd like to see the prisoner," Estin told them. He held up a mandolin secured in the case he'd managed to procure. "He likes to play."

"Yes, Your Highness," one of the guards, the taller and older of the two agreed. He opened the door into a narrow corridor lit by *diptha* lanterns mounted to the wall. An iron-barred window at the far end provided further illumination, although with night having fallen, all that could be seen was golden Fulsom and a patch of clouds.

But the weather and sights outside didn't hold Estin's interest. Instead, it was the four stout wooden doors facing the hall. Cinder was in one of them, and Estin furtively licked his lips. *Here it goes.* He'd be risking much to go against his mother's wishes, all to free a human everyone knew he loathed.

But he had to. If Cinder was who he and the *Lamarin Hosh* suspected, then he had to help. But that supposition alone wouldn't have been enough to earn Estin's aid.

It had been Mahadev. Cinder's destination, where he would prove himself as Shokan. Or not. The prophecies in the true renditions of *Forever Triumphant* stated the Lord of the Sword would pilgrimage to Mahadev, the ancient city of the Mythaspuris, the city collapsed long ago to evil. Mahadev and Cinder's plan on going there were the main reasons Estin had called on the Seconds, demanding their help in freeing Cinder.

Their response had been wary silence. None of them—Riyne included—had trusted his intentions, and they had stared silently at him, like a pride of lions judging prey. It had been humiliating, but somehow, Estin had managed to sway his fellow Seconds of his sincerity.

Or rather, it had been Lisandre. The ranger had unexpectedly arrived at their barracks and quickly deduced what was being discussed.

His surprising declaration of support for Estin's plan had convinced the others to follow through with it.

As to why Lisandre had shown up when he had and said what he did—it was a question for another time.

Right now, the important part began here, with distracting the guards, the taller and older of whom had entered the hallway, and the shorter and younger of whom stood well back, maintaining his post in the small room outside the cells.

If all went well, a Blended Sriovey and Riyne should be on their way to the prison, ready to deliver a dose of winter's breath—an odorless, tasteless medication—into the guards' food. Once consumed, the sentries would be asleep inside of ten minutes. No one would know Cinder had escaped, not until the next shift change, which was hours away.

Then would come the tricky part of the escape. A ship was ready to leave for Swift Sword with the rising tide, not too long from now. They needed to hustle Cinder to the docks, unnoticed and unseen, and get him aboard in that span of time.

The tall guard peered inside the nearest cell and grunted. "He's in there," he said, opening the door and stepping inside to where Cinder was shackled to the wall.

Estin blinked.

Except Cinder wasn't shackled. Yes, he was in the cell, but his shackles had been pulled free from the wall. *How?*

The tall guard tried to shout even as he attempted to back away, but a swing of the chains clocked him in the head. He collapsed bonelessly to the ground.

Estin Shielded right before he caught Cinder's eye. "Wait!" he whispered, holding up the mandolin case as if it were another shield. "I'm trying to break you free, and—"

Cinder either didn't hear him or didn't believe him, and Estin never saw the kick that launched him like a catapult out of the cell. His Shield protected him from the worst of it, but he still slammed into the wall, hitting with a dull thump before sliding down.

He groaned, watching as Cinder stepped past him. The shorter guard had stepped into the hallway, a look of dismay on his face. He tried to scramble back and lock the door, but Cinder was on him too quickly. How the fragging hell did he move so fast?

Estin chuckled to himself. He was cursing like the human.

The second guard was shortly down, unconscious as well.

Estin creaked himself upright, his chest and back throbbing. "Will you stop fighting for a second," he called out hoarsely. "Sriovey is coming. He'll Blend you. We're trying to get you out of here."

Cinder glanced at him, his eyes cold. "I don't need Sriovey to Blend me. I can do it myself, and it also looks like I got free on my own."

Estin closed his eyes, praying for patience. "Can you please shut the fuck up and just accept some help. Once you get out of the fort, where will you go, stupid?"

Finally, a wary acceptance firmed across Cinder's bull-stubborn features.

"We've already got everything planned." Estin hobbled down the hall, clutching his ribs. One of them was sure to be cracked. *Damn Cinder.*

"I'm sorry," Cinder said, sounding genuinely contrite.

"Shut up, moron," Estin growled. "Just follow my lead."

Seconds later, the door to the guards' room opened and closed on quiet hinges. No one was there. But an instant later, Sriovey and Riyne flickered into view, both their mouths agape.

"The hell did you two do?" Sriovey demanded.

Estin chuckled bitterly. "I didn't do anything. The dumbass did."

Riyne shook his head, probably in disbelief. Either that or he was trying to rid his sight of whatever disaster he had walked in on. "Is the plan still the same?"

"It is if Anya's already on the ship," Estin answered.

"She is," Riyne replied. "Same with Fastness and her gelding. We're all set to go."

"You planned all this for me?" Cinder asked, his voice soft.

Estin glanced at him in incredulity. *What an idiot. If he's Shokan,*

Devesh help us all. "Why else do you think I'm here?"

Cinder stared back, his head tilted in bewilderment and abashment. "I don't know."

"Because it's necessary," Estin said. "Now hurry up. You have to hustle along with Sriovey and Riyne. They'll fill you in on the rest of the plan. I'll go back to the cells and pretend you knocked me out, too." He pressed the mandolin case into Cinder's hands. "And take this with you. I know how much you like to play."

Cinder glanced at the case, and then at the chains dangling from his wrists. "Err. Who has the key to these?"

"They should be in the cabinet over there." Estin pointed, and Cinder quickly found the keys and got rid of his chains.

"Now get going." Estin made to hobble back down the hall, but Cinder's voice halted him.

"Looks like neither of us wins the wager."

Estin eyed him in confusion. *What wager?*

"At the end of the year, we were supposed to duel. Both of us going with everything we had. Whoever loses had to call the other one *Exalted Lord and Master.*"

Estin recalled the bet now, and he waved it aside. "We both know you'd win."

Cinder started, apparently not expecting Estin's response. Well, well. It seemed the human didn't know everything.

"Thank you, Estin." Cinder eventually said, his voice contrite.

Estin spoke over his shoulder. "You're welcome. And if you don't mind, lock the doors behind you so it's harder for the guards to spread the word of your escape."

The closing and locking of the hallway door was his only reply.

49

In the end, getting Cinder out of Fort Carnate proved anti-climactic, at least as far as Sriovey was concerned.

Estin's plan had been a good one, and things had worked out even better than expected. What with Cinder clobbering the guards with his shackles. No one could definitively claim any of the Seconds had helped him escape. And with luck, no one would learn of Cinder's jailbreak until early tomorrow morning. Sriovey didn't like or trust the prince, but he had to admit, Estin had done right tonight. Devesh knew why the prince wanted to help Cinder, but whatever the reason, Sriovey would take it, and he was glad for the simple plan Estin had dreamed up.

Once Cinder was out of his cell, all Sriovey had to do was Link a Blend with Cinder and Riyne—who wasn't half bad now that he wasn't acting like an asshole—and sneak Cinder out of the guard room and through the rest of the fortress. From there, they met Ishmay and Bones at a predetermined location near the front gates where the two humans distracted the sentries.

It was simplicity itself slipping out of the fortress and hurrying on over to the docks.

They halted at the gangway to their vessel, a small, gnarly boat that somehow still had undeniable charm to it. The ship would carry them from Carnate to Swift Sword.

However, there was no time to linger because Anya was waiting for them at the gangplank. She took over the Blend hiding Cinder and hustled him into the cabin the two of them would be sharing.

The jailbreak was complete, and in the shadows of the ship, where no one would notice, Sriovey let go of his Blend. He shared a triumphant grin with Riyne.

"Stay in touch," Riyne said, and Sriovey found himself receiving an unexpected hug. "And stay safe."

"I will," Sriovey growled. "It would have been a lot safer if there had been a ship to carry us straight to Surent Crèche from here, but beggars can't be choosers and all that."

Riyne grinned. "No, we can't."

Sriovey hesitated. "And give my best to Estin. He did good."

Riyne nodded. "I will."

Jozep and Derius, who had also already boarded, were peering down the gangplank.

"Captain says we're shoving off in a few minutes," Jozep said. "You better get aboard."

Sriovey inclined his head in a final farewell to Riyne before striding up the gangplank. He and the other two dwarves immediately headed for their cabin. This was a human ship, so unlike on an elven vessel where they might have received sneers of superiority, this crew dipped their heads in respect as the dwarves passed them by.

Once in their cabin, Sriovey Blended again, and he indicated for the others to do the same. There was a delayed discussion they had to have, one of the utmost importance, and Sriovey didn't want anyone to overhear them.

"What happens now?" Jozep asked.

"We need to figure out what the fuck to do about Cinder," Sriovey said. "The wisdoms believe he might be the Fated Foe."

Jozep started. "The Fated Foe? That's not possible. We know Cinder. We know who he is and everything about him. He's a kind person, steadfast and true." The young dwarf's face grew earnest. "He's accepted us as his brothers. How many dwarves in all of history can make that claim? He can't be the Fated Foe."

Sriovey privately agreed with the younger dwarf's assessment, but it didn't mean they could simply disregard the judgment of the wisdoms. He left it to Derius to explain.

"Cinder has abilities that surpass our own," Derius said, holding up a single finger as if making a point.

"How do you know that?" Jozep asked.

"I felt his Blend," Sriovey said. "It was when we were creeping through the fortress. It's deep. Damn deep, and richer than anything I can create. Probably deeper and richer than any I've ever encountered. And you've seen how fast and strong he is. It's not natural."

Derius continued. "And as it is stated in *Crèche Prani*, "*The Fated Foe will know your powers better than you know them yourselves. He will pretend weakness, but mastery of all arts will come to him as easily as breath. He will wield* Jivatma *and proclaim affection and brotherhood, but behind his cunning smile watches the* Elonic Ciprion." He held up a second finger as if making another point. "By his own admission, Cinder can wield *Jivatma*. He possesses two of the attributes that the *Crèche Prani* warns about regarding the Fated Foe."

"He also is a man without memory," Sriovey said.

Jozep faced him with an unhappy frown. "Which means what exactly?"

"I don't know," Sriovey replied, "but it's another fucking oddity about him. And it means once we get to Swift Sword, our work isn't done. We have to watch him. Anya, too."

"We truly were lucky there were no ships headed for Surent Crèche," Derius said. "It gave us a needed excuse to take the same ship as Cinder and Anya."

"You think it's lucky we might have to kill our brother?" Jozep asked.

"I don't like this any more than you do," Derius growled. "But our home—the whole world—is in danger, and we need to understand everything we can about Cinder Shade."

Jozep shook his head. "I already understand everything I need to about Cinder Shade. He's my brother, and I won't help you hurt him."

"Will you try and stop us if we have to?" Sriovey demanded, glaring now at the younger dwarf. Most times he found Jozep's innocence charming. This wasn't one of them.

Jozep answered by crossing his arms over his chest and glaring right back. "Cinder saved my life from an *aether*-cursed bear. What do you think I'll do?"

It wasn't much of an answer, and Sriovey threw up his hands in disgust.

Quelchon Ginala awoke with a start. For weeks now, she'd felt an itch in the back of her mind, a barely perceptible warning that she'd overlooked something important.

But she could never determine what it meant.

She could now, and fear and fury filled her. Everything had been going according to plan. The months of work setting the empress to a panic-stricken state. Soon the sithe would be at a boil, ready to come apart at the seams, and all the sacrifices Ginala had made to bring forth the dreams of her Master were coming to fruition.

Even Shet's recovery was of minimal concern. She had felt the roiling of the world's *aether* when the so-called god of the *rahaasras* had awoken from his millennia-long sleep and clawed his way out of his imprisonment. In the end, it mattered not. The Master would see to Shet. There was no one who could defy the true ruler of this Realm; not the woven, Mahamatha, or even an upstart god.

But there was someone who could possibly deny her Master his proper place. Someone she had never before met, but whose presence she knew. The color and scent of his *lorethasra* had been imprinted upon her mind many thousands of years ago.

But over time, those memories had grown dim and distant. She remembered them now, remembered them with perfect clarity. She recalled the feel of his *Jivatma* and the scent of his *lorethasra*. She remembered, and now she knew fear.

Shokan reborn. He was the only one who had even the slightest chance of hindering her Master, and her orders about him had been quite clear: kill Shokan no matter the cost. His death was needed so her Master, the true Zahhack, could rise unimpeded in his power and drag this realm to the dark reaches of absence and His father, the Empty One.

And she could have followed through with those orders—if she had recognized Shokan.

Ginala swung ancient, shriveled legs over the edge of her bed and sat up. Her breathing trembled, and her heart took the pace of a beating drum. She had encountered Shokan, and she had not noticed him. He had been so weak—his puissance not yet manifested—and her pride had made her arrogant. Ginala had actually touched him, seen him, pretended to recite him, and through it all, she'd overlooked her greatest enemy.

Fool.

Only now, tonight, during a bitter evening of harsh rain had she pierced the shawl of forgotten truths.

How could she have been so stupid? The boy, Cinder Shade, had deceived her with his play at being innocent. It made Ginala want to howl in outrage. She wanted to kill Cinder Shade, tear him into small pieces and put him back together again so she could tear him apart anew.

Shokan was reborn, and he was currently far, far from her reach. Orders had been sent to arrest him and bring him straight to Revelant as soon as he arrived at Fort Carnate, but Ginala couldn't leave this to chance. What if Shokan somehow escaped?

She took a long breath, stilling her thoughts and began considering options.

After hours of contemplation, her lips curled in a moue of distaste.

The only means to ensure Shokan's death was to share the glory of his killing with her sister, Sheoboth, the Webbed Queen, the mother of the spiderkin. Heremisth, their Rakshasa sister guarding the anchor line to the darker realms of Zahhack's rule, would also have to be informed.

Shet gave a testing tug on his spiritual chains. They had been clamped to his wrists by none other than the mighty Indrun himself, the greatest of the Mythaspuris.

But Indrun wasn't the one who Shet despised above all others.

That special hate was given over to Sapient Dormant and Manifold Fulsom. The two necrosed had once been his slaves, but somehow, they had overcome their bondage, supposedly in the Realms of the Rakshasas.

He didn't know how, nor did he care. The only thing that mattered was that it had occurred, and the two had brought war to him here. They had come to Seminal as Mythaspuris, engaging in battle against Shet and helping to defeat and shackle him.

He would never forgive them, no matter that his counterthrust to their betrayal was to destroy their fabled city and bind them to this world. They were trapped. Not for them was the singing light they claimed called the faithful home to Devesh. Not for them was the possibility of ascension on the Wheel of Life. They would never again be reborn in any useful form or in any other realm.

Shet snorted in derision. Not that he believed in rebirth.

There was no such thing as reincarnation, just as there was no Loving Lord named Devesh or a terrible Demon of Consumption, the supposed Empty One or his son, Zahhack. There was only force and will, and any who said otherwise were the worst kind of deluded fools—they were cowards.

And Shet wasn't a coward, nor was he deluded or a fool. He was an agent of utmost force and will, and this time, with no Mythaspuris to defy him, no Shokan and Sira to stand athwart his destiny, he would remake Seminal in his own image. He would force this world to bow before his godhood.

The same as Earth, the realm of his birth. He had unfinished business there, work that would ultimately save Seminal itself.

It was fate. After all, the girl had seen him, and he knew from whence she hailed. She would take the tidings of his resurfacing to her people, and they would know fear and terror and devotion.

As it should be. For his glory was meant to be made manifest.

Shet once again stretched the smoky chains binding him to the Piercing Heart, and while doing so, he pushed against the barrier of blue-and-green lightning denying him his *Jivatma*. There was pain in doing so, and he gladly accepted it. He had mastered pain long ago, when Shokan had burned his face.

He grimaced a moment later. He had been unable to penetrate the lightning, only being able to conduct the slightest dregs of his *Jivatma*. He had to make it enough.

Shet prepared his will, and when he was primed, he drove out his call. It sped as swiftly as thought, twisting and shifting until it found its target.

In a far-off land across the world and next to the sea, in a long-forgotten temple, crusted in vines and empty of a roof, Shet felt the response of one of his Titans, the greatest of them. Sture Mael breathed to life and cracked open his eyes.

Their cabin was tight, with room enough for only a single bunk, an overhead *diptha* lantern, a small desk and chair, and nothing else. But from what Anya had told him, it was better than what the three dwarves had to share. Cinder smiled. There had to be a funny story in there somewhere.

It was grim kind of humor he felt right now, though. Cinder was tense. He stared out the porthole, and it wasn't until after their ship slipped the docks that he found himself able to relax. He watched

Carnate recede in the distance, watched the city dim and disappear in the night. All the while, he kept thinking about Estin. Why had the prince helped him? They had been enemies for so long. It made no sense for Estin to have come to his aid.

"Why did your brother help me?" Cinder at last asked Anya.

She moved to stand at his side, her cinnamon scent noticeable over the briny wash of the Sentient Sea. "I don't know," she said, shrugging minutely. "He said he made a vow to some secret society. It sounded like that was the reason, but he wouldn't tell me what it meant."

Cinder grimaced. He had so many worries on his mind and trying to decipher Estin's motives was an unnecessary weight. "I wish elves were easier to figure out."

Anya offered a low chuckle. "Sometimes I feel the same way, but at least we're safe. You don't need to be afraid." She tugged on his hand, pulling him away from the porthole. "Sit down."

Cinder took the chair by the desk while Anya sat on the bunk. He felt it when she wove a Blend, and he cocked his head in question.

"No one knows you're onboard," she explained. "And no one can know. The less wagging tongues who might recognize either of us, the better."

Cinder nodded agreement. They had talked about this when she'd led him aboard and down to their cabin.

The easiest way to reach Mahadev would be to take a ship from Swift Sword to the rough port of Drow in the Wilding Forest and from there, travel west to the lost city. They would need supplies, maps, and a ready explanation for why a Yaksha elf had journeyed so far from home. Or better, lie and claim Anya was from Apsara Sithe. No need to make it easy to track them, and Cinder had no doubt they would be tracked.

There was no chance Anya's mother wouldn't figure out that he had help in his escape and that her daughter had likely played a key role. The empress would send her ships after them, after any hint or sighting of them. They had to travel fast and evade capture, which meant they couldn't afford drawing attention to themselves.

Fewer questions would likely have been raised if they went through Surent Crèche, but such a path was no longer an option. It would take too long. Travel through the Dagger Mountains wouldn't be easy or safe enough, and Cinder thought the danger was likely to be increased even further since Shet had largely broken free of his prison.

Speed was of the utmost importance now.

"It will take us eight days to reach Swift Sword," Anya said, somehow guessing the direction of his thoughts.

"How long will it take to find a ship heading in our direction?"

Anya shrugged. "Your guess is as good as mine."

"Should we—"

Anya held up a hand, interrupting what he had been about to say. "You just escaped Fort Carnate's prison. Relax and enjoy the moment."

"But we have to—"

"Tomorrow will come when it does," she cut in. "We have eight days to plan our next steps, but I have to say that traveling hidden and alone for all that time, brooding and worrying, won't make for a fun voyage."

Cinder flashed a sudden grin. "Well, I'm sure we'll find something to keep ourselves occupied." His grin faded as he realized how his words could be interpreted.

Anya, however, hadn't dropped her gaze. She smirked knowingly at him. "And I'm sure I know exactly what activities you're hoping will keep you occupied."

Cinder blushed. His mouth was always getting him in trouble around her.

Anya pealed laughter. "I was talking about music," she said, holding out the mandolin case. She arched her eyebrows. "What did you think I meant?"

Cinder knew better than to argue. It would only lead to more trouble. "Nothing," he grumbled, taking the case and opening it.

Inside was a mandolin. Made of cherry wood, it was of higher quality than the one he'd left behind at the Directorate. He gave it an experimental strum, listening for the correct tune. A few more strums, a couple of turns of the tuning pegs, and he had it sounding right. It had a lovely sound, warm and resonant.

He glanced at Anya. "Will your Blend hide the music?"

She nodded. "It should be fine, but it would be better if you sat closer." She shuffled over on the bed, making room for him.

Cinder controlled a grin threatening to spill across his face. He had a notion of saying how Anya just wanted to get him in her bed. He was wise enough to keep his mouth shut.

Something in his face must have given him away, though because Anya rolled her eyes. "Get those thoughts out of your head right now. I could always make you sit on the floor."

Cinder didn't bother arguing. He simply accepted her words with a shallow incline of his head and took a place next to her on the short, narrow bed. He began playing then, a song of longing and loss, of meaning and family, and all the work a person might put into achieving a life worth living. It was about some nights of waking, seeing a ghost, and hearing a swan's song.

It felt apropos to where he and Anya found themselves, and it surprised him when she began singing along with the music. Her throaty alto carried him along the tides of the lyrics, and he closed his eyes. The images of the woman with honey-blonde hair passed over him like the caress of a soft breeze.

He recalled her, remembered her, remembered her passion and promise. A million memories lurked behind her smile and in the depths of her glorious eyes, but he couldn't keep hold of any of them. All he knew was his love for her. For Anya.

When the song ended, he opened his eyes. Anya met his gaze. A faint smile lit her features, her expression knowing yet inviting, and her emerald eyes arresting. Cinder's mouth went dry, and his breathing went tight. Between the glory of her golden hair, the warmth of her wry smile, and the way her camouflage ranger's garb perfectly fit her tall, lean form, he was lost. He couldn't find himself, not even if zahhacks threatened to tear down the cabin's door.

He unconsciously leaned in toward to her.

"Cinder," Anya breathed. "If you move any closer to me, I'm afraid

I'll kiss you."

Cinder blinked, unsure what to do.

"Cinder. Move closer."

Anya shifted, bending toward him, and Cinder met her in the middle. He kissed her, softly at first. His arms went around her waist and shoulders, pulling her forward, and she drew him closer as well, the back of his neck was held in the crook of her elbow. Their kiss deepened, and for a timeless moment, all the turmoils, troubles, and terrors haunting him for the past several months melted away in the safety of her embrace. All he knew was the heady aroma of her cinnamon scent, the feel of her in his arms, and the softness and taste of her lips and tongue. His heart pounded.

It wasn't enough, but after an unknown period of time, Anya pulled back from their kiss. She breathed heavily, her forehead still pressed against his, her hands resting on his thighs.

Cinder lifted her chin, forcing her to meet his gaze. "I love you, Anya Aruyen." He needed her to hear the words again.

"I love you, too, Cinder Shade," she replied. "Or Rukh or Shokan or whoever we are. I love all of you."

Cinder had hoped to hear her say it back, expected it, but still, he was relieved. "What happens next?"

Anya grinned, a flash of her white teeth. "This." Her arms went around his neck, and she kissed him again, drawing him closer, tugging gently at him, urging him. He melted with the motion, easing down with her against the small cot.

THE END

A Final Note

Thank you for reading what I've written. Without people taking an interest in my books, I'd have little-to-no chance at doing what I'm doing. I am humbled and gratified beyond measure that there are so many of you who are willing to give my words and worlds a chance.

I'd also be grateful if you decided to add a review for the book. Those social proofs are pretty much the lifeblood of an author.

In addition, if you're really feeling ambitious, please consider signing up for my newsletter. It includes all of latest news, and while there's usually not a lot to tell, hey, at least you'll be up to date with what I'm doing.

As for Cinder and Anya, their story continues in *A Necessary Heresy*.

Glossary

Absin Morewe: Weapons master at the Third Directorate.

Aether: Akin to *lorethasra*, but it is the magic imbued in the world at large. Also known as *lorasra*.

Aia: Mythical steed of Shokan. Thought to be of a species of cat called Kesarins.

Antalagore the Black: Mythical black dragon.

Apsara Sithe: An elven empire known for their agriculture and horses. They are perpetually infuriated that their horses are not a match for the Yavanas.

Anya Aruyen: Younger princess of Yaksha Sithe. She is the first and only elven woman to attend and graduate from the Third Directorate. She is also a ranger.

Avan Aruyen: Consort to Sala Yaksha, empress of Yaksha Sithe. Anya's father.

Bharat: Powerful island nation of the rishis, who claim to be direct descendants of the Mythaspuris.

Bishan: General definition means student, but in *Shevasra* it translates as *'incompetent person who has potential*

Bones Jorn: Human warrior. Cadet at the Third Directorate and in the same class as Cinder Shade. He was formerly a student of

Steel-Graced Adepts.

Breech: A holder who protects the troll, Maize Broad.

Brow Cowl: Human warrior. Cadet at the Third Directorate and defeated by Cinder Shade in the Maker's Tournament. A former student of the *Jasmine Water* martial academy.

Braid: Also known as a weave. A practical use of *lorethasra*.

Brilliance: An *aether-cursed* snowtiger.

Capshin Sonsing: Lieutenant and master/instructor in History at the Third Directorate.

Cariath Gelindun: Elven cadet at the Third Directorate who is in the same class as Cinder Shade.

Certitude: City in Yaksha Sithe. It is closely aligned with the Third Directorate.

Chakras: Potential loci of power, possibly within all beings, and it allows more instinctual control of weaves and braids.

Cinder Shade: Human. An unusual warrior of superlative skill. He has no recollection of his past.

Crail Valing: Elven cadet at the Third Directorate and was in the same class as Cinder Shade. Killed in the Unitary Trial.

Crèche Prani: Holy text of the dwarves.

Depth Knarl: Human warrior. Cadet at the Third Directorate and in the same class as Cinder Shade.

Derius Surent: Dwarven cadet at the Third Directorate and in the same class as Cinder Shade.

Devesth: The capital city and name of one of the Sunset Kingdoms. It is the home of the famed Yavana horses.

Dorcer Surent: Dwarven cadet at the Third Directorate and was in the same class as Cinder Shade. Killed during the Unitary Trial.

Dorr Corn: Former student at *Steel-Graced Adepts*.

Drak Renter: One of Shet's Titans.

Duchess of Certitude: Hereditary position and currently held by Duchess Marielle Cervine. Historically, the Duchess of Certitude is also a high-ranking member in the succession for the imperial throne of Yaksha Sithe.

Enma Aruyen: Elder princess and heir to the throne of Yaksha Sithe.

Estin Aruyen: Prince of Yaksha Sithe. He is also an elven cadet at the Third Directorate and in the same class as Cinder Shade.

Fain Kole: Journeyman at *Steel-Graced Adepts*.

Farin Eshanwe: Elven cadet at the Third Directorate and was in the same class as Cinder Shade. Killed in the Unitary Trial.

Fastness: A white Yavana stallion.

First Directorate: Yaksha Sithe's shadowy organization of spies.

Forever Triumphant: Elven holy text.

Gandharva Federation: A human nation. It is allied with Yaksha Sithe and Rakesh.

Garad Lull: One of Shet's Titans. Like the other known Titans, he lives in a statue-like state and is currently kept within the Quad at the Third Directorate.

Garlin Fairsent: Warrior of Rakesh. Defeated by Cinder in the Maker's Tournament.

Genka Devesth: Warlord from the Sunset Kingdom of Devesth. He believes himself the heir spoken of in the *Medeian Scryings* and intends on recreating Shang Mendi, Mede's ancient empire.

Gorant Sin Peace: Student at *Steel-Graced Adepts*.

Halin Dorund: Cavalry master at the Third Directorate.

Holder: A species of woven who are the pre-eminent warriors in all of Seminal. Little is known about them other than they have no known lands of their own and are entirely devoted to the protection of yakshins and trolls.

Indrun Agni: A Mythaspuri.

Isha: Common definition is 'instructor', but in *Shevasra*, it means 'master'.

Ishmay Sensow: Human cadet at the Third Directorate and in the same class as Cinder Shade. Originally from the Gandharva Federation.

Isthrim: A type of *aether*-infused dwarven steel that is able to kill vampires and necrosed.

Jameken Battalion: Veteran battalion of Yaksha's imperial army. Colloquially known as the 'James'.

Jasmine Water: A martial academy in Swift Sword.

Jine Kole: Master at *Steel-Graced Adepts*.

Jivatma: Supposedly the soul. Largely thought to be mythical, although some accounts of the Mythaspuris indicate it was the source of their power.

Joria Javsheck: Human cadet at the Third Directorate and was in the same class as Cinder Shade. Killed in the Unitary Trial.

Jovick Sonsen: Unarmed combat master at the Third Directorate.

Jozep Surent: Dwarven cadet at the Third Directorate and in the same class as Cinder Shade.

Koran Yaksha: Founder and first empress of Yaksha Sithe.

Lamarin Hosh: Secret society in Yaksha Sithe. They seek to discover and aid the reborn Shokan and Sira. Founded by Duchess Sarienne Cervine of Certitude, who was a quelchon.

Lerid File: Owner/master of *Steel-Graced Adepts*.

Liline Salt: Known as Water Death. One of Shet's Titans. Along with Rence Darim, they are the only two female Titans. She is also frozen in a statue-like state and housed in a courtyard in Apsara Sithe.

Lisandre Coushinre: An elven ranger and occasional instructor at the Third Directorate. Brother to Riyne Coushinre.

Loial Company: Small unit decimated during a recent Unitary Trial.

Lor Agni: An ancient holy text centered around the proper means of righteous living and the worship of Devesh. Mostly limited in importance to Gandharva and Rakesh (translated as *the Secret Fire* in *Shevasra*).

Lorasra: Synonym for *aether*, although the term has fallen out of favor and is rarely used any longer.

Lorethasra: A mystical source of power by which woven are able to create weaves and braids that impact the world.

Loriam Stilwen: Elven cadet at the Third Directorate and in the same class as Cinder Shade.

Mahadev: The fallen city of the Mythaspuris.

Maize Broad: A troll who meets Cinder Shade at the Third Directorate and recognizes him.

Manifold Fulsom: Along with Sapient Dormant, one of the leaders of the Mythaspuris.

Marielle Cervine: Current Duchess of Certitude and the leader of the Lamarin Hosh.

Mede: Ancient warlord from Parn, who set out to conquer the world. He was largely successful, and his empire was known as Shang Mendi. However, upon his death, his empire quickly fell apart into strife and civil war.

The Medeian Scryings: Holy text written by Mede and said to be inspired by the voice of Devesh. Much of the book is a biographical account of Mede's life and conquests as well as his philosophical beliefs.

Mirk Bassang: Human student at *Steel-Graced Adepts.*

Mohal Holwarein: Elven cadet at the Third Directorate and in the same class as Cinder Shade.

Molni Cirnovain: Master librarian at the Third Directorate.

Mother Ashoka: Mother to all the Ashoka trees and yakshins on Seminal.

Mythaspuris: Powerful humans who entered Seminal during the *NusraelShev* and are thought to have turned the tide in the battle against Shet.

Naraka: Shet's ancient empire.

Nathaz Surent: Dwarven cadet at the Third Directorate and was in the same class as Cinder Shade. Killed during the Unitary Trial.

Nuhlin Genhin: Master/instructor of Tactics and Strategy at the Third Directorate.

NusraelShev: Translated as *the Disastrous Submission* in *Shevasra*. The ancient war against Shet and his forces.

Pitch Shade: Brother to Cinder Shade.

Quelchon: A rare woven who can 'recite' a person and thereby learn a hint of their future.

Quelchon Ginala: Elderly elf with the power of a quelchon. She is not what she appears.

Rakesh: A human nation. Allied with the Gandharva Federation and essentially a vassal state to Yaksha Sithe.

Redwinth Wheat: Prince of Apsara Sithe and presumed fiancé to Enma Aruyen of Yaksha Sithe.

Rence Darim: Known as the Illwind. One of Shet's Titans. Along with Liline Salt, they are the only two female Titans.

Revelatory Dreams: A set of scrolls written by the trolls and yakshins. Translated from *Shevasra*, and there are conflicting versions.

Rishis: Rulers of Bharat, who claim to be the human descendants of the Mythaspuris.

Riyne Coushinre: Elven cadet at the Third Directorate and is in the same class as Cinder Shade. Brother to Lisandre Coushinre.

Rorian Molinking: Human cadet at the Third Directorate and was in the same class as Cinder Shade. Killed in the Unitary Trial.

Sala Yaksha: Current empress of Yaksha Sithe.

Sapient Dormant: Along with Manifold Fulsom, one of the leaders of the Mythaspuris.

Sash Slice: Human student at *Steel-Graced Adepts*.

Savage Kingdoms: Group of rival human kingdoms that were formed from the remnants of Shand Mendi, Mede's empire, in the far northeast of the world.

Serwil Opturund: Archery master at the Third Directorate.

Shadion Carrend: A dwarven spy from Surent Crèche. He often pretends to be a merchant and has a donkey named, Pretty.

Shalla Valley: Home of the yakshins.

Shaloce Astreas: Colonel and commander of Jameken Battalion.

Shet: A self-proclaimed god, who battled much of the world three thousand years ago in the *NusraelShev*. He was supported by seven Titans.

Shokan: A mythical human warrior. Along with his wife, Sira, they are said to be Shet's greatest foes and are collectively known as the Blessed Ones.

Shon: Mythical steed of Sira's. Thought to be of a species of cat called Kesarins.

Simone Trementh: Dowager Duchess and aunt to Marielle Cervine.

Sira: A mythical human warrior. Along with her husband, Shokan, they are said to be Shet's greatest foes and are collectively known as the Blessed Ones.

Sriovey Surent: Leader of the dwarven cadets at the Third Directorate who are in the same class as Cinder Shade.

Sture Mael: The greatest of Shet's Titans.

Sunset Kingdoms: Group of rival human kingdoms that were formed from the remnants of Shand Mendi, Mede's empire, in the far northwest of the world.

Surent Crèche: Dwarven crèche and somewhat allied to Rakesh and Yaksha Sithe. By tradition, surnames are taken from the mother's side of the family, but to everyone not of the crèche, the surnames are always told as being 'Surent'.

Swan Yaksha: Second empress of Yaksha Sithe.

Swift Sword: Capital of Rakesh.

Sylve Arwan: General and commandant of the Third Directorate.

Taj Wada: Complex of buildings that comprise the imperial palace of Yaksha Sithe.

Third Directorate: Yaksha Sithe's pre-eminent military academy.

Tomag Jury: Known as the Shield Render. One of Shet's Titans. Twin brother to Tormak Jury.

Tormak Jury: Known as the Sword Breaker. One of Shet's Titans. Twin brother to Tomag Jury.

Trolls: A species of woven known for their ability to apply Justice, a type of braid/weave by which they allow the truth of a matter to be truly known and never forgotten. They are also the only woven who procreate by parthenogenesis

Vampires: Species of woven who are beholden to Shet. They have a type of flight and gather blood slaves as a means to acquire power.

Wark Nil: Human warrior. Cadet at the Third Directorate and in the same class as Cinder Shade.

Weave: Also known as a braid. A practical use of *lorethasra*.

Woven: General name for all self-aware beings on Seminal other than humans.

Wraiths: Twisted humans, who apparently have the means to source either *lorethasra* or conduct *Jivatma*. They are universally insane and lust for flesh and brains.

Yakshins: Tree maidens. A type of woven known for their deeply held bonds to trees and nature.

Yavanas: Finest breed of horse in the world. They only breed true in the Cord Valley or Devesth, one of the Sunset Kingdoms.

Zahhack: Name given to the woven who are beholden to Shet. It is also the name of a mythical being of whom very few know, who is reputedly the son of the Empty One, Devesh's great foe.

About the Author

Davis Ashura is a legend...in his own mind. He resides in North Carolina, sharing a house with his wonderful wife who somehow overlooked Davis' eccentricities and married him anyway. As proper recompense for her sacrifice, Davis then unwittingly turned his wonderful wife into a nerd-girl. To her sad and utter humiliation, she knows *exactly* what is meant by 'Kronos'. Living with them are their two rambunctious boys, both of whom have at various times helped turn Davis' once lustrous, raven-black hair prematurely white (it sure sounds prettier than the dirty gray it actually is). And of course, there is the obligatory strange, calico cat (all authors have cats – it's required by the union). She is the world's finest hunter of socks, be they dirty or clean. When not working – nay laboring – in the creation of works of fiction so grand that hardly anyone has read a single word of them, Davis practices medicine, but only when the insurance companies tell him he can. Visit him at www.DavisAshura.com and be appalled by the banality of a writer's life.

Made in the USA
Monee, IL
12 September 2023

42643386R00392